EAGLE-SAGE

EAGLE-SAGE

BOOK III

of

The LonTobyn Chronicle

DAVID B. COE

TOR®

A Tom Doherty Associates Book / *New York*

EAGLE-SAGE

This book is printed on acid-free paper.

Edited by James Frenkel

Maps by Ellisa H. Mitchell

A Tor Book
Published by Tom Doherty Associates, LLC
175 Fifth Avenue
New York, NY 10010

www.tor.com

Tor® is a registered trademark of Tom Doherty Associates, LLC.

Library of Congress Cataloging-in Publication Data

Coe, David B.
    Eagle-sage / David B. Coe.—1st ed.
        p. cm.—(LonTobyn chronicle; bk. 3)
    "A Tom Doherty Associates book."
    ISBN 0-312-86791-3 (alk. paper)
        I. Title.

PS3553.O343 E26 2000
813'.54—dc21

99-089861

Printed in the United States of America

0 9 8 7 6 5 4 3 2

For Alex and Erin,
who, in ways they don't even know,
add light and magic to my world.

Acknowledgments

If an author is fortunate enough to surround himself with caring, supportive people, his or her acknowledgments tend to grow terribly redundant. So it is with mine.

Once more, I would like to thank Harold Roth, my agent and life-long friend; Tom Doherty, for continuing to believe in me and my work; Jim Frenkel, my editor, for his friendship, his wisdom, and his humor; Jim's terrific staff, especially Kristopher O'Higgins and Seth Johnson; Karen Lovell, Jennifer Hogan, Jim Minz, and all the other great people at Tor; my friends, Alan Goldberg and Chris Meeker, who, as always, read early drafts of this book; and my siblings, Bill, Liz, and Jim, and their families, who continue to give me the love and encouragement that have, for as long as I can remember, made our family so special.

As always, my deepest thanks are reserved for my wife, Nancy Berner, and our (now) two daughters, Alex and Erin. Nancy is my most astute critic, my best friend, and the source of my greatest inspiration. Without her love, her laughter, and her unwavering support, LonTobyn would still exist solely in my mind. Alex and Erin, on the other hand, are almost totally clueless as to what it is Daddy does for a living. But they seem to love me anyway, and for that, I am grateful beyond words.

—D.B.C.

Dhaalmar Shallows

the Boreal Stand

Dhaalmar Mts.

MOUNTSEA R.

Dhaalmar Spur

Three Fools Lakes

Oerellan Harbor

DEEP CANYON R.

VRULDAN R.

VRULDAN R. EAST FORK

Oerellan Peninsula

Oerella Nal

Lake of the Matrons

Point of the Sovereigns

Gold Inlet

Ari...

S...

GLACIER GAP R.

Oerellan Green

Bay of Storms

Lake of the Clouds

THREE NALS R.

Bragory Wood

Western Ocean

DARKWATER R.

Median Range

THE RIVER WANDERER

Gold Palace

Gu...

REIVDRAH R.

Bragor-Nal

Lake Merrie

BRAGORY R.

Gulf of Dalrek

VIHIR R.

Cape of Stars

Gulf of Dalrek

Einar's Fen

Greenwater Range

Guards Swam...

Stib

Grove

Stony Harbor

LITTLE GREENR.

Cape Lon

Stib-Nal

Gulf of the Gods

Stib Bay

Isthmus Point

Lon-Ser

Duc...

Abborij

Tobyn-Ser

Forests of Leora

Abborij Strait

Hawksfind Wood

Brisalli

Accalia

Taima

Greenbough

Dacias Lake

Amarid

Upper Horn

Northern Plains

Prannal

Tobyn's Wood

MOUNT R.

North Shelter

LITTLE R.

DHAALISMIN R.

River Haffe

PARNE HOME MTS.

PURFALL R.

LARIAN R.

Arick's Wrath

Seaside Mts.

Wadd's Mist Lake

South Shelter

Riversmeet Traverse

SAPPHIRE R.

Lastri

Emerald Hills

Phelan Spur

Lower Horn

Lake of the Dunes

Sern

Kaera

Sunfury Harbor

Great Desert

Watersbend

LonTobyn Isthmus

Tobyn's Plain

Southern Swamp

MORIANDRAL R.

TONG R.

Dacias' Tears

Riversend Harbor

Firegrass Lake

the Shadow Forest

Therons' Grove

Necklace

Gulf of Ceryllon

the Sawblade

Ceryl Cavern

Ceryllon

Southern Archipelago

Bragor-Nal

EAGLE-SAGE

1

Even with the establishment of commerce between our two lands, even with seven years having passed without additional conflicts, the people of my land remain deeply distrustful of Lon-Ser. They accept the goods you send, but only because these goods ease the burdens of their daily chores. They are curious about your land and eagerly seek knowledge about your customs and society. They even acknowledge that our languages are similar and that this implies a shared ancient history. Still, they remain convinced that war with Lon-Ser is not only possible but perhaps inevitable. Many of us in the Order have tried to convince them that this is not the case, that we have little to fear from you, but even the people who live in Order towns remain skeptical. More than ten years have passed since the outlanders burned our villages and killed our people, but the scars are still fresh.

> —Hawk-Mage Orris to Melyor i Lakin, Sovereign and Bearer of Bragor-Nal, Winter, God's Year 4633.

He is standing in a field he does not recognize, squinting up into a bright blue sky. Above him, two birds do battle, wheeling and stooping, talons outstretched and beaks open. They are enormous, and framed as they are against the sun and the blue, they appear almost utterly black.

For one terrifying instant he fears that the outlanders have returned. But the outlanders' birds would not fight each other, and both of these creatures are crying out stridently, something the mechanical hawks from Lon-Ser never did. So he watches, marveling at the size and grace of the winged combatants, though troubled at the sight of their slashing claws and beaks. Yet, even with his eyes riveted on the struggle taking place above him, he senses another presence in the clearing.

Tearing his gaze from the birds, he sees a woman standing on the far side of the field. She has straight brown hair and pale eyes, and there is something vaguely familiar about her. For a disorienting moment he wonders if this is his daughter, grown suddenly into a woman. But when he hears her laugh, malicious and bitter, he knows that this cannot be. He opens his mouth to ask her name, but before he can he hears a piercing wail from above.

The two birds are locked together now, their talons digging into each other's flesh and their wings beating desperately though in unison, as if even in the throes of battle they are working together to keep themselves aloft. But their efforts are in vain. Toppling one over the other, they fall to the ground, landing at his feet. They are dead, though whether from the impact or the damage they have inflicted on one another, it is impossible to tell. And seeing them at last, their carcasses bathed in the sunlight that had obscured their color and features just seconds before, he cries out in despair.

Jaryd awoke with a start and found himself immersed in darkness. He heard Alayna beside him, her breathing slow and deep, but otherwise all was still. Lying back against his pillow, he took a long, steadying breath and closed his eyes. He knew better than to try to go back to sleep. His heart was racing, and his hair was damp with sweat. He was awake for the day. He opened his eyes again and stared up toward the ceiling, although he could see nothing for the darkness.

"You up again?" Alayna asked him in a muffled, sleepy voice.

"Yes," he whispered. "Go back to sleep"

She said something in reply that he couldn't make out, and a moment later her breathing slowed again.

He couldn't remember the last time he had slept through the night. It wasn't that he slept poorly. For the first several hours, he slept like the dead. But every day for weeks on end he had awakened before dawn, sometimes spontaneously and other times, as today, out of a dream. At first he had taken his sleeplessness as a sign that something was coming; that perhaps, not too long from now, he would bind again, and end this interminable wait. But slowly, as each day passed without a new familiar appearing, he began to accept that there was nothing more to it than the obvious: he was just waking up too early.

Usually during these predawn hours he tried to clear his mind using the exercises he had first learned so many years ago, when he was a Mage-Attend to his uncle Baden. If he wasn't going to sleep, he reasoned, he might as well prepare himself for his next binding. But invariably, rather than quieting his emotions and taming the confused thoughts that came to him in the darkness, the exercises only served to heighten his feelings of loss.

His hawk, Ishalla, was gone. She had been since late summer. And though he had hoped that the agony of losing his first familiar would begin to abate with time, he was forced to admit that it hadn't. He had so much in his life: a cherished wife and daughter, a brother and mother to the north whom he loved, and friends throughout the land for whom he would gladly have given his life. He had served the communities on the western shores of Tobyn-Ser for nearly a dozen years, and in return he enjoyed the respect and affection of many of those who lived there. And yet, with all this, Ishalla's absence still left a void within him that he could scarcely fathom. Even the death of his father had not affected him so.

Time and again, he had watched people he loved, Baden, Trahn, Rodomil, cope with the loss of their familiars. Orris had lost two familiars in the time Jaryd had known him, both of them as a result of violence. The first, a large impressive hawk, had been killed at Theron's Grove by the great owl carried by the traitor, Sartol. And the second, a dark falcon, died just over three years ago during one of Orris's many battles with members of the League, who had decided long ago that the burly mage deserved to die for what they viewed as his betrayal of the land.

Most recently, Alayna had lost Fylimar, the great grey hawk who had looked so much like Jaryd's Ishalla, that many in the Order had said that in sending them such similar familiars, the gods had marked Jaryd and Alayna for each other. Like Ishalla, Fylimar had died a natural death, one she had earned after a life of service to the land. This, of course, had not softened the blow for Alayna, any more than it had for Jaryd. But Alayna found a new familiar quite soon after Fylimar's death.

And what a binding it had been. She had left their home early in the day, leaving Jaryd to care for Myn, their daughter, and when she returned late that afternoon, she bore on her shoulder a large, yellow-eyed owl with great ear tufts. It was the same kind of bird to which Sartol, her mentor, had been bound, and it occurred to both Jaryd and Alayna that the gods were offering her a chance at redemption. "Sartol failed the land," they seemed to be saying. "Go now and make right all that he made wrong."

The others had bound again as well. Indeed, Trahn's binding to an owl had come just a few days after the death of his hawk, prompting Orris to suggest that owls had actually been waiting in line to become

Trahn's familiar. Orris, too, had found his new familiar rather quickly. He was bound now to another falcon, this one larger than his last bird and as white as snow.

None of his friends had spent more than a season unbound. Yet here was Jaryd, still without a familiar after nearly half a year. Alayna assured him that, notwithstanding her experience or Trahn's, being unbound for long stretches was a normal part of being a mage. And Baden, who communicated with him periodically using the *Ceryll-Var*, reminded him during one merging that Owl-Sage Jessamyn, Myn's namesake, who had been leader of the Order when Jaryd received his cloak, had spent more than a year unbound.

Such reassurances helped, but only a little. Certainly he didn't begrudge the others their bindings. He was deeply proud of Alayna, who had become the youngest Owl-Master within memory. But he could not help but wonder if he was ever going to bind again, or if he was destined to die unbound and become yet another victim of Theron's Curse.

He had spoken with Phelan, the Wolf-Master. He had endured the terrors of Theron's Grove, and he now carried Theron's staff as his own. He had seen what it was to be unsettled, and the very idea of it filled him with a cold, penetrating dread. But after all this time without finding a new familiar, Jaryd was forced to acknowledge that this might be his fate, that the sense of foreboding that hovered at his shoulder all day, and followed him to bed at night, might carry the weight of prophecy.

After struggling with his fears privately for some time, he mentioned this possibility to Alayna, who reacted predictably.

"That's ridiculous," she told him. "We're all afraid of Theron's Curse. That's just part of being a mage. It certainly doesn't mean that you're fated to become one of the Unsettled."

He nodded silently, accepting the logic of what she said. But later that day he noticed her watching him, concern etched on her delicate features. And he knew what she was thinking. *He has been unbound for such a long time . . .*

Oddly, Jaryd found comfort not in anything Alayna or Baden said to him, but rather in a lesson he had learned long ago from his father. Jaryd had never been very close to his father, and the distance between them had only increased after Jaryd became a mage. But while Bernel had been brusque and taciturn, he also had possessed a pragmatic wisdom that had manifested itself late in his life in terse, pointed maxims that he offered without warning to anyone who cared to listen.

One of these Jaryd heard for the first time when he took Alayna and Myn to Accalia so that his mother and father could meet their granddaughter for the first time. During the journey, Myn slept poorly, often refusing to nurse, and Jaryd and Alayna worried that something might be wrong with her.

"Worrying's a fine way to waste some time," Bernel finally said, after listening to them fret for an entire afternoon, "but it sure doesn't accomplish very much, except to annoy the rest of us."

Alayna had taken offense, prompting Drina to scold her husband for the balance of the day. But lying now in his bed, watching the room he and Alayna shared brighten slowly with the first grey glimmerings of daylight, Jaryd could only smile at the memory.

He glanced over at Alayna, who was still asleep. Her long dark hair was streaked with strands of silver, and her face was leaner than it had been when they first met eleven years ago. But the passage of the years had not diminished her beauty.

I can worry about becoming one of the Unsettled, Jaryd told himself. *Or I can enjoy what the gods have given me until they decide that I'm ready for my next binding.*

He smiled in the silver light. It didn't strike him as a difficult choice.

He leaned over and kissed Alayna lightly on her forehead. Then he lightly slipped out of bed, dressed, and wrapped his green cloak tightly around himself. Spring was approaching, but there was still a chill in the air.

He started toward the common room, intending to light a fire in the hearth, but as he walked past Myn's room he glanced inside and saw his daughter sitting beside her small window, bundled in a thick blanket, and reading a worn book of Cearbhall's fables.

"Good morning, Love," Jaryd said in a whisper.

She looked up from the book and smiled at him. With her long chestnut hair, perfect features, and dazzling smile she was the image of Alayna. All except her eyes, which were pale grey, just like Jaryd's and those of his own mother.

"Good morning, Papa!" she said.

Jaryd held a finger to his lips and pointed back toward his bedroom. Myn covered her mouth, her eyes wide.

"What are you doing up so early?" he asked her quietly.

"I always wake up when you do," she whispered.

"How do you know when I wake up?"

She shrugged. "I don't know. I just do."

Jaryd gazed at her for several seconds, then nodded. That she showed signs of having the Sight, already, at the age of six, did not surprise them. Both he and Alayna had understood from the beginning that their child would not be ordinary. But she was attuned to both of her parents in strange and wondrous ways, some of them remarkably subtle and completely unexpected.

Jaryd stood in her doorway for another moment, watching her and grinning. She just looked back at him, saying nothing.

"I was going to make a fire and have some breakfast," he finally told her. "Are you hungry?"

She nodded, put the book on her bed, and, keeping the blanket around her shoulders as if it were an overly large cloak, followed him into the common room.

After lighting the fire, Jaryd cut two large pieces of the dark currant bread he had made the day before and covered them with sweet butter. They sat in the kitchen, and as they ate, Myn told him about the fable she had been working her way through when he found her. She was just learning to read, and Cearbhall's work was not the easiest to figure out. The fable she had been reading, however, was one of his favorites, *The Fox and the Skunk*, and he had read it to her many times when she was younger.

"It was smart of you to start with one you know already," he said, still speaking in a whisper.

She smiled, her mouth full of bread. "Mama picked it out."

Jaryd laughed. "Well, then it was smart of her."

He got up to cut some more bread, and as he did he heard the rustling of blankets in the other room.

"I think your mother's awake."

"She has been for a little while," Myn said. "I think she was listening to us."

Jaryd turned to look at her again.

"How did you know that, Myn-Myn?" Alayna asked, appearing in the kitchen doorway with Wyrinva, her great owl, sitting on her shoulder.

Myn looked at her mother and then at Jaryd, a shy smile on her lips. "I just know," she said, seeming embarrassed. "I can feel it when you're awake. Both of you."

Alayna glanced up at Jaryd and grinned.

"Is it bad that I can tell?"

"Not at all," Jaryd said.

"Does it mean I'm going to be a mage?"

Jaryd suppressed a laugh.

"I'd be very surprised if you weren't a mage," Alayna said, her eyes still on Jaryd. "And so would everyone else in Tobyn-Ser."

This time Jaryd couldn't help but laugh out loud. Since before she could walk, Orris and Baden had been saying that she was destined to be Owl-Sage, and though Jaryd and Alayna were determined to let Myn find her own path, neither of them doubted that she would bind someday, probably to Amarid's Hawk, just as they both had. The question was: would she join the Order or the League? Indeed, Jaryd could not even be certain that both would still exist by the time Myn was ready to choose. He shook his head. It was not a line of thought he cared to pursue just then.

"Good," Myn said. "I want to be a mage. I like going to Amarid."

"I'm glad you like going there," Alayna said, crossing to the bread and picking up the knife to cut herself a piece. "We like it, too."

"That's why I'm happy today."

Alayna turned to look at Myn, the knife poised over the loaf. "What do you mean, Myn-Myn?"

"I'm happy because we're going to Amarid soon."

"No, we're not, Love," Jaryd said gently. "It's still winter. The Gathering isn't until summer."

Myn smiled at him as if he were a child. "I know that. We're going anyway."

Alayna walked to where the girl was sitting. She squatted down and looked Myn in the eye. "What makes you think we're going to Amarid, Myn?"

"I saw us going there in a dream."

Alayna's eyes flicked to Jaryd for an instant, and then she forced a smile. "There are different kinds of dreams, Myn-Myn. Your Papa and I have explained—"

"It was a real dream, Mama," Myn said earnestly. "I promise."

Jaryd took a deep breath. Myn's Sight had grown stronger over the past year. He and Alayna had learned to trust her visions almost as fully they trusted their own. He had no idea why they would need to undertake the journey to Amarid so suddenly, but neither did he truly doubt that they would. "How soon, Love?" he asked her. "When do you think we'll be going?"

Myn looked at him and wrinkled her forehead in concentration "Tomorrow, I think," she finally said. "Maybe the day after"

He faced Alayna again and saw his own concern mirrored in her expression. What had happened? What would lead Owl-Sage Radomil to summon the mages of the Order to Amarid for a Gathering? Had something happened to Radomil himself? Had he fallen ill or died? Jaryd looked at his staff, which was leaning against the wall near the door of their small home. The sapphire stone mounted atop the ancient charred wood still glowed steadily. Neither Radomil nor First of the Sage Mered had awakened the Summoning Stone yet. If one of them had, Jaryd's stone, as well as that of every other mage in Tobyn-Ser, would have been flashing by now.

"We've still got some time," Alayna said, as if reading his thoughts. "We should probably let Narelle know."

Jaryd nodded. Narelle was the leader of the town council in Lastri, the nearest of the villages located along the shores of South Shelter. Or rather, the nearest of those villages that remained loyal to the Order rather than the League. Narelle needed to know that Jaryd and Alayna would be departing for Amarid, leaving Lastri and the other villages without their services for some time.

"I'll go and tell her," Jaryd said. "And I'll also get us some food. You and Myn can start closing up the house."

Alayna sighed. "All right," she said. "This is the last thing I was expecting."

"I know. Me too."

"I'm sorry," Myn said, her voice quavering slightly.

Jaryd and Alayna both looked at her.

"For what, Love?" Jaryd asked.

Myn shrugged, refusing to look up. A single tear fell off her cheek and darkened the table.

Alayna placed a hand on her shoulder and bent to kiss her forehead. "It's not your fault that we have to go, Myn. Just because you have a vision, that doesn't mean you make it happen. We've told you that before. Remember?"

"Yes," the girl said softly, wiping another tear from her face.

"So we don't blame you. In fact, it's better that we know now, so we can get ready and warn the people in town."

Myn looked up. "Really?"

Alayna nodded and cupped Myn's cheek in her hand. "Really. Now go get dressed and wash up, and then we'll get to work."

"All right, Mama," Myn said. She stood, pulling her blanket around her shoulders once more, then returned to her bedroom.

"You don't have any doubts, do you?" Alayna asked Jaryd, staring after their daughter.

Jaryd shook his head. "No. A year ago I might have, but every vision she's had since last spring has been true. I don't see any reason to start doubting her now."

Alayna passed a hand through her hair. "Neither do I."

He let out a sigh. "I guess I'll go put a saddle on one of the horses."

"You can't," she said, grimacing "I promised Myn I'd start teaching her to ride today."

"This isn't the best time, Alayna."

"I know, but I've been promising her since midwinter. And now that we're going to Amarid, who knows when I'll have another chance?"

"She'll be riding every day for the next fortnight," Jaryd said.

"But with one of us sitting behind her. You know that's not the same."

He stared at her for several moments, shaking his head. The sunlight shining through a small window behind him made her eyes sparkle. Brown and green they were, like a forest in midsummer.

"Do you know how beautiful you are?" he said, smiling and kissing her lightly on the lips.

She gave a wry grin. "Does that mean you'll walk to the village?"

"What choice do I have?" he answered, laughing.

"Then you'd better get going. We have a lot to do today."

She pushed him toward the door, but not before letting him kiss her again.

He put on his leather shoes, which had been sitting on the floor beside the door, and stepped out into the cold morning air. A light westerly wind stirred his cloak and hair, carrying the familiar scents of brine and seaweed. A few featherlike clouds floated overhead, but otherwise the sky was nearly as blue as his ceryll. In winters past, on a morning like this one, he might have taken Ishalla to the water's edge and watched her fly or hunt.

He shook his head. "You're not doing yourself any good," he said aloud. He let out a long breath and started toward town.

The walk to Lastri usually took him nearly an hour. Once it had been a pleasant journey along a narrow trail that wound among towering forests of oaks, maples, ashes, and elms. Occasionally, the path angled toward the coast and the woods thinned, allowing a traveler to catch glimpses of Arick's Sea pounding endlessly at the rocky shoreline below.

Over the past few years, however, the trail had changed, as had everything else in Tobyn-Ser. Vast stretches of the magnificent forest had been cut down so that the wood could be shipped to Lon-Ser, or in some cases, Abborij. Where the trees had been there was now little more than bare patches of exposed rock and dirt. Only the mangled roots and stumps left behind by the woodsmen gave any indication of what once had stood there. The trail had been widened and straightened into a broad, rutted road, so that the timber could be hauled to town in large carts drawn by teams of horses. And Lastri itself had become heavily dependent upon the wood trade. From all that Jaryd and Alayna had heard, Lastri was one of the largest wood ports in Tobyn-Ser. Many of its people had grown wealthy as a result, and it was hard to find a single family in the town that did not prosper in some way from the cutting of the forests. So whenever he visited the town, Jaryd tried to mask his distaste for what had been done to the landscape.

Not all the trees were gone. There were still sections of the journey that remained just as Jaryd remembered them, except for the road itself, which was wide and relatively straight all the way to town. But the areas of forest seemed smaller each time Jaryd saw them, and recently he had realized that there were now more stumps to be seen along the way than there were trees.

Indeed, he had last made the journey only a fortnight ago, and yet on this day, as he walked to Lastri wondering what crisis would compel them to Amarid, Jaryd could see that there had been even more cutting done during the interval. It was frightening how quickly the trees were disappearing.

His one consolation was that there were no woodsmen at work as he made his way to town. Not that they had ever treated Jaryd or Alayna with anything but courtesy and respect. In fact, several of them now greeted Myn by name when she made the journey with one of her parents. But they seemed to know how Jaryd and Alayna felt about the work they did, and they regarded the mages with suspicion.

More than that, the woodsmen had been hired by the Keepers of Arick's Temple, who now owned much of the land on either side of the path and who had profited more than any other group from Tobyn-Ser's recent forays into transisthmus commerce. Everyone in Tobyn-Ser was aware of the hostility that had existed since the time of Amarid between the Keepers and the Order. The emergence of the League and, more recently, of a growing number of so-called free mages, had done nothing to lessen this animosity, and it seemed to Jaryd that the Temples' commercial ventures had actually deepened it. Even if the woodsmen understood nothing of the issues that had divided the Children of Amarid and the Children of the Gods for a thousand years, they must have sensed that by working for the Temples they had made themselves parties to the feud.

Or perhaps Jaryd was merely imagining it all. Perhaps the woodsmen were just uncomfortable around the mages because, like so many of Tobyn-Ser's people, they were awed and a bit frightened by the power he and Alayna wielded. Or perhaps they supported the League rather than the Order. In a way it didn't matter. Whatever the reason, Jaryd was just as happy to find himself alone on the road. It gave him time to think.

The Summoning Stone hadn't been used in some time, not since the death of Sonel's owl necessitated the election of a new Owl-Sage nearly four years ago. Before then, it hadn't been used since just before the sundering of the Order, when Owl-Master Erland demanded that Sonel convene a Gathering so that he could accuse Orris, Baden, and others of treason.

Even before Erland and his followers formed the League, use of the Summoning Stone was limited to dire emergencies. But with the Mage-Craft divided, use of the stone all but ceased. For in altering the giant crystal and tuning it to the cerylls of every mage in the land, Amarid and Theron had not allowed for the possibility that the Order might someday be challenged by a rival. While the mages of Tobyn-Ser were divided by personal resentments and profound differences over matters of conduct, they were still united by the stone. And each time the great ceryll was used to call together what remained of the Order, every free mage and every member of the League saw his or her ceryll flash as well.

Which meant that whatever it was that would cause Radomil or Mered to convene the coming Gathering would have to be grave indeed.

Driven by the thought, Jaryd glanced at his stone again. Nothing yet. But turning his gaze back to the path, he spotted something out of the corner of his eye that made him freeze in the middle of his stride.

He was in an open area, where the trees had long since been cut and hauled off to Lastri. One of the few remaining forested sections loomed before him. And just beside the path, only a few feet in front of this next stand of trees, an enormous dark bird sat on a scarred stump. Its feathers were rich brown, save for those on the back of its neck, which shone in the bright sunlight as if they were made of gold. Its dark eyes regarded Jaryd with an unnatural intelligence that made the mage shiver. It almost seemed to him that the bird had been waiting for him, that it had known he would be coming.

He knew, of course, what it meant, what the gods and this bird expected of him. And he shook his head.

More than anything in the world he wanted to be bound again. But even this longing had its limits. He didn't want a familiar this badly.

"I don't want this," he said, his voice sounding small.

The great creature stared at him impassively.

Jaryd turned away. He wanted to run, to turn his back on this gift from the gods, if such a binding could even be considered a gift. *What would happen if I were to refuse a binding?* he wondered briefly. *Would the gods ever favor me with a familiar again?* He shook his head. Probably not. Because in this case, refusing the binding meant far more than defying the gods. It meant breaking his oath to serve Tobyn-Ser and its people.

The gods had sent him an eagle. And though his blood ran cold at what that meant, Jaryd knew that he had no choice but to accept this binding and all that came with it.

He took a long, steadying breath, readying himself for the onslaught of images and emotions he knew would come as soon as he met the eagle's gaze again.

I've been through this before, he told himself, remembering his binding to Ishalla. *I know that I can do it.*

He took another breath, then faced the great bird once more.

Their eyes met. Jaryd had time to remark to himself that this was the most magnificent bird he had ever seen. And then it hit him.

For any ordinary binding, his experience with his first familiar might have been ample preparation. But this was an eagle, and, Jaryd realized in that final instant of clarity, there would be nothing ordinary about their time together. It was his last rational thought for some time.

Visions and memories suddenly coursed through him like the flood-waters of the Dhaalismin: hunting along the crest of the Seaside Range; flipping over in mid-flight to ward off the attack of two smaller hawks; swooping and diving with another, smaller eagle in what he recognized instinctively as a courtship flight; pouncing on a rabbit, digging his talons into its soft fur and flesh, killing it with a quick slash of his razor beak.

He reached for the eagle, feeling her presence in his mind and remembering that he had done this with Ishalla. But the bird resisted him, as if she were not ready to accept him yet. *There is more,* she seemed to be telling him. *It is not yet time.*

The images continued to cascade through him so swiftly that he barely had time to make sense of them. The next one seemed to begin before the last was done. He saw the eagle's parents, its siblings, all the creatures it had ever killed, all the rivals it had ever fought off. He saw its one mate, and he saw that bird die with a hunter's arrow in its breast. He saw the eagle's entire life pass before him in a spiraling procession of memory, thought, and emotion. Yet, dizzying and bewildering as this was, he had expected it. The pattern was familiar in a way. He had shared his consciousness with a bird before. And so he resisted the overwhelming urge to fight against this tide of thought. Instead he allowed the eagle's consciousness to carry him where it might.

But despite his experience, despite his attempts to heed the lessons he had learned from his first binding, what came next shocked him, humbled him, frightened him. Abruptly, he wasn't an eagle anymore. Or rather, he wasn't *this* eagle anymore.

He was circling above a tall, powerfully built mage to whom he was bound. And as he watched, two armies approached each other under a hazy sky. One army flew the flag of ancient Abborij. The other was led by a phalanx of mages. In the distance, beyond the warriors, he could see the waters of the Abborij Strait, and he knew that he was on Tobyn-Ser's Northern Plain, watching the first war with Abborij. The armies came together amid shouts of death and fear, and almost immediately the Abboriji army fell back, their weapons shattered by magic.

An instant later, he was bound to a different mage, this one a woman, tall and hale like the man who came before her. Her silver hair flew in a stiff, cold wind, and the cerylls of her fellow mages glittered in the bright winter sun. Again an army approached across the plain, a larger force this time. It marched under a flag different from the first, but still recognizable as a banner of Abborij. And once more the soldiers of Abborij were no match for the mages of Tobyn-Ser.

A third mage, this one also a woman. She was young and small of stature, though no less fierce than her predecessors in her defense of the land. The army approaching her through a fine grey mist was larger than the first two combined, and the magic of the mages she commanded took far longer to prevail. But prevail it did. He saw the people of Tobyn-Ser rejoicing in their victory even as they wept for the dead. He saw Glenyse hoisted onto the shoulders of an enormous, bearded man who wielded an ax and bore welts and bloody gashes on his forehead and arms. This man walked with the mages and held a ceryll, but he carried no familiar on his shoulder. And in the remote corner of his mind that was still his own, Jaryd recognized this man as Phelan, the Wolf-Master, who had lost Kalba, his one familiar, just before the third Abboriji invasion, and who had vowed never to bind again.

Other images washed over him. Lifetime after lifetime after lifetime. It almost seemed that he was binding not to one bird, but to many, each carrying its own memories and those of the mage it had loved. He saw scenes from the lives of the three Eagle-Sages who had come before flashing through his mind so swiftly that he had no time to interpret them, no time even to divine from whose life they had come. He kept waiting for a pattern to emerge, for the flood of images to begin again, as it had during his binding to Ishalla. But there was no ending here; there was nothing to grasp. Yes, he had been through a binding before. But nothing could have prepared him for this. He was being carried away by the deluge. He was drowning.

And in that moment, when at last he saw a familiar image and sensed that a pattern had finally emerged, that there was an ending after all, he was very nearly too exhausted to assert his own consciousness again.

Jaryd felt the eagle touch his mind once more, nudging him as if to awaken him from slumber. This time, when Jaryd opened himself to her, offering her his memories and emotions as she had done for him, she accepted. Once more, he saw her flying, hunting, fighting, but this time his own life was interwoven with hers. The images of the Abboriji wars did not return, and seeing the images of her life again, Jaryd understood why. They had not truly been her memories to give. This was not the same eagle who had bound to Fordel, Decla, and Glenyse, the three Eagle-Sages. But somehow, this eagle—*his* eagle, who now named herself to him as Rithlar— carried those memories within her. It was impossible. The wars had taken place hundreds of years ago. But Jaryd knew what he had seen.

Rithlar seemed to sense his doubts, for a moment later he saw the armies again, and the sequence of events repeated itself in his mind, exactly as it had a short time before. Then he understood.

"This is how it was given to you," he said aloud.

His voice appeared to break the spell woven by their binding. Suddenly he was standing in the clearing again. It was over. He felt the eagle's presence in his mind, and he knew that they were bound to each other.

Jaryd continued to gaze at the bird, who still had not moved from her perch beside the road. He felt awkward in a way. The instant he bound to Ishalla, he loved her as he had no other person or creature. Even his love for Alayna, powerful as it was, did not exceed his feelings for his first hawk.

But he knew already that he and Rithlar would have a different kind of relationship. She was an eagle, and because she had chosen him, he would be the fourth Eagle-Sage in the history of the land. The gods had brought them together for one reason: Tobyn-Ser was destined for war. Soon. Theirs was not to be a binding based upon love or even friendship, although in time it might come to be characterized by those things. Theirs was a bond born of necessity and forged by their devotion to the land. He wondered briefly, if it might have been otherwise had he not at first resisted the binding, but he sensed no resentment in the bird's thoughts. Only a reserved pride and the same preternatural intelligence he had seen in her eyes when he first encountered her. Had it been this way for Glenyse and the others?

Thinking this, he began to tremble. *I am an Eagle-Sage*, he told himself. *I'm going to lead Tobyn-Ser into a war*. But against whom? There had been no new conflicts with the outlanders since Orris returned from Lon-Ser over six years ago. Certainly Abborij posed no threat—Tobyn-Ser had been at peace with its northern neighbor for more than four centuries.

"At least now I know why we have to go to Amarid," he said grimly.

That of all things caused the great bird to stir. She opened her wings and let out a soft cry. Jaryd walked to where she was sitting and held out his arm for her. Immediately she hopped to it, and Jaryd gasped with pain. Not only were her talons considerably larger than Ishalla's and just as sharp, she also weighed far more than his first familiar. Her claws stabbed through the skin of his forearms like daggers. He quickly conveyed to her that she should move to his shoulder, where his cloak was reinforced with leather. Even this did not help much, however. The padding on his shoulder was as effective as parchment against those talons.

"We're going to have to do something about that," Jaryd said, wincing as he resumed his journey to Lastri. After only a few steps though, Jaryd realized that he could not carry Rithlar the way he had Ishalla. The eagle was simply too large and heavy. Every step he took caused her to grip his shoulder, and he could feel his shirt and cloak becoming soaked with blood.

I'm sorry, he sent, *but you'll have to fly*.

She sent an image of herself gliding above him as he walked to show that she understood, and Jaryd braced himself, knowing that when she leaped off his shoulder, her claws would gouge him again. Instead, however, she hopped down to the ground and then took off with great, slow, sweeping wing beats. And as Jaryd started to walk again, entering one of the few remaining wooded sections of the road, Rithlar soared overhead, just above the tops of the bare trees.

In flight she appeared even more enormous than she did when she was sitting. The combined length of her wings easily exceeded Jaryd's height, and he was by no means a small man. When the mage stepped back into an open area, she swooped down low and circled just above him, and he marveled that so great a creature could move with such grace.

It was not the binding he had expected or hoped for. In truth the implications of the eagle's appearance terrified him. But Jaryd could not help but smile as he watched her fly. It had been so long since he had shared his thoughts with a familiar, or felt the enhanced awareness of his surroundings that came with being bound. For the first time in longer than he could remember, he felt like a mage again.

2

Your concern for my safety is appreciated but unnecessary—and you can tell Jibb that I'm not yet ready to resort to employing a bodyguard. This is not to say that the conflicts between the Order and the League have ceased or that I am any less a target of the League's enmity. Quite the contrary: the mages of Tobyn-Ser remain hopelessly divided, and I still spend much of my time looking over my shoulder for would-be attackers.

In a sense, though, I am resigned to this. It strikes me as a fitting punishment for my defiance of the Order's will. The land has suffered greatly as a result of my actions; that I should suffer too, seems just. Don't be alarmed: I have no intention of allowing myself to be killed. My guilt does not run that deep. But just as the gods appear to have ordained that I shall never bind to an owl, the League has determined that I shall never know peace. And I am prepared to accept both decrees.

—Hawk-Mage Orris to Melyor i Lakin, Sovereign and Bearer of Bragor-Nal, Winter, God's Year 4633.

By the time Jaryd and his eagle reached Lastri it was past midday. Jaryd gathered food as quickly as he could and then went in search of Narelle, the leader of the town council. He found her by the piers arguing with an Abboriji sea merchant.

Narelle was a stout woman, with steel grey hair and overlarge features. She had a deep, powerful voice, and pale blue eyes that flashed angrily as she spoke to the merchant.

"If you unload your cargo, you pay the town docking fees!" she told the man, as Jaryd approached. "If you don't wish to pay the fees, that's fine! You can take your ship and everything on it somewhere else!"

The man shook his head. "But as I told you, I have no choice but to unload here. My client—"

"And as I've told you," Narelle said, "that is not my concern! If you use Lastri's piers, you pay Lastri's fees."

She turned away, effectively ending their discussion, and almost bumped into Jaryd.

"Hawk-Mage!" she said pleasantly. "How nice to see you!"

Jaryd had to fight to keep from laughing. He had seen Narelle do this before: she could be unyielding and hostile one moment, and effusive and charming the next. As far as he could tell, neither was done for effect; it was just her way.

"It's good to see you as well, Narelle," Jaryd replied. "Better for me, it would seem, than for that merchant."

She laughed and waved her hand, as if she could dismiss the matter of the docking fees with the gesture. "That was nothing," she said. "I must have the same conversation five times a day." She started to walk back toward the town square, indicating to Jaryd that he should follow. "Everyone wants to do business here, but only on their terms. They don't understand that I have a town to run. Those new piers didn't just emerge from the sea. We built them, and it cost us a good deal of gold to do so. But these merchants don't seem to understand that. As far as they're concerned, we owed them the piers."

Jaryd smiled, remembering the first time he saw this town, soon after he and Alayna arrived on the shores of South Shelter a decade ago. At that time, the entire town had consisted of one street and two or three storefronts, and the villagers had stowed their fishing boats on a sandy beach because there were no docks at all. Commerce had been limited to whatever Lastri's people could get for the fish they caught and the baskets they wove.

"I know what you're thinking," Narelle said, looking at him sidelong. "But even if we weren't sending timber to Lon-Ser, we still would have needed the docks."

"Actually," Jaryd told her, "I was just thinking back to my first visit to your town."

"Ah," she said, nodding. "I think of that now and then, too. There wasn't much to see back then, was there?"

Jaryd forced a smile, but said nothing, and they continued in silence for several strides.

"You have blood on your cloak!" Narelle said with alarm, stopping suddenly and pointing to Jaryd's sleeve. "Are you all right?"

"I'm fine. I have a new familiar, and she has quite a powerful grip." He glanced up at Rithlar, who was circling above them.

Following his gaze, Narelle gave a small gasp. "She's beautiful, Hawk-Mage! I've never seen a hawk so large!"

He didn't bother to correct her. No doubt she was familiar enough with the history of Tobyn-Ser to know what the appearance of an eagle meant, and he didn't wish to frighten her.

She looked at Jaryd again. "So how can I help you, Hawk-Mage? You must have come to see me for a reason." She glanced at the sack of food he was carrying and frowned slightly. "This is not good," she said. "Whenever I see you with provisions it means my people will be doing without your services for some time."

Jaryd laughed. "I'm afraid you're right. Alayna and I will be leaving for Amarid in the morning. I'm not certain how long we'll be gone." He thought about saying more, but again he thought better of it. He and Alayna would not be back for some time. He was to be Eagle-Sage, which meant that they would be living in the Great Hall until whatever crisis awaited them had passed. But he couldn't tell her that either. He looked around at the town, noting the faded green flags that flew above the doorways of every home and building. This was an Order town largely because he and Alayna lived nearby. Even with the anti-Order sentiment fomented by Erland and his allies when they formed the League, the people of Lastri had remained loyal to the Order because they knew and trusted the young mages who lived just outside of town. But Jaryd wondered now whether that loyalty would survive their departure and the arrival of a new mage in the area.

"Is everything all right, Hawk-Mage?" Narelle asked. "You look troubled."

"Everything's fine, Narelle," he said, his assurances sounding hollow to his own ears. "I just wanted to let you know that we'd be going."

She frowned again, furrowing her brow. "Well, do you know why you're needed in Amarid?"

"No," he said, although he could not keep his gaze from wandering up to Rithlar. "I have no idea."

He thought he was lying to her. It was only later, as he walked back through the forest, that he realized how much truth there had been in his answer. Even knowing the land was destined for war, he had no sense of why this should be so or who their enemy would be.

He arrived back home just as the sun was disappearing behind the Lower Horn on the far side of South Shelter. Stopping by the front door, he waited for Rithlar to settle to the ground beside him. He squatted and stroked the feathers on her chin.

You are the most glorious creature I've ever seen, he sent. *I don't know why you've come, or why you chose me, but I'm sorry I refused you at first. And I promise that no matter what it is that brought you here, we'll face it together.* By way of reply, she nuzzled him gently with her huge hooked bill. In spite of everything, Jaryd laughed. Perhaps he could love her after all. He stood, opened the door, and stepped inside, motioning for Rithlar to follow him.

Three saddlebags sat near the door in the common room. Two of them had been filled and strapped shut. The last, obviously intended for the food, was still open and was empty save for some rope, a few eating utensils, and some of Myn's favorite playthings.

Jaryd heard Alayna and Myn laughing from one of the back rooms.

"I'm back," he called.

"We're in Myn's room," Alayna answered. "What took you so long?"

He looked at Rithlar, who had been surveying her surroundings with a critical eye. Now she bounded into the kitchen, hopped onto a chair, and jumped from there onto the table.

"Come out and take a look," Jaryd said, following the eagle into the kitchen. "I think I've figured out why we're going to Amarid."

"How could you have?" Alayna called back. "Radomil hasn't even figured it out yet." She appeared in the doorway with Myn behind her. "Our cerylls still aren't—"

She froze, her eyes widening as the color drained from her cheeks. "By the gods!" she whispered.

Myn stepped past her and walked right to the edge of the table, staring at the great bird. Rithlar gazed back at the child, her head tilted to the side slightly, and they remained that way for several moments, neither of them looking away.

"What is it, Papa?" the girl asked.

"It's an eagle, Love. Her name is Rithlar."

"That's a funny name."

"Actually," Alayna said quietly before Jaryd could respond, "it's the name of every eagle that has ever bound to a mage."

Jaryd looked at her sharply. "Are you sure?"

She nodded.

"I guess I shouldn't be surprised," he said, facing his familiar again. "She carries their memories. I saw the Abboriji invasions during our binding."

Alayna pushed her hair back from her forehead with a rigid hand. "You have to contact Radomil," she told him. She looked pale, and her voice sounded tight. "He has to summon the others."

"I know."

"Did you see Narelle?"

"Yes."

"And had you already been bound?"

"Yes, but don't worry. Narelle just thought I'd found a really big hawk."

Alayna gave a small laugh, although she grew serious again almost immediately. "An eagle, Jaryd," she said, shaking her head in disbelief. "Do you know what that means?"

"What does it mean, Mama?"

Alayna glanced quickly at Jaryd and then looked down at Myn, making herself smile. "Well, Myn-Myn, it means that . . ." She trailed off, her eyes meeting Jaryd's again.

"It means," Jaryd said, "that I'm going to be the new leader of the Order, so we'll be living at the Great Hall for a while."

Myn stared at him in amazement. "You're going to be Owl-Sage?"

"In a sense, yes," Jaryd told her. "But I'll be called Eagle-Sage. And since we'll be living in Amarid, and we won't be back here for a long time, I want you to go check your room to see if there's anything else you want to bring with us. All right?"

"All right, Papa," she answered, already running to the back of the house.

"Thanks," Alayna murmured, staring after her.

"We'll have to tell her eventually," Jaryd said. "She's going to figure it out when she sees the way other people react."

Alayna faced him again and nodded. "I know." She stepped forward and wrapped her arms around him, resting her head on his shoulder. "Are you scared?"

"Yes, but not as much as I was this morning."

"At least you've bound again."

She pulled back and gave him a wry look, which he returned. Again, though, her smile faded quickly.

"I don't envy you," she said.

"It's not just me," he replied. "You're going to be First of the Sage."

She put her head on his shoulder again. "Wouldn't you rather have Orris?"

He kissed the top of her head. "Orris's hair isn't as soft as yours."

"How do you know?" she demanded, feigning jealousy.

Jaryd grinned.

"I think I'll check on Myn," Alayna said. "She's probably trying to pack her bed."

Jaryd nodded, taking a long breath. "I'll contact Radomil."

He stepped outside again with Rithlar following close behind. It was almost dark. Only the western horizon was still tinged with yellow and orange, and several stars had already emerged in the deep indigo overhead. Jaryd's breath hung before him in clouds of steam, and he shivered slightly in the cold, still air.

He had not attempted to use the Mage-Craft since Ishalla's death, and faced now with the prospect of attempting the *Ceryll-Var*, one of the most complicated and draining tasks any mage could undertake, he felt unsure of himself.

"I haven't done this in a while," he said to the eagle.

She merely stared at him.

He sat on the ground beside her and, closing his eyes, reached for the connection they had forged that morning. He felt her presence instantly, and as he began to send his consciousness eastward toward Amarid, where Radomil now lived, he felt power flowing through him like the icy waters of a mountain stream. The sensation was both familiar and alien, for while Ishalla's power had also run cool and swift through his body, his first hawk had never been this strong. Within seconds Jaryd had found Radomil's ivory ceryll in the vast blackness in which one traveled for the stone merging. He projected his own sapphire into the Owl-Sage's stone and then waited for Radomil to reach back. The entire process had been nearly effortless.

Jaryd? Radomil sent.

Yes, Owl-Sage. I'm here.

This is a surprise. I didn't know you had bound again. Congratulations.

Thank you, Owl-Sage. Jaryd couldn't help but smile. He had known Radomil since his childhood. The rotund Owl-Master had once served Leora's Forest in northwestern Tobyn-Ser, where Jaryd's home village of Accalia was located. And even now, after the two of them had served in the Order together for a dozen years, Jaryd still sensed an almost fatherly pride in Radomil's thoughts as the Owl-Sage congratulated him on his binding.

Have you bound to an owl? Mered and I have assumed since Alayna's binding that you would.

Jaryd sighed. This was not going to be easy.

No, Owl-Sage, it wasn't an owl.

Jaryd sensed Radomil's embarrassment. *I'm sorry, Jaryd. I didn't mean to presume . . .*

Please, don't apologize, Jaryd sent. There was no way to cushion it. *I've bound to an eagle, Owl-Sage. That's why I've contacted you. I thought you should know.*

The Sage offered no response for some time. Indeed, had not Jaryd still felt the Sage's shock and fear, he might have thought that their connection had been broken.

Arick guard us all, the Owl-Sage finally sent. *Have you told Baden yet?*

No. Aside from Alayna, you're the only one who knows. I assumed you'd want to convene a Gathering to inform the others and decide what we should do next.

What I want is irrelevant. You lead the Order now.

Jaryd sensed no bitterness in Radomil's thoughts, no anger at having his rule ended so abruptly. He was merely acknowledging what both of them knew to be true.

Would you like me to use the Summoning Stone, Eagle-Sage?

Eagle-Sage. Jaryd felt his mouth go dry. He wasn't ready for this.

Jaryd?

Yes, he sent at last. *Yes, I guess I would.*

Very well. If you'd like, Mered and I will remain in the Great Hall until you and Alayna arrive—I assume Alayna will be your First.

That will be fine. Thank you, Radomil. Jaryd felt himself growing light-headed. Perhaps it was the strain of using the Mage-Craft for the first time in so long. Or perhaps it was the realization of what he had become. It was hard to tell just then. But he felt his connection with Radomil growing weaker.

I don't want anyone to know yet, Radomil, he sent, desperately trying to keep his thoughts coherent. *Only you and the First. And Baden, but I'll tell him myself. I don't want to cause any panic. If anyone asks, just tell them I've requested a Gathering.*

I understand, Radomil replied, his thoughts seeming increasingly distant with each moment. *Arick guard you on your journey, Eagle-Sage. And may he bring you to us quickly.*

An instant later, Radomil was gone. Jaryd opened his eyes to a starry sky that appeared to spin like a child's top. He sensed no fatigue from Rithlar, nor had her power wavered even for an instant during his exchange with the Owl-Sage. But he was exhausted from channeling the magic she gave him. And not for the first time that day, he wondered why the gods had chosen him for this binding.

"There must be others who are better prepared for this," he said to the darkness. "There must be others who are stronger and wiser."

Rithlar nuzzled him, again, as she had earlier in the evening. *I've chosen you,* she seemed to be telling him. *For better or worse. I've chosen you.*

Jaryd stroked her chin, and then gazed up at the stars again. The dizziness was beginning to pass, and he could see the constellation of Arick overhead, his hand raised to smite the land.

"There is a war coming," Jaryd whispered, feeling cold and terribly young. "And I am to be the fist of the gods."

He was a migrant. He always had been, and he had no doubt that he would remain one for the rest of his life. The way of the nester had never appealed to him. The very idea of it made him restless. He had only known two women in his life who, given the chance, might have convinced him to settle in one place and make a home. One of them was now the wife of his best friend, and the other lived hundreds of leagues away, on the far side of Arick's Sea, in a land so alien that even the stars looked different in the night sky.

Every mage in the land knew that Alayna and Jaryd belonged together. The gods had made that clear by sending them identical birds for their first bindings. And Orris would never have begrudged his closest friends their happiness, particularly not after the birth of their beautiful daughter.

As for Melyor, who now ruled Bragor-Nal as Lon-Ser's first Gildriite Sovereign, Orris was too wise a man to pine for her. Notwithstanding the narrow isthmus that joined their two lands, they lived in utterly different worlds. It didn't matter that they loved each other. They had their letters and, Orris knew, that was all they could have, at least for now. And though he would never have said that the letters were enough, they were something. They were the only things that even allowed her to be a part of his life in Tobyn-Ser.

He accepted that as part of the price he paid for the power the gods had given him, just as he had reconciled himself to the fact that his endless solitude was a natural outgrowth of being a migrant mage. No one had forced him to live this way; it had been his decision. And he had pledged himself to the Order and to the land long before he had fallen in love with Bragor-Nal's Sovereign. But though he accepted the choices he had made, he was forced to acknowledge that he had never expected his travels to become as frenzied and relentless as they had in the past few years. Even in his youth, when he had wandered the length and breadth of the land, intent on proving to the older migrants of the Order that he was hardier than they, he had not covered as much territory as quickly as he did these days. Because while he had been driven as a young man by arrogance and misguided zeal, he had never been hunted, as he was now.

It sometimes seemed to Orris that there was no place where he could rest. Everywhere he went, the mages of the League of Amarid found him. Sometimes it took them a few days, on rare occasions a week. But eventually he would be forced to move on. The only real peace he had known for the past several years had come during his visits with Jaryd and Alayna on the shores of South Shelter. There, either the League mages couldn't find him, or more likely, they were unwilling to take on Jaryd and Alayna as well. But though his friends had always welcomed him and had never placed any constraints on the length of his stays, Orris was unwilling to impose upon them for very long. They had Myn to take care of, and though the League mages had left him alone during his visits thus far, he had no guarantee that they wouldn't be bolder the next time.

So after a short rest, usually no more than three or four days, he would leave them and resume his journeys, watchful once more for any sign of attack. He did everything he could to avoid confrontations. Given the choice between fighting and fleeing, he invariably chose the latter. Clearly the League mages had found some way to reconcile their attacks on Orris with their pledge to uphold Amarid's Laws, but Orris had vowed not to use the Mage-Craft against another mage, and he intended to do everything he could to honor that vow.

On those occasions when he had no choice but to fight, he did so defensively, using his power only to shield himself until he could slip away. He had yet to kill one of his attackers, despite being injured several times himself. And though he would have liked to hunt down the man who had killed Anizir three years ago, he knew that his adherence to the oath he had taken would not allow him even that satisfaction.

There was nothing for him to do but continue his wanderings and, when possible, offer his services to those who would accept them. Of course, even that was made more difficult by the existence of the League. Over the past few years he had been in every region of Tobyn-Ser. He had stopped in literally hundreds of towns and villages and had seen the blue flags of the League flying in roughly half of them. Somewhat fewer remained loyal to the Order, and a growing number wished only to be served by those mages who claimed to have no ties to either body.

These so-called free mages were a relatively new phenomenon, but they struck Orris as far more dangerous than the League. They answered to no one. If a mage of the Order attempted to use the Mage-Craft to gain wealth or power, or to harm in any way the people of Tobyn-Ser, he or she would be tried and punished by the rest of the Order. And though the leadership of the League appeared to be encouraging or at least tolerating the attacks on Orris, as far as he knew they dealt with other violations of Amarid's Laws just as the Order did. In practice, there had been few violations of the First Mage's Laws over the course of the last thousand years, and in the most serious case, the treachery of Owl-Master Sartol, the Order had been agonizingly slow to act. But in theory at least, the mages of both the League and the Order were held accountable for their actions. The free mages, on the other hand, were subject to no laws of conduct. They took no oath, and they had no procedure for disciplining renegade mages. Orris shuddered to think of what would have happened if Sartol had been given the opportunity to be a free mage rather than a member of the Order.

He had been walking northward along the eastern edge of Tobyn's Plain, and he paused now, looking west to watch as the sun, huge and orange, and partially obscured by a thin line of dark clouds, began to slide below the horizon. Almost immediately, the wind sweeping across the grasses and farmland turned colder. Orris shivered within his cloak and started walking again, immediately falling back into the rhythm that came to him so naturally. He could see the God's wood before him, perhaps a league away. It would be dark when he got there, but the moon was up in the eastern sky, yellow and almost full. It would light his way once the daylight vanished, and if it failed him, he could always summon mage-light from his ceryll. He glanced at the stone and grinned, his thoughts traveling west again to Lon-Ser. Once he had carried a crystal that shone with an amber light. But seven years ago, in Bragor-Nal, he and Melyor had used his stone and hers to fool Cedrych, the Overlord who was responsible for the outlanders' attacks on Tobyn-Ser. Their ruse worked for only a moment, but that was long enough. In the battle that followed, they killed Cedrych, sending him toppling from the window of his opulent quarters to the avenue far below. But Orris's staff fell with him, and the mage's ceryll shattered into thousands of pieces.

After returning to Tobyn-Ser, Orris traded for a new ceryll with his friend Crob, an Abboriji merchant. But when Crob placed the new stone in Orris's hand, the light that burst from the crystal was different from the hue of the mage's first ceryll. It was a subtle change. Few people other than Orris would have noticed. And thinking about it afterward, he soon realized that he shouldn't have been surprised. Since finding his first stone in the caverns of Ceryllon he had grown wiser, more patient, and more compassionate. But he also knew from looking at the new ceryll that there was more to it than that. His ceryll-hue had gone from amber to russet. It almost seemed as if some of the red from Melyor's stone had found its way into his. Again he smiled. He still wasn't entirely certain what it meant, but it pleased him.

He continued northward as darkness spread across the plain and the constellations began to take shape in the night sky. A town appeared in the distance, ahead of him and slightly to the west, its small houses glowing warmly with candlelight and hearth fire, but he didn't alter his course. He had been there before. Its name was Woodsview, and it was a League town.

Seeing the lights of the village, Orris felt himself growing tense. His grip tightened on his staff, and he found himself scanning the horizon continuously and glancing over his shoulder periodically to make certain he wasn't being followed. Kryssan, gliding above him, seemed to sense the change in his mood, and she flew higher so that she could better survey their surroundings. He looked up at the white falcon and nodded with grim satisfaction. They weren't likely to be surprised out here on the plain. Once they reached Tobyn's Wood, they'd be more vulnerable to an attack, but he and his falcon had been in hostile areas before. They were more than capable of defending themselves.

At times he grew tired of living like an Abboriji war general, planning for battle every time he walked into a new village or crossed unfamiliar terrain. But he was used to it by now, and considering how many times a little bit of foresight had saved his life, it seemed a small enough price to pay. Still, he had made the mistake once of complaining about it to Melyor in one of his letters. She had replied rather unsympathetically by pointing out that she had been living this way since the age of fifteen, when she had become a break-law. "Such is the nature of life in Bragor-Nal," she had reminded him. "If you can live that way in Tobyn-Ser, perhaps you are ready to return to Lon-Ser and be with me." He had not complained about it again, nor had she raised again the prospect of his joining her in Bragor-Nal.

Skirting Woodsview, Orris and Kryssan soon reached the edge of the God's wood. The gentle radiance of the moon had been enough to light their way as they covered the last league of the plain, but as they stepped into the brooding shadows of Tobyn's Wood, Orris was forced to draw more light from his ceryll. He did so reluctantly, knowing that it announced their presence to anyone within sight of the wood. Their only other choice, however, was to spend the night on the plain, where the chill air would have required that he start a fire. At least the wood offered shelter from the wind and the opportunity for an inconspicuous retreat.

They walked some distance into the forest, only stopping when Orris could no longer see any sign of Woodsview. Even then, Orris took the added precaution of finding a small hollow in which to make camp and build his fire. Kryssan flew to a high branch that afforded her a view of the hollow and the surrounding forest, and she began to preen. Orris gathered a pile of wood, started his fire, and sat back against the trunk of an enormous oak to eat some of the smoked meat and dried fruit that he carried in pouches within the folds of his cloak.

He had eaten well earlier in the day on a large grouse killed for him by his falcon, and he ate only a few bites of meat and fruit before putting the food away. He briefly considered working on his current letter to Melyor, but tired as he was, he decided against it. Instead, he laid his staff across his legs where he could reach it easily and settled back against the tree again with his eyes closed. When he was younger, he would have found it impossible to sleep this way. But as in so many other ways, the exigencies of his life had demanded that he adjust.

He was certain that he had fallen asleep quickly, because the next thing he knew, Kryssan was waking him silently, sending him the image of an approaching mage. Orris sensed an eager tension in the falcon's thoughts, but no panic. The mage often wondered if she actually enjoyed these encounters.

He closed his eyes again and, reaching for the falcon with his mind, looked upon the approaching mage a second time. It was a man, bearded and slight, with youthful features. He carried a sea-green ceryll and was accompanied by a small grey woodland hawk. Orris didn't recognize him, but he knew from the stranger's blue cloak that he was a League mage, and therefore an enemy. He could also tell from the way the mage carried himself—his staff held out before him, his body in a fighter's crouch, his steps light and careful—that he was ready to fight. He knew Orris was there.

Opening his eyes once more, Orris glanced quickly toward the fire. It had burned down to little more than a bed of glowing orange coals that crackled and settled loudly in the stillness shaped by Tobyn's Wood. Still, in the darkness, Orris could see that the embers offered a would-be attacker ample light. And the thin line of pale grey smoke that rose from the fire and drifted, as it happened, back toward the plain and Woodsview, could easily have served as a beacon to someone tracking him from that direction.

Cursing his own stupidity, Orris considered smothering the remnants of his fire, but in that moment he heard the footfalls of the stranger. The man was close; Orris didn't even have time to flee. Kryssan dropped silently to the ground beside him and the mage did the only thing he could. He crawled into the shadows on the far side of the small clearing and waited for the League mage to come into view.

He took position behind a jagged stump among tangles of bare vines and brush. He could already see the sea-green glow of the man's ceryll seeping into the darkness around him like a slow summer tide advancing on the dark sands of the Upper Horn. He held his breath, remaining per-fectly still. He again reached for Kryssan with his mind, readying her for what he intended to do, and felt once more the eagerness for battle that he had sensed when she awakened him.

Do you hate them so? he asked her, chiding her slightly with his tone.

She nuzzled him gently in response, and Orris allowed himself a momentary smile.

Then he saw the young stranger who wished to kill him, and his mood grew dark. The man's bird was perched on his shoulder, and for just an instant Orris thought of avenging Anizir. It would have been so easy.

"I have sworn an oath," he reminded himself.

It was only when the man froze, looking frantically in his direction, that Orris realized he had spoken aloud. Before his would-be attacker could do anything, Orris uncovered his ceryll for just a second and sent a beam of rust-colored fire hissing past the stranger's head. The man dived for cover, and his grey hawk darted up into a nearby tree, crying out repeatedly. An instant later the mage sent his own mage-fire back in Orris's direction, although his volley did not come very close to where Orris was hiding.

Orris grinned in the darkness. The stranger was new to battle.

"Have you come to die, Mage?" Orris called out.

Another stream of sea-green fire crashed into a nearby tree trunk, closer this time. Orris crouched a bit lower.

"I can see your little hawk, Mage," Orris goaded. "Shall I kill her now?"

No mage-fire this time, but the woodland hawk did hop higher into her tree, positioning herself on the far side of its trunk, which was just what Orris had been hoping for. As long as she was hiding, she couldn't offer her mage any information on Orris's position.

"Come now, friend," Orris called. "Surely you don't wish to die here, far from your home and—"

Two more beams of fire sliced through the darkness, one of them actually striking the tree stump that Orris was using for shelter. Orris retreated a bit farther into the brush. Perhaps the stranger wasn't as callow as he had seemed at first.

"I'm not afraid of dying!" the man threw back at him, contempt in his young voice. "At least not in a battle with you. Word of your cowardice has spread through the land, Mageling! And if your first attempt on my life in any indication, I have nothing to fear from you!"

I was trying to miss, you idiot! Orris wanted to shout back. Instead, he took a steadying breath. This was a tactic the League mages had used repeatedly in their recent encounters with him. They could not keep him from fleeing, and they had trouble tracking him when he did, so they had taken to trying to provoke him into staying and fighting.

"If I had wanted to kill you with my first volley, you'd be dead," Orris said evenly.

The stranger fired again, hitting the stump a second time and igniting a small fire. "Well, here I am, traitor!" he answered. "Why don't you kill me now?"

Orris shook his head, though the man couldn't see him. "I'm not in the habit of killing children." He regretted his choice of words the instant he spoke.

"No!" the man cried out, pouncing like a wildcat. "You're too much of a coward even for that! Instead, you give aid to those who kill children! You take them from their prison cells and return them to the comfort of their homes!"

Orris closed his eyes and gritted his teeth. How much abuse could the gods ask him to endure? How much longer could he be expected to honor his oath? Yes, he had taken Baram from his prison cell and returned him to Lon-Ser. He would even admit that by doing so he had contravened the will of the Order, although there had been no formal vote on the matter. But he had done so to save the land, not to betray it. And Baram had died in Bragor-Nal. Orris could still see the outlander's smile as he released his hold on the window ledge outside Cedrych's office and began to fall to the pavement far below. The outlander was dead. Wasn't that what they had all wanted in the first place?

Yet another shaft of green power flew from the man's ceryll, this one soaring just past Orris's head. Glancing up, Orris saw that the small grey hawk was in the open again and no doubt could see just where he and Kryssan were hiding. Uncovering his own stone again, Orris sent two small bursts of fire at the branches above and below the bird.

The creature leaped into the air, screaming again, and began to circle far above the treetops, her plaintive cries sounding small and distant.

The stranger fired again, but his volleys passed harmlessly over Orris's head.

"You'll attack my bird, but you're afraid of me, eh, traitor?"

He had suffered the League's attacks and insults for several years, repeatedly resisting the urge to lash out with the violence that had once been so much a part of him. And yet it was this last comment that finally broke his resolve. He could accept what they had done to him. He could accept that they wanted him dead. But they had killed Anizir. And now this man had the gall to accuse Orris of cowardice because he had thrown two balls of mage-fire in the direction of the stranger's bird, intending to miss with both. This was too much.

Orris stood, beckoning Kryssan to his shoulder with a thought. Immediately, the League mage sent a beam of fire at him, but Orris shielded himself with a wall of russet power and began advancing on the man. The young mage fired a second time, his eyes widening and his mouth hang-

ing open with fear and disbelief. Again, Orris blocked the attack with little effort. The stranger was new to his power and not terribly strong.
Orris, on the other hand, had been battling mages for a long time. He
grinned and continued to stride toward his attacker.

The man scrambled to his feet to flee, whistling for his bird as he broke
into a run.

Get him! Orris commanded.

Kryssan flew from Orris's shoulder, overtaking the mage in a few seconds and knocking him off-balance with a blow to the back. Orris's bird
then circled back and, ignoring the cries of the smaller woodland hawk,
dived at the mage's head. The man cried out and stopped to shield himself from Kryssan's assault. When Orris caught up with him, he was still
guarding his face and head with both arms.

Seeing Orris approach, the mage tried to get off one last volley of
mage-fire. Before he could, though, Orris smashed his own staff into the
man's shoulder, sending the young mage sprawling to the ground and his
staff hurtling end over end into the forest. Orris dropped his staff and
lunged for the man, picking him up by the collar of his blue robe and
knocking him back to the ground with a fist to the jaw.

Then he retrieved his staff and leveled it at the prone man, making the
rust-colored ceryll blaze menacingly.

"I—I thought you took an oath!" the League mage said, staring fear-
fully at the glowing stone. A small line of blood trickled from his mouth,
mingling with his beard.

"My oath didn't include putting up with the likes of you!" Orris
growled in reply.

The man's hawk called out in alarm, and Kryssan responded with a
fierce hiss that silenced the smaller bird.

"They all said you wouldn't fight! You never fight!"

"And that gives you license to attack me?" Orris demanded, his voice
rising. "To try to kill me? That gives you the right to call me a traitor and
a coward?"

"No, Mage!" the man said, despite his obvious fright. "You earned
those names a long time ago!"

Orris exhaled angrily and thrust his ceryll closer to the man's face. The
mage flinched and closed his eyes for a moment. But then he opened
them again and met Orris's glare.

"You have some courage," Orris said grudgingly. "When you tell the
story of this night to your children, you can say it was that, as much as
anything, that saved your life."

He started to turn away, but the League mage spit on the ground at
Orris's feet.

"You weren't going to kill me," the man said, sneering at him. "You haven't the nerve."

Orris almost did kill him then. He spun back toward the man, laying his ceryll against the side of the mage's throat and baring his teeth in a venomous grin. But in that very instant, even as he reached for Kryssan with his mind to draw the killing power from their bond, he saw something that stopped him cold.

His ceryll had begun to pulse like a heart. For a single dizzying moment he thought that it was a sign from Amarid himself that he should reconsider and spare the man's life. But then he understood. Someone had awakened the Summoning Stone.

The League mage was staring at Orris's ceryll in amazement. "What does it mean?" he asked, his voice barely more than a whisper.

"You don't know?"

"I'm new to the League," the mage admitted. "I've never seen this before."

Orris gave a small laugh and shook his head, turning away once again. "Go home and ask your masters," he told the man. "They can tell you what it means. I promise you, it's all they'll be talking about."

He started to walk away, but he stopped himself and returned to where the man still sat on the ground.

"Tell your masters this as well: you are the last."

The mage narrowed his eyes. "The last what?"

"The last survivor. The next mage they send against me I'll kill. I swear it in Amarid's name."

The man opened his mouth to fling back a retort, but Orris stopped him with a raised finger and a look of steel in his eyes.

"Not a word! I've chosen you to be my messenger, but your corpse can make my point just as effectively."

The mage stared at him for some time, saying nothing. Finally, the man nodded once. Orris turned and walked away, leaving him there on the forest floor.

Kryssan flew to Orris's shoulder, but she continued to glance back at the League mage and his hawk for some time as Orris made his way northward through the wood.

Don't worry, he sent soothingly. *He won't be following us. We may yet have other attacks to deal with, but not from that child, not tonight.*

He glanced at his stone. It was blinking steadily now, a general summons. Something important had happened. With the thought, an image of Jaryd and Alayna entered his mind. And Myn, of course. He smiled. At least he'd be seeing the three of them soon. Regardless of what crisis the Order might face now, he would look forward to that.

3

I am glad to hear that you and Shivohn are pleased with the trade that has developed between our two lands over the past several years. I wish that I could share your enthusiasm. The fact is, however, that Tobyn-Ser's recent involvement in transisthmus commerce has had unintended and, in my opinion, undesirable consequences for our people, our land, and our culture. Even our language has changed. I had never heard the word "transisthmus" until a few weeks ago and it still sounds strange to me. It does not even describe accurately the nature of our trade, given that ships are used to transport all the goods that travel in both directions between Tobyn-Ser and Lon-Ser. Yet the term persists, and I grow more confused by the day.

No doubt you are laughing at me now, amused by my inability to adapt to these changes I describe. In spite of everything, that is a sound I would love to hear. Still, I find it hard to see the humor in this new world, that I helped to create. I fear that while the tools and devices you send us may indeed save us time and effort, as you say, they are still going to bring great hardship to my land.

> —Hawk-Mage Orris to Melyor i Lakin, Sovereign and Bearer of Bragor-Nal, Winter, God's Year 4633.

Baden stood in the doorway of their small house and gazed out into the night. Four years ago, when he and Sonel first came to this cottage, they could see nothing from here save the small garden they had carved out of the God's wood and the elms and maples that grew around it. Even now, in the summer months that was still the case. But the cutting that had been done left sizable tracts of forest with no trees at all and a lattice of wide roads for removing the harvested timber, destroying the essence of Tobyn's Wood. This winter, when the trees were bare and the air was clear, as it was tonight, Baden could see the Emerald Hills from their doorway. Or rather he could see fires smoldering on the hilltops where once trees had covered the hills.

He was tired and he felt the cold air reaching through his cloak like an icy hand, but he couldn't tear his eyes from those distant fires. He heard the door open and close behind him, and a moment later he felt Sonel's hand on his back.

"Longing for your migrant days again?" she asked, standing beside him.

He glanced at her and saw a gentle smile playing at the corners of her mouth. There were more lines on her face now than there once had been, and her wheat-colored hair had broad streaks of silver that shone in the moonlight. But she still remained much as he remembered her from their first meeting so many years ago: straight-backed and tall, with a youthful oval face and those stunning green eyes. Looking at her made him feel old and ungainly, and not for the first time, he wondered why she still loved him.

"Hardly," he finally answered, placing his arm around her shoulders.

"Then what?"

He shrugged. "I'm just watching the fires."

She gazed up at the hills and frowned. "There are so many of them. It seems like there are more every night."

Baden nodded. "There are."

"There are limits to how much they can cut, Baden," she assured him, beginning again a conversation they had repeated several times in recent months. "The Temples don't own everything in the hills."

"It's not just the Temples anymore," he said more sharply than he had intended. "Sure, they were the first, and they still own more land than anyone else. But there are lots of people logging now."

"I know," she said quietly.

"I'm sorry, Sonel," he whispered, kissing her brow. "I just wish Radomil would do something about it."

"He can't act alone, Baden. He needs the Order's support."

"He's got it!" Baden said, shaking his head. "Between us, Jaryd and Alayna, Orris, Trahn, Mered, and a few others, he's got the votes."

"You know better than that. If he pushes an issue like this with a bare majority, he'll drive more mages to the League. He needs to do this carefully. He can't rush it."

Baden looked up at the hills again. "He doesn't have that luxury."

She nodded grimly. "I agree." Then, her mood brightening slightly, she added, "But maybe that's what this is all about. Maybe he finally has the support he needs to act."

Baden looked down at his staff. The orange stone mounted on top of it had been flashing for nearly an hour.

"Maybe," he said, though he could not keep the skepticism from his voice.

"Are you humoring me?" she demanded with a smile.

Baden laughed in spite of himself. "Yes, I'm afraid I am."

"Don't you know that it's a violation of Amarid's Laws to humor a former Owl-Sage?"

"No, I didn't know that," Baden said, raising an eyebrow.

"Well, it's one of his lesser-known laws," she explained airily. "You don't hear of it much, because there aren't that many of us."

He grinned at the understatement. There was one, to be exact. Sonel had lost her owl four years ago and was forced by the rules of the Order to relinquish her position. The previous four Sages had died during their tenure in the Great Hall, including Baden's friend, Jessamyn, Sonel's immediate predecessor, who had been killed at Theron's Grove by the renegade, Sartol.

Thus, Sonel was something of an oddity: a living former Sage. She and Baden had often remarked on how lucky she was to have been succeeded by Radomil, a man whose modesty and lack of ambition allowed him to see her as a friend and advisor rather than as a threat to his authority. For now that she was bound again, there was nothing to stop her from asking to be considered for the position again if Radomil lost his familiar or died. She claimed to have no interest in returning to the Great Hall in that capacity, and she had given Radomil no reason to doubt her word. But another Sage might have seen such claims as disingenuous and taken her expressions of support as a calculated attempt to curry favor.

"Come on," Sonel coaxed softly. "It's late, and we have a long day ahead of us."

"I'll be along in a minute." He gave her arm a squeeze.

She smiled sadly and nodded. She had known him long enough to recognize his mood. If he followed her in now, he wouldn't be able to sleep anyway.

"Don't be too long," she called over her shoulder.

"I won't be."

A moment later he heard the door open and close again, and he looked up at the hills once more. He reached for Golivas with his mind and found her asleep in her usual spot, on the top shelf in the kitchen. She slept more and more these days. He had been with her for more than ten years, and she probably didn't have many Gatherings left.

And how many bindings do you have left, Mage? he asked himself, gazing at the stars overhead. A cold breeze stirred the bare limbs of the trees around him and Baden shivered. He didn't feel old, although he knew that he was considered one of the senior members of the Order. Despite the cold, he and Sonel planned to walk to Amarid, as they still did for every Gathering. And while he was no longer a migrant, he still ranged far from their cottage during the summer months, covering not only the hills and much of Tobyn's Wood, but also most of the Northern Plain, where he still had many friends.

But though he was youthful for his age, he was no fool. He didn't expect to live forever. And more than anything, before he died, he wanted to see the Order restored to its rightful place as the land's sole body of mages and masters. He had repeated this wish to many of his friends within the Order, always keeping his tone light and confident. But he had seen enough towns with blue flags hanging on their homes and shops to know that even if the conflicts dividing League mages from Order mages could be overcome, the Order had much work to do to regain the trust of Tobyn-Ser's people. Too much, in all likelihood.

He shook his head, as if he could fling these dark thoughts from his mind with the motion. He knew he should go to sleep. Sonel was right: they had a long journey ahead of them and a good deal of preparation to see to before they left. But something was keeping him out in the cold night air with the stars and the subtle scent of smoke that rode the wind. He couldn't name it, but he had been a mage long enough to trust his instincts in such matters.

So when at last Jaryd's blue appeared for a second in the flashing orange of his ceryll, Baden was not surprised. Reaching for Golivas and closing his eyes, he extended his awareness back to the west, toward the Seaside Mountains.

He found his nephew waiting for him just above the trees.

Hello, Jaryd, he sent.

I'm sorry to contact you so late at night, Baden, the young mage returned. *I would have done this earlier if I'd been able.*

Baden sensed Jaryd straining to maintain their connection, and he remembered belatedly that his nephew had been without a familiar for many months.

You've bound!

Yes.

Baden almost congratulated him, but the uneasiness he read in Jaryd's thoughts stopped him. *What's happened?* he asked instead.

I've bound to an eagle, Baden.

Baden had wielded the Mage-Craft for nearly forty years, and, because his mother and grandmother had both been mages, he had attended Gatherings and been acquainted with the Order and its ways for most of his life. He had spoken with Phelan, the unsettled Wolf-Master, he had unmasked a traitor to the land, and he had fought against outlanders who had come to Tobyn-Ser to destroy the Order. He had spent the better part of three years interrogating the one outlander who survived the battle at Phelan Spur, learning from him of a people who could create weapons and goods that mimicked nature with mind-numbing accuracy. He had seen the Order sundered and supplanted in the hearts of Tobyn-Ser's people by a rival body. And he had seen the land itself scarred beyond recognition by men and women chasing a dream of wealth. Few things surprised him anymore. Fewer still shocked him speechless.

Yet he could think of nothing to say in response to Jaryd's news. An eagle. They were destined for war. And Jaryd was to be their Eagle-Sage.

When? Baden finally managed to ask.

Today. This morning.

So that's why Radomil summoned us.

Yes.

Baden took a long breath. *Are you all right?*

It's been a long day, Jaryd replied. *I'm exhausted. And I'm frightened.*

You should be. We all should be.

What do you think it means, Baden?

You mean aside from the obvious? I really don't know.

He could feel Jaryd's fatigue growing by the moment, and he wanted desperately to end their connection with a word of encouragement. But nothing came to him. Even having access to Jaryd's thoughts, he couldn't even begin to imagine what his nephew was feeling. He sensed the young mage's apprehension, his self-doubt, and his bewilderment. But the link they had forged in the night did not allow him to divine much more than that.

If I can help you in any way, Jaryd, he began, knowing how inadequate that must have sounded. He didn't even bother to finish the thought.

I know, Baden, the mage sent back. *Thank you. Before this is over I'm certain I'll need the counsel of every mage in the Order.*

Their connection was weakening. In another moment, Jaryd would be gone. So Baden offered the one assurance he could. *The gods wouldn't have chosen you if they doubted your ability to lead the Order, Jaryd. Remember that, if you start to question yourself.*

I will. Thank you. Arick guard you, Baden. And Sonel, too. We'll see you soon.

Arick guard you as well! Baden tried to send in reply. But his nephew was already gone. The Owl-Master opened his eyes and immediately his gaze was drawn back to the fires burning on the Emerald Hills. "Arick guard our land," he said out loud. He watched the fires for several moments longer before finally turning and stepping into the warmth of the cottage.

They awoke early the following morning to prepare for their journey to Amarid. As they ate a modest breakfast, Baden told Sonel of Jaryd's binding and saw the shock and fear he had experienced the night before mirrored in her eyes.

"An eagle!" she breathed. "That's the last thing I was expecting this Gathering to be about."

Baden nodded. "I felt the same way."

"I'm not happy with all that's come of our trade with Lon-Ser," she went on. "But I thought the threat of war had passed a long time ago."

"So you think we're going to war with Lon-Ser?"

"Who else would it be?" she asked with genuine surprise.

He shrugged. "I'm not sure. But I think it's dangerous to jump to conclusions."

Sonel fell silent for several moments. "I suppose you're right," she said at last, "though I don't see any other possibilities. Certainly Abborij wouldn't attack us."

"Probably not."

There was another possibility, Baden knew, one that frightened him far more than war with Lon-Ser, but he wasn't willing to give it voice. Not yet, not even with Sonel.

Sonel regarded him keenly, her gaze expectant. But he said nothing more and she didn't push him on the matter. Throughout the rest of the morning, as they prepared to depart for Amarid, they spoke little.

Just after midday they took the narrow path from their garden through the surrounding forest until they reached one of the many logging roads that now ran through the God's wood. Stepping onto the road, they exchanged a look and then a smile, as they often did now when they made this journey. Neither of them approved of the roads, or, for that matter, of the timber trade that they made possible. But the Owl-Masters could not deny that the wide thoroughfares made the journey to Amarid faster and easier than it had ever been before. It was an irony they had acknowledged to each other on a number of occasions.

In recent months they had also been forced to admit that many of the towns engaged in the sale of timber seemed to have benefited from it. The homes and shops in these villages looked sturdier, the people appeared well fed and well clothed, and in those villages where the blue flags of the League flew, Baden and Sonel sensed a slight but unmistakable easing of the people's hostility toward the Order. Prosperity, it seemed, was a balm for a variety of the land's ailments.

This was not to say that Baden and Sonel welcomed the timber trade's astonishing growth. As they had discussed the previous evening, they both wished the Order could take some action to limit the scope of the logging taking place under the supervision of the Temples. But unlike a number of their colleagues in the Order, including Trahn and Ursel, they did not view Tobyn-Ser's burgeoning commerce as totally evil.

Still, they could not help but be disturbed by what they saw as they made their way through the southern portion of Tobyn's Wood. Barely half a year had passed since the Midsummer Gathering, and yet, in that brief interval, enormous swaths of the forest had been stripped of every tree. No attempt had been made to repair the land or to leave saplings that might someday replace the giant oaks, maples, and elms that had been cut. There were stumps, mutilated shrubs, a few forgotten branches, and nothing more. The very sight of it pained Baden's heart and left him wondering if any amount of wealth or prosperity could be worth such a price.

The two Owl-Masters came to the southern bank of the Dhaalismin ten days after leaving their cottage, and, turning to the southeast, they followed the river for two days before coming to a bridge. Even along the river, the forest had suffered at the hands of the Temple's woodsmen, and the waters of the Dhaalismin had been muddied by soil from the cleared areas and choked with tangled tree limbs and brush. Where once the river had been a torrent, its waters were now sluggish and meek.

Several days after crossing the Dhaalismin and turning once more to the northeast, as they began to hear the roar of Fourfalls River echoing through the wood, Baden and Sonel came to a small village nestled within the trees. Though not terribly far from one of the larger timber cuts they had encountered thus far, the forest surrounding the town appeared undisturbed, save for a small clearing a short distance from the village where one of Arick's Temples stood, austere and weatherworn. Intending to replenish their supplies, if this was an Order town, Baden and Sonel left the logging road and turned onto a narrow footpath that led to the cluster of shops and homes.

But as they drew nearer to the town, a strange scene unfolded before them. A number of people had gathered outside the front gates of the town and were standing in a long curving line with their backs to a sizable, dense grove of oaks and maples. Facing them were perhaps a dozen woodsmen, carrying axes and saws, and seven other men, all of them tall and muscular with dour expressions on their faces. All the men were dressed in identical bulky grey shirts. Between the woodsmen and the townsfolk stood three mages, none of them wearing a cloak, and another man, tall and heavyset, wearing a silver-grey robe that marked him as a Keeper of Arick's Temple. The mages and the Keeper were engaged in a heated argument, and the people of the town appeared quite agitated.

"The land surrounding the village belongs to the Temple!" the Keeper was telling the three mages, as Baden and Sonel halted within earshot. "You have no right to come here and stir up trouble!"

"The people of Prannai asked for our help!" one of the mages said. He was tall as well, although far leaner than the Keeper and younger-looking. "They've seen what the Keepers have done to Tobyn's Wood, and they don't want their piece of the God's forest destroyed to fill the Temple's coffers!"

"Do not presume to lecture me about the people of Prannai!" the Keeper answered, raising his voice and gazing past the mages toward the villagers. "I've known most of you for the better part of your lives!" he said, a plea in his words. "Do you really think I'd do anything to hurt you or this town?"

"Your men are killing the wood!" a woman cried out from the crowd. "We've asked you to stop them, but you won't listen to us!"

The other townsfolk shouted their agreement, drawing satisfied smirks from the mages.

"It is our land!" the Keeper told them again, his round face reddening. He paused, as if trying to compose himself. "We understand that the changes that have accompanied our new prosperity are . . . unsettling to some of you," he began again. "But surely you see the benefits as well. The timber trade is bringing wealth to Tobyn-Ser that none of us ever imagined possible. And Prannai will see more than her fair share of that wealth. But we must do our part as well."

"What if we don't want your riches, Keeper?" a man shouted. "What if we just want our homes and our trees to stay as they are?"

The Keeper straightened and stared grimly at the townspeople. "In that case," he said, his voice suddenly cold, "I will remind you once again of what we all know to be true: they are not *your* trees. They belong to the Temple, as does all the land surrounding the village."

"That land was entrusted to the Temple by our forebears hundreds of years ago!" replied the woman who had spoken earlier. "The Keepers were to care for the land, not destroy it!"

"The Children of the Gods have tended this land for generations," the Keeper said. "We have always acted in the best interests of Prannai and its people, and we continue to do so today. In your hearts you know that to be true." He indicated the three mages with a disdainful gesture. "But these strangers have thrust themselves into our affairs and filled your heads with nonsense! They are the problem, not the Temple!"

The tall mage bristled. "As I told you before, the people of your town sought our help! They asked us to come, because they believe that the Temple and its Keeper have betrayed their trust!"

"Careful, Mage!" the Keeper said, his tone low and dangerous. "Meddling is one thing. Accusing the Temple of betrayal is quite another."

The mage bared his teeth in a harsh grin. "Your actions invite the words, Keeper."

The Keeper glared at him for another moment before spinning away with a swirl of his silver robe. "I won't listen to this anymore!" He faced the woodsmen. "Cut the trees!" And then, turning to the burly men standing beside the loggers, he added, "Make sure no one gets in their way."

Immediately, the seven men, their faces still grim and their feet planted solidly, pulled strange-looking objects from beneath their bulky shirts and pointed them toward the crowd. The Keeper gave a satisfied nod.

The three mages stared at the Keeper's men, their eyes wide and their faces turning pale. Behind them, the people of Prannai began to whisper to each other.

"I had heard tales of such things," the tall mage breathed, "but I didn't want to believe them."

Baden had not heard any of these tales, and he didn't know what the men were holding. But he had an idea, and he had seen enough.

"Perhaps we can be of assistance!" he called out, striding forward with Sonel close behind.

None of them had noticed the Owl-Masters until now and all of them, including the villagers, regarded Baden and Sonel with expressions that ranged from thinly veiled mistrust to open hostility.

"The Order has no business here," the Keeper said. His tone was icy, though the expression on his face betrayed his discomfort. "I'd suggest you move on."

"We're on our way to Amarid," Baden said, ignoring the man. "We've come to Prannai to replenish our supply of food. In exchange for our service, of course."

"This is not an Order town," the tall mage told him, his voice carrying little more warmth than that of the Keeper.

"I see that," Baden replied. "But I see nothing to suggest that it's a League town either. Perhaps your people are ready to embrace the Order as an ally, at least for the time being."

"Such arrogance!" one of the other mages said, stepping forward to stand beside the tall man. She was a young woman with light brown hair and grey eyes. She bore a large brown-and-white hawk on her shoulder, and like her two companions, she wore no cloak over her woolen shirt and trousers. "You assume that the Order and the League are their only choices. What if they want nothing to do with your petty quarrels? What if they prefer mages with no ties to either the League or the Order?" The woman shook her head and regarded the Owl-Masters with disgust. "The Keeper's right: you should go."

"Well, at least we got them to agree on something," Sonel muttered under her breath.

"What's your name?" Baden asked the woman, not bothering to respond to Sonel's comment.

The mage narrowed her eyes. "Why do you want to know?"

"Because I wish to speak with you," Baden answered, impatience creeping into his voice. "And I prefer to know someone's name when I carry on a conversation with them."

She pressed her lips into a thin line and glanced at her companions. "Tammen," she finally said. "My name's Tammen."

"Well, Tammen, before you tell me with such certainty what the people of Prannai do and don't want from us, wouldn't it be a good idea to ask them? And before we ask them, wouldn't it also be a good idea to tell them just what those men are holding in their hands? We want them to make an informed choice, don't we?"

"You're wasting our time, Owl-Master!" the Keeper broke in. "I've asked you to leave, and so have these mages. None of Prannai's people have asked you to stay. The only one who seems to think you belong here is you. Now I will say this one last time: leave us!"

"I would think, Tammen," Baden said, glaring at the Keeper, "that with the Keeper so anxious for us to leave, you'd want us to stay."

"We don't need your help!" the taller mage said, sounding unsure of himself.

Baden turned to the man slowly. "And your name is?"

The man hesitated for a moment. "My name is Nodin."

"And have you ever seen, Nodin, what the weapons of Lon-Ser can do to one of our villages?" Baden glanced at the Keeper. "Those are from Lon-Ser, aren't they?" he demanded.

The Keeper's face reddened. "Yes, they are," he said. "So are the chairs in my quarters at the Temple. What of it?"

"Your chairs aren't used to kill people!" Sonel answered.

The Keeper raised a finger as if in warning. "No one's been killed, Owl-Master! You'd do well to remember that!"

"But what they're saying is true, isn't it, Keeper?" one of the villagers called out. "Those are the weapons the outlanders use. And you were going to have your men use them on us."

"I did not order these men to use their weapons on anyone!" the Keeper insisted, his voice rising. "These mages, all of them, have put ridiculous notions in your head!" He pointed to the armed men. "The Temple hired these men solely to protect our woodsmen. As long as no one interferes with the logging on our land, no one will get hurt."

"So it comes back to that," Nodin said.

The Keeper gritted his teeth. "It is our land!"

"That may be," Baden told him. "But I don't think you'll be cutting any trees today."

The Keeper looked at him, a challenge in his eyes. "Do you plan to stop me, Mage? I gather that you have seen what these weapons can do. Do you honestly think that you can stand against me?"

Baden allowed himself a dark smile. "Yes, Keeper, I do. You see, I was at Phelan Spur when six mages of the Order did battle with thirteen out-landers who were, I guarantee you, far more skilled with their weapons than your men are with theirs. We prevailed then, and I have no doubt that my friend and I, along with these three mages, can defeat you now."

"I don't get the feeling that these three mages like you very much, Owl-Master. What makes you think that they will fight by your side?"

"Against you and your mercenaries," Nodin broke in, stepping forward to stand next to Baden and Sonel, "I would join forces with Theron himself." He made a small gesture, and Tammen and the third mage moved to stand beside him.

The Keeper stared at the mages for what seemed to Baden an eternity. The Owl-Master honestly believed that five mages were more than a match for the Temple's men, but he had no desire to test that belief. There were too many people here. Someone was bound to get hurt, even killed. Nor did he want to kill these men, even if they were armed and in the service of this Keeper.

Fortunately, the Keeper was no more willing than he to press the matter. "Very well, Owl-Master," he finally said, meeting Baden's glare. "Our trees will stand for another day. If your flashing stone is any indication, you're anxious to get to Amarid. You won't guard this grove forever."

Baden offered no response, and the Keeper grinned broadly. He glanced at Nodin and the other mages, nodded once, and then turned and walked toward the path leading back into the village.

"We'll be here, Keeper," Nodin called after him. "If you want to cut those trees, you'll have to deal with us first."

"I was counting on it, Mage," the Keeper replied, not even bothering to look back. He made a single gesture, and immediately the woodsmen and the guards fell in behind him.

Baden and the others watched as the Keeper and his men returned to the Temple. Only when they were out of sight did Baden finally turn to the three mages.

"We were lucky that time," he said grimly. "He won't give in so easily tomorrow."

"That's our concern, Owl-Master," Nodin told him, "not yours."

Sonel gaped at him. "You can't be serious! Baden just saved your life and quite possibly that of every other person here! And now you're telling us that it's not our concern? How dare you!"

"We didn't ask for your help!" Tammen said. "We've dealt with the Temples before without any interference from the Order! We would have dealt with them today, with or without you!"

"Have you faced those weapons before?" Sonel demanded. "Would you have known how to guard yourself and the people over there, who are counting on your protection?"

Tammen hesitated, drawing a smile from the Owl-Master.

"I thought not," Sonel said. "Perhaps you need us more than you think."

"We have no need of the Order or the League!"

"It's not your decision to make," Baden broke in. "Nor is it ours."

He looked over at the villagers and walked to where they stood. Most of them wore anxious expressions, although one, the woman who had argued with the Keeper, stepped forward confidently to meet him. She was small and thin, with white hair and dark brown eyes. Her face was deeply lined, giving her a severe appearance, and though she smiled at Baden, the look in her eyes remained reserved.

"I am Maira," she said, bowing her head slightly. "I lead Prannai's Council of Elders."

"I'm Baden."

"My people and I are grateful for your help, Owl-Master," she said. "That Keeper is new to our Temple. The old Keeper never would have tried such a thing."

Baden nodded soberly. "Tobyn-Ser is changing. None of us is immune from the effect of those changes."

"True."

"But perhaps, working together, we can make sense of them. We can help each other adapt."

Maira smiled thinly. "We have no desire to adapt, Owl-Master. We have no intention of changing."

Baden stared at her, not knowing what to say.

"You think us mad."

"Not mad," the Owl-Master said cautiously. "But the entire land—"

"We don't care what others do," Maira told him. "We're not foolish enough to believe that we can keep the rest of Tobyn-Ser from changing. But we plan to resist that change for as long as we can. We see strange goods made by outlanders flooding our land. We hear others talking of minting coins for use throughout the entire land, as if we lived in Abborij. We encounter strangers just outside the gates of our village who speak not a word of our language. And now we have seen the Keeper of our Temple threaten us with outlanders' weapons. We want no part of this new world that seems to be intoxicating the rest of the land. We don't want wealth, or Lon-Ser's notion of comfort and luxury. We just want to live our lives as we always have."

She paused, shaking her head slowly. "You protected us today, and for that we thank you. But the Order has done nothing to guard Tobyn-Ser from these larger intrusions."

Baden opened his mouth to argue, but she stopped him with a raised hand.

"I know, Owl-Master: neither has the League. Which is why we want nothing to do with either of you." She indicated Nodin and his companions with a gesture. "The free mages listen to us. They share our concern for what's happening to the land, and they do not act on the assumption that they know us better than we know ourselves." Again, she smiled sadly at him. For all the severity he had noted in her features a few moments before, Baden was struck by how the smile softened her face.

"No doubt you deem us strange, Owl-Master. I'm sorry for that. You and your companion seem to be decent people. For all I know, you were among those who advocated executing the outlander held by the Order all those years ago. Perhaps if the other mages had listened to you then, we would not be where we are now."

Baden offered no reply at first. As it happened, he and Sonel had been almost entirely responsible for keeping Baram alive. He had argued repeatedly against Baram's execution, believing that the Order had too much to learn from the outlander to throw his life away for the sake of vengeance. And when at last the Order voted to kill Baram anyway, Sonel, Owl-Sage at the time, overruled the vote, as was her right in such cases. But Baden saw no sense in correcting Maira on this matter. "I doubt that listening to us would have made much difference one way or another," he said instead. "I believe that some changes are just inevitable."

Maira raised an eyebrow, but said nothing.

"As to whether I think you're strange or not," Baden went on, "I don't believe that I'm in a position to judge you. This isn't the first time I've heard your point of view."

"Nor will it be the last," the woman said pointedly. "Mark my word, Owl-Master: the People's Movement is growing, as is the stature of the free mages. The Order and League ignore us at their own risk."

Baden narrowed his eyes. "The People's Movement?"

"That's what they call themselves," Nodin said.

Baden turned to look at the mage. "Who?"

"Those in other villages who feel as Maira and her people do."

"You've spoken to these people?" Baden asked.

"Yes. Many of them."

Baden began to nod, comprehension coming to him with the force of a thunderclap. "How fortunate then that you and your friends should be here just at the time when Prannai's people are feuding with their Temple." He stared at the mage, daring the man to meet his gaze. "Was that merely a coincidence, or was it something more?"

Nodin stared back at him silently for a few seconds before looking away.

"The people of this village asked us to stay with them and join their cause," Tammen answered, taking up the fight. "I heard no such invitation extended to you and your friend."

"And how long do you plan to stay around?" Baden asked her. "Will you see this through to the end? Or do you prefer to move on before things get too ugly?"

"I don't know what you're implying, Owl-Master," Maira said, "but we had no intention of allowing the Temple to cut those trees, even before these mages came and told us of the Movement. You may think us too simple and weak to take up such a battle on our own, but I assure you, we don't lack for courage! And just because the Order and the League have proven themselves adept at manipulating the people of Tobyn-Ser, that doesn't mean that the free mages are guilty of this as well!"

Baden sighed and glanced at Sonel. She was watching him, a pained look in her green eyes. She shrugged slightly, then shook her head.

"I assure you, Maira," Baden said, turning back to the white-haired woman, "I meant no offense."

Maira regarded him dubiously. "Perhaps not, but I still think you and your friend should leave. There's an Order town several leagues east of here. You can reach it by nightfall without adding much distance to your journey. I'm sure they'll be happy to give you what provisions you need." With that she turned away and rejoined the other villagers.

Baden faced the free mages again. They were already watching him, looked smug. "Let's go," he said to Sonel.

He started back down the narrow path that led to the logging road. Sonel fell into step beside him. After a few strides, however, he stopped and looked back at Nodin. The mage was still watching him, as were the others.

"Their weapons are powerful," Baden called. "But a shield of power can block their fire. Conserve your strength though; use a shield only when you need it. The weapons don't get tired."

Nodin gazed at him for several moments, as if unsure of what to say. Finally, he nodded. "Thanks," he said.

Baden and Sonel continued on in silence, saying nothing until they were back on the logging road and had put several miles between themselves and Prannai.

"Those mages are going to get them all killed," Baden said at last, shaking his head with disgust.

"You think Maira and the others should just let the Temple cut the trees?"

He glanced at her briefly. "No. But I'm not sure that the trees are worth dying for, either."

Sonel shrugged. "That's not your choice to make."

"Isn't it?" Baden demanded. "I can protect them. We can protect them. That's what we're supposed to do, right? 'I shall serve the people of the land,' " he recited, quoting the oath every member of the Order took when receiving his or her cloak. " 'I shall use my powers to give aid and comfort in times of need.' "

"You can't protect people who don't want to be protected, Baden," Sonel said gently. "We can offer our service, but if the people say no, we have to accept that."

Suddenly he felt cold, though the day was mild and sunlight filtered through the bare limbs of the wood. "When did all this happen, Sonel? How is it that the people of the land hate us so much that they'd rather die than accept our help?"

"I don't know," she answered in a low voice. "But the gods have sent us an Eagle-Sage, so they must think we still have a role to play in guarding the land."

Baden nodded and took her hand. She smiled at him, and they walked on toward the First Mage's city. She was right, he knew. The appearance of Jaryd's eagle was double-edged: it meant war, but it implied as well that the Order was still Tobyn-Ser's guardian.

Or did it? There was another possibility, he suddenly realized, one that terrified him more than anything, more even than the prospect of war with Lon-Ser.

4

I continue to be amazed by the changes that have come to Bragor-Nal over the past seven years. The constant warfare among Nal-Lords and break-laws that once threatened to plunge the entire Nal into chaos is now largely over. Firefights still break out occasionally, and assassinations continue to claim the lives of a few Nal-Lords each year. But I have made it clear to my Overlords that I will not tolerate such activities, and they have conveyed this message to their underlings. Advance-

*ment, I have told them, will be based upon production, efficiency, and
Nal maintenance. Those who resort to violence even once will be punished; those who return to it again and again will be stripped of their
authority and jailed . . .*

*As I say, I have made my policy on this matter quite clear, and my
subordinates appear to have taken it to heart, with one notable exception: while they have stopped trying to kill each other, some among
them—I have yet to learn who—have redoubled their efforts to have
me killed.*

—Melyor i Lakin, Sovereign and
Bearer of Bragor-Nal to Hawk-Mage
Orris, Day 4, Week 8, Winter, Year
3067.

The sound of the explosion jolted Melyor awake, her heart hammering within her chest, and her ears ringing. For one horrible,
disorienting moment, she was eleven again, waking in the small bedroom
of her childhood to the sound of the blast that killed her father. But the
memory was fleeting. She was in her quarters in Bragor-Nal's Gold
Palace, and this bomb had been meant for her.

Shards of glass lay scattered across the wooden floor and on the satin
coverings of her bed, and smoke was beginning to drift in through the
shattered windows, acrid and thick, mingling with the cold air of the late-
winter morning. She could hear men shouting outside, below her window. Jibb's men. She might even have heard Jibb himself. She couldn't
be certain, not with the ringing in her ears.

She checked herself for injuries and found none, although she felt
something moving high on her cheek. She touched it and then looked at
her hand. Blood. Probably a cut from the flying glass.

"Bastards!" she said, swinging herself out of bed and throwing on her
silk robe. She stepped to the mirror on the far wall of her chamber, which
hung crookedly but had survived the blast, and examined the cut on her
cheek. It was nothing, barely more than a scratch with a smudge of blood
beneath it. But she was furious. "Bastards!" she said again. She took a
deep breath and realized that she was trembling.

There was a knock on her door.

"Come in!" she said, thrusting her shaking hands into the pockets of
her robe.

The door opened and Jibb walked in. Melyor still found it strange to
see him in the stiff, pale blue uniform of SovSec, though he had been the
head of her security force for nearly seven years. She still thought of him

as a break-law, just as she still thought of herself as a Nal-Lord, rather than as Sovereign and Bearer of the Stone. It didn't help that in most respects, he looked just as he did more than ten years ago, when she first encountered him in a bar in Bragor-Nal's Fourth Realm. He was still powerfully built and graceful. His shaggy hair remained dark, unmarked by the silver that had already begun to appear in her own amber waves, and his face was still round and youthful. He was more reserved than he used to be, and perhaps a bit more cautious. But that had as much to do with changes in their relationship as it did with the passage of time. In other ways, he was still the same, except that now he was personally responsible not only for her safety, but for maintaining order throughout the Nal.

"Sovereign!" he said, striding into the room and looking toward her bed. He halted when he saw she wasn't there, and quickly scanned the room. His eyes widened when he finally spotted her. "You're hurt!" he said, approaching her.

She frowned. "Hardly. Report, Jibb. What happened?"

"We should call a doctor," he insisted. "You're bleeding."

She laughed, though she kept her hands hidden and had to fight a sudden chill that ran down her spine. How many assassination attempts could a person tolerate? "I'm fine, Jibb. I promise. Just tell me what happened."

He stared at her for another moment, then shook his head slowly, his face wearing a look of resignation that Melyor knew all too well. A few years ago she would have teased him about it, delighting in his frustration and telling him that if she made it too easy for him to do his job, he'd grow bored and leave her. Such had been the nature of their friendship.

All that changed a few years ago, however, when Jibb finally admitted that he was in love with her and asked her to marry him. They were walking the grounds of the Gold Palace at the time, enjoying the cool breezes of an early-autumn evening. At first she thought he was joking, but when her flippant response elicited only silence and a pained expression in his dark eyes, she understood her error. Fighting a sudden wave of panic, she tried to explain to him that she didn't love him in that way and didn't think she ever could.

"You're my closest friend," she told him. "But that's all I can give you."

Jibb, though, refused to be dissuaded. He tried to convince her that, given some time, her feelings might change. In the end, she had no choice but to tell him the one thing she knew would hurt him most, even as it put the matter to rest.

"I can't love you," she finally said, surprised to find herself crying, "because I'm in love with someone else. I'm in love with Orris."

Jibb stared at her for a long time, holding himself perfectly still. At last he nodded and walked away.

Melyor feared that in the wake of their conversation, Jibb would resign as commander of SovSec. But he was in his office the following morning, making her security arrangements and dispatching a group of men to deal with the aftermath of a firefight in the Seventeenth Realm. They never spoke of the matter again. Melyor tried to once, but Jibb made it clear that he would not discuss it. Instead, they both tried to pretend that nothing had changed.

Nonetheless, their friendship had not been the same since. Their conversations suddenly became strained and awkward. Where once Melyor had talked with him freely about almost everything and joked with him without a second thought, she now found herself watching every word for fear that she would hurt his feelings, or worse, give him cause to think that she had reconsidered her rejection of his proposal. She was profoundly relieved by his willingness to stay on as head of SovSec, but she knew beyond a doubt that the ease of their friendship was gone forever. She saw him every day, and yet she missed him the way she missed her father.

Once in a great while, when they were working out security logistics or discussing strategies for the next meeting of the Council of Sovereigns, Melyor could almost convince herself that their relationship was back to the way it had been years ago, when they were still working out of her flat in the Fourth Realm. But standing now amid the shards of glass that littered the floor of her sleeping quarters, with smoke stinging her eyes, it seemed to Melyor that the gulf between them was as wide and deep as Arick's Sea.

"The boomer was hand-detonated," Jibb said, his voice flat, "apparently by someone dressed in a SovSec uniform. He got as far as the steps leading to the palace entrance before my men noticed him. Their thrower fire took him down, but he managed to set off the explosion."

Melyor nodded. It was an old tactic, but an effective one. Give an assassin mind-mastering drugs, strap explosives to the inside of whatever disguise you wanted him or her to wear, and send the poor fool to die, hoping that he or she would take out your target as well. Cedrych, who was Overlord of Bragor-Nal's First Dominion, was almost killed this way, and he bore the scars of that assassination attempt for the rest of his life. And in the last year alone, Melyor had survived four such attacks. *Now five*, she told herself, conscious once more of the cut on her cheek and the trembling of her hands.

She and Jibb still had no idea who was behind them. After the first attempt, they had received reports that Enrik, one of Melyor's Overlords, was responsible. Under questioning from Jibb's men, the Overlord admitted as much and was thrown in prison. But the attacks continued—from all that Jibb could learn, all four assassins had used the same type of explosive and the same type of casing. That, combined with the similarity of their tactics, convinced both Jibb and Melyor that the same person or people had sent them all. After the last bombing, Jibb questioned Enrik a second time, but while the Overlord admitted that he had received instructions from another source, and more than enough gold to convince him to follow these instructions, he claimed that all of this had come through intermediaries. Jibb had used every method at his disposal—even now, Melyor could not help but shudder at the implications of that phrase—to get Enrik to reveal the identity of his backer, but the Overlord told them nothing.

"He doesn't have much tolerance for pain," Jibb said at the time. "So I'd guess that he really doesn't know."

Who could be doing this? Melyor asked herself, as she had so many times over the past year. She had no shortage of enemies, she knew. Glancing over at her staff, with its glowing red stone, she smiled sadly. As Sovereign, she was a natural target for for assassination. Despite all the changes she had brought to Bragor-Nal, she could not alter the one essential truth of the Nal's system of government: peace and stability tended to limit opportunities for advancement. The violence of the Nal, which Melyor and Jibb had worked so hard to curb, did have a practical side. It enabled break-laws to become Nal-Lords and Nal-Lords to become Overlords. And if this violence managed to claim the life of the Sovereign, as it had seven years ago when Cedrych murdered Sovereign Durell in this very room, the effects rippled through the entire system, creating openings for a few lucky people at every level of the Nal hierarchy.

But Melyor believed that this was only part of the reason for the repeated attempts on her life. She was more than just Bragor-Nal's Sovereign. She was also Bearer of the Stone and the first self-acknowledged Gildriite in the Nal's history to wield any authority at all, much less occupy the Gold Palace. Because of their Sight—their ability to divine the future—her people had been persecuted for a thousand years. And as the most prominent and powerful Gildriite in all of Lon-Ser, Melyor could not help but become a target for the fear and hatred that the Gildriites had endured throughout their history.

"Are you sure you're all right?" Jibb asked her, looking at her closely.

She managed a smile. "Yes, thanks."

"We'll find out who's behind this, Sovereign," he said confidently, holding her gaze. "I give you my word. I've already got Premel working on it, and with the additional evidence from this attempt, he should have something for us very soon."

"I don't doubt it for a moment," Melyor replied.

"But something's troubling you."

She smiled, ignoring another chill. "This wasn't the nicest way to wake up."

"Of course not, Sovereign." He looked away. "You probably need some time alone. I'll leave you."

She shook her head. "That's not what I meant, Jibb—"

"It's all right. I should oversee the sweep-up anyway. I don't want them to lose anything that might help Premel."

Melyor took another breath and nodded.

"Let us know if you need anything, Sovereign."

Sovereign. *Call me Melyor!* she wanted to say. *You're my best friend!* Instead, she merely nodded a second time. "I will."

He turned and left the room, closing the door behind him.

Melyor pulled her hands from her pockets and ran them through her hair. The smoke had thinned a bit, leaving just a fine grey haze, but her quarters looked like a quad bar the morning after a firefight. It would take most of the day just to clean it up and replace the windows. None of that, of course, was her concern; a Sovereign had stewards to see to such things. But it did mean that her room, and the study that adjoined it, which, she could see, had also been damaged, would be inaccessible until the evening.

She walked to the small sink by her bed, wiped the fragments of glass from its edge, and then splashed cold water on her face. The water stung the cut on her cheek, but it made her feel better, so much so that she abruptly made a decision. Stepping out of her robe, she quickly dressed and pulled on her boots. Sovereigns of Bragor-Nal were expected to wear the golden robe; it was as much a token of a Sovereign's position as the palace itself. But Melyor had never felt comfortable in anything but her loose-fitting black trousers and ivory tunic, and she continued to wear them, along with the thrower that she still strapped to her thigh, even to meetings of the Council of Sovereigns. Marar, the leader of Stib-Nal, Bragor-Nal's inconsequential southern neighbor, had made it quite clear that he found her lack of decorum offensive. Even Sovereign Shivohn of Oerella-Nal, who had played such an important role in the events leading to Melyor and Orris's confrontation with Cedrych, had often commented, with more seriousness than she could mask with a smile, that Melyor looked like a Nal-Lord rather than a Sovereign.

Melyor, of course, didn't care what her fellow Sovereigns thought of her attire. She was a Gildriite, a Bearer; she was bound to be different. But more than that, she ruled a Nal famous for its break-laws and firefights. It wouldn't do for the first female Sovereign in its history to put away her thrower and dress in a pretty robe.

Strapping on that thrower now, and picking up her staff, Melyor left her bedchamber and made her way downstairs and outside, where Jibb and his men were examining the damage caused by the explosion. The marble stairs leading to the palace entrance, which had once been golden, were now blackened and covered with glass and other debris. Most of the steps were fractured beyond repair, and the second, third, and fourth steps from the bottom had been completely obliterated. The gilded facade of the palace was blackened as well and pitted with jagged pieces of marble.

Approximately a dozen of Jibb's men lay on the ground near the entrance, their blue uniforms stained with blood. A few had already been bandaged while others were still being tended to by the crisis meds. Three men had already been covered with white sheets so that Melyor could see only their black boots and the crimson streams of blood that flowed from their bodies. There seemed to be nothing at all left of the assassin.

Those of Jibb's men who had come through the attack unscathed were searching the front grounds of the palace for boomer fragments or anything else that might tell them something about the assassin. Several others were carefully extracting debris from the palace facade. Jibb stood at the base of what was left of the steps, speaking in low tones to Premel. If Melyor found it difficult to see Jibb as head of SovSec, she found it even more disorienting to think of Premel as second-in-command of the security force. With his clean-shaven head and the large gold hoop in his ear, he still looked too much like a break-law, even in the pale blue uniform. In spite of the carnage around her, Melyor could not help but smile. It seemed at times that they were all just children, pretending to be Sovereigns and soldiers.

"Sovereign!" Jibb said with surprise, noticing her in the doorway. "Did you need something?"

"No. I just thought I'd offer you some help."

He narrowed his eyes. "Excuse me?"

"I used to be a pretty good Nal-Lord, remember?"

"Of course. But—"

She walked down the stairs, nimbly jumping over the steps that were too damaged to support her. She stopped in front of him and met his gaze evenly. "I may be Sovereign," she said with quiet intensity, "but that doesn't mean I'm not capable of sifting through rubble, or doing any of the other things that you and your men do."

"I know that, Sovereign," Jibb replied, lowering his voice as well. "But it does mean that you're even more of a target than you used to be. And who's to say that there isn't a second assassin in the area."

She smiled. "You're right. Good thing the commander of SovSec is nearby."

Jibb shook his head. "This isn't funny, Sovereign."

"No, it's not," Melyor agreed, her smile fading as she surveyed the carnage around them. "Someone killed three of my men today, and I'd like to know why." She looked at Jibb again. "As to the rest, I'm still better with a blade or a thrower than any man here. Including you Jibb. Never forget that."

He grinned at her in a way that she hadn't seen in years. "I never have," he said. "I'm glad you haven't either."

She frowned, uncertain of what he meant.

"Come with me," he said, gesturing toward a small pile of debris that sat a short distance from the palace entrance. "Let me show you what we've found so far." They squatted next to the pile and began to examine the blackened fragments of rock, clothing, and metal. A moment later Premel joined them.

"In most ways we're finding just what we found the last four times," Jibb told her, looking closely at one piece of metal for a few seconds and then tossing it casually back onto the rest of the debris.

Melyor gave a rueful grin. "In other words: nothing."

The security chief shrugged and then nodded. "But it's the same nothing each time."

Premel made a loud snorting sound. It took Melyor a moment to realize that he was laughing. But when she glanced at the bald man she saw little mirth in his pale eyes.

"That's worse than nothing," Premel said. "It's like they're taunting us."

"So you agree with Jibb," Melyor said. "All the bombs were sent by the same person."

It took him a minute. "Or people," he corrected. But then he nodded. "Yes, I guess I do."

"Well, that's something." She faced Jibb again. "So what do we know about them?"

Jibb shook his head. "Not much. There's rarely anything left for us to look at. A few pieces of bomb casing, some clothing from the assassin. They make good bombs, and they're more than willing to sacrifice a few men if it means killing you. But beyond that . . ." He trailed off, shrugging again.

"You haven't learned anything from the casing or clothing?"

Jibb shook his head. "Not yet, no. But this boomer might offer a bit more."

"What do you mean?"

He picked up another scrap from the pile of debris and handed it to her. It was black and jagged, and it was barely larger than the palm of her hand. "You may not believe this," he said, "but that's the biggest scrap we've gotten from any of the boomers."

Melyor turned it over and, seeing nothing distinguishing on either side, handed it back to him. "That's not much to go on."

"No, but there are several other fragments that are nearly that size. Apparently, this bomb wasn't as well made as the others. We might find something more."

"And if we don't?" Premel asked.

The three of them stood, but before Jibb or Melyor could answer, one of the men scanning the facade of the palace called excitedly to Jibb. He was holding something in his hand, and he bounded down the stairs and rushed to where the three of them were standing.

"What is it?" Jibb asked.

The man grinned. "I think it's the detonator."

He held it out, and Jibb grabbed it from his hand. The security chief examined it for several moments before looking up at the man again. "Well done," he said with a single nod.

The man's smile deepened. "Thank you, sir." He turned away and hurried back to the palace.

"Well?" Melyor asked Jibb.

The big man gazed at the object again. "He's right. It is the detonator." He handed it to Melyor. "Take a look," he said grimly.

It was a small metal cylinder, dented on one side and blackened like the other fragments. There were two holes near one end of the cylinder probably for the wires leading to the explosive, but otherwise the object was unmarked. And yet this single piece of metal told Melyor all that she needed to know about her would-be assassin.

She was no expert on boomers. Even in her younger days, when she had killed with some frequency, she had preferred the precision of her thrower and blade to the unpredictability of explosives. But her life in the quads had demanded that she learn something of bombs. Indeed, on more than one occasion, her survival had depended upon her ability to disable timed boomers. So she knew that the detonators on most of the boomers used by break-laws and Nal-Lords were far cruder than the one she held in her hand. The man who had tried to kill her this morning had been sent by someone with the resources to supply him with a sophisticated device.

But that was secondary. Boomers made in Bragor-Nal had squared detonators. All of them. It was required under the provisions of the Green Area Proclamation signed by the Sovereigns of Lon-Ser's three Nals in 2899. All of the Nals were required to standardize certain components of all of their advanced goods. The provision was designed to enforce the ban on exporting advanced goods by making each item traceable to its source. It covered a wide range of essential parts for carriers, manufacturing devices, speak-screens and other everyday items, and, of course, weapons. Including detonators.

"What do you think?" Jibb asked, watching her closely.

Melyor took a breath. "This wasn't made in Bragor-Nal."

"No, it wasn't," he agreed.

She stared at him for another moment and then, handing the device back to him, spun on her heel and started back toward the palace.

"Where are you going?" Jibb called to her.

"To my office!" she replied over her shoulder without breaking stride. "I need to speak with Shivohn!"

"Good morning, Sovereign!" one of the laborers called as Shivohn stepped onto the low terrace overlooking the empty flower beds and precise, curving hedgerows.

She waved and smiled, her crimson robe and light hair stirring in a soft wind. Several of the other men and women called greetings to her, and she waved to them as well.

It was cold still. She knew that if they moved the flowers from the growing house to the gardens today, they risked losing them all in a hard frost. But winter's grip was loosening, and she was impatient to see the blooms opening beneath the Oerellan sun. Besides, she had always followed her instincts when it came to the gardens. And in all her years as Sovereign, she had never lost a single bud to frost.

She descended the narrow staircase that led from the terrace to the garden and began to stroll along the meandering pathways defined by her well-groomed hedges.

Most aspects of her life as Sovereign had grown stale over the years: the isolation, the constant fawning of her underlings, the pomp of ceremonies that held no interest for her anymore. She had grown impatient with the ever-worsening strife among her Legates. She understood it, of course: they all wished to be Sovereign, someday, and she was getting old. But she was weary of their ambition and dismayed by the bitterness of their rivalry.

Even the meetings of the Council of Sovereigns, which she had attended with renewed interest and enthusiasm when Melyor was invested as leader of Bragor-Nal, had grown tedious once more. Marar, the Sovereign of Stib-Nal, showed little interest in bringing genuine change to Lon-Ser, and Melyor, though savvy and well-intentioned, still had much to learn about running a Nal and building relations with Bragor-Nal's neighbors.

She knew that there was an opportunity here for Oerella-Nal. Stib-Nal remained weak, and Bragor-Nal's leader lacked experience. Ten years ago a younger Shivohn would have found a way to exploit such a circumstance, and perhaps Wiercia, or one of the other Legates, could have done so now. But this older Shivohn, who shivered slightly within her crimson robe, was tired, and with Durell gone, and with him, the threat of war, she no longer felt the urgency that had once driven her.

The only thing that held her interest anymore was the garden. Here she could act, boldly filling her flower beds as if daring the winter to provoke her. This was her battlefield, and these laborers were her soldiers.

She walked among them now, peering over their shoulders, occasionally offering a word of advice or instruction. Most of them she had known for years. Old Tiran had been here longer than she, and Krid, Lirette, and Affren, had arrived soon after her investiture. Several others had been hired more recently, and though she didn't know their names, she recognized their faces. And, as there seemed to be each year, there was a new face as well, a woman she had never seen before who was walking in her direction now. Shivohn smiled. The new ones always liked to meet her.

"Sovereign!" She turned and saw Lirette motioning for her to come and look at something. Shivohn nodded and started in that direction. The new woman would have to wait.

"Yes, Lirette," Shivohn said as she reached the stout woman, who was turning the soil in a large section of flower bed. "Is there a problem?"

"There certainly is, Sovereign!" Lirette answered, her blue eyes blazing as she laid down her hoe. "They've got your lobelia and your hibiscus going in right next to each other! Never mind that I don't care for the color combination! But the hibiscus is just too tall! By midsummer it will be shading the other something fierce!"

Shivohn suppressed a smile. Lirette had never been shy about expressing herself, and while she was respectful of Shivohn's position, she had never left any room for doubt: the garden was her domain.

"I see your point, Lirette," Shivohn said with appropriate gravity. "Make any changes you feel are necessary."

The woman smiled. "Thank you, Sovereign."

Shivohn nodded and resumed her strolling. Then, remembering the new woman, she paused and scanned the garden for her.

Before she found her, however, she heard someone else calling for her. Sighing heavily, she turned back toward the terrace and saw one of her bodyguards beckoning her back to the palace.

"What is it?" she called impatiently.

"Your speak-screen, Sovereign!" the man answered. "Sovereign Melyor wishes to speak with you!"

Shivohn made a sour face. "Very well."

She turned to follow the shortest path back to the terrace, and nearly bumped into one of the laborers. An instant later she realized that it was the new woman.

"Oh, hello," Shivohn said, as pleasantly as she could manage. She tried to step around her. "I'm afraid our introductions will—"

She stopped, gaping at the woman's eyes. Her pupils were enormous, leaving just a thin ring of pale grey around the fathomless black.

She's been drugged, the Sovereign realized, fear gripping her heart. She tried to back away, knowing with sudden, mind-numbing clarity why the woman had come, but there was a hedge just behind her.

No one else had noticed. She was going to die within shouting distance of a dozen laborers and an entire unit of security men, and there was nothing anyone could do about it.

"Why?" she asked, her voice barely more than a whisper.

But she knew that the woman could not answer.

The woman raised her hand slightly, and Shivohn saw the morning sun glint off the metal of the square-edged detonator. The Sovereign opened her mouth to scream, but before she could, the assassin moved her thumb.

5

I have never made any secret of my feelings for the League. Indeed, I'm sure that you would be happy if you never read another word about that body or its members. I find it hard to imagine forgiving any of them for the harm they have caused me, and harder still to pardon what they have done to the Mage-Craft. You know all of this, of course. I've written it all before.

So it may come as something of a surprise to you that there is one member of the League for whom I hold no animosity, and with whose rejection of the Order I cannot find fault. No doubt it will surprise you further to learn that this person is considered one of the leaders of the League—for all I know, she is one of those who has ordered the attempts on my life. Even if this were the case, however, it would not matter. . . .

Her name is Cailin, and she suffered so at the hands of the outlanders when she was but a child that I can scarcely fathom how she has managed to survive to adulthood. That she holds the Order responsible for its failure to protect her seems to me entirely justified, and convinces

me that as long as she serves the League in any capacity, there will be
no reconciliation between our two groups.

> —Hawk-Mage Orris to Melyor i
> Lakin, Sovereign and Bearer of
> Bragor-Nal, Winter, God's Year
> 4633.

Cailin dried her eyes a second time and smiled apologetically at Linnea.

"I'm sorry, Eldest," she said, her voice still unsteady. "This is all so new to me. Every time I start to talk about it, I feel like I've lost him all over again." She swallowed, fighting back another wave of tears. Marcran had been dead for nearly a fortnight; the numb, empty feeling in her chest seemed as familiar to her now as the small falcon's presence in her mind had felt just a short time ago. And yet, each time she spoke of his death, which had come gently, as he slept, she felt the pain of losing him once more, as vivid and debilitating as it had been that first day.

Linnea had been standing by the window in her dimly lit chamber, her bulky frame appearing almost black against the silver-grey of another rainy afternoon. But now she stepped to where Cailin was sitting and placed a hand on the young woman's head.

"There's no need to apologize, Child," she said softly. "Not to me. I'm just sorry that I can't help you more. I can tell you that being unbound is part of being a mage, but that's not likely to help you very much." She moved a small wooden chair next to Cailin's and lowered herself into it. "Isn't there anyone in your League who can help you?" she asked. "Someone who's been through this before."

Cailin shrugged. "I suppose there are a few I could talk to," she answered without enthusiasm. "Most of them are afraid of me."

"Afraid of you?" Linnea repeated with a breathless laugh. "They must not know you very well."

Cailin looked at the woman and grinned. Linnea had aged considerably over the past few years, particularly since she had given up leadership of the Temple just over two years ago. Her hair was white now, and her once round cheeks looked hollow and were marked by deep lines. And though she was still a large woman, she appeared frail somehow, as if her silver-grey robe was draped over bones and skin and little else. Recently, Cailin had begun to fear that the Eldest might be ill. Still, while the rest of her seemed to be failing, the woman's pale blue eyes remained as bright and sharp as ever. They sparkled with the light from the window and the flashing golden glow given off by Cailin's ceryll.

"You may not find me frightening, Eldest," Cailin said, using Linnea's old title as much out of habit as out of deference. "But to the mages of the League, especially the younger ones, I'm . . ." She hesitated, feeling herself starting to blush.

"A legend?" Linnea ventured, completing the thought.

Cailin nodded sheepishly. "Yes. Not that I've ever wanted to be treated that way, but that's what I've become." She pushed her long brown hair out of her face and shrugged again. "Anyway, to answer your question," she told the Eldest, "I'm certain that there are those in the League who'd be willing to help me, but none whom I'd feel comfortable asking."

"I would guess," Linnea said, "that your ties to the Temple are little help in this regard."

Cailin laughed. While the League and the Temples had been allies for a brief time after First Master Erland formed the League seven years ago, the tensions that had developed between them in recent years already ran nearly as deep as those between the Children of the Gods and the Order. "Actually they don't create as many problems as you'd expect," she said. "Being a legend has certain advantages."

"I'm glad to hear it," Linnea replied with a smile. "I'd hate to think that our friendship might keep you from becoming First Master when you bind to your owl."

"Since when are you so ambitious for me?" Cailin asked, ignoring the pang in her heart. She still was troubled by the notion of binding to a bird other than her beloved Marcran.

The Eldest smiled enigmatically. "So what of Erland in all this? Is he of any help to you?"

The young mage shook her head. "You never have liked him, have you?"

"I don't know what you're talking about," Linnea insisted, her eyes widening with feigned innocence. "I merely asked a simple question."

"Indeed."

Linnea gave a small laugh and stood, stepping once more to the window. "It's not important, Child," she said, her voice subdued suddenly. "I just wondered if he could help you."

Cailin stood as well. "Look at me, Linnea."

The Eldest turned at the sound of her name.

"Look at me," Cailin repeated.

She watched the older woman's face, seeing Linnea's pale eyes soften as she looked Cailin up and down.

"I'm not a child anymore. I'm not even certain that I ever was one. Certainly I wasn't after Kaera. But the point is, I'm grown now. I'm eighteen. If I was just an ordinary woman rather than a mage, I'd be joined by now; I'd probably have children. Yet everyone still treats me as if I'm the little orphan who survived the outlanders and bound to the pretty falcon."

Linnea frowned. "Cailin, when I call you 'Child' I—"

"I don't care what you call me, Eldest," the mage broke in, shaking her head. "But how am I to convince the League to take me seriously as one of its leaders if I can't even get you to talk to me honestly about Erland?"

The Eldest stared at her for several moments, saying nothing. Finally, she inclined her head slightly. "I see your point."

"Good. Then tell me why you hate Erland so much."

"I don't hate him. We of the Temple do not direct hatred at individuals; to do so is to repeat the wrongs of Tobyn and Lon and thus risk provoking Arick. You should know that after living among us for so long."

"Of course, Eldest," Cailin said. "I'm sorry."

"You needn't apologize, Ch—" She grinned, her cheeks coloring for just a moment. "I don't hate him," she continued after a brief pause. "I just don't trust him. I never have."

"But didn't you ally the Temple with him when he split from the Order?"

"We supported the League. We hoped that maybe, if the Mage-Craft was controlled by a body other than the Order, this ancient feud of ours might finally end. And at the time, I suppose, supporting the League meant supporting Erland." She made a sour face. "But even then, I didn't trust him."

"Why not? Because he used me? Because he needed a symbol for his new League and chose me?"

Linnea regarded her with unconcealed astonishment.

"Yes," Cailin said, smiling again. "I knew. Not immediately, of course. I was too young and too taken with the idea of being First Mage of the League." She still remembered the day Erland came to her in the clearing above the Temple where she liked to fly Marcran, and offered her the chance to wear the blue cloak. The League was new to the land then— she had never even heard of it. But in a vision that had come to her nearly two years earlier, she had seen herself in a blue cloak, killing the men who had killed her parents. And so she accepted his offer, believing that the gods had ordained that she should serve the League. "But it didn't take me long to figure out why Erland was being so kind to me," she went on. "I could see it in the way the other mages treated me."

Linnea narrowed her eyes. "How did they treat you?"

"Like a child."

"Do they still?"

"Not all of them. The younger ones look to me for direction during the Conclaves. But Erland and his allies still see me as little more than a trophy."

The Eldest nodded. "I see."

"So is that why you don't trust him?"

Linnea gazed at her without responding for several seconds. "You really want to know what it was?" she asked at last.

Cailin nodded.

"It was the ceryll."

"My ceryll?" Cailin asked incredulously, her gaze falling on the golden stone. Erland had given it to her that day in the clearing, a gentle smile on his lips and a look of kindness in his dark blue eyes. And as soon as he placed it in her hand, a brilliant light had burst from it like a flame. "You now possess everything you need to be a Hawk-Mage," Erland told her that day. "The power you carry within you, your familiar and your stone." It was, to this day, the finest gift anyone had ever given her. In the years that followed, as her awareness of the motives of those around her grew, she had clung desperately to the memory of that single moment. It was the one act of genuine kindness that Erland had shown her; it was a gift of such surpassing generosity that, in this one instance, she had refused to question his motives, ignoring all that she knew of him.

"I've troubled you," Linnea said with concern. "I'm sorry, my dear."

"It's all right," Cailin answered in a small voice, her eyes still fixed on the flashing golden crystal. With an effort she made herself meet the Eldest's gaze. "Tell me about my ceryll."

Linnea took a long breath. "You remember Sonel, who led the Order when you first bound to your falcon?"

"Yes."

"Despite the animosity that exists between the Temple and the Order, I often spoke to her of your progress in mastering the Mage-Craft. She made it clear to me that until you had matured and learned to control your power, it would be dangerous to give you a ceryll."

"And you believed her?" Cailin asked dully, grasping for anything that might preserve her memory of Erland's gesture. "Could she have been trying to keep me from coming into my power?"

Linnea shook her head. "I don't think so. I sensed no malicious intent. I think this is what she honestly felt was best for you and for those of us who were caring for you."

"Did you try to keep Erland from giving it to me?"

"No," Linnea said with a thin simile. "I didn't know he intended to until it was too late."

"And you think he gave it to me as a way of luring me into the League." Cailin offered it as a statement. It made sense really. Given reason to doubt the trust she had placed in the white-haired Owl-Master, she had found herself in recent years re-examining all the kindnesses he had shown her since their first meeting. Every one of them, she had come to realize, could be interpreted as an attempt to deceive and influence her. Why should the ceryll have been any different?

"Yes," the Eldest said. "He needed you. Your presence in the League immediately made it a legitimate alternative to the Order. Without you it would have taken him years to win the support of so many of the land's villages and towns. He as much as told me that he had purchased the ceryll for just that reason."

Cailin felt herself blanch. "He told you that?" she whispered.

"Yes. Why?"

The mage gave a small, mirthless laugh. "He made it sound as though it had been lying around his home gathering dust for years."

Linnea sat beside her again and put her arm around Cailin's shoulders. "I'm so sorry, my dear."

"Don't be," Cailin said. "I needed to know this." She glanced at the Eldest and made herself smile. "As I said before, I'm not a child anymore. And actually, it explains a great deal."

"In what way?"

She pushed the hair from her face again. "At the last two Conclaves I've spoken against some of Erland's actions, most importantly against his endorsement of the attacks on that man in the Order."

"The one he believes is a traitor?"

"Yes. Those attacks are a direct violation of Amarid's Third Law, no matter how our bylaws might justify it." The bylaws of the League, adopted at the body's first Conclave, expressly amended Amarid's Third Law, which prohibited mages from using the Mage-Craft against one another. Such attacks, the amended law stated, were justified if they were necessary to protect the land. In the years since, Erland and his supporters had used this law to explain away their attacks on the Order mage. "How can the League hope to maintain the people's faith in the Mage-Craft," Cailin asked, "if we can't even abide by its oldest laws?"

Linnea grinned, shaking her head slightly. "You see the irony?" she asked.

"Yes," Cailin said, smiling for a moment as well. As a young girl, newly bound to her falcon and still haunted by the memory of her parents' death, she was so resentful of the Order for its failure to protect her family that she refused to take the oath to abide by the First Mage's Laws. As she grew older and came to recognize the importance of the laws, she realized how foolish she had been. In her mind, though, the ultimate irony lay not in her own belated adherence to the laws, but rather in the disregard for the laws shown by her older colleagues.

"So, Erland objected to your opposition?" Linnea prompted, bringing them back to subject at hand.

"That's an understatement. I always believed that as a member of the League I had the right to speak my mind, and much of what I said drew support from the younger mages. But after the first time I opposed him on this matter, Erland told me that he expected me to endorse all of his decisions. I told him I couldn't do that, and when I disagreed with him again at the most recent Conclave, he acted as though I had violated some unspoken agreement. He stopped speaking to me, he refused to recognize me during formal deliberations, he even tried to exclude me from the closing ceremonies, although the others wouldn't allow that."

Linnea shook her head. "It sounds to me as though your League needs a new leader, or at least someone who's willing to stand up to Erland."

"I agree," Cailin said. "But there's little I can do about that. Especially now."

Linnea frowned. "What do you mean?"

"When I lost Marcran, I also lost my status as First Mage."

"But Erland lost his owl a few years back," Linnea said, her voice rising. "He managed to keep his position."

Cailin nodded. "I know. He maneuvered to have the man who replaced him as First Master designated as an interim leader. But he's already named my successor. And he made it clear that she'll continue to be First Mage long after I find my next familiar. I can still speak against him, but I don't have the standing within the League that I used to."

Linnea sighed. "It's unfortunate that Erland has remained your leader for so long."

"Perhaps," Cailin agreed. "But it seems that changing leadership carries risk as well."

"Ah," the Eldest said with a wan smile. "So we're speaking of the Temple now, are we?"

"You have to do something, Linnea," Cailin told her. "The Temple lands are being destroyed, and the people in the League villages are growing frightened."

The older woman made a small, helpless gesture with her hands. "What can I do? When I stepped down as Eldest, I relinquished my hold on the Temple."

"You still have influence though. You must."

"Less than you'd think," Linnea said grimly. "Too much has changed over the past few years." She smiled. "It's ironic, really: you have the support of the younger mages, and I still have some influence with the older Keepers." The smile fled from her lips. "But not the young ones. All they can think of is gold and power. The Temples have never had so much gold, and yet all they want is to cut the forests and get more. Several of us have called for an end to the cutting, at least for a time. But the rest of them don't listen. As far as they're concerned, we're too old to understand this new world created by our trade with Lon-Ser. And with Brevyl as Eldest, they don't have to listen to us. He's more obsessed with gold than any of them."

"Is it true that the Temples have been trading for weapons as well?"

Linnea nodded, her face going white. "Brevyl didn't even ask us about that," she said. "He just announced one day that the weapons had been purchased. As far as I know, they haven't been used yet," she added quickly. "Brevyl says he needed them to protect the loggers."

Cailin felt her expression harden. "Come now, Linnea. You know better than that. Even if they haven't been used yet, it's only a matter of time before they are. Someone is going to get killed."

The Eldest stared at her with wide eyes, looking for all her white hair and facial lines like a child. "You're right," she whispered. "I know you are. But what can I do?"

"I don't know, Eldest," Cailin said in the same hard voice. "Something. Anything. You have to try."

They sat for some time, saying nothing and avoiding each other's gaze. Cailin had never spoken to Linnea in that manner, and though she felt her words were justified, she was afraid of how the Eldest might respond. In the end, however, Linnea surprised her.

"You know," the older woman finally said, laughing nervously, "it might help me if I could take you with me to the next Assembly of Keepers."

Relieved, Cailin allowed herself to smile. "Only if you'll come to the next Conclave," she replied, laughing as well.

Linnea indicated Cailin's ceryll with a nod. "Perhaps we should both journey to Amarid and join the Gathering that Radomil has summoned."

Cailin glanced down at the stone again. It had been flashing for well over a fortnight, having begun to do so just days before Marcran's death. In the aftermath of losing her familiar, Cailin had given little thought to why the Summoning Stone might have been used. But now, prompted by the Eldest's comment, she began to wonder.

"Do you have any idea what's happened?" Linnea asked, as if reading her thoughts.

"None." She looked up from the stone to meet the older woman's gaze. "I've been too consumed with losing Marcran." She paused for a moment. "Maybe something's happened to Radomil."

The Eldest shook her head. "No. This is a general summons. If they just needed the Owl-Masters to choose another Sage, the interval between the flashes would be much longer."

Cailin narrowed her eyes, staring at the Eldest. "How do you know so much about the Order?"

Linnea gave a sly smile. "It's always wise to know something of one's adversaries."

Cailin considered this for several moments. Then she pointed at her stone. "So this means that the entire Order has been called to Amarid?"

"Yes."

"How often do they use the Summoning Stone in this way?"

"Very rarely," Linnea said. And then, seeming to anticipate Cailin's next question, she added, "It was rare even before the formation of the League."

Cailin felt a wave of apprehension wash over her, like the frigid waters of Arick's Sea in winter. "Did they use it when the outlanders came?" she asked, her voice barely more than a whisper.

Linnea looked at her with a pained expression. "Honestly, Child, I don't know. But I don't think we have anything to fear from the outlanders anymore. At least not in the way we did when you were a child."

The mage heard the truth in what the Eldest had said, and she tried to take solace in it. But her fears clung to her heart as if they had talons. Her ceryll was flashing. *Something* had happened, even if it had nothing to do with the outlanders.

"Have you ever thought," she asked, gazing wistfully into the flickering ceryll, "that if you and I could just sit down with the leader of the Order—just the three of us—that we could solve all of these problems, end the fighting and the distrust?"

"All the time," Linnea answered in a tone that made Cailin look up from her stone.

The mage felt her pulse quicken. "So how do we make that happen?"

Linnea shrugged, although her pale eyes remained locked on Cailin's. "I'm not sure. So much needs to happen. I would have to be in a position where I could count on the support of at least some of the younger Keepers."

"And I'd have to be bound again, preferably to an owl."

"We'd need a different Sage as well," the Eldest added. "From what I know of Radomil, I believe him to be a decent man. But he's very cautious."

"What is it we're talking about?" Cailin asked, feeling strangely giddy as she leaned forward.

Linnea grinned. "You tell me. It was your idea."

"It wasn't an idea, it was a fantasy, an idle thought."

"Then why do you look so exhilarated?" the Eldest asked with intensity. "Why is my heart pounding so?"

"I don't know."

"Well, I'd suggest," Linnea went on, a warning in her tone, "that you not share such fantasies with anyone other than me. Your fellow mages in the League might be disturbed by the direction your mind takes in its idle moments."

Cailin nodded and swallowed. The Eldest was right, of course. Not that it mattered: the entire notion was ludicrous. Linnea, the Owl-Sage, and herself meeting in secret to save the land? Such a thing would never come to pass. And yet, for some reason, Cailin could not bring herself to dismiss the idea, nor, she knew, could Linnea.

They sat in silence for some time, Linnea staring at her hands and Cailin gazing once more into her ceryll. Eventually, the Eldest asked her about a Keeper in Tobyn's Wood, a friend of Linnea's Cailin often saw during her travels. And for what remained of the afternoon, they spoke of other things, avoiding further mention of political matters.

But late in the day, as Linnea led Cailin to the front gates of the Temple, she returned to the topic once again.

"I don't know how long I have before Arick and Duclea call me to their side," she said, taking Cailin's hand in her own.

Cailin felt her blood turn to ice water. "Are you—"

The Eldest stopped her with a raised finger and a quick shake of her head. There was a single tear running down her cheek. "Let me finish. I don't know how long I have, and, of course, neither of us knows how long it will be until you bind again, be it to a hawk or owl. But as absurd as it sounds, I think that the two of us have as much chance as anyone of bringing an end to the conflicts that have plagued Tobyn-Ser. Even before you said what you did about the two of us meeting with the Owl-Sage, I had a feeling about this."

"Eldest," Cailin said, "do you mean to tell me that you have the Sight?" She tried to keep her tone light, but Linnea's words from a moment before kept repeating themselves in her head. *I don't know how long I have until Arick and Duclea call me to their side . . .*

"Me with the Sight?" Linnea answered, coloring to the tips of her ears. "Don't be ridiculous! I just think that the gods have marked you for an auspicious binding. And I think it will come soon. Perhaps as one who has given her life to the gods, I'm able to, glimpse such things."

"And what of your role in this new world we're going to create?" the mage asked. "Have you seen that future as well?"

"On the contrary," Linnea said, shaking her head. "I've seen the past, and I don't like it. You're right: it's time for me to reassert myself in the assembly. I still have allies, people who are no happier than I with what Brevyl has done in the name of the Temple. It's time we made ourselves heard."

Cailin stepped forward and put her arms around the older woman. The thought of her life without the Eldest frightened her deeply. She knew what it was to lose people dear to her, and she was not at all ready to lose Linnea as well.

"Don't be frightened, Child," Linnea whispered. "I have some time left yet."

"Are you ill?" Cailin asked, feeling herself start to cry. "Can I heal you?" She stepped back and looked the Eldest in the eye. "All you have to do is ask."

Linnea smiled. "I know that. If I thought it was within your power, or anyone else's for that matter, I would ask. I'm afraid, though, that there's nothing to be done, except wait, and make good use of the days I have left." She wiped the tears from Cailin's face and kissed her forehead. "Are you sure you won't stay the night? There's room, and we have plenty of food."

The Eldest's offer was tempting, particularly now that she knew her time with Linnea was limited. But since leaving the Temple three years ago to begin her life as a migrant mage, she had taken shelter only on the coldest of nights. A mage belonged in the forests and mountains and plains, she had decided long ago. Serving the land meant living on the land. And though her heart was heavy with the knowledge of Linnea's illness, and the rain was still falling, she could not in good conscience sleep anywhere but in Hawksfind Wood. In an odd way, she felt that she owed that much to Marcran.

"Thank you," she said. "But I'm sure. I'll visit again soon, though. I promise."

"Very well, my dear," Linnea said, kissing her a second time. "Arick guard you."

"And you, Eldest."

She turned quickly and walked from the Temple. She was crying again, her tears mixing with the cold rain that stung her face, and she did not look back, although she knew that Linnea was still watching her from the gates. *I don't know how long I have . . .*

"Not her, too," she whispered to the trees and the rain, feeling Marcran's absence like a wound on her heart. "I'm not ready to lose Linnea, too."

In the distance she heard the ring of a woodsman's ax against still another tree, and she shuddered. She pulled her cloak tight against the cold and glanced at her flickering golden ceryll. Something was happening in Amarid, and she burned to know what it was.

Everything was so much easier when she first joined the League, so much clearer. She grinned in spite of the rain. More likely that had been an illusion, too, like Erland's generosity. As she told Linnea a short time ago, she hadn't been a child since Kaera. But she had been young, and too quick to believe in Erland and his promises, too eager to blame the Order for all the land's troubles. They had let the outlanders come. They had let her parents die. Nothing else mattered. The Keepers hated the Order and had raised her after her parents died. Linnea hated the Order and loved her almost the way her mother and father had. Erland hated the Order and gave her a ceryll. It all seemed so simple, so clear.

Except that now the Temples were destroying the land's forests, Erland was treating her like an enemy, and Linnea was dying. And in Amarid, just a few leagues from here, the mages of the Order were gathering in response to the call of the Summoning Stone. The Order wasn't evil—it never had been. She knew that now. It was nothing more or less than the League: a collection of men and women who wielded the Mage-Craft, most of them well-intentioned, all of them fallible. She had come to this realization slowly, and it had made coping with her past, with the distant memory of her parents and her childhood, more difficult, not less. A part of her didn't care whether it was all an illusion; she wanted to be eleven again. She longed for that clarity. But another part of her knew better. If she was to lead the League and prove to Erland that he could not ignore her any longer, she had to accept the ambiguities that came with being an adult.

"I'm not a child anymore," she had told the Eldest. Right. Then it was time to stop seeing the world through a child's eyes.

The path she was on met a logging road and, on a whim, she turned northward. There were fishing villages on the coast above Hawksfind Wood. That was as good a place as any to offer her services, limited as they were just then.

Once more she thought of Marcran, her eyes stinging at the memory of his brilliant colors and breathtaking flight. But a moment later she remembered what Linnea said just before she left the Temple. *The gods have marked you for an auspicious binding. And I think it will come soon.*

Cailin halted, knowing as she did that her new familiar was here, on this road, watching her. Suddenly her heart was hammering at her chest so hard that she could actually see her cloak move. She felt the creature's presence as if it was already perched on her shoulder, and she readied herself for what she knew would happen as soon as her eyes met those of the bird. She still remembered her binding to Marcran as if it had happened yesterday. She had nearly lost herself in the maelstrom of memories and emotions that he had conveyed to her. That had been years ago, of course. She was merely a child then, new to the ways of the Mage-Craft. In the years since, she had grown accustomed to sharing her thoughts with a wild creature, and though she knew that binding to a new bird was no trifle, she also knew that she was ready for this.

Taking a breath and turning slowly, she looked up toward the low perch where she knew the bird was sitting.

And seeing her new familiar, she felt her head spin, as if the world itself had shifted. She heard Linnea's voice in her mind again, speaking to her of the binding that she had foreseen.

But not this! Cailin had time to think before a flood of images hit her. *Surely she didn't mean this!*

6

The emergence of the People's Movement is a relatively new development although not a surprising one. With both the Order and the League looking for ways to temper the effects of Tobyn-Ser's new commercial activity, and the Temples driven only by their lust for gold, there has been no organized attempt to end the trade with Lon-Ser altogether. Until now. From what I have heard, it seems that the People's Movement wishes to reverse all that has happened to our land since my journey to Bragor-Nal. It goes without saying that they want to end our trade with your land. But they go much further than that. They want to destroy all of the advanced goods that have come into our land and they wish to expel those citizens of Lon-Ser who have tried to settle in our seaports. Some have even gone so far as to suggest that we should end our trade with Abborij, which has been ongoing for centuries.

And yet, as extreme as their demands may sound, I find nothing inherently dangerous in the existence of this movement. I see it merely as

an inevitable consequence of the vast changes that have come to Tobyn-
Ser in the past several years. I am frightened, however, to learn of the
alliance being forged between the People's Movement and the free mages.

> —Hawk-Mage Orris to Melyor i
> Lakin, Sovereign and Bearer of
> Bragor-Nal, Winter, God's Year
> 4633.

Tammen smiled grimly as she surveyed the scene before her. Notwithstanding the Temple's men with their large weapons and the fearful expressions on the faces of the townspeople, she felt confident. For the past six days, the people of Prannai had joined her and her fellow mages in opposing the keeper and his mercenaries. The townsfolk had been reluctant at first. Perhaps the presence of only three mages had not been enough to embolden them. Nodin, Henryk, and she were certain of their ability to defend the town against the Temple, but it had taken some time to convince Maira and the rest of the Elders that their village would be safe. And in the end, the Keeper's inability or unwillingness to act, not anything that the mages did, won over the villagers.

It began with their first encounter, when the two Owl-Masters from the Order intervened, and Keeper Padgett backed down. Each day since then had been pretty much the same except that no more mages from the Order had come through the village. The Keeper and his woodsmen, accompanied by their armed escort, approached the grove only to be confronted by the villagers and the three free mages. Padgett threatened to have his men kill anyone who interfered with the woodsmen, but when Maira and her people, supported by Tammen and her friends, refused to allow the woodsmen to cut the trees, he did nothing. Perhaps he feared that Tammen and her friends would retaliate by killing him, or perhaps he merely lacked the nerve to resort to violence. Whatever the reason, six days later, the forests still stood.

And with each day, the confidence of the villagers grew. Tammen could see it in their faces, she could hear it in their cheers each afternoon when the Keeper and his men finally retreated to the Temple. Eventually—quite soon, really—Tammen, Nodin, and Henryk would have to move on. There were other towns and other forests. If the movement was to succeed, none of the land's dozen or so no-cloaks, as the free mages called themselves, could remain in any one place for very long. And with their cerylls flashing in response to the summons of the Order's Owl-Sage, Tammen and her companions knew that they could not tarry in Prannai for much longer. *Something* was happening, and Tammen was determined that the Movement would have a role to play in whatever changes were coming to Tobyn-Ser. Fortunately, she no longer doubted that Maira and her villagers would keep up the fight once she and her fellow mages were gone. The weapons carried by the Keeper's guards still scared them, of course. That was to be expected. And it didn't help that Padgett had increased the number of armed guards accompanying his woodsmen from seven to fourteen. But even that could not alter the one essential truth of what had happened during their six days of confrontation. Here in Prannai, the People's Movement had taken hold.

There was a part of her that wondered if once she and her companions were gone, Padgett would allow his men to use their weapons. But such concerns were, Tammen believed, beside the point. As she saw it, the free mages were responsible for bringing the People's Movement to the towns and villages of Tobyn-Ser. It was up to Tammen and those like her to organize the townsfolk and to make them believe in their ability to end the destructive transformations that they saw taking place all around them. But once the no-cloaks did this, it fell to the villagers themselves to sustain the Movement, even if that meant risking their lives to do so. This was, in a sense, a war for the future of the land. There were bound to be casualties.

"Here he comes," Nodin said in a low, tight voice.

Immediately, Tammen looked toward the Temple and saw the Keeper striding in their direction, his silver robe rustling in the light wind, and his round face looking flushed beneath his steel grey hair.

"He looks different," Henryk said under his breath. "Something's happened."

Tammen heard the tension in his words, and for a moment she thought she might laugh. "He looks beaten," she told him. "He knows we've won."

"Maybe," Nodin said cautiously. "I agree with Henryk: he does look different somehow. But I'm not as sure of the reason."

"I just told you," Tammen said impatiently, shaking her head. She knew that Nodin considered himself a man of some importance among the free mages; certainly he saw himself as the leader of their little group, and Henryk treated him that way. But despite his swagger and his posturing, the tall mage was neither bold nor particularly brave. He had some wisdom, Tammen had to admit, but if it wasn't for her, he would have given up on Prannai after their encounter with the two Owl-Masters. And even then, he had only listened to her because he was half in love with her.

"You heard what Baden said about those weapons!" he fretted at the time. "We could get these people killed!"

"He was trying to scare us," Tammen had replied. "He wants us to leave. And even if all he told us is true, he also said that we can block their fire."

"For a time," Nodin had said. "But not forever."

She had come close then to just throwing up her hands in disgust and striking out on her own. She didn't need Nodin or Henryk. If this was how they planned to advance the Movement, she wanted no part of them. But in the end, she decided that three mages could accomplish more than one, and, though it took her much of that night, she did manage to convince them that they should stay in Prannai for just a few days more. The success they had enjoyed since then had only served to prove how right she had been. Again.

Watching Padgett approach for yet another day of confrontation, Tammen could not help but think back once more to their first encounter. The Keeper had been so smug that day, as if he himself had been holding a weapon. To see him now, his fat face looking red and blotchy in the morning sun, made her feel giddy. *This is our first victory,* she realized, a smile springing to her lips. *The Movement is truly on its way.*

"Good morning, Padgett!" she called out, not bothering to conceal her glee. "Have you come to dismiss your mercenaries? Or shall we shout insults at each other for another day?"

The Keeper stopped in front of the three mages and looked at them gravely. He did not look well. There were dark circles under his green eyes, and he was sweating, although the morning air was cool.

"I have tried to reason with you these past several days," he said. And even Tammen could hear the plea in his voice. "I have tried to tell you that I wish the people of this village no harm, that I hope and expect that they will profit from the timber trade even as the Temple does." He paused and swallowed.

Tammen wondered briefly if he was going to be ill.

"But now," he went on, "I'm asking you—begging you, in fact—to tell these people to step out of our way."

"Why?" Tammen asked. "So that you can destroy this forest? So that you can steal this land from Prannai's people? Haven't you been listening to us? Haven't you been listening to Maira?"

"Yes! I've been listening!" Padgett shot back with uncharacteristic fervor. "But clearly you haven't! None of you have!" he added, glancing at Nodin and Henryk. "*This is not their land!* It's not my land, either! It belongs to the Temple, and so is subject to the decisions of Eldest Brevyl! You must understand that!"

Tammen laughed harshly. "And you must understand that—"

"What does Brevyl have to do with this?" Nodin broke in, silencing Tammen with a glare.

The Keeper hesitated, licking his lips. "I received a dispatch from him this morning. He is on his way to Tobyn's Wood so that he can see for himself how the harvesting of Temple lands is progressing. According to his message, he left Hawksfind Wood nearly a fortnight ago. He will reach Prannai within the next day or two."

"I don't believe you," Tammen said.

Nodin turned and glared at her. "Be quiet, Tammen!"

She felt her color rising. She was certain that Henryk was watching her, that all-too-familiar amused expression in his dark eyes, and she had to resist an urge to spin around and slap him.

"What's your point, Keeper?" Nodin asked, facing Padgett again. "What happens when Brevyl arrives?"

Padgett took a slow breath. "That depends. If the forests haven't been cut yet, he'll cut them, regardless of the cost in human life."

"That's quite a statement to make about the leader of Arick's Children," Nodin said, raising an eyebrow.

The Keeper shrugged. "I'm merely telling you what I know to be true. The Eldest is a decent man, but like any person in a position of such importance, he's used to having his orders followed. He has little patience with delay and less still for frivolous challenges to his authority." He gazed beyond Nodin and Tammen toward the townspeople. "I have done all that I can to spare the lives of these people because I care about them. I care about Prannai." He looked at Nodin once more. "Brevyl has no such sentiments to stay his hand."

Nodin nodded, as if weighing this. "So what do you propose?" he finally asked.

"Let us cut the forest now, and we'll only cut half of it. When Brevyl arrives I'll tell him that we're in the process of harvesting the rest. He'll move on, satisfied with our progress, and he'll never know of the bargain we've struck."

"You're not really listening to him, are you?" Tammen asked, unable to contain herself any longer. "He's lying! He doesn't care about these people! He's just worried about what will happen to him when Brevyl sees that we've beaten him!"

Nodin passed a hand through his short dark hair. "She makes a good point," he told the Keeper. "How do we know that Brevyl is really coming? And even if he is, how can we be sure that once you've cut half the forest, you won't just come back for the rest later?"

"As to Brevyl's visit," Padgett answered, "I can show you the dispatch. The rest you'll just have to take on faith. I'm a man of my word: if I tell you that I'll only cut half the forest, I'll only cut half the forest."

" 'I'm a man of my word,' " Tammen mimicked, her voice tinged with contempt. "That's it? That's the best you can do?"

"Can you offer us any other guarantee?" Nodin asked mildly, as if he hadn't heard what Tammen said. "For instance, would you be willing to cede the uncut land to the village?"

Padgett glared at Tammen for several moments before finally responding. "I'm afraid I can't do that" he said, clearly struggling to control his anger. "Only the Eldest can acquire or bestow lands in the Temple's name. And as I've tried to explain to you, Brevyl would not be willing to do that."

Tammen shook her head. "So you're not really offering us anything, are you? You want us to give way so that you can cut half the forest immediately, and all you offer in return is an empty promise that you won't take the rest when the mood strikes you."

"Perhaps, Mage," the Keeper said, his anger rising again, "you should ask Maira and the others what they think of my offer before you dismiss it out of hand! And when you do, tell them that the alternative is to have us cut it all right now, with our weapons trained on their hearts!"

"Be that as it may, Keeper," came a voice from nearby, "we will not tolerate the cutting of even one tree."

They all turned to see Maira standing a short distance away. She looked small and somewhat frail beside Nodin and the heavyset Keeper. Her white hair shifted in the light wind, and her arms were crossed over her chest as if she were cold. But there could be no mistaking the look of resolve in her brown eyes and her set jaw.

"These mages have filled your head with foolishness, Maira," Padgett said with disgust. "They've convinced you that there's some great movement out there, when in reality there's nothing. Just a few mages who are looking to make a name for themselves. They've deluded you, and they're going to get you and your people killed."

"We're not doing this because of the mages, Keeper," she said evenly. "And we're not doing it for the Movement. You may think we're simple, that we're not capable of thinking for ourselves, but you're wrong. We're doing this because someone has to stop the Temples before they destroy every forest in the land. We're doing this for our children."

"You see, Padgett?" Tammen said with satisfaction. "As we've been telling you all along: the people of Prannai want nothing of your gold or the future you want to buy with it, so take your men to another village!" she went on, raising her voice so that the rest of the townsfolk could hear. "Prannai's forests are not for you!"

A loud cheer greeted her words.

The Keeper glanced at Nodin, who shrugged.

"Ultimately, this is Maira's decision," the tall mage said. "Hers and the rest of the Elders. We serve the village."

"You serve yourselves!" The Keeper regarded them all with a bitter expression on his face. He was shaking his head slowly, and his face had reddened again. "Fine!" he said at last. "But I've warned you!" He started to walk back to where his men were standing, but then he stopped himself and faced the crowd of villagers. "I've tried to tell Maira and the mages that this is your last chance!" he called to them. "I've tried to tell them that Eldest Brevyl is on his way to Prannai. I have no choice. I must begin the harvest today. If you try to stop me, you'll die. But if you allow us to cut the trees, I promise that we'll only take half of them. The rest of the forest will stand for as long as I'm your Keeper."

"And what did Maira say to that?" a man called out.

"She said that she'd rather die than give up a few trees," the Keeper answered.

"Good for her!" the man said, drawing nods and murmured agreement from the other townsfolk. "That's just what I would have told you!"

Again, Padgett shook his head. "You're all mad!" he said. He glanced over his shoulder at Nodin. "This is on your head, Mage. Remember that."

The Keeper approached the woodsmen and their guards and spoke to one of the armed men for several moments. Then he started back toward the Temple.

"Where's he going?" Tammen asked in a low voice.

"I'm not sure," Henryk answered. "But if I had to guess, I'd say he's going somewhere where he won't have to watch."

She knew that he was right as soon as the words left his mouth, and she felt her stomach clench itself into a fist. Sensing her tension, Othba, her splendid brown hawk, gripped her shoulder tightly.

It's all right, Tammen sent, but she didn't believe it herself. Othba's talons dug deeper into her flesh. "What are they going to do?" she whispered.

Nodin looked at her grimly. "They're going to cut the trees. The question is, what are we going to do?"

As if on cue, the woodsmen stepped into the nearest grove and the guards brandished their strange weapons.

"Well?" Maira demanded, eying Tammen and her companions expectantly. "Are you going to stop them?"

Tammen looked beyond the white-haired woman to the villagers. A few of them were watching the woodsmen unsheathe their axes, their eyes wide with fear, but the rest were looking at the mages with expressions that mirrored Maira's.

"Well?" the woman said again.

Henryk and Nodin were staring at each other, both of them looking pale and uncertain. Neither of them said anything, and Tammen could tell they had no idea what they should do.

One of the woodsmen had chosen a tree. He planted his feet, hefted his ax, and swung it back to strike his first blow.

There was only one thing Tammen could do. She raised her staff and, with barely an effort, sent a ball of pale blue fire at the man. Her timing and aim were perfect. Her mage-fire crashed into the head of the man's ax just as he paused before swinging it forward. The force of the blow ripped the ax from his hands and snapped it in two. The handle landed a few feet from where the woodsman stood, its wood splintered and charred, while the metal blade, smoking and blackened, flew several yards before burying itself harmlessly in the ground.

A cheer went up from the villagers, but it was followed almost immediately by a collective gasp as the guards aimed their weapons at Tammen.

"Don't do it!" Nodin shouted at the men. "We don't want to hurt you!"

"We have our orders!" the guard to whom Padgett had spoken replied. His voice sounded unsteady, and his eyes flicked nervously from the three mages to the townspeople.

"Do your orders include dying for the sake of a few trees?"

The man hesitated. "Yes," he finally said. "They do."

A second woodsman stepped forward, selected a tree, and readied his ax. And before he started his swing, four others had done the same. The three mages leveled their staffs at the men and sent streams of fire at their axes. Nodin found his target, but Tammen and Henryk missed and hit the men instead. Two woodsmen fell to the ground writhing and screaming, one of them with his shoulder blackened and bloody and the other with his hand severed at the wrist.

Immediately, the guards opened fire, sending beams of sizzling red flame at the mages. Tammen raised a shimmering shield of blue power that was joined an instant later by Nodin's violet and Henryk's sea green. And though the force of the guard's fire staggered Tammen and Nodin and knocked Henryk to one knee, the curtains of magic held.

But at the same time, the rest of the woodsmen started hacking at the trees, and before the mages could stop them, the villagers surged forward. Some of them were carrying hoes, shovels, or other farming tools. A few had axes of their own. And they ran at the woodsmen with their weapons held high.

Seeing this, the guards trained their weapons on the villagers.

"*No!*" Tammen screamed sending a torrent of blue power at one of the guards. Her mage-fire stuck the man full in the chest, throwing him backwards as if he was made of rags and engulfing him in flame. Two other guards fell as well as shafts of violet and green sliced through the morning air.

Two of the guards faced the mages once more, firing their weapons and forcing Tammen and the others to guard themselves before they could throw their power again. And the rest of the guards began to fire their weapons at the people of Prannai. Screams of pain and terror echoed off the trees as men and women fell to the ground with smoking black wounds.

"Henryk!" Nodin cried. "Shield us for as long as you can! Tammen and I will try to protect the villagers."

Henryk nodded and gritted his teeth, and in the next instant the sea green of his shield brightened.

Acting in perfect unison, Nodin and Tammen thrust their cerylls out before them and sent rivers of power toward the villagers in an attempt to cloak them in magic. Violet and blue, their power appeared to meld together into a gleaming wall of lavender light that succeeded in blocking the first volleys of red fire. But the weapons of the guards were too strong, and the townsfolk were so far away. Tammen's arms were already trembling with fatigue. Her back and shoulders ached, and she feared her legs would give way at any moment. She could feel Othba's exhaustion as deeply as she felt her own, and though she hadn't the energy even to glance at Nodin, she had no doubt that he and his familiar were fading as well. It would have helped if they could have moved closer to the villagers, but to do so would have stretched Henryk's power and endangered their lives.

Another barrage of weapons fire from the guards carved through their shield as if it wasn't even there, striking several of the villagers.

"Fist of the God!" Nodin spit.

"Do something!" Maira screamed at them, as the cries of her people and the smell of burning flesh filled the air once more.

Nodin and Tammen exchanged a silent look. There were tears in the tall mage's eyes and as Tammen held his gaze, he began to shake his head slightly.

It was up to her, and in Tammen's mind there seemed to be only one choice. Two of the guards continued to fire their weapons at the mages, but Henryk's barrier of sea-green magic still held. The rest of the guards were too occupied with firing on the villagers to notice her. Taking a breath, she raised her staff again and began to throw mage-fire at the guards. She tried to hit their weapons, but she was tired, and her aim was not as true as it might otherwise have been. And when all of the guards turned their weapons on her, she had to bolster Henryk's shield with her own magic and throw fire at the guards when the opportunity arose. In the end, she killed three of them and maimed four others before the rest fled, with the woodsmen close behind, scattering into the forest like frightened rabbits.

She stared after them for a long time, her arms hanging at her sides and her face and cloak soaked with sweat. She sensed Nodin beside her, and, with an effort she turned to look at him. His face was damp as well, but with tears rather than perspiration, and his eyes had a wild, terrified look that made her shudder. He hadn't done a thing to help her in her battle with the guards. He hadn't even raised a shield to protect himself. It was remarkable that he had survived.

"It wasn't supposed to happen like this," he whispered, tears still pouring down his face. "We weren't supposed to kill anyone."

"We had no choice," Tammen said in a flat voice. "They were killing the villagers."

"We're mages!" he said, whirling toward her. "Amarid's Laws forbid us from using our powers this way! 'We shall use our powers to give aid and comfort in times of need!' " he recited. "We're not supposed to kill!"

"We never took an oath, Nodin! We're no-cloaks! We haven't violated any laws! We did what we had to do! No one can blame us for that! Besides," she added, looking away, "you didn't kill anyone. You just stood there like a statue of Amarid."

"I did before," he answered, his voice low once more. If he heard the accusation in her tone, he showed no sign of it. "I killed a guard earlier."

She nodded, remembering. "That's right. You did."

Tammen heard a footfall nearby and turning, saw Maira approaching. Her face was ashen and the look in her eyes resembled the expression in Nodin's.

"Sixteen of my people are dead," she said, her voice cracking. She swallowed. "Nearly three dozen are wounded and require your aid."

"Of course, Maira," Tammen said. "Right away."

But the older woman didn't move. "How did this happen?" she asked after a lengthy silence. "How could such a thing happen?"

"It shouldn't have," Nodin answered. "It was a terrible mistake."

"No!" Tammen found herself saying. "No, it wasn't a mistake! It was unfortunate, perhaps even a tragedy. But it was not a mistake."

Nodin opened his mouth to say something, but she cut him off with an abrupt gesture.

"We came here to keep the Temple from killing this forest," she said. "Did you really believe that the Keeper would give up the gold he'd get for these trees without a fight?"

"An hour ago you told us that Padgett was beaten," Henryk reminded her. "Or have you forgotten that already?"

"No, I haven't forgotten," she said, her cheeks burning as if he had struck her. "I was being foolish, just as Nodin is now." She looked at Henryk for a moment, but he merely stared back at her, his expression unreadable. "This is more than just a movement," she said, facing Nodin once more. "This is a war, and we've just fought the first battle."

"Perhaps, Mage, you should have told us that earlier," Maira said severely. "We might not have been so quick to join you had we known that you considered us foot soldiers in your conflict with the Temple."

"You and your people were more than willing to accept our protection, Maira," Tammen said, ice in her voice. "You asked us for no explanations, and we put no conditions on our offer of aid. Don't think that you can absolve yourself of responsibility in this matter. You can't. You're to blame for this as much as we are, and it ill behooves one who calls herself a leader to run and hide as soon as things turn a bit ugly."

Maira glowered at her. She was breathing heavily, and her hands were clenched in white-knuckled fists. "How is it possible for one so young to be so cold?" she asked at last, her voice barely more than a whisper. "Has life been so cruel to you?"

Tammen looked away. The woman's questions struck a bit too close to her heart. "Your people need healing, Maira," she said. "Why don't you take us to them?"

The white-haired woman stared at her for several moments more, but Tammen refused to meet her gaze. Finally, without another word, Maira turned and led the three mages to where the dead and wounded lay.

Light. Pale yellow, like the color of sand on the shores of Duclea's Ocean. That was all he could see. Sometimes it seemed that it was the sum of his entire existence. Light, the weight of a hawk on his shoulder, and the burning memories of his life and death. The radiance stabbed into his eyes like daggers. He could close his eyes against it, but after so many years, it even seemed to follow him into this haven. One of the others—a young one, a woman of no consequence—had described it as living in one's ceryll, which was perfect. He was trapped in a prison of light and magic. It might as well have been his ceryll. Or perhaps, he thought with a bitter smile, the Summoning Stone, which he had come so close to making his own.

The bird on his shoulder ruffled her feathers and began to preen, and he stroked her chin absently. This was not Huvan, the great owl who had been with him in the time of his power, and who he had killed at the end to win for himself a measure of immortality and one last desperate chance to wreak his revenge. This was Miron, the pale brown hawk of his youth. And though the accursed light kept him from seeing anything of his surroundings during the day, he knew that he was on the Northern Plain, where, on a grey afternoon countless years ago, he first bound to her.

He remembered that day more clearly now than he had during the later years of his life—what else did he have other than his memories? He had been little more than a child then, overwhelmed by the myriad possibilities embodied in this beautiful bird. There had been so many paths laid out before him, and all had seemed destined to lead him to power and glory.

That had been before the reprimands and indignities heaped upon him by his fellow mages in the Order. Then he had been only Hawk-Mage Sartol. He had little influence or fame, he knew nothing of the Mage-Craft. And yet it was, he realized, noting the irony, the only time in his life when he had been truly happy. All too soon after he had become Sartol, who extracted payment for his service to the people of the plain; Sartol, who was censured by his fellow mages; Sartol, who was passed over by his fellow Owl-Masters each time they were called upon to choose a new Sage. Finally, in death, he became Sartol, the murderer and traitor, who was killed by the collective might of the Order. Today, he was Sartol the Unsettled, more hated even than Theron.

Even in his prison of light and magic, he knew what they said about him. Like all the Unsettled, he was Mage-Craft incarnate. He still had the Sight and more, for, he had learned, as a victim of Theron's Curse, he could see much that went on throughout Tobyn-Ser. So he knew. Sometimes he actually heard Baden and the rest speak of him.

More than anything, he wanted to destroy them, to avenge his defeat in the Great Hall, to make them pay for what they had forced him to do to Huvan. Not only Baden, whom he hated more than any of the others, but also Jaryd and Alayna, the whelps. They were the ones who had stumbled upon him as he stood over the bodies of Jessamyn and Peredur. They were the ones who somehow managed to survive Theron's Grove when he was certain that they would die there. They were the ones whose appearance in the Great Hall during the trial of Baden, Orris, and Trahn destroyed all for which he had worked so long and so hard. Before this was over every mage in Tobyn-Ser would suffer for what had been done to him, but none more than those three: Baden, Jaryd, and Alayna.

He had tried the very first night of his eternal unrest. When Phelan, Theron, and the rest of the Unsettled offered aid to the mages in their battle with Calbyr's band of outlanders, Sartol used all of his power to hinder their efforts. And, though new to the ways of the Unsettled and unfamiliar with the workings of the Mage-Craft in this strange realm, he did manage to keep Phelan and the others from taking away the outlanders' weapons. As a result, Niall died and Baden was rendered unbound.

But that did little to satisfy his hunger for vengeance, and it cost him a good deal. From that time on, he was ostracized by the rest of the wandering ghosts. He became an exile among outcasts. Except for Miron, he was utterly alone. It was funny in a way: in punishing him the rest of the Unsettled were also giving him the freedom and privacy he needed to plot his revenge. Among the ghosts of Tobyn-Ser, thought was communication. Had Theron or Phelan or one of the others deigned to speak with him, had they even come just to revile or taunt him, they would have divined his thoughts and found a way to stop him. But instead, out of spite and stupidity, they isolated him.

So he waited and watched, biding his time, which was the one thing he had in abundance. He saw Jaryd and Alayna in their home by South Shelter and he watched the birth of their little brat of a child. He knew of Orris's defiance of the Order, and he looked on with interest and satisfaction as Erland and his allies formed their little League and sundered the Mage-Craft. And most recently, he watched the so-called free mages struggle to make their mark on the land, seeing in their repeated failures and their growing desperation the opportunity he had been waiting for.

So much still had to happen, he had to remind himself again and again. So much remained beyond his control.

Even now, he saw cerylls flashing throughout the land, and though he had yet to learn why, he wondered if there was an opportunity here as well. They were using his stone after all. He had Seen patterns emerging. In the waking world of dream and thought that passed for sleep in the realm of the Unsettled, he had glimpsed the future. Or more precisely, he had envisioned one possible future among many. And he saw in it a path to redemption and retribution. He had learned all he could of the power he still possessed as one of the Unsettled. He knew its limitations as well as its possibilities. When the moment came, he would be ready. He had only to wait and be patient. For time was the one thing he had in abundance.

7

In your last letter you expressed surprise that I would inform you in such detail of the political maneuvering within the Council of Sovereigns and in each of the Nals. As you put it, "I am satisfied in knowing that you and Shivohn remain in control of your respective Nals and allied with each other. Little of the rest concerns me."

I could not disagree more. It seems to me from what you have told me in the past that you have railed against your colleagues in the Order for expressing a similarly narrow view of the world. In light of Tobyn-Ser's expanding commerce, its leaders must pay heed to all that affects the governance of its trading partners, no matter how arcane such matters may seem. Just as you seek to know all you can about the internal workings of the League, you must keep abreast of all that happens in Lon-Ser.

—Melyor i Lakin, Sovereign and
Bearer of Bragor-Nal to Hawk-Mage
Orris, Day 1, Week 11, Winter, Year
3067.

"I'm sorry, Sovereign," the woman said, grinning at the speak-screen in a way that told Melyor she wasn't sorry at all. "Sovereign-Designate Wiercia cannot speak with you right now. She's terribly busy with plans for her investiture. Perhaps if you contact her again after—"

Melyor shook her head, her frustration mounting. "It can't wait!"

The woman's expression hardened. "I'm afraid it will have to!" She reached forward as if to switch off her screen.

"No!" Melyor said quickly, drawing another grin from the woman. Melyor closed her eyes and took a slow breath. *She's a Legate*, she told herself. *Treat her that way.*

"Please," she began again. "This is very important. I understand that Wiercia has much to do, but this is about what happened to Shivohn."

The Legate narrowed her eyes. "We know what happened to Sovereign Shivohn. Sovereign-Designate Wiercia intends to raise the matter at the next meeting of the Council."

"She can't do that!" Melyor said.

"Of course she can. I'm certain that Marar will be fascinated to learn that a Bragory assassin killed Sovereign Shivohn."

Melyor shook her head again. "That's not what happened." But she knew that she had no chance of convincing the woman. She had been through this same conversation a number of times over the past several days with a number of different Legates. Perhaps she had even spoken with this woman before. It was hard to tell. With their faces framed by the black headpieces, all of Oerella-Nal's Legates looked the same: dour and cold. Certainly they were all equally adamant in their unwillingness to listen to her or allow her to speak with Wiercia.

In all likelihood she would have no more success with Oerella-Nal's new leader if she ever got the chance to speak with her, but she had to try. There was too much at stake not to.

She could still hear in her mind the explosion that killed Shivohn as it had sounded over the speak-screen. And she could still see the expression on the face of the young woman who had answered her call, and who, after an agonizingly long interval, returned to Shivohn's quarters to inform her that the Sovereign was dead. Coming as it did less than an hour after the attempt on her own life, Shivohn's assassination struck Melyor as too improbable a coincidence to be believed.

Her suspicions were confirmed two days later, when she received word through Jibb's intelligence network that the detonator of the boomer that killed Shivohn had been found and identified as coming from Bragor-Nal. Two bombs, one with a detonator from Oerella-Nal that almost kills Bragor-Nal's Sovereign, and the other with a detonator from Bragor-Nal that kills the Sovereign of Oerella-Nal. So clumsy a plot could only have been initiated by one man: Marar, Sovereign of Stib-Nal. Who else had so much to gain from a conflict between Oerella-Nal and Bragor-Nal? Since Melyor's investiture, the centuries-old antagonism between Lon-Ser's two largest Nals had been replaced by an unprecedented period of accord. As a result, the perquisites Stib-Nal had enjoyed as Bragor-Nal's ally within the Council, meager though they were, had vanished, leaving Marar's diminutive territory as little more than a political irrelevancy. Of course he was behind the bombings. It seemed so transparent that it was almost laughable. At least it did to her.

But Wiercia and her Legates remained unconvinced. Melyor had shown them the detonator from the boomer that damaged the Gold Palace, holding it up before the speak-screen so they could see. But all the Legates to whom she had spoken had dismissed the item as nothing more than a prop in Bragor-Nal's elaborate scheme to kill Shivohn. As if Melyor had nothing better to do with her time than stage attempts on her own life and kill the single most powerful ally she had in all of Lon-Ser.

It was ludicrous. And yet, for all its gross heavy-handedness, Marar's ploy was working. In the course of a single morning, he had managed to end nearly seven years of cooperation between his two giant rivals. Wiercia and her underlings believed that Shivohn had been killed by agents of Bragor-Nal, and Melyor didn't know how to convince them that they were wrong.

"Look," she said dully, gazing at her speak-screen again, "there was an attempt made on my life the same day Shivohn was killed. We found the detonator from the bomb and—"

"Yes, I know," the Legate broke in, sounding unimpressed. "The detonator from that bomb came from Oerella-Nal. We've heard this before, Sovereign. You and I spoke just a few days ago. Sovereign-Designate Wiercia will consider your evidence at the next meeting of the Council."

Melyor exhaled through her teeth and rubbed a hand across her brow. She had never suffered fools well and was about to tell the Legate as much, when a thought occurred to her. She had little expectation that this gambit would work, but she had long since exhausted her other options. "Tell Wiercia that I wish to congratulate her myself on her impending investiture, and that I want to do so not only as Sovereign of Bragor-Nal, but also as Bearer of the Stone and emissary of Lon-Ser's Gildriites."

The Legate looked at her skeptically for several moments.

"Tell her as well," Melyor added, casually picking up her staff with its glowing crimson stone and laying it on her desk where it could be seen through the speak-screen, "that I also wish to convey a message of goodwill from the Order of Mages and Masters in Tobyn-Ser."

The woman's eyes widened and, after another moment's hesitation, she nodded and stepped away from her speak-screen.

Melyor waited for what seemed a long time, and as the minutes passed, she began to wonder if her gambit had worked. But at last, just as she had convinced herself that Wiercia had refused to speak with her once more, the Sovereign-Designate stepped in front of the speak-screen and sat down.

Melyor had only met Wiercia once before, seven years ago when, along with Gwilym, Bearer of the Stone, and Orris, she was arrested and thrown in an Oerellan jail. Desperate to speak with Shivohn and enlist her aid in their struggle against Cedrych, the Bragory Overlord who was behind the attacks on Orris's land, Melyor had told the guards that the three of them were in Oerella-Nal as Shivohn's guests. She had been lying, of course, but perhaps because of the sheer audacity of the claim, Shivohn sent Wiercia, at the time a Legate, to investigate.

Wiercia had not changed much in the intervening years. There might have been a few more lines around her blue eyes and her wide mouth and a few more wisps of grey in her golden hair. But otherwise her face was just as Melyor remembered: square, attractive in a severe way, and wearing a cold, thin smile. Melyor also noticed that even though she had yet to be invested, Wiercia was already wearing the crimson robe donned by all of Oerella-Nal's Sovereigns.

"Hello, Wiercia," Melyor said with exaggerated enthusiasm. "How kind you are to speak with me."

"You've finally gotten my attention, Melyor," the woman replied indifferently. "Don't waste my time with sarcasm. What is it that you want?"

"As I told your Legate, I only wish to congratulate you on behalf of my people and my friends in Tobyn-Ser."

"Yes, so she told me. Mentioning your sorcerer friends did just what you wanted it to: it got me here. Now, I'll give you one last chance. What do you want?"

"How goes your investigation of Shivohn's assassination?" Melyor asked.

Wiercia's eyes flashed dangerously. "How dare you!" she breathed. "I will not sit here and be mocked by you of all people!"

"The question was intended seriously," Melyor told the woman, struggling to keep her own temper in check.

"This charade of yours has gone on long enough!" Wiercia sat forward so that her face came close to the screen. "Shivohn's lone fault was her overriding desire to see the good in people. You may have fooled her into believing that you had reformed your ways and changed Bragor-Nal into a place of peace and respectability. But I know better. The detonator from the bomb that killed the Sovereign only proved what I've suspected all along. You're still just a miscreant who happens to rule a den of hoodlums."

"Careful, Wiercia," Melyor said. "You don't want to make me angry. If I deny your petition for entry to the Council, your Legates will have to choose someone else. Surely you don't want that, do you?"

The woman's face blanched. "You wouldn't dare! The petition is a formality, nothing more! You can't deny it!"

Melyor gave an icy smile. "Can't I? If I was willing to kill Shivohn, as you believe, why should I even hesitate to do this?"

Wiercia glared at her, the muscles in her jaw clenching. "What do you want?" she asked once more, although this time there was a note of resignation in her voice.

"I just want you to listen to me with an open mind," Melyor said. "Put aside your suspicions for a moment and hear what I have to say."

She smiled again. "That's a small price to pay for admission to the Council, don't you think?"

The woman said nothing, but after several moments, she gave a small nod.

Melyor took a breath. This was to be her only chance, she knew. She needed to choose her words carefully. "I don't expect you to believe this right away, but I considered Shivohn my friend."

Wiercia let out a high, disbelieving laugh.

"You agreed to listen!"

"I expected more than lies!"

That almost ended it. Melyor was already reaching for the speak-screen to switch it off when a voice in her mind stopped her. Shivohn's voice. *Don't let it end this way*, she heard the Sovereign say. *Don't let them win, not without a fight.*

Pulling her hand back, Melyor exhaled slowly. "Do you think I'm a foolish woman, Wiercia?"

The woman blinked. "What?"

Melyor grinned. "Do you think I'm foolish?"

"No," Wiercia replied after a brief pause. "I think you're dangerously clever."

"Then why would I have Shivohn killed?"

She hesitated, and Melyor could see from the uncertainty in her pale eyes that she had never stopped to consider a motive for Shivohn's murder. "Well . . ."

"You yourself just said that Shivohn had been too willing to trust me; that she was too eager to believe I had changed," Melyor went on pressing her advantage. "Why would I want to see her replaced by someone who'd be less likely to trust me?"

Wiercia stared blankly at her speak-screen.

"It doesn't make any sense, does it?"

For a long time, the Oerellan leader said nothing, and when she finally spoke, her reply surprised Melyor. "I'm listening," she said simply.

"If it wasn't for Shivohn, I would never have become Sovereign. In fact, I probably would have died at the hands of Cedrych's assassins. And even though we didn't agree on every issue that came before the Council, we did work well together. Indeed, I'd guess that relations between our Nals have never been so good."

"I suppose that's true."

"Which begs the question," Melyor continued, "who has the most to gain from putting an end to our cooperation?"

Wiercia seemed to consider this for some time. "I'd have to say Stib-Nal."

Melyor nodded. "Very good." She held up the detonator from the boomer that damaged the Gold Palace. "This came from a bomb that went off just outside my bedroom window less than an hour before Shivohn was killed. Do you recognize the shape?"

"Yes," the woman said evenly. No doubt her Legates had prepared her for this. "It's one of ours."

"Doesn't that tell you something?"

"Not necessarily," Wiercia said with a shrug. "You could easily have smuggled that into Bragor-Nal and staged the attempt on your life."

"Yes!" Melyor said impatiently. "Just as you could have with the device that killed Shivohn!"

"*Me?*"

Melyor almost said the obvious: that Wiercia had more to gain from Shivohn's death than anyone else in the Matriarchy. But she knew that such a statement would do far more damage than good. Wiercia had no more to do with Shivohn's death than Melyor. "Not you personally," she said instead. "Someone. Anyone. The point is that while Shivohn's assassination and the attempt on my life could have been carried out by people from either of our Nals, it strikes me as too much of a coincidence that such similar attacks should take place in a single morning."

"And it strikes me as absurd that Marar would try something so clumsy and transparent."

Melyor closed her eyes and rubbed a hand over her face. Wiercia was right. It *did* sound absurd. But she had thought it through again and again. This was the only explanation that made any sense at all. "Do you know Marar, Wiercia? Have you ever met him?"

"No," the woman admitted.

"Well, I've known him for several years. You can't serve on the Council with someone for that long without gaining an understanding of how his or her mind works. Before I became Sovereign, Marar played a crucial role in maintaining Bragor-Nal's supremacy within the Council. And as such he wielded a certain amount of power and influence. He lost all that when Shivohn and I became allies, and he's been looking for a way to get it back!"

"I'm sure he has. But this is . . ." Wiercia opened her hands and shook her head. "Even Marar wouldn't be this inept."

"Inept?" Melyor repeated. "Don't you see? It's working. You think I killed Shivohn. It took days before you would even talk to me. Imagine if I had died, too. Our Nals might already be at war." She smiled grimly. "It may have been heavy-handed, but Marar's plan has proven itself anything but inept."

Again Wiercia fell silent, and she sat perfectly still, staring at her hands. "If you're right," she began at last, "what can we do?"

"I'm not sure yet," Melyor admitted, gazing at her glowing red stone. "I need to know if he's going to try to have me killed again immediately, or if he'll be satisfied for now with driving a wedge between the Matriarchy and Bragor-Nal." She looked up again, her eyes meeting Wiercia's. "In the meantime though, we can at least keep speaking to each other. We can't let Marar think he's winning."

"Why not?" the woman asked. "If he's convinced that he's broken the Oerellan-Bragory alliance, maybe he won't come after you again at all."

Melyor felt herself break into a grin. Perhaps she could work with this severe woman after all. "That's an interesting point. Although I don't think it would save my life."

"Why not?"

She held up her staff. "I'm a Gildriite, a Bearer no less." She shrugged. "Marar has never trusted me. Eventually he'll come after me again. But you may be right: we can at least buy ourselves some time by making him think that his plan is working."

"And how do we do that?"

"By making a show of not trusting each other." She smiled. "It should be easy for you."

To Melyor's surprise, Wiercia smiled in return. "Too bad," she said. "I like a challenge." A moment later though, her smile vanished. "You realize that if you turn out to be right, we have another problem."

Melyor held herself perfectly still and waited. She knew what Wiercia was going to say, for she had been thinking the same thing for several days. Marar was the least of their worries.

"If Marar really did smuggle these bombs into our Nals," the woman was saying, her square features growing pale as if she was hearing her own words for the very first time, "then we've both got traitors in our security forces. Which means that both of our lives are in danger."

"I know," Melyor said, nodding slowly. "Be careful whom you trust."

Wiercia gave a small, mirthless laugh. "Those are unsettling words coming from you."

"I don't doubt it," Melyor answered, trying unsuccessfully to smile. "Welcome to the Council of Sovereigns."

At first he had been livid. He was paying the guard handsomely—a good deal more than he had paid Shivohn's security man—and in return for all of that gold he expected efficiency and competence. He had spent too much time and far too much money putting this plan in motion to have it spoiled by one man's carelessness. He had told the guard as much that very night, while the rest of Melyor's men were still repairing the facade of Bragor-Nal's Gold Palace. And he had been pleased to see the man flinch at his raised voiced and his threats of punishment for further failures.

Melyor and Shivohn thought him a poor leader, he knew. They thought him a fool. But even if Stib-Nal was the smallest and weakest of the Nals, becoming its Sovereign had been no small accomplishment. Marar was fairly certain that Melyor's path to power and his own had been rather similar. Like Bragor-Nal, Stib-Nal was governed by a strict hierarchy within which advancement resulted from guile and strength and, yes, just a little bit of luck. The Bragory system operated on a much grander scale, but the similarities were too significant to be ignored. Those in Stib-Nal who had underestimated him had wound up dead. Just like Shivohn. In many ways, he and Melyor had much in common.

Which was why, after a few days' reflection, his ire had begun to fade. He had wanted her dead. She was a Gildriite and he was more than a little afraid of the powers embodied in that glimmering crystal she carried with her. But she also had ties to the mages of Tobyn-Ser, and no matter what she had become in recent years, once upon a time she had been as ruthless and ambitious as any of Bragor-Nal's lords. If the alliance between Oerella-Nal and Bragor-Nal could be broken, and if Melyor could be convinced once more that the path to power and gold led through Tobyn-Ser, the guard's failure might prove to be a stroke of enormous good fortune. Her connections to Tobyn-Ser's Order of Mages and Masters would be invaluable if combined with the relations Marar himself had cultivated with that land's clerics. The possibility remained remote of course. But he still had the guard. If things didn't work out, he'd just send another bomb for Melyor.

He had first learned of the Tobyn-Ser Initiative seven years earlier during that extraordinary meeting of the Council when Shivohn confronted Durell with her knowledge of the plan to subjugate the mysterious land across Arick's Sea. Marar had been so shocked by her revelations, and so frightened of their implications, that he actually opposed Durell openly, something he had never done before. He had feared that the Bragory Sovereign would punish him in some way for his effrontery, but Durell didn't even survive the night. Cedrych, the renegade Overlord, killed him and petitioned for admission to the Council, only to be killed himself by Melyor and her sorcerer before Marar and Shivohn could reply.

In the years since, however, Marar had come to recognize what he might gain from the conquest of Tobyn-Ser. From all he had heard from

Abboriji merchants, the land of the Hawk-Magic had in abundance all the raw goods that Lon-Ser's Nals had exhausted: timber and minerals, as well as clean water and air and room to expand. Which was why, when those same merchants told him that Tobyn-Ser's clerics sought weapons in exchange for gold, Marar jumped at the chance to arrange a series of clandestine weapons transactions. It was an opening. Nothing more, he knew. Stib-Nal had neither the resources nor the technology to defeat the sorcerers' magic, even with the clerics' help. But apparently this Cedrych had once believed that he did. And since he had chosen Melyor to be the leader of the band that traveled to Tobyn-Ser, it followed that she knew what Cedrych had in mind.

Marar nodded to himself and smiled. For now at least, Melyor was worth far more to him alive than dead. And if she proved uncooperative, she could be killed; then he'd approach the new Bragory Sovereign about Tobyn-Ser. The beautiful Gildriite had made much of the changes she had brought to Bragor-Nal, but Marar suspected that Stib-Nal's northern neighbor remained much as it had been. Melyor's appetite for gold might have ebbed, but her replacement was unlikely to be so principled.

He took a breath and sat before his speak-screen. In the interim, he had another assignment for the Bragory security man. Melyor wasn't the only threat he faced in Bragor-Nal.

Premel was in a security meeting when the summons came. Jibb, who was reviewing what they had learned about the boomer that damaged the palace was in mid-sentence when the beeping interrupted him.

"What was that?" he asked, glancing up from the papers in front of him and scanning the room.

"It was nothing, General," Premel answered, fighting to keep his voice steady. "Just a remote signal from my speak-screen." Jibb narrowed his eyes slightly, and Premel forced a smile. "Probably just the girl I was with last night."

The security chief gave him a wry grin and resumed his briefing. But Premel heard little of what Jibb said for the rest of the hour, and by the time he returned to his quarters his hands were shaking with rage and another thing that he didn't care to name.

Switching on the screen on his desk, he immediately found himself face-to-face with the Sovereign of Stib-Nal.

"Ah, at last," Marar said, a hollow smile spreading across his thin, bony features. "I was beginning to think you were ignoring me."

"I was in the middle of a briefing!" Premel flung at him. "I thought you were only going to contact me after hours."

The Sovereign shrugged his narrow shoulders with annoying indifference. "I needed to speak with you," he said. "And I suggest you watch your tone. I'm paying you, remember?"

Premel glared at the man, but offered no reply. He had been growing increasingly uncomfortable with their arrangement. There was no denying that the rewards were great, but the risks were growing all too rapidly. It had started innocuously enough: standard intelligence gathering, logistical information, and a few details on weapons technology. None of it had seemed overly threatening to his own safety or that of his friends in SovSec.

But then the assassination attempts began. Premel, either by unconscious choice or sheer stupidity, had been slow to make the connection, but when Marar started asking him questions about security response times to the attacks, he could no longer ignore the obvious.

Even then, though, he had found a way to justify his betrayals and the riches they brought him. Melyor was a Gildriite; she had no business running Bragor-Nal. One had only to look at the things she had done as Sovereign to understand that. The Nal system had always been based upon a strict hierarchy that rewarded strength and resourcefulness. It was violent, perhaps even cruel to those who were too weak to advance. But it worked. It had for centuries. And she knew that as well as anyone, because she had been as fine a Nal-Lord as Premel could have imagined. But that stone she carried had changed her. It had made her squeamish. Her efforts to rid the quads of violence had only weakened Bragor-Nal. And even worse, she had forged an ill-conceived and dangerous alliance with the Oerellan Matriarchy that threatened to compromise the Nal's military and economic supremacy.

So when Marar instructed Premel to arrange the next attempt on Melyor's life, the security man hesitated, but only briefly. He was doing it for the good of the Nal, he told himself. No Sovereign as weak as she would have survived this long under the old rules. If Bragor-Nal was to remain the strongest Nal in Lon-Ser, she had to die.

But while Premel had long since made peace with his decision to betray Melyor, his betrayal of Jibb still bothered him. In his opinion, Jibb should have been Sovereign. The security chief still understood the way the Nal was supposed to work, and he would never have allowed Bragor-Nal's position in Lon-Ser to be weakened. Only his unflagging devotion to Melyor kept him from saying as much openly. And though Premel didn't quite understand Jibb's continued loyalty to her, he could not help but admire the man for it. Jibb was a unique blend: he was strong enough to survive the Nal system and yet honorable enough to earn the trust and respect of the men who worked under him. Jibb would have been disgusted by Premel's betrayal. But as Premel saw it, this was his chance to set things right, his chance to make Jibb Sovereign.

The trick was to keep Marar happy at the same time that he pursued his own goal. So for the time being, he had resolved to accept the Sovereign's condescension with equanimity. When Jibb became Sovereign and Premel the leader of SovSec, they'd get their revenge.

"What is it you need, Sovereign?" Premel asked with as much courtesy as he could muster.

Marar grinned. "That's better."

Premel merely waited, refusing to react to the Sovereign's remark.

"I've been thinking, Premel," Marar began again a moment later. "Your failure the other day may have been fortuitous. I've come to think that I was a bit rash in trying to have Melyor killed just now. She is, I've concluded, far more valuable to me alive than dead."

Your failure. Premel had to bite back a retort. It hadn't been his fault. For some reason, whether because he was too drugged to know better, or too stupid to care, the assassin had deviated from their timetable. Not by much to be sure, but enough. Premel had explained that to Marar several times already, but the man refused to listen.

"I'm glad to hear that, Sovereign," Premel managed. "Is that why you contacted me? To put my . . . concerns to rest?"

"Hardly," Marar replied, smiling thinly. "No, I have another task for you."

Premel felt the color drain from his face. If he didn't want Melyor dead right then, what else could he ask—

"I want you to get rid of Jibb for me."

Premel stared at the screen. "You can't be serious," he finally said, the words coming out as little more than a whisper.

"I'm not a man given to jests, Premel."

"But Jibb—" He faltered. "Why?"

"Any number of reasons," Marar said breezily. "At some point I will want Melyor dead. And when I do, it will be much easier to kill her without Jibb by her side. Besides, you know as well as I that if word ever got back to Jibb that I'd been responsible for Melyor's death, he'd see to it that I died as well." The Sovereign narrowed his eyes. "Is there a problem, Premel?"

He licked his lips but it did no good. His mouth was as dry as a quad avenue in midsummer. "Killing Jibb could be . . . could be complicated."

Marar chuckled. "No more complicated than killing Melyor certainly." He furrowed his brow, though a smile lingered on his lips. "Come now,

Premel. I expected you to relish this assignment. You told me yourself that if Jibb ever left SovSec, you'd replace him as head of security. Here's your chance."

Premel exhaled through his teeth and closed his eyes briefly, cursing himself for confiding such a thing to this man. "I can't do this," he said, opening his eyes once more. "Jibb is my friend. He's a good man." *He's going to be Sovereign.* "I can't do this," he repeated.

"Sure you can," Marar told him, his tone hardening. "You will, and soon."

Premel swallowed, gathering himself. "And if I refuse?"

"I don't think you will," the Sovereign said. "I think you have too clear a notion of what Jibb and Melyor would do to you if they learned of your disloyalty."

Premel opened his mouth to speak but found that he couldn't think of anything to say. For the first time in more years than he cared to count, he felt like crying.

"Life is about choices, my friend," Marar was saying, although Premel could barely hear him. "Some time ago, you chose wealth. You must have known that such a choice would carry a price. You're lucky really. As it happens, you not only get gold, you also get power. SovSec will be yours. Considering that, it seems to me that Jibb's life is a relatively small price to pay."

Premel stared at his desk—he couldn't bear to meet the Sovereign's gaze—and he kept silent.

"Think of this as your chance to redeem yourself," Marar went on. "I'll expect to hear from you when this is taken care of."

There seemed to be a windstorm in his mind. Marar's words were coming to him from a great distance. But he made himself nod once. The Sovereign would be expecting at least that much.

"Don't fail me again, Premel. Or I'll be forced to expose you and find another man in SovSec who's more committed to carrying out the tasks I assign."

An instant later, the Sovereign's bony face was gone. Still, Premel just sat there, unable even to muster the energy to switch off his screen.

He had more gold than he had ever dreamed possible. SovSec was his if he wanted it. And he had never in his life felt so helpless. Marar had trapped him with bait that he had been all too willing to take. There was no one to whom he could turn.

That thought stopped him cold, for there was one person. Remarkable and strange as it seemed, he suddenly knew with shocking certainty that he was not without hope. He had never dreamed that he could even consider such a thing, but neither had he ever expected that he would be in a predicament like this.

Life is about choices, Marar had said.

Premel nodded, and leaning forward, he finally turned off his screen. Perhaps this once he had made the right one.

8

As I see it, the appearance in Tobyn-Ser of these free mages is danger-ous for a number of reasons. Indeed, the concern that I expressed to you in my last letter—that they do not answer to any central authority, as the mages of both the Order and League do—is but one of my objec-tions, and not even the greatest. . . .

For the first time in a thousand years, the Mage-Craft is con-trolled by two bodies rather than one. The Order's relationship with the Keepers remains strained at best, and, from what I have heard, it seems that the early cooperation between the Temples and the League has given way to conflict and distrust. Add to that the new People's Movement, which professes hostility toward the League, the Order, and the Temples, and the result is more instability and a greater like-lihood of violent conflict than this land has ever seen.

Right now a delicate balance exists, maintaining a fragile peace among all these bodies. But it will not take long for the free mages to realize that they have the power to tip that balance one way or another. And I fear that when they recognize this, their hunger for power will lead them to throw the whole land into chaos and ruin.

—Hawk-Mage Orris to Melyor i Lakin, Sovereign and Bearer of Bragor-Nal, Winter, God's Year 4633.

Tammen sat across from him, staring at the fire, her face looking young despite the lines around her mouth and the scowl that she always seemed to be wearing these days. The light of the flames and her flashing blue stone shimmered in her pale eyes, and her light brown hair fell attractively over her brow. Nodin thought that she had never looked so lovely.

He looked away and stroked the chin of his hawk who sat beside him on a wide log. Tammen didn't care for him in that way, he knew, and though he could still feel his heart tighten when he thought of it, for the most part the pain of her rejection had healed. He could not bear, however, to have her think of him as a coward, as she clearly had since the incident at Prannai several days before. He could hear it in her voice when she spoke to him. He could see it in her eyes on the rare occasions when she allowed herself to look at him. *It's not my fault!* he wanted to tell her. *I didn't want anyone to die.* But he knew that wasn't the issue. It no longer mattered how it had begun, or what they had intended. There had been a battle, and he had merely watched from behind Henryk's shimmering green shield as she killed the Temple's men. It hadn't been cowardice. He really wasn't certain what it had been. But it had earned her contempt.

"Perhaps we should go back," he suggested, gazing at her through the firelight. He glanced at Henryk, who was leaning against a tree a short distance from the fire, his eyes closed, his feet resting on a broad, flat rock. "Padgett might try something again. Maira might need our help."

"We've been through this," Tammen said wearily. "Maira asked us to leave. And besides, I don't think the Keeper is about to go after the trees again."

"But what if he does? We should—"

"Stop it, Nodin!" she said, her voice like a blade. "It's over, and we have other things to worry about! What happened in Prannai doesn't matter anymore!"

He felt his face turning red and was grateful for the darkness and the uncertain light of the fire. He looked at Henryk again and saw that the man was watching him, the expression in his dark eyes unreadable.

"I'm sorry," Nodin murmured.

Tammen dismissed his apology with an impatient gesture and picked up her staff. "I wish I knew what they were up to," she said, gazing at the flashing blue ceryll. "I don't trust them. I don't care if the League has more members at this point. The Order is the real danger. They're the ones we have to watch."

Nodin shot a look toward Henryk, who merely shook his head. She had said such things before, and though neither of them agreed with her, they both understood why she felt as she did.

Tammen was one of the few survivors of the outlanders' infamous attack on Watersbend, the last of Tobyn-Ser's villages to be ravaged by the raiders. Her parents and sisters died that night years before, as did most of her neighbors and friends, and though she had known for years that the attackers had not truly been mages, she had never stopped blaming the Order for what had happened.

"Why would they have a Gathering now?" she asked, her eyes still on her stone.

"We'll find out soon enough," Henryk said, sounding worn. "It's probably just something having to do with the League. It's nothing for us to worry about."

"No," Tammen said. "It's more than that. I'm sure of it. You can't trust them."

Nodin and Henryk exchanged a second look, but said nothing more.

They sat in silence for some time, Tammen still staring at her ceryll and Henryk sitting forward to stir the coals with a long narrow branch. Nodin tried desperately to think of something to say. He was the oldest member of their trio. He had been bound to this, his second bird, for nearly as long as his companions had been bound to their first familiars. It fell to him to come up with a plan of some sort. At least it should have. But ever since Prannai . . .

"So where are we going next?" Henryk finally asked, settling back against his tree.

"That's really not the issue," Tammen answered. "It doesn't matter where we go, or who we encounter. We need to find a way to make ourselves stronger. We can't afford a repeat of what happened in Prannai."

"I promise it will be different next time," Nodin told her.

She shook her head. "I'm not talking about you, Nodin! I'm talking about all of us, the entire Movement!"

"I don't understand," Henryk said.

"How many free mages would you say there are in all of Tobyn-Ser?" she asked him.

The dark-eyed man shrugged. "I don't know. Ten. Maybe a dozen."

"Right. And that's less than half the membership of the Order or the League."

"I think our numbers will grow," Nodin said. "It may take some time—"

"We don't have time!" she broke in. "The People's Movement is looking to us for leadership and protection. If we can't help them now, it won't matter how many no-cloaks there are next year. A few more episodes like the one in Prannai, and the Movement will be dead. No one will trust us to help them anymore."

"What's your point?" Henryk asked.

"My point is this: the League and the Order outnumber us, apparently the Temples have access to the outlanders' weaponry, and it's only a matter of time before they're too powerful for us as well." She paused and regarded them both. "We need a weapon as well. We need something that will allow us to contend with the numbers of the League and Order, and the weapons of the Keepers."

Nodin stared at her. "You may be right, but what?"

She hesitated, suddenly appearing uncomfortable. She glanced briefly at Henryk, but then faced Nodin again. "We need help," she said, sounding far less certain of herself than she had a moment before. "And I haven't been able to think of anyone who'd be willing to help us." She took a breath. "At least no one who's living."

"No one who's living?" Henryk repeated, a quizzical expression on his angular face.

But Nodin already understood. It almost made sense really. Everyone knew that the Unsettled had helped the Order defeat the outlanders at Phelan Spur twelve years ago. Obviously they still possessed power of a sort. And if they could be convinced to aid the no-cloaks, the People's Movement might be able to overcome the advantages enjoyed by its rivals. Nodin could not help but see the logic in what Tammen was suggesting.

But neither could he ignore the cold dread that had taken hold of him as soon as the words passed her lips, as if one of the ghosts had wrapped an icy hand around his heart. Theron's Curse was no trifle; no mage who had spent even a single day unbound could ever doubt that. And those who had fallen victim to the Curse, those who Tammen sought to enlist in their cause, included some of the most formidable and . . . malevolent . . . figures in the land's history.

"You can't be serious!" Henryk said breathlessly, his dark eyes wide as he finally grasped what she had suggested. "You want us to go to the Unsettled for help?"

"Yes," she answered defiantly. "I've been thinking about this for several days, and I don't see any other way for the Movement to survive."

"But it makes no sense! Why would they even help us? All of the Unsettled were once members of the Order. They have no interest in helping us or the Movement."

"Some of them do," Tammen said pointedly. "Some of them care nothing for the Order."

Henryk leveled a rigid finger at her. "I'm not going to Theron's Grove!"

"No one's asking you to, Henryk!" she replied.

"Then who's going to help us?"

Nodin knew what she would say even before she spoke the name. She had been at Watersbend. And just as that meant that she would never trust the Order, it also meant that where the rest of the land saw a traitor and a murderer, she saw a redeemer, a man who had saved her life and what remained of her home.

"Sartol," Tammen said.

The very sound of the Owl-Master's name made Nodin shudder. It didn't matter that Sartol had killed the outlanders at Watersbend in order to keep his treachery a secret. It didn't matter that he had given aid to the outlanders, that he had helped make the attack on Watersbend possible in the first place. All that mattered to Tammen and the others who had survived that night of horror and flame was that Sartol had ended the attack and avenged the lives of those who died. To them, Sartol was a hero. They didn't care what the rest of Tobyn-Ser thought.

"*Sartol?*" Henryk said. "The man was a traitor! He helped the outlanders! He's not interested in helping the Movement!"

Tammen regarded him coldly. "You sound like an Order mage, Henryk."

Henryk leaped to his feet, his eyes flashing with firelight and ceryllglow. But somehow he managed to keep his temper in check, and when he spoke, his voice was surprisingly calm. "I'm only telling you what I know to be true. Sartol betrayed the Order and Tobyn-Ser. He killed the Sage and her First." He opened his hands as if pleading with her. "These things are a matter of history, Tammen. They aren't stories made up by the Order. They're facts."

"And I can tell you for a fact that he saved my life. If it wasn't for Sartol my entire village would have been destroyed, and I would have died, just as my parents did. Just as my sister did."

Henryk opened his mouth to say something but then stopped himself. For a long time he just looked at her, a sad expression in his eyes. "I won't do this," he finally said. "I know that you trust him—perhaps I even understand why—but I know what he was in life, and I won't go to him for help, even now."

"We have to!" Tammen insisted. "We need help!"

"You may be right," Henryk answered. "But we don't need it from the Unsettled!"

She threw up her hands in frustration. "Then who? How else can we match the strength of Lon-Ser's weapons and the number of mages in the Order and League?"

Henryk looked away. "I don't know. But this is insane! It's too dangerous!"

"So, you admit that you're scared."

"Yes," Henryk said, meeting her angry gaze again. "I'm scared. I'm afraid of the Unsettled. And I'm terrified of Sartol."

"And you're willing to let your fears destroy the Movement."

She offered it as a statement, and though Henryk turned away again, he didn't argue the point.

"And what about you?" she demanded, facing Nodin. "Are you afraid as well?"

Like you were in Prannai? She didn't say it of course. She didn't have to. Nodin heard the insinuation in her voice, saw the challenge in her grey eyes. He glanced at Henryk and saw that the dark-eyed man was watching him, too, his expression no less intent than Tammen's. Finding a compromise that both of them would accept wouldn't be easy.

Fortunately, probably without meaning to, Henryk had given him an opening of sorts. "I agree with Henryk that Sartol is not to be trusted," he said. "The risks are too great. But," he added quickly, seeing Tammen sneer in disgust, "I'm not ready to dismiss the idea of seeking the aid of the Unsettled. I don't expect them to help us, but we need to do something." He shrugged. "Maybe they'll surprise us."

"All right," Tammen said grudgingly. "But if not Sartol, then who?"

"I had forgotten this until Henryk mentioned that Sartol had killed the Sage and her First all those years ago," Nodin replied. "But the First was a man named Peredur, and he was rendered unbound before he died. He found his first familiar along the western edge of Tobyn's Wood. It's only six or seven days from here if we make good time."

"How do you know this?" Henryk asked.

"I was raised not far from there," he said. "Peredur and my father were friends."

"So he might listen to you."

"Possibly. It can't hurt to try." Nodin looked at Tammen. "I believe there are some free towns in that area. Perhaps they'll be open to joining the Movement. Even if Peredur won't help us, the journey won't be for nothing." It came out as more of a plea than he had intended, but at that point he didn't care. In spite of all that had passed between them, he still wasn't ready to lose her.

"To the west, you say?" she asked, seeming distracted.

He nodded, and then said "Yes," because she didn't appear to be looking at him.

"Near the Northern Plain?"

"Within two leagues of it. You know the place?"

Tammen shook her head. "No." A moment later she shook her head a second time, as if clearing her sight. "All right," she said. "We'll speak with Peredur." She smiled at him. She actually smiled. "It's a good idea."

Nodin grinned in return—how could he help it?—and he turned to face his other companion. "Henryk?"

The man looked from Nodin to Tammen, his dark eyes grim. "I don't like this," he said. "I'll do it, but I don't like it."

Nodin nodded, still smiling. "Good." Henryk's fears were probably well-founded, but he couldn't bring himself to think of that right then. They had a plan, one that kept them together for a while longer. And she had smiled at him.

Jaryd, Alayna, and Myn came within sight of Amarid late in the morning. From where they stood, on a stone outcropping in the lower foothills of the Parneshome Range, the First Mage's city resembled a sprawling quilt of white, grey, and green. The crystal statues of the Great Hall sparkled in the sunlight and, farther in the distance, the white and blue spires of Amarid's Assembly, the meeting place of the League, gleamed like blades.

It would have taken them but a few hours to reach the Great Hall, but Jaryd and Alayna thought it best to wait until nightfall, when Rithlar was less likely to be noticed. They had avoided villages and towns during their journey across Tobyn-Ser and, when encounters with strangers appeared inevitable, Jaryd had instructed the great eagle to fly off rather than allowing her to be seen in the company of a mage. Too many of Tobyn-Ser's people knew what the appearance of an eagle meant, and the last thing the mages wanted to do was cause the people of the land to panic.

During their journey, they had managed to explain all of this to Myn in a way that did not raise the child's fears, but as her excitement at seeing Amarid grew, so did her impatience to reach the great city. And in this instance, finally, Jaryd and Alayna's casual explanations did not satisfy her. In the end, Jaryd felt he had no choice but to tell her the truth, at least in part.

"We need to wait until nightfall, Myn, because we don't want anyone to see Rithlar."

"Why not?" the girl asked, looking puzzled.

"People might be scared of her," he said, glancing up at the bird, who was circling high above them, a dark speck in a brilliant blue sky. "Sometimes people are scared of eagles."

"Do they think eagles are mean?"

Jaryd took a breath and glanced at Alayna. He wasn't handling this very well.

"People are afraid of eagles," Alayna explained solemnly, "because usually eagles only bind to mages when there's a war."

"A war?" Myn whispered, her face turning pale. "Is there a war now?"

Alayna smiled. "No, Myn-Myn. There's no war."

Jaryd made himself smile as well, hoping Alayna's answer would satisfy his daughter. A year ago it might have.

"Is there going to be a war?"

Alayna's smile vanished, as did his own.

"We don't know, Myn," he told her. "We've come to Amarid so that we can work with Uncle Baden, and Trahn, and Orris, and the rest of the mages to prevent a war. But for now we don't want to scare the people in the city by letting them see Rithlar. Do you understand?"

The girl nodded, her pale eyes wide, and her long chestnut hair stirring in the mountain wind. "Who would we fight in a war?" she asked a moment later.

"I don't know, Love," Jaryd said quietly. "None of us knows."

They spent the rest of the day playing beside a remote corner of Dacia's Lake at the base of the foothills, the respite serving as a distraction for Jaryd and Alayna as well as their child. Only when the sun disappeared behind the mountains did they finally start toward the First Mage's city.

They reached the bank of the Larian several hours later, crossed one of the small, ancient bridges into the old town commons, and made their way quietly to the Great Hall. Myn, who was sitting in front of Alayna on Alayna's horse, had long since fallen asleep, and even after Alayna handed her down to Jaryd, she did not wake. With Rithlar bounding along beside him and his staff with its sapphire ceryll tucked under one arm, Jaryd carried the girl to the large wooden doors of the domed building and knocked once. Several moments passed before one of the blue-robed stewards of the Hall answered his summons. She was young-looking and her face was puffy with sleep, but she seemed to recognize him immediately.

"Hawk-Mage!" she said with genuine surprise. "Can I help you?"

"Hawk-Mage Alayna and I need a place to sleep," he answered. And then, grinning and glancing at Myn in his arms, he added, "As does our daughter."

She furrowed her brow. "I don't understand. The inns are full?"

Apparently, Radomil had kept Jaryd's secret all too well. "Perhaps you should summon the Owl-Sage," Jaryd said gently. "He'll know what to do."

"The Sage is sleeping, Hawk-Mage," the woman told him, looking at him now as if he had lost his mind. "Everyone in the Hall is asleep."

Jaryd stared at the woman for several seconds and then, taking a slow breath, he summoned a bright light from his crystal so that its glow fell upon Rithlar, who now stood beside him on the threshold of the Hall.

Seeing the great bird, the woman let out a startled gasp and jumped back. "Fist of the God!" she breathed. "That's the biggest hawk I've ever seen!"

"That's because she's not a hawk," Jaryd replied. "She's an eagle."

At first the woman did not seem to have heard what he said. She continued to stare at the bird with unconcealed amazement. But after several moments her eyes suddenly flew to Jaryd's face. "An eagle?" she repeated.

Jaryd nodded.

By this time Alayna had joined him at the doorway, and she glared at the woman with manifest impatience. "I believe Eagle-Sage Jaryd asked you to wake the Owl-Sage," she said with asperity. "Please, don't make us ask you again."

"Of course, Owl-Master!" the attendant said, nodding eagerly before spinning away. "Please, enter!" she called over her shoulder. "The Sage will be here shortly!"

The woman vanished behind a door, but almost immediately several stewards appeared in her place, and within a few minutes the entire Hall was bustling with activity. Attendants appeared carrying plates of food that they placed on the council table in the middle of the Gathering Chamber. Jaryd glimpsed others carrying bed linens to a small room in the back of the Hall, and an older man, also wearing a blue robe, told him that their horses had been taken to a nearby stable where they would be fed and brushed.

Myn awoke, and seeing the small feast that had been prepared for them, announced that she was too hungry to sleep. Alayna took her from Jaryd's arms and carried her over to the food, for at that moment, Radomil emerged from his chambers, accompanied by Ilianne, his wife.

"Eagle-Sage!" he called in his deep voice, striding across the Hall's broad marble floor. "Welcome to Amarid!"

Jaryd felt himself blush. "It's just me, Radomil."

The heavyset man gestured toward the enormous golden brown bird standing by Jaryd's side. "And are you not bound to that magnificent creature?"

Jaryd conceded the point with a grin and an embarrassed shrug.

Stopping in front of him, Radomil wrapped Jaryd in a fierce embrace. "I'm glad to see you," he whispered, pounding Jaryd's back. "Even under these circumstances, I'm glad to see you."

A moment later Radomil released him and turned toward Alayna and Myn. "Hello, Alayna!" he said cheerfully. "Who's this young woman sharing your meal with you?"

Myn looked at him with wide eyes. "It's me, Owl-Sage!" she said. "Myn!"

"Myn?" Radomil said with an exaggerated frown. "Impossible! Myn is just a babe! You're much too old to be her."

"No, really," the girl insisted. "It is me!"

The Sage squatted down next to her. "Are you sure?" he asked.

She nodded, and Radomil began to laugh. "Very well," he said. "I believe you." He stood again and embraced Alayna. "She looks just like you, Alayna." He glanced at Jaryd mischievously. "Lucky child."

Alayna laughed, as did Jaryd and Radomil.

"Don't listen to him, Jaryd," Ilianne said, a smile on her round, pleasant face. "I see as much of you in Myn as I do Alayna. Actually the one she really favors is your mother."

"I know," Jaryd agreed. "She has my mother's temper as well."

Radomil laughed again, but an instant later his mirth vanished, leaving him grim-faced. He looked old, Jaryd realized. There was more grey than black in his goatee and mustache, and even puffy with sleep, his face appeared lined and drawn. The Sage regarded Rithlar a second time and then approached her cautiously.

"Will she let me touch her?" he asked over his shoulder, his eyes never leaving the eagle.

"Yes," Jaryd replied. "She's not as ferocious as she looks."

The Sage nodded. "I've never been this close to an eagle," he whispered, squatting again so that he could look at her closely. "I never imagined they could be so large. Or so beautiful," he added quickly, looking back at Jaryd for a second. He stroked the bird's chin, and she closed her eyes and stretched out her neck obligingly. "What's her name?"

"Rithlar."

Again the Sage nodded. "Like all the others."

Radomil looked over his shoulder at Ilianne, and the two of them shared a look.

After several seconds, she nodded. She might even have smiled. "Myn," she said, "why don't you and I go put the linens on your bed. We have a special room set aside for you."

Myn glanced up at Alayna, a question in her pale eyes.

"It's all right, Myn-Myn," Alayna said. "I'll be along soon."

Myn took Ilianne's hand and the two of them started toward the back of the Hall, where the living quarters were.

"Ilianne and I will be out of the Sage's quarters tomorrow," Radomil said, standing again and smoothing his cloak. "We weren't certain when you'd be arriving. Mered has already vacated the First's quarters. That's where we assumed you want Myn to be, so we prepared the room for her ahead of time."

Alayna smiled, looking tired. "Thank you. That will be perfect for her.

As to the rest, we're in no rush to get into your quarters. If you need more time, take it."

"Absolutely," Jaryd agreed. "We'll be fine anywhere."

"You're kind," Radomil said. "But with all the gods have placed on your shoulders, you shouldn't have to worry about your comfort as well."

"Have the rest arrived already?" Alayna asked.

"Most, yes. Trahn arrived several days ago, as did Orris. Baden and Sonel have been here for some time as well." The Sage smiled. "Basically, we've been waiting for you. Mered and I have done as you asked: no one knows of your binding. All we've said is that you asked for a Gathering."

"Thank you. That must have raised some eyebrows."

"It did," Radomil said with a grin. "I seem to recall Orris's response being particularly spirited."

Alayna laughed. "He probably hasn't left Baden alone for a minute."

The three of them laughed briefly before growing serious again.

"What do you intend to do, Jaryd?" Radomil asked.

Jaryd pushed his hair back from his brow and took a slow breath. "I'm still not certain," he admitted. "There's too much we don't know about why Rithlar has come. And even with that information, I don't feel qualified to make these decisions on my own. I need advice from all of you."

"I understand," Radomil said, nodding. "Truly, I do. I never felt that I was particularly well-suited to leading the Order, and I never had to face the burden of being bound to an eagle. I don't envy you."

"We need sleep," Alayna said after a brief silence. "At least I do. We can't decide anything tonight anyway."

"You're right," the Sage said, suppressing a yawn. "Let me show you where you'll be sleeping tonight."

Jaryd and Alayna followed the Sage to their room and within a few minutes had climbed into bed and fallen into a deep slumber. They awoke early the next morning and after eating a quick breakfast, had one of the attendants call the Order to the Gathering Chamber by ringing the bells mounted atop the Great Hall.

They waited with Radomil in the Sage's quarters for the mages to arrive. Better to field everyone's questions at once, Jaryd and Alayna decided, than to answer them repeatedly as the membership of the Order trickled into the Hall. The wait seemed interminable to Jaryd, although he knew that it lasted only a short while. Faced now with the prospect of assuming leadership of the Order, he felt all of his fears and doubts returning. *I'm not ready for this*, he said to himself. *Why would the gods choose me?*

Alayna took his hand, seeming to read his thoughts, and Rithlar sent him an image of their binding, as if to say that she had truly been meant for him.

"It's time," Radomil said quietly, standing to face Jaryd. He smiled reassuringly. "Lead the way, Eagle-Sage."

Fighting back a wave of nausea, Jaryd stood as well and tried to return the Sage's smile. He called Rithlar to his arm, wincing as her talons gripped him. Even with the padding he had added to his sleeves, he still felt as though she was shredding his skin. But in this instance, he wanted her on his arm. With one last glance back at Alayna, he stepped to the door, opened it, and entered the Gathering Chamber.

The others in the Hall turned to look at him, the rustle of their cloaks echoing with unnatural loudness off the domed ceiling of the chamber. His footsteps, and those of Alayna and Radomil behind him, resonated through the room as well, but no other sounds reached him. Unmoving and silent, his fellow mages merely stared at him, or rather at the great bird that gripped his forearm, her talons piercing his flesh. Baden and Orris were there, as were Sonel and Trahn, Mered, and Ursel. They were his friends, the people who had taught him to be a mage, and somehow he was supposed to lead them. He saw the fear in their eyes—how could he miss it?—and as he had so many times since binding to Rithlar, he had to struggle to control the panic rising within him.

Reaching the Sage's chair—his chair now—he stopped and looked around the council table. It had been many years since Erland and Arslan led their followers out of the Great Hall and created the League, and yet Jaryd was still not accustomed to seeing the long table with so few seated around it. Strangely, he found himself thinking about the size of the meeting table in Amarid's Assembly. Did Erland find a smaller table, or did he expect that someday the Assembly would accommodate all of Tobyn-Ser's mages?

Alayna and Radomil stopped on either side of him, and a deathlike stillness fell over the Great Hall. The building itself seemed to be holding its breath, as if waiting to see what would happen now that an Eagle-Sage had appeared again in the Gathering Chamber. The only one who seemed unaffected was Rithlar, who turned her head from side to side, staring avidly at the other birds arrayed around the table.

"The gods have sent us an Eagle-Sage," Radomil announced, at last. "Jaryd leads the Order now, and he has chosen Alayna to be his First." The ghost of a smile touched his lips. "I would think it a good choice even if she wasn't his wife."

Everyone in the chamber laughed, and much of the tension that had gripped the room a moment before vanished. Jaryd grinned appreciatively at the portly mage, thinking to himself that despite Radomil's comments to the contrary, the Owl-Master was a fine leader.

"I will leave it to our Eagle-Sage to convene this Gathering," Radomil said, his smile lingering. "Thank you all for the wisdom and respect you've shown me during my time as your Sage." He gripped Jaryd's shoulder briefly and nodded once to Alayna, before making his way to what had been, prior to his term as Owl-Sage, his customary position at the table.

Alayna reached over and gave Jaryd's hand a squeeze. Then she lowered herself into the First's chair.

Jaryd looked around the room and took a steadying breath. "This is Rithlar," he said, indicating the eagle with his free hand. "I bound to her several weeks ago and immediately contacted Radomil to request that he summon all of you to Amarid." *Why would the gods choose me?* "I'd be grateful for any advice you can offer. I don't know why this bird has come to me rather than to one of you, but we all know what the appearance of an eagle means."

He looked around the table, inviting the others to speak. At first no one did, but then Trahn sat forward, looking from Jaryd to the other mages.

"Do we really know?" he asked. "Certainly in the past, they have been harbingers of war. But does Jaryd's binding mean that war is inevitable or only that it's possible?"

"I'm not sure that it matters," Orris replied grimly. "We have to assume the worst and make our preparations accordingly."

Sonel nodded. "Orris is right. I hope that war can be avoided, but we'd be foolish to allow such hopes to interfere with our planning."

"But how do we prepare?" Ursel asked. "We don't even know who our enemy is."

"Of course we do!" said Tramys, one of the newer members of the Order. "It's the outlanders. It must be."

"We've had no trouble from the outlanders for several years," Orris said. "What makes you think that they're suddenly interested in a war?"

"They've attacked us before!" Tramys answered. "Recently. I know that things have improved since your journey there, Orris. But you can't expect them to have changed entirely. Not this soon."

The burly mage shook his head. "I don't believe we have anything to fear from Lon-Ser."

Another of the young mages stood, a woman named Orlanne. "What about the stories we've heard of Temple guards carrying weapons from Lon-Ser?"

"I'm alarmed by that, too," Orris said. "But it doesn't mean that the Sovereigns want war."

Tramys opened his arms wide. "But who else could it be? The Abborijis? We've enjoyed peaceful relations with them for hundreds of years."

"There is a new Supreme Potentate in Abborij," Mered observed. "Perhaps she's not as committed to peace as her predecessors."

"We should also remember," Trahn added, "that the other three Eagle-Sages fought against Abborij. Based on those experiences, we're ready to assume that the appearance of an eagle inevitably means war. Isn't it just as possible that it inevitably means war with Abborij?"

"Regardless of who our enemy is," Alayna said, "I think we need to recognize how limited our power is. If we're to fight a war, be it against Lon-Ser, or Abborij, or some other enemy, I think we need to consider approaching the League and the Temples. We can't do this alone."

"If the Temples are indeed getting weapons from Lon-Ser," Orlanne said, "we should consider the possibility that they've already joined forces with our enemies."

Tramys and the other young mages nodded in agreement.

"Even so," Jaryd said, "Alayna's point is well taken. We should go to the League and tell them of my binding. If we're destined for war, we'll need all of Tobyn-Ser's mages. And who knows?" he added. "Maybe this will begin our reconciliation with the League."

"Nothing would make me happier," Baden commented, speaking for the first time since Jaryd entered the chamber. "But I think we need to consider another possibility."

Everyone had turned toward him.

"This eagle may have come because we're on the verge of a civil war."

9

I have not the time to write a lengthy letter, and even if I did, I do not believe that I could find the words to convey this news gently. So I will just write it and be done, knowing as I do that it will take some time to reach you.

Shivohn is dead, killed by an assassin's bomb. I have my suspicions as to who is responsible, but I will not commit them to paper, for if I am right, our correspondence may not be as privileged as we once believed. I will write at length when I am able, but for now let me leave you with this warning: Lon-Ser may be moving toward a period of profound unrest, perhaps even civil war. It is only a matter of time before this conflict, if it comes, spills over into your land and Abborij. For all I know it has already.

Guard yourself, Orris, and do not allow the vigilance with which

*you and your fellow mages protect Tobyn-Ser to slacken for even a
moment.*

> —Melyor i Lakin, Sovereign and
> Bearer of Bragor-Nal to Hawk-Mage
> Orris, Day 6, Week 4, Spring, Year
> 3068.

Watching Wiercia pace the length of the Council chamber, her
long legs carrying her from one end of the room to the other in
just a few strides, Melyor could not help but question her memory of
their conversation from a few days before. She had switched off her
speak-screen that day convinced that somehow she had managed to win
at least a measure of Wiercia's trust. They had a long way to go before
they could be allies, she knew, and probably she would never be as close
to Wiercia as she had been to Shivohn. But she felt that they had reached
an understanding. And yet now, listening to the tirade of Oerella-Nal's
new Sovereign, as the surf of Arick's Sea pounded the Oerellan shore just
outside the windows, she wondered if she had imagined it all.

True, they had spoken of the need to make Marar believe that he had succeeded in driving a wedge between the Matriarchy and Bragor-Nal. If that
was what Wiercia was doing, she was making an awfully good show of it.

"I may be new to your little Council," the tall woman was saying, her
crimson robe rustling as she turned at the far wall and started back toward
the end of the table at which Melyor and Marar were seated. "But I will
not allow Oerella-Nal to be bullied! Bragor-Nal will accept suitable punishment for its crimes, or we will be forced to retaliate in kind! I have the
support of my Legates on this, Sovereign!" she said, her eyes blazing as
she glared at Melyor. Her face was flushed, and she was gesturing sharply.
"If Bragor-Nal wants a war, then by the gods we'll give you a war!" She
turned her hot gaze on Marar. "And lest you think that Stib-Nal would
stand to gain from such a conflict, Marar, think again! Any interference on
your part—any at all—will be taken by the Matriarchy as an act of war!"

Melyor glanced at Stib-Nal's Sovereign and found that he was already
looking at her, a slight smirk pulling at the corners of his mouth. He held
himself with an air of confidence she had never seen in him before: he
wasn't sitting as hunched as usual; his shoulders didn't look quite so narrow.

You bastard, Melyor thought. *Shivohn's dead, and you think you've
won.*

She looked at Wiercia again, but the Oerellan Sovereign had already
made her turn and was walking away from them.

"Don't you have anything to say for yourself, Melyor?" Wiercia demanded over her shoulder. "Or do you just plan to hide behind the shameless lies you've told my Legates since Shivohn's death?"

It was an opening, whether or not that was now Wiercia had intended it, and Melyor had little choice but to play along. "Perhaps we should allow Marar to judge what I have to say, Sovereign," she said with a frosty smile. "What the Matriarchy dismisses as lies may carry some weight with the good people of Stib-Nal."

Wiercia halted her pacing and turned to look at Melyor, her expression revealing little.

Her eyes fixed on the tall woman's face, Melyor pulled out the detonator from the boomer that had damaged the Gold Palace and tossed it onto the table. "This is from an explosive device that came frighteningly close to killing me. As you can see," she added, turning briefly to Marar, "it was made in Oerella-Nal."

"When did this attack occur?" Marar asked, not bothering to hide his amusement.

"As it happens," Melyor answered, watching him closely, "the same day Shivohn died."

A smile broke over his face, as if he could no longer contain his delight at all he had wrought. "My, but the two of you have been busy," he said, looking from one of them to the other.

Wiercia took a step forward and leveled a rigid finger at Marar. "I have done nothing! That detonator proves nothing!"

"It proves no less than the detonator you found from the bomb that killed Shivohn!" Melyor fired back. "You can't have it both ways, Wiercia! If Bragor-Nal is guilty, then so is the Matriarchy!"

"You're forgetting one important difference, Melyor," the woman returned. "You survived. How do you explain that?"

Melyor swallowed. Wiercia was really quite good at this. She hoped. "I guess I was lucky."

Wiercia gave a high, mirthless laugh. "Lucky? You expect us to believe that?" She shook her head. "I think it much more likely that you had Shivohn assassinated and then staged the attempt on your own life to confuse us."

"I must say," Marar broke in, the grin still on his bony face. "That's the way it looks to me as well."

Melyor looked at Wiercia, gauging her reaction. And what she saw chilled her blood. The Sovereign's pale eyes gleamed triumphantly, and she wore a fierce, predatory smile on her lips.

Melyor felt her stomach knotting. What of their conversation? What of their agreement that Marar had everything to gain from a conflict between their Nals?

"Marar, would you excuse us for a moment?" she managed to say. Her mouth had gone dry. "Sovereign Wiercia and I need some time to work this out in private."

"I'll do better than that, Melyor," the man said smugly. "I'll give you all the time you need." He rose smoothly and stepped away from the table.

"I do not need to be alone with this criminal for even a moment!" Wiercia raged, her eyes fixed on Melyor again. "Anything you and I have to say to each other can be said in a meeting of the full Council! You tried this before, Melyor. All those attempts you made to contact me by speak-screen should have told you something! I will not be manipulated and I will not be intimidated!"

Too late, Melyor realized her error. It was all an act. Incredible as it seemed, Wiercia was doing just what they had agreed. Even as she kicked herself for failing to recognize this sooner, Melyor could not help but smile to herself. Wiercia was really quite good at this. Better than Melyor herself, as it turned out.

Wiercia continued to glare at Melyor for another moment, as if chastising her. Then she turned to Marar. "Please stay, Sovereign," she said warmly. "The people of Oerella-Nal would appreciate your insight on this matter."

"You're very kind, Wiercia," Marar answered. "But it seems quite obvious to me that this is a dispute that has nothing to do with the people of Stib-Nal." He smiled and opened his hands slightly. "I would just be getting in the way were I to remain." He glanced at Melyor. "Sovereign," he said mildly, with a single nod.

A moment later he was gone. Wiercia and Melyor stared at each other, but they said nothing until they heard Marar's air-carrier rise above the ancient palace in which they were sitting and fly off toward Stib-Nal.

"You idiot!" Wiercia said, practically shouting it at her. "What were you thinking?"

Melyor shrugged slightly. "I wasn't really sure what to think," she admitted. "With all that you were saying—"

"I was doing exactly what you told me to do! I thought you wanted to convince Marar that he had turned us against each other!"

Melyor grinned. "I did. I just didn't realize that you'd be so good at it."

Wiercia stared at her for several moments. Then she began to shake her head, laughing quietly. "Well, let that be a lesson to you, Sovereign: never underestimate me, or my people."

"I'll try to remember that."

"Good." The tall woman smiled and, after a moment, she sat down. "So what do we do now?"

"We wait. In light of your performance, I doubt we'll have to wait very long."

Wiercia inclined her head slightly, acknowledging the compliment. "What do you think Marar will do next?"

"I expect he'll contact one of us, offering an alliance in exchange for some exorbitant reward."

Wiercia arched an eyebrow. "Ah, but which of us?"

Melyor considered this briefly. "It depends. He has to decide which of us can offer him the most, which of us needs him the most, and which of us will be the easier to control." She paused again. Finally, she smiled. "Me," she said. "I expect he'll contact me."

"Why you?"

"Because he knows me, and because he'll expect you to be too principled to join forces with him. I'm a Gildriite, and that will give him pause, but I was once a Bragory Nal-Lord. He understands me—at least he thinks he does. Stib-Nal isn't all that different from what Bragor-Nal used to be." Melyor nodded at the soundness of her own reasoning. It all made so much sense. She smiled to herself. In spite of all the changes she had brought to Bragor-Nal, there were times when she longed for the simple, brutal clarity of the old ways. "He'll contact me," she repeated, nodding again. "Probably this evening."

Wiercia grinned. "That's fine with me," she said dryly. "I can't stand the man."

Even by air-carrier, the trip from the Point of the Sovereigns, on Oerella-Nal's eastern shore, back to his palace in Stib-Nal took several hours. And Marar smiled the whole way. He couldn't remember the last time that had happened. Probably it never had. As much as he still rued the passing of the days when he and Durell had stood together against Shivohn, he knew that even then he had been unhappy. Durell might have needed him, but the Bragory Sovereign had never respected him, and neither, Arick knew, had Shivohn.

But all of that was about to change. Sitting at his desk in the Grove Palace, staring out at the Greenwater Mountains, which were shrouded in the cool blue shadows of early evening, Marar grinned. How could he help it? He had seen fear on Melyor's face today, and there had been barely checked rage in Wiercia's every gesture. And he had seen as well that they were both putting on a show for his benefit. It was obvious. Both of his rivals had figured out that he was responsible for Shivohn's death and the attempt on Melyor's life. Perhaps they had done so together. It really didn't matter.

For in seeing beyond their deception, Marar had also seen the limits of their newly fledged alliance. Melyor's fear was real. She still wasn't certain that she had won Wiercia's trust. And though the Oerellan Sovereign had been feigning her outrage, the lie came to her too easily. Clearly, she still half believed that Melyor had been involved in the plot to kill Shiv-ohn. Yes, the two women were working together—he was certain of that—but neither of them was happy about it. And each was still more than willing to believe that the other was the enemy.

Which suited his needs quite well. He had to drive a wedge between them, and already he knew the points at which their relationship was weakest. It might have been easier if he had been interested in a partner-ship with Wiercia. Her doubts about Oerella-Nal's alliance with Bragor-Nal ran far deeper than did Melyor's. And, of course, she wasn't a Gildriite. But neither did she have any knowledge of Tobyn-Ser's sorcer-ers.

He glanced down at the papers that Gregor, his First Minister, had just put before him and found that he was grinning again. He could hardly help it. Earlier that day, he had received a shipment of gold from Tobyn-Ser's clerics that had exceeded even his most fanciful expectations. There were riches in that strange land that were ripe for the taking, and as wary as he was of doing business with Melyor, he understood that he had little choice in the matter. Perhaps soon, if Stib-Nal's trade with the clerics continued to expand, he would not need her anymore. At which point he would have her killed. But for now, he had to content himself with what he had accomplished thus far: Shivohn's death, his discovery of a new, seemingly endless supply of wealth, and the recruitment of well-placed security men in both Bragor-Nal and Oerella-Nal. All that remained for him to do was complete what Shivohn's assassination had begun: the destruction of the Oerellan-Bragory alliance.

Reaching for his speak-screen, he pressed the yellow button that con-nected him with Bragor-Nal's Gold Palace, although not before he took the usual precautions to be sure that his conversation was not being recorded or monitored. An instant later, the face of one of Melyor's guards appeared before him. Marar didn't recognize him.

"Yes, Sovereign," the man said with proper courtesy. "How may I help you?"

The Sovereign glanced down at his desk again, as if already bored with their conversation. "I wish to speak with your Sovereign."

The man nodded. "Of course. One moment please."

The guard reached for a button on the console, and the screen went blank for several moments. The next face that appeared was Melyor's. She was dressed as she had been earlier in the day—as she was every time

Marar saw her—in an ivory tunic and dark loose-fitting trousers. He couldn't see her thigh, but he assumed that she had a thrower strapped to it. She always did. Many thought her beautiful, he knew, and he could see why.

As soon as she appeared, a light on Marar's console began to flash.

"You have a recording device," Marar said, with a smile.

The woman nodded. "Yes I do. Is that a problem?"

"I'd like you to turn it off."

"Why?" she asked with a coy grin.

Marar shrugged, feigning indifference. "As a rule, I don't allow my conversations to be recorded. If we're to talk, you'll have to turn it off."

"You contacted me, Marar. What makes you think I'm interested in talking to you?"

"Perhaps you're right. How presumptuous of me. Shall we speak another time?"

She regarded him for several moments, her expression neutral. Finally, she reached forward and pressed a button on her screen. The light on his console stopped flashing.

"Thank you," he said, smiling.

"What can I do for you, Marar?" she asked with manifest impatience.

"Can't I contact you just to chat?"

"You never have. And besides, I said everything I needed to in the Council meeting."

He raised an eyebrow. "I sincerely doubt that."

"Meaning what?" Melyor demanded, narrowing her eyes.

"Just that there seemed to be a great deal that went unsaid in today's meeting."

"I don't understand."

For a second time, Marar smiled. It was clear from the look of alarm in her eyes that she did understand. "Let's dispense with the games, Melyor. They insult both of us."

She stared at him for some time, saying nothing. Then she nodded once, as if coming to a decision. She might even have grinned for an instant—it was hard to tell. "All right, Marar," she said. "What is it you're after? Why did you have Shivohn killed, and why did you send that assassin after me?"

He raised an eyebrow. "Do you think I was responsible for all that?"

"I thought you didn't want to play games."

"I don't." He paused briefly, then smiled. "Let's do it this way: speaking hypothetically, were I to have done all that you say, I'd still have trouble replying honestly to your questions."

She looked at him skeptically. "Why?"

"You make it sound as though they all can be addressed with one answer," he said. "They can't. What do I want? Why would I have Shiv-ohn killed? Why would I try to have you killed? Those are three separate matters."

"Three or two?"

Marar gave a small laugh and inclined his head slightly, conceding the point. "All right, perhaps two."

"Then give me two answers," Melyor said, sitting back in her chair and crossing her arms over her chest. "But they'd better be good ones, Marar. Technically, what you've done is an act of war, and regardless of whatever advances you feel Stib-Nal has made in the past few years, I shouldn't have to remind you that my military is still far more powerful than yours."

Marar smiled disarmingly. "Of course, Sovereign." *And you would do well to keep in mind,* he wanted to say, *that if I was able to kill Shivohn, and if I came so close to killing you once, I can do it again.* But such brazenness would have been a bit premature. "Please keep in mind that we're still speaking hypothetically," he said instead.

She nodded and made an impatient gesture, as if urging him to go on.

"As to what I'm after, as you put it," he continued, "that should hardly come as a shock to anyone. I want wealth, and I want power."

"You have both of those already," she said. "You're Sovereign of Stib-Nal. You answer to no one, and surely your position brings you ample amounts of gold."

He nodded. "That may be true, Melyor, but let me ask you this: would all I have satisfy you?"

"What?"

"You've ruled Bragor-Nal for nearly seven years now. You know what it is to command the land's greatest army, to call yourself Sovereign of the land's largest Nal, to have at your disposal the land's richest treasury. Would you trade that for what I have?"

She hesitated, and Marar smiled.

"Of course not," he said, answering his own question. "Neither would I, were I in your position." He sat forward, resting his elbows on the arms of his carved wooden chair and peering into the screen. "But I'm not in your position, am I? I don't have all that you have. I don't even have what Wiercia has. I'm not even close."

"So it's not really power or wealth you're after, is it Marar?"

His turn to hesitate. "I don't follow."

"Listen to yourself," she said with unsettling equanimity. "You're not interested in gold or influence. You're just jealous. You want what we have. Probably you always have, but you never had the wherewithal to go after it until now."

"That's ridiculous!" he said.

"Is it? It also seems to me that this explains Shivohn's assassination and the boomer you sent to the Gold Palace." She gave a thin smile. "You may enjoy sounding mysterious and complicated, but when it comes right down to it, you're a child. You want everything that your playmates have, and if you can't have it, then you'll find new playmates."

"How dare you!" he sputtered. "Who do you think you're talking to?"

Her smile vanished, and she glared at the screen with hard green eyes. "I'm talking to the man who tried to have me killed, and who has violated more provisions of the Cape of Stars Treaty than I care to count! It would be within my rights under both the Treaty and the Green Area Proclamation to invade Stib-Nal tomorrow. Or Wiercia and I could simply have you removed from the Council. Don't push me too far, Sovereign!"

He opened his mouth to fire back a threat of his own. In that instant he wanted nothing more than to see her dead. But once again he resisted the urge to give too much away. He clamped his mouth shut, struggling to regain his composure.

Melyor seemed to read his thoughts anyway. She reached to the side and a moment later produced her staff with its brilliant red stone. "In case you plan on trying something again, Marar," she warned, "you should know that Gildriites are seldom taken by surprise twice."

"I appreciate the advice," he managed to say. He reached for his screen to end their communication.

"Are we finished already?" she asked.

He stared at her, his hand poised above the console. She had him off-balance, he knew. If this had been a street fight, he would have been dead by now. But she still had so much to offer him: her knowledge of Cedrych's plan to conquer Tobyn-Ser, her ties to the sorcerers there, and, remote as the possibility seemed right now, all the resources she could bring to an alliance between Bragor-Nal and Stib-Nal.

"You contacted me for a reason, didn't you, Marar?" she coaxed. "We still have much to discuss."

He pulled his hand back slowly and regarded her for some time. "Like what?" he finally asked.

She smiled indulgently, as if he really were a child and she a lenient parent. "You tell me. You sent assassins after both Shivohn and me. That's bold. A leader with your experience doesn't take such a step on the spur of the moment. You must have had something in mind; a plan that you were carrying out."

"Perhaps," he said. "What of it?"

"It may be that I can help you with it." Her smile deepened as she traced an idle finger along the edge of her glowing crystal. "That is why you contacted me, isn't it? To gain my trust?"

He licked his lips nervously. Abruptly he wasn't certain why he had contacted her.

"Both of us know that you don't want me as an enemy," she went on. "Stib-Nal can't possibly be prepared to go to war with Bragor-Nal. But by the same token, you're wise enough to recognize my value as a potential ally." She paused briefly, as if giving him time to consider what she had said. "So tell me: why did you contact me?"

She was offering him what he wanted. Indeed, it was practically all he had thought about since he had first heard of Premel's failure. And yet, in that moment, something stopped him. It might have been the sight of her staff and the ancient fears it aroused within him. It might have been intuition—at one time, when he had still been a minor lord making a name for himself in the quads, his instincts had been quite good. Perhaps it was merely that her offer was too perfect, too close to being exactly what he needed. Whatever the reason, he could not bring himself to trust her. She was powerful and brilliant and rich beyond all measure, but she was also ruthless and a Gildriite. Most importantly, though, she was his enemy, and nothing would ever change that. He had been a fool to think otherwise, even for just a moment.

"No," he said, shaking his head for emphasis. "Contacting you was a mistake. I'm sorry to have bothered you, Sovereign." He sounded ridiculous he knew. He certainly wasn't fooling her. But he needed to extricate himself from the conversation before he ruined everything. Obviously he had underestimated her. He had contacted her so that he might lure her into an alliance, and instead he had nearly been trapped himself.

"You want me to believe that you summoned me by mistake?" she asked with unfeigned surprise.

"Yes."

Her expression hardened. "And did you send the assassin by mistake as well?"

He said nothing, but reached once more to switch off his console.

"Think carefully, Marar," she warned. "If you end this conversation now, you'll be all alone. No one in Lon-Ser will be able to help you."

He hesitated, but only for an instant. "I'll have to take that chance." He switched off the speak-screen and fell back heavily into his chair, his eyes closed.

A moment later, however, he leaned forward again, turned on the recording safeguards, and punched in the code for Premel. His speak-screen beeped for several minutes before the security man's sharp features finally appeared before him. Premel looked angry—probably he had been in the middle of another briefing—but Marar didn't really care.

"Yes, Sovereign," he began impatiently. "What do you—?"

"Is Jibb dead yet?" the Sovereign demanded.

Premel looked away briefly before meeting Marar's gaze again. "No," he answered, his voice flat.

"Well, kill him. Soon. And Melyor, too."

Premel stared at him, his pale eyes widening. "Now you want both of them dead?"

"Yes."

"But the other day you told me—"

"I know what I said the other day! Now I'm telling you to kill them both! And I expect it to be done!"

Marar jabbed his finger at the console button, terminating their connection before Premel could say anything more.

Slumping back into his chair once again Marar took a long breath. He felt better already. Melyor had unsettled him greatly, but knowing that she would soon be dead did much to calm his nerves.

There was still one more conversation he needed to have, however. Melyor, he realized belatedly, had been a poor choice from the start. She was too shrewd to be manipulated by anyone, and too dangerous to be embraced as an ally for any length of time. But if the Bragory Sovereign could not be turned to his purposes, perhaps the Oerellan Sovereign could.

Wiercia was already speaking with Melyor when her speak-screen beeped for a second time.

"One minute, Melyor," she said, interrupting the other woman's description of her conversation with Marar. "I've got another summons coming in."

"It's him," Melyor said with such surety that Wiercia knew she had to be right.

"What should I do?"

The Bragory Sovereign shrugged. "Talk to him. See what he wants. You and I can speak later."

"All right," Wiercia said. "Later, then."

She pressed a button on her screen to switch views and, just as Melyor had predicted, found Marar waiting for her, a sour smile on his narrow face.

"Marar," she said, trying to keep her tone light. "What a pleasant surprise."

"I doubt that," he replied.

She felt her pulse quicken. "What do you mean?"

"I would guess that you were already speaking to Melyor. No doubt you knew it was me before you switched views."

She stared at him for several moments. Perhaps Melyor and she had given Stib-Nal's Sovereign too little credit. She abruptly felt beyond her depth. The other two Sovereigns had been playing these games far longer than she. She straightened in her chair and met his gaze as steadily as she could. "You're right. I did."

His smile broadened at that until it looked almost genuine. "Excellent," he said. "I appreciate your candor."

She heard the goad in his words, but she ignored it. "What do you want?"

"What did Melyor tell you about our conversation?"

He wants candor? she thought. Fine, I'll give him candor. "We only spoke briefly before you interrupted us," she said. "But she did tell me that you had confessed to killing Shivohn and sending an assassin to the Gold Palace."

Marar began to laugh—he had a surprisingly deep laugh for a man of his meager stature—and he nodded, as if acknowledging a good jest. "That was very amusing, Sovereign," he said after some time. "I wouldn't have thought you the joking sort."

Fighting to ignore the tightening knot in her stomach, Wiercia merely sat there, gazing placidly back at the screen until finally Marar's mirth subsided, and he regarded her with narrowing eyes.

"You are joking, aren't you?" he asked.

"No. And I don't find your dissembling very convincing."

What remained of his smile vanished from his face. "She really told you that?"

"Yes."

"And you believed her?"

Wiercia faltered. "I suppose I—"

"Do you really think me that stupid?" he demanded. "Do you honestly believe that if it was true, I would admit it to Melyor?"

"She made it sound as though you had little choice," Wiercia said defensively.

He nodded. "Yes, I'll bet she did." he looked away for a moment, his lips pressed together in a tight line. "Did she bother to tell you," he asked, facing her again, "that she had mentioned the possibility of an alliance between Bragor-Nal and Stib-Nal?"

"You're lying!" Wiercia said with more vehemence than she had intended.

"I believe she said that I was wise enough to recognize her value as a potential ally, or something to that effect."

Wiercia's hands were trembling, and there was a sound in her ears like wind rushing through the quads of Oerella-Nal. She wanted desperately to terminate their communication, but she couldn't bring herself to do it. He was lying. He had to be lying. But what if he wasn't? What if Melyor had been misleading her all this time, getting her to believe that Marar was behind Shivohn's assassination, when in fact it had been a Bragory plot all along?

"I think you're lying," she said warily.

Marar nodded gravely. "Yes, you said that. But think for a moment: if I had gone to so much trouble, if I had sent assassins after both Shivohn and Melyor, why would I then turn around and blurt out my plans to one of those I wanted dead? What kind of a fool would do such a thing?"

"But she said—"

"I assure you, Wiercia, regardless of what Melyor told you, I never said that I was responsible for these attacks."

Wiercia stared at him in silence for some time. She wasn't sure what to believe anymore. "Do you admit that you contacted her?"

He nodded.

"Tell me why."

He shrugged. "For the same reason I've contacted you: to discuss today's meeting of the Council." The Sovereign gave a sad smile. "It wasn't one of our best. I fear that you and Melyor are moving toward some kind of armed conflict, and I want to do everything I can to prevent it."

"How noble of you," she said.

"Hardly," he replied, his tone icy. "I'm thinking only of my people and myself. A Nal as small as mine could easily be crushed in such a conflict, even if we're not party to it."

He was right, of course. Had she been in his place, she would have been worried as well "Then an alliance with Bragor-Nal should be quite attractive to you," she said. "Which leaves me wondering why we're even speaking."

"To be honest," Marar said, "if Bragor-Nal was led by anyone else, we wouldn't be. I would have already pledged my aid to the Bragory Sovereign and we'd be busy making preparations for war."

"Go on," Wiercia said after a brief pause.

"Melyor frightens me. I'm not ashamed to admit it." He sat forward, bringing his thin face close to the screen. "Leave aside for a moment the fact that she was once an outlaw, that she's killed more times than you and I can imagine. She's also a Gildriite. I don't trust her at all, not as an enemy, and certainly not as an ally."

"Is this your way of saying that you do trust me?"

"It's my way of saying that I'm willing to try. Provided you are as well."

Wiercia held herself very still and continued to stare at Marar's face. She didn't trust him. She wasn't sure that she ever could. But neither was she certain that she had been wise to place so much faith in Melyor. Much of what the Bragory Sovereign had said had sounded quite plausible at the time. Perhaps a bit too plausible. She seemed to have an answer for everything. It did strike Wiercia as overly convenient that Marar should confess to the crimes the very first time Melyor spoke with him alone.

And then there was Melyor's ancestry. Wiercia did not like to admit it, not even to herself, but she, too, found the notion of being allied with a Gildriite . . . distasteful. It was not that she lacked tolerance. She just preferred to do business with people she understood, people, who were like her. It was quite possible that she had been too quick to trust Melyor. The Bragory Sovereign was a murderer and a Gildriite. True, Shivohn had trusted her, but Shivohn was dead. This was no time to rush into anything. Nor was it time to rule anything out.

"You understand," she said at last, "that I bring far less to a potential alliance than Melyor. Oerella-Nal is strong and prosperous, but we're no match for Bragor-Nal."

At that Marar smiled broadly, exposing bright white teeth that appeared too large for his narrow face. "I'm aware of that, Sovereign," he said. "But I believe you'll be surprised by how much Stib-Nal can bring to such a partnership."

10

I have heard little from you since the colder months and less still from Shivohn. I hope you both are well and that your sudden silence is not a harbinger of bad tidings to come. Indeed, your lack of communication is particularly worrisome now because of recent developments here in Tobyn-Ser.

My friend, Jaryd, of whom I have told you so much over the past few years, has bound to an eagle, becoming the land's first Eagle-Sage in more than four hundred years. Throughout Tobyn-Ser's history, the binding of a mage to an eagle has presaged the coming of war, and my fellow mages of the Order fear that this time will be no different.

Many are convinced that Lon-Ser is to be our enemy in such a conflict, and though I have assured them that we have nothing to fear from the Nals, I find myself wondering what would happen to the amicable relations between our two lands should something happen to Shivohn or, Arick forbid, to you. I know that this message will, not reach you for some time, and I am reasonably certain that some correspondence from you is already on its way across Arick's Sea. But if one is not, please write as soon as you can so that I can put my fears, and those of my colleagues, to rest.

—Hawk-Mage Orris to Melyor i Lakin, Sovereign and Bearer of Bragor-Nal, Spring, God's Year 4633.

It was well past dusk when they finally adjourned for the night, discouraged and subdued. Jaryd wished that he had something to offer them. It was his responsibility, he knew. He was their leader. The future of the land rested on his shoulders. But there was still much that they didn't know. Just over a fortnight had passed since his arrival in Amarid, and he still had received no responses to the missives he sent to First Master Erland and Brevyl, Eldest of the Gods. There was nothing for the Order to do but wait and wonder if Baden was right in believing that their enemy was not a foreign one, but rather one or more of the Order's rivals here in Tobyn-Ser.

Hence, their daily discussions had become little more than somber vigils kept for the messengers of the League or the Temple. And yet, when Jaryd offered his fellow mages the choice of not meeting until some word came, they were nearly unanimous in refusing.

"We should remain close to the Great Hall," Baden had said, speaking for the vast majority of them, "just in case we need to take swift action."

So they convened, and they sat, and when the stewards of the hall brought food, they ate. But they said little and did less, and with each day that passed, Jaryd's frustration mounted. The mages had managed to keep Jaryd's binding a secret, although in recent days rumors of a new Sage had begun to spread through the city. But even this small success struck Jaryd as hollow; it was just a matter of time before someone learned that Tobyn-Ser had an Eagle-Sage. And as of yet, Jaryd had no answer for the panic that he knew would follow. He didn't want to believe that their war would be fought with the League or the Children of the Gods, but neither could he ignore the implications of Erland's and Brevyl's silence.

"It probably doesn't help that I'm so young," he said to Alayna, as they walked slowly back to their quarters in the rear of the Hall. "A more experienced Sage might have gotten an answer by now."

She shrugged. "You're our leader. They have no more right to ignore us because you're young than you do to ignore the League because Erland's old."

Jaryd grinned. "He's not old, he's venerable."

"He's old," she said. "He was old ten years ago, which makes him older than old. They don't even have a word for how old he is."

Jaryd laughed and shook his head. "You're a cold-hearted woman. I hope I don't get old and decrepit before you do."

"You'd better not," she said. "I like my men young."

They were met in front of the doorway to Myn's room by Valya, the townswoman who took care of their daughter when Jaryd and Alayna were occupied with their duties.

"She's already asleep," the grey-haired woman whispered as they stopped in front of her. She gave a toothless grin. "She tried to wait up for you, but she was too tired."

"Thank you, Valya," Alayna said quietly. "We'll see you tomorrow. Sleep well."

"And you, First." She nodded to Jaryd. "Sage."

As the woman shuffled off, Jaryd and Alayna opened Myn's door slowly, allowing the muted light of their cerylls to spill across the room. The girl was sprawled in her bed, soundly asleep. Alayna grinned and they both stepped into the room to fix Myn's blankets and kiss her cheek.

"This is the third night in a row that we've done that," Alayna whispered as they left the room and closed the door behind them. "I hate not saying good night to her."

"I think she understands."

Alayna nodded. "I'm sure she does, but I still don't like it. Let's try to adjourn a bit earlier tomorrow."

"All right," Jaryd said, taking her hand. "If it's at all possible, we will."

They made their way back to their own quarters, closing the door behind them and lighting several candles. Jaryd tossed himself onto the bed as Rithlar took her usual spot atop the large mantel over the hearth. Alayna sat beside him and took his hand, but neither of them spoke. Jaryd was too tired to say anything, although he doubted very much that he would be able to sleep. He hadn't had a decent night's rest since before their arrival in Amarid.

"What if it doesn't mean anything, Jaryd?" Alayna asked without preamble.

He opened his eyes and looked at her. "What?"

"What if your binding doesn't mean anything? What if we're doing all this for nothing?"

"Do you really think that's a possibility?"

She shrugged and pushed her dark hair back from her brow. "I don't know anymore," she said. "I—"

She stopped at the sound of voices coming from the Gathering Chamber. They exchanged a look.

"It might just be the stewards," he said, sitting up.

Alayna shook her head. "I barely hear them during the day. They wouldn't be making so much noise at this hour without a reason."

She was right, of course. Jaryd swung himself off the bed and started toward the door, but before he reached it someone knocked. He halted and glanced back at Alayna. Again she shrugged.

"Yes?" he called, facing the door again.

The door opened, and one of the attendants peered around its edge tentatively.

"I'm sorry to trouble you so late, Eagle-Sage," the woman said in a soft voice. "But there's someone come to see you."

"Who is it, Grieta?" Alayna asked.

"A woman, Owl-Master. I believe she's from the League of Amarid. She wears a blue robe."

"Did she give her name?" Jaryd asked.

"No, Sage, she didn't." The attendant faltered. "She's asking to speak with the Owl-Sage, and I wasn't certain what to do."

Jaryd tried to smile. "It's all right," he said. "Tell her we'll be out in a moment."

The woman nodded and closed the door again, leaving Jaryd and Alayna alone.

"It's awfully late for an envoy," Jaryd said, as their eyes met.

"I agree. You think it's someone who wants to cross over?"

He shook his head. "I don't know. I guess that's possible. It's also possible that she's an assassin."

"You don't really believe that, do you?"

"I'm not sure what to believe anymore," he said.

She stepped forward and took his hand again. "Do you want me to come with you?"

"I think you'd better. I'm not ready to let a League mage see Rithlar, and I don't want to face her without access to the Mage-Craft."

She nodded, and the two of the walked out into the Gathering Chamber, Alayna with her great owl on her shoulder, and Jaryd beside her, carrying his staff and acutely aware of Rithlar's absence.

But when he reached the great wooden doors of the Hall, he found that their visitor was not carrying a bird either. She was a young woman, with long brown hair that hung straight to her shoulders and delicate features that resembled Alayna's. She carried a plain staff crowned with a brilliant golden stone, and she wore the blue cloak of a League mage. But her eyes drew Jaryd's attention. They were as blue as the sky on a cool autumn morning and carried within them a wisdom and an awareness of life's capriciousness and cruelty that went far beyond the girl's years. He had seen these eyes before, years ago, when this woman was just a girl, newly orphaned by invaders from Lon-Ser and distrustful of anyone wearing the forest green cloaks of the Order, and so he knew her name before she spoke it.

"I'm Cailin," she said.

"Yes, Cailin," Alayna replied. "We remember you."

The young mage narrowed her eyes. "Have we met?"

"Once," Jaryd said. "A long time ago, when you were still living in the Great Hall." *Just after your parents were killed along with every other person in your world.*

Cailin looked from one of them to the other. "You're the ones who went to Theron's Grove, aren't you?"

Alayna nodded. "Yes."

"Which staff was the Owl-Master's?" she asked, her voice suddenly tinged with awe.

"This one," Jaryd answered.

He held out his staff for her to take and examine, but though she stepped forward to look at it closely, she seemed reluctant to handle it.

"My name is Jaryd. This is Alayna." He indicated the council table with his hand. "Would you like to sit?"

"Thank you, no." She took a breath. "Which of you is the new Sage?"

Again, Jaryd and Alayna looked at each other. "I am," Jaryd said after a moment. "Alayna is First of the Sage."

"We had heard that the Order had a new leader," Cailin told him. "I hope nothing has happened to Owl-Master Radomil. From what I've been told, he seems a decent man."

Jaryd forced a smile, although he felt his stomach tightening. "Thank you for your concern," he said. "Radomil is fine."

"Then why are you Owl-Sage now?"

"Are you sure you wouldn't like to sit, Cailin?" Alayna broke in. "If not here, then in our quarters?"

Cailin gave a thin smile. "There's little more trust here than there is at the Hall of the League," she said, as much to herself as to either of them. "I appreciate your courtesy," she continued an instant later, looking at them both again. "But I doubt that you'll want to sit with me once I explain the reason for my visit."

She walked to the Hall's entrance, opened the heavy wooden doors, and gave a single whistle, sharp and brief.

Almost immediately, Jaryd heard the sound of flapping wings, and in the next instant, he saw something that caused his entire world to shift in ways he had never anticipated. Standing in the doorway, taller and more majestic than any bird he had ever seen save one, stood an eagle. Like Rithlar, she was deep brown except for the back of her neck, which was washed with gold. The bird's eyes were dark, giving her a look of ferocity and intelligence that would have shocked him had he not seen precisely the same expression in his own familiar. Looking at the eagle, wrestling with the implications of its mere presence, Jaryd found himself remembering the strange vision that had haunted his sleep before his own binding. He had realized some time before that Rithlar was one of the eagles he had seen fighting to the death in the sky above him. Here, it seemed, was the second bird. He looked at Cailin once more, wondering if she was the woman he had seen. But though she resembled that woman, she was not the one. There was still a piece missing. It had not been a true Seeing. He had known that at the time. But seeing this second eagle, he was forced to consider the possibility that his dream carried at least some grain of truth.

"I know this must come as a shock to you," he heard Cailin say, although in truth he was barely listening to her. "It did to me as well. To be honest, I haven't been sure what to do about it. But Erland has summoned the mages of the League to Amarid in response to your use of the Summoning Stone, and so I felt that I had to do something. And I thought I should come here first, since traditionally an Eagle-Sage becomes leader of the Order."

Jaryd glanced at Alayna, but she had her eyes locked on the bird, and didn't seem to notice.

"What's her name?" Jaryd managed to ask, staring at the eagle once more. He didn't know for certain what the binding of a second mage to an eagle meant, but he had some ideas, and none of them was terribly appealing.

"Rithel."

"And when did you bind to her?"

"Just over two fortnights ago."

After my binding, he thought, although that did little to ease his mind.

"I don't know how you want to handle this," Cailin began again with obvious discomfort. "Do you want to tell the other mages of the Order or do you want me to?"

At that, Alayna finally looked up. "Tell them what?"

Cailin blinked. "That there's an Eagle-Sage, of course. That I'm to lead the Order."

"That's why you came here?" Alayna demanded. "Because you think that we're just going to step aside and let the League take over the Order?"

Cailin's expression hardened. "That's not what I said!" She stopped herself and took a long breath. "Look," she said in a calmer voice, "for better or worse, the gods have sent me an eagle, and we all know what that means. Tobyn-Ser is destined for war. This is no time for pettiness and rivalry. For now at least, we need to work together. Once our enemy is defeated, you're free to choose your own leader again."

"Do you have any idea who our enemy is?" Jaryd asked.

Cailin looked away. "No. I'm hoping that Erland and the others will have some idea." A moment later she met his gaze again. "I'd welcome your thoughts as well, and those of your colleagues."

Jaryd started to respond, but then he stopped himself, remembering something from before. "Did you say that you came to us first?" he asked.

"Yes, I—"

"So Erland and the rest don't know about this yet?"

Once again, she looked away. "No, they don't. My standing in the League is . . . not what it once was."

"And you thought that taking control of the Order would put you in a better position," Alayna said.

"That's not why I came!" the young woman insisted again. She stood very still for several seconds, glaring at Alayna. Then she shook her head. "I should never have come at all."

She turned away from them and started back toward the door.

"Cailin, wait," Alayna called.

Cailin turned with obvious reluctance and faced Alayna again. She wore a sour expression, but she said nothing.

Alayna smiled. "I'm sorry. But we had to be sure."

"Sure of what?" Cailin asked with manifest skepticism.

"This is yours to tell," Alayna said, turning to Jaryd. "But I don't think we have much choice."

"I agree," he said, nodding. He looked at Cailin. "Come with me, and bring your bird."

Cailin glanced at Alayna with uncertainty, but then she began to walk with Jaryd toward the back of the Hall.

"Please speak quietly back here," Jaryd said as they approached Jaryd and Alayna's quarters. "Our daughter is sleeping in the next room."

Cailin smiled. "How old is she?" she asked in a lowered voice.

"She's just turned seven."

The woman's smile abruptly faded, and Jaryd remembered that she had been seven when the outlanders attacked her home.

Reaching their quarters, Jaryd pushed open the door and gestured for Cailin to enter. Hesitantly, she stepped past him, and he followed her inside. Rithlar, still perched on the mantel, remained utterly motionless, eyeing Cailin warily.

At first Cailin didn't even notice her. "What am I looking for?" she asked, scanning the room. "I don't—" Seeing the great eagle at last she let out a loud gasp and jumped back toward the door, nearly crashing into Jaryd. "Fist of the God!" she whispered. She spun to look at him, her eyes wide. "How did—" She stopped herself as her own eagle glided into view, landed at the threshold of the room, and stared up at her impassively. She spun again to look at Rithlar. "Fist of the God!" she said once more.

"Her name is Rithlar," Jaryd said. "I bound to her a short time before you bound to Rithel."

The young mage nodded, although she still stared at Jaryd's eagle. "That explains your use of the Summoning Stone."

"Yes."

She continued to look at Rithlar for some time, saying nothing, and not even appearing to move. Finally, she turned to face Jaryd. "What do you think this means?"

"I wish I knew. The most obvious conclusion would be that the League and the Order are destined to battle each other."

Cailin's face paled and she shook her head. "I don't want to believe that."

Jaryd smiled wanly. "Neither do I."

"Then don't allow it to happen," came a third voice.

Jaryd and Cailin turned toward the doorway, where Alayna stood watching them. "You're Eagle-Sages, both of you," she went on. "You lead the Order, Jaryd, and, Cailin, soon you'll lead the League. Not even Erland would deny your claim under these circumstances. So it lies within your power to prevent a war."

"Does it?" Cailin asked. "The gods sent us eagles. If their wishes lie elsewhere, we may be helpless to deny their will." She paused, averting her gaze. "I'm not even certain that I can control the rest of the League, and you want me to defy the will of the gods?"

"I don't think you'll have to," Alayna said, her voice gentle. "The gods have always sent eagles to protect Tobyn-Ser, not to destroy it. And I don't think this time will be any different."

Cailin looked up. "What are you saying?"

"The gods have sent two eagles, one to you and one to Jaryd. I think this is their way of telling us that the League and the Order need to come together, that whatever enemy we're about to face can only be defeated by the combined power of all the land's mages."

"You take comfort in that, don't you?" Cailin asked.

A small smile flitted across Alayna's features. "Yes, I do."

"As do I," Jaryd said. "Shouldn't we all?"

Cailin shook her head. "If you knew Erland as I do, you wouldn't. He hates the Order with more passion than you can imagine. He'll never allow the League to be allied with you for any cause."

"That's all the more reason," Alayna said, "for you to assume your rightful place as leader of the League as quickly as possible."

"You don't understand the League," Cailin replied, walking to the hearth and looking up at Rithlar. The eagle regarded her coolly, and then began to preen. "Erland is to the League what Amarid once was to the Order. He created it, he leads it, he controls it. Even the younger mages, whom you might expect to oppose him on so many issues, defer to him more often than not."

"But they must feel the same way about you," Jaryd said. "When you joined the League seven years ago, everyone in Tobyn-Ser assumed that the Order would be gone within a year."

She turned at that, the ghost of a smile on her lips. She looked so young, barely more than a girl really. And yet, like him, she was an Eagle-Sage. "You're right," she said. "That is what they thought. Even Erland did. That's why he worked so hard to get me to join. But that's not what happened, is it? The Order is still here, not as strong as it was, but not as weak as it might be either." She made a small sound that might have been a laugh, but an instant later her smile vanished. "I've been a disappointment to them. They've made that very clear. Especially Erland. He won't give up power, at least not to me."

"But you've bound to an eagle," Jaryd said. "It doesn't matter what they think of you. You're their Eagle-Sage. Nothing can change that."

Cailin made an impatient gesture. "The League isn't the Order. You can't just assume that your rules apply to us."

"But still—"

"No," she said, shaking her head vehemently. "You don't understand! Even when his owl died he managed to remain First Master. The eagle means nothing. That's why I came here first. My one hope was that I could go to the Conclave having assumed leadership of the Order."

"Well obviously that's not going to happen," Alayna said.

Cailin nodded. "I can see that."

"So you have to find another way."

"Have you heard anything I've said?"

Alayna's dark eyes flashed angrily. "Yes, everything. But you're not a child anymore, Cailin. You're a mage who's bound to an eagle. And that carries a great deal of responsibility. The gods have chosen you, so they must think you're ready. But now it's up to you."

Cailin glared at her wordlessly for several moments. "There may be some truth in what you're saying," she said at last. "Perhaps more than I'd like to admit. But if you know anything about me at all, you know that I was never a child. I never got the chance."

The two women stared at each other for another few seconds before Alayna looked away.

"I'll do what I can," Cailin said, her tone icy. She glanced at Jaryd. "Arick guard you, Eagle-Sage. I hope that we can stand together before all of this is over."

"Be well, Cailin," Jaryd replied. "If we can be of help in any way, let us know."

Cailin nodded and left their quarters. For several moments Jaryd and Alayna stood silently, listening as Cailin's footsteps echoed off the domed ceiling of the Gathering Chamber. When she was finally gone, Alayna turned to him, her expression grim. "I shouldn't have pushed her so hard."

Jaryd shrugged. "It's hard to know. She's so young."

"She's no younger than we were when we went to the Grove."

"I know," he said with a smile. "Remember how young we were then?"

Alayna gave a small laugh, but she quickly turned serious again. "If I'm right, and we can't defeat this enemy alone, she's going to have to find a way to overcome Erland's influence."

"Yes," Jaryd said, nodding. "And as Order mages, that's the one thing we can't help her with at all."

"I don't like this," Henryk said for what must have been the thousandth time. "I don't like this at all."

Tammen glanced at him for just an instant, before turning her attention back to the cluster of trees in front of her. "So you've told us," she said, not bothering to mask her disdain. "If you want to leave, I won't stop you."

The dark-eyed mage shifted his position slightly, but he didn't go. Tammen wasn't sure whether she was relieved or disappointed.

They were on the western fringe of Tobyn's Wood, less than a day's walk from the Northern Plain and, if Nodin was to be believed, within shouting distance of the place where First of the Sage Peredur bound to his first familiar over sixty years ago. As of yet, however, they had seen no sign of the Owl-Master's unsettled spirit.

"You're sure this is the right place?" she asked Nodin, briefly meeting his gaze, which, in recent days, seemed to be fixed on her constantly.

He frowned. "I thought I was. It's been a long time since I was in this part of the wood. I know we're close, but this might not be the exact spot."

She rolled her eyes and propelled herself off the large, decaying tree trunk on which they had been sitting since dusk. "And when were you planning on mentioning that?"

"It had just occurred to me when you asked," he answered, sounding defensive.

She exhaled loudly. "So do we need to move?"

Nodin surveyed the forest, his uncertainty written plainly in his pale eyes. "I'm not sure," he admitted. "I don't think we're that far from where we should be, but—"

"But you don't really know, do you?"

"This was a bad idea to start with," Henryk said, shaking his head. "We should just—"

"Henryk!" Tammen said, whirling toward him. "If I hear one more word from you . . ." She stopped herself. This wasn't getting them anywhere.

"What, Tammen?" Henryk demanded, getting to his feet.

Nodin stood as well. "Stop it, both of you."

"No," Henryk said. "I'm tired of her making me feel like a coward. You're not afraid of the Unsettled," he said, offering it as a statement. "Not at all."

She held his gaze as steadily as she could. "I'm here because I believe the Movement needs help," she answered at last. "That's all that matters. Being afraid or not being afraid is beside the point."

"And what about you?" Henryk asked, facing Nodin. "You're not afraid either?"

Nodin's eyes flicked momentarily toward Tammen. "Like she said," he began in a low voice, "the important thing is that the Movement needs help."

Henryk looked away. "Right. The Movement."

He turned back a moment later as if intending to say something more, but in that instant a strange pearl-colored light began to seep through the forest, like torchlight in a coastal mist.

The three mages turned toward it, all of them falling silent. Tammen's heart was pounding so hard she thought she could hear it, and her stom-

ach felt cold and heavy. Even Othba, her beautiful brown hawk, who usually sat so composed on her shoulder, was crying out softly and digging
her talons into Tammen's shoulder.

As the light approached and grew brighter, Tammen began to see a
figure walking at the center of it. He was tall and lean, and he walked
with long, confident strides. He bore a staff in his right hand and, as he
drew closer still, Tammen saw that he carried a small woodland hawk on
his shoulder. His eyes were as bright as stars, and his face, though lined
with age and framed by white hair, looked young somehow, as though
the light shining from him had chased away the years.

He stopped before the three mages, regarding them coolly. When his
eyes came to rest on her, Tammen felt as though a frigid wind passed
through her, chilling her heart. A moment later he turned his gaze to
Nodin, and she allowed herself to breathe again.

"You're Prin's boy, aren't you?" the spirit said in a voice that sounded
like a high wind moving through trees.

"Yes, First," Nodin answered, his voice sounding leaden and awkward.
"My name is Nodin. With me are Hawk-Mage Tammen and Hawk-
Mage Henryk. We're honored by this meeting."

Peredur looked at Henryk and then Tammen, before facing the tall
mage again. "Where are your cloaks?"

Nodin swallowed and glanced as his companions. "We wear no cloaks,
First. We're free mages."

"What does that mean?" the ghost asked, his bright eyes narrowing.

"It means," Tammen broke in, "that we don't belong to either the
Order or the League. We merely serve the people."

The ghost lanced her with his glare. " 'We merely serve the people,' "
he mimicked. "What do you think I did for fifty-two years? And I did
belong to the Order!"

"Yes, First," Nodin said quickly. "Of course you did."

"What in Arick's name does the land need free mages for, anyway?"

Nodin looked at Tammen for just an instant before answering. "Perhaps you know something of the feud between the League and the
Order," he said.

The spirit made a sour face. "Yes, I do. It's all nonsense."

"It is to us as well," Tammen said, allowing herself a smile. "How can
mages serve the land if they're so busy fighting each other?"

Peredur regarded her skeptically, as if not quite comfortable with the
fact that he agreed with her. "Go on."

Tammen shrugged. "We've found another way. We serve the land, but
we have no part in their quarrel."

"And who keeps watch on your kind?" the spirit asked. "Who makes certain that none of you is violating Amarid's Laws?"

"We hold each other to the laws," Tammen answered. "Just as the Order and League do."

The Owl-Master's ghost took a step forward. "That's not good enough! You have no formal body, so you have no method for imposing discipline or punishment. I was killed by a renegade, a man who betrayed not only the Mage-Craft and the Order, but the entire land. And even with all the rules and processes we had in place to deal with such things, in the end it took the combined might of all the mages of the Order to stop him. How could you possibly stop one of your 'free mages' who did something similar?"

Sartol. He was talking about Sartol. Tammen had to fight an urge to fling back an angry reply.

"The free mages are committed to serving and guarding the people of Tobyn-Ser, Owl-Master," Nodin said, his voice tinged with so much pride that Tammen could not help but smile. "We are part of a great Movement—the People's Movement—that seeks to rid Tobyn-Ser of the foreign influences that have already done such damage to the land." He glanced at Tammen again, and seeing that she was smiling, he smiled himself.

"I've heard nothing of this," the spirit said. "I've seen the trees cut, and the strange weapons in the hands of the Temple's men. But a People's Movement?" He shook his glowing head.

"But if you've seen the rest," Tammen said, "the weapons and the destruction of Tobyn's Wood, then surely you see the good that could come from our Movement."

The ghost hesitated. "Perhaps," he acknowledged at last. "What of it?"

Nodin took a long breath, as if gathering himself. "Our Movement needs help, First. We free mages are badly outnumbered by both the League and the Order. There are too few of us to do battle with the Temple's men now that they carry weapons from Lon-Ser. We have much support among Tobyn-Ser's people, but we can't defend those who stand with us." He swallowed, and even in the strange light given off by their cerylls and by the unsettled spirit before them, Tammen could see his face growing pale. "Just a few days ago, in a village called Prannai, sixteen people died because we weren't strong enough to protect them."

Peredur stared at them all, his expression as cold as a winter wind. "If you cannot protect them, you have no right to involve them in your cause! As mages you should know that!"

"They asked for our help!" Tammen said.

"You should have refused!"

Tammen started to respond, but Nodin stopped her with a hand on her shoulder.

"You may be right, First," he conceded. "In our desire to preserve the land, we may have acted rashly. We're young, and we're still learning. But that merely proves our point. We not only need help, to make us stronger, but also guidance, to show us how best to serve the People's Movement."

Tammen nodded. When he wanted, Nodin could be exceptionally clever. "Nodin's right," she said. "We have much to learn from you and the other Unsettled. And," she added, dropping her eyes diffidently, "I apologize for the way I spoke to you earlier."

The spirit looked at her briefly, his expression revealing nothing. Then he turned to Henryk. "What of you, Mage? Your companions seem to be doing all the talking. You haven't said a single word. Are you ready to ally yourself with the Unsettled as well?"

The dark-eyed man glanced sidelong at Tammen and Nodin, looking uncomfortable. "I support the Movement with all my heart," he finally answered, meeting the spirit's bright gaze. "If the Unsettled can help us achieve our goals and guard the land, then yes, I'm ready to accept you as an ally."

Peredur grinned. "Deftly handled, Mage." He faced Nodin again. "You have a fine companion here. He has grave doubts about what you're doing, but he's willing to support you. It's too bad his sense of loyalty has won out over his common sense."

"I don't follow."

"You're attempting to harness powers you can't possibly understand, all for the sake of a movement that will ultimately do more harm than good."

"You don't know that!" Nodin said.

"Don't I? You don't fool me with your flattery and your obeisance. You care nothing for guidance. You want the aid of the Unsettled so that you can match the power of the League and the Order, and the weapons of the Temples. That's all that matters to you. As it is, this land is headed for violence and upheaval. Your little band of free mages is just going to make matters worse. Even if I could help you, I wouldn't."

"Even if you could?" Tammen repeated. "What does that mean?"

"It means that the Unsettled have little access to power in your world. There's actually very little that I can do for you without the help of all the other Unsettled, and ever since Sartol became one of us, there's been no chance of that."

"So there's nothing that you can do? There's no way for an unsettled mage to affect our world? I don't believe you."

"Believe what you will," the spirit said. "The paths to power open to a single unsettled mage are not paths that I care to take. If you want help from one of us, you'll have to find it elsewhere."

Tammen suppressed a smile. That was the confirmation she had been seeking. There was a way, and here on the northwest fringe of the God's wood, they were only a few days' walk away.

"Leave me now," Peredur commanded. "I don't wish to be disturbed anymore."

"But, First," Nodin pleaded. "We need your help. The land needs your help."

"I've served the land," the spirit said, turning away. "For more than half a century I guarded the people, healed them, mended their broken fences and their shattered homes. And I always did so with a clear conscience, because I knew that as a member of the Order, I was following in Amarid's footsteps." He turned to face them once more, and his eyes appeared more radiant somehow, as if they were cerylls, and he had summoned from them a brighter light. "I'll not undo a lifetime of faithful service for the likes of you." He turned a second time and walked away, not bothering to look back at them again.

They watched as he walked away, his pearly glow retreating into the darkness like a fog, until they were alone, the only light in the wood coming from their cerylls. Tammen felt something loosen in her chest as the ghost vanished amid the tree trunks and branches, and not for the first time, she wondered if she was up to the task that had really brought her to this part of Tobyn-Ser.

"So what now?" Henryk asked, running a hand through his dark curls.

Nodin shrugged. He looked tired and beaten. "I don't know. There are some free towns in the area. I suppose we should see if we can enlist them in the Movement." He looked off in the direction the spirit had gone. "I really thought he would help us. Not before tonight, mind you," he added, facing Tammen and Henryk again. "But when he said that the feud between the League and the Order was nonsense, I started thinking that this might work."

"And what if it had?" Henryk asked. "You honestly believe that the three of us would be capable of controlling the Unsettled, of wielding them as if they were a weapon?"

"I wasn't looking for a weapon," Nodin answered. "I was looking for an ally. And if you had so little faith in what we were trying to do, maybe you shouldn't have come."

Henryk recoiled as if he had been struck, and his face turned bright red. He stood saying nothing for several seconds. Then he turned on his heel and walked away.

"Henryk!" Nodin called after him. "I didn't mean . . ." He trailed off. Henryk wasn't coming back, at least not tonight. He looked back at Tammen and shook his head. "I shouldn't have said that."

"It doesn't matter," she told him. Actually, she was glad he was gone. What she had to do next would probably be easier without Henryk around arguing against it.

"So where do you think we ought to go from here? There are free towns to the south and west."

"I think we should go north," she said.

"North? Why?"

She took a breath. "Peredur isn't the only unsettled mage in this area. And it's possible that a different spirit will give us a different answer."

It took a minute. And then suddenly his eyes widened, and he actually took a step back away from her. "You mean Sartol?"

"Yes."

He shook his head again, vigorously this time, and he licked his lips nervously. "No," he finally said. "It's too dangerous. You heard what Peredur said: Sartol killed him, rendered him unbound. He betrayed the land."

"He saved my life! He saved Watersbend! I saw him do it! I saw him kill the men who killed my parents!"

"I know," Nodin said. "But he did that to save himself."

Tammen turned away from him. "That's the Order talking."

"Tammen—"

"No," she said, "it doesn't matter. Henryk will never agree anyway. I'll go by myself. You and he can go to the free towns."

Nodin said nothing for a long time and Tammen stood motionless, with her back to him, waiting. In truth, she didn't want to do this alone. For all her insistence that Sartol would help them, that he was not the figure of pure evil that the Order mages said he was, she was frightened. Confronting Peredur's spirit had been unnerving enough, and Sartol in life had been a far more formidable figure than the First.

Nodin was still there behind her. She sensed his uncertainty and his unwillingness to leave her side. Before this his affection for her had been a nuisance, but now she saw in it an opportunity.

Turning again, she stepped close to him, raised herself onto her toes, and kissed him lightly on the lips, allowing her breasts to graze his chest as she did. "Be well, Nodin," she whispered, pulling away. "I'll miss you."

She started to walk away, but he barely allowed her to take a step.

"Tammen, wait."

She faced him, suppressing a smile. Perhaps she could have convinced him some other way, and perhaps what she had done was wrong. But she had to acknowledge that she did care for him. And she certainly preferred being with him to being on her own.

"I'll go with you," he said. "I wouldn't want you to do this alone."

How wrong could it be? she asked herself, seeing the smile spread across his face. How much harm could it do to let him take care of her for a short while?

"Thank you, Nodin. I'll be glad to have you with me."

His smile broadened. How wrong could it be?

11

For several years now, the members of my Order have been acting under the assumption that we seek reconciliation with the League. All of us recognize the dangers inherent in having control of the Mage-Craft divided, and there is as well a sense among many of us that we allowed the Order to be sundered and that, therefore, it falls to us to set things right. I am forced to acknowledge, however, that if I was given today the opportunity to unify the Mage-Craft once more, I would have strong reservations. After all that I have been through, I find it hard to imagine ever thinking of a League mage as a friend, or even a peer. And while others in the Order have not been persecuted by the League as I have, I am certain that I am not alone in feeling this way.

It remains to be seen if this will be an issue in my lifetime. The mages of the League have shown in more ways than I can count that they want nothing to do with the Order. But should the occasion arise, either in the near future, or many years from now, I believe that those pushing to reunite the League and the Order will face resistance from within both bodies.

—Hawk-Mage Orris to Melyor i Lakin, Sovereign and Bearer of Bragor-Nal, Spring, God's Year 4633.

Baden sat staring at Jaryd and Alayna, too astounded to speak, and wondering if it was possible for two people to share a delusion. Judging from the utter stillness of those around him, the Owl-Master guessed that others in the Hall shared his astonishment. He shifted his gaze to the enormous brown bird perched on the back of

Jaryd's chair and shook his head slowly. To have an eagle bind to a mage—and not just any mage, but his own nephew—was incredible enough. But for there to be two Eagle-Sages in Tobyn-Ser at one time defied comprehension. He didn't know whether to be terrified or elated, but in an odd way he couldn't help but be awed. He had never thought that he would live to see such times.

"You're certain that your binding came first?" Tramys asked, breaking a lengthy silence. "You established that?"

"I don't see what difference that makes," Orlanne said, before Jaryd could reply. "If we're to go to war with the League, it really doesn't matter who bound first."

"But if we're to go to war with Lon-Ser," Tramys replied, an earnest expression on his youthful face, "it makes a great deal of difference. The mage who bound first will command our land's army." He faced Jaryd again. "Wouldn't you agree, Eagle-Sage?"

Jaryd took a breath, his face wearing a sour expression. "I hadn't really thought that far ahead."

Another of the younger mages stood. "If the gods intended us to fight alongside the League, they wouldn't have sent two eagles. They would have sent only one. This must mean that we're destined for a civil war, just as Baden suggested a few days ago."

"Nonsense!" Mered said, standing as well. "They may have sent two eagles because our enemy this time is more powerful than any we've faced before. Certainly that would be the case if we were to fight Lon-Ser."

Others nodded.

"Maybe it's a sign that we face more than one enemy," Neysa added. "Perhaps we'll be faced with threats from Lon-Ser and the Temples. The Children of the Gods have been acquiring weapons."

Mered looked at her skeptically. "Would the gods favor us with even one eagle if our fight was with the Keepers?"

The tall woman nodded. "If, in their pursuit of gold, the Children of the Gods have abandoned the people of Tobyn-Ser, then I believe they would."

Several mages voiced their agreement, and almost immediately arguments began to break out all around the council table.

"This is premature," Jaryd said loudly, halting the discussions as quickly as they had begun. "We don't know enough to draw any conclusions. This kind of speculation gets us nowhere."

"What did you and Cailin have to say about your bindings?" Baden asked. "You've told us of her eagle, but I'm more interested in your conversation."

The Eagle-Sage gave a small smile and inclined his head slightly, as if thanking Baden for the question. "It wasn't an easy one," he began, glancing briefly at Alayna. "Cailin is willing to believe that the Order and the League are destined to be allies in a coming war, but she's not at all convinced that the rest of the League will accept such an arrangement. She's not even sure that Erland will step aside and allow her to lead them."

"They haven't made her Eagle-Sage yet?" Sonel asked with amazement.

"They don't even know that she's bound to an eagle."

Baden's eyes widened. "What?"

"Well," Jaryd amended, "they may by now. But they didn't as of last night."

Sonel shook her head. "How is that possible?"

"It seems that Cailin's influence within the League is not what it once was," Alayna explained. "Erland is still revered by even the youngest Hawk-Mages, and Cailin has fallen out of his favor."

"But why?" Sonel persisted. "At one time she was everything to them." She had met Cailin years ago, Baden remembered, when she was still Owl-Sage, and though Cailin had been but a child then, newly bound to her first hawk, Sonel had been quite impressed with her.

Alayna gave a wan smile. "Apparently the mages of the League, particularly Erland, blame Cailin for the fact that the Order has survived these past seven years."

"That's ridiculous," Sonel said.

"Perhaps," Radomil agreed. "But it's not surprising. I've never really understood Erland's reasoning on any subject."

"So how did you leave matters with Cailin?" Baden asked, looking at Jaryd again.

The mage shrugged. "We reached no agreements, if that's what you mean. I certainly wasn't going to commit the Order to anything without consulting the rest of you, and Cailin was in no position to speak on behalf of the League. She has a great deal of work to do before she can claim to have any authority at all."

"Is there anything we can do to help her in that regard?" Trahn asked, scratching the chin of his large, round-headed owl.

"I doubt it," Jaryd said. "Her loss of standing is tied almost entirely to the fact that this body still exists. Any help we might try to give her would probably do more harm than good."

"Why would we want to help her?" Tramys asked. "I don't care if Erland has lost faith in her and—forgive me, Eagle-Sage—I don't care that she's bound to an eagle. She's no less a League mage than the rest of them."

Orlanne nodded. "I agree with Tramys. I know she went through a lot as a child, but I still don't trust her. Why did she come here, anyway?

What did she hope to get from us that she couldn't get from the League?"

Jaryd hesitated, his eyes flicking in Baden's direction, as if he was looking for help. "She didn't know of my binding," he said, his voice subdued. "And since Eagle-Sages have traditionally become leaders of the Order simply by virtue of their bindings, she came here thinking that she would assume leadership of the Order and then go to Erland."

A shocked silence fell over the Gathering Chamber. Even Baden felt his mouth drop open, although he recovered quickly. It made a great deal of sense really. What better way to win the support of her fellow mages in the League?

"What arrogance!" Tramys breathed. "She honestly believed that we'd just ignore the color of her cloak and accept her as our Sage?"

"Why not?" Orris demanded, speaking for the first time that morning. Everyone turned to face him. "If we didn't already have an Eagle-Sage, we'd be debating the matter right now. There has never been an Eagle-Sage who didn't lead the Order." He pointed in Jaryd's direction. "Under any other circumstances, she'd have a very powerful claim to sit in that chair. It seems to me a measure of the extraordinary times we're witnessing that we can dismiss her claim out of hand."

"But, Orris," Tramys said, "this is Cailin we're talking about. She practically founded the League with Erland. You, of all people—"

"Yes, Tramys. I, of all people can find it within myself to understand her and accept what she did. Doesn't that tell you something?"

The younger man said nothing, and after a moment he lowered his gaze.

Orris swept the chamber with his dark eyes, as if daring someone else to challenge him. "It may be that we can't help Cailin, at least not yet. As Jaryd said, the rest of the League expected her to destroy the Order simply by donning a blue cloak. But at some point that may change, and if it does, I think we should be willing to help her in any way we can."

"Even if that means helping the League as well?" Orlanne asked.

"Yes. Even then."

The young woman shook her head, the expression in her pale eyes growing cold. "I don't know if I can do that. Frankly, I'm amazed that you can even contemplate such a thing. They've been stalking you for years. By the gods, they killed your familiar!"

Baden saw Orris clench his jaw. This wasn't easy for the burly mage, he knew. Several years ago, Orris would have been siding with Tramys and Orlanne. Actually, Baden thought, smiling inwardly, he would have been leading them. It was an indication of how much Orris had matured over the years that he was capable of forgiving the League. Baden wasn't certain that any other mage in the chamber could have done it. Including himself.

"I know what they've done to me, Orlanne," Orris finally said, his voice low. "And I'm not ready to make overtures of any sort to Erland. But to me, Cailin is a different matter, especially given that she's an Eagle-Sage. For all we know the League is destined to be our enemy in the coming war. But if the gods have sent these birds as a sign that the Order and the League must work together to save Tobyn-Ser . . ." He shrugged. "I'm not so vain that I'd defy the gods to satisfy my own hunger for vengeance." He glanced at Baden and grinned. "At least not anymore."

Baden laughed, as did several of the other mages. But the Owl-Master noticed that Orlanne and Tramys did not.

"Do you know what I see, when I look around this Hall?" Tramys asked, his tone severe despite the sad look in his green eyes. "I see mages who still carry feelings of guilt for having allowed Erland to leave all those years ago. You still see this Order as incomplete; you believe that it won't be whole again until we've reunified the Mage-Craft." He shook his head. "Those of us who joined the Order after the split did so because we regard the Order as the true guardian of Amarid's legacy. We chose the green cloak. That's why we're here. We don't blame you for what Erland did, and we have no desire to see League mages around this table. To us, the League is a fraud. If its members truly honored Amarid's memory, they would abide by his laws." He turned to Orris. "I'm sorry, Orris, but that's how I feel. Even if you can forgive them for what they've done to you, I can't." He regarded the rest of them again. "But while we hate the League, we also accept that it's here to stay, and the time has come for the rest of you to do the same. This reconciliation you're waiting for is never going to happen. The League mages don't want it, and even the appearance of a hundred eagles wouldn't change that."

Baden could hear the truth in Tramys's words. Looking across the table at Sonel, he saw from her expression that she had heard it as well. He could think of nothing to say.

He could only nod in silent agreement when Alayna, staring at Tramys with a bleak expression on her beautiful face, gave voice to her own fears. "I can only hope, Tramys," she said, "that the mages of the League can find it within themselves to see beyond their hostility for the Order. Because if you're right, and they can't, our people are doomed."

She briefly considered going to Erland first. *Perhaps,* she thought, *if I can speak with him alone, when the rest aren't watching, I can get him to see my eagle as something more than a threat to his standing within the League.* It didn't take her long, however, to dismiss the idea. He had never been any more honest with her in private than he had been in front of the others. It would be better, she finally concluded, to catch him unawares, with the entire membership watching.

So the morning after her unsettling visit to the Great Hall, Cailin watched from afar as her fellow mages, dressed in their bright blue cloaks, entered the Hall of the League to begin the Conclave. Only when she was certain that the rest were inside, did she leave her hiding place in the narrow alleyway and approach the great doors of the hall with Rithel gliding easily above her.

Despite the best efforts of Erland and the rest, the League's meeting place had, in the end, come to resemble the Great Hall of the Order in most respects. Both buildings were oval, with blue-domed roofs and large arching wooden doors. The Hall of the League had marble statues atop its roof, instead of the dazzling crystal figures that were mounted on the Great Hall, and the windows of the League's building were decorated with panels of brilliant stained glass, but in every other way, the buildings were quite alike. Cailin thought it an irony, one that became more and more poignant with each year that passed.

Reaching the wooden doors, she took a steadying breath, opened them, and stepped inside. Rithel walked in behind her and then hopped to her arm, the iron grip of her massive talons causing Cailin to wince.

Erland was standing at the far end of the long wooden meeting table, speaking to the rest of the mages, a broad smile on his ruddy face. He was tall and still carried himself like a young man, so that his silver beard and white hair, rather than making him appear aged, gave him an almost regal aspect. Regardless of what he had done to her, or what she thought of the decisions he had made as leader of the League, Cailin could not deny that he looked and sounded just like a First Master should. She felt herself starting to tremble, and she fought to calm her nerves. But she was, in that instant, intensely aware of her own youth and her slight frame.

I've bound to an eagle, she reminded herself. *The gods have decreed that I should be leader of this body.*

"Cailin!" Erland said, gesturing toward her with an open hand. The rest of the mages turned in their chairs to face her. "How nice to see you! We had started to wonder if you were planning on coming at all."

She started to respond, but before she could, Erland's eyes widened slightly.

"I see you've bound as well. Splendid! We had heard of Marcran's death, but we didn't know—"

He stopped abruptly, and Cailin noted with satisfaction that all the color drained from his face.

She stepped closer to the table as a flurry of whispered conversations filled the room.

Still Erland did not speak, but at length, Arslan stood, the sunlight from one of the windows lighting his red hair like a flame. "You've bound to an eagle!" he said, his voice tinged with wonder.

Cailin smiled. Of all the mages in the League, Arslan had been kindest to her, offering her encouragement as Erland's words to her grew harsher, and defending her openly when others questioned her loyalty. "I have," she answered. "Her name is Rithel, and she came to me two fortnights ago."

Vawnya, another of the younger mages, stood as well, a look of astonishment in her green eyes. "The gods have sent us an Eagle-Sage!"

"That is an Order term!" Erland said, his tone severe.

"An Eagle-Master then," Vawnya replied. "It's still wondrous."

Erland regarded Cailin skeptically. "Is it?" he asked. "Or is this some kind of trick?"

"Yes, Erland," Cailin said, unable to stop herself. "It's a trick. She's not really my familiar; she's just a bird I coaxed onto my arm to stir up some excitement."

"Such a tone dishonors yourself and this body, Mage."

She glared at him. He had treated her like a child for long enough. "I am properly addressed as Eagle-Master, Erland!"

"And I am properly addressed as First Master! You would do well to remember it!"

"I haven't forgotten, but it may be that your time as First Master is coming to an end."

The white-haired man narrowed his eyes. "Meaning what?"

Cailin glanced around the vast chamber, hoping that someone might take up her cause; she didn't want to have to do this alone. But no one showed any signs of wanting to help her. Even Arslan avoided her gaze. She had only been in the hall for a few moments, but already it seemed she had pushed her claim too far. She thought briefly of her conversation with the Eagle-Sage and his First the night before. If only they could see her now, they might understand what she had been trying to tell them about the League.

"Meaning," she said at last, "that every mage in this room knows what it portends when the gods send us an eagle. There is a war coming, and it falls to he or she who has bound to the eagle to lead Tobyn-Ser in that war." She was misleading them, she knew, but her one hope was that Erland would take the bait she was dangling before him.

"We haven't had an Eagle-Sage for over four hundred years," said Stepan, one of Erland's staunchest supporters among the older masters. "The appearance of an eagle might not mean a thing anymore."

Arslan shook his head. "You don't really believe that, do you Stepan?"

The older man shrugged. "I don't know what to believe. I do know that there is nothing in the League bylaws that compels Erland to step down in Cailin's favor." He looked at Cailin, a sneer on his broad, pasty face. "That is an Order tradition."

"Cailin wasn't suggesting that Erland relinquish power," Arslan said. "She was just suggesting that she—"

"Actually, Arslan," Cailin broke in, "that's precisely what I was suggesting."

The red-haired mage frowned at her and shook his head.

"As Stepan just reminded us," Erland said, "there's nothing in the bylaws that supports your claim to my chair. This is nothing more than a blatant attempt to seize power, and it's not going to work. Perhaps Order mages would allow you to get away with this, Cailin, but we won't." He grinned. "That is an idea though: why don't your take your eagle to the Order; perhaps they'll make you Eagle-Sage."

Stepan laughed, as did a few others, but most of the mages kept themselves perfectly still, as if waiting to see how this latest confrontation between the League's founders would turn out.

For her part, Cailin allowed herself a smile as well. Erland was a formidable man, but he was also unimaginative. It had been almost too easy leading him to this point. "Going to the Order is a fine idea, Erland. Indeed, I already have."

His grin vanished, and he stared at her with avid interest. "And?" he said, suddenly breathless.

"They already have an Eagle-Sage."

She had expected that this news would be greeted by an explosion of shouted questions and denials, and she was not disappointed. She had also expected, however, that Erland would be the most vocal in calling her a liar, but the older man surprised her. He seemed to sense somehow that she was telling the truth, and though his face turned deep red, his voice when he spoke remained level. Still, it cut through the din like a blade, silencing the other mages.

"Who is it?" he demanded. "Tell me it isn't Baden."

"No, not Baden. A younger man named Jaryd."

"Jaryd?" Arslan said, his eyes growing wide. "Is Alayna his First?"

"Yes."

"Jaryd," Erland repeated quietly. "He told us something like this would happen."

"Who did, First Master?" Stepan asked.

"Baden, of course," the white-haired man mumbled. A moment later, Erland shook his head and looked around the room, as if suddenly remembering that the rest of them were there. "This is an interesting turn of events," he said. "I'll admit that. But it changes nothing."

"Doesn't it?" Vawnya asked. "The Order has an Eagle-Sage, and yet the gods have chosen to send an eagle to one of us as well. That has to mean something."

"I agree."

Everyone looked to a chair at the far end of the table, just beside Erland. And for the first time that day, Cailin felt a surge of hope.

"You, Toinan?" Stepan asked, his voice tinged with amazement and, Cailin thought, more than a bit of despair.

Toinan had been Sonel's First of the Sage before the creation of the League, and as such, had long been, aside from Erland, the most respected mage to wear a blue cloak. With her support, Cailin might have a chance.

"Yes," the old woman said. She stood, leaning heavily on her staff. She had grey hair and dark blue eyes that had grown rheumy over the past few years. But her voice remained strong, and she commanded the attention of everyone in the hall. "I've lived a long time—longer than any of you, I daresay—and I've never seen even one eagle on a mage's arm. And now there are two?" She shook her head and tried to smile, but was stopped by a spasm of coughing. "The gods would not have done such a thing lightly," she continued when she could speak again. "There's a warning in this, a hint at the power of the enemy we face. We ignore it at our own risk."

"Does that mean," Arslan asked, "that you believe Cailin should lead us?"

Erland gestured impatiently and stepped away from the table. "This is not a matter for Toinan to decide," he said, and then, turning back to the table, he quickly added, "or any individual mage for that matter."

"Of course it's not," Arslan agreed. "But I'd like to hear what the Owl-Master has to say." He smiled, although not with his eyes. "We should all be heard on a matter of such importance. Don't you agree, First Master?"

"What are you implying?" Erland asked in a low voice.

Arslan shook his head. "Nothing at all. But this is an issue that transcends the personal interests of any one member of this body. Even you, Erland." He took a breath and ran a hand through his unruly hair. "Most of us in this hall followed you out of the Gathering seven years ago because we agreed with your criticisms of Baden, and of what he and Orris had done. You must know how hard that was for us to do. But we trusted you, and given the chance to relive that day, I wouldn't hesitate to follow you again. I doubt any of us would. But you led us out of the Great Hall because Baden and the others had come to care more about their own concerns and well-being than they did about the land and its people. And I won't stand by and let any member of this League do the same thing. Not Cailin, and not you."

Erland surveyed the room, as did Cailin, and it seemed from his reaction that he saw the same resolve in the faces of their fellow mages that she did.

"Very well," the First Master said, returning to his chair. He sat and looked around the room a second time, his expression grim. "Very well," he said again.

"Toinan?" Arslan said, facing the old woman again.

The Owl-Master gave a slight shrug. "As Erland said, this is not a matter for me to decide. But I will say this: we have a First Master whom we respect, and an Eagle-Master who comes to us bearing a harbinger from the gods. Having two such leaders can only strengthen us."

Toinan sat back down, a small smile on her wizened face.

For a moment there was silence, and then an instant later, there seemed to be arguments everywhere.

And yet, Cailin knew that Toinan had found the solution. It might take the mages of the League the rest of the day to come around to it, but she had heard the prophecy in the old woman's words.

Looking across the table at Erland, she found that he was already watching her, as oblivious as she to the clamor around them. She saw resignation in his dark blue eyes, and then, to her surprise she actually saw him nod to her, as if he already recognized the inevitability of this.

As Cailin expected, the rest of the mages accepted the change far more slowly. Too slowly, as far as she was concerned. Everything the League did in recent days seemed to spark a fight. Their deliberations, she had realized recently with some alarm, resembled the descriptions she had heard of the last days of the Order before Erland led his followers out of the Great Hall.

In the end, the mages did agree, which was something. Cailin was to be Eagle-Master, and Erland would remain First Master. And until whatever crisis that presented itself had passed, they would rule the League together, with the consent of the rest.

It was a fine start, she thought, leaving the Hall long after dusk, and returning with Rithel to the peace and solitude of Hawksfind Wood. But it was nothing more than that. She and Erland had been thrown together into what promised to be a difficult partnership. He had agreed only to share power with her, not to listen to her, and certainly not to follow her.

On those occasions when they disagreed—and there would be many—Cailin had little doubt as to whose side the others would take. In a way she almost hoped that their conflict would be with the Order, because she knew that she would never convince Erland and his followers to accept the Order as an ally.

Reaching a secluded clearing along the banks of the Larian, Cailin stopped and sat on a low rock. Rithel glided to the ground beside her, and Cailin leaned over to scratch the bird's chin. She pulled from her cloak a pouch of dry bread and hard cheese, and began to eat. But before she could take a second mouthful, she heard a man's voice calling her name.

Cailin stood, her blood suddenly coursing through her veins like the glacial waters that raced over stone and silt beside her. *I'm bound again,* she reminded herself. I may be alone, but I have nothing to fear. A moment later a ceryll came into view, and then the man who carried it.

"Cailin," Stepan called again, drawing closer.

She thought about retreating into the forest. Even if she trusted him, she had little desire to speak with him. But she was Eagle-Master and he a member of the League. She had responsibilities now. She raised her staff over her head and brightened the golden glow of her ceryll so that it illuminated the wood.

A few seconds later he stood before her, breathing hard. Even had it not been for the red light of his stone reflecting off his perspiring face, the older man would have appeared alarmingly flushed. He bent over with his mouth open, as if trying to catch his breath. If he had come to kill her, he'd need to rest first.

"What are you doing here, Stepan?"

Rithel hopped forward to stand with her and let out a small hiss. Stepan's small owl hissed in return.

The Owl-Master straightened and regarded her coolly. "I've come to talk."

I don't believe you, she wanted to say. *And even if I did, I wouldn't want to listen to you.* "About what?"

"You handled things poorly today. You shouldn't have challenged Erland the way you did."

"Ah, I see," Cailin said with a nod. "You've come as Erland's lackey."

The Owl-Master smiled thinly. "Hardly. If Erland knew I was here, he would be . . . disappointed."

She looked at him skeptically.

"You don't believe me."

"Why should I?"

He allowed the point with a small shrug.

They stood in silence for several moments, Stepan watching her with a neutral expression on his pale face. Finally, Cailin exhaled heavily.

"All right, Stepan," she said, her voice flat. "What should I have done differently?"

He gestured toward the rocks on the riverbank. "Let's sit."

She didn't move, and after some time, he shook his head. "As you wish, but I intend to sit."

He walked over to the riverbank and lowered himself gingerly onto one of the large stones. "You've been a mage for some time now, Cailin, and you've been a part of the League from the beginning. All of us know how special you are, and all of us recognize that you're wise beyond your years. But you still have a good deal to learn about using your influence and authority."

"Do I?"

"You wasted an opportunity today. You've bound to an eagle, Cailin, and you had the good sense to conceal that from us until your arrival in the hall today. But then you squandered the advantage you'd gained by demanding immediately that we choose between you and Erland."

She stared at him, not quite believing what she was hearing. "And what should I have done?" she asked.

"You should have given those who might have been inclined to support your claim a chance to help you."

"I don't understand."

He looked down, wiping a hand across his damp brown. "You know what Erland means to us," he said, meeting her gaze again. "None of us who followed him out of the Order will ever do anything to embarrass or hurt him."

"I wasn't asking you to."

"Yes, Cailin, you were. And I understand why. He hasn't treated you well in the past year." He looked away again. "None of us have. But when you turned your claim to leadership into an assault on Erland, you made it impossible for anyone to support you. Frankly, you were lucky that Toinan said what she did, or you might have left the hall with even less than you did."

She sat down on a stone near his. "Why are you telling me this?"

Stepan hesitated. "Because I'm scared," he finally said. "I never thought I'd see one Eagle-Sa—" He stopped himself and grinned, although only briefly. "I certainly didn't think I'd ever see two mages bound to eagles at one time. Notwithstanding Erland's denials, or my own for that matter, that has to mean something. The gods wouldn't send two such birds without reason."

"So you think I should be leading the League."

The Owl-Master stood abruptly. "I didn't say that."

Cailin threw up her hands in frustration. "Then what are you saying? If you're so frightened, why did you oppose me today?"

"I told you why: Erland is my friend, and he's First Master of this League. I won't allow him to be humiliated by you or anyone else." He swallowed. "Perhaps you should be leading us, at least until we know why your eagle has come. But you're going to have to find a way to assert your will in more subtle ways. You can't win the support you need by fighting with Erland."

"But Erland and I are bound to disagree. Are you saying that I always have to give in?"

"Not at all. I'm merely saying that you have to argue your point of view carefully."

Cailin shook her head. "But how—"

"It's not my place to tell you how to lead, Cailin," he said, his voice almost kind. "No doubt, there will be times when I'll oppose you, and I have no intention of helping your cause any more than I have to. But you're an intelligent young woman. I have confidence in your ability to figure this out on your own."

They both fell silent again. It was getting cold. Cailin suddenly was anxious to light a fire, and to consider in solitude what Stepan had told her.

"I should leave you," the Owl-Master said at last. He hesitated, and then said, "I would prefer that you speak to no one of our conversation. I don't want Erland to learn that I came to you." He gave a thin smile. "It seems that I've given you something to hold over me, should you ever have need."

Cailin stood and looked at him. "I won't tell anyone," she said, her eyes locked on his. "I swear it to you on the memory of my mother and father."

His eyes widened at that, and after several seconds he nodded.

She made herself smile. "Thank you for your advice, Stepan. I think I have some idea of what it took for you to come to me like this. I'm in your debt."

"I did it for the League and for Tobyn-Ser," he said brusquely. "And I suppose I did it for Erland as well."

She smiled again, and this time she meant it. "Whatever your reasons, I'm grateful. I'll try to find a way to put your counsel to good use."

"Good night, Eagle-Master." He glanced at Rithel, who stood on the ground at Cailin's feet, gazing up at him avidly. And it seemed to Cailin that the Owl-Master nodded to the bird before turning and starting back toward Amarid.

When she could no longer make out the red glow of Stepan's ceryll through the forest, Cailin set about searching for dead tree limbs with which to make her fire. But she didn't search long. She was tired and she reconciled herself to a small blaze and the completion of her modest meal. Stepan had been right about one thing at the very least: she was inexperienced in the ways of leadership and persuasion. And there in the darkness of Hawksfind Wood, alone save for the great bird to whom she was bound, Cailin could not help but wonder if her ignorance would bring ruin to all of Tobyn-Ser.

12

With all the changes that have come to my land—and there have been many—I am forced by recent events to admit that some among the lords and break-laws of the Nal remain wedded to the old ways. The continued attempts on my life offer clear evidence of this, as do the skirmishes that still break out with annoying regularity in various realms. As I have told you on more than one occasion, I see real progress in this regard. I take great pride in accomplishments, but I must also acknowledge the limits of my success.

. . . The danger of course, is that something will happen to one of us before the transformation of Lon-Ser is complete. Jibb's death or my own, or even Shivohn's, could have devastating consequences for every person in every quad in all three Nals. Progress is steady, but the danger of falling back into chaos and violence is constant as well. All it would take is one well-placed explosive, one brief volley of thrower fire, one unseen dagger. . . .

—Melyor i Lakin, Sovereign and Bearer of Bragor-Nal to Hawk-Mage Orris, Day 1, Week 11, Winter, Year 3067.

They were in the tunnels again, making their way to the Fourteenth Realm to quash yet another skirmish that had broken out between two rival Nal-Lords. Melyor could tell the lords and their underlings how to run the realms, she could tell them how to do business with each other, but she could not force them to change their very nature. And so it fell to the men of SovSec to enforce the Sovereign's decrees, regardless of whether they agreed with the laws or not.

Under normal circumstances, Premel wouldn't have minded. He usually enjoyed these forays into the quads. It felt good to be forced once more to rely on his instincts and his extensive knowledge of the streets and byways. He was in his element, as was Jibb. The security chief would never have admitted it to anyone, Premel knew. Jibb would have considered such an admission a betrayal of Melyor's trust. But one needed only to look at the man as he loped through the tunnels, his thrower in hand, his dark eyes watchful, his teeth bared in a fierce grin, to see that his heart was still in the quads. Indeed, his mere presence was an acknowledgment of the obvious. Slevin, his predecessor as head of SovSec, never would have gone on a mission of this sort, leaving it instead to his subordinates. But not Jibb. And under normal circumstances, Premel would have been glad to have the dark-haired man along.

But these were not normal circumstances. Marar expected Premel to kill both Jibb and Melyor within the next day or two. And truth be told, this mission presented Premel with his best opportunity yet to carry out the first half of that assignment. They were bound to run into resistance when they reached the Fourteenth. Were a stray blast of thrower fire to hit Jibb, it would arouse no suspicions. Things of that sort happened all the time in Bragor-Nal. There might even be a way to do it that would allow Premel to blame someone else—another guard, or perhaps even one of the breaklaws. Logistics weren't the problem.

He had never had an older brother, but he felt about Jibb the way he imagined his own younger brother had felt about him before dying several years ago in a firefight in the Twelfth. He couldn't stomach the idea of losing a second brother. And yet, by refusing to kill Jibb, he made his own life forfeit. He had thought of one possible solution after one of his recent conversations with Stib-Nal's Sovereign, but it had been so drastic and so risky that he had quickly lost his nerve. Then Marar had contacted him again, with that half-crazed look on his narrow face, and demanded that Premel kill both Jibb and Melyor. They had spoken once more since then, albeit only long enough for Marar to ask whether the assassinations had been carried out, and for Premel to explain that the occasion had not yet arisen. Marar accepted this grudgingly, but Premel had little hope that he could put the Sovereign off again. One way or another, he'd have to act soon.

Ahead of him, Jibb raised a hand, pulling Premel from his dark musings. The security chief turned to face them and pointed to a small blue light mounted on the curved cement ceiling. They had reached the edge of the Fourteenth. Premel and the other ten guards gathered in a tight ring around Jibb.

"Stay alert now," the big man whispered. "Gribon's men could be anywhere, and at last report Tullis's invaders were in this part of the Realm."

The others nodded, as did Premel after a moment's hesitation. He took a deep breath, trying to clear his head. He needed to concentrate. A man could get killed in the tunnels if he wasn't paying attention.

"Should we split up, General?" one of the other men asked in a low voice.

"I've been trying to decide that," Jibb said. He glanced at Premel. "What do you think?"

If we split up, there's no way I can kill you. "I'm not sure. It might be a good idea."

"But?"

The man was unnervingly perceptive. Premel cleared his throat, forcing his mind past his own problems. "But we have a better chance of ending their conflict by finding one of them and persuading him to break off. And we can only do that if the one we find is convinced that SovSec is here in force."

Jibb seemed to weigh this for several moments until, finally, he nodded. "That makes sense. We'll stay together."

He started forward again and Premel followed, unsure whether to feel relieved or dismayed.

"You all right?" Jibb asked as they stole through the passages.

No, I'm a traitor. "Yes, fine."

"I thought you'd be glad to be back in the quads."

Unnervingly perceptive. "I am. It's just been a while. I'm still trying to make the adjustment." *And I'm trying to decide whether it would be easier to kill you or just get myself killed and be done with it.*

Jibb grinned. "Well don't take too long. Tullis and Gribon aren't likely to be as patient as I am."

Premel tried to smile, but judging from the frown that appeared on Jibb's face, he knew that he'd failed. Jibb faced forward again, and they continued through the tunnels, taking a fork to the right and then a second several moments later.

Jibb glanced back at him a second time and opened his mouth to say something. But in that instant a man stepped into view at the end of the corridor, and though the tunnels were dimly lit, and the man appeared as little more than a shadow, Premel could see that he had a thrower in his hand. Without pause, in a motion so fluid he must have done it a thousand times before, the man raised his thrower and fired, red flame leaping from his weapon. Without even a thought, Premel did the only thing he could, the only thing he had ever really been capable of doing. Crying out a warning, he leaped forward, knocking Jibb to the cold cement floor with his left forearm while at the same time firing his own weapon at the break-law.

Premel heard Jibb grunt with pain, and he wasn't certain whether he had been hit by the thrower fire or had just had the wind knocked out of him by his fall. But in the next moment it hardly mattered. The man in front of them was joined by several of his comrades, all of them armed. Using the corner of the corridor for protection, they took turns pouring their thrower fire into the passageway and then ducking back for cover.

Premel and the other guards were well-trained and highly skilled with hand weapons. But in the narrow passageway they had nowhere to hide and could do little to protect themselves. At least five of them fell in the first volley—it was hard for Premel to get an accurate count, draped as he was over Jibb. Judging from the angle of their return fire, the rest seemed to have dropped to the floor to use the bodies of the dead for protection, but they could not hold out for very long.

"Use your hand boomers!" Jibb said through clenched teeth, his voice strained. The break-law must have gotten him with his thrower, Premel thought, starting to tremble.

"Of course," Premel answered. "Hand boomers!" he called out for the rest to hear. "Quickly!"

For several seconds nothing happened, and the men in front of them continued their assault. Then one of the guards shouted out a warning from behind them. And an instant later the tunnel rocked with the force of an explosion.

Bits of cement fell on Premel's back and head, and smoke began to fill the corridor. But the firing stopped, and, despite the ringing in his ears, he could hear screams coming from where their attackers had been.

"Take them forward," Jibb said in the same tight voice. "Don't let the break-laws get away."

"But you're—"

"I can protect myself. I still have my weapon and one good arm."

One good . . . "Is that where you were hit?" Premel asked, climbing to his feet and helping Jibb into a sitting position. "Your arm?"

"My left shoulder."

Premel looked more closely, and even in the faint light he could make out the sheen of blood on Jibb's pale blue uniform. For a moment he wondered if he was going to be ill. He was trembling again, and he wasn't sure why. He was a soldier—before that he had been a break-law—things like this weren't supposed to bother him. But this was Jibb who had been hurt. This was Jibb whom he was supposed to have killed.

"Could you tell whose men they were?" Jibb asked, wiping sweat from his brow with his good hand.

"No."

Jibb closed his eyes and leaned his head back against the stone wall. "Well you'd better get going. I don't want them getting away."

Premel swallowed, nodded. "We're moving!" he said to the rest, a slight flutter in his voice. "After them!"

The others started forward, but Jibb reached out for Premel's leg, stopping him.

"Premel."

"Yes."

"Thanks."

Premel nodded again—somehow he couldn't bring himself to say anything at all—and then he followed the rest of Jibb's men.

The boomer had killed three of the attackers and driven the rest off. And as Premel's hearing slowly returned, he could make out the sound of their footsteps retreating down the passageway in front of them. Apparently the rest of the men heard them as well, because one minute they were stepping gingerly over the rubble left by the explosion, and the next they were sprinting down the corridor, weapons drawn.

They couldn't see the break-laws, and while they were running they couldn't even hear them, but Premel could tell that he and his men weren't getting any closer to them. When the tunnel forked, as he knew it would, they'd lose them. It happened even sooner than he'd expected. Rounding a bend in the passageway, they came to a second corridor that veered off sharply to the right. They stopped, and Premel held up a hand indicating that the guards should remain silent.

"There!" he said after several seconds. "Footsteps to the right!"

They started after them again, but almost immediately they saw flashes of red light reflecting off the walls.

"Thrower fire!" one of the other guards shouted.

"I see it!"

They slowed again, peering ahead cautiously until, finally, the break-laws came into view. They were crouched at the mouth of yet another fork in the tunnels, firing their weapons at some unseen enemy and occasionally ducking for cover to avoid the bursts of red flame that streaked past. So far they had not noticed Premel and the other guards, and Premel scanned their faces in an effort to figure out whose men they were. To his great surprise, he soon spotted Tullis himself, taking aim with the rest of them, and giving commands in sharp, silent gestures.

Thus far, Premel and the others had not used their hand lights—Jibb had feared that they would alert the break-laws to SovSec's presence before the guards could get close enough to do any good. But now Premel pulled his light from his belt and pointed it directly at Tullis.

"Drop your weapons!" he shouted. "And stay right where you are!"

Tullis whirled toward them and fired, as did several of his men.

Premel dived for cover, spitting a curse. This was no way to run a Nal. Better to let them fight it out.

"SovSec!" he heard Tullis call out. "Run!"

The Nal-Lord, following his own advice, took off down the left-hand passageway, twisting once to fire wildly over his shoulder. Premel fired at him three times, and though he missed, the shafts of fire came close enough to the Nal-Lord's neck and cheek to send him sprawling to the floor, his arms wrapped around his head.

"Stop firing!" he cried. "I give up!"

Several of the guards fired warning shots over the heads of Tullis's men, and the break-laws threw down their weapons. If Tullis was willing to cower for his life, they seemed to decide, they weren't about to risk theirs defending him.

Premel strode across the corridor to where Tullis still lay and hauled him to his feet.

"The Sovereign would like a word with you, Tullis," he said, turning the man around and looking him in the eye.

"What about Gribon?" the Nal-Lord asked petulantly.

"We're in Gribon's Realm. He's not the aggressor here."

"He started this fight! I was just defending myself! If I hadn't attacked first, he would have!"

"Tell it to the Sovereign," Premel said, shaking his head. "I'm really not interested."

"That Gildriite bitch wouldn't know—"

Before Premel knew it he had hammered his fist into the man's gut, doubling him over. He had no idea why. He had called Melyor much the same thing in his own mind more times than he could count.

"That's the Sovereign you're talking about!" he growled.

But Premel was trembling again. First he had saved Jibb's life, and now he was defending Melyor as if she were his sister. He felt as though he was losing control of himself.

He yanked on Tullis's arm. "Let's go."

"What about the rest of them?" one of the guards asked, gesturing toward the break-laws they had captured.

"We'll take them to the general and see what he says."

The guard nodded.

Glancing back over his shoulder down the other corridor, Premel saw several of Gribon's men watching them, their weapons held casually at their sides. "Take them back to Jibb," Premel commanded, facing the guard again. "I'll be along soon."

"Yes, sir."

Turning again, Premel approached Gribon's men, making a point of putting his weapon away as he did.

"What do you want?" one of the break-laws asked, as Premel drew near. "We heard what you said to Tullis, and you were right: he started this, not us."

Premel opened his hands and smiled. "I just want to talk."

"We have nothing to say to SovSec."

Premel's grin vanished as quickly as it had come, and he twisted his fist into the man's shirt, pulling him close. "Well SovSec has something to say to you, or rather to your boss. Tell Gribon that he's getting off easy right now. The Sovereign is willing to assume that he was just defending himself. But any retaliation, any move at all against the Fifteenth, and she'll strip him of his Realm, arrest all of his men, and let the rest of the Nal-Lords in the dominion carve up his wealth. Understood?"

The man met Premel's gaze with a smirk on his lips, but he said nothing.

It wasn't an uncommon reaction among gangmen. They were afraid of SovSec, even if they didn't admit it to each other, but seeing the stiff blue uniforms seemed to make them bold, to a point. Premel had been like that himself when he was still a break-law, and he had seen it many times over the past few years. But after all that had happened this day, and with all that preyed on his mind, his rage finally exploded like a hand boomer, sudden and uncontrollable.

Still gripping the man's shirt with one hand, Premel pounded his other fist into the break-law's stomach, much as he had done to Tullis a few moments before. But this time, when the man doubled over, Premel drove his knee up into the break-law's face and then, almost in the same motion, flung him headfirst into the tunnel wall. The break-law hit the cement with a sickening thud and then crumpled to the floor like a child's doll.

"Fist of the God!" one of the other break-laws breathed, staring at Premel as if he were some creature out of a nightmare. "I think you killed him!"

Premel looked at the one who had spoken, and then at the other two who remained standing. "I asked him to deliver a message. He refused. Now is one of you going to volunteer to do what he wouldn't, or do I have to do this to all of you?"

"No!" the first one said quickly. "We'll tell Gribon, just like you said."

Premel nodded. "Good." His anger had sluiced away, leaving him badly shaken and terrified that he had in fact killed the man. When the break-law stirred and let out a low groan, he breathed a ragged sigh of relief.

"Get your friend to the meds," he said, "and keep out of the tunnels." He didn't wait for a reply. He just left them there and walked back toward Jibb and the others. He felt sick. It wasn't as though he had never beaten a man before. He had done far worse as a break-law many times. But somehow this was different. He hadn't planned to do it at all. He just attacked, without thinking, without being able to stop himself.

"I don't even know who I am anymore," he mumbled in the dim corridor. And a voice in his mind answered, *You're a traitor. You'd kill your Sovereign and your best friend for gold.*

He shook his head. "No." He said it aloud, so that it echoed off the walls.

Then you're a dead man, Marar will see to that. Those are your choices traitor or corpse.

"No." There had to be another way. Which of course led him back to the one alternative he had thought of, the one that had come to him the night he spoke with Stib-Nal's Sovereign. It wasn't much of an option. Just the idea of it made his skin crawl, and it carried grave risks. But it was all he had. He had wracked his brain trying to come up with other choices, but there were none. Marar had him trapped.

"No," he said to the darkness a third time. "You did this to yourself."

He saw the rubble from the hand boomer in front of him, scattered around the bodies of the break-laws who had died in the explosion. At the same time, the sound of voices reached him, and stepping over the debris, and turning the corner, he saw Jibb. The security chief was still sitting with his back against the wall. He was speaking to two of the guards, who stood over him gesturing toward the other survivors and the bodies of the guards they'd lost. He turned at the sound of Premel's approach and beckoned to him with his good hand, before looking up at the guards again.

"We'll have the bodies taken to the coroner in this Realm," he said. "The Sovereign will send for them later."

"Very good, General," one of the guards said, before they both moved off.

Jibb turned to Premel as he drew closer. "There you are," he said. His voice sounded stronger than it had before. "What took so long?"

Premel stopped before him and squatted down to take a closer look at Jibb's shoulder. "I had to give Gribon's men a message for their leader. I don't want to have to come back here anytime soon."

"Good thinking."

"We need to get you to the meds. This doesn't look too good."

Jibb made a sour face. "It's fine. I'll be fine."

"I didn't say you wouldn't be. But you still need to get that worked on."

The general indicated the other men with a bob of his head, as if he hadn't heard. "They told me how you captured Tullis. Well-done."

Premel felt his face reddening. "Thank you, sir."

"First you save my life and then you grab a renegade Nal-Lord. You're turning into quite the hero, aren't you?"

He looked away, unwilling to meet Jibb's gaze just then. "We should be going." He stood and gently pulled Jibb to his feet.

"There's blood on your uniform," the general said, gritting his teeth as he stood. "Are you all right?"

Premel looked down at his shirt, spotted with blood in several places. It must have come from the break-law he had beaten. "Yes, I'm fine. One of the break-laws I talked to was less cooperative than I would have liked."

Jibb raised an eyebrow. "You've been busy."

He tried to force a smile, but failed.

"You're sure there's nothing wrong?"

"Yes, General. But we should get you back."

This time Jibb nodded.

Premel snapped his fingers and waved two guards over to assist the general. A moment later his companions set off down the corridor, but Premel lingered briefly, glancing one last time at the mess they had made of the tunnel and shaking his head. It could have been far worse, he told himself. Jibb could have been killed. *You could have killed him.* He shook his head a second time, trying to clear his mind. Then he followed after the others.

But even as he walked, all he could hear was Jibb's voice. *You're turning into quite the hero, aren't you?*

He couldn't possibly have been further from the truth.

There was still daylight coming through her windows, but already Melyor was on her third glass of wine. She didn't usually drink so early, or so much, but this had been an extraordinary day. Never mind that Wiercia was refusing to speak with her again, or that she had received intelligence reports indicating that Marar was accumulating gold and new weapons at an alarming rate. Those were secondary.

Jibb had nearly been killed. The injury to his shoulder was severe, according to her personal surgeon, to whom she had sent the security man as soon as she learned that he had been hurt. The physician had gone so far as to caution that Jibb might never have full use of that arm again. True it was his left arm, but still . . .

And then, of course, there were the five men who hadn't returned at all.

She drained her glass and poured another.

It wasn't supposed to be like this. She had devoted herself and all the resources available to her as Sovereign to changing Bragor-Nal, to ending the violence. People spoke of the Consolidation, the prolonged period of civil conflict that had consumed the land for over a century several hundred years ago, as a tragic episode in Lon-Ser's history. And yet, in effect, Bragor-Nal had been experiencing its own consolidation ever since. How else could one describe the constant warfare that had raged unabated among the Nal's Overlords, Nal-Lords, and break-laws? Was she the only one who understood how dangerous it was? Was she the only one who wanted to see it end? Certainly it seemed that way at times. Despite all her efforts, too many Nal-Lords and break-laws stubbornly held to the old ways. Her Overlords, Dob, Bren, and Bowen claimed to support her efforts to end the bloodshed, but if they really meant it, they wouldn't have tolerated so many skirmishes. Dob was the only one who seemed sincere in his agreement and, unfortunately, he had little influence with his peers.

She ran a hand through her amber hair and took another sip of wine. She'd strip Tullis of his Realm and throw him in jail for ten years, she'd throw each of the break-laws they had captured in jail for five years, and she'd divide Tullis's wealth among Tullis's neighbors, including Gribon, she decided with some reluctance. She also would make a point of withholding some gold from Bowen, Tullis's Overlord, when she next paid out the Dominion allowances. All of this didn't amount to much, she knew, especially since five of her guards had been killed, but it was something, and Melyor felt it important that she show everyone in the Nal that the old ways didn't pay anymore, but instead carried a cost.

Glancing at her staff, which leaned against the wall beside her desk across the room from where she stood, the Sovereign couldn't help but wonder if she'd have had more success if she weren't a Gildriite. If she were just Melyor i Lakin trying to change the Nal, rather than Melyor i Lakin, Bearer of the Stone, might they listen to her? The question was moot of course, but she found some solace in the notion that they opposed her, and wanted her dead, because of their prejudice rather than because they thought her vision of the Nal was flawed.

She raised her glass to her lips again, but stopped herself before drinking anymore. This maudlin self-pity was getting her nowhere. Setting the glass on a low table by her bed, she crossed to her desk and the speaker that connected her with Jibb's office. From the sketchy reports she had received from the surviving guards, it seemed that Premel had not only saved Jibb's life, but had also been responsible for the arrest of Tullis and his men. For some reason, the tall man hadn't reported directly to her, but it was time she thanked him. If Jibb's injuries prevented him from continuing as head of SovSec, Premel would replace him, and ever since she had become a Bearer, their interaction had been difficult.

Before she could turn the speaker on, however, she heard a knock on her door.

"Who is it?" she called.

"Premel."

She grinned, stepped to the door, and pulled it open.

The security man stood before her, looking pale and younger than she had seen him look in many years. He still had blood on his blue uniform, and he glanced at her only briefly before looking down to avoid her gaze. Jibb, Melyor knew, was Premel's closest friend—it was one thing that she and Premel had in common. No doubt, the general's injury had the man worried.

"May I speak with you a moment, Sovereign?"

"Of course, Premel. Come in."

He looked around him, as if checking to see if anyone was watching from the hallway, and then he entered her chamber.

"I was just going to call for you," Melyor said, closing the door behind him. "It sounds like you had quite a day."

"Yes, Sovereign." He was wandering around the room, still avoiding her gaze. He came to her desk, and stopped for a moment to stare at her staff and the glowing scarlet stone it held.

"I want to thank you, Premel. According to the reports I received, you saved Jibb's life."

He looked up at that, his eyes wide, as if she had caught him in a lie.

And suddenly, Melyor felt her stomach tightening. Something wasn't right here. Her hand moved involuntarily to her thigh and the thrower that was strapped there. Fortunately, Premel had looked away again and didn't notice.

"I can't thank you enough," she went on, trying to keep her tone casual. "I care about Jibb a great deal, Premel. Perhaps as much as you do."

Finally, he met her gaze. "I know you do, Sovereign. I believe you would have done the same thing if you had been there instead of me."

"That's kind of you to say."

He dismissed the comment with a small gesture and began wandering around the chamber again.

Moving slowly, so as not to betray her suspicions, Melyor began to wander as well. She needed to be at her desk, just in case she had to call for security.

"So how can I help you, Premel?" she asked. "You did come to me, after all."

He stopped walking and looked at her again. He was breathing hard, and Melyor half expected him to go for his thrower in the next instant. But instead he averted his eyes again. "I'm not sure," he said, his voice barely more than a whisper.

She put her hand on her weapon. "Not sure of what?"

He shook his head. "Of anything: why I'm here, whether you can help me. Anything."

Melyor just waited, saying nothing. She wasn't sure what to make of Premel's odd behavior, but she could see that his confusion was genuine.

"I need your help, Sovereign," he said after a long pause. He stopped pacing and met her gaze again. "I've gotten myself into some trouble."

"I'll help you in any way I can, Premel. You know that I've always taken care of the men who work for me."

He gave a brittle laugh and shook his head. "I wouldn't be so generous if I were you. Not yet."

"I don't understand."

He took a long breath. "Perhaps you've wondered how the assassin who died on the steps outside your window managed to get so close to the palace."

She stared at him. A moment ago she had wondered if he planned to kill her. She shouldn't have been surprised at all. But this was different. In a way it was worse. She knew she should have said something, but she found that she could barely speak. "You?" she finally managed.

"Yes."

Somehow she had her thrower in her hand, and she waved it at a chair near her bed. "Sit," she commanded, her tone icy.

He obeyed her without a word, his eyes never leaving her face.

"Why, Premel?"

"I was offered a great deal of gold, more than I ever imagined I—"

"Was it Marar? Was he the one who recruited you?"

Premel swallowed. "Yes."

Melyor sat on the corner of her desk and shook her head, exhaling slowly. "You still haven't told me why," she said after some time.

"Yes, I did. The gold—"

She silenced him with an abrupt gesture. "That's not what I mean. Marar offered you gold to help him kill me, and you wanted to be rich. I understand that. What I don't understand is why you wanted me dead." For an instant she thought she might cry, but she thrust the emotion away. *This isn't the time,* she told herself. *Later, when you're alone.* "What have I ever done to you," she pressed on, "except give you a job when no one else would, and take you with me to the Gold Palace when I became Sovereign?"

He looked away. "It's difficult to explain."

"Try."

He shifted in his chair. "When you became a Gildriite—"

"I've always been a Gildriite, Premel. Getting this staff didn't change anything. It just told everyone else what I'd known all along."

"No!" he said. "You're wrong! It did change you! You started trying to make the Nal into something it's not! It was like you wanted us to become another Oerella-Nal."

"Would that be so bad?" she asked.

He looked at her with disgust. "The Melyor i Lakin I pledged myself to all those years ago would never think to ask such a question."

She started to argue, but then stopped herself. After several moments she gave a single nod. "You're right, she wouldn't have. I guess I have changed, and I've tried to change the Nal with me."

"It didn't need changing."

"No? You saw the old ways at work today, Premel. Did you like what you saw? We lost five men; Jibb was almost the sixth. We killed three of Tullis's men, and I haven't even gotten the count on how many died in the firefight between the break-laws. Is that the way you want to live?"

He looked like he wanted to say something, but Melyor wouldn't let him.

"What's it going to take, Premel? How many have to die before you're willing to give this a chance to work? Or isn't it a matter of numbers? Would Jibb's death have done it?"

His eyes flashed angrily, and he looked for just an instant like he wanted to strike her. But then he looked down at his hands. "Yes, that might have done it," he said quietly.

She nearly laughed aloud, although she couldn't say why. "Great," she said, shaking her head.

He said nothing, and they sat that way for a long time.

"So why did you come to me, Premel?" she finally asked. "You said you were in trouble, that you needed my help. Why should I help you after all this? You've gotten all that gold; why don't you just buy your way out of trouble?"

"It's not that easy. Marar has me . . . trapped. This thing has gotten out of control, and I don't know how to get myself free of it."

"And why should I care? Why shouldn't I just cut you loose and let Marar do what he wants with you?"

"Because," Premel said bitterly, looking up at her again, "if you cut me loose, Marar will find someone else. I'm not the only one in SovSec who'd be willing to help him in this way."

Melyor felt an aching in her chest, and for a second time she thought she'd cry. He was right, of course. She was certain of it. "All right. But you still haven't told me why you've come to me. What kind of trouble are you in?"

Premel hesitated, but only briefly. "Marar wants me to kill Jibb, too. He says that if Jibb ever learned that he'd had you killed, his own life would be in danger. Jibb would never rest until he'd avenged you." He paused again, his eyes remaining locked on hers. "He's right. I think you know that."

She nodded. It all made a great deal of sense, really. "So you were willing to have me killed, but you got squeamish over killing Jibb?"

His face reddened.

"Never mind," she said. "You don't have to answer that. Tell me though: what do you expect me to do? How am I supposed to help you with this?"

Premel shrugged. "Just by knowing. Marar threatened to expose me if I didn't kill both of you. Now that you know, his threat means nothing. In a way, I'm already out."

"Except that I may have you killed as a traitor."

He was brave, she had to give him that. He didn't look away. He didn't even blink. "If that's what you choose to do, I'll gladly die. At least I'm the one who told you. At least I didn't let Marar win."

She smiled. Trying to keep Marar from winning had become something of a hobby of hers recently. She was ready to tell him as much, when she was stopped by another knock on her door.

Premel's eyes flew to the door, and the color drained from his features.

"Who is it?" Melyor asked.

"It's me." Jibb's voice.

She stood. "Come in."

The door opened, and the big man walked in. His arm was in a sling, and he was wearing quad clothes rather than his uniform: dark pants, an ivory shirt, soft leather shoes. He looked pale, but he was smiling. And his grin broadened when he saw Premel.

"I was hoping I'd find both of you."

"How are you?" she asked, not bothering to mask her concern.

He shrugged, winced. "Surgeon said I'm all right for now. He's still not certain how the shoulder's going to heal, but he said that he was more confident now than he was when they first brought me in. Still, I won't be going out on any security details for a while." He turned to Premel. "Which I believe makes you acting head of SovSec." He grinned. "How does that sound, Colonel?"

Premel lowered his gaze and licked his lips nervously. He glanced at Melyor for a moment, a plea in his eyes.

"No," she said. "This is your story to tell."

"What's going on?" Jibb demanded. "What story—" He stopped, noticing for the first time that Melyor held her thrower in her hand. "What is all this?"

"Tell him," Melyor said. "You want my help? First you tell him."

Premel stared at her for another moment before giving a single nod.

"Tell me what?" Jibb's voice had grown cold, and he was, looking from one of them to the other.

"That I'm a traitor," Premel said. "That I was recruited by Marar to help him assassinate the Sovereign. That I was responsible for allowing the bomber to get so close to the Gold Palace."

Jibb gaped at Premel as if the guard had disfigured himself in some way, as if he had severed his arm from his shoulder and left it bleeding on the floor. After a long time he looked over at Melyor. "Is he telling the truth?"

She nodded.

Facing Premel again, the general took an awkward step forward, so that he was standing right in front of the man. "Stand up," he commanded.

Premel shot Melyor a look and then did as he was told. When both were standing, Premel was slightly taller than Jibb, but at that moment, the general seemed the larger man. They stood that way for some time, staring at each other. And then, with such swiftness that it actually made Melyor start, Jibb hit him. Premel staggered backward but quickly righted himself, a bright red welt appearing almost immediately high on his cheek. An instant later Jibb struck him again. This time Premel fell to one knee. He was bleeding from the corner of his eye, and he blinked several times, as if attempting to keep his head clear. But after a few seconds he struggled to his feet and stood before Jibb once more. And again Jibb hit him, Premel fell to the floor bleeding from a cut on his cheekbone as well. He lay still for a moment and then fought to raise himself onto one elbow.

"Get up!" Jibb said.

Melyor found herself trembling, her arms folded over her chest. "Jibb, that's enough."

"*Get up!*" he repeated, ignoring her and balling his fist again.

"I said that's enough, General!"

At that, Jibb looked at her. "You and I agreed a long time ago that I was to have free rein disciplining my men."

She remembered. It had been years ago, the day she met him, when she was just an inexperienced Nal-Lord, and he a brash independent. This had been the one condition he had set when he agreed to work for her. "Yes, I did," she conceded. "But—"

"Then let me do my job!"

"No, not this time."

He started to protest, but she stopped him with a raised finger.

"He tried to have me killed, Jibb. Marar hired him to have me killed."

"Yes! And he deserves to be beaten for that! He deserves to die!"

"Maybe," Melyor said. "But not yet. I need him to help me get at Marar."

Jibb held himself utterly still for some time, his dark eyes locked on hers. Finally, he exhaled, and it seemed like his entire body sagged. He dropped himself into the chair that Premel had occupied a few minutes before and, after another moment, he nodded. "All right."

Premel sat up slowly and dabbed gingerly at the cut on his eye. "How?" he asked, looking at Melyor. "I'll do anything you want, but how are we going to get him?"

She shook her head. "I don't know yet." She was tempted to just take an army across the Greenwater Range and crush Stib-Nal like a bug. But the last thing she wanted was war with Oerella-Nal, and she had no doubt as to how Wiercia would respond to such an aggressive move. "I don't know," she said again. "But I'll think of something. One way or another, I'm going to destroy him.

Jibb glanced up at that, an eager look in his dark eyes that Melyor hadn't seen since their days in the quads.

13

Despite the concerns of my fellow mages, and your recent silence, I remain convinced that Lon-Ser presents no threat to our land. Jaryd's eagle, I believe, has come to help us defeat some other enemy. But who? If the gods have sent an eagle, this foe must be formidable indeed.

Many in the Order have even speculated that we are destined for a civil war, much like your Consolidation, a viewpoint that has been reinforced by the appearance in Tobyn-Ser of a second eagle. She is bound to Cailin, the young woman of the League about whom I have told you so much.

The presence of two Eagle-Sages is unprecedented in our history. Most cannot even begin to imagine what it might mean. But I believe that I know. I believe that Tobyn-Ser faces an enemy so overwhelming in its power and destructive capacity that the gods determined that one eagle would not be sufficient. . . . If I am right, then it becomes more vital than ever that the League and the Order reach some sort of accommodation. For if the Mage-Craft is divided against such an enemy, no number of eagles will save us.

> —Hawk-Mage Orris to Melyor i Lakin, Sovereign and Bearer of Bragor-Nal, Spring, God's Year 4633.

As a boy, Nodin had traveled the length and breadth of the Northern Plain with his uncle, a peddler whose company he had much enjoyed. They spent time in all sections of the plain, including the eastern corner adjacent to Tobyn's Wood and just north of the Dhaalismin River, which Nodin remembered as being no different from the rest: populated by hardworking farmers and marked by low rolling hills and small clusters of windswept oaks.

Looking around now, as the sun dipped low in the western sky toward the distant peaks of the Seaside Range, Nodin thought to himself that these plains still looked much as they had all those years ago. They still possessed a subtle, haunting beauty; tall grasses still swayed in the constant wind, and small towns with their modest, low-roofed homes still dotted the landscape.

The difference was that now, the towns had been abandoned, the homes left to decay, the fields neglected. Because eleven years ago, one hundred leagues from here, one man, on the verge of being killed by the mages of the Order, rendered himself unbound and thus became one of the Unsettled, fated to wander the nights in eternal unrest with the spirit of his first familiar. It was an accident of history and nothing more, that drove the people of the eastern plain from their homes. For decades before this man's death, he had bound to his first hawk on this spot. So it was that this land, once a home to the people of Tobyn-Ser, now belonged to the wind by day, and to Sartol's ghost by night.

"You're certain that this is the right place," Tammen said, a simple statement.

Nodin shook his head. "No. I'm not. I never claimed to know very much about Sartol. I thought you'd know."

She pressed her lips into a thin line, but said nothing.

It had been like this all day. It almost seemed to Nodin as if the previous night had never happened, that it had been but a dream. Except that his memory of their lovemaking was far too vivid to have been a vision. He could still feel her lips on his, he could still taste her skin and see her face illuminated by the firelight, eyes closed, mouth opened, as his lips traveled her body. The rhythm of their movements was as much a part of him this day as the beating of his heart and the measure of his breath. Yes, it had been a dream, but a waking one. It had been real.

She was using him. He knew it. She needed him for this journey—she was afraid to face Sartol without him. That was why she had allowed him to love her, not because her feelings had changed. He was too wise not to see through her pretense, and even if he hadn't been, Henryk, who had accompanied them after all, had been quick to point it out before stalking off into the night to give them their privacy. But if this was the only way he could have her, then so be it. He had denied himself for too long. Perhaps, with time, she would learn to love him as he loved her.

"So neither of you knows if this is the right place?" Henryk asked, sounding impatient and disgusted, just as he had nearly every day since Prannai.

"It's the right place," Nodin said, his voice low. He indicated the abandoned farmhouses before them with a wave of his hand. "Look around. These people were driven away, and not by the weather." He glanced at Tammen. "Are you sure you want to do this?"

She nodded, although he noticed that she had her arms folded in front of her, as if she were cold.

"All right. Then let's start a fire and eat something. The sun will be down soon."

Neither their meal nor their fire amounted to very much. None of them was terribly hungry, and with little wood to be found on the plain, and the god's forest at least an hour's walk back to the east, they had to content themselves with burning a few planks from the dilapidated fences nearby. They briefly considered taking wood from one of the abandoned houses, but Henryk argued against it.

"I know they're probably not coming back," the dark-haired mage said, "but it just wouldn't be right."

Tammen said that he was being foolish, but Nodin agreed with Henryk. They left the houses alone.

Sitting beside the small fire in anxious silence, the three mages watched the sun disappear behind the mountains and stars begin to emerge above them in a sky of deep indigo.

"What are we going to say to him?" Nodin finally asked.

Tammen shrugged. "The same thing we said to Peredur, I guess."

Henryk shook his head and gave a high harsh laugh. "Right, because it worked so well the first time."

"That had nothing to do with what we said," Tammen shot back. "He wouldn't have helped us under any circumstances. He was First of the Sage in the Order. He'd have seen any help he offered us as a betrayal." She ran a hand through her light brown hair and twisted her mouth in annoyance. "He was a bad choice."

"No," Henryk said. "This is a bad choice. We shouldn't be here. I think our lives are in danger."

"We've been through this," Tammen told him. "If you don't want to be here, leave. But I don't want to talk about it anymore."

For a moment, Henryk looked as though he might actually go, but then he sighed heavily and threw the last scrap of wood on the fire.

Nodin looked to the west, where the last vestiges of daylight still glowed orange, like embers in a dying fire. His grey hawk gave a soft cry and he scratched her chin. She cried out a second time, and Nodin felt a sudden cold dread that made him shudder. *He's here.*

He heard Tammen draw breath.

"Look," Henryk whispered.

Turning to look east, toward Tobyn's Wood and the advancing night, Nodin saw a glowing figure in the distance, picking its way among the remains of the farming community. He could tell that it was a man, tall and graceful, with a large hawk on his shoulder and a staff in his hand. He and his bird were both suffused with a pale yellow glow, the color of sand touched by the golden light of a setting sun. As the man, or rather, as Sartol's ghost came closer, Nodin found that he could see more of his face, just as he had with the spirit of Peredur a few days earlier.

With all that he knew, or thought he knew, of Sartol's life, Nodin had expected his appearance to be harsh and forbidding. This was, after all, the man who had killed Peredur and Sage Jessamyn, the man who had given aid to the outlanders. He hadn't expected to see this handsome mage who was approaching them, his dark hair flecked with grey and his chiseled features weathered like those of a seaman. The spirit was smiling broadly, his arms opened in greeting, belying his reputation. Only his eyes gave Nodin pause. They glowed bright and hot, like torches, making it impossible to see what lay behind the smile. It had been much the same way with Peredur's ghost, Nodin realized, except that the First's eyes had been whiter in color. But it hadn't bothered him as much that night, perhaps because he knew Peredur from his youth, or perhaps because he had heard so much about the evil that dwelled within Sartol.

He looked briefly at Tammen beside him, but he could read little on her face. She was watching Sartol walk toward them, just as he was, and though she appeared to be trembling slightly, her expression remained neutral. Henryk, on the other hand, looked frightened, his dark eyes wide, and his face pale in the ceryll-glow and the spirit light. He looked toward Nodin for a moment and shook his head, seeming to say one last time that this was a bad idea. Then they both faced forward once more.

She was a child again, the burns on her neck throbbing, her face grimy with tears and sweat, the image of her parents and sisters burning like wood in a hearth seared on her mind forever. She could smell the fires. Flesh, wood, her own hair. Everything seemed to be burning. Someone was carrying her, running so that she bounced in his arms. She knew it was a man; she still didn't know who.

But suddenly they stopped, despite the mages and dark birds pursuing them. For standing before them were two more mages, one of them lean and balding, and the other dark-haired and powerfully built, like a hero out of one of Cearbhall's dramas. And like a hero, this mage did what the other had been unable or unwilling to do. Thrusting forth his staff, summoning from his stone a brilliant yellow fire, he smote the men who had destroyed her village and killed her parents.

Again and again she saw it in her mind: the way the fire forked at the last instant, smashing the attackers to the ground and consuming them in flames. She could hear the cries of the other townspeople—she heard herself crying out as well, though she didn't know why—and she saw them gather around this man, pressing close to thank him for saving them and avenging their loved ones.

She had seen all these images a thousand times, in dark dreams that thrust her from sleep sweating and panting. But never had they come to her so clearly, so completely. Because never, in all the years since that horrific night, had she seen that man again, that hero, that tall, dark-haired mage.

Until tonight. He glimmered with a soft yellow light, as if he were mage-fire itself. And the bird on his shoulder was not the great owl she remembered from Watersbend. But she would have known his face anywhere. This was the man who had saved her life.

She held herself perfectly still as he approached, fearing that if she even allowed herself to exhale, she would weep. Often she had wished that she could see her parents once more before she died. This was the next best thing.

"Greetings!" the spirit of Sartol said, his arms still spread wide. The great hawk on his shoulder regarded Tammen and her companions coolly. "We've been expecting you."

Henryk and Nodin exchanged a look.

"You have?" Nodin asked.

"Of course. After your conversation with Peredur went as it did, I guessed that you would be coming to me next."

Tammen smiled, though her heart was hammering in her chest, and her hands were shaking. "Then you know why we've come," she said, a flutter in her voice.

"Yes, I do. I must say, I think Peredur was a poor choice. A man of his temperament would never embrace a movement such as yours. He could never be so bold, so courageous."

She could scarcely believe what he was hearing.

"You know of our Movement?" Nodin asked. "How is that possible? Peredur knew nothing of it."

"Those of us who choose to keep watch on the world of the living have the ability to do so. I've been aware of your Movement for some time now. You deserve praise for what you've done; I think you're providing the people of Tobyn-Ser with a valuable alternative to the Order and the League."

"How convenient," Henryk said under his breath.

The smile on the spirit's face widened. "Ah, you don't believe me."

"I just find it strange," Henryk answered. "Peredur had no knowledge of the Movement, and yet you claim not only to know of us, but to be an admirer of our work."

"There's nothing strange about it," Sartol said. "I longed for an alternative to the Order throughout my service to the land, but the opportunity never presented itself. As for Peredur," the spirit added with a shrug. "Well, even in life, the First was not a man given to bold thinking."

"Is that why you killed him?"

"Henryk!" Tammen snapped, spinning to face him.

Sartol's smile vanished, and the fire in his glowing eyes appeared to brighten. "Remember to whom you're speaking, Mage!" he said, his tone as hot and hard as newly forged iron. "I may not have been a Sage, or even a First, but I was an Owl-Master before you were born, and in my time I was as powerful as any mage who has ever walked the land!"

"Our apologies, Owl-Master," Tammen said quickly, her voice still unsteady. "He meant nothing by it. We've come to you in friendship. We have no wish to give offense."

Sartol glared at Henryk for another moment, before turning his gaze to Tammen. "Of course," he said, the smile touching his handsome face again. "I understand really. No doubt all of you have heard . . . things about me, about what I was supposed to have done. It took great courage for you to have come here."

"Actually, Owl-Master," Tammen said, "I've wanted to come for some time. I was at Watersbend. I saw you save our village from the outlanders."

"Did you?" Sartol asked kindly. "So then you know that the mages of the Order told the most horrible lies about me so that they could conceal their own treachery."

She nodded. "That's why we've come to you. You of all people might understand our opposition to the Order, and to the League." She hesitated. "Maybe you'd even be willing to help us."

"Help you?"

"The People's Movement has support throughout the land, but there are only a few free mages. We're no match for either the League or the Order, and now that the Temples are getting weapons from Lon-Ser, we can't even be sure of equaling their strength."

The spirit nodded. "Ah yes, the Temples. I had seen something of this as well."

"Then you know how desperate our need is."

Sartol furrowed his brow and walked off a few steps, seemingly lost in thought. He stood that way for several moments, his back to them, his head bowed slightly, and his hand gripping his staff tightly. His hawk sat perfectly still on his shoulder, and even the wind that drifted across the plain did not ruffle the bird's feathers or the mage's hair.

Tammen held her breath. Without Sartol, she wasn't certain what they would do.

"Very well," he said at last, turning to face them again. "I'll help you."

"Thank you, Owl-Master," she said, feeling her relief like a cool wind on a summer afternoon. "I knew you wouldn't refuse us."

"I'm glad to be able to further your Movement, my dear. What better way for me to use those powers that I still possess."

"How are you going to help us?" Henryk asked.

Sartol frowned slightly, as if puzzled by the question. "In any way I can, of course."

"That's not what I mean. Peredur told us that the Unsettled are limited in their ability to affect the living world, and that what little they can do must be done together, with the consent of all. He even implied that since you became one of them, such cooperation among your kind has become next to impossible."

"Peredur is a fool," Sartol said, sounding annoyed. "And as I told you before, he was never terribly clever or creative."

"So there are ways for you to help us?" Tammen asked.

"Yes."

She looked at Nodin, smiling triumphantly. "I knew it!"

"I will need your help though," the spirit added.

Tammen faced him again. "What do you mean?"

"Peredur is right in part. I can't use my power the way I could when I was alive. It's not that easy."

"But you said—"

He smiled disarmingly. "I said I would help you, my dear. And I will. But I'm not a mage anymore. I'm one of the Unsettled, and my kind are constrained not only by Theron's Curse, but by the very nature of the Mage-Craft."

"So what is it that you need from us?"

Sartol's smile broadened. "A trifle, really. Nothing more."

Nodin felt suddenly and inexplicably as though his entire world was balanced on the edge of a blade. Watching the spirit intently, waiting for him to respond to Tammen's question, he saw Sartol struggling with something. It took him a moment to figure out what it was. But then he knew. The ghost was fighting an urge to laugh, straining to control a wave of giddiness. Nodin felt a chill run through his body, as if one of the Unsettled had run a finger down his spine. He wanted to warn Tammen. He wanted to grab her hand and lead her away from here at a dead run. But he knew that it was too late. They had set a series of events in motion, and he had no idea how to stop them. All he could do was watch and listen, and hope that Tammen would realize their error in coming here.

The spirit still had the same benign smile on his lips, and now he took a single step forward. It covered little distance, but Nodin suddenly felt an urge to back away.

"I need access to your ceryll," Sartol said.

Tammen stared back at him, as though not quite believing what she had heard. "Our cerylls?"

"Not all of them, just one."

"You can't be serious," Henryk said. "You can't really expect that we'd allow you to use our cerylls for anything."

The smile faded from the ghost's face. "I do expect it. You came to me seeking my help, and I'm happy to give it. But I can do little without receiving help from you in return. As I told you a moment ago, there are limits on my powers. If you want me to help you, you're going to have to help me first, so that we can overcome these limits." He regarded the three of them somberly. "Besides," he went on, "why should I trust any of you if you show so little trust in me?"

Henryk gaped at him. "*What?* You want us to believe that you're worried about our trust?"

"That's enough, Henryk!" Tammen said. She turned to Sartol and took a long breath. "What exactly do you mean when you say that you need access to one of our cerylls?"

"It's difficult to explain," the spirit replied. "We who are unsettled exist as Mage-Craft, and nothing more. We are the embodiments of power, but we are also tied by Theron's Curse to the places of our first bindings." He gestured toward his own ceryll. "In my realm, this ceryll is real, but it doesn't exist in your world. So I need your ceryll to focus the power that I still possess. Without it, I have no way to use my power in your world, and I have no way to leave this place."

"Tammen," Henryk said, a plea in his voice, "you can't really be considering allowing him to do this."

"What's to stop you from just using our cerylls without our consent?" she asked, ignoring Henryk.

Sartol shook his head. "Nothing. Nothing at all." He smiled at her. "If I really were the monster your friend thinks I am, I would have done it already."

Tammen glanced at Henryk and then Nodin, with a look that seemed to say, See? I told you we could trust him.

"Would you mind, Owl-Master," Nodin asked, "if we took some time to discuss this among ourselves? You've given us a good deal to think about, and we'd like to give your offer the consideration it deserves."

"Yes," Henryk agreed. "I might be more amenable to all this if I have a chance to speak with my friends about it."

Tammen opened her mouth, no doubt to object, but Nodin silenced her with a glare before facing Sartol again.

The spirit was watching them with narrowed eyes. Nodin could see him clenching his jaw, but otherwise he offered no response for what seemed a long time. "Very well," he finally said, with a thin smile. "You know where to find me."

He turned and walked off through the ruined village, his yellow glow fading into the night as the sun had done some time ago.

Nodin turned and started in the opposite direction, signaling that his companions should follow, but saying nothing until they were a good distance from the old farmhouses and could no longer see Sartol's ghost.

"What in Arick's name was that all about?" Tammen demanded, whirling on them both when they finally halted. "He was ready to help us!"

"I don't know what he was ready to do," Henryk said. "But I got the feeling that helping us was the least of his concerns."

Nodin nodded. "I agree. He's plotting something. I'm sure of it. He was just too eager to get at our cerylls."

"You idiots! Didn't you hear what he said? If he had wanted to use our cerylls he could have done so at any time."

Nodin hesitated, but only for a moment. "Yes, Tammen. I heard him. But I didn't believe him."

"Well, I did! And I don't care what you do or do not believe! I'm going back to find him before he changes his mind about helping us."

"Tammen, don't!" Henryk said. "I know that you think of him differently, that where we see a villain, you see a man who saved your life. But didn't it strike you as a bit too convenient that he should know so much about us, and that he should be so willing to help us, and that he should know of a way to get around all the limitations that Peredur mentioned? It was all just too perfect. Didn't you see that?"

She stared at him, looking pale and young in the strangely colored light from their cerylls, and then she began to shake her head slowly. "You know what I think?" she said at last, a look of defiance in her grey eyes. "I think that the two of you are afraid of succeeding?"

"What?" Nodin said. "That makes no sense!"

"Doesn't it? Here we are, on the verge of joining forces with someone who can put the Movement on an equal footing with the Temple, the League, and the Order, and it seems like the two of you are searching for reasons to refuse his aid!"

"That's not true," Nodin said. "We're just not certain that it's wise to give Sartol a way to use his power in our world." He placed a hand on her shoulder, but she shook it off. "I know that you trust him," he continued, trying to ignore the sudden ache in his heart. "I even understand why. But Henryk and I can't just ignore everything else that we know about him. He killed Peredur and Jessamyn, and he helped the outlanders. Can you really blame us for being cautious?"

Their eyes met, and Nodin found himself holding his breath. *I love you,* he wanted to say. *I don't want to risk losing that.* But he kept silent and waited.

"No," she finally said. "I don't blame you. But I know that you're wrong about him, that the things the Order said about him aren't true. And even if you can't bring yourselves to accept his help, I can."

With that, she started away from them as if she was going back to Sartol.

"Tammen, no!" Nodin said, grabbing her arm.

She looked down at his hand, her expression hardening. "Let go of me!"

"No. I won't let you do this."

She gave a short, harsh laugh. "You won't let me? Who do you think you're talking to? One night together doesn't make you my husband or my master! You can't keep me from doing anything!"

Nodin felt his face redden. Suddenly he was intensely aware of Henryk standing beside him watching their exchange. He closed his eyes briefly. "Tammen—"

"No!" she said, wrenching her arm out of his grasp. "I'm going! You two can do as you wish."

She began striding away from them, and Nodin followed. She spun around and leveled her staff at him, making her blue ceryll gleam menacingly. "Don't, Nodin! I won't let you stop me, so you might as well just let me go."

He saw that her hands were trembling, but no more than his own. After several moments, he opened his arms in a placating gesture, and nodded once, cursing the single tear that he felt running down his cheek.

She seemed to see it, because a moment later, she allowed herself a sad smile. Nodin thought that he might even have seen tears in her eyes as well. It was hard to tell. But she gazed at him briefly, and then she whispered, "I'm sorry," so softly that if he hadn't seen her lips move, he might have thought it just the wind moving over the grasses of the plain.

Then she turned and started once more to make her way back to Sartol.

Nodin stood watching her go, feeling like someone was kneeling on his chest. *I love you.*

"We're just going to let her do this?" Henryk demanded. "We're just going to let her give him her ceryll?"

"What are we supposed to do?" he answered, his voice subdued. "It's her life. We can't keep her from doing it if that's really what she wants."

"You're wrong!" the dark-haired man said with such fervor that Nodin turned to face him. "It may be her life, Nodin, but if she gives Sartol access to her ceryll, she's endangering every person in Tobyn-Ser!"

He was right. Nodin knew it immediately. "But how do we stop her?"

"Any way we can."

"I can't hurt her, Henryk. And I can't allow you to either. Do you understand that?"

Henryk looked away, but nodded. "We'll just have to find some other way."

A moment later they were sprinting through the grasses after Tammen, back toward the place where they had encountered Sartol's ghost. But they hadn't gone very far—not nearly as far as they should have—when they saw the glowing figure of the Owl-Master standing before them. Tammen was already with him.

"I thought we had gone much farther than this," Nodin said.

Henryk was breathing hard, struggling to keep up with Nodin's longer strides. "We had," he managed. "Sartol must have followed us."

They ran on, closing the distance between themselves and the ghost as swiftly as they could. But somehow Nodin knew that they wouldn't get there in time.

And just then, as if to prove him right, Sartol stepped toward the woman, his hands extended toward her ceryll.

"*No!*" Nodin cried out.

But it was too late. In the next instant, a brilliant flash of yellow light brightened the plain, as though the sun itself had fallen from the sky and landed in front of them. Nodin and Henryk stopped running to shield their eyes. And when they looked again, the spirit was gone. Tammen stood alone amid the crumbling farmhouses. Her great brown hawk was nowhere to be seen, and Sartol's glowing bird sat on her shoulder, as if it had been there all its life.

He had known they would come. With each day that passed in his prison of light, his certainty had grown, until the feeling was so strong upon him that the hours between dawn and dusk became unbearable. He had tracked their progress through Tobyn's Wood after their conversation with Peredur, screaming within his mind for them to move faster. His interminable waiting was coming to an end at last, and yet these final few days seemed to pass slower than had the preceding eleven years.

He knew from the vague images he had seen and the fragments of conversation that had reached him through the web of consciousness that linked the Unsettled to each other, that they were free mages, and that they sought help for their precious Movement. But he had not realized until they reached the Northern Plain that there was a woman in their party. And he had not realized until he began speaking with them that she was the one.

It was like an unexpected gift. A woman would arouse far less suspicion than a man, she would allow him to carry his plan much further before he had to betray himself by using his power. That the woman had

been at Watersbend seemed to him an almost uncanny stroke of good
fortune. That she was exceptionally attractive made the prospect of what
was coming that much more enticing. Had he not known better, he
would have sworn that the gods were with him.

Her companions were an annoyance, but nothing more. Under different circumstances, their abrupt departure would have alarmed him. But
this woman—Tammen—had long since made up her mind. Long ago, he
had saved her life, and tonight he had won her trust with his careful use
of partial truths and modest lies. He had been following their Movement
for some time, although only because he viewed it as a means for further-
ing his own ambitions. The limitations placed upon him by Theron's
Curse did necessitate his use of her ceryll, although not in the way she
thought, and not so that he could help them fight the Keepers and the
land's other mages. And he could have used their cerylls at any time, but
only to destroy them where they stood. In order to gain the type of
access he needed, she had to give it to him freely.

But she believed him, or rather, she believed in him, and nothing her
companions might say could dissuade her from giving herself to him. He
had only to give her the opportunity. So he followed them, at a distance
to be sure. He was no fool. But he followed, and soon he saw her walking back toward him, a look of grim resolve in her grey eyes.

She slowed when she saw him approaching, and she seemed to waver
slightly.

He smiled and raised a hand in greeting. "I was hoping you'd come
back." He frowned. "Where are your friends?"

"They're not coming," she said in a quavering voice.

"I'm sorry to hear that. I hope I didn't give offense." He stopped just
in front of her. Her light brown hair stirred slightly in the wind, and her
eyes shone with his glow. She really was quite beautiful.

She looked back over her shoulder briefly, as if she expected them to
appear on the horizon at any moment. "No, Owl-Master, you didn't,"
she said, facing him again and taking a breath. "They just . . . aren't certain that we can trust you."

"I see. And what about you?"

She shrugged and tried to smile. "I'm here."

"Indeed." So beautiful.

"So what do we do now?"

He fought to suppress a wave of giddiness. He had waited eleven
years for this. Eleven years of isolation and tedious light. "It's very simple. When you're ready, I'll lay my hands on your ceryll, and by so
doing, place my essence, my very existence now that I'm Mage-Craft
and nothing more, within your stone." Partially true he actually

planned to channel his power through her stone and thereby take possession of her body. "At that point you and I will be linked to each other in a way that few people have ever been." True, but not as he intended her to understand it. "I will no longer exist independent of you. My life will be inextricably bound to yours." Again, true. Her body would become a vessel for his power and his consciousness. As long as she lived, he would dwell within her. And she would live forever.

Tammen shuddered slightly.

"Are you all right?" he asked.

"Yes. Fine." She chewed her lip. "And once this is done, you'll be able to leave this place? You'll be able to help us?"

"My dear, once this is done, you and I will be able to go anywhere in Tobyn-Ser, and all the power I possess will flow through your ceryll." All true.

She considered for another moment. And as she did, he became aware of her companions approaching. They didn't have much time.

Hurry! he wanted to rail at her. *I will not let you ruin this!*

But in the next moment she nodded; she even managed a small smile. "All right," she said. "I'm ready." She was brave. He had to give her that.

"Close your eyes. And hold your ceryll out to me."

She did as she was told. The other mages came into view.

"Do you grant me access to your ceryll, freely and without reservation?"

"Yes."

He reached for the glowing blue stone.

"No!" one of the mages cried.

He laughed. There was nothing they could do now.

Tammen's eyes flew open, but even she was powerless to stop him now. She had given her consent. He laid his hands on her crystal, and yellow light exploded from it so suddenly and so brilliantly that even he had to close his eyes, he who had known nothing but light for so long.

And using the ceryll as a portal to her mind, he entered her. She screamed and reached for her hawk, attempting to use her power to ward him off. But she was too late. Again he laughed, and using his power, sending it through her ceryll, he killed the bird with a blast of power that was so intense it left nothing, not even ash. Just as the fire that killed him in the Great Hall all those years ago had left nothing.

A moment later, as darkness returned to the plain, Miron, the bird of his youth, settled on his shoulder. Or rather, on Tammen's shoulder. They were one now. He felt her struggling against him. He heard her screams, although he did not allow her to give them voice.

You cannot fight me, he told her. *This body is mine now. It will never die, it will never even suffer pain. But it will never be yours again.*

Why are you doing this? she sobbed.

He watched her friends approach, deciding that he would indulge her until they reached him. After that, he would not even allow her to communicate with him. *Because I can,* he answered. *Because you let me. And because this was the only path I could find to vengeance.*

But—

Your friends are almost here, and I can't afford to have your voice in my head once they reach us.

You'll never silence me, she told him. *Not for good. I don't care if you were once the most powerful mage in the history of Tobyn-Ser, you won't defeat me. I'll find a way to—*

Enough! he snapped, bringing the full weight of his power down upon her mind. *I have defeated you. There's nothing you can do to save yourself. And just so we're clear: I wasn't the most powerful mage in the land's history during my life—my first life, that is—but I will be before long. And all the mages in Tobyn-Ser will not be able to stand against me. Thanks to you. I have nothing to fear from anyone.*

He didn't even allow her to respond. Surely she was sobbing again, begging him for mercy. But never would he listen to her thoughts again.

Her friends were almost upon him, and he smiled, watching them draw near.

You should tell them to run, he taunted, flaying her mind with his laughter. *You should tell them to save themselves while they still can.*

He nearly laughed aloud. He was going to enjoy this so. And this was but the beginning, the first steps down a path that would lead eventually to Baden and Trahn and Orris, and, of course, to Jaryd and Alayna. *But I'm getting ahead of myself,* he told her. *All that will come in good time. First these two. After eleven long years, vengeance is finally mine.*

She couldn't do anything. She couldn't even cry. It was like Sartol had buried her mind and heart beneath boulders. Except that she felt everything—pain, grief, humiliation. She felt Sartol's laughter as a blade slashing at her chest. But she could not give expression to any of it. Othba, the only familiar she had ever known, was dead, wiped from the face of the earth by a blast of power from her own ceryll. And she couldn't even shed a tear for him.

You'll never silence me, she had told him vainly. *You won't defeat me.* She would have laughed at her foolishness, if she could. She was silenced, and she was defeated. By the man who had saved her life. She was his now. Utterly. He was inside her, raping her body and her mind.

And all she could do was obey his every command as if she were a child's puppet.

Sartol had saved her life and her village. He had killed the outlanders who killed her parents, and he had done so despite the fact that his companion, an Order mage, tried to stop him. Because of him, Tammen had become a free mage, making something positive of her hatred of the Order and allowing her to overcome the loathing she had felt for herself when she first became a mage. Everything she was today, everything she had accomplished in her life, could be attributed to three people: Sartol, and her parents, whose lives he had been unable to save.

In mere moments, the Owl-Master's spirit had succeeded in shattering everything she believed in, everything she thought she had known about what happened that night in Watersbend eleven years ago, about her parents' fate, about the Order and the outlanders, about the Mage-Craft, and most of all, about herself. She wanted to destroy him. She wanted to scream. She wished that she could take her own life, rather than become the agent of his conquest of Tobyn-Ser.

Nodin and Henryk were almost upon them, and they regarded her warily. She wanted to shout a warning to them, to tell them to run and let the whole world know that Sartol was coming. Instead, she raised a hand in greeting.

What are their names? the Owl-Master demanded.

She tried to close her mind to him, and a moment later she was in agony, her mind seared by the spirit's fire. And, she knew, there was a smile on her face.

Don't resist me. It does you no good, and it will bring you great suffering. As if to prove his point, he hurt her again, until she wanted to claw at her eyes to get at the pain.

And then it stopped. *Nodin and Henryk. Thank you.*

She didn't even know she had told him.

"Nodin, Henryk, how nice to see you again."

"Tammen?" Nodin said, narrowing his eyes. "Is that you?"

"In a sense, yes."

"What have you done with her?" Henryk asked in a hard voice. "What happened to her hawk?"

He killed her! Just as he plans to kill you! Get away from here! Get help!

Even Sartol couldn't hear her. She was close enough to Nodin to take his hand, but she might as well have been a thousand miles away.

"Sartol and I are joined now," she heard herself say. She tapped the side of her head. "His knowledge and his wisdom are here, and his essence is contained within my ceryll—see how it's changed?"

She wanted desperately to know what Sartol meant, and as if reading her thoughts, or perhaps thinking it another way to torment her, he let her look down at the stone. It was blue still, virtually unchanged from how it had been. But at its very center, burning like a small candle in a blue mist, was a spark of yellow light. She wanted to cry out. First Othba, and now her stone. He had truly taken everything from her.

"As for my hawk," Sartol went on, pretending to be she, "she's fine. She's left me. Even though Sartol and I are two, as long as we're linked, we can only be bound to one bird. So we let Othba go."

Nodin and Henryk exchanged a look.

"So," she said brightly, "where are we going next? We have Sartol on our side now; what should we do?"

"No," Henryk said flatly. "We're not going anywhere. I don't believe you. I see Sartol's light in your eyes, Sartol's bird on your shoulder, Sartol's ceryll hue in your stone. And yet you want me to believe that you're still just Tammen? Forget it. It's not going to work. Now tell me what you've done with her."

She shrugged. "Fine," Sartol said, sounding bored. "This would have been easier with the two of you traveling with me. But I'm perfectly capable of doing it alone."

Tammen felt herself raise her staff, and instantly a bolt of fire, banded yellow and blue like ribbons in a little girl's hair, blasted Henryk in the chest, smashing him to the ground. Tammen knew without looking that he was dead.

Nodin cried out and thrust forth his ceryll. With no effort at all, Sartol raised a shield of power that shimmered blue and yellow, like the sea beneath a midday sun. But Nodin's blast never came. There were tears on his face, and rage in his eyes. But, Tammen knew, he still saw her standing before him, and he loved her.

Instead, the mage spun away to flee, his grey bird leaping into the air. And casually, as though she had all the time in the world, Tammen, with Sartol's will guiding her, aimed her staff at the creature and destroyed it with a second burst of power.

"Where did you bind to your first bird, Nodin?" she heard herself call. "Where will you spend eternity?"

The tall mage was running as fast as he could toward the river, but he had so far to go, and on the plain there was no place to hide.

Tammen was helpless, and she thought it would drive her mad. She had never been in love with Nodin. Both of them knew that, and it had been a source of much pain for him. But, she now realized, she had loved him in her own fashion, and in that moment, she would gladly have given her life to save his.

For a third time, Sartol made her raise her staff. Tammen tried to close her eyes and, failing that, close her mind to what she was about to do. But even that solace was denied her. A third bolt of fire flew from her ceryll, crashing into Nodin's back and driving him to the ground in a whirlwind of flame. The last thing Tammen saw before Sartol turned her away and started walking east toward Tobyn's Wood was Nodin flailing about like a fish on land, trying to put out the flames that had engulfed his cloak and his hair.

You're probably wondering where we're going, he sent to her as she walked, his words buffeting her mind like storm winds. *We're on our way to Amarid. There are people there I've dreamed of killing for many years, and there's a stone there that almost belonged to me once. It's time I made it mine.*

14

After taking precautions to ensure that our correspondence remains secure, I can tell you what has been happening here for the past few days. Shivohn has been succeeded by Legate Wiercia as Sovereign of Oerella-Nal. You may remember Wiercia as the rather severe-looking woman who escorted us from the Oerellan prison to Shivohn's palace seven years ago. Wiercia and I have gotten off to a difficult start, and I fear for the Oerellan-Bragory alliance. In large part, the tensions in our relationship stem from the circumstances of her rise to power and the successful efforts of Shivohn's assassin to make it appear that Bragor-Nal was responsible for the Sovereign's death.

I have believed all along that Marar, Sovereign of Stib-Nal, was behind the bombing that killed Shivohn as well as the attack on the Gold Palace that almost killed me, but I have been unable to prove this. Until now. One of Jibb's men has confessed to being an operative for Stib-Nal and has told me of orders he received to kill both Jibb and me. Unfortunately, I cannot get Wiercia even to speak with me, much less consider this evidence of Marar's duplicity. I do not know what Marar hopes to gain from my death, or from the hostility he has fostered between Bragor-Nal and Oerella-Nal. I only know that he is proving to be a far more formidable foe than I previously thought.

—Melyor i Lakin, Sovereign and Bearer of Bragor-Nal to Hawk-Mage Orris, Day 1, Week 7, Spring, Year 3068.

They were sitting together by the window in her quarters looking out on the palace courtyard, where Premel was leading the guards in their daily drills. She could feel Jibb growing tense, and she knew it was only a matter of time before he resumed pacing.

"You still haven't heard from Wiercia?" he asked abruptly, breaking a lengthy silence.

Melyor shook her head. "Not since that evening after the Council meeting." She exhaled through her teeth. "I haven't heard anything from Marar either. For all I know, they're allies now, making plans for a war with us."

"I doubt that," Jibb said. "Wiercia's too cautious, and Marar has shown no sign that he's ready to do anything that bold. He's content to recruit traitors and assassins. That's much more his style."

An instant later, he propelled himself out of his chair and began stalking around the room again. "He shouldn't be out there," he muttered, gesturing violently toward the window. "He should be in prison, and every one of those men he's ordering around should know what he did. We owe them that much."

"You're right, we do owe them that. And perhaps at some point we'll tell them. But what about Premel, Jibb? What do we owe him?"

The general looked at her as if she were insane. "Premel? We don't owe him anything! Except maybe an execution!"

"He saved your life. And he confessed to me, rather than follow Marar's order to kill you. That must count for something."

"He almost managed to get you killed," Jibb said. "And if Marar hadn't been afraid of me coming after him, Premel would still be trying to find a way to kill you. For all we know, he would have succeeded by now."

She smiled. "Oh, I doubt that. I hear the head of SovSec is very good at what he does."

"I'm serious, Melyor. It's one thing to keep him out of jail, but it's quite another to put him back out there among the men, much less as their interim leader. For all we know this whole thing was a ruse that he and Marar thought up to get us to relax."

"I guess that's possible," she said with a shrug. "But I didn't get the feeling that he was putting on an act when he confessed. That felt real. As for the rest," she went on, glancing out the window again, "I really had no choice. I don't want Marar to know that we suspect anything, at least not yet. And we don't know how good his intelligence is." It was enough to know that he still had other operatives working in Bragor-Nal, including the ones who had transported Marar's gold to the Nal and given it to Premel. She and Jibb knew their names now, but they couldn't risk arresting them either. "If he learned that you were wounded," she concluded, "and that I'd given SovSec to someone other than Premel in your absence, it would make him suspicious."

The big man flexed his shoulder gingerly, as though her mention of his injury had reminded him that he was in pain. "I still can't believe that bastard actually hit me."

"It could have been worse, Jibb," she said. "If Premel hadn't been there, it would have been."

"Why are you defending him? He betrayed you!"

She stood and walked to her desk where, as usual, her staff leaned against the wall. "Do you think I've changed much, Jibb?" Picking up the staff, she turned and faced him. "Do you think I'm very different now from the way I was before I met Gwilym and Orris?"

His face colored slightly at the mention of the sorcerer's name, and he looked away. "I don't know. I guess."

"It's all right. I want to know."

He met her gaze again and took a breath. "Very well. Yes, you've changed. A great deal."

"For the worse?"

"I'm not sure that I can answer that. You're not as reckless as you used to be. You control your temper better. You're wiser. Those are all good things."

"But?"

He looked away for just an instant, an embarrassed smile tugging gently at the corners of his mouth. "But you've also grown cautious. Too cautious. You're so concerned about doing the right thing all the time, about making certain that nothing you do is at odds with the changes you're trying to bring to the Nal, that you seem . . . indecisive, maybe even weak."

She nodded, trying not to let him see how much his words had hurt her. After all, she had asked him to be honest. "And what about those changes? Do you disapprove of them as well?"

He frowned. "I don't disapprove of anything you do, Melyor. It's not my place, and even if it were, I wouldn't presume to do so. You should know that by now."

"But you think that trying to change the Nal was a bad idea."

"Actually, no. I think the Nal needs to change if it's going to survive. The old ways, Cedrych's ways, were destroying us. And if we really care about preserving our peace with the sorcerers in Tobyn-Ser, we have to find another way."

She could scarcely believe what she was hearing, and she desperately wanted to accept that he was telling her the truth. "Thank you," she said. "I needed to hear that."

"That's not why I said it."

"I'm glad to know that."

"If I'm going to be completely honest with you, I also have to say that I think you expect too much change too quickly. You can make new laws, and hold people responsible when they break them, but you can't force people to change their attitudes. You need to be patient. The men in the quads have lived their whole lives under one set of rules, and now you've gone and changed them. It's going to take them some time to adjust. Some of them never will."

She nodded, looking out the window again. "You're right. I'll try to remember that."

"You still haven't answered me, though," he reminded her. "What does all this have to do with why you're defending Premel?"

She ran a hand through her hair. "He told me that he helped Marar because he thought I was ruining the Nal. He said I was trying to make it into Oerella-Nal. And he also said that there were others in SovSec who felt the same way."

Jibb gave a reluctant nod. "That's probably true. But that doesn't excuse what he did."

"No. But maybe it means that I'm partially responsible. Maybe I have expected too much of them."

"That's ridiculous. Premel is a traitor. He doesn't deserve your understanding or your guilt. Certainly he's done nothing to earn your protection."

"You're wrong," she said, looking at him. "He saved your life. I can never repay him enough for that."

Jibb dismissed the remark with a wave of his hand, but once more he averted his gaze.

"You can't ignore that, Jibb. Whatever you may think of what he's done, you can't deny that he cares about you."

"He's got a strange way of showing it," Jibb said, a pained expression in his dark eyes. "You weren't the only one he betrayed."

"In a way I was. The one thing that's absolutely clear to me is that the thought of killing you was too much for him. In these three days since you learned of what he had done, have you stopped to consider how hard it must have been for him to confess to me?"

He stared at her. "No," he finally admitted. "I guess I haven't."

"Maybe you should. Maybe that would give you some sense of what you mean to him."

Jibb shook his head, looking uncomfortable. "I'd rather not think about it. It would be easier if we could just punish him and be done with it."

Melyor smiled. "When was the last time I made anything easy for you?"

Jibb laughed.

"Think about it, Jibb. Talk to him. In spite of all he's done, I think he's basically a decent and loyal man. And I'm convinced that before all of this is over, we'll need his help."

He pressed his lips into a thin line, just as he did every time she asked him to do something he didn't want to do. It wasn't really fair of her, she thought with an inward grin. He never could refuse her. "All right," he finally said. "I will think about it."

"Thanks." She smiled at him again. "You know," she said, "I'm almost glad you got hurt."

He raised an eyebrow. "Excuse me?"

"This is the longest conversation you and I have had in years. I've missed this. I've missed you, Jibb."

"I know," he said quietly. "I've missed it, too."

She walked to where he stood and took his hand. "Are you ever going to forgive me?"

His brow furrowed. "Forgive you for what?"

"For loving Orris."

"I forgave you a long time ago," he said, looking down at their hands. "I just never stopped loving you."

She took a long breath, not knowing what to say. It would have been easier if he had just been angry with her. "I'm sorry," she whispered after some time.

Their eyes met, and he smiled. "Don't be."

Standing there in silence, they heard Premel give the command ending the training exercises.

"He'll be coming back up," Jibb said, releasing her hand as his expression soured again. "I'm not sure that these interrogations are doing us any good. We haven't learned a thing from him."

"No, we haven't," she agreed. The interrogations had been her idea, a compromise of a sort intended to appease Jibb after she refused to have Premel thrown in jail. Whenever Premel was off duty, he was expected to report to Melyor's quarters for questioning. "But at least we always know where he is," she pointed out after a brief pause. "I'd have thought you'd want to continue meeting with him just for that."

Jibb inclined his head slightly, conceding the point.

"Besides," she went on with a grin, "I get the feeling that these sessions leave Premel feeling like some fledgling break-law arrested on a carousal charge. And there's something to be said for that."

He grinned as well. "Yes, there is."

A moment later there was a knock on the door.

"Come," Melyor called.

The door opened, and Premel walked in. His face was flushed, his uniform darkened with sweat. He glanced uncomfortably at Melyor as he crossed to the chair he usually sat in for questioning. But he said nothing, and he didn't even look at Jibb.

"How did the exercises go?" Melyor asked.

"Very well, Sovereign," he answered, lowering himself into the chair.

"Good." She looked at Jibb and raised her eyebrows. "Where should we begin today?"

The general shook his head. His expression had grown grim with Premel's arrival. "I don't know," he said in a flat voice.

"Let's go back to the gold," Melyor suggested after a brief silence. "How much have you received from him so far?"

"Twenty-two bars, Sovereign."

"Twenty-two bars," she repeated in a low voice. He had told her this before, a day or two ago, but she still had trouble believing it. It was far more than she paid Jibb in an entire year, and from what Premel had told her, she gathered that Marar had also recruited a man in Wiercia's security force. No doubt Stib-Nal's Sovereign was paying him nearly as much. She walked to the window, absently tracing a finger along the edge of her glowing red stone. "Where is he getting all that gold?"

"I don't know," Premel answered.

She looked up at that. "I didn't think you would. I was thinking out loud." She paused, thinking back to her last conversation with Marar. He had spoken of wanting more wealth, of being dissatisfied with his position in Lon-Ser. *I don't have all that you have,* he had said plaintively. *I don't even have what Wiercia has. I'm not even close.* And yet he was throwing gold around like a drunken Nal-Lord. She looked at Premel again. "You said yesterday that Marar changed his mind about killing me, that he decided that I was more valuable to him alive than dead, right?"

"Yes, Sovereign."

"Did he tell you why?"

"No, he didn't. He rarely explains anything to me. He gives me orders, and he gives me gold. But that's all."

"Are you complaining?" Jibb demanded harshly.

Premel was rubbing his hands together nervously, and he looked down at them now. "No, General. I'm just answering the Sovereign's questions."

"Well, do it without the self-pity. We're not interested."

"Yes, General."

Melyor wished Jibb would ease up on the man, but she wasn't about to say anything to him in front of Premel. And at the moment, her mind was focused elsewhere. The gold was the key to everything, she realized with sudden certainty. She didn't know where these flashes of intuition came from, but in the years since she had gotten her stone, she had come to trust them nearly as much as she did her Sight. They were, she had decided long ago, just another part of what it meant to be a Gildriite.

"What is it?" Jibb asked, looking at her intently.

"I'm thinking about Marar. I last spoke with him just after the Council meeting, and he contacted me. I hadn't given it much thought until now, but I think he was going to propose an alliance."

"An alliance?" Jibb asked, sounding skeptical. "But he tried to kill you."

"Yes. And then he decided that it had been a mistake." She looked at Premel. "Right?"

The man nodded. "That's what he told me."

"If we could just figure out why he changed his mind," she said. "If I just knew why he contacted me that—"

She stopped, interrupted by a beeping sound coming from Premel's belt. She and Jibb both stared at the man, whose face had gone white as the walls in her chamber.

"What was that?" she asked.

Premel swallowed nervously before removing a hand communicator from his belt and giving it to her.

It beeped a second time.

"This isn't one of ours," she said.

"No, Sovereign," Premel said. "It was given to me along with my first payment. This is how Marar contacts me."

Jibb grabbed the front of Premel's shirt and yanked him out of the chair. "Why didn't you tell us about this before?"

"I didn't think of it," the man said, sounding surprisingly calm. "I wear the thing on my belt. Most of the time I don't even remember it's there."

"I don't believe you!"

"It's all right, Jibb," Melyor said.

Jibb shot her that look and opened his mouth to argue. But instead he just glared at Premel again and shoved the man back into his seat.

"So what's supposed to happen now?" Melyor asked.

Premel licked his lips. "That's a summons. Normally I'd return to my quarters and use my speak-screen to contact him."

"Then let's go," she said, starting toward the door.

"Wait!" There was a look of panic on Premel's face. "He's going to want to know if you're dead yet." His pale eyes darted nervously to Jibb. "Both of you."

"I'm not dead yet," Melyor said. "Are you?"

Jibb shook his head.

She faced Premel again. "It doesn't strike me as a very complicated question."

"But—"

Melyor felt her patience waning. "Make something up, Premel. Lie to him. It shouldn't be that hard. You've been lying to us for long enough."

The guard looked down again. "Yes, Sovereign," he said sullenly.

"Or better yet," she said, an idea coming to her in that moment. "Tell him that you have it all worked out. That you're going to take care of both of us tomorrow."

"Tomorrow?" the two men said simultaneously. They looked at each other and Jibb frowned.

Melyor had to suppress a smile. "Yes. Now let's get to Premel's quarters. And think quickly, boys. We need a plan."

The wait seemed interminable to Marar, although by now he should have been used to it. Premel had been responding to his summonses quite slowly recently. It was not a trend that pleased him. He needed to impress upon the man that if he was no longer eager to earn Stib-Nal's gold, some other member of Melyor's security force would be.

It had started, the Sovereign realized, when he instructed the man to kill Jibb. Apparently, Premel just wasn't up to the task. Perhaps, in light of his failure to kill Melyor the first time he tried, Premel wasn't capable of taking care of the Gildriite either. Marar had been so pleased by his ability to recruit Melyor's third-in-command that he hadn't even stopped to wonder if Premel was the right man for these jobs. The guard had been happy enough to take the gold, and had professed a deep resentment toward Melyor, but he had been a part of Jibb's security team for more than ten years. One could not help but build up a certain level of loyalty in that much time, more perhaps than even gold could overcome.

It was disappointing, because in other ways his plans were progressing quite well. He had spoken with Wiercia twice more since the evening of the Council meeting, and though the Oerellan Sovereign had yet to pledge herself to an alliance, she had shown ever-increasing interest in the idea. And she showed no sign of gravitating back toward Melyor. Add to that the continued attentiveness of the Oerellan security man he had recruited—just in case Wiercia proved too intransigent in the future—and, as evidenced by the latest figures Gregor had given him, the steady flow of gold from Tobyn-Ser, and Marar could barely contain his delight. Except with respect to Premel.

As if in response to that final thought, Marar's speak-screen suddenly, finally came to life, revealing the guard's face. He looked even paler than usual. There was an anxious look in his grey eyes, and he looked surprisingly young and vulnerable, as if the big gold hoop in his left ear had been placed there as a joke. Something had happened.

"You summoned me, Sovereign?" he said.

"Some time ago, yes," Marar answered, not bothering to mask his impatience.

"Yes. I-I'm sorry. I had some trouble getting away."

"Premel, I find myself forced to wonder if you're still the right man for this job. Should I be looking for someone new to help me?"

The man shook his head and swallowed. "No, Sovereign. I'm fine. Everything's fine."

"Good. Then I don't expect to be kept waiting the next time I want to speak with you."

Premel nodded, but said nothing.

"So?" Marar said, after a brief silence. "Report. Have you taken care of them yet?"

"Not yet. But they should be dead by this time tomorrow."

The Sovereign raised his eyebrows in unfeigned surprise. "Tomorrow?"

"Yes. Jibb and Melyor will be going into the quads to speak with a Nal-Lord who's been giving the Sovereign some trouble. I've been in touch with some independents who are going to start a firefight, and I'll be there to make certain that Melyor and Jibb don't survive."

"But Jibb's hurt, isn't he? Why would he be going?"

"Actually, Sovereign, it's because Jibb is hurt that Melyor will be going. Otherwise, he'd go on her behalf. But with me in charge of SovSec, she didn't feel comfortable staying behind. And wherever she goes, Jibb goes."

Marar nodded, considering all this. "I must say, Premel, I'm pleasantly surprised. After our recent conversations, I had come to believe that you were unwilling or unable to carry out my orders." He smiled. "I'm delighted to find that I'm wrong."

The corner of Premel's mouth twitched, but otherwise he offered no response. And for the second time, Marar had the distinct impression that something wasn't right.

"What is it, Premel?" he asked. "Is there something you want to tell me?"

"No." The guard made a sour face. "I still don't like this, that's all. I don't see why you're so eager to have Jibb killed, or Melyor for that matter. A week ago you wanted her alive."

"You needn't worry about my reasoning, Premel. That's not your place. You just do as I ask, and enjoy your gold, and we'll get along quite well. Is that clear?"

"Perfectly. But all I'm saying is that it would be easier for me to follow your orders if I understood them. Doesn't that make sense?"

The Sovereign narrowed his eyes. Something was definitely wrong. "No, it doesn't. This has never been an issue before."

Premel hesitated, then shook his head and tried weakly to smile. "You're right. Please forget that I even mentioned it."

Not likely. "Of course, Premel."

Marar leaned forward to turn off his screen.

"Sovereign."

He stopped, leaned back again. "Yes, Premel?"

The guard took a breath. "I haven't been paid in a long time. I believe . . . I believe you owe me three bars of gold."

Marar smiled. So that was it. "Yes, I know. As I told you, I'd been worried about your performance recently. You've allayed my fears somewhat in this conversation though."

"So, you're going to pay me now?"

"Soon. As soon as I know that Jibb and Melyor are dead, I'll send what I owe you. You can think of it as a reward for a job well-done."

"But that wasn't our arrangement. We worked out a schedule of payments."

Marar felt his features harden. "Premel, you seem to be under the impression that you're indispensable to me. You're not. It would be nothing for me to expose you to Melyor and find someone to take your place. I'd suggest that you remember that the next time you feel the need to complain to me about changes in our arrangement." He leaned forward again and held his finger over the console button. "Do we have anything else to discuss?"

Premel glared at him for several moments, his face reddening as if Marar had chastised him in front of his closest friends. But when he spoke, it was in a low, meek voice. "No, Sovereign."

"Good. I'll speak with you again when they're dead. And not before."

The Sovereign jabbed at the screen keypad, terminating their connection. Then he sat back in his chair again, shaking his head. He didn't have time for such nonsense, and he didn't like what he had just seen in Premel. The man had behaved strangely. Probably the guard was merely upset about his payment, but the story he had told about going into the Nal with Melyor and Jibb left Marar somewhat skeptical. It seemed almost too easy to be believed.

The Sovereign was forced to consider the possibility that Premel would have to be replaced, regardless of whether he actually succeeded in killing them. The guard was becoming too unpredictable. He was asking too many questions and challenging too many orders. And he had yet to prove himself useful enough to justify all the gold he had received.

Marar nodded to himself. The time had come to make a change. Fortunately, he already had the names of several men in Melyor's SovSec whom he believed he could turn.

There was also the other man he had recruited several months before. He wasn't a security man. He didn't have Premel's skill with weapons. But Marar had no doubt that he would be useful in his own way. Perhaps it was time to speak with him as well.

His screen went blank, and Premel fell back against his chair, closing his eyes and taking a long breath. He felt drained, the way he did after an intense firefight.

"I don't think we fooled him," he said, his weariness seeping into his voice. "I'm pretty sure that he suspects something."

"He might," Melyor agreed. "But your complaints about the gold seemed to confuse him. Certainly it gave him something to which he could attribute your nervousness. That was quick thinking, Premel. Well done."

"Thank you, Sovereign." He had to suppress a smile—strange that her praise could still please him so—and he glanced at Jibb.

The general, however, wasn't even looking at him, which wasn't very surprising. That was how it had been since he confessed. Except for hitting him or threatening him, Jibb appeared to want nothing to do with him. And in truth, Premel could hardly blame him. Melyor, on the other hand, had treated him astonishingly well. It almost seemed that she accepted what he had done, that she understood his reasons and was willing to look beyond his crimes. A few days ago he would have scoffed at such compassion, seeing it as further proof of her weakness. A true Sovereign of Bragor-Nal would have executed him and been done with it. Only a Gildriite would have gone so far out of her way to spare not only his life, but also his feelings. This at least is what he would have told himself.

But having received her compassion, her mercy, and—dare he think it—her forgiveness, he could not dismiss her so easily. Perhaps the changes he had seen in her over the past few years hadn't weakened her after all. Certainly the way she had treated him these last three days didn't make him think less of her. On the contrary: it humbled him. He had betrayed her. Yet rather than punishing him, she had found a way to turn his betrayal to her advantage. And in doing so she had offered him a gift of surpassing generosity: a chance to redeem himself. He couldn't have done the same thing, and neither, it seemed, could Jibb. Maybe, just maybe, she was stronger and wiser than both of them.

The very idea of it staggered him. It turned his entire view of the world on its head. And it forced him to consider that the changes she was trying to bring to the Nal might not be so foolhardy. Which, if it were true, would mean that he had truly been an idiot for betraying her.

And perhaps that was the point. By not punishing him, she had allowed him to reach this conclusion on his own. She could have had him killed, or she could have imprisoned him—either course of action would have been well within her authority as Sovereign. But his public execution would have further angered those who also opposed her. And in jail, he would have brooded, his hatred for her growing, and with it his belief that he had been right to betray her. Instead, she had begun to earn his respect. Again. He was far taller than she, and more powerfully built, but in that instant he felt like a child beside her.

"So what do we do now?" Jibb asked, breaking a brief silence.

Melyor shrugged. "We need to stage a firefight. And I suppose we have to make it look like you and I are dead."

"You can't be serious!" the general said. "How far are we going to carry this? Do we make Premel Sovereign and let him forge an alliance with Marar? Maybe we should just let the two of them attack Oerella-Nal and plunge the whole blasted land into civil war!"

Melyor gave him a sour look. "Settle down, Jibb. I'm not going to let this get out of hand. But I want Premel to get paid again, so that we can grab the courier. I need to know where that gold is coming from."

"Isn't it coming from Stib-Nal?"

"I doubt it," the Sovereign said. "When I pay operatives in the other Nals I do it through merchants and other operatives. I rarely send the gold myself."

Jibb grinned. "Sovereign!" he said in mock horror. "You have operatives in other Nals?"

She gave a wry grin, but it vanished quickly. "So who's our troublesome Nal-Lord?" she asked. "Any ideas?"

Jibb didn't even hesitate. "Someone in Dob's Dominion. He's the only Overlord I'd trust to find us one."

Premel smiled inwardly. Seven years ago, in Melyor's absence, Dob had attacked Jibb and taken the Fourth Realm from him. He had done so with help from Cedrych, the Overlord who almost succeeded in taking over the Nal and killing Melyor, but that didn't change the fact that Jibb blamed Dob and wanted desperately to kill the man. It was a measure of how much things had changed between them that Jibb should now consider Dob the most trustworthy Overlord in Bragor-Nal. There was a lesson there, Premel realized. Yet another one about the virtues of change.

"I agree with you," Melyor said. "I'll contact Dob and arrange things. In the meantime, I need you to select two units of your best men for this. We're going to be playing a very dangerous game, and I don't want anybody making any mistakes."

Jibb nodded. "Of course."

Melyor started toward the door, but then stopped herself and faced Jibb again. "Take Premel with you. He's going with us tomorrow; he should be there with you when you put together the units."

The general glanced at him with obvious distaste. "I don't see why," he said. "We might be giving him a chance to bring along one of his fellow traitors."

"We both know better, Jibb. Even if there are others in SovSec on Marar's payroll, he wouldn't tell Premel who they are. It's much safer for Marar if each operative thinks he's the only one. Besides, Premel knows the men almost as well as you do. He can help you choose."

"But—"

"The men will expect him to be there with you, Jibb, especially since you're hurt. If you don't bring him along, it will raise their suspicions. And one of those other traitors you're so worried about might report back to Marar."

Jibb pressed his lips together. But after a moment he nodded.

Melyor smiled, though not with her eyes. "Good. Report to me when you're done. By then I should know whose Realm we'll be visiting."

A moment later she was gone, and for the first time since admitting that he was traitor, Premel was alone with Jibb. Realizing this, he felt his mouth go dry, and he looked up at the general.

He found that Jibb was already watching him, his round features looking uncharacteristically severe, and for just a second, Premel wondered if the dark-haired man was going to kill him. They said nothing for what seemed to Premel a long time, and their eyes remained locked on each other.

Finally, Jibb looked away. "Get up," he said.

Premel rose from his chair, his legs feeling unsteady.

The general motioned sharply toward the door, and the two of them left Premel's quarters and walked wordlessly down the corridor toward the lifter that would take them back to the palace's training levels. Waiting for the lifter seemed to take forever, and even after it came and began to carry them up from the guards' housing level, they did not speak.

But just before they reached the training level, Jibb abruptly pressed a button on the wall, halting the lifter.

"Why did you do it?" he demanded, spinning toward Premel so swiftly that the guard actually backed away. "Why would you turn on her after all these years?"

Premel stared at him bleakly. "I don't know."

"You don't know?" Jibb repeated contemptuously.

"That's not what I mean," Premel said, closing his eyes for a moment. "Of course I know. I did it because of what she was trying to do to the Nal, and because she's a Gildriite. But I can't justify it with those reasons anymore."

"Why not? She's still a Gildriite. She's still trying to change the Nal."

"I know. But those don't seem like such bad things now."

Jibb turned away. "I don't believe you. At this point you'd say anything to save yourself."

"I don't expect you to understand," Premel said quietly.

"If you didn't like what she's doing, you should have quit SovSec and gone back to the quads. A man with your skills could have found work in any Realm in the Nal. Even if things are changing, a Nal-Lord or Overlord can always use someone who's good with a blade and thrower. But selling yourself to Marar." Jibb faltered and shook his head. "All I could think while you were talking to him just now was, 'He betrayed Melyor for this bastard?' "

"I didn't do it for Marar. I did it for gold."

"Marar's gold!" Jibb snapped, whirling on him again. "This is about more than greed! It's worse than that! You betrayed all of us! Melyor, me, the rest of the guards!" He shook his head a second time. "How are we supposed to trust you now?

I saved your life, Premel wanted to say. *Doesn't that mean anything?* He didn't, of course. He didn't dare. Instead, he just looked away, and murmured, "I'm not sure."

"Neither am I, Premel. You were the best man I had, and you threw everything away."

They stood there for some time, each seeming to wait for the other to say something.

"Can I ask you a question?" Premel finally said.

Jibb stared at him for a moment. "I suppose."

"If you didn't love her, would you approve of the way she's running the Nal?"

Jibb's face turned red, and he balled his hands into fists, but for some time he didn't answer. And when he finally did, his voice was surprisingly subdued. "Yes," he said. "But it took me a long time to come around to it. She's smarter than the rest of us, Premel. You should know that by now. She sees things that the rest of us miss. That's why she was able to beat Cedrych all those years ago. That's why she's Sovereign."

Premel nodded and actually managed a smile. "It's taken me a while, but I'm starting to see that."

"It's a little late."

"Is it, General?" Premel ventured. "The Sovereign doesn't seem to think so. Just you."

Jibb glared at him. "The Sovereign tends to be too lenient at times like these."

Premel shook his head defiantly. "No. You can't have it both ways. If she's right about the Nal and about changing from the old ways, then you have to accept that she's right about this, too."

"Don't you dare tell me what I have to do!" Jibb said, his voice rising. Once more Premel wondered if the general was going to hit him, but instead the big man started to pace the length and breadth of the small lifter, his gestures sharp, and his dark eyes focused on the floor. "You're a traitor! You almost got Melyor killed—you're partially responsible for the deaths of three of my men! And you wonder why I'm not ready to forgive you?"

"I also saved your life, and when Marar told me to kill you I chose instead to admit what I had done."

Jibb stopped in front of him, and this time he did strike him, across the cheek with the back of his good hand. Premel staggered back, but quickly straightened.

"Never speak to me again of saving my life!" Jibb said, leveling a rigid finger at him. "This isn't about me! This is about Melyor and what you did to her!"

"Then why are you taking it so personally?"

Jibb took a menacing step toward him, but Premel held his ground.

"Because she's my Sovereign," Jibb told him. "And she's my friend. And because she's been both of those things to you as well, and still you chose gold over her. I can never forgive you for that, even if she can." He paused, running a hand through his unruly dark hair. "But more than that, you were my friend. I trusted you with her safety because you knew how much she means to me, and because I thought that you would die to save her, just like I would."

Premel stood utterly still, fighting to keep from crying, and searching desperately for something to say. But there was nothing, or at least nothing that would make any difference. In the end, it didn't matter if Melyor was willing to give him another chance. It was Jibb whose respect he wanted, and that was gone forever.

"So that's it?" he finally managed, forcing the words past the lump in his throat. "That's all there is to say? There's no way I can win back your trust?"

Jibb stared at him for several moments, then finally shook his head. "None that I can think of."

Premel nodded and swallowed. "All right. Can you at least treat me with . . . courtesy, just in front of the men?"

"I'll try."

Premel nodded again, before gesturing vaguely toward the lifter control panel. "We'd better get going."

Jibb regarded him for a few seconds more before pressing the stop button a second time. The chamber jerked upward, and a moment later it stopped again, and the doors slid open. Still, neither of them moved.

"For what it's worth, Jibb," Premel said, "I am sorry."

The general looked away. "I wish I could believe you."

Jibb stepped out of the lifter and started down the corridor toward the training rooms. And Premel followed, not knowing what else to do. His face still stung from where the general had hit him, and he could imagine the welt that was forming there on his cheek for all to see, like a sign reading, "I'm a traitor. I betrayed you all." It was appropriate, really. It was a badge he had earned, just as he had earned Marar's gold.

15

My friend Crob, the Abboriji merchant whom I have mentioned to you before, is standing beside me as I finish this missive, waiting to take it on the first leg of its long journey to Bragor-Nal. It pleases me to know that it will be on its way so quickly, and yet it reminds me once more of something I often try to forget: you and I are separated by too great a distance. This bothers me not only for the obvious reasons, but also because I need your help with a matter of great urgency, one that requires your immediate attention.

Someone in your land is providing the Temples of Tobyn-Ser with weapons. From all that you have told me of Lon-Ser's advanced goods, I am reasonably certain that this is a violation of your laws. Yet the weapons keep coming. They have been used to kill our people and to guard the Keepers as they defile our land. . . . .

I do not believe that you or Shivohn would allow something of this sort to happen, but the leader of Lon-Ser's third Nal, whose name I have forgotten, strikes me as the kind who would. Obviously it falls to my fellow mages and me to keep the Temples' men from doing more

damage. But unless you and Shivohn can stop these weapons from leav-
ing your land, our efforts here will do little good.

> —Hawk-Mage Orris to Melyor i
> Lakin, Sovereign and Bearer of
> Bragor-Nal, Spring, God's Year
> 4633.

"There's an Eagle-Sage! The Order is led by an Eagle-Sage!"

"So then it's true. We're to go to war!"

A third voice. "That's not all. I hear that the League has an Eagle-Sage, too. And that the League mages and the Keepers have joined forces to destroy the Order."

"So it's to be civil war!"

"That's insane!" The first voice. "Erland and Cailin wouldn't do that!"

"Wouldn't they? They've been trying to get rid of the Order for years now."

Sitting in the back of the Aerie, listening to the conversations that buzzed around the tavern like flies in a stable, Orris didn't know whether to laugh at what he was hearing, or hurry back to the Great Hall and warn Jaryd of the panic mounting in the streets of Amarid.

Actually, he was fairly sure that Jaryd already knew. They had spoken earlier that day, when Orris had gone to ask Jaryd for permission to send his letter to Melyor. Normally, of course, he wouldn't have bothered asking; he would have just sought her help. But these were dangerous times, and they still didn't know for certain whom they were destined to fight in the coming war. Indeed, if it had been left to the entire membership of the Order, Orris believed that he wouldn't have been allowed to ask for Melyor's help. But Jaryd didn't give the others a chance to prevent it.

"Some things are best decided by the Eagle-Sage," he said at the time, his youthful features looking pinched and weary. "You trust her." He offered it as a statement, but Orris could tell that he needed confirmation.

"Yes," Orris said. "Even if our enemy is from Lon-Ser, it's not Melyor. I promise you."

Jaryd nodded. "All right. Send your letter. And let me know as soon as you hear something."

"Of course." Orris smiled at him, but Jaryd seemed too weary even to smile back. "Are you all right?" the mage asked, his smile fading.

"I'm fine. I'm just tired."

"Where's Alayna?" Orris asked, glancing around the Sage's quarters.

"She's with Myn. I think they went to the old town commons. I would have liked to go with them—I haven't had any time with Myn since we got here—but I didn't feel right leaving the Hall." He shrugged. "Just in case."

"You need to get out of here occasionally, too. You're no good to us if you're too exhausted to lead."

"You're right. I've been reluctant to take Rithlar out into the streets, but I'm not sure that matters anymore."

At the time, Orris hadn't given Jaryd's last comment much thought, but now, listening to the conversations taking place around him, he understood.

"Pardon me, Hawk-Mage," said one of the men who had been speaking before. "We were wondering if you might tell us what you know about the Eagle-Sage."

Orris looked up from his ale at the three men sitting at an adjacent table. Two of them were young, one of them dark-skinned with dark brown eyes and long black hair, and the other heavier, with pale features and hair as yellow as Orris's. The third man also had yellow hair, but it was streaked with silver, and his face was lined and leathery, as if he had spent most of his life working in the sun. It was this older man who had spoken.

"What is it you want to know?" Orris asked.

The older man shrugged. "His name, to start."

They were going to know eventually. Everyone was. And better it should happen this way, in casual conversation, than in a time of crisis, when the League or the Temples or someone else might have a chance to spread lies about him. "His name is Jaryd. And his wife, Alayna, is First of the Sage."

"Jaryd and Alayna," the man repeated softly. "They're the young ones aren't they? The ones who spoke with Theron?"

"Yes, that's right."

"We always said they were destined for great things."

Orris smiled at the man. "So did we."

"Is it true that the League has an Eagle-Sage as well?" the dark-skinned man asked.

The mage hesitated, but only for a moment. "Yes. But I believe they call her Eagle-Master."

"It's a woman?"

"It's Cailin."

"Cailin?" the older man repeated, his eyes widening. "But she's so young! Both of them are for that matter." He sighed. "My time is passing before my eyes. There are two Eagle-Sages in the land, one of them young enough to be my child, and the other almost young enough to be my grandchild."

Orris offered a sympathetic smile. There had been times recently when even he felt old, and this man was at least twenty years older than he.

"Do you expect the League and the Order to go to war?" the second young man asked.

Orris looked at him for several seconds, gauging what he saw in the man's pale eyes. It was he who had been telling the wild tale of an alliance between the League and the Temples, and Orris could see that he was enjoying himself. "I believe that Jaryd and Cailin will do everything in their power to prevent that."

"But if the gods have decreed—"

"And have they?" Orris asked. "Do you have knowledge of such things? Because I certainly don't."

"Well, no," the man began, abruptly sounding nervous. "I mean, I don't know anything for sure. But the gods have sent two eagles. That must mean something."

"I agree," Orris said. "And the mages of both the League and the Order are still trying to figure out what that might be. Until we do, I think we'd all be best served by avoiding any wild tales. After all, we wouldn't want to frighten people unnecessarily, would we?"

The man hesitated, then shook his head.

"Do you have any ideas of what two eagles might mean, Hawk-Mage?" the older man asked after a brief, awkward silence.

Orris kept his eyes on the young man for a moment longer, watching him grow increasingly uncomfortable. "I have some," he said at last, facing the older man. "But they're only that. Ideas. It wouldn't be any more appropriate for me to speak of them than it would be for your friend here."

The older man nodded. "I understand. Can you at least tell us who you think our enemy might be?"

Orris frowned. "I could, but that would be little more than a guess, as well."

The man glanced at his companions and made a sour face.

"I don't mean to be evasive," Orris told them. "Honestly, I don't. We just don't know yet."

The three men appeared unconvinced.

"I will say this though," Orris went on an instant later. "Cailin and Jaryd have spoken to each other twice now, and they plan to meet again soon. And I've been in touch with people in Lon-Ser whom I know to be our friends. It may be that the eagles were a warning of sorts, and that having received that warning, and having reached out to old enemies, we've managed to avoid a war." He wasn't sure that he believed this, but it had occurred to him in recent days that the appearance of Jaryd and Cailin's eagles had done more to improve relations between the Order and the League than anything else that had happened over the past seven years. That wasn't saying much—all that had happened really was that the two Eagle-Sages were talking to each other. But that was something at least. He just hoped that the men at the next table would not take note of the one potential enemy he had failed to mention. He should have known better.

"What about the Keepers?" the dark-skinned man asked. "Who's talking to them?"

Orris considered a lie, but quickly thought better of it. "I don't know," he admitted. "I'm not sure anyone is."

The older man raised an eyebrow. "Someone should be if the stories I've heard are true."

"You mean because of the weapons," the yellow-haired man said.

"Yes, Tret," the older man replied, a note of impatience in his voice. "Because of the weapons." He faced Orris again. "Are those tales true as well?"

The mage nodded. "I'm afraid so."

"So then your friends in Lon-Ser aren't as reliable as you'd like us to believe."

Orris stared at the man, wondering if he was trying to start an argument. But that didn't seem to be his way. He was making a statement, and nothing more. And, truths be told, he had a point. "That's not exactly right," Orris said, picking his words carefully. "My friends are quite reliable, but Lon-Ser is a vast land, and they have enemies whom neither they nor I can control."

The man held his gaze. "I see. I appreciate your candor, Hawk-Mage. My name is Delsin, and I must tell you that I'm a League man from a League town. But I respect someone who's honest with me no matter the color of his cloak."

"Thank you, Delsin," the mage said, trying to smile. The men's questions alarmed him, and the more he turned them over in his mind, the more frightened he became. As far as he knew, no one was talking to the Keepers, and if they had access to weaponry from Lon-Ser, they would quickly become every bit as great a threat as the League and the free mages. The mage suddenly felt a need to discuss this with Jaryd, and to prevail upon him to broach the subject with Cailin.

He stood abruptly. "I should be going. I've enjoyed speaking with you. My name is Orris, and if there's ever anything I can do for you, please let me know."

Delsin furrowed his brow. "I hope I didn't give offense, Hawk-Mage."

Orris sighed. He'd never been very good at dealing with people. "Not at all, but you've given me much to think about, and I'd like to discuss it with the Eagle-Sage."

The man fairly beamed at that. "Thank you, Hawk-Mage. I'm glad to have been of help."

"And my thanks to you, sir. Arick guard you." The mage nodded a farewell to the two younger men and then, calling Kryssan to his shoulder, he hurried out of the tavern. It was late—Jaryd, Alayna and Myn were probably eating supper—but with the days lengthening, there was still enough light to make his way through the alleys and byways without brightening his ceryll. He walked quickly, anxious as he was to speak with Jaryd. His conversation with the three men kept repeating itself in his mind, and he barely paid attention at all to where he was going. He had followed the twists and turns of this path dozens of times before; they came to him almost without thought.

It was only when he had walked a good distance from the Aerie that realization struck him. He halted abruptly, his heart suddenly pounding in his chest. He was quite alone in a small courtyard among the narrow passages, too far from the tavern, and yet not close enough to the Great Hall. He had been limiting his movements since his arrival in Amarid, making sure to remain in open areas and, when possible, traveling with other mages from the Order. For the League was here, and despite his stern warning to the young League mage he had encountered in Tobyn's Wood several weeks earlier, he had little doubt that Erland and his allies still wanted him dead.

He looked around quickly, trying to get his bearings and find the quickest route to the city's main thoroughfare. But by then it was too late.

"I smell a traitor," came a man's voice from behind him.

Orris whirled and saw a mage in a blue cloak approaching him from another alleyway. The man had long, dark hair and an angular face that bore a malicious grin. His ceryll was deep orange, the color of an autumn moon hanging low in the sky, and the large, dark falcon perched on his shoulder looked very much like Anizir, whom a League mage had killed several years before.

"I smell a coward," a second man said.

Orris turned again. Two more Leagues mages stepped into the byway from the same direction he had come. Apparently he had been followed. Both of them were young—indeed, he recognized one of them as the man from Tobyn's Wood—and they were grinning as well.

He had brought this on himself, he knew. He could still hear himself telling the young man that he was to be the last, that the next League mage who came after him would die. Orris almost laughed at the memory and at his own stupidity. It hadn't even occurred to him that they'd send three.

Kryssan let out a low hiss and raised her wings. One of the men laughed.

"Your bird looks scared, Mage," said the one with the orange stone. He laughed again, softly. "You do, too."

"I find this very interesting," Orris said, pleased to hear that his voice remained steady. "League mages are always calling me a coward, and yet it's the League that sends three men to attack one." He glanced at the young mage he had bested in the God's wood. "I guess that was quite a beating I gave you."

The man's face turned crimson, and he took a threatening step toward Orris.

"Hold!" the first mage said. "He's trying to bait you. We'll do this as we agreed: together."

"I can defeat him alone!" the young mage answered, his eyes still fixed on Orris.

"I believe we already established that you can't," Orris said with a grin. "Remember?"

The man leveled his staff at Orris, and brightened his sea-green ceryll. Orris dropped into a crouch, and Kryssan hissed again, drawing a harsh cry from the man's small grey hawk.

"I told you to stop!" the other mage called.

For a moment the young mage hesitated, but then he lowered his staff again, a look of barely checked rage in his eyes.

Orris spun to face the man with the orange stone. "What about you then?" he demanded. "Do you have the courage to fight me, or do you need help from these children?"

The man bared his teeth in a fierce grin. "I would give anything to fight you on my own. Killing you would be one of the great joys of my life." He exhaled through his teeth. "But I have my orders."

"Whose orders?" Orris asked. "Who's telling you to do this?"

Again the man smiled. "The Eagle-Master of course. Who else?"

Orris's mouth dropped open. *Impossible,* he wanted to say. *Cailin wouldn't do this.* He had nothing on which to base such an assertion. All he knew about her was what he had heard from others. They had never even met. But he had come to think of her as someone who could change the League, who could overcome all that Erland had done to tarnish Amarid's legacy. That she would send these men after him seemed unthinkable.

He was about to say this to the long-haired mage, but before he could speak, the man nodded once to his two companions and then thrust his staff out before him, sending a beam of orange mage-fire surging in his direction.

Orris started to dive out of the way, but remembering the two mages behind him, thought better of it. Instead, he surrounded himself and Kryssan with a barrier of russet power. The orange flame crashed into his shield with such force that he nearly fell to the ground, and in the next instant green and silver flames from the other two mages hit the barrier as well. Orris fell to one knee, gasping at the effort it took to block their assault, and Kryssan let out a sharp cry. But their shield held.

"How long can you hold us off, Mageling?" the long-haired mage called to him, mockery in his voice. "Mind you, we're in no rush."

Orris said nothing. He just closed his eyes, pouring every bit of his strength into blocking their mage-fire. And already he knew that it wouldn't be enough. The younger ones weren't very strong—he could have defeated either of them with ease, perhaps he could have beaten them both. But the mage with the orange ceryll was another matter. He would have been a difficult opponent on his own. With his companions, he was far more than Orris could handle.

Kryssan let out a second cry and Orris opened one eye to look at her. Her mouth was open, as she was panting, and she sat hunched, her feathers slightly ruffled and her eyes nearly closed. She was tiring quickly.

And he was as well. Sweat poured from his face and arms, soaking his hair and his cloak. The muscles in his legs and forearms were starting to quiver, and he felt light-headed.

"Give up, Mageling!" the leader of League mages said. "You can't possibly win."

"Never!"

"If you give up now, and let us end this, I promise you that no harm will come to your bird."

Orris opened his eyes. "You mean that?"

The man flashed a smile, and his eyes gleamed with mage-fire. "Yes. We'll let her go."

But seeing the expression on the man's face, Orris knew better. He intended to kill Kryssan first and send Orris to the Unsettled, to wander eternally in the company of Theron and Phelan.

"You lie!" Orris roared. "You'd better hope that you kill me, because if you don't, I'll hunt you down like an animal!"

"An idle threat, traitor. You know it as well as I do."

The man was right. Even as Orris gathered himself to cry out a denial, he felt his shield failing. The heat from their fire was already starting to burn his face and hands.

I'm sorry, my love, he sent to Kryssan. *I've failed you.*

She nuzzled him weakly and sent in return an image of their binding place on the northern coast of Leora's Forest.

Orris opened his eyes again, looking quickly at the three mages and wondering if there was a way to take at least one of them with him when he died.

And so it was that he saw the three men from the tavern approaching through one of the alleys.

"What's going on here?" Delsin shouted, rushing forward into the courtyard. "Why are you attacking this mage?"

"This doesn't concern you, old man!" the long-haired mage said, not bothering to break off his assault. "Now leave, before you and your friends get hurt, or worse."

"Are you threatening me, Child of Amarid?"

This time the mage did lower his staff, and a moment later his companions did the same.

Exhausted nearly to the point of collapse, Orris dropped his shield. He kept a wary eye on the other mages, but even if they renewed their attack, he wasn't certain that he could have mustered the strength to raise the barrier again.

"I meant no offense, sir," the League mage was saying, his face wearing a smile that wouldn't have fooled anyone.

"Perhaps not," Delsin said. "But you certainly seemed intent upon killing this mage."

"He's a coward and a traitor!" said the young mage Orris had bested in the wood. "He deserves to die!"

The older man shook his head. "Killing him is a violation of Amarid's Laws. Even I know that."

"That's not entirely true," the long-haired mage said. "The bylaws of the League allow us to use our powers against other mages when doing so is consistent with our oath to serve the people of Tobyn-Ser."

Delsin narrowed his eyes. "I've heard nothing of this."

"It's true," Orris said. "It's one of the things that distinguished the League from the Order. Where we seek to uphold the First Mage's Laws, they look for ways to bend them so that they can justify their crimes."

The younger mage glared at him. "Shut your mouth, traitor!"

"Even if what you're telling me is true, I don't see how killing this man serves the land."

"I'm not going to waste my time explaining it to you," the long-haired mage said. "This is no concern of yours."

"Well," Delsin told him, "I'm making it my concern."

The mage glared at him, his grip on his staff tightening until his knuckles turned white. Then he turned to Orris. "So now we see the extent of your cowardice, Mage. You'd let these men risk their lives to save yours."

"No," Orris said evenly. "I'd die before I allowed you to harm them. But I'm guessing that even the League's bylaws don't allow you to harm innocent people."

"You bastard!" the mage said. And moving so quickly that Orris had no time to defend himself, the League mage swung his staff, striking Orris in the side.

He fell to the ground, gasping for breath, and the League mage moved to hit him again.

But Delsin stepped in front of him. "Enough!" he said. "You've done enough. Now go!"

The mage bared his teeth again, and Orris feared that he would strike Delsin down. But after several moments he looked away. He nodded to the other mages, and they began to walk away. Just as he reached one of the alleyways, however, he looked back at Orris. "This isn't over, Mageling! We'll find you again. You have my word on it."

He turned again, and the League mages walked away.

Orris got to his feet slowly and took a long, deep breath. His side ached, but he didn't think that the man had broken any of his ribs. "Thank you," he said, looking at Delsin. "I'm sure that you saved my life."

"They were wrong to attack you like that. It saddens me that League mages would do such a thing." He glanced at Orris's side. "Are you hurt badly? Do you want us to get you help?"

"No, thank you. I'll be fine."

Delsin nodded. "Very well." He hesitated, and then he looked Orris in the eye. "Why do they call you a traitor?"

The man had saved his life, and he had spoken to Orris a short time ago of honesty and respect. What choice did the mage have? "I was the one who took the outlander back to Lon-Ser. I needed him as a guide and, I thought at the time, as proof that the men who attacked our land came from Lon-Ser." He shrugged. "Erland and his friends saw this as a betrayal, and they branded me a traitor."

Delsin's eyes widened at Orris's admission, but otherwise he offered no outward response. His two companions exchanged a brief look, but they, too, kept their expressions neutral.

They remained silent for what felt like a long time, looking at him appraisingly, as if they had never seen him before.

"It took courage to tell us that," Delsin finally said.

"It took courage to stop those men from killing me. I felt you deserved no less in return."

The man nodded. "Can we escort you to the Great Hall, Hawk-Mage?"

Orris smiled. "That's kind of you, but—"

"Those mages are still out there," Delsin said. "You shouldn't be alone."

He was right, and though Orris felt foolish accepting his offer, he would have been a greater fool to turn it down.

"Very well. Thank you."

They said nothing as they covered the rest of the distance. By the time they reached the Hall, the silence had grown awkward, but still Orris was grateful for their company.

"Thank you, again," the mage said, standing on the steps outside the domed building. It was hardly adequate given what the man had done for him, but he wasn't sure what else to say.

"Arick guard you, Hawk-Mage," Delsin said. "If there are more like you in the Order, I may have to rethink my support of the League."

"Arick guard you as well, Delsin. And your friends."

Orris turned to climb the stairs, but before he could take a step one of the other men called to him. He faced the men again and waited.

"We were told that the outlander died in Lon-Ser," the dark-skinned man said. "Were you the one who killed him?"

Orris sighed. It was an old wound, but it still hurt. He had wanted to save Baram's life, and yet it was his death that had made his defiance of the Order acceptable to some. "The outlander killed himself," he said. "I saw him fall, but I didn't kill him."

The man stared at him, considering this. "At least he died," he said at length. "You saw to that." He stood there for another moment before nodding a farewell and walking away with his friends.

Orris watched them go, stroking Kryssan's chin and shaking his head sadly. It still pained him so, even after so many years. After some time he looked around, as if expecting to see the League mages again. But the street was empty. He rubbed his side gingerly and then climbed the steps to the Great Hall. He had much to tell Jaryd.

Cailin sat staring at her hands which were folded in her lap. The two eagles sat together on the giant stone mantel above the Sage's hearth, as still as statues, eyeing each other warily and yet each seemingly comforted by the other's presence. *Very much like the mages to whom they're bound,* she thought, suppressing a smile.

A part of her still felt that her conversations with Jaryd amounted to a betrayal of the League. It was not that she told him anything that was meant to remain secret. Indeed, she told him nothing that didn't pertain directly to her duties as Eagle-Master. Still, she knew that Erland and the others wouldn't have approved of their conversations had they learned of them. And she didn't enjoy skulking about like a bandit every time she and the Eagle-Sage were supposed to meet.

But she also knew how important it was that she and Jaryd share with each other all that they knew about who their enemy might be and how the mages of the League and the Order were responding to having two eagles in Amarid. And she had to admit that she enjoyed speaking with him. Despite the different colors of their cloaks, they had much in common. She believed that the Eagle-Sage harbored no ill will toward the League, and after spending more time with Alayna, she had come to the same conclusion about her. At times it seemed to Cailin that she had more in common with the Eagle-Sage and his First than she did with anyone in the League. Certainly they shared her belief that war between the two bodies could lead only to disaster. Erland and the others did not.

Which was just what she was on the verge of telling Jaryd.

"Cailin?" he said, looking concerned. "Are you all right?"

She made herself smile. "Yes. Fine. What is it you were asking?" She remembered his question, but she was none too eager to answer it. Once again, as she had been so many times in recent months, she was embarrassed to be wearing a blue cloak.

"I asked you whether Erland had been receptive to the idea of getting all the mages of Tobyn-Ser together to discuss the possible meanings of our bindings. It seems foolish for each body to have the same debate separately. And this might be a way to begin building some trust between the League and the Order."

"Have the mages of the Order already agreed to this?" she asked.

He hesitated. "No, not yet."

"Have you discussed it?"

Again, he seemed to falter. "I've mentioned the possibility to several mages individually. But I was waiting to hear from you before I brought it up before the full membership."

She grinned. "Well then you might want to wait a bit longer."

"He didn't like the idea?"

"I haven't even mentioned it to him." The Sage opened his mouth to say something, but she stopped him with a raised finger. "I've tried to explain this to you before, but you just don't seem to understand. Erland isn't interested in improving relations with the Order. Few mages in the League are. They don't trust you."

"They don't trust me?"

Cailin shook her head. "Not you specifically. All of you, anyone in a green cloak. Since its creation the League has defined itself by its enmity for the Order. It exists to keep watch on you, to prevent the Order from becoming too powerful. You can't expect them to just turn around and embrace the Order as an ally because you and I have bound to eagles."

Jaryd regarded her for several moments. "And what about you?" he asked at last. "You refer to Erland and the others as 'them.' Does that mean that you trust us?"

She shrugged and looked away. "I'm here, aren't I?"

"Yes. But you're not comfortable with that."

"Does it matter?"

"Yes, Cailin, it does."

She looked at him again.

"Alayna and I haven't broached the idea of meeting with the membership of the League because we don't think a majority of the Order mages will agree to do it. Distrust of the League runs as deep in the Order as distrust of the Order does in the League."

"I doubt that," she said. But she was shivering. This was the last thing she had expected to hear.

"All right," Jaryd admitted. "That may be an exaggeration, but not by much. The distrust exists on both sides, and if we're to overcome it, you and I have to be committed to keeping the peace."

"I am."

"But you're still worrying about what Erland and the others would say if they saw you here."

She shifted uncomfortably. "So? Shouldn't I worry? You're telling me to betray the League, and yet I see no willingness on your part to do the same to the Order. You haven't even talked to them about meeting with us, and you're judging me?"

"I'm not asking you to betray anyone, Cailin," he said gently. "And I'm certainly not judging you. I'm just asking you to put your love of the land ahead of your concerns about what Erland is going to think of our meetings. There are those in the Order who feel that I've betrayed their trust, but I don't care. I meet with you anyway, and I report to the Order on each of our discussions. I wouldn't ask you to do anything that I'm not willing to do myself. But," he said with a sigh, "I realize that our circumstances are different, and I won't deny that you're in a more difficult position than I am."

Cailin said nothing. She had heard her voice rising a moment ago. She sounded young and peevish, not at all like an Eagle-Master ought to sound, a fact that was made that much more obvious to her by Jaryd's calm. At that moment, she would have given anything to be elsewhere, and she chose to say nothing rather than embarrass herself further.

He seemed to misunderstand her silence. "I know how hard this must be for you Cailin. I'm not trying to deny that."

She smiled at that and shook her head. "No, Jaryd, I don't think you do know how hard this is. Nobody does. Nobody could." She stood and walked to the mantel. "You know that I grew up hating the Order," she said, gazing up at Rithel. "Everyone knows that." She turned to face him. "But did you know that I hated it so much that I despised myself for binding to my first familiar?" Her eyes stung at the memory. She could see Marcran sitting before her, his brilliant feathers glimmering in the autumn sunshine as they had the day of their binding. "Did you know," she went on, heedless of the tears on her cheeks, "that I refused to use my powers for months because I thought becoming a mage would mean that I had forsaken the memory of my parents?"

She could see the grief in his eyes, and she had to stifle a sob. Right now, she couldn't even bear his sympathy.

"Cailin—"

She shook her head so hard that the tears flew from her face. "Don't. It doesn't matter. There's nothing you can say to make it better." She swallowed, struggling to compose herself. "But don't tell me that you know what I'm feeling, or that you understand how hard this is for me. You don't. Nobody does. Because nobody has ever been through what I've been through."

She knew that she sounded hopelessly self-pitying. But she also knew that it was true.

He opened his hands in a helpless gesture. "I don't know what to say."

"That's all right," she managed, shrugging again. "You don't have to say anything." She wiped her sleeve across her face, drying her tears, and she willed herself to stop crying. "I should go."

"Won't you stay and eat with us? Alayna and Myn should be back soon. I'm sure that Myn would love to meet you."

Cailin shook her head. "Thank you, but I'm meeting someone." It was a lie, but the last thing she needed right then was to spend time in the company of a seven-year-old girl.

Jaryd smiled at her. "I understand."

And she saw that he really did. Was she that obvious?

"Come back soon," he said. "Please."

She nodded, and started toward the door.

But before she reached it, she heard voices coming from outside the chamber. "I'd rather not be seen," she said, turning back to Jaryd again.

"It's probably just Alayna and Myn."

But even as he spoke, they heard a man's voice echoing loudly off the domed ceiling of the Hall.

"I'll go and see," he said.

He stepped past her out into the larger meeting room, closing the door behind him, and she heard him call out a greeting to whoever had come. For a moment she remained where she was, but then, unsure as to why she was doing it, she walked over to the door and pressed her ear against the wood.

". . . Three of them," she heard the stranger say. "All of them from the League. If it hadn't been for some men I had been talking to in the Aerie, they probably would have killed me. As it is, I could use some healing."

"Where?" Jaryd's voice, sounding alarmed.

"My side."

The rustling of cloth. A sharp intake of breath.

"It looks worse than it is," the man said. "I don't think he broke any bones. He hit me with his staff."

"I can see that from the bruise. Weren't you protecting yourself?"

"They had already attacked me with mage-fire. He hit me after the men I mentioned intervened. I wasn't ready for it."

Cailin had heard enough. She pushed the door open and stepped out into the hall. "Who hit you?" she demanded. "Who were these men?"

Jaryd looked up, a startled expression on his face, but Cailin was intent on the other man. He was solidly built, with long yellow hair, dark, angry eyes, and a short, bristling beard. He had taken off his cloak and shirt, and she could see the long dark bruise snaking around his side.

"Eagle-Master Cailin," Jaryd said, "this is Hawk-Mage Orris. He's a good friend and a man who can be trusted."

It took her a moment. "Orris?" she repeated, her eyes flying to Jaryd and then coming back to the burly man. "You're Orris?"

He regarded her warily. "Yes, Eagle-Master."

"You're the one who took the outlander back to Lon-Ser."

She saw something flit across his features, a look of pain, or perhaps longing. It was hard to tell, and it vanished as quickly as it came, leaving only weariness.

"Yes," he said, his voice low. "I'm the one."

She wasn't sure what moved her in that moment. Maybe it was what she had seen in his dark eyes, eyes that weren't so angry after all, or perhaps it was her knowledge of what the mages of her League had done to this man. But she surprised even herself with what she said next. "Then we have you to thank for the peace we now enjoy with Lon-Ser."

It almost seemed that Leora herself had laid her hands on the man's face, his expression brightened so. "I never thought I'd hear that from a League mage," he whispered. "Thank you."

She shook her head. "Please don't thank me. Just accept my apologies for what the League has done to you these past years." She felt her expression harden. "The men who attacked you tonight, did one of them have long hair and a sharp, narrow face?"

"Yes."

"I thought so. His name is Kovet. And if I'm not mistaken, he was with Brinly and Dirss."

Orris gave a small shrug. "I don't know their names, although one of them tried to kill me once before, early this spring, in Tobyn's Wood."

She nodded. "That's Brinly. I heard about your encounter with him. That's why they sent three this time."

He gave a rueful grin. "I assumed as much. I won't be so boastful next time."

She smiled, although she couldn't help but think that her betrayal of the League was now complete. This man before her was the body's most hated enemy, and here she was chatting with him about the League mages who attacked him tonight. If Erland had walked in at that moment, he wouldn't have known which of them to kill first.

"You should also know this, Eagle-Master," the burly mage went on a moment later, eyeing her closely. "Kovet claimed that you gave the order to attack me."

Cailin abruptly felt herself growing hot with rage, as if there was mage-fire rather than blood coursing through her body. But she did her best to hide her anger from the others. This was a matter to be discussed within the Hall of the League, not here among Order mages.

"I swear to you on the memory of my parents, it's not true," was all she said.

Orris smiled. He was actually quite handsome when he wasn't scowling. "I never truly believed him."

Jaryd had called his eagle to him, and was now laying his hands on Orris's side. "From now on, I don't want you traveling in this city alone," the Sage said as he healed the man. "You should always have someone from the Order with you."

"Is that a command, Eagle-Sage?" Orris replied, sounding amused.

Jaryd's face colored, and he grinned. But he also nodded. "Yes, it is. And if you defy me, I'll send Alayna after you." He stepped away from Orris, and Cailin saw that the man's bruise was gone.

"Now that's a threat," Orris said to Cailin, winking at her.

"I heard that!" Alayna stepped into the hall from another room with her daughter in tow. "And if you're foolish enough not to listen to Jaryd, you'll deserve what I do to you."

Orris raised an eyebrow, and Cailin found herself smiling in spite of everything. She was supposed to hate them, all of them. And she couldn't do it.

"All joking aside," Alayna went on a moment later, looking at Jaryd and then Cailin, "the two of you might want to consider the fact that with Orris accompanied by Order mages, and bands of League mages roaming Amarid looking for him, this city could easily turn into a battleground."

"There may be a way to prevent that," Cailin said.

They all looked at her, but she kept her gaze fixed on Orris.

"You said that some men saved you from Kovet and the rest."

"Yes."

"Did they actually witness the attack?"

He nodded.

"Good. Do you think you could find them again?"

The mage hesitated. "Maybe. They were in the Aerie, but I don't know if they were staying there. And I don't know how long they'll be in Amarid. I got the feeling that Delsin was a peddler."

She chewed her lip for a moment. "It may not matter, but just in case, I'll have to move quickly." She glanced at Jaryd. "I should be going," she said for the second time that night. "I hope we can speak again soon."

"So do I."

"Before you go," Orris said, "Delsin and his companions wanted to know if anyone from either the League or the Order had been in touch with the Keepers. It struck me as a good question."

Jaryd exhaled through his teeth. "It is a good question, but I have to admit that I have few ties to the Keepers. Leaders of the Order have seldom been popular with the Gods' Children."

"I may be able to help with that, too," Cailin said.

Jaryd smiled. "For someone who professes to be an ineffective leader, you certainly seem to be shouldering a good deal of responsibility. Thank you, Eagle-Master."

Cailin felt herself blush. She turned away and whistled for Rithel. But before the eagle reached her, Cailin felt a tugging on her cloak. She looked down and saw Jaryd and Alayna's daughter standing before her. She was a beautiful girl, with long dark hair like her mother's and grey eyes like Jaryd's.

"Are you the other Eagle-Sage?" she asked.

Cailin glanced up at Jaryd, feeling awkward. Children made her uncomfortable. "Yes, I am."

"What's your name?"

"Cailin."

The girl continued to look at her, and after a few seconds, Cailin cleared her throat. "Uh . . . what's your name?"

"I'm Myn. Do you think that you and my daddy are going to have a war?"

"Myn," Jaryd said, coming forward and placing a hand on the child's shoulder, "that's not really a fair question, Love."

Myn twisted her head around to look up at him. "But you told me what eagles mean, and I just thought that I should ask her if she thinks you're going to be enemies."

The Eagle-Sage opened his mouth to say something more, but Cailin stopped him with a raised hand and a shake of her head.

"It's all right." She looked down at Myn and smiled. "The answer is no. I don't think your daddy and I are going to be enemies. Actually it's too late for that." She looked up at Jaryd and then glanced back at Orris and Alayna as well. "We're already friends."

16

Thinking back on my recent correspondence I realize that most of what I have written will have left you with the impression that the goods sent here from Lon-Ser have brought nothing but heartache and turmoil. This is not the case. Many in Tobyn-Ser have come to admire and enjoy the things you send us. Children now play with toys the likes of which their parents could not even have imagined. Men and women enjoy tools that make meal preparation, farming, and countless other tasks far simpler than they have ever been. Chores that once took hours to complete now take only minutes, thanks in great part to the items that have come to us from Lon-Ser.

From all that you have told me, and all that I saw during my time in your land, I know that the things you have sent us are primitive by your standards. Indeed, I would guess that you are prohibited by law from sending us more advanced items. It doesn't matter. To us, these tools and toys are marvels, and despite all the difficult changes that have come to our land in recent years, I believe that most of my people would now be reluctant to do without them.

—Hawk-Mage Orris to Melyor i Lakin, Sovereign and Bearer of Bragor-Nal, Spring, God's Year 4633.

Lessa was walking as quickly as she could, the muscles in her arms burning with the weight of the two water buckets until she thought that she would have to drop them. But her house was only a few painful strides away, and with the cold rain stinging her eyes and soaking through her clothes, she couldn't bear to stop. Reaching the single step that led into her home, she finally put down the pails and slowly straightened her cramping fingers. Then she pushed open the door and hoisted the buckets into the house one at a time.

Entering the house and shutting the door behind her, she immediately noticed that the common room was far too dark. *The fire!* She spun toward the hearth and, as she had feared, saw that the fire had died again. There wasn't even any smoke rising from the rain-soaked wood.

"Fist of the God!"

Adlyr and the boys were still at the smithy, but it was getting late. At this rate, supper wouldn't be ready until well after dark.

She pushed her damp hair back from her brow and knelt before the hearth, shivering slightly with the cold. She still had plenty of twigs and birch bark with which to light the wood, but there wasn't even a spark left in this fire. It had been Telar's day to bring in the wood, but in his excitement at going with his father and older brother to the smithy, he had forgotten. The logs were soaked from the rain. Lessa was going to have to start over completely. She closed her eyes and exhaled heavily, and then reached for her flint.

"Where's a mage when you need one?" she muttered under her breath, as she prepared to strike the stone.

She paused on that thought, glancing over at the small box that still sat on the floor beside the woodpile, just where Adlyr had first put it over a fortnight ago. The flamesticks from Lon-Ser. Adlyr had used them a number of times now to light his pipe. But Lessa had yet to even touch them. It wasn't that she disapproved, although she knew of several people in Greenbough who did. She just was not sure that she wanted to use them yet, and, to be honest, she was more than a bit afraid of them. They smelled strange, and they flared suddenly and quite brightly when struck against stone.

But she was cold, and it was growing late, and she had already tried to light the fire with her flint four times this day.

She leaned over and picked up the box, hearing the flamesticks rattle around inside. Her heart was pounding, and her hand might have trembled slightly as she lifted the lid. Even now, before she had lit one of them, she could smell them, acrid and yet not entirely unpleasant. She had watched Adlyr closely when he lit his pipe and so she knew to grip the stick tightly and scrape it along the stone of the hearth. But still, when the bright fire burst from the stick's yellow top, she gave a small gasp and dropped the stick on the floor. Breathing hard, she picked it up immediately, but then realized that she had forgotten to prepare the kindling. Reluctantly, she blew out the flame and began piling the bark and twigs beneath the damp logs, carefully hiding the wasted stick within her pile. Adlyr was a kindly man and patient, but he would have been angry with her for wasting one of the sticks. They had been costly, and he hadn't gotten many of them.

Taking a second stick from the box, she again swiped it against the stone, this time fighting the urge to drop the stick when the flame appeared and the blue smoke swirled up to the ceiling. She held it to the kindling and couldn't help but smile as the twigs and bark caught fire and began to crackle.

For several minutes Lessa added more kindling, until she was certain that the flames had taken hold and the room glowed again with firelight. The logs continued to smoke and sputter from the dampness, but soon steam was rising from the water for her stew and the room started to grow warmer. *Perhaps these advanced goods are not so bad,* she thought with another smile. *I could grow accustomed to this.*

She crossed to the eating table and began to cut roots and greens for the stew, but after only a short time, she heard a knock at the door. Wiping her hands on the front of her dress, she pulled the door open.

It had stopped raining, but she hardly noticed. For there standing before her, was a woman with long brown hair that was still wet, and pale grey eyes that had a somewhat wild look to them, as if what she looked at and what she saw were not the same. She carried a staff with a bright blue ceryll at its top, but she wore no cloak, indicating to Lessa that she was a free mage. However, there was no bird on the woman's shoulder, and Lessa wondered if she was unbound.

"I am Hawk-Mage Tammen," the woman said. "I was traveling through the wood and noticed your village."

"Greetings, Hawk-Mage," Lessa replied, feeling awkward. "I'm honored by this meeting. How may I help you?"

"What is this place?"

"This is Greenbough, Hawk-Mage, a free town. Are you with the Movement?"

The mage hesitated, but only for an instant. "Yes, I am. There are several of us in this area, all of us stopping at towns like yours to encourage you to join the Movement."

"I see," Lessa said with a nod. "If you'd like I can arrange for you to speak with the village elders. They'd—"

"No. That won't be necessary. You can tell them I was here. That will suffice."

Lessa stared at the mage, not quite believing what she had heard. "I know little of your Movement, Hawk-Mage, and even less about the politics of the Order and League. I'm not certain that I'd be the best person to speak to the elders for you."

Tammen smiled, although the unnerving look in her eyes remained. "You'll be fine. Can I impose upon you for some food? This body—" She stopped herself and smiled again. "I'm hungry. And since I lost my familiar, I haven't had a decent meal."

"Of course, Hawk-Mage. I'm still preparing supper, but you're welcome to eat with us."

"No," the mage said again, even more quickly this time. "I can't stay that long. I should be moving on. Just some cheese or dried meat would be fine."

Lessa frowned for a moment, but then nodded. "Very well, Hawk-Mage. I'll see what we have. But I'm afraid it won't be much. You might want to check with the merchant in the village commons. He's likely to have plenty."

"Thank you. I'm sure whatever you can spare will be sufficient."

Lessa stepped back into her home, feeling uncomfortable and keenly aware of the mage's presence just behind her. It was growing dark outside, and Lessa had yet to light any candles. The only light in the house came from the small windows in the common room and the flickering flames in the hearth. She wished Adlyr and the boys were home.

A year ago she would have had little to offer the mage, but with the arrival in Tobyn-Ser of covered glass containers from Lon-Ser, she had two blocks of cheese, and several pieces of dried fruit, in addition to the dry breads she normally kept on hand.

"Here you go, Hawk-Mage," she said, handing Tammen one of the pieces of cheese, and all of the dried fruit. "I wish I had more to offer, but I have two growing boys, and more often than not, I have even less in my pantry."

Lessa smiled, but the mage offered no reaction.

"This will do," she said. "My thanks."

The woman turned to go.

"You're certain you won't stay for supper?"

"Quite certain," the mage answered, shaking her head. She cast an anxious glance toward the window. "It's getting late. I must find a place to pass the night."

"We haven't much room, but you're welcome to stay here."

Tammen faced Lessa again and smiled, but there was a brittleness to her expression, as if she were desperate to be on her way. Her eyes appeared even more wild than before. "You're very kind. But I can't stay."

Lessa forced a smile as well. "I'm sorry to hear that." A lie. She was profoundly relieved. She had never met a mage like this one. Indeed, it occurred to Lessa that being rendered unbound might have driven the mage mad. She had never heard of such a thing happening before, but it was certainly possible. Mages were said to be quite close to their birds, and of course, those who were unbound had Theron's Curse to worry about. Tammen appeared quite young—perhaps too young to cope with her grief and her fear. What other explanation was there for her strange behavior?

The mage put the food into a pouch that hung on her belt and started once more toward the door.

"What would you like me to tell the elders?" Lessa asked.

Tammen stopped again, just on the threshold of the door. Lessa saw her ball her fists for just an instant, before she glanced back over her shoulder, the same thin smile on her face.

"Tell them that the Movement needs all the support it can get. They should do everything they can to convince other towns in this part of the wood to join us. Tell them as well that at some time in the near future, the leaders of all the free towns will be contacted and told what they should do. Can you remember all that?"

Lessa nodded.

"Good. And now I really must be going."

Without another word, the mage hastened out of the house and disappeared from view.

Lessa hurried to one of the windows and saw Tammen striding quickly away from the village and back into the shadows of Tobyn's Wood. She soon lost sight of the mage, although she was able to track the woman's progress by the glowing blue ceryll she carried. And just before the mage vanished entirely, Lessa thought that she caught a glimpse of a glowing yellow form on Tammen's shoulder. An instant later, she could see nothing of the mage at all, and she was forced to wonder if it had just been an illusion, a trick played on her eyes by the light from her fire and the uneven glass of the window. No doubt that was what it was. It had to be. Except that the form had looked just like a hawk.

She shivered slightly and realized that the door was still open. She walked to it intending to pull it closed, but as she did she heard Adlyr's voice and the laughter of her boys.

"And dinner's not even cooking yet!" she said under her breath.

She rushed to the fire and placed another damp log on it, and then she returned to the table and resumed her cutting. She paused briefly, as her men drew closer, and glanced out the window, wondering if she could catch another glimpse of the mage. But seeing nothing, she turned her attention to dinner. It was going to be so very late.

"With all due respect, Eldest," Linnea said, her voice rising, "all your assurances and apologies cannot change the fact that people have died. For the first time in the history of this land, men and women of Tobyn-Ser have perished as a direct result of the Temple's actions. Someone must answer for that."

Brevyl shifted uncomfortably in his chair, but gave no other indication that he was alarmed by what he was hearing. "I've already told you, Linnea: if you seek someone to blame for this unfortunate incident, I suggest you look to the free mages who instigated the confrontation in the first place." He opened his meaty hands, as if in a plea. "These deaths are on their heads. Our men merely sought to protect themselves and the woodsmen they were hired to guard."

Linnea struggled to keep her temper in check. She had been hearing the same nonsense from Keepers throughout eastern Tobyn-Ser. Brevyl had been all too effective in conveying his message to all the land's Temples and keeping his supporters in line. Which was why she was back here, in this chamber that had once been hers, arguing with the man who had succeeded her as Eldest of the Gods. Normally, she and Brevyl avoided each other, which was not always easy, given that she still lived in the main Temple of the Children of the Gods. But on this day she had sought him out, swallowing her pride to request an audience. She knew that she would have no success turning the others against him, so she had little choice but to try to change his mind. And already she knew that she was going to fail at this as well.

"The mages were there at the request of Prannai's people," she said through gritted teeth. "And if your men hadn't been carrying those weapons, they would never have attacked."

"Linnea," he said, smiling at her as if she were simple, or a child, "you don't really believe that do you? You, of all people? These free mages are as bad as the Order. They may even be worse. You know what it's like dealing with them. It wasn't that long ago that you were sitting where I am." His smile deepened. It was the third time in this discussion that he had said something to remind her that he was now her superior. "To be honest," he went on a moment later, "I'm surprised to hear you saying such things."

"As am I, Brevyl."

"You see? You're just a bit out of sorts. With all that's been going on recently I'm not at all surprised. We all are to some extent."

She shook her head. "That's not what I meant. I'm surprised, because I never thought I'd have to confront an Eldest of this Temple on such a matter. You've disgraced us, Brevyl."

The Eldest launched himself out of his chair, his round face turning crimson. "How dare you!" he said. He was standing over her, holding a rigid, trembling finger just inches from her face. "I am Eldest of the Gods! No one speaks to me that way! Not even you!"

"Perhaps that's the problem," Linnea said, refusing to be cowed. "You have all of the Keepers so afraid of you that no one is willing to question any of your decisions."

"My decisions don't need to be questioned!"

"Don't be ridiculous, Brevyl," she said, sounding, she knew, as condescending as he had a few moments before. "You're not perfect. Don't let your title and that pretty robe of yours convince you otherwise." He started to say something, but she stopped him with a raised hand. "Hear me out. I know a great deal about the dangers of believing oneself to be infallible. Every day you're told that you speak with the tongue of the gods, that you are the instrument of Arick on this earth. And hearing this, it's easy to forget that the gods are imperfect, just as we are. Lon and Tobyn bickered like children, Leora, in her vanity, fueled their rivalry, and Arick, in a fit of pique, sundered the land."

He turned away from her and walked to the chamber's only window. "I'm no child, Linnea," he said, his voice sounding tight. "I know the gods; I daresay I'm as familiar as you are with their glories and their shortcomings."

"Then pay heed to what they tell you."

He faced her again, his dark eyes narrowing. "Meaning what?"

"You make mistakes, Brevyl, just as the rest of us do. And lately you've made more than your share."

"I don't see it that way."

"Then you're blind. People are dead, Brevyl, the land is scarred, there's talk of civil war."

"That last is certainly not my fault! You can't blame me for the fact that mages are binding to eagles!"

Linnea shook her head. The man was hopeless. "I'm not trying to, Eldest. I'm just pointing out to you that these are dangerous times, and anything that the Temple does to heighten that danger must be questioned."

Brevyl stared at her for several seconds, his expression thoughtful. Perhaps she had been too quick to judge him.

Perhaps not. "You're right: these are dangerous times. But am I to be blamed for wanting the Temple to take advantage of current circumstances?" He returned to his chair and pressed his thick fingers together. "Isn't it my responsibility, as Eldest of the Gods, to do all that I can to assure that the Temple emerges from this coming crisis in the strongest position possible? Would you have done otherwise, Linnea?" he asked, raising an eyebrow.

She hesitated, and Brevyl grinned.

"Of course not," he said, sounding pleased with himself. "It's only now, after you've relinquished power, that you start to think this way." He leaned forward. "It's understandable really: you haven't much to fill your days anymore, and that can't be easy for someone who was once the most powerful person in the Temple. But don't expect me to take your criticisms seriously, Linnea. You'd find fault with me no matter what I did. If I was doing what you suggest right now, you'd be in here wondering why I wasn't arming the guards and harvesting more of the forest."

"That's not true!" she said. But she could hear how defensive she sounded, and she knew that she had no hope of convincing him. He had made up his mind about the weapons, and he had made up his mind about her.

"Will you at least allow me to raise these issues at the next Assembly of Keepers?" she asked him, resignation in her voice. She knew before he answered what he would say.

"We've a long time to wait until the Autumn Assembly, Linnea. I can't even begin to imagine what we might be discussing." He smiled at her in a way that told her all she needed to know. "But if we have time for it, I won't stop you from broaching the subject."

Brevyl glanced toward his desk before facing her again, the same thin smile on his lips, and Linnea knew that their meeting was over.

"Forgive me," he said, "but I have a great deal to do this afternoon. I'm sure you understand."

"Of course."

Linnea forced herself out of her chair, wincing at the pain. The illness was in her bones now, like an animal gnawing its way through her body. Despite all the assurances she still offered to Cailin, she knew that she had little time left.

"Are you all right, Eldest?" Brevyl asked, with unconvincing concern. "Can I get you anything?"

I'm dying, you bastard. Can't you see that? Hasn't it been clear all this time? "No, Brevyl. Thank you. I'm fine. Just a little stiff from sitting too long."

"I'm glad to hear it. We'd hate for anything to happen to you. You're a rarity in the Temple, Linnea: an Eldest who relinquished her power rather than carrying it to her deathbed. I can't recall the last time that happened. None of us can."

Linnea stared at him, ignoring her pain for the moment. "What is it you're trying to tell me, Brevyl?"

He opened his hands and raised his eyebrows in what must have been an attempt to look innocent. The effort was wasted. "I'm merely saying that you occupy a special place in all of our hearts."

"And?"

He hesitated, but only for an instant. "Well, it does make one wonder why you did it? Especially since you seem so eager to criticize all that I do."

Linnea took a long breath. She had no desire to share her reasons with this man, but he was right. She had no right to criticize him in light of the decision she had made. He was Eldest now, and though she believed that he was bringing ruin to the Temple and, potentially, to the land as well, it was not her place to judge him. At least not openly.

"I did it," she said at last, "because I grew weary of the bickering and the politics, and because I wanted to have a little time to enjoy my life before . . ." She paused and swallowed. Strange that she should manage to be so stoic around Cailin, but that talking to this man made her heart ache with grief for herself. "I had a premonition that I hadn't much time left. So I stepped down."

Brevyl was gaping at her, an appalled look on his round face. And once more, Linnea was forced to wonder if she had judged the man too harshly.

"Do you mean—?" He closed his mouth. Blinked. "Do you mean to tell me that you're dying?"

"Yes," she said, her voice even.

"Have you seen the Temple's healers?"

She actually laughed. "The healers gave up long ago."

"And what about Cailin?"

The question surprised her. Brevyl and she had rarely spoken of the young mage, and when they had, he had made it quite clear that he disapproved of Linnea's relationship with her. Now that he was Eldest, he had suggested during one of their more heated discussions of the topic, it was improper for her to meet with any members of either the League or the Order, even Cailin. Naturally, she had chosen to defy him, and this had only deepened their mutual distrust. But after some time, Brevyl let the matter drop.

"What about Cailin?" Linnea asked cautiously.

"Can't she heal you?"

"She's offered to try. I declined."

"But why?" he asked, his eyes widening. "If she—"

She averted her gaze again. His question struck her as far too similar to those she continued to ask herself. There had been a time when Cailin might have saved her, when the power of the Mage-Craft might have been a match for the animal inside her. But how did one who had spent her life opposing the Order on behalf of the gods accept such healing with a clear conscience.

"It's my time, Brevyl," she said at last. "Even if Cailin could help me, I'm not sure I'd want her to. Arick and Duclea have called me to their side. Who am I to keep them waiting?" She forced herself to smile. "Your concern surprises me," she said, trying to keep her tone light. "I'd have thought you'd be glad to be getting rid of me."

"That's an ugly thought, Linnea," Brevyl said, looking hurt. "It does an injustice to both the Temple and me."

She lowered her gaze. She had never been very good with people, which was why the bond she had somehow managed to forge with Cailin was so special to her. "You're right, Eldest. Please forgive me."

Brevyl waved off her apology with a dismissive gesture. "I really have much to do," he said, his tone gruff.

He wasn't very subtle, and yet she lingered, suddenly unwilling to leave him after such an exchange. "I'm truly sorry if I've hurt you, Brevyl. That wasn't my intention."

"Does it matter, Linnea? It seems a fitting way to end our conversation, regardless of your intent."

He sounded surprisingly sad, and Linnea considered saying something more. But the distance between them was too great to be bridged now. A year ago, perhaps. But not now.

Instead, she nodded, and then, without another word, she left him and started back toward her modest quarters at the far end of the Temple grounds.

She was tired, and she moved stiffly across the stone courtyard in the middle of the grounds, feeling each step as if it were a hammer on her tender bones.

I need to rest, she told herself, smiling grimly at the double meaning of the thought. Soon, she told herself. Very soon.

But when she reached her quarters, she found Cailin waiting for her.

The mage rose from the corner chair when Linnea opened the door, a smile on her youthful face.

"I let myself in. I hope you don't mind, but I didn't want any-one . . ." She trailed off, her smile giving way to a look of concern, and then fear.

"You look terrible," she said coming forward to help Linnea into the room. "Come and sit down."

"I'm fine, my dear," Linnea told her, hearing the lie in her own words. "Just a bit tired."

"Where have you been?" Cailin asked, obviously unconvinced.

"Speaking with Brevyl."

"About the weapons?"

"Yes."

"And it didn't go well."

Linnea allowed herself a wan smile. "To say the least."

"Have you told him how sick you are?"

"I did today," Linnea said, lowering herself slowly onto her bed. "I thought that giving him the good news would smooth things along. But it didn't work."

At least this time the joke got a laugh, although it brought tears as well.

"I hate him," Cailin said, returning to the chair and dabbing at her eyes with the sleeve of her cloak. "Why couldn't he be the one to get sick?"

Linnea frowned. "That doesn't become you, Cailin. You know better than to wish such a thing on anyone."

The mage gave a rueful grin. "Yes, Eldest."

They sat in silence for several moments, Linnea with her eyes closed feeling her pain recede slowly, like an ocean tide.

"So what brings you to the Temple?" she finally asked, opening her eyes and facing Cailin. "Are you here as Eagle-Master or just as Cailin?"

"Both, actually. I wanted to see how you were doing, but I also needed to ask you some questions. Hearing about your conversation with Brevyl, however, tells me most of what I need to know."

"About what?"

"About whether the Temples can be persuaded to stop arming their woodsmen and, if possible, to cease their cutting of the forest altogether."

The Eldest shook her head. "I doubt it. I've spoken with Keepers throughout Hawksfind Wood, the eastern halves of Tobyn's Wood and Tobyn's Plain, and even a few on the northern edge of Phelan Spur—"

"No wonder you look so tired! Linnea you're in no con—"

"Let me finish," Linnea said. "None of the Keepers I've spoken to is willing to defy Brevyl. And Brevyl made it clear to me today that he has no intention of backing down."

"Doesn't he realize how close this land is to a civil war?" Cailin asked. She pushed herself out of the chair and started to pace the floor of the small room. "Doesn't he see the danger?"

"Yes, he does. But to him, that danger justifies what he's doing. He sees the League and the Order at each other's throats, he sees the free mages aligning themselves with the People's Movement, and he feels that the Temples should be able to defend themselves as well."

Cailin halted and stared at her, a look of incredulity on her face. "You almost sound like you agree with him."

"I wouldn't go that far," Linnea said. "But I do understand him. And I think that if I was still Eldest—and if you and I weren't friends—I might be following the same course."

"Linnea! You can't be serious!"

"Perhaps I wouldn't be cutting so many trees, but think about it, Child! The Mage-Craft and those who wield it have been enemies of the Temples for a thousand years. And now, suddenly, we face not one enemy, but three. Granted, none is as powerful as the Order was when it was united, but still, we are surrounded by foes, and, as you say, Tobyn-Ser may be on the verge of civil war."

"So is that what I am? An enemy?"

"Come now, Cailin. You're being childish. Of course you're not an enemy. But if you're to be lead the League, you must have the ability to view the world as it's seen by those who would oppose you, be it mages of the Order, free mages, or even Keepers of the Temple. And what I'm telling you is that, though I disagree with what Brevyl is doing, I under-stand it. Can you see the difference?"

For several seconds, Cailin merely glared at her. The mage's cheeks were bright red, almost as if she had been slapped on either side of her face, and her blue eyes blazed defiantly. But then she took a long breath and nodded. She might even have smiled. "Yes, Eldest," she said at last. "I see the difference."

"Good."

"But that still leaves us without a solution."

Linnea conceded the point with a slight bob of her head. "Do you have any news? What of Erland in all of this? And the Eagle-Sage?"

"Nothing has changed with Erland. And for that matter, nothing has really changed with the Order either, although the Eagle-Sage and I seem to agree on a good deal, far more than I ever expected we would."

"You trust him?"

"Yes," Cailin said, surprising Linnea with the surety of her reply. "I trust him and his friends more than I do most members of the League."

Linnea raised an eyebrow. "Are you considering changing the color of your cloak?"

Cailin smiled. "No. I think I can do more good in the League. What I said before about Erland wasn't really true. Something has changed. He and some of his friends got careless and may have violated the bylaws of the League."

Linnea looked at her keenly. "Can you prove this?"

"Yes, but it might take the testimony of an Order mage. And not just any mage: the one who took the outlander back to Lon-Ser."

Linnea gaped at her. "Would the mages of the League even allow him into their hall?"

The young woman shrugged. "There were other witnesses, but I haven't found them yet."

"I think you'd better."

"Probably," Cailin said with a wry grin.

Linnea tried to stifle a yawn, but failed. She smiled apologetically.

Cailin leaned forward and squeezed her hand. "I should go."

Normally Linnea would have insisted that she stay, but today she didn't even have the energy for that. "Come back soon, all right?"

"Of course."

Cailin stood and stepped to the door. As she placed her hand on the door handle however, Linnea stopped her, calling her name. The mage turned to face her again.

"I'm sorry I failed with Brevyl," the Eldest said weakly. "I'm sorry I couldn't stop him."

Cailin smiled reassuringly, although the expression in her eyes remained grim. "There's no need to apologize, Linnea. We'll just have to find another way."

The Eagle-Master returned to Amarid by late afternoon, but not before leaving Rithel, her cloak, and her staff in a remote clearing in Hawksfind Wood. She needed help, but she had to be circumspect in how she got it, both for her own sake and that of the person whose assistance she needed.

The tavern he was said to frequent sat on a narrow byway only a short walk from the Hall of the League. It was possible, she knew, that other League mages would be there as well, and would recognize her even without her cloak and ceryll. But she had to take that chance. There seemed little chance that he would come to her in the forest again.

Checking herself once more to make certain there was nothing upon her that made her appear to be anything more than a poor young woman, Cailin entered the tavern.

The barkeep called to her almost immediately, just as she had expected.

"Hey, you! We don't serve children in here! You trying to get me closed down?"

Cailin suppressed a smile. "I'm not here for a drink," she said, as meekly as she could. "I'm looking for my uncle. Please! I need to speak with him! It won't take but a moment."

The man frowned and looked around the room, which was almost empty. "All right," he muttered. "But make it quick."

"Yes, sir. Thank you."

She hurried to the back of the tavern, scanning the dimly lit tables until she spotted Stepan sitting against the back wall, reading from a scroll. She walked to his table, sat across from him, and cleared her throat quietly.

The Owl-Master looked up at her. "Yes? Is there something—?"

He stopped, his eyes widening, and then he glanced nervously around the tavern. "Are you insane?" he whispered. "Do you know what Erland will do if he finds me talking to you?"

"Nobody will recognize me without my cloak, Stepan. The barkeep thinks I'm your niece."

"My niece?" he repeated, his voice rising.

"Besides, what can Erland do? I'm Eagle-Master, you're a member of the League. We're not allowed to talk?"

"You know what I mean. Now leave me alone."

She shook her head. "No, not yet. I'll go in a minute, but first I need your help."

"You must be joking."

"Do I look like I'm joking?"

He stared at her for several moments, his pale face looking even more ashen than usual. "All right," he finally said, his eyes flicking around the tavern again. "What is it you want?"

"You heard about Kovet, Dirss, and Brinly?"

He let out a short laugh, though his expression remained grim. "Fools," he said. "It's bad enough that they tried to kill Orris here in the city, with every League mage and every Order mage within shouting distance of where they attacked him. But to threaten those men . . ." He shook his head. "What a disaster."

"You see a disaster," Cailin said. "I see an opportunity."

"I don't understand."

"These men violated Amarid's Laws and our bylaws, and they did so following Erland's orders."

"You can't prove that."

"I don't have to, Stepan. Everybody knows it. He's been obsessed with Orris for seven years. We all know that Kovet and the others were doing what Erland wanted them to do. If I wanted to, I could have them expelled from the League, and I could use this incident to embarrass Erland enough to ensure that he'd never lead the League again."

"You wouldn't," Stepan breathed.

"I would, but I don't want to. You were right in what you told me that night in the forest. For the good of the League, I need to find a way to lead us without weakening us. And as much as I hate to admit it, that means keeping Erland's standing intact."

He raised an eyebrow and nodded. "I'm impressed. I wasn't sure you were listening." He regarded her for another moment, as if weighing his options. "So what is it you want from me?" he finally asked.

"I need you to find the men Kovet threatened. I haven't been able to, and you know this city far better than I do."

"But why do you need them? You just said—"

"I said that I would try to do this without destroying Erland. But I need him to believe that I can destroy him, and in order to do that, I need to be able to prove just what happened that night."

His eyes narrowed. "How do I know that you won't turn around and use these men to destroy Erland after all?"

"You don't, Stepan," she said, not bothering to mask her anger. "You're just going to have to trust me. You're the one who came to me and told me that I needed to find more subtle ways to assert myself within the League. Well, that's what I'm trying to do. One way or another, I'm going to lead us through this war. Now you can help me do this quietly, by allowing me to go to Erland with all the information I need to win his cooperation, or you can force me to take this fight to the entire Conclave, in which case Erland will be humiliated."

They stared at each other across the table, neither of them looking away.

"What if you can't convince him?" Stepan asked at last. "You know how stubborn he can be."

"If he believes that I know where those men are, he won't have any choice but to back down."

The Owl-Master smiled sadly. "You don't know him very well. He doesn't like to give in under any circumstance."

"Actually, I know him better than you think. Find those men for me, Stepan. I'll do the rest."

He hesitated, but only briefly. "All right. Give me a day or two."

She smiled, surprised by how relieved she felt. "Thank you."

"Don't thank me. As I've told you before, anything I do on your behalf, I do for Tobyn-Ser, the League, and Erland."

"Yes, I know," she said. "And as I've told you before, I'm grateful anyway."

The older man smiled at that. "I hope this works. Truly, I do."

She stood and started to walk away.

"Arick guard you," he called after her. "Niece."

17

I do not know how much news you receive of events in Lon-Ser other than those tidings that I send. Before your journey to my land you received none; this much you have told me. But with merchants traveling regularly between Tobyn-Ser and Lon-Ser that may have changed. For all I know, you had learned of Shivohn's death long before you heard of it from me.

It is for this reason that I send this brief note, which so quickly follows my last one. Much is happening here that I cannot yet explain to you, but I want you to know that not all of what you hear from others about events in Bragor-Nal is true. At least for now, believe nothing unless you hear it from Jibb, Premel, or me. I apologize for being so mysterious. I hope that you will trust me when I say that it is absolutely necessary.

Arick guard you, Orris. Always remember that I love you.

> —Melyor i Lakin, Sovereign and
> Bearer of Bragor-Nal to Hawk-Mage
> Orris, Day 4, Week 7, Spring, Year
> 3068.

Honid wouldn't have been his choice. In fact, Jibb could think of at least three other Nal-Lords in Dob's Dominion who were smarter, braver, and more skilled with a weapon. But it hadn't been his decision to make; Melyor had left it to Dob, and Dob had chosen Honid.

In at least one way it did make sense. Honid controlled the Second Realm, which bordered Melyor's old Realm, the Fourth. It was familiar territory for all of them, but not so familiar as to raise Marar's suspicions. Dob had also gone out of his way to assure Melyor and Jibb that Honid was the most honorable Nal-Lord in the Dominion, and though Jibb wouldn't have thought it possible a few years ago, Dob's word on such matters now carried a good deal of weight with both of them.

Still, Honid? He didn't like it. Of course, he didn't like the entire plan, but that was another matter.

"You're awfully quiet," Melyor said, sitting beside him in the long, black carrier as it sped northward along the Upper. "Something on your mind?"

Jibb shrugged and opened his mouth to reply. But noticing Premel, who was sitting in one of the seats across from them, he thought better of it. "No," he said in a low voice. "Nothing at all."

Premel stared at him for a moment before shifting in his seat to face the window.

"All right," Melyor said in an offhand way, "but if you're going to be sullen and moody, this is going to be a very boring day."

"Boring?" Jibb repeated, not believing what he was hearing. "Are you kidding me? We're going into the quads to stage—"

He stopped, feeling his face grow hot. She was laughing at him, as she always seemed to be at times like these.

She shook her head slowly, a smile lingering on her face. Why did she have to be so beautiful? "You have got to stop being so serious all the time," she told him. She glanced at Premel. "He's always been like this: so earnest, so duty-bound."

Not always, he wanted to say. *Only since I've been with you. Only since you put your life in my hands.* But he kept silent. He knew what she was trying to do, and he was determined not to let it work. He and Premel had said all that they needed to say in the lifter the other day.

Premel appeared to feel the same way. He laughed politely at the Sovereign's remark, but he made no effort to prolong the exchange. And after another moment, he turned back to the window.

Melyor looked at them both, and then, pressing her lips into a thin line, she shook her head again. "Fine," she muttered at last. "I don't care what you do. As long as SovSec continues to function up to my expectations, I really couldn't care less."

Jibb glanced at Premel again, but the guard kept his gaze fixed on the Nal as it hurtled by outside the carrier. The welt on Premel's cheek had begun to fade, but it was still quite noticeable, and seeing it, Jibb couldn't help but grimace. He knew that it had raised eyebrows among the men, and Melyor, who had no doubt as to how it had gotten there, had been infuriated. Jibb realized how stupid it had been—if he was going to hit the man, better to punch him in the gut, where no one could see. Not that he cared about humiliating Premel, but he couldn't afford to put Melyor's safety at risk by alerting other traitors to the possibility that something was amiss. He had apologized to her profusely, and she, of course had forgiven him. But he couldn't stop worrying that the damage might already have been done.

They rode without speaking for what seemed like an eternity, all of them staring out their windows. After some time, Jibb leaned his forehead against the cool glass and closed his eyes, trying without success to sleep.

"You're both clear on what we'll be doing?" Melyor asked, abruptly ending the silence.

"I'm clear on it," Premel said, as Jibb turned to face them. "But I don't like it."

Jibb looked at him quickly, then looked away. He had wanted to say the same thing.

"That's too bad," the Sovereign said. "We're doing this my way, whether you like it or not. If it wasn't for you, we wouldn't be in this mess in the first place."

Premel's face colored, and he turned toward the window again without offering a reply.

"Can you believe him?" she asked Jibb.

The general cleared his throat. "Actually," he began, feeling awkward. "I'm not sure about this either."

"Great," Melyor said. "You haven't said two words to each other in days, and the only thing you can agree on is that I'm doing this wrong."

Jibb shook his head. "I didn't say that. Regardless of what I think of the plan itself, I'm not sure that Honid and his men are up to this."

"Dob says that Honid is as trustworthy a man as there is in the entire Dominion."

"That may be true," Premel said. "But we need someone who's more than just honest." Again his face reddened, and he looked to Jibb for help. He was really in no position to be arguing this point.

"I think what Premel means, is that Honid and his men are going to have to be extremely precise with their thrower fire, and that while neither of us questions their loyalty, they may not be good enough with their weapons to make this work."

"Exactly," Premel added.

Melyor looked at them both, as if weighing what they were telling her. "Well," she finally said. "I guess that's why I brought the two of you along."

"The two of us may not be enough," Jibb said. "I've only got one good arm, and he's—" He clamped his mouth shut.

"He's what, Jibb?"

"He's a traitor," Premel said, completing the thought.

"And are you intending to betray us again?"

"No, Sovereign, I'm not," Premel said. "But no matter what assurances I give you, you'd be foolish to trust me, particularly under these
conditions."

She regarded him for a moment before facing Jibb again. "Is that what
you were going to say?"

"Essentially, yes."

She nodded and gazed out her window. They were drawing near the
enormous glass buildings of the Farm. It wouldn't be long now.

"I'm not worried about Honid and his men," she said after a lengthy
silence. "I trust Dob's judgment on this. I'm not worried about your arm
either, Jibb. I'd trust you to protect me even if both your arms were use-
less. And maybe I'm crazy, but I don't think that Premel will betray me
again." She shook her head. "No, none of that worries me." She faced
them again, her face looking pale. "What does worry me is the fact that
the two of you aren't speaking, because if something goes wrong, and we
need to act quickly, that could cost all of us our lives. So you two can
spend the time we have left considering how you might live with yourselves and with each other if your stubbornness and your pride get me
killed."

Once more she turned away from them, and Jibb found that he and
Premel were staring at each other, their eyes locked.

"You remember what we talked about in the lifter a few days ago?"
Jibb asked at length.

"Yes."

"Maybe I can bring myself to trust you, at least with regard to this."

Premel nodded. "All right."

"If you disappoint me, Premel—if you give any sign at all that you plan
to betray us again—I'll kill you on the spot, just as I should have the first
time."

This last Jibb said for Melyor's sake, but she showed no sign that she
had even heard him.

"I understand," Premel said, nodding a second time. "And what if I
don't disappoint you? What if I do just what you and the Sovereign
expect of me? Will I start to earn back your trust in other ways as well?"

If Melyor hadn't been there, he would have hit the man. Here he was
offering Premel a way to redeem himself, at least to some extent, and
Premel was already reaching for more. He glared at the guard, allowing
him to see how angry he was, but he offered no answer. After several
moments, Premel lowered his gaze.

A short time later, Melyor's driver steered the carrier off the Upper
and down into the crowded quads of the Second Realm.

Jibb sat up, suddenly alert and watchful. He glanced back through the rear window to be sure that the larger vehicle behind them, which was carrying two units of his best men, had followed. Seeing that it had, he nodded and faced forward again. His hand wandered to the thrower on his thigh, and he felt reassured by the feel of the cold metal. Premel, he noticed, was sitting more erect as well, and Melyor had both hands on her staff, as if the red stone mounted upon it could guard them from those who might attack the carrier.

Their driver pulled off the main avenue almost immediately and followed a series of turns through narrow alleys until they reached the back entrance to Honid's flat. The second carrier stopped just behind them.

Dob wasn't there yet, at least there was no sign of his carrier or his men, and Jibb felt his apprehension mounting, and with it, his anger. Who was Dob to keep the Sovereign waiting, especially under these circumstances, when she was exposed like this?

"It's all right," Melyor said quietly, placing a hand lightly on his arm. "He'll be here."

And in the next instant, as if her reassurances had been prophecy, two more carriers entered the passageway, both of them large and black. They pulled up alongside Mclyor's carrier and the one holding Jibb's men, and Dob climbed out, accompanied by a dozen of his men, all of them in black uniforms.

Seeing Dob, Premel abruptly turned pale. "Does he . . . ?" He hesitated, as if he didn't know how to continue.

Melyor smiled gently. "All he knows is that there have been attempts on my life, and that we're here to stage this firefight. I told him nothing else."

"Thank you, Sovereign," Premel breathed.

Melyor nodded. "I'm ready when you are," she said to Jibb.

He pulled his pocket communicator from his coat and pressed a button on its side. "The Sovereign is ready," he said. "Take positions."

Immediately, the doors of the carrier behind them opened, and twelve men in the light blue uniforms of SovSec emerged from the vehicle and formed a semicircle around Melyor's carrier.

"We're ready, General," one of the unit commanders told him over the communicator.

Jibb turned to Melyor. "They're in position, Sovereign."

She took a breath and flashed them both a smile. "Let's get started." She opened her door, but then paused. "Watch yourselves," she said, her voice suddenly low. "Just in case."

The three of them stepped out of their carrier and into the alley. Jibb scanned the rooftops and windows for assassins, and, he noticed, so did Premel.

"Hello, Dob," Melyor said. "It's nice to see you again."

"The pleasure and honor are mine, Sovereign," Dob said, smiling and bowing formally at the waist. He was an Overlord now—not Melyor's strongest, but not her weakest either—and he was dressed elegantly in black, just as an Overlord should have been. His long black hair was touched with narrow streaks of silver, and he wore it tied back. He had added a beard since the last time Jibb saw him, silver and black like his hair, and, the general had to admit, it looked quite dignified. But to Jibb, Dob would always be the overreaching break-law who, with Cedrych's help, had taken Melyor's Realm from him.

Apparently, Dob felt the same way, because when he next turned to Jibb, he appeared decidedly less sure of himself. "Good morning, General," he said, not quite meeting Jibb's gaze. "We're honored to have you in our Dominion."

"Thank you, Dob. I'm delighted to be here."

"You remember Premel, don't you, Dob?" Melyor said, indicating the guard with a casual gesture. "Jibb's second-in-command?"

"Yes, of course."

"Premel is interim head of SovSec until Jibb's arm heals."

"Right," Dob said, with a nod. "I had heard of your injury, General. I'm sorry. I also heard," he added, turning to Premel, "that we have you to thank for saving the General's life."

Premel grimaced but didn't look away. "That's a bit of an exaggeration."

"No, it's not," Melyor corrected, her eyes flicking for a moment toward Jibb. "Premel's just being modest, Dob. Don't pay any attention to him."

"What's the situation, Dob?" Jibb asked, in an attempt to change the subject.

Dob kept his eyes on Melyor and Premel for another moment, before turning to answer the question. "Honid and his men staged a raid on the Third Realm last night. They killed several men, did a good deal of damage to the infrastructure, and captured a large cache of hand boomers and throwers."

Most of this was true, Jibb knew. They had staged the raid the night before to give Melyor an excuse to come here. Little had been explained to Carden, Nal-Lord of the Third Realm. He had been warned that the raid would take place, and he had been promised generous compensation if he allowed it to succeed with an impressive but ineffectual defense. From all reports, he had made a good show of it. The corpses had been faked. Melyor had insisted on that. And though they had succeeded with this aspect of the ruse as well, Jibb had no desire to know how they had done it.

"This is why you called the Sovereign and the General here?" Premel demanded, also making a good show of it. "To deal with a renegade Nal-Lord?"

Dob glared at him. "No. I called in the Sovereign because Honid did something else as well—something that concerns her."

"And that is?" Jibb asked, allowing a touch of impatience to creep into his voice.

"He also struck at a meeting of the Network. It seems he and his men killed nine Gildriites."

For several seconds none of them spoke, although Jibb could hear a few of Dob's men whispering among themselves.

"Why would he do this?" Melyor finally asked. She looked pale, and she appeared to be trembling.

Jibb had to suppress a grin. It shouldn't have surprised him; after all, she was ridiculously good at everything else she did. Why not this as well?

Dob shook his head. "I don't know, Sovereign. That's why I contacted you. Honid seems determined not only to defy you, but to flaunt that defiance by attacking your people. I thought you'd want to speak with him yourself."

It wasn't the story Jibb would have used. There were too many holes in it, starting with the obvious: why not have Dob and his men capture Honid themselves and then escort the renegade to the Gold Palace? But Melyor had been determined to find out immediately what Marar was up to, leaving them with little time to prepare. And this was the best of the options they had considered.

"Very well," she said with a nod. "Dob, I want your men positioned around the flat. Nobody comes in or leaves until I'm done in there. Understood?"

"Yes, Sovereign."

"Jibb, Premel, you and your men come with me. We're going to take the building. Once Honid's men have been disarmed, the guards will take up positions on the first floor while the three of us and Dob speak with our rebellious Nal-Lord."

"Me?" Dob said, his eyes widening in a display of alarm that had been rehearsed as well.

"Yes, Dob. I'm here because you failed to control one of your Nal-Lords. It only seems right that you should face him as well."

"But—"

"Jibb?" Melyor said sharply.

In response, Jibb nodded once, and Premel pulled out his thrower and leveled it at Dob's heart.

"All right!" the Overlord said quickly. "All right."

The Sovereign nodded once and glanced around at the men standing with her in the alley. "You all know what to do. Let's get this over with."

Premel barked a command, and a moment later a phalanx of guards led Melyor, Jibb, Dob, and Premel into the rear entrance of the flat. Almost as soon as they crossed the threshold into the building a shaft of red fire sliced across through the air from above.

"Ambush!" one of the guards cried out. Instantly guards dived for cover and began returning fire.

Honid's men continued to fire as well, although they did a remarkable job of keeping themselves concealed, and for a few minutes the building seemed to be consumed by thrower fire.

Jibb kept low to the floor and remained close to Melyor. After a time, he began to feel something burning in his chest, and he realized that he wasn't breathing. This was the most dangerous part of their scheme. His men had no idea that this was being staged—if there was a second traitor among them, it was crucial that he believe that what was happening was real. As long as Honid's men managed to stay hidden, and didn't actually kill any of the guards, this would work and no one would get hurt. But as soon—

"There!" one of the guards cried out, pointing at something above them. Instantly, three more of his men began to pour their fire in the direction indicated by the first.

"Hold your fire!" came a cry from above.

"Not until you surrender and lead us to Honid!" Premel answered. "The Sovereign herself has come to speak with him!"

"The Nal-Lord's gone!" came another voice. "He took to the tunnels as soon as you came in! Hold your fire!"

"Throw down your weapons!" Premel commanded.

The weapons' fire ceased, and a moment later Jibb heard the sound of throwers clattering down the stairs and onto the ground floor.

"Gather them up!" Melyor shouted, sprinting toward the tunnel access on the far side of the building. "Don't let any of them escape, but don't harm them! Jibb, Premel, and Dob, you're with me!"

All three of them had anticipated the order and were already following her, but Jibb knew that there was nothing suspicious about that. Anyone who knew them would have expected it. So far, unbelievably, their plan was working.

Reaching the low door, Melyor threw it open and plunged into the darkness with her staff held out before her. The three of them followed, charging down a long flight of stairs into the rank, still air of the tunnels.

When they got to the base of the steps, they turned right and sprinted to the first sharp turn. But there they stopped. Honid was waiting for them, his shiny bald head glinting in the dim light, and a crooked smile on his square face.

"Welcome to the tunnels, Sovereign. I'd guess it's been some time since you were here."

Melyor regarded him coolly. "You've done well so far, Honid. Don't ruin it all now by being presumptuous."

The man's smile vanished abruptly. "My apologies, Sovereign. I didn't mean to give offense."

"You spoke about this to no one, correct?"

"Only the five men in the flat, Sovereign. And I'll personally vouch for their discretion."

"And if they betray your trust?"

Honid smiled again. "I've promised each of them a slow, painful death."

Melyor stared at him for several moments, until his smile faded once more and he began to fidget. "Very well," she said. She turned to Jibb. "As of right now, you and I are dead." She glanced back over her shoulder. "Honid, I'm afraid you're a corpse as well, at least for the time being. Premel here has killed us all, and he and Dob have reached an agreement. Premel will take control of SovSec and, when the time is right, he'll throw the full weight of the security force behind Dob's effort to become Sovereign." She turned to Dob. "That at least is the story I want making its way through the quads over the course of the next day or two."

"All right," Dob said. "But we're going to a great deal of trouble to fool someone. I'd like to know who it is."

"That's none of your business."

Jibb winced at Melyor's tone and, looking quickly at Dob, he could see, even in the dim light, that the Overlord's face had reddened.

Melyor seemed to notice as well. "I'm sorry, Dob," she said, taking a long breath. "That wasn't fair of me after all you've done. You deserve an answer, as does Honid, but I have to ask you both to be patient. I can't say right now. The fewer people who know, the better."

Dob held himself perfectly still, refusing to look Melyor in the eye.

She stepped forward and placed a hand on his arm. It may have been a trick of the light from the glow of her red stone, but this appeared to make the Overlord even more uncomfortable. "I promise you, Dob: as soon as I can tell you I will. Please understand."

He gave a reluctant nod and allowed his gaze to touch hers for just a moment.

She smiled and gave his arm a squeeze. "Thank you."

"So what do we do now?" Premel asked.

"First, you and Dob should fire your weapons for a while, just up and down the tunnels. There should be some blast points on the walls, and your weapons should be warm. After all, you were in a firefight." Again she smiled, though only for a second. "Then the two of you will go back up to Honid's flat and tell everyone there what happened." She turned to Honid. "Your men have been instructed to make a show of positioning themselves to take your place, right?"

"Yes, Sovereign."

"Good. Premel, I want you to take control of the situation. Act as though you've been intending to take Jibb's place all along. If any of the men challenge you, assert yourself; make it clear to them that SovSec is yours now. Obviously you shouldn't allow anyone else down here—tell them that you'll be handling the official inquiry into our deaths. Don't worry about it looking suspicious. That could actually work to our advantage."

"How are you and Jibb going to get back to the palace?"

"You're going to take us."

"In your carrier?" Premel asked. "What about your driver?"

"Vian?" Melyor said. "What about him?"

"Do you trust him?"

"Absolutely. Vian's been with me longer than any of you. Even Jibb."

"Being with you a long time doesn't necessarily mean anything," Jibb said pointedly.

Premel clenched his jaw, but otherwise offered no reaction.

"Don't worry about Vian," Melyor said. "Just do what I've told you." She faced Premel. "You should be the last to leave Honid's flat. Seal it for the coroner—he's already been paid—and make certain nobody else comes in. Then take my carrier; we'll meet you four quads east of here in the middle of the byways."

"It almost sounds too easy," Premel said.

Melyor grinned. "That's fine for you to say. You're not dead like the rest of us."

They all laughed, but only briefly.

"Get going," Melyor said a moment later. "And don't forget to fire your weapons a few times."

"Yes, Sovereign," Premel said. "We'll see you soon." He turned to Jibb, his expression growing solemn. "General."

Jibb said nothing, but after a moment he gave a single nod.

Premel opened his mouth as if to say something, but then he appeared to think better of it, and instead, he and Dob just walked away, discharging their weapons at the tunnel walls as they did.

"We have plenty of time," Melyor said, turning to face Jibb, "but I wouldn't mind starting toward the meeting place now. We might have to take some detours to avoid being seen."

"All right." Jibb glanced around him, trying to get his bearings.

"This way," she said, pointing to the right with her staff. It wasn't the direction he would have taken, but he was sure she was right. He had spent a lot of time in the tunnels as a break-law, and he had learned to travel them long ago. But, like most, his navigation of the tunnels was approximate, not exact. Melyor was the only person he had ever met who always seemed to know precisely where she was. During her days as a Nal-Lord, her ability to navigate within the tunnels had been legendary, enhancing her already formidable reputation.

"What would you like me to do, Sovereign?" Honid asked, as Jibb and Melyor started to walk away. Jibb had forgotten that he was even there, and it seemed that Melyor had as well.

"A good question, Honid. I guess I just need for you to disappear for a while. Just for a couple of days."

The Nal-Lord nodded, although he didn't look pleased. "Do you want me to stay in the tunnels?"

"Only as a last resort," Melyor said, frowning. "You must have places to hide, someplace you go when things get too hot."

He stared back at her, wearing a puzzled expression. "I had some when I was a break-law," he said at last. "But I haven't been to any of them in years."

"You don't have even one?"

"Why would he need one?" Jibb asked gently. "Being a Nal-Lord isn't like it used to be. The Nal has changed."

She looked at him sharply, as if she thought he was criticizing her. But a moment later, she tipped her head slightly, conceding the point. She might even have grinned.

"Well, that does present Honid with a bit of a problem, doesn't it? It wouldn't be right of us just to leave him to fend for himself in the tunnels."

"I suppose it wouldn't," Jibb agreed. "We could take him back to the palace with us. He'd certainly be safe there."

Melyor's face brightened. "That's a great idea. Have you even been a guest of the Sovereign?" she asked the Nal-Lord.

Honid smiled sheepishly. "No, never."

"Then it's decided. You'll come with us."

"Thank you, Sovereign, General."

They walked for perhaps an hour, following the twists and turns of the tunnels, but making their way steadily westward. And when Melyor finally led them up a stairway, perhaps the fifteenth they had seen since leaving Honid's flat, Jibb was amazed to find that they were just where they were supposed to be. The Nal-Lord was utterly speechless.

"H-How?" he finally managed to ask Jibb in a whisper.

The general shrugged. "She's Melyor i Lakin," he said, as if that could explain everything.

Honid didn't look satisfied.

"From what she'd told me, there's a pattern to them."

"A pattern? Not that I've ever seen."

"I haven't found it either. Apparently it repeats itself every six quads or so. The secret is figuring out just where you are in the pattern and keeping track of your direction."

The Nal-Lord shook his head. "A pattern," he said again. "I guess that's why she's Sovereign."

Jibb laughed. "Now you know how I feel every day."

The three of them waited in the doorway to the alley for nearly another hour before Melyor's carrier finally came into view. Looking around them to be sure that they weren't seen, they hurried into the vehicle.

"Go!" Melyor called to the driver almost before Jibb had closed the door behind them. The carrier lurched forward out of the byway, and in a few moments they were climbing back onto the Upper and speeding toward the Gold Palace.

"Report," the Sovereign commanded as she settled back into her seat. "Did everything go all right?"

"It seemed to go fine," Premel said, sounding surprised. "I did just as you told me to. Nobody challenged my claim to SovSec, and I think they all believed the story. Dob was a big help. He was very convincing." He glanced at Honid. "Has there been a change in our plans?"

"Not in any way that concerns you," Melyor answered. "Honid just needs somewhere to hide for the next few days."

"Is my flat sealed?" the Nal-Lord asked.

"Yes, and your men assured me that they'd keep watch on it."

Honid nodded, although he looked a bit uneasy. Jibb sympathized. Even with the changes taking place in the Nal, no Nal-Lord liked to be away from his flat or his Realm for very long. Even the most trustworthy break-laws had been known to betray their lords under such conditions.

"Now what?" Premel asked, looking at Melyor again.

"We'll talk back at the palace," she said, her eyes flicking briefly in

Honid's direction. "Suffice it to say that we have to begin spreading the word. Do you take my meaning?"

Premel paled noticeably. "Yes, Sovereign."

The rest of their journey back to the Gold Palace passed without conversation. Honid and Premel appeared to be too preoccupied to speak, and though Jibb would have liked to talk to Melyor about Marar, and her plans for Premel once all of this was over, he couldn't very well bring those matters up in front of the other two men.

Upon returning to the palace, Melyor, Jibb, and Honid snuck in through an air-intake port. Premel used the main entrance. After leaving Honid in a small room on the subfloor, Melyor and Jibb made their way to Premel's chamber and immediately had the guard contact Marar.

"What should I tell him?" Premel asked. He actually looked scared.

"We've been through this, Premel. It's not going to be that hard. Just tell him Jibb and I are dead, demand your gold, and end the conversation. It couldn't be easier."

The guard smiled at that, as did Jibb. It would be easy for her maybe. Just like everything else. But, in spite of his feelings toward Premel, Jibb couldn't help but feel a bit sorry for him. He wouldn't have wanted to make this call either, particularly with his Sovereign and his commander sitting just on the other side of his desk.

"All right," Premel said, as much to himself as to Melyor. He leaned forward to punch Marar's code into his speak-screen.

"Premel," Melyor said, stopping him.

He looked up at her and waited.

"Have fun with this. Regardless of what comes after, this is your chance to get back at this man. Do it for me, and for Jibb."

Premel nodded. Then, looking at the screen once more, he entered the code.

Jibb and Melyor sat in silence nearby. Jibb's heart was beating so hard that he almost worried about Marar hearing it, and it was all he could do to keep himself from standing and pacing the length of the room.

It was several minutes before Marar finally answered Premel's summons. "Yes, Premel. What is it?"

The guard flashed a smile. "You don't sound very happy to see me, Sovereign."

"Should I be? I think I told you that I didn't want to hear from you again until you had done as I instructed."

"I remember that as well."

A pause, and then, "So you're telling me—?"

"They're dead, Sovereign. Officially, they died earlier today, in a firefight with a renegade Nal-Lord, who, as it happens, also died. Obviously, you can confirm that they're dead with whatever sources you care to consult."

"And I will," Marar said, sounding amazed. "Nobody saw you do it?"

"One man did. Dob, an Overlord who wishes to succeed Melyor as Sovereign."

"Do you trust him?"

"I trust no one," Premel said, baring his teeth in a harsh grin. "Not even you, and certainly not Dob. But he needs help from SovSec to become Sovereign, and I control SovSec now."

"Well, Premel, I must say that for a man who seemed reluctant to carry out my orders, you certainly have moved quickly to take advantage of the situation."

"I won't lie to you, Sovereign, I was frightened. I did this for gold, but you were offering me much, much more. You were giving me an opportunity to fulfill all my ambitions, and it scared me. But I realized after our last conversation that I'm tired of being afraid, I'm tired of being used and manipulated by other people, including you."

"Meaning?"

"Meaning that I'm head of SovSec now, and I want my gold. And if there are any more delays in delivering it to me, I'll use all the resources that are now at my disposal to get it."

Melyor and Jibb exchanged a look. Premel's approach carried risks, but it was also quite believable. And the guard sounded far more convincing than he had the other day when Marar contacted him.

"I certainly understand your eagerness to receive your payment, Premel. You must understand though, that I have to verify what you've told me before I can pay you."

"Of course, Sovereign. You have one day."

Marar laughed. "One day? That's hardly enough time to verify your story, much less get in touch with my couriers."

Melyor sat forward.

"I'll need at least three days," the Sovereign went on. "And even that will be a stretch. Besides, if you're head of SovSec now, what difference could my gold make to you? It's nothing compared to what you're about to have."

"Perhaps you're right. But I see it as a test of your good faith. You owe me this money. Regardless of what I am now, or even what I'm to become, we had a deal. And I expect you to honor it. I'll give you two days."

"Premel, this is no way to begin this new phase of our relationship."

"What new phase?"

"Before, I was your employer. I'd like to think that we're ready now to become partners."

"With all due respect, Sovereign, I'm about to enter into a partnership with the new Sovereign of Bragor-Nal. What could you possible have to offer me that would match what he can give?"

Again, Melyor and Jibb looked at each other, and this time she was grinning, her eyes wide with astonishment at the direction Premel had taken their conversation.

There was a long pause, and Jibb held his breath waiting for Marar's response. Premel, he could see, was doing the same.

"Let me ask you something," the Sovereign finally said. "Did you ever meet the sorcerer, the one Melyor knew?"

"The sorcerer?"

Melyor's face turned ashen, as it always seemed to when someone spoke of Orris. But she nodded so that Premel could see without taking his eyes off the screen.

"Yes," Premel said. "I met him."

"Would he remember you? Would he trust you?"

Again she nodded.

"I believe so, yes."

"In that case, I can offer you riches beyond your wildest imagination."

Premel smiled. "Come now, Marar. Bragor-Nal's Sovereign can offer me far more gold than Stib-Nal has in all—"

"This gold isn't coming from Stib-Nal, Premel. It's coming from Tobyn-Ser, and there's more to be made than you can conceive."

Jibb saw Melyor's jaw drop.

"Tobyn-Ser?" Premel said. "How?"

"Never mind that for now. Are you interested in a partnership or not?"

Premel looked away from the screen as if pondering the offer, and he waited for Melyor's signal. After a moment she nodded once again. The guard delayed his response several seconds more for effect, then turned back to Marar.

"Yes," he said. "I'm interested. Get me my gold, and after I've received it, we can discuss this further."

"Very well."

An instant later, Premel fell back into his chair and closed his eyes.

"That was masterfully done," Melyor told him, although she clearly was preoccupied. "You were very convincing."

"Thank you, Sovereign."

Premel glanced at Jibb, and the general forced himself not to look away.

"Well done," he said grudgingly.

Premel grinned, looking more pleased than he had any right to look.

Jibb thought about saying something to deflate him just a bit, but
instead he turned his attention back to Melyor. She was shaking her
head, her flawless features still looking pale, and her eyes wide with
worry.

"What would he want with Orris?" she asked in a low voice. "Who in
Tobyn-Ser would give him gold?"

He could scarcely believe it. Naturally, he'd have to have it confirmed by
other operatives, but Premel wouldn't have lied to him about something
like this, no matter how much he wanted to disentangle himself from
their relationship.

Melyor was dead. And for the first time in his reign as Sovereign of
Stib-Nal, he had a true ally in the Gold Palace. To be sure, Premel
didn't like him, but a few extra bars of gold would help smooth things
over. That was a small price to pay for the cooperation of SovSec's
leader.

Marar smiled—he could hardly help it—and he got up from his desk
and began wandering around his office. It would have been far easier had
Premel chosen to become Sovereign rather than head of SovSec. In that
case, Marar could have ended his frustrating efforts to win Wiercia's trust
and concentrated instead on improving his rapport with the Bragory
guard. But now he had to wait and see who ascended to the Gold Palace.
And even if it was this Dob of whom Premel had spoken, there was no
guarantee that he would be any easier to control than Melyor had been.
He shook his head. No, Wiercia couldn't be jettisoned just yet.

Pausing by one of his windows, Marar stared out at his gardens. The
last rays of sunlight were angling sharply across the blossoms and shrubs,
giving everything a bright, golden glow, and the laborers who remained
were working in shirtsleeves.

He couldn't remember the last time he had taken a stroll through the
rows of flowers laid out before him or, better yet, through the gently
winding trails of Stib Grove. He had been planning for so long that it
sometimes seemed that his entire life had become a series of speak-screen
conversations: giving Premel his orders, making arrangements to have
gold delivered, arguing with Melyor, negotiating with Wiercia. He
needed rest. He needed time to relax. And what better time than now? It
was almost dusk, his favorite time of the day.

He nodded, as if reaching a decision. He even took a step toward the
communicator he used to summon Bain, his security chief. After what he
had done to Shivohn, he wasn't about to go on such an outing without a
security detail.

But then he stopped himself. First he needed to speak with Wiercia. It was quite possible that Melyor's death would be the event that cemented their alliance. The possible benefits of an alliance between the Matriarchy and Stib-Nal might never look so enticing again.

Returning to his desk, he tapped the button that summoned her to her speak-screen and settled back into his chair.

A moment later, she appeared before him.

He fought to keep from smiling. It wouldn't do to seem too pleased. "Good afternoon, Sovereign."

"Hello, Marar," she said, sounding far from thrilled to see him on her screen.

"You're well I trust."

"Quite. What do you want?"

"You haven't heard?" It was so hard to keep a straight face.

She sat forward, narrowing her eyes. "Heard what?"

"Melyor is dead."

"What?" she said, her voice suddenly a whisper. She shook her head. "How?"

"I believe she was killed in a firefight. She went to see some renegade Nal-Lord and never returned."

She shook her head a second time. "I've heard nothing of this. When did it happen?"

"Just this morning."

"Strange that you should know of it already."

Marar hesitated, and from a distant corner of his mind he suddenly heard a voice calling to him, telling him that this was a mistake, that he needed to end this conversation immediately. "My intelligence officer briefed me just moments ago."

"Really?"

Turn off the screen. Just turn it off. "Yes. He said he came to me immediately upon learning of it."

"And you felt compelled to inform me as soon as he left."

This is madness! Tell her that one of your Quad-Lords is here; tell her you have to contact her again later. "I thought you'd want to know. If I was mistaken, forgive me." He reached forward to switch off the speak-screen, cursing the trembling of his hand.

"Wait, Marar."

He stopped and, after a moment, reluctantly withdrew his hand.

"I want to know the real reason you contacted me."

"I just told you. I th—"

"I don't believe you," she said. She pressed her fingers together, as if lost in thought.

Marar opened his mouth to tell her that he had to go, but she raised a finger before he could say anything and shook her head. He felt his left eye starting to twitch, and he had to resist the urge to rub it.

"You thought that this would convince me, didn't you. You thought that hearing of Melyor's death would make me join forces with you."

"I merely thought that you should know what happened, Sovereign," he told her. He tried to sound indignant, but it merely came out peevish. *This was a mistake.*

"Did you think it would scare me, Marar? Did you mean to imply that I'd suffer the same fate if I refused you?"

"I don't know what you're talking about!"

"You killed her, didn't you?"

"Of course not! I already told you, she died in a firefight in Bragor-Nal!"

"But you arranged it." She gave a small mirthless laugh. Her square face looked pale, but there was no fear in her blue eyes. Only rage. "She was right all along, wasn't she? You sent the bomb that killed Shivohn, and the one that almost got Melyor. And today you finally succeeded in killing her."

"Don't be ridiculous!" He sounded desperate.

"You led me to believe that she assassinated Shivohn and then staged the bombing of the Gold Palace. But now she's dead. And what am I to believe? That she staged this, too? Or that she was telling the truth? That it was you this whole time, trying to kill them both."

"You're obviously distraught, Wiercia," he said, trying to salvage some small shred of his dignity and credibility. "I'll speak to you in the next few days, after you've managed to calm down."

"Don't bother, Marar. I'll see you at the next Council meeting, and we can discuss all of this with Bragor-Nal's new Sovereign."

She switched off her console, and his screen went black.

"Fist of the God!" he muttered, turning his console off as well. He rested his elbows on the desk and dropped his head into his hands. All the work he had done, trying to win Wiercia's trust. And he had destroyed all of it in a matter of moments. How stupid could he be? Now he'd have to kill her, too.

A moment later the screen beeped at him. He would have liked to ignore it, but . . . It beeped again. He jabbed at it with a rigid finger. Missed the button. Jabbed again.

For just an instant, he didn't recognize the face that appeared before him. They had only spoken once, several months before, when the man first agreed to work for him. He hadn't done much since—occasionally he gave Marar a scrap of information for which the Sovereign paid him a bar or two of gold. Only recently had Marar begun to think of him as someone who could help him in a meaningful way. Because only recently had the Sovereign recognized the importance of having Jibb killed as well.

And this man hated Jibb. Marar wasn't clear on exactly why. Something about a half brother whom the security man had killed in the quads a year or two ago.

"What do you want?" Marar asked.

"I have news, Sovereign."

Marar rubbed a hand over his face. "I've already heard. Melyor and Jibb are dead. I won't be needing—"

"No," the man interrupted. "They're alive."

The Sovereign gaped at him. *"What?* That's impossible!"

"I assure you, it's true."

"But Premel said . . ." He trailed off. Premel. Of course. "You know this for a fact?" he demanded a moment later. "You've seen them?"

Vian grinned. "Seen them? I drove them back to the Gold Palace. How else do you think they got home?"

Marar closed his eyes. She was alive. Which meant that she knew. Somehow, Premel had won her trust and then told her everything. And Marar, in turn, had given it all away. He had revealed himself to Wiercia. But worse than that, he had mentioned to Premel—and, no doubt, to Melyor as well—that he was getting gold from Tobyn-Ser. He felt ill.

Opening his eyes again, he saw Melyor's driver staring at him, waiting. He looked away, toward the window. The sun was dipping down below the horizon, casting shadows across the Nal, its last light reflecting off windows and the moving steel of carriers on Stib-Nal's Upper.

I should have taken my walk, Marar thought. I just should have done it when I had the chance.

18

That Kovet, Dirss, and Brinly attacked the Order mage Orris is not in dispute—they admit that much. Nor is this fact the reason for my submission of this formal accusation, though I remain convinced that their actions violate the spirit, if not the letter, of our bylaws. These charges stem instead from their interaction with three men of Tobyn-Ser whom they endangered with their reckless attack on Orris, and then threatened, in direct violation of Amarid's First Law. Their actions have disgraced themselves, this body, and the memory of the First Mage, whom we seek to honor through all that we do.

No violation of our bylaws should be taken lightly; no one who defies Amarid's Laws should escape punishment. But coming at a time when our land stands at the brink of civil war and our need of the peoples' support is most pressing, the offenses of these mages seem particularly egregious. For that reason, I believe that this matter should be addressed by this body immediately.

> —Formal charges submitted to the Seventh Conclave of the League of Amarid by Eagle-Master Cailin, in accordance with the Bylaws of the League of Amarid, Spring, God's Year 4633.

Erland slumped back into his chair and closed his eyes. He had read Cailin's charges a second time, looking for something— anything—that would allow him to salvage at least a small victory from what promised to be a nightmarish debate. But there was nothing there. Nothing at all. He was tempted to throw the parchment into the flames that crackled in his hearth, just for the satisfaction of making her scribe the document a second time. But instead he took another sip of his *shan* tea and began to read it through a third time.

It was, he had to admit, a brilliantly conceived document. She had been careful not to predicate her charges on the attacks on Orris, although neither did she concede their legality. Instead, she merely used the opportunity created by Kovet's actions to criticize the attacks, which were already becoming a point of contention within the League. Arslan and his followers were bound to be sympathetic, as were those who already supported Cailin over Erland. And due to the sheer stupidity of what Kovet and his companions had done, Erland had little doubt that even his strongest allies would support some sort of punishment for them, possibly even expulsion from the League. Which would deny Erland three dependable votes on all subsequent matters.

"Idiots," he muttered under his breath, sipping his tea again. What could have possessed them to threaten those men? What could they have been thinking? He had summoned Kovet to the hall to ask him just those questions, but the mage had yet to respond. No doubt he knew what his conversation with the First Master would be like. Erland could hardly blame him for avoiding the encounter.

He raised the cup to his lips again, but before he could drink, someone knocked at his door.

"Yes?" he called.

The door opened, and one of the hall's attendants poked her head into his quarters.

"The Eagle-Master is here, First Master," the woman said. "Shall I tell her you wish to speak with her?"

"Thank you, no," Erland answered, getting to his feet. "I'll ask her in myself."

The woman inclined her head slightly. "Very well."

He made himself smile. "Thank you," he said again, feeling awkward. He should have known her name. He had resided in the Hall of the League for six years, and this one had been here almost from the beginning.

She offered a thin smile and withdrew.

He stood where he was until he could no longer hear the woman's footsteps, and then he waited a few seconds more, not wishing to appear too anxious. Cailin was probably smart enough to know when she had the upper hand, but just in case she didn't, he would do nothing to give himself away.

He took a quick, deep breath, fixed a smile on his lips, and strode purposefully into the central chamber of the hall.

He had hoped to give the appearance of being on his way somewhere, but Cailin was standing at the far end of the meeting table, staring at him as if she knew better.

It was an unusually cold morning for so late in the spring, and her cheeks were still flushed, making her youthful face seem almost childlike. Her great eagle sat on her arm, dwarfing her, and making her look even younger and less imposing. And yet there was something in the way she carried herself and bore the bird who had chosen her that left Erland feeling insignificant and just a bit intimidated.

Why would the gods have chosen someone so young? he found himself wondering. Why did they choose her instead of me?

"You've been waiting for me?" she said, her blue eyes locked on his.

What was the point of lying? "Yes."

"To discuss the charges against Kovet and the others?"

"Yes."

She gestured toward the door through which he had just come. "After you."

Erland retreated into his chamber with the Eagle-Master behind him.

"Please sit," he said, waving at one of the large chairs by the hearth and closing the door. "Can I offer you some tea?" It was his room, by the gods, and regardless of the situation he resolved to take control of their discussion, as was fitting given his age and his position in the League. Pride demanded no less.

And yet, Cailin seemed determined to deny him even this small victory.

"I'm fine, thank you," she said, standing by the fire, as her eagle hopped from her arm to the mantel and began to preen. "Let's just be done with this, Erland. You wanted to talk to me. So talk."

The First Master swallowed and lowered himself into his chair. He had been planning what he would say to her for the better part of an hour. He had decided upon a tone of voice, a bargaining position, a set of concessions he was prepared to offer, and a second set he was determined to demand of her. But abruptly he felt far less sure of himself.

"These are very serious charges, Cailin," he began, willing his voice to remain steady. "If these men are found guilty and punished in accordance with the bylaws, it could weaken the League. As you point out yourself, we're living in dangerous times. We can ill afford to have our standing in the land damaged just now."

"You should have thought of that before you sent Kovet and his friends after Orris."

"Orris is a traitor! He deserves what he gets!"

"That may be. But if your obsession with him harms the League, you'll have no one to blame but yourself."

Erland narrowed his eyes. "So this is about Orris."

"No," she said quickly. "It's about what Kovet did to the peddler and his friends."

"Yes. You make that very clear in your allegations. But you and I know better, don't we? You want to end the attacks on Orris. That's your aim in all of this."

"The attacks on Orris are hurting the League, Erland. We both know that." She pushed her hair back from her forehead in a gesture he had often seen her make when agitated. "They've done nothing for us, and in fact they continue to divide us and hinder our ability to serve the land."

He smiled, sensing that she no longer had quite the advantage she had enjoyed a few moments before. "Nonsense," he said. "We may not all agree on this matter, but I don't think our pursuit of justice has hurt us at all. In fact, you're the only person I've heard say such a thing." This was a lie, of course, but he gave her no chance to say so. "Why is that, Cailin? Why are you so concerned with Orris? Could it be that your meetings with the Eagle-Sage have become more than that?"

Her mouth dropped open.

"Yes," he said, still smiling, "I know of your surreptitious journeys to the Great Hall. I've said nothing before now because I thought some good might come of them." And because he had not been willing to admit that he was having her followed. "But it seems that I was wrong.

All that's happened is that you've compromised your oath to the League."

"I've compromised nothing," she said, her voice even. If he had managed to shake her composure, the effect was fleeting. "I tell Jaryd nothing of our Conclaves, and I've never forgotten the color of my cloak."

He started to challenge her, but she raised a finger, stopping him.

"But neither have I forgotten," she went on, "that the gods have favored me with an extraordinary binding, one that carries responsibilities to the land that go far beyond my oath to this League. I meet with Jaryd because doing so may help us avoid a civil war, and I'll continue to meet with him as long as our conversations remain amicable and productive."

"And what of Orris?" Erland asked bitterly. "Have you met with him, too?"

She hesitated, but only for an instant. "He came to the Great Hall the last time I was there. He had just come from his confrontation with Kovet."

"And that's when he prevailed upon you to submit these charges."

Her eyes blazed. "No one prevailed upon me to do anything!"

"I don't believe you," he said, shaking his head. "Someone must have forced you to do this. Because the Cailin I know would never have turned against her own this way."

"The Cailin you knew was a child, Erland. And she ceased to exist years ago, just around the time she realized that you had been lying to her and using her from the very start."

"I don't know what you're talking about." He said the words forcefully enough, but he couldn't keep himself from looking away.

"Of course you don't," she said softly.

They both lapsed into silence so that the only sound in the room was the crackling of the fire. After some time he chanced a glance in her direction, but she was looking up at her eagle and gently stroking the bird's feathers. Soon they began to hear voices in the central chamber of the hall—the other mages arriving for the day's session—but still neither of them spoke.

Finally, he drew a long breath and faced her again. "So how do you want to do this?"

"I've submitted my charges, Erland. I intend to pursue them. How far this goes is really up to you."

"Up to me?"

"Yes. If you want to turn this into a discussion of the attacks on Orris and my conversations with Jaryd, that's your decision. But I promise you that if you do, I'll beat you. It may take some time, and it may do a good deal of damage to the League, but I will win. I think we both know that."

He was less certain of this than she seemed to be. And even if he had agreed with her fully, he wouldn't have admitted it. But there could be no denying that the prospect of this fight daunted him.

"The men Kovet threatened," he said, his voice low, "you've spoken with them? You know where to find them?"

"Yes."

She might have been lying; it was hard to tell. A year ago the very notion wouldn't have even entered his mind, but Cailin had learned the art of politics all too well.

"You don't believe me," she said.

"I'm not sure," he admitted.

She smiled, looking quite suddenly like a child playing a game. "Good." An instant later though, her expression turned grave again. "It's certainly possible that I'm trying to deceive you, Erland. Amarid is a big city—finding those men would not have been an easy task. It's possible that I searched for days without success and finally gave up, choosing instead to lie my way through this." She shrugged, appearing maddeningly calm. "Then again, I may have found them after all. I'm not one to play games, Erland." She smiled again. "At least I didn't used to be. You have to decide from what you know of me whether you think that I would go so far as to submit these charges if I didn't know where the men were. And then you have to ask yourself," she went on, the smile lingering this time, "whether you can afford to assume that I haven't found them. Because if you're wrong, and I do know where they are, Kovet, Dirss, and Brinly will never wear the blue cloak again."

She was giving him an opening, he knew. Even as she was threatening him; she was also holding out the hope of a compromise.

"But how am I to decide all this?" he asked, not quite willing to give in just yet. "Certainly you don't think that I can read your mind." He made himself smile as well. "My powers run deep, my dear, but not that deep."

"You play Ren-drah, don't you, Erland?"

He nodded, then licked his lips, which had suddenly gone dry. He played, but he wasn't very good at it.

"Well, this is much the same thing. You have to decide what you're willing to risk based upon what you know of your strengths and weaknesses, and what you can divine of mine."

But I can divine nothing about you! I didn't even know that you were capable of placing me in such a position! "The affairs of the League are hardly a game, Cailin. They shouldn't be treated as such."

"Nonsense!" she snapped, her smile vanishing abruptly. "You've been playing games of this sort for years. How do you think I learned to play?" She stared at him for a moment longer before, shaking her head. "Fine. If this is the way you want to do it, I'm happy to oblige." She turned toward the mantel and raised her arm for her eagle, as if readying herself to leave his chamber.

Erland closed his eyes and made his decision. Better to surrender now than to be beaten in front of the entire League. "What is it you want, Cailin?"

She glanced back over her shoulder at him. Her bird had yet to move, and he had to wonder if she had ever intended to leave. Not that it mattered anymore. Whatever games she had learned from him she had mastered in ways he had not. "I want your cooperation. I want you to stop turning every issue into a test of the League's loyalty to you."

"All right."

She turned to face him again. "The attacks on Orris have to stop immediately."

"You can't expect me to control the actions of every mage in the League, Cailin. And you certainly can't expect me to control those whom we expel." He wasn't going to concede everything to her.

"I do expect it, Erland. If you tell them to leave Orris alone, they will. And as to the rest, I think we might be able to find a solution to this business with Kovet and his friends that stops short of expulsion."

"I believe," Erland said, trying not to sound to eager, "that such a solution would be in the best interests of the League. This is no time to be pushing our mages toward the Order or the People's Movement."

"I agree. I'd hate to have to take their cloaks from them."

He gritted his teeth. "And what will it take to keep that from happening?"

"A promise from you that I'll have your full cooperation on all matters pertaining to the Order, the free mages, and the Temple."

"You can't be serious!" he breathed. "You're asking me to just give you control of the League!"

She shrugged, her expression neutral. "I wouldn't go that far."

"How is it different? You want me to defer to you on all matters of importance."

"Only for a while. Only until this crisis—in whatever form it takes—has passed."

Erland hesitated, tempted once more by the promise of what she wasn't saying. "And then?"

"From all that I've heard of Tobyn-Ser's previous Eagle-Sages, it seems that once the need for an eagle has passed, the birds move on, leaving their mages unbound."

Erland nodded. "I've heard much the same thing."

"So then once this crisis is over, the League will be yours again. An unbound mage can't be First or Second Master."

"But you won't be unbound forever," he said, regarding her skeptically. "Are you telling me that you have no ambitions to lead this body?"

"No, Erland, I'm not saying anything of the sort. I'm reminding you of what we both know to be true: I have plenty of time. I'll be First Master someday. And I'm willing to wait."

"How do I know that you'll keep your word?" he asked. "It's not easy to relinquish power once you've had it."

She nodded sagely. "So I've seen."

He felt the blood run hot to his cheeks, and he looked away.

"You're just going to have to trust that I'll step aside," she added a moment later. "I'm afraid you have little choice."

"I could fight you." He pointed toward the door leading to the central chamber. "I could make you convince them to side against me."

"You could. But as I told you before, you'd lose."

"You don't know that."

The eagle abruptly hopped to Cailin's arm, and she started toward the door. "You're right. Let's go find out, shall we?"

He didn't stop her immediately; he wanted to see how far she'd go. But when she grasped the door handle and started to pull, the door open, he had little choice but to call to her.

She pushed the door closed again and turned to face him.

"All right," he said. "I pledge my cooperation. But in return, I'd ask that our arrangement be kept secret. Call it vanity if you like, but I'd rather no one knew about this conversation."

"You have my word," she said solemnly.

"And I also have your promise that Kovet, Dirss, Brinly will not be punished?"

She shook her head. "Oh, no. You have no such thing. They will be punished. I just promise you that I won't have them banished from the League."

"But you said—"

"I promised no more than this, Erland. And you should count yourself fortunate that I've given you this much. Your friends will be allowed to keep their cloaks and attend our Conclaves, but they're to say nothing and have no vote for a year."

"A year?"

"Yes. That should teach them a lesson, and it should also keep you from breaking the promises you've made to me today."

"We're only talking about three men, Cailin. That may be enough to defeat me on a few matters, but not all. If you try to do anything foolish with this power I'm granting you, or if you stray too far from what I believe to be the wisest course, I'll stop you. And there won't be anything you can do about it."

Her features grew pale, leaving her looking young, and, for the first time that day, just a bit frightened. "So in other words, you have no intention of honoring our agreement."

Erland shook his head. "I didn't say that. Despite what you may think of me, Eagle-Master, I am true to my word. I've agreed to your terms, and I trust that you'll live up to the promises you've made to me. We each have some advantage over the other, some threat that we can use to compel each other to keep our promises. But in the end, Cailin, it comes down to trust. I have to believe that you'll relinquish power when the time comes, and you have to believe that I'll support you until that time comes." He opened his hands. "Have I really given you so much cause to doubt me?"

For several moments she said nothing. She merely stared at him, her sapphire eyes locked on his. "Do you remember the day you gave me my ceryll, Erland?" she asked at last, surprising him.

It was hardly something he was likely to forget. He would remember until he died the brilliant golden light that burst from the stone as soon as she laid her hand upon it. It had almost seemed as though Leora herself had been in the clearing with them, laying her hand on the crystal at the same time, and filling the stone with her radiance. But even more than that, Erland would always recall the joy he had felt at winning Cailin over to his cause. Until that moment, he had doubted whether his League, and the challenge to Baden, Sonel, and the rest of the Order that it embodied, would amount to anything more than a dream, or, worse, a tavern joke. But when Cailin agreed to join him, he knew that it would succeed. Indeed, he convinced himself that the League would supplant the Order within a year or two. The day to which she was referring had been, quite possibly, the happiest day of his life.

"Yes," he told her. "I remember."

She nodded, as if she was reliving the moment. "It was the finest gift anyone had ever given me," she said. "In many ways, it still is."

"I'm glad."

"But I know now why you gave it to me. I know that it wasn't just gathering dust in your home as you claimed, that actually you bought it so that you could use it to lure me into the League."

He considered denying it, but only briefly. There was no sense in it really. She wouldn't have believed him, and it would only serve to erode further the fragile bond that still tied them to each other. "I'm sorry," he said instead. "We needed you, and I did what I felt was necessary to get you to join us."

She nodded again, but she kept silent.

"So that's why you don't trust me? Because of the ceryll?"

Cailin gave a small, brittle laugh. "That's just one reason among many. Neither one of us has done much to strengthen our friendship in recent years."

He gave a rueful grin. "True. But then perhaps this can be a new beginning for us."

"Perhaps," she said, holding his gaze.

They stood looking at one another for a few moments more. Finally she pulled the door open again, and they walked together into the central chamber of the hall.

He drove her as an Abboriji warrior might have driven a stallion, pushing her body beyond endurance, and resting just often enough to keep her from failing. He did his best to keep her fed and watered, and when she grew too weak, he bolstered her strength with his power. But he had need of haste, and he refused to allow the frailty of Tammen's flesh to slow him. Not now, not when he had gotten so close.

He would have preferred to find a mount and travel that way. It would have shortened his journey significantly. But a mage on horseback, particularly a free mage, would have drawn attention. Sartol had no choice but to content himself with the progress he could make on foot. He passed through a number of free towns along the way—Greenbough, Starview, Vilpar, Kittran. There were more of them than he had ever imagined; the Movement was spreading. And in all of them he managed to replenish his food stores and leave before dusk revealed Miron's ghost on his shoulder.

His days were long. He walked from first light until nightfall, pausing only long enough to drink some water and eat a few bites of cheese or dried fruit. On a few occasions, when he felt certain that he would not encounter any strangers along the path, he ate a light supper as the sun set, and then pressed on toward Amarid. The darkness posed no problem for him; actually, even looking at the world through Tammen's eyes, he could see more at night than he could during the day. On those nights when he didn't press on toward Amarid, he allowed Tammen to sleep and let his own mind wander, as the Unsettled did when they sought rest. Sometimes, though, before he gave Tammen's flesh over to sleep, he made her remove her clothes and he touched her in ways he had never thought he would touch a woman again. It had been so long, and this was his body now, to do with as he pleased.

Five days after Greenbough, he came within sight of the Parneshome Range. Beyond the snowy peaks and green valleys, he knew, lay Amarid. And in the city stood the Great Hall, and within the Hall, resting in its stand, dormant and huge, was the Summoning Stone. It had almost been his once. He had come so close to mastering the great crystal that it had taken every mage in Tobyn-Ser to defeat him. And if he was right, if he had interpreted correctly all that he had learned about the Unsettled and their powers, it followed that the stone would respond instantly to his touch. What had been within his grasp in life, remained his in death. It was merely a matter of getting there, of laying his hands—Tammen's hands—upon it.

But first things first. He still had food enough for a day or two, but not enough to get him through the mountains. Fortunately, there were several towns and villages strung along the base of the foothills, and after searching for the better part of the morning, Sartol finally found one that flew the brown flags of the People's Movement. Striding into the town, with Tammen's staff grasped firmly in her slender hands, he felt a wave of giddiness pass over him. This was his last stop before Amarid. Whatever food he found here would be enough to see him the rest of the way to the Great Hall. Usually when he entered a town he forced a smile onto Tammen's lips—there was no sense in drawing attention to himself by appearing surly. But today it required no effort; he could barely contain his glee. Until he reached the village commons. And by then it was too late.

There were three of them, all of them free mages. They were speaking with a group of older men and women, no doubt the village's elders. Sartol considered turning on his heel and taking the shortest path out of the village and back into Tobyn's Wood. But in the next instant one of the mages, a thin bald man with a dark beard, spotted him—or rather, her—and beckoned him over.

"Greetings!" the man called out. "Have you come to join us?"

He wanted to run, to tell them that he had no desire to have anything to do with them or their Movement. But he was carrying a staff, and he wore no cloak. Under the circumstances, making a show of joining them was the only thing he could do without arousing their suspicions.

"Perhaps," Sartol said, stopping in front of the man as the others looked at Tammen appraisingly. "I had heard that there was a group of free mages in the area. If it turns out we're headed in the same direction I'd be happy to join you."

"Wonderful!" the man said, looking and sounding so enthusiastic that Sartol found himself wondering idly how long it had been since the man last passed a night with a woman. "My name is Hywel." He gestured toward the other two mages. "With me are Shavi and Ortan."

Sartol glanced at the two men briefly and made Tammen smile. One of them was thin and of medium height, with curly yellow hair and blue eyes. The other was taller, with long silver and black hair that he wore tied back.

"It's a pleasure to meet you all," he said. "My name is—"

"Tammen."

Sartol looked sharply at Ortan, who had spoken. He saw now that this man was older than his companions and more solidly built. He had a scar on his temple that had healed poorly, and his eyes were dark and difficult to read. Sartol noted as well that the man carried Amarid's hawk on his shoulder.

"Yes," Sartol said. "That's right. Have we met?"

"Once, long ago. You were traveling with Nodin then, and another man whose name I forget."

He searched Tammen's memory. "Henryk?"

The man grinned, although not with his eyes. "Yes. Henryk. How is Nodin? I always liked him."

Sartol shrugged. "It's been some time since I last saw him. We were spreading word of the Movement on the Northern Plain. I assume he's still well."

"Why did you part company?"

"It's a long story. We parted as friends, I assure you, but beyond that I don't really care to discuss it."

"You'll have to pardon Ortan," Hywel broke in. "He's prone to asking too many questions. He tends to be suspicious of strangers. But don't let it put you off. We're very happy to have you with us. We can always use another mage, even one who's between bindings."

"Thank you," Sartol said. He cast another glance at Ortan and saw that the man was still eyeing Tammen closely, although he gave no indication that Hywel's comment had angered him.

"We were just asking the village elders where we might find the next free town," Hywel went on. "The people here are committed to the Movement, but other towns might not be so well informed." He flashed a smile at the elders.

"I'd suggest you head south along the edge of the foothills," one of the older men said. "You're more likely to find free towns in that direction than to the north."

Hywel nodded. "Thank you. That's what we'll do then."

The elders and the mages began to bid each other farewell, but Sartol stopped them. "I'm sorry to be a burden," he said to the elders. "But is there someone in town who might be willing to give me a bit of food in return for my services?" He looked at Hywel and gave an embarrassed smile. "Without my familiar, I've been forced to eat roots and greens for too long."

"We can help you," Hywel told her. "You needn't trouble anyone here."

"I appreciate that," Sartol said, fighting a surge of anger. "But as it turns out I won't be traveling with you. I'm headed east, across the mountains to Hawksfind Wood. I'm sorry."

"As am I," Hywel said, looking genuinely disappointed. "Still, we can help you, and perhaps in doing so, we can convince you to stay with us for a time."

If they had been alone, Sartol would have killed the man on the spot. He couldn't afford to stay with them past sunset, and at this point he had no tolerance for delays of any sort. But what could he do?

"Thank you, Hywel. You're very kind."

A few moments later the mages said good-bye to the elders and made their way out of the village and into the shadows of the God's wood.

"So where are you going, Tammen?" Hywel asked, as they walked. "Why are you so reluctant to travel with us?"

Sartol made himself laugh. "Don't be silly. I'd be delighted to travel with you. But I'm on my way to Amarid."

"To Amarid?" the one named Shavi repeated, his eyes widening. "Why?"

Sartol made Tammen shake her head. "Never mind. You'd think I was foolish."

"No, we wouldn't," Hywel assured her. "Please tell us."

"Well, the Movement needs more mages, doesn't it?"

"Of course. We all know it does."

"Exactly. And right now, the mages of both the Order and the League are all in Amarid. So I want to see if I can convince some of the cloaked mages to join us."

Shavi halted and gaped at her. "You must be joking! Everyone knows what the cloaks think of us. They'd never leave their halls."

The rest of them stopped walking as well.

"You may be right," Sartol answered. "But the Movement needs help. If we don't get more mages, it's going to die before it ever has a chance to succeed."

"Is this why Nodin isn't traveling with you anymore?" Ortan asked. "Because he didn't approve of what you want to do?"

Sartol hesitated and looked away. "Yes," he said at last.

"I can't say that I blame him," Shavi said. "This will never work. The Movement has no place in Amarid. It exists out here among the villages and towns. That's the whole point. We don't belong there any more than the cloaks belong out here."

Ortan nodded. "I must say, I agree with him. I think this is a bad idea."

Sartol suppressed a grin. *Good. Then take your pitiful little Movement to the next free town and leave me alone.* "I'm sorry to hear you say that. But nonetheless, I'm going to do this, even if I have to do it alone."

"You won't," Hywel said. "I'll come with you."

"*What?*" Shavi hissed. "You're going to leave us? Just like that?"

Hywel faced him. "I'd rather not. I'd rather you and Ortan came with us. But I think Tammen's idea has merit, and I don't think that she should have to do this alone. If it comes to a choice between making her do this on her own and separating from the two of you for a short while, I'll do the latter."

"Well, then, that's what you'll have to do," Shavi insisted. "Because I'm not going to Amarid."

Hywel turned to Ortan, as did Shavi.

"I'll go with Shavi to the next town," the dark-eyed man, said evenly. "I hope you'll find us again soon."

Hywel nodded once, but he said nothing, and Sartol could see from the way the muscles in his jaw were working that he was unhappy.

"I don't want to be responsible for breaking up your group," Sartol said, looking at each of the mages in turn. His gaze finally came to rest on Hywel. "I'll be fine on my own. I have been for a long time now." *Keep away from me. Go with your friends if you want to live.*

"My mind is set, Tammen. Yours is a worthy endeavor, and I want to be a part of it. And when you and I are done, we can rejoin Shavi and Ortan, accompanied by the new no-cloaks we'll have convinced to join the Movement."

The bald man smiled at her and Sartol made himself smile in return. "Thank you, Hywel. I'll be glad to have you with me." *And I'll enjoy killing you.*

"I can't believe you're doing this," Shavi said, his voice thick with resentment. "After all the time we've been together . . ." He trailed off, shaking his head and refusing to look at Hywel.

"We'll be back before you know it, Shavi. I promise."

The yellow-haired mage offered no reply, and Hywel turned to Ortan. "Do the two of you have enough food?"

"Yes. We'll be fine. Arick guard you, Hywel. Return to us soon." Ortan glanced at Tammen and essayed a thin smile. "Be well, Tammen. Perhaps we'll meet again."

He turned, placed a hand briefly on Shavi's shoulder, and began to walk away. Shavi faced Hywel for a moment and shook his head one last time before turning and following Ortan. He didn't even look at Tammen.

"He'll be fine when we rejoin them," Hywel said, after the two mages had disappeared from view. He flashed a smile at Tammen and gestured toward the path. "Shall we?"

They began to walk, heading generally eastward and, after only a few moments, beginning the slow climb into the foothills.

"Have you been unbound long, Tammen?" Hywel asked after a lengthy silence.

"Not very, no."

Another silence.

"Where are you from?"

"Tobyn's Plain. A town called Watersbend."

Silence.

"How long have you been a mage?"

And so it went throughout the rest of the day. Hywel would ask her a question, Sartol would give a terse response, and they'd walk in silence until the free mage could think of something else to ask. Sartol was so furious with himself for allowing his encounter with the mages to happen in the first place that he couldn't bring himself to sustain a conversation. And Hywel was too much of a fool to give up trying. Until at last, late in the afternoon, as they crested yet another hill and finally saw the Parneshome Mountains looming before them, Sartol decided that the time had come to end their time together.

"So how did you lose your hawk?" Hywel asked, apparently too desperate at this point to realize how rude his question had been.

"Actually," Sartol said, stopping in the middle of the trail and turning to face him, "I killed her."

Hywel gave an awkward laugh. "I—I'm sorry if my question was inappropriate."

"Not at all. If I had thought it inappropriate, I wouldn't have answered."

"But surely you didn't mean . . ." He licked his lips. "You weren't being serious."

"Of course I was."

Hywel stared at her, his face turning white. "You killed your own familiar."

Sartol smiled. "Well, she wasn't really mine."

"Not yours? I don't understand."

"The bird belonged to Tammen, as did this body you see before you."

The man's eyes widened and he took a step back. But before he could take another, Sartol reached out with Tammen's hand and, grabbed him by the throat. The mage's small falcon leapt into the air and started to cry out, but Sartol silenced her with a single burst of blue-and-yellow flame. She fell to the ground in a smoldering heap.

"You shouldn't have come with me, Hywel. And you shouldn't have asked me so many questions." He lifted the mage off the ground and tightened his grasp.

"Who are you?" Hywel managed, his eyes beginning to bulge from his head and his hands clawing vainly at Tammen's wrist.

Sartol pulled the man's face close to Tammen's. "Look into my eyes," he commanded. "What do you see?"

The man looked and an instant later his eyes widened even further with recognition. He made a sound that might have been a gasp had he been able to breathe.

"You see it don't you. Tammen's not alone in here."

"Who are you?" Hywel mouthed again, although by now he couldn't make any sound at all.

"My name's Sartol. Perhaps you've heard of me." He squeezed Tammen's hand nearly to a fist, crushing the mage's throat as one would dry leaves in autumn. After a few moments more, Hywel went limp and Sartol carried him some distance off the trail and dropped him in a thicket of pines. He took the man's food pouch from his belt and then, as an afterthought, retrieved the carcass of Hywel's bird and tossed it among the trees as well. Probably no one would have noticed it, but he wasn't willing to take that chance.

It was only when he was walking again, watching the sky darken gradually overhead, that Sartol realized what a terrible mistake he had made. Indeed, he realized with a start, stopping in his tracks, he had made the same mistake twice: once with Nodin, and now again with Hywel.

He had sent them to the Unsettled. And in doing so, it was possible that he had alerted Theron, Phelan, and the others to his plans.

Idiot! he raged at himself. *Fool!*

A moment later, Miron appeared on his shoulder, yellow and spectral, like moonlight in a summer haze. She stared at him for a moment, then began to preen her ghostly feathers.

It's done, she seemed to be telling him. *Make your peace with it and move on.*

"You're right," he said aloud. He even smiled. He had seen no sign that Theron and the others were aware of his plan, and Nodin had been dead for days.

"They're the fools, not I."

And saying that, he continued on toward the great city and Amarid's Great Hall, vowing not to rest again until he stood before the Sammoning Stone.

19

I have written to you at great length about the free mages and their strengthening ties to the People's Movement. I'm sure that you are tired of hearing about them by now, and if this is so, I apologize. And yet here I sit, writing of them again. I have been thinking about them a great deal recently, trying to remember how they first came to play a role in the increasingly intricate politics of my land. My friends in the Order and I cannot recall precisely when we first heard someone speak of a "free mage"; the term seems to have entered our language while no one was looking.

I am certain, however, that despite their present close ties, the free mages and the People's Movement arose separately from each other, with the free mages appearing first by as much as a year or two. Originally, I believe, these mages were men and women who refused to be drawn into the bitter rivalry that had grown between the League and the Order, and who chose instead to serve the land on their own terms. And who could blame them? It might surprise you to hear this from me, but I think their original purpose was a noble one. It was only later, when their solution to the problem failed to catch on with others and they found themselves alone, in numbers too small to be taken seriously, that they turned to more dangerous and questionable activities.

—Hawk-Mage Orris to Melyor i Lakin, Sovereign and Bearer of Bragor-Nal, Spring, God's Year 4633.

He was alive. For reasons he couldn't fathom, he had survived Sartol's assault. His body was covered with burns, but with his beloved hawk dead there was little he could do to heal the oozing wounds or ease the pain than knifed through him with each movement. He had managed, with an effort that nearly killed him, to crawl to the houses and barns that stood abandoned on the plain, as if they were monuments to Sartol's malevolence. And rummaging through the homes, which had been left in haste, as though the terror brought upon the villagers by the Owl-Master's ghost had brooked no delay, Nodin found salves and bandages to put on his blistered skin. He found clothes to replace the blackened tatters of what he had been wearing when the ghost of Sartol threw Tammen's fire at him. He found an old hat to protect his burned head from the sun, whose once gentle caress now felt like raking talons on his scalp.

He found food as well, or at least something that used to be food. None of it was fit to be eaten. So after drinking greedily from a rain-filled trough in one of the farmyards, he left the village, abandoning it once more to the wind and the grasses. He made his way eastward, as Sartol had done in Tammen's body two nights before. While he had the strength and could bear the pain, he walked. But that didn't last long. By late afternoon, he was on his hands and knees, his eyes fixed on the trees of Tobyn's Wood, which still seemed impossibly far away. Walking with Tammen and Henryk a few days ago, it had taken him but an hour to walk from the wood to Sartol's binding place, but now he wasn't sure that he could make it back to the shelter of the trees before nightfall.

Perhaps Sartol killed me after all, he thought, his heart aching with a grief that made his physical pain seem as nothing. The Owl-Master's spirit had two days on him, and Tammen was strong. She could carry Sartol swiftly across Tobyn-Ser to wherever it was he was going. Amarid, probably. That's where the Order and the League were. If Sartol wished to defeat them and make himself sole master of the Mage-Craft, he would have to start there.

Nodin didn't know how to stop the Owl-Master's spirit. He was unbound and half-dead from his injuries. And he knew better than to think that he could save Tammen. He had seen Sartol's yellow fire in her eyes just before she raised her staff and tried to kill him. She was gone already.

But he had loved her, and she had cared for him in her own fashion; their one night together had convinced him of that. So, he had to try. He owed her that much. And even if he didn't, he owed it to himself. He refused to allow the history of Tobyn-Ser to show that Tammen had allowed Sartol to destroy the land.

And so he crawled, the sun behind him, casting his own animal-like shadow before him, too low now to score the wound on his back where Sartol's fire had hammered into him. He held his staff against his body with one arm, stopping frequently to switch it to one side or the other so that he didn't lean on either hand for too long, but always keeping his violet stone in front of him, as if its continued glow offered some reassurance that he was still alive. Every part of his body hurt. His knees were just about the only parts of him that weren't burned, and they grew increasingly sore with every minute that he crawled. And his hands, which were charred almost beyond hope of recovery, throbbed with such intensity that even if he had found food in the village, he probably would have been unable to keep it down.

He felt the hoof beats before he heard them. They drummed through the soil of the plain like a pulse, flowing up into him through his knees and his hand.

He stopped crawling and raised himself with an effort that tore a gasp from his chest so that he knelt upright. The horseman was to the south, heading toward the wood as well, and seemingly unaware of Nodin. The mage raised his staff over his head and reached for what little power he had left to make his ceryll gleam.

Almost immediately, the rider turned toward him, and within moments he had dismounted and was kneeling by Nodin's side.

"Fist of the God!" the man whispered. His face and voice were youthful, but Nodin noticed little else about him. "What happened to you, Child of Amarid?"

The mage hadn't even thought of what he would tell anyone. On some level he had never believed that he would speak to another living man. Would people believe him? Would they think him mad with pain and lack of food? And if they did believe him, would the news that Sartol was wandering the land again, freed from the constraints of Theron's Curse and armed once more with the Mage-Craft, send panic through Tobyn-Ser?

"I was attacked by a fellow mage," he finally said, struggling to make himself heard. "She's mad, and I need to find her before she does this to others."

"You need a healer, Mage," the man told him. "Or better yet, another of your kind who can tend to you. The rest can wait."

"No!" Nodin winced. Even speaking pained him. The man was right. "My apologies," he breathed. "I appreciate your concern, sir, and I'd be grateful if you could get me to a healer. But we have need of haste. This mage must be stopped."

The man nodded. "Can you stand?"

"With your help."

"And can you ride?"

Nodin swallowed. He knew what it would cost him, but he knew as well that he had little choice. "I'll try."

As it turned out, the jarring of the mount was so painful that Nodin passed out practically with the beast's first stride. It was a blessing of sorts. When he awoke next, he was on a bed in a small room, lying on his side. It was night still; the only light came from his ceryll, which lay beside him, and a candle burning on a nearby table. The rider was there, standing beside a young woman who appeared to be his wife. An older woman, her brow furrowed and her mouth set in a thin line, sat on the bed laying pungent poultices on Nodin's burns.

"Your touch is deft, Healer," he told her, trying to smile. "But your herbs smell like a stable."

"It may not be my herbs, Mage," she returned drily. "When did you bathe last?"

It hurt to laugh, and Nodin squeezed his eyes shut against the pain that knifed through him. "Please, Madam," he whispered, "spare me your humor."

She placed one last poultice on his back and stood. "Those should remain in place for at least two days. Preferably longer." She turned toward the rider and his wife. "Feed him stews and water. Nothing solid until his strength returns. Send for me if he worsens."

"I need to be going," Nodin told her even as he felt himself drifting back toward sleep. "I have to find the mage who did this to me."

The woman faced him again, arching an eyebrow. "Why? So that he can finish you? Don't be a fool. He's but one mage. Others will deal with him. Count yourself lucky that he didn't kill you."

She started to turn away.

"Listen to me!" he said with all the force he could muster.

The healer halted and waited.

"This is not just any mage." He took a breath and glanced briefly at the man and woman before fixing his eyes on the healer again. They might think him crazed, but he had to take that chance. "Her name is Tammen. She . . . she was a friend. But we sought help for the People's Movement from the Unsettled." It occurred to him that he didn't even know whether this was a free town, but that hardly mattered anymore. "One of them refused us, and so we went to Sartol. He has her now. He controls her, and somehow he's used her to gain access to the Mage-Craft and leave his binding place. It was he who did this to me, not Tammen."

They were staring at him, and he feared that they did indeed consider him a madman. The healer stepped forward and placed a cool hand against his cheek.

"He's feverish," she said over shoulder, although she kept her eyes on Nodin.

"This is not my fever talking, Healer. I promise you: what I'm telling you is true. Sartol is roaming the land again in the guise of a mage named Tammen."

She chewed her lip for several moments and continued to stare at him. "He seems to have his senses still." She glanced back at the others. "I'm not certain what to think."

"Stop talking about me as if I'm not here and listen! My name is Nodin. I'm a free mage. I was rendered unbound and burned over most of my body. I couldn't heal myself, but I managed to find some bandages and salves in the abandoned homes on the plain and I used them to treat my wounds. Now do those sound like the recollections of a man crazed with fever?"

The healer crossed her arms over her chest. "No," she admitted.

"Then hear what I'm telling you. Sartol convinced Tammen to give him access to her ceryll, and in doing so, he managed to make her body a vessel for his spirit. He is free. He's found a way to escape his binding place, and Arick knows what he plans to do next. We're the only people who know of this. I'm sure of that. We have to warn the leaders of the Order and the League."

She regarded him for a few moments longer. "How long ago did you say this happened?"

"Two nights."

"And do you know where Tammen is now?"

"You mean Sartol. No, I don't. I would guess that he's headed east, toward Amarid."

She nodded. "I suppose that would make sense." She seemed to consider something for a moment. "Was he on horseback?"

"Not that I know of. The three of us came to the plain on foot."

She narrowed her eyes. "There were three of you?"

"Yes. Tammen, myself, and a mage named Henryk."

"And where is Henryk now?"

"Dead. Killed by Sartol."

Again she nodded. "You should rest," she said after a brief pause. "I'll consider what you've told me. And I'll inform the village elders. They should know about this."

Nodin sat up, gritting his teeth against the pain. "I don't have time to rest, and I can't wait while you and the elders ponder all this. Haven't you been listening to me?"

"Yes, Mage," she said sternly, "I've been listening. And I've heard an incredible tale about an unsettled spirit taking control of a living mage, of a long-dead villain threatening us from the grave, all from a man who's been without food for days, who's more dead than he is alive, who's flushed with fever, and who's lost his familiar and his friends and is probably half-crazed with grief. Pardon me for being skeptical."

He looked beyond the healer to the rider and his wife. "Do you think I'm mad? Do I sound crazed to you?"

The man cleared his throat. "Forgive me, Child of Amarid, but I'm not a healer. I know nothing of such things."

"It doesn't matter what he thinks," the healer said. "You're in no position to be going anywhere. So you might as well wait until the morning. I promise you that I'll relate your story to the elders first thing."

"And I promise you that as soon as you leave this room, I'll be going as well. Sartol is days ahead of us already. I have to go after him."

"You won't get far," she said, as if daring him to try.

"I had crawled most of the way to Tobyn's Wood by the time this kind man found me," Nodin told her. "Go ahead and ask him. If I have to, I'll go all the way to Amarid on my hands and knees. But I will be going."

The healer exhaled through her teeth. "You're a fool. I should let you go. If you're so determined to kill yourself, I should just let you do it."

"You're too good a healer for that. I can tell."

She looked at him, saying nothing. He could see from the working of her jaw and the intensity of her gaze that a battle waged within her.

"Help me, Healer. Help me stop him."

"You're a fool," she said again. "And I must be an even bigger fool."

Nodin smiled, his relief as much a balm for his burns as the healer's poultices.

"Farrek," the woman said, turning once more to the rider. "Do you still have that cart that you used to take your goods to market last summer?"

"Yes, Healer, of course."

"And can you spare a plow horse for a time?"

"A plow horse?" Nodin broke in before the man could reply. "You can't be serious! How are we supposed to catch up to Sartol with a plow horse and cart?"

"I'd rather be placing you on a cart than on a pyre!" the healer said, whirling on him. "Farrek here told me that you passed out as soon as he placed you on his stallion. Is that true?"

Nodin gave a reluctant nod.

"I thought so. Now I'm willing to take you to Amarid, but we're going to do this my way. You may be trying to save the land, Mage, but I'm determined to save you, with your help or without it."

"You're right, Healer," he said, still not meeting her gaze. "My apologies and my thanks."

"Hitch the beast to your cart, Farrek," she instructed, as if she hadn't heard Nodin at all. "And pack up whatever food you can spare."

"You're leaving now, Healer?"

"You heard him. If we try to wait until morning, he'll be crawling through the wood like a worm all night, upsetting all my poultices and bandages." She shrugged. "I can't abide the waste."

"Yes, Healer," the man said, hurrying out the door. "Right away."

She looked at Nodin again and shook her head. "Arick help you if it turns out you're crazed."

As it happened, Nodin couldn't even stand the pain of being carried from the bed to the pallet they prepared for him in the cart. He passed out again as they carried him and did not awaken until morning. It was only then that he became convinced that the healer believed his tale, for if she hadn't, they would surely have returned him to the small bedroom as soon as he lost consciousness.

The pallet was made of straw, but it was uncommonly thick and comfortable. The forest path they were on was rough, and the wooden cart bounced constantly and swayed from side to side. And yet Nodin felt little of it.

"Awake at last," the healer said in a flat voice, not even bothering to look at him.

"Yes," he answered. He sat up gingerly, and though his burns still throbbed painfully, he was at least able to move his limbs. "You do good work, Healer. Your poultices seem to be working."

"There's broth in a skin back there," she said. "It's not very warm, but it will have to do."

He found the skin wrapped in several pieces of cloth and took a long drink. It was salty and delicious, and though it wasn't hot, it hadn't turned cold yet either. "Thank you," he said after taking a second pull from the skin. "It's very good."

"Finish it. There are three more skins full of it, and when that's gone we'll stop at an inn and get you more."

"Do you know of other free towns in the God's wood?"

At that, she did turn. "Does it matter?"

"I just meant that a free town will gladly give us the food. That's all."

"Ours was an Order town, and I'm doing this for you. Do you really think that any town regardless of its loyalties would deny food to someone in your condition?"

He said nothing, and after a moment she shook her head and faced forward again.

"We'll ride for a few miles more," she said without even looking back over her shoulder. "Then we'll stop so that I can check on your burns. In the meantime, you should sleep some more."

He nodded, and then, realizing that she hadn't looked for a response, he said, "That sounds fine. Thank you, Healer."

"My name is Ianthe."

"All right. Thank you, Ianthe."

She glanced back at him. "And yours?"

"Nodin."

She gave a single nod, then clucked at the old plow horse. He watched her for another minute or two and then lay back down on his side and closed his eyes to sleep. At this pace it would be at least a fortnight before they reached Amarid, but he could hardly complain. He was lucky to be alive and luckier still to be pursuing Tammen at all.

Sartol, he told himself. You're pursuing Sartol. Tammen is dead. If the gods know anything at all of mercy, she's dead.

Rhonwen knew that another had joined them the moment it happened. It was as if a dozen voices whispered the news in her mind in unison. It was as if she was part of a great circle that suddenly opened itself a bit wider to admit another. Neither image, she knew, was terribly far from the truth. In this place where light was power, and thought was communication, there were voices in her head, and her circle, the circle of the Unsettled, had just grown larger.

She still remembered her first day as an unsettled mage with a vividness that constricted her heart. Trevdan, whose ghost now sat on her shoulder preening, had been killed a few months before by a hunter's arrow. It had been an accident; the man had meant no harm. He had been in tears as he apologized to her again and again. And though she had grieved, she had always assumed that she would soon find a new familiar, that she would serve the land for a lifetime. But when the fever took her, she lacked the power to heal herself, and she hadn't enough strength to return to Amarid in search of aid from other mages.

Before she understood what had happened, she found herself surrounded by a light so dazzling that it nearly blinded her. Trevdan was with her again, which should have told her everything. But only when Theron came to her, cold and distant, and yet repentant in his own way, did she fully comprehend her fate.

She was a ghost, denied the solace of rest and the comfort of the gods' embrace by Theron's Curse. She would spend eternity immersed in light—teal, like the color of her ceryll—and she would wander the shadows of Tobyn's Wood within earshot of the River Halcya and within sight of the Parneshome Mountains. At least that's how she remembered this spot, the place of her binding to Trevdan, her one and only familiar. She heard many things, and she could see much that went on throughout the land, but she could take no pleasure in the music of the river or the beauty of the mountains. Such sights and sounds were beyond her reach. She was in a radiant prison; she was dead.

And so too was another mage. A new one. Hywel, the voices in her head whispered. His name is Hywel. He was in Leora's Forest now, the place where he had bound to his first hawk, although he had died elsewhere. She would go to him when the time was right. Not now, not today, or even tomorrow. Theron would speak with him first. Theron spoke to all of them first, as was appropriate. His curse, his circle. And when Theron was done, when his emerald glow withdrew, leaving the newest of the Unsettled alone with his fear and his despair, Phelan would go next, to give what reassurance he could, and to offer some kindness in a place that was endlessly cruel.

It was much the same for all the new ones. It was a ritual of sorts, though a strange one to be sure. Theron and Phelan. One was the most reviled man ever to have walked the land, and the other was beloved and revered more than any figure in Tobyn-Ser's history except Amarid. Yet in her time with them as one of the Unsettled, Rhonwen had come to see that there was both more and less to them than their legends could convey. They were men, or rather, the ghosts of men. And like all men, they had their faults and their virtues.

Theron was arrogant and gruff. Even sharing his thoughts, she sensed that there was a remoteness to him, a desire to distance himself from all others. He seemed incapable of warmth or kindness. But he was not evil, as she had once believed. Though he was loath to admit it, he felt remorse for what he had done to the others in this circle. He knew the Curse had been a mistake, and while the greeting he offered to the new ones carried no apology, or even sympathy, the gesture itself, she had come to understand, was intended as an expiation.

Phelan, on the other hand, was kindness personified. Just the sound of his voice, which was as gentle and deep as a morning tide, had given her some relief that first day. He had been so gracious with her, so polite, that she had been embarrassed to be treated so by a man as great as he. And yet the assurances he had given her, though kindly meant and welcomed at the time, had been empty. It didn't get any easier; there was no relief from the tedium and the loneliness and the regret. He, who had chosen to become one of the Unsettled so that he could spend eternity with his beloved wolf, had no idea what it meant to be ensnared by Theron's Curse against one's will.

So she would wait her turn, and when the time came, she would speak with Hywel, who was only the second mage to join their circle since her death. And she would tell him what little she had learned about their existence in this realm of light and death. That the greatest suffering came not from the Curse itself, or from Theron, but rather from the regrets and the lost loves that he brought with him. That even with the voices that would gather in his mind as he learned to hear them, there was no companionship here, no comfort or friendship or love. There were only light and memory, and it never got any easier.

Except that in the next moment, there was more. Abruptly the whispers in her head changed, taking on an urgency that Rhonwen had never heard before. Even when the voices argued, even when there was discord among the Unsettled, there was an order to the voices that allowed her to follow what was being said, or, to be more precise, thought. It was, in that way, not unlike attending a Gathering in Amarid's Great Hall. But now, in the aftermath of whatever had happened, that order was gone, replaced by a clamor that left her dazed and frightened. She could make out little of what the others were saying; all she knew was that they were angry and afraid. Then a word reached her through the bedlam in her head. One word that the others cried out repeatedly. Sartol.

Sartol. The one voice that she had never once heard in her head. The one mage among all the Unsettled whom they had told her was never to be addressed. She knew who he was, of course. Everyone did. And having been a member of the Order, even though it was only for a few months, she probably knew more than most people in Tobyn-Ser. She knew of his betrayal, of his alliance with the outlanders, and of how close he had come to having others in the Order punished for his crimes. And she knew that in his first day as an unsettled mage, he had defied Theron and Phelan and nearly succeeded in bringing ruin to the living mages who battled the outlanders at Phelan Spur. For this, he had been isolated from the rest. She had been instructed by Theron himself never even to think of Sartol.

"As far as I am concerned," the Owl-Master had once told her, "he does not exist. Let him spend eternity utterly alone. He has earned that in life and in death."

Now, however, something had changed. Because all of them were thinking of him. All of them were shouting his name until it seemed to echo within her skull like thunder rolling through a mountain pass.

"*Enough!*" Theron finally roared, his voice crashing down upon their minds like a wave, silencing them all.

"Can you tell us what's happened, Owl-Master?" Phelan's voice, deep and calm, even now.

"The traitor has freed himself from the Curse. He is loose upon the land again."

"How?" several cried out at once, like a chorus from one of Cearbhall's tragedies.

"I cannot explain it," Theron rumbled. "At least not yet. Somehow he is using the body and ceryll of a living mage. He has left his binding place and is on his way to Amarid."

"The Summoning Stone." Rhonwen didn't know that she had allowed the others to hear her thought until Theron addressed her.

"Yes, Mage. I agree. It was almost his once. He must believe that he can control it still."

"Can he be stopped?" Phelan asked.

Theron didn't answer, and for what seemed to Rhonwen a long time, there was utter silence in her mind. She couldn't remember the last time she had experienced such a thing. She sensed the others waiting, just as she was, wondering what Theron was doing.

"I have seen his binding place," the Owl-Master announced, abruptly entering their thoughts again. "I understand what he has done."

"And?" Phelan said.

"We can do nothing."

Chaos. Cries of despair. Questions flying at Theron from all over the land.

"He has done nothing to alter the Curse," Theron told them, silencing them again. "He has merely found a way to use the power he has." He paused, and then, "I will show you."

An instant later an image entered Rhonwen's mind, and immediately she understood. It was brilliant, though so ruthless and twisted that it nearly defied comprehension. The image Theron sent was of a remote spot on the Northern Plain—the place of Sartol's first binding. Except that rather than seeing the Owl-Master's spirit, as she should have, she merely saw his ghostly staff planted in the ground. And from the ceryll mounted atop the wood, light flowed like blood, running down his staff into the rich, dark soil and coursing eastward toward Tobyn's Wood and Amarid. By day, no living man or woman would have seen anything, and even at night, a passerby would have seen the staff, and perhaps a small puddle of yellow light at its base where Sartol's power soaked into the ground, but little more. Only the Unsettled could see all of it and divine from this vision what Sartol had done.

He was rooted to this spot on the plain by Theron's Curse, but using the ceryll of the unfortunate mage he had mastered, he had found a way to extend his reach across the land. Any of them could have done it, because all of them were manifestations of the Mage-Craft. But in order to do it, they would have had to be capable of the worst kind of violation. This was rape, certainly nothing less. A man capable of doing this . . .

She didn't allow herself to complete the thought. True, she was dead, a ghost and nothing more. But she still loved the land and she still believed in the Mage-Craft and all that it represented. To have it perverted in this way seemed to her something akin to blasphemy.

And there was nothing they could do.

"If he had altered the Curse in some way," Theron told them all, "he might have freed us to alter it as well. Then perhaps we could stop him. But unless one of us is willing to do what Sartol has done, we are powerless."

"Can we at least warn someone?" Rhonwen asked, "so that they can tell the Order and the League that Sartol is coming?"

"Of course," Theron said. "But as always they must come to us first. We have no way to reach out to them."

"We are power incarnate," one of the others said bitterly. "And yet we are powerless."

Rhonwen shook her head in frustration. She wanted to cry, but her rage would not even allow that. Instead she just stared into the brilliant teal light that surrounded her. And for just an instant, she thought she heard laughter coming to her from a great distance.

"I'm hungry, Mama," Myn said, as Alayna led her through the maze of merchants in Amarid's old town commons.

Alayna was looking for one peddler in particular, a man who was selling a shirt that she wanted for Jaryd. His birthday had already come and gone, but with all that had been happening, they had done little to celebrate.

"I know, Myn-Myn" she said. "Me too. I just want to find this one peddler and then we'll get something to eat, all right?"

"Can I get a sweet?"

Alayna laughed. "Maybe. After we have our meal."

They walked on for a few minutes more, Alayna searching for the merchant and Myn humming a song to herself.

"I had a dream last night, Mama," the girl said after some time.

"What was it about?" Alayna asked absently, frowning as she looked around them. The man couldn't have moved on already. It was still too early in the year for the old town merchants to be leaving Amarid for the smaller towns.

"It was about a man who's coming here."

Alayna stopped and looked down at her daughter. They had tied back the girl's hair today, and with her hair pulled away from her brow, and the sunlight sparkling in her grey eyes, she looked just like Jaryd's mother.

"What kind of a dream was this, Myn-Myn?"

"A real one. The kind you and Papa sometimes have."

A vision. Alayna felt her heart racing suddenly, and she had to fight to keep her voice steady. "Myn, this is very important: do you remember anything about the man in your dream?"

"I didn't like him very much."

"Why not?"

Myn shrugged. "I think he was mean. And I don't think you and Papa like him either."

"What makes you say that?" Alayna asked, squatting beside her.

"I'm not sure. You looked kind of angry when you saw him."

"Did he say anything? Or did we say anything to him?"

Myn looked at her feet and shrugged again. "I don't know, Mama. I made myself wake up too soon. I didn't like looking at him."

"Did he scare you a little, Myn-Myn?"

She nodded.

"Then you did the right thing waking up." She hesitated. She didn't want to make Myn recount anything that would frighten her, but she also knew how important it was to know as much as they could about this man. "Do you remember what he looked like, Myn? Can you tell me a little bit about him?"

"Yes. He was a mage, and he was big."

"Was his hair silver?" Alayna asked, thinking that perhaps the girl had dreamed of Erland.

"No. It was dark, but there was a little bit of silver in it."

Alayna shuddered slightly but then smiled at her own foolishness. She knew of one mage who fit this description, but it couldn't have been he.

"Was he wearing a blue cloak?"

"No, green."

"And what color was his stone?"

"Yellow."

She shuddered again. Myn was describing Sartol.

"Are you sure this was a real dream, Love? Are you sure it just wasn't so scary that it felt real?"

"I'm sure, Mama. I saw this man in the Great Hall. I promise."

Alayna didn't want to believe her. Sartol was dead. He walked with the Unsettled now, which meant that he was tied for all eternity to the Northern Plain. But Myn was old enough and familiar enough with the Sight to know a vision when she had one.

"What did his bird look like?" Alayna asked, unable to keep her voice from quavering.

"It was a hawk, a big one, and I don't think it was a kind I've seen before."

Alayna racked her brain trying to remember what kind of bird Sartol's first familiar had been. He had told her once, during her apprenticeship, back when they were friends. Back before she learned that he was a traitor and a murderer. So much had happened since then; so much had changed. She couldn't remember anymore.

"Are you scared, Mama?"

She had learned long ago that it was impossible to lie to Myn. The child was far too perceptive. "A little bit, Myn-Myn. The man you've described is not someone I'd care to see again."

"Is he dead?"

The mage felt the blood drain from her face. "Why would you think that?"

"Because of the way his eyes looked," Myn said in a small voice.

"How did his eyes look?" she asked, not really wanting to know.

"Sort of like they were on fire."

Alayna nodded, knowing precisely what the girl meant. She had seen Theron, after all, and Phelan as well. She knew what it was to look into the eyes of the Unsettled. Standing and taking Myn's hand in hers, she started back toward the Great Hall.

"What about Papa's shirt?"

"We'll get it another day. Right now, I want you to tell your papa about your dream."

"Slow down, Mama," Myn said. "You're going too fast."

"I'm sorry, Myn-Myn."

She made herself walk more slowly, but she kept glancing over her shoulder and peering down alleyways, as if she expected to see Sartol's ghost coming after them.

As soon as they reached the Great Hall, Alayna took Myn back to see Jaryd and had her repeat to him what she had seen in her vision. When Myn left out details, Alayna prompted her, but otherwise she merely allowed her daughter to recount the dream as she had the first time. For a long time after Myn finished, none of them spoke. Jaryd and Alayna exchanged a look, and Alayna knew from what she saw in the Eagle-Sage's eyes that he recognized the man Myn had described.

"Myn-Myn," Alayna finally said, "why don't you go to the kitchen and get something to eat. Your papa and I need to talk."

"All right," she said quietly, starting toward the door. But when she reached it she stopped and faced them again. "I'm afraid to be alone, Mama. I'm afraid of that man."

Alayna went over to her and gave her a hug. "How about if I call for Valya? Will that make you feel better?"

Myn nodded, and Alayna led her into the kitchen. After getting the girl some food and waiting until Valya, the townswoman who had been taking care of her arrived, Alayna returned to their quarters and sat down in one of the large chairs. Jaryd hadn't moved from where she had left him. He was standing in the middle of the room, staring at the empty hearth while his enormous eagle sat, as always, on the mantel.

"What do you suppose it means?" he asked, as Alayna closed the door behind her.

She shook her head. "I wouldn't even want to guess. I don't even know whether I believe it was a true Seeing."

"I thought of that," he agreed. "But we've never told her about Sartol. How could she have described him so accurately if this wasn't a vision?"

"I don't know. But I also don't know how it's possible for him to be coming here. The Curse ties him to his binding place."

"Is it possible that this wasn't Sartol? That we're allowing our own memories and fears to make her vision into something that it wasn't?"

Alayna pushed her hair back from her forehead. "I'd like to believe that. But you heard what she said about his eyes. She saw an unsettled mage. And based upon everything else she told us, I have to believe that it's him."

"And why would he be coming here? Revenge?"

"That. And the Summoning Stone."

Jaryd's face turned ashen. "I had forgotten about the stone."

"I haven't forgotten any of it."

He gave her a sympathetic look. "It wasn't your fault. You should know that by now."

"I do." It was true in the strictest sense. For a long time after he was revealed as a traitor, she had blamed herself for not being able to see beyond his deceit. But finally she had come to see that she was no more to blame than any other mage in the Order. Sartol had deceived all of them, and when she had been his Mage-Attend and had known him best, she had also been most susceptible to his lies. She had looked up to him. He had been like a second father to her. And she had taken all he told her not just as truth, but as lessons to be learned. But now, thinking of him again after so long, feeling the old fear of what he had become well up within her once more, she could not help but feel some of her guilt returning as well.

And knowing her as well as he did, Jaryd saw this. He crossed to where she was standing and took her in his arms. "So you know that it wasn't your fault, but you still feel guilty about it."

She gave a wry smile. "Yes. Something like that."

He smiled and kissed her. But then his expression grew grave again. "We'll stop him, Alayna. We stopped him once before, and we'll do it again."

"How?" she asked, shaking her head and feeling herself begin to tremble. "If he's managed to alter Theron's Curse, and he's confident enough in his powers to come after us as a ghost, what makes you think that we can defeat him?"

"The eagles. Now we know why they've come. They're here to unite us, to bring the League and the Order together to face him, and to give us the strength and the courage to destroy him."

"All of us were just barely enough last time," she said. "What if he's stronger now?"

"We'll have to be stronger, too. What choice do we have?" He had always been strong-willed and passionate. It was part of what had made her fall in love with him so many years ago. But gazing into his grey eyes now, Alayna saw a look of resolve and certainty that was unlike anything she had ever seen in him before. "All of Tobyn-Ser is depending on us," he told her. "But more than that, Myn is depending on us. I'll destroy him myself if that's what it takes to save her."

20

Obviously, the leaders of all the great Nals of Lon-Ser have an interest in maintaining stability and order. We live in unsettled times, as the recent assassination of Oerella-Nal's Sovereign Shivohn demonstrated so vividly. Now, with the tragic death of Sovereign Melyor i Lakin, Bragor-Nal has suffered a similarly debilitating loss. This is a time of mourning and reflection for Bragor-Nal's people. It is a time to remember our fallen leader and to honor all that she accomplished.

But it is also a time of fear, a time of uncertainty. Bragor-Nal needs a leader who can lead it through this time of crisis, who can offer the people of the Nal the reassurance that comes with continuity and familiarity.

For this reason, and in accordance with the procedures established by the Cape of Stars Treaty of 2802, I hereby formally petition Lon-Ser's Council of Sovereigns to recognize my claim to the position of Sovereign of Bragor-Nal by admitting me to its ranks.

> —Formal petition for admission to the Council of Sovereigns, submitted by Dobir i Waarin, Overlord of Bragor-Nal's First Dominion, Day 1, Week 8, Spring, Year 3068.

Wiercia still wasn't sure why she had agreed to this. She had been fooled once by Marar, and it seemed quite possible that the ease with which she had been duped had cost Melyor her life. And yet here she was, only days after the Bragory Sovereign's death, consenting to a face-to-face meeting with Dob, the Sovereign-designate. She knew little about him, just that he was an Overlord, and that he had once been a break-law, just like Melyor.

Which perhaps was the point. She had failed Melyor dismally, allowing Marar to trick her into abandoning the friendship she and the Gildriite woman had begun to forge. In a sense, meeting with Dob was her way of making amends. Unfortunately, the gesture came a good deal too late.

Dob had suggested that they meet at the Monarch's residence on the Point of the Sovereigns, where the Council of Sovereigns usually met. It was, she had decided, quite presumptuous of him. His petition for admission to the Council had yet to be approved, and here he was inviting her to a clandestine meeting as if he had been a Council member for years. But it was the very audacity of his invitation that had convinced her to accept. Obviously he had something important to discuss, and in light of what she now knew about Marar, Wiercia had little choice but to find out what it was.

But as her air-carrier drew closer to the old residence, she began to have misgivings. What if Dob thought that she was somehow responsible for Melyor's death? Or what if he merely wanted to throw Oerella-Nal into turmoil as a prelude to invasion? She knew nothing about him, at least nothing of substance. What if this was a trap?

Shivohn would have shaken her head at such thoughts. "The world is a lonely place for suspicious people," she had once told Wiercia, when, as a Legate, Wiercia had expressed doubts about Melyor. "If you go looking for enemies, you'll never find any friends."

Of course, Shivohn was dead now, killed by an assassin whom she allowed to get too close. Wiercia rubbed a hand across her brow and shook her head. She was not a trusting person; she never had been. And recent events had reminded her once more of why: she was not a good judge of people. She had mistrusted Melyor because she feared the woman's Gildriite powers and could not forget that she had once been a break-law. Yet she had nearly agreed to an alliance with Marar, who she now believed had been behind Melyor's death, and who had probably been responsible for Shivohn's as well.

"We'll be at the residence in just a few moments, Sovereign," the carrier pilot informed her over the speaker console.

She almost told him then to turn the carrier around and take her back to the palace. She actually had her finger on the console button before she stopped herself.

If you go looking for enemies . . .

She pressed the button after all, but only to thank the pilot.

The carrier landed a few minutes later, and Wiercia saw that the air-carrier of the Bragory Sovereign was already there. She smiled to herself. At least the man was being as presumptuous with his own people as he was with her.

She took her time leaving the carrier and walking into the residence. He might have called the meeting, she decided, but she was the only true Sovereign there. And she was determined to make him understand this. She had also brought an unusually large contingent of guards, along with the two Legates who usually accompanied her, and she had the soldiers form a tight diamond cluster around her, just in case.

As soon as she entered the residence, however, she realized that there was more to Dob's invitation than she had divined. First, rather than waiting for her upstairs in the Council meeting room, Dob was standing in the entrance foyer of the residence. And he was alone.

"Greetings, Sovereign," he said, his tone crisp. "You and your attendants are free to go up to the Council chamber, but your guards will have to remain here with me."

"What?" she said. "Why should I—?" She stopped abruptly, as the full import of what he had said reached her. "Remain with you? I thought I was here to meet with you."

"You'll understand shortly, Sovereign." He gestured toward the curving staircase. "Please. We're pressed for time."

She stared at him for several moments. "I'm not sure I trust you," she admitted.

He grinned, his blue eyes dancing beneath a shock of unruly black hair. He was quite handsome in a rough way. She couldn't help but think that he must have been a very good break-law. "I don't blame you," he told her. "But that's why I stand before you, alone and unarmed. If any harm comes to you, your guards will be able to exact a measure of revenge by killing me."

She stood regarding him for a few seconds longer, then nodded. "Watch him," she said, turning to the captain of the guard. "But unless something happens, don't touch him."

"Yes, Sovereign."

She started up the stairs, motioning for her Legates to follow. There was really only one explanation for this, and she wasn't entirely certain how she felt about it. On the one hand she was relieved, more so than she would ever have believed. Yet she was also angry. How much trickery could she be expected to tolerate from her fellow Sovereigns?

Though she was prepared, however, her Legates were not, and when they walked into the Council chamber and saw Melyor sitting in her customary place, very much alive, with an enigmatic smile on her lips, they gasped in unison.

"Funny," Wiercia said drily, "you don't look dead."

Melyor's smile broadened. "I'll take that as a compliment."

"I'm not sure how you should take it. By the gods, Melyor, what is all this? What are we doing here? Why are you pretending to be dead?"

The Bragory woman indicated Wiercia's chair with an open hand. "Please, sit," she said. "I'll answer all your questions, but it could take a while."

Wiercia took her seat reluctantly, glancing around the room as she did. There were two men sitting with Melyor. One of them was her security chief, Jibb, whom Wiercia had met several times before. But the other was a man she did not know. He was long-limbed with a thin face and pale, nervous eyes that flicked to Wiercia's face for just an instant before darting away again. He wore a uniform like Jibb's, so he had to be a security man as well, but unlike Jibb he carried no weapons that she could see.

As usual, Melyor was armed. Her thrower was strapped to her thigh, and she was dressed as always in dark, loose-fitting trousers and an ivory tunic. The only thing that distinguished her from an ordinary break-law was her staff, which lay across the table, its crimson stone glowing brightly, as if to remind Wiercia of why she didn't trust this woman.

"First of all," Melyor began, regarding her solemnly, "please accept my apologies for the deception. I assure you it was absolutely necessary. I want Marar to believe I'm dead, and since I don't know which of my men he's recruited as spies, I need for all of them to believe it as well."

"Well, I can tell you that Marar is convinced," Wiercia said. "He contacted me a few days ago to tell me, and he was positively giddy. At least he was at first."

"And then what happened?"

"I asked him how he had learned of your death so quickly, and when he hedged, I accused him of having you killed and of sending the assassin for Shivohn as well."

Melyor raised an eyebrow. "Is that really what you think?"

Wiercia shrugged, her gaze wandering to Melyor's stone again. "I don't know what to think anymore. Frankly, I don't trust either of you."

"Would it help if I could offer you proof that Marar tried to have me killed?"

"What proof?" Wiercia asked, looking at Melyor again.

"Tell her," Melyor said over her shoulder.

The bald guard cleared his throat and shifted in his chair. He had a large golden hoop in one ear that she hadn't noticed earlier. "Me," he said. "I'm the proof. I'm a traitor. Marar hired me to kill the Sovereign and the general, and he paid me a great deal of gold."

Wiercia looked at the man for a long time, until a muscle on the side of his face began to jump, and he looked away. He could have been lying. She wouldn't have put it past Melyor to get him to say these things in order to win Wiercia's trust. *The world is a lonely place for suspicious people. . . .* The fact of the matter was, he didn't appear to be lying. And neither did Melyor. She looked over at Jibb and saw that his shoulder was bandaged.

"What happened to your arm?" she asked.

"I was trying to tame a renegade Nal-Lord and ended up in a firefight." He shrugged. "It's not as bad as it looks."

"Premel here saved his life," Melyor added.

Jibb made a sour face, but said nothing.

There was far more to this story than they were telling her, Wiercia realized, but little of it concerned her. The important thing was, she believed them. And in that moment she wouldn't have traded places with the one named Premel for all the gold in Lon-Ser.

"So what do you want from me?" Wiercia asked, shifting her gaze back to Melyor.

The woman smiled, her relief written so plainly on her face that Wiercia had to grin as well. "Thank you," she said.

"I haven't done anything yet."

"Actually, you've probably done more than you think. If Marar believes that he's made an enemy of you, he's more likely to strike a deal with Dob, which is exactly what we want him to do."

"I'm surprised you haven't just gone into Stib-Nal and gotten rid of him."

"I would have," Melyor admitted, "but I was afraid that would lead to a war with the Matriarchy."

Wiercia considered this briefly and conceded the point with a nod. "It probably would have."

"Besides," Melyor continued, "Marar is up to something. He told Premel that he's getting gold from Tobyn-Ser, and I want to know how that's possible."

Wiercia shot a look toward the security man. "He really told you that?"

Premel nodded.

"Did he say anything else?"

"No," Melyor answered. Wiercia faced her once more. "Jibb and I were in the room during their conversation," she explained. "He was very vague. That's where you can help us. In addition to playing along with all of this—acting as if you believe I'm dead, considering Dob's petition, all of it—you can also have your Legates talk to some of the merchants that frequent your ports. Find out if any of them have noticed any unusual activity between Stib-Nal and Tobyn-Ser."

"All right. What else?"

Melyor thought for a moment. "It might also help matters along if you play up this meeting you were supposed to have had with Dob today. Make it sound as though the two of you established a strong rapport. If we can scare Marar enough, he might make a mistake. Be on your guard, though. If he decides that you've become a threat, he won't hesitate to send another assassin to your palace."

"I know," Wiercia said with a nod. "Security at the palace has never been so tight."

They sat in awkward silence for several moments. There wasn't much left to say, and the two of them had never been very good at making conversation.

"So what are you going to do next?" Wiercia finally asked.

"Marar still owes Premel some gold. We're going to collect it today."

"Why bother?"

"I want to interrogate the couriers and find out if they know which merchants are supplying the gold. And I want to know who else in my palace they've been paying."

Wiercia nodded slowly, pondering this. She had little doubt that there were traitors in the Matriarchy as well, and she would have given a good deal for similar information. "Let me know what you find out," she said.

Melyor smiled. "I will."

After another brief silence, Wiercia stood, as did her Legates. "We should be going," she said.

"Very well. We'll wait until you and your men are gone. It would be best if your guards didn't see me."

"They'll know that I never spoke with Dob. Some of them may get suspicious."

Melyor pressed her fingertips together and frowned. "I suppose they might." She sat perfectly still for some time and then finally shrugged. "There's really nothing to be done. Explain it to them as you wish. If you trust them, I have little choice but to trust them as well. If you don't, find a way to keep them from contacting anyone, at least for the next few days."

"All right," Wiercia agreed, a bit unsure of what she would do. She had trusted them enough to bring them with her, but trusting them with a matter of this importance was another thing entirely. She would have to ponder the matter on the way back to the palace. She met Melyor's gaze and made herself smile. "Don't worry about this," she said. "One way or another, I'll keep your secret safe."

"I had no doubt," Melyor said, smiling as well. "Arick guard you, Sovereign."

"And you."

Wiercia led her Legates toward the doorway, but she stopped on the threshold and looked back at Melyor. The woman had her eyes closed tightly, and she was rubbing her brow, as if her head hurt. Seeing Wiercia turn, Jibb cleared his throat. Instantly, Melyor was looking at her again, a smile on her lips.

"Was there anything else, Sovereign?"

"No," Wiercia said softly. She had a sudden urge to tell Melyor to be careful, but their relationship had never allowed for such things. Besides, Melyor hadn't gotten as far as she had without learning to avoid careless mistakes. "No," she said again. "I'll see you soon."

But as she descended the stairs and made her way back to her air-carrier, Wiercia could not help but wonder if she'd ever see Melyor again.

When they returned to the Gold Palace, Premel and Dob made a great show of entering the building together, distracting the guards long enough to allow Melyor and Jibb to sneak in through the air-intake port and make their way back to Melyor's quarters. Once there, they had little to do but wait. All the arrangements for the coming meeting with the couriers had been made by Premel, while Melyor looked on, watchful, but unseen.

They were to meet them about an hour after nightfall, in the tunnels just two quads due south of the palace. It promised to be a fairly simple encounter. The couriers would be armed, but not heavily. Most of the couriers Melyor used tended to carry two throwers, one of them concealed, and perhaps a hidden blade as well. But that was all. More weaponry than that would call attention to them, and given the amount of gold they generally carried, that was the last thing they wanted. From what Premel had told her, Melyor gathered that Marar's couriers took a similar approach.

"So then why am I so nervous?" she said, pushing herself out of the chair in which she had been sitting, and beginning to pace the length of her chamber.

"What?" Jibb asked, not even bothering to open his eyes. He was lying on her sofa as if he actually believed that he could fall asleep.

"How can you just lie there?"

He opened his eyes. "What's the matter?"

"I don't know. I have a bad feeling about tonight." Her palms were wet and she wiped them on her trousers.

"What kind of a bad feeling?"

She shrugged and crossed her arms over her chest as she continued to pace.

Jibb's eyes strayed to her stone, which was leaning against the wall by her bed. "Have you . . . have you seen something?"

"No. Nothing like that. It's just a feeling."

"Maybe we shouldn't go. We can always—"

"No," she said, halting in front of him. "We're doing this tonight. We're too close to stop now."

He ran a hand through his dark curls. "All right," he sighed. "But then I don't know what to tell you."

"I know." She resumed her pacing. "I'm being foolish. Go back to sleep, Jibb. I'll be fine."

"I have a better idea," he said, getting to his feet. "Why don't I leave you alone, and you can sleep?"

She stopped again. "No. I mean, maybe you're right. I'll lie down for a while, but I'd prefer it if you stayed. I'd rather not be in here alone."

He smiled and sat back down on the sofa. "As you wish."

She crossed to her bed and lay down. And though she didn't sleep, she found some peace in staring out her window and watching the afternoon gradually give way to night. Jibb did fall asleep, and she found some comfort as well in the slow rhythm of his breathing. It was almost as if his mere presence offered her a measure of safety.

It's too bad I can't bring myself to love him, she thought. *At least he's here.*

And with that, of course, an image of Orris's face entered her mind, and the old pain rose in her chest again.

Fortunately, Premel knocked on her door a few minutes later, rousing Jibb from his slumber, and forcing her to move past her melancholy.

"It's almost time, Sovereign, General," the security man said, poking his head into the room.

Melyor sat up and pushed her hair back from her forehead. "Thank you, Premel. I'll be ready shortly."

"Of course," he said. "I'll be waiting in the next room."

He withdrew and closed the door.

"I'll give you a minute or two," Jibb said, stretching and then making his way to the door. "Call if you need me."

A moment later he was gone, and Melyor was left to prepare herself as best she could. She stood, strapped her thrower to her thigh, slipped her dagger into its sheath in her right boot, and, as an afterthought, took a second thrower from her desk drawer and put it in one of the inner pockets of her overcoat.

Satisfied that she was ready, she started toward the door. But as she reached it, she heard a beeping sound coming from her desk. At first she thought it was her speak-screen, and she decided not to answer. There was no telling who it could be. It might have been Marar, looking for Dob. But then she realized that the sound was coming from her pocket communicator, the code to which few people had access.

Returning to her desk, she picked up the device and turned it on.

"Yes?" she said.

"I just wanted to let you know that I'm ready to go when you are, Sovereign." It took her a moment to recognize the voice as that of her driver.

"Excuse me?"

"I have the carrier ready," Vian told her, his voice sounding thin and strange through the small speaker.

"We're taking the tunnels," Melyor said, wondering how he even knew about this excursion. Jibb, Premel, and she had decided to tell no one. Not even Dob.

"General Premel led me to believe that you'd changed your mind."

"Well, I haven't. It'll be safer to do this underground."

"You're sure, Sovereign? I can have you there in no time at all."

"I'm quite sure," she said. "But thank you." She switched off the device, and as she did, there was a knock at her door.

"What is it?"

Jibb pushed the door open. "We should get going."

She nodded and followed him out of the room. She'd mention the driver's call to Premel later.

They made their way to the sub-ground floor of the palace by way of the lifter shaft and entered the tunnels through an access that dated back, she had been told, to the earliest days of the Consolidation. From there, it was a small matter to navigate the tunnels to the meeting place, which was at the northern edge of the Sixth Realm. The tunnels in this part of the Nal were rarely used and poorly lit. Premel and Jibb were forced to carry hand lights, and she, of course, used the light from her stone, but they made their way through the passageways somewhat slower than Melyor would have liked.

When they came within a turn or two of the meeting place, Premel went ahead to find the couriers. Jibb and Melyor were to wait for a signal, a single flash of Premel's light, before coming into view. But only moments after Premel left them, he returned.

"They're not here yet," he said quietly, a frown on his thin face.

"Have they ever been late before?" Melyor asked.

"No. Usually they're waiting for me."

She chewed her lip for a moment. "Well, let's give them a few minutes. I'd rather not have to do this again."

Both men nodded, and they waited there in silence for a time, listening for voices or footsteps.

After a few minutes, Melyor remembered the driver's call. "Why did you tell my driver that we'd need him tonight?" she asked Premel. "I thought that we decided to use the tunnels days ago."

"I didn't tell the driver anything about this," Premel said, looking surprised. "I haven't even spoken to him."

Melyor looked at Jibb. "You?"

"I haven't talked about this with anyone except Dob."

"Dob? Why did you tell him?"

"Because I wanted someone to know where we were going."

"Do you think he would have mentioned it to the driver?" Premel asked.

Jibb shook his head. "I made it clear to him that he wasn't to speak with anyone about this."

"The driver told me it was you," Melyor said, facing Premel again. "I'm sure of it."

"Then the driver was lying."

"Was he?" Jibb demanded, eyeing Premel with obvious distrust.

"Yes."

"Because if he wasn't, and you've done anything to tip off those couriers—"

"Quiet!" Melyor hissed. "Did you hear that?"

Jibb and Premel immediately fell silent, and Melyor strained her ears to hear the sound again. It had sounded like a footfall, soft and slow, as if someone was approaching cautiously. But something about it was odd. She just couldn't put her finger on what it was.

They waited for what seemed an eternity. Before they finally heard it again, still soft, but unmistakable. It was a footstep. But rather than coming from ahead of them, where the couriers should have been, it came from behind them, as if they had been followed.

And suddenly, although too late by far, all of it made sense to her: the ease with which they had been able to set up this meeting, Vian's call, the couriers' failure to show up, all of it.

"Ambush!" she had time to cry out, grabbing for her thrower. "Cap and strike! The cap man's behind us!"

An instant later, the tunnels came alive with thrower fire. Shafts of scarlet light carved through the darkness, bringing clouds of smoke and showers of sparks when they hit the stone walls, and hissing like fat on a griddle. Melyor, Jibb, and Premel dropped to the floor and fired back, but they were in the middle of a straight corridor with nowhere to hide, and their attackers had taken positions at the corners at either end of the hallway. The only thing that saved the three of them from a quick death was the small, dim chamber just a few feet from where they had been standing. And if it hadn't been for Premel, Melyor never would have even known it was there.

Shouting for Jibb and her to follow, Premel leaped into the room. Jibb managed to crawl in as well, and Melyor, diving forward into a roll, fired once at the two assassins in front of her, and then rolled a second time into the chamber, just as two red beams crashed into the doorway over her head.

Miraculously, none of them had been hit, but their situation had not improved by much. The chamber offered them some cover, but its entrance was barely wide enough for two of them to fire their weapons at the same time. They were trapped there. It was all they could do just to keep their attackers from advancing on them. Escape seemed out of the question.

With only two of them able to fire at any given time, they took turns resting. Because of Jibb's injury, he could only fire in one direction, which made the rotation a bit awkward. But they managed to maintain a fairly constant barrage, thus forcing the assassins to remain hidden.

For their part, the attackers had all the time in the world, and they seemed to know it. They fired sporadically, establishing no rhythm with which Melyor and the others could time their salvos. At one point, Melyor stuck out her head and arm to fire, only to see a shaft of flame immediately burst from a thrower. She barely ducked back into the room, yanking Premel back with her, before the fire sliced through the chamber entrance.

After that, the three of them varied the heights from which they fired, sometimes squatting or kneeling, sometimes standing, and at times even lying on their bellies. But the longer the firefight dragged on, the worse their chances of surviving it grew. Close calls like the one Melyor had occurred with ever-increasing frequency. Their chamber began to fill with smoke, and their throwers got hotter and hotter until Melyor began to wonder if they would cease working altogether.

"We've got to do something," Jibb finally said in a hoarse whisper, as he poured his fire into the corridor.

Premel, who was firing as well, opened his mouth to respond but began to cough instead. In the end he merely nodded his agreement.

"Ideas?" Melyor asked, looking from one of them to the other.

"I suppose," Premel said through another fit of coughing, "that this would be a bad time to ask them if they have my gold."

Melyor and Jibb laughed so loudly that the assassins momentarily stopped firing. A few seconds later, however, after their laughter had subsided, the attackers resumed their attack, driving Jibb and Premel back into the room.

"Have you noticed," Jibb asked, "that the fire coming from the right is far weaker than the fire from the left?"

"Of course," Premel said. "There's only a single attacker to the right: the cap man. The two deep men are on our left."

"That's not what I mean. Not only is the cap man alone, he's also not as good with a thrower."

Melyor nodded. She had noticed this as well, although she hadn't given it much thought.

"I bet the cap man's your driver," Jibb went on. "Which means that while he's armed, he's not trained."

"So what do you suggest?"

"One of us should rush him."

"You must be insane!" Premel said. "Whoever does it will get killed before he takes two steps!"

"Or she," Melyor corrected. "And that won't happen if the two who remain throw enough fire their way."

Jibb grinned at her. "Exactly. You two get into position and when you start shooting, I'll charge him."

"You're not going anywhere," Melyor told him. "Not with only one good arm." She pulled her second thrower from her coat, and then, as an afterthought, took the coat off.

"I won't let you do this," Jibb said.

Before Melyor could respond, they heard a footstep in the corridor. Immediately, Jibb and Premel jumped back to the entrance way and fired their weapons, driving the assassins back.

"You can't do this!" Jibb called over his shoulder as he continued to fire. "If you won't send me, send Premel. But—"

"I'm not arguing about this, Jibb. Neither of you is as good as I am with a thrower, and neither of you is as skilled with a blade. And on top of that, I'm Sovereign. It's my decision to make."

She could see the muscles in his jaw tightening as he fired his weapon, but after a moment he glanced at her and nodded once.

She crossed to the entrance and crouched down by Premel's legs. There was a good deal of smoke in the corridor by then, but that actually worked to her advantage.

"When I give the word, Premel," she whispered, "I want you to turn your weapon on the deep men with Jibb. Don't give them a chance to throw any fire at me. I don't want to get hit in the back."

"What about the cap?" Premel asked in a low voice.

"I'll be using both my weapons. That should keep him pressed against the wall long enough for me to reach the end of the corridor."

"And what then?" Jibb asked

"At that point we should be on equal footing, and if that really is my driver, he won't have a chance."

"And if it's not? If it's really another assassin?"

She looked up at Jibb and smiled. "I still like my chances. Don't you?"

The big man grinned and shook his head. "Watch yourself."

She nodded. "I'll see you in a few minutes."

Turning her attention back to the corridor, Melyor squeezed between her two companions, remaining in a low crouch. She adjusted her grip on the two throwers and, taking a deep breath, stepped into the corridor.

She assumed that Premel turned as she had instructed and started firing at the deep men. Certainly he wasn't firing this way anymore. But she was, with both weapons, as she ran through the blue-grey smoke, still in her crouch. She knew that the cap man, whoever he was, could hear her footsteps, but there was little she could do about that.

She hadn't thought that the end of the hallway was very far, but it seemed an impossibly long way now. With each step she expected to feel an explosion of pain in her back. But none came, and just before she came to the end of the tunnel, she heard voices shouting from behind her. Somewhere in a remote corner of her mind, she wondered what she was hearing and whether Jibb and Premel were all right. But she didn't hesitate even for an instant.

Just as she reached the corner, without breaking stride, she dived and tucked, rolling on her shoulder and coming up on one knee with both throwers ready and firing, the left one aimed low, the right one aimed high. Both volleys of fire found their mark, sending the man sprawling backward, although not before he managed to get off a blast of his own.

And as he fell onto the floor, screaming in pain, Melyor felt white heat stab into her thigh like a knife. Gasping, she dropped one of her throwers and grabbed at the wound. The man in front of her—it was her driver after all—tried to raise himself up to fire again, but she fired first with the thrower she still held, catching him in the wrist and sending his weapon and much of his hand flying against a nearby wall.

Lowering herself onto her back, Melyor squeezed her eyes shut and gritted her teeth against a wave of nausea. She felt herself growing dizzy, and for a moment she thought she might pass out. But then she opened her eyes again, and forced herself to crawl toward Vian. He was writhing around like a wounded animal. His shooting hand was little more than a bloody stump, and he had blackened, bloody burns on one knee and on the upper part of his chest.

"Was it Marar?" she asked him, her voice sounding thick and unsteady. "Did he tell you to kill us?"

He glanced at her through half-closed eyes, but said nothing.

She pounded her fist into his injured knee and he screamed.

"Answer me!" she demanded. "Was it Marar?"

"Yes," he managed.

"And did he want all three of us dead?"

"Yes. All three of you."

"Where are the couriers?"

He shook his head.

She raised her fist again. "You don't know, or you won't say?"

"I don't know. I swear."

"Why did you do it, Vian?" she asked, her fist still poised over his knee.

"Ask Jibb."

She shook her head. "What?"

"I said, 'Ask Jibb.' Ask him about Selim."

She didn't understand what he was saying, but she hadn't the strength to pursue the matter.

She lowered her hand and leaned back against the wall. She was starting to shiver with cold. Her lips were trembling.

She heard someone running toward them and with an effort she lifted the hand that held her thrower. But then Jibb came into view, and she let her arm fall to the floor again.

"Fist of the God," he whispered, rushing to her side. "Premel!" he shouted, his voice cracking slightly.

She heard a voice call back, as if from a great distance. She felt faint.

"Call for meds!" Jibb yelled.

"I'm all right," she said, closing her eyes again and swallowing.

"No, you're not. You need a doctor."

"Are you all right? Is Premel?"

"We're both fine. Premel's with Dob and the others."

She opened her eyes. "Dob?"

"He came up from the south and surprised the deep men. Like I said, I wanted someone to know where we were going." He smiled, though there was an anxious look in his dark eyes.

"Are the assassins dead?"

"One of them is. We grabbed the other one so you could question him."

She nodded, allowing her eyes to close again. "Good. Make sure Vian lives. I want to talk to him, too."

He brushed a wisp of hair from her brow and kissed the top of her head. "Don't worry about that," he whispered. "Don't worry about anything. Just rest now."

She nodded again. "Yes. I'll rest. And then I'm going to kill Marar."

21

At this point it is the waiting that disturbs me most. The bindings of Jaryd and Cailin tell us that war is inevitable. That at least is what history teaches us, and certainly most in this city have taken that lesson to heart. So we sit and we wait, seeing enemies everywhere. Will the League fight the Order? Will the mages unite to fight the Temples, or will the Temples join forces with one body to do away with the other? Will the People's Movement and its free mages go to war with the God's Children, drawing the guardians of the Mage-Craft into the conflict in some way? Or is our fight with some foreign foe: Abborij, or Lon-Ser?

This is all we ponder; it is all we discuss. Today Jaryd and Alayna informed the mages of the Order that their daughter, Myn, who in fairness to them has shown signs of possessing the Sight, dreamed of Sartol, an unsettled mage who has been dead now for eleven years. Based on this child's nightmare, they fear that Sartol may have found a way to alter Theron's Curse, and make himself a threat to our land again. I fear that we have allowed ourselves to be consumed so by our anticipation of war, that we have lost our senses. And I wonder if, when the time comes, we will still be capable of distinguishing our true enemies from those with whom we will need to ally ourselves in order to prevail.

—Hawk-Mage Orris to Melyor i Lakin, Sovereign and Bearer of Bragor-Nal, Spring, God's Year 4633.

It had taken Jaryd a long time to conquer his doubts, to stop wondering why the gods and Rithlar had chosen him over every other mage in the Order. For weeks after their arrival in Amarid, he had worn the title "Eagle-Sage" uneasily. He thought of the other Eagle-Sage's in Tobyn-Ser's history—Fordel, Decla, Glenyse—and he knew that he did not deserve to have his name mentioned in the same breath as theirs. They were legends, heroes. They had saved the land. And he was but a mage. Nothing less, certainly, but nothing more either.

On more than one occasion, as they lay together in their bed in the Great Hall, Alayna had assured him that such doubts were to be expected.

"I'd have them, too," she had said more than once. "Any of us would. I'd be more worried about you if you didn't feel this way."

Though it had taken a long time, he had finally come to recognize the wisdom in her words. He had, at long last, learned to live with his doubts and to accept that the gods had chosen him for a reason, for something that they saw in him, even if he didn't, see it.

And he had done so, at least in part, because of the faith in his leadership shown by the other mages of the Order. Their belief in his abilities had, in turn, nurtured his own. If they think I'm worthy of being called Eagle-Sage, he had told himself, then perhaps I should believe it as well.

All of which had made the doubts that he saw now written across their faces that much more disturbing.

He and Alayna had just finished telling the gathered mages of the Order about Myn's dream, making it clear that they believed the girl's vision to be prophecy.

"Over the past few years, Alayna and I have learned to trust Myn's Sight almost as completely as we trust our own," he had concluded. "We believe her. We don't know how it's possible for Sartol to be coming here. Obviously it means that something has happened to change the nature of Theron's Curse, or to allow Sartol to escape the limitations that the curse imposes."

At first, the other mages said nothing, and an uncomfortable silence settled like a heavy fog over the Gathering Chamber. The mages shifted noisily in their seats, clearing their throats or casting furtive glances at those sitting next to them. The only thing they didn't do was look Jaryd or Alayna in the eye. After all, Jaryd was their Eagle-Sage, and Alayna his First, as well as his wife. How could the others say that they didn't believe what the two of them were saying? How could they say that where Jaryd and Alayna saw prophecy, they saw merely the dark side of a child's imagination?

Most disturbingly, it didn't appear to be just a few of them who felt this way. All of them did, even Orris and Radomil and Sonel. Even Baden.

Baden was the first to respond to what Jaryd had said. "None of us doubts that Myn is an extraordinary child, Jaryd," he began, rising slowly from his seat. "And all of us expect that she'll be a mage someday, a powerful one at that. With you and Alayna for her parents, she could be no less. But right now, she's only a child. She's barely old enough to know the difference between what is real and what is fantasy. You can't expect us to believe that she can tell the difference between visions of the future and simple dreams."

"Baden's right," Orris added. "It's not always easy for mages to decide whether or not we've had a Seeing. Trusting a child's judgment on such a thing, even if it is Myn, is just too risky."

Alayna tried to tell them that they were wrong, that even a child of Myn's age had a better sense of what was and wasn't real than they thought. And on this point, Trahn, who had two girls of his own, offered some support. But the others remained unconvinced.

"It makes no sense," Radomil told them, a pained expression on his round face. "Don't you think that if the Curse had been altered in some way that someone would have noticed?"

"Not necessarily," Trahn answered. "It's not as though any of us spend a good deal of time with the Unsettled. Unless we have need of them, we avoid contact with them. And Tobyn-Ser's people still fear them. I'm not sure I believe that anything has happened to change the Curse, but I'm certain that no one would notice if something had."

"And even if someone had noticed," Alayna said, "how would they let any of us know? If we were out there, wandering the land, speaking with the people the way we usually do, that would be one thing. But we're here, hundreds of miles away from Sartol's binding place. If something had happened, we'd be the last to know about it."

"You're right," Orris agreed. "And perhaps that's the problem. Perhaps we've been here for too long, talking about war, planning for war, wondering whom we're going to face in a war. Maybe it's clouding our judgment."

"You mean our judgment, don't you," Jaryd corrected. "Alayna's and mine."

The burly man shook his head. "I didn't say that."

"But you thought it, didn't you?"

"None of us is questioning your judgment, Jaryd," Baden broke in. "Or Alayna's either. But the two of you have been bearing an enormous burden for quite some time now. Were any of us in your position, we might find ourselves getting a bit carried away from time to time as well."

"Carried away?" Jaryd shot back at him. "Is that what you think?"

Sonel placed her hand on Baden's and rose to stand beside him. "I think what Baden means is that, even in the best of times, and even for the most experienced leaders, it's not always easy to sift through all the possible threats and problems we face and separate the more serious ones from the less serious ones. The two of you have done a fine job so far, under terribly difficult circumstances, and we all believe that you'll continue to. But in this one instance, your perceptions may be clouded by the fact that Myn is your daughter."

Jaryd stood and picked up his staff. "If that's what you want to believe, that's fine. You can dismiss all that we've told you. Yes, we're tired, and we're concerned. And yes, Myn is our daughter, and we love her more than anything else in this world. But even if she was a stranger, I'd think very carefully before I rejected her vision out of hand. Alayna and I have never told her anything about Sartol. I'd be surprised if she had ever heard his name before all this began. But yesterday this child, who does have the Sight, and who knew before Alayna and I did that we'd be coming to Amarid to take our places at the head of this table, described him to us as if she had just been standing beside him. Now if any of you can explain that to me in a way that puts my fears to rest, please do. But until one of you can, it's my responsibility to assume that Sartol is on his way here." He paused, sweeping the table with his glare. And none of them said a thing. "We're adjourned," he said, spinning away from the table with a swirl of his cloak. "I'll see all of you tomorrow morning."

He didn't look back at them, although he did glance to the side to see Rithlar bounding along beside him. When he reached the door to the Sage's quarters he merely stepped inside and closed it, not loudly, but not gently either. He had left Alayna out there to deal with them, and he felt guilty about that, but he was fairly certain that she would understand.

Orris, he knew, was afraid that they were all panicking. Jaryd feared that the opposite was true: that they were growing complacent again, that the longer they sat here waiting for a war that never began, the less prepared they would be when it finally did. He couldn't allow that to happen, not so long as Rithlar stayed with him.

He could hear them talking in the Gathering Chamber, arguing about what he had just said and done, and about the possible meanings of Myn's dream. A part of him wanted to return to the council table and join in those discussions. But he had walked out for a reason. For now there was nothing to do but wait for Alayna to return to their chamber, and tell him about it. And that wouldn't happen until after all the others had gone.

The wait proved to be shorter than he had expected. Within a half hour, the last of the voices ceased, and he heard the sounds of Alayna's footsteps echoing off the domed ceiling of the Great Hall as she approached.

She entered the room, looked at him, and rolled her eyes. "What a morning. They were terrified that they had really offended us. I've never had so many people say so many nice things to me about Myn at one time." She let out a long, slow breath. "I'm exhausted."

He came forward and put his arms around her. "I'm sorry to have done that to you. I shouldn't have abandoned you that way."

"Don't apologize. I'm glad you said what you did. If you hadn't, I would have. But I think it was better coming from their Eagle-Sage."

"Did you end up convincing any of them?"

She shook her head. "I don't think so. They've been expecting our enemy to be the League or the Temples, or, in Orris's case, the free mages for so long, that they refuse to accept that it could be someone else."

"Particularly Sartol."

"Right," she said with a thin smile. "Do you think we gave too much credence to Myn's dream?" she asked a moment later, her smile vanishing. "She is just seven. Maybe we've been wrong to place so much faith in the strength of her Sight."

Jaryd shrugged. "I suppose it's possible. But her description of him was so precise. Even the color of his ceryll was right." He threw up his hands and shook his head slowly. "I don't know what to think anymore."

"Maybe we should talk to her again. Later, after she's finished with her lessons."

"All right. In the meantime," he said, "I've been thinking that I should tell Cailin about the dream, just so she knows what we're thinking about right now."

"You don't want to wait until we've spoken to Myn again?"

Before Jaryd could answer, someone knocked on their door. The two of them exchanged a look and then Alayna called for whoever it was to enter. One of the hall's attendants stuck her head into their room.

"I'm sorry to disturb you, Eagle-Sage, First, but there's a mage here to see you. One I've never seen before."

Jaryd felt his stomach start to tighten. Glancing at Alayna, he saw that her face had turned pale. "What does he look like?" he asked. "What color is his cloak?"

"It's a woman, Eagle-Sage. And she's not wearing a cloak. She doesn't even have a bird. The only way I knew she was a mage was from her staff and stone. She's asking to speak with the Owl-Sage. I wasn't sure what to tell her."

Jaryd felt himself start to relax again. A woman, and a free mage at that. It was strange to be sure, but that was all. "It's all right," he said, smiling. "Send her in. We'll speak with her in here."

The woman nodded. "Very good, Eagle-Sage."

Alayna called her owl to her shoulder while the attendant went to get their visitor. "What about Rithlar?" she asked. "Shouldn't she stay out of sight?"

Jaryd shook his head. "Word of the eagles has spread throughout the city. It's probably starting to move through the rest of the land by now. There's no sense in hiding it anymore."

She nodded. "I suppose you're right."

There was a second knock at the door and a woman stepped into their chamber. She was young, perhaps a year or two older than Cailin, but no more. She had light brown hair and pale eyes and a face that would have been pretty had it not appeared so severe. Like other free mages Jaryd had encountered over the past few years, she was dressed plainly in brown trousers and a lighter shirt. The attendant had been right: without her bird there was nothing to mark her as a mage except for her ceryll, which was blue, much like his own.

When she saw Jaryd and Alayna, she seemed to freeze momentarily, as if surprised by their very presence. Then she continued to scan the room, and seeing Rithlar she started, her eyes widening and then flying to Jaryd.

"Is she yours?" the woman asked.

"Yes. My name is Jaryd. I'm Eagle-Sage of the Order. This is Alayna, First of the Sage, and my wife."

The woman smiled and nodded, although she didn't approach them to clasp hands. "My name is Tammen." Her gaze returned to the eagle, and for several moments she said nothing.

"Would you care to sit?" Alayna asked, indicating one of the large chairs by the hearth.

"Of course," Tammen said, crossing to the chair, but staring first at Jaryd and then at Alayna.

It almost seemed to Jaryd that she recognized them from a previous meeting, and in truth, she looked somewhat familiar to him as well. "Is something troubling you, Tammen?" he asked. "Perhaps you had expected to find Sage Radomil instead of us."

"Yes, Radomil. He was Sage the last I had heard." Once more her eyes strayed to Rithlar. "And I knew nothing of the eagle."

"I assure you," Jaryd told her, trying to ignore his memory of Radomil's comments during that morning's session, "I speak for the Order just as he did, and I have, in almost all respects, continued on the path that he and his predecessors set out for us."

Tammen smiled again. "I'm sure you have." She glanced at Alayna and then quickly looked away. "How long have you been . . . I mean when did you bind to your eagle?"

"Near the end of winter."

She nodded and looked at the bird yet again, as if trying to divine its meaning.

"How can we help you, Tammen?"

She faced him again, although she appeared distracted. "My apologies." She shook her head slightly, as one might when trying to clear away stray thoughts. "I've come to you," she began at last, "to discuss a possible alliance between the Order and the People's Movement."

"Really?" Jaryd replied with unfeigned surprise. "I was under the impression that the free mages wanted nothing to do with either the League or the Order."

"Yes, well that was before the Temples starting receiving weapons from the outlanders. We now find ourselves in a position where we cannot hope to match the strength of any of our potential rivals. Both the Order and the League have far more mages than we do, and with their weapons, the Keepers have become far too formidable a foe."

"So why the Order?" Alayna asked. "Why not go to the League? They have more mages than we do, and I've always heard that the free mages hate the Order more than anything, more even than they do the League."

Tammen hesitated, but only for an instant. "I disagree. Even before the Movement contemplated this alliance, it always viewed the Order as a more legitimate guardian of the Mage-Craft than Erland and his crowd."

"What would the Order gain from such an alliance?" Jaryd asked. "Are the free towns willing to accept service from Order mages? Are you and your fellow mages willing to work with the Order to end your conflict with the Keepers?"

"Yes, we'd be willing to do all of that, and more. We'd be willing to join forces with you. Wouldn't it be helpful to have additional mages for any future conflict you might have with the League?"

"We're hoping there will be no conflict with the League, Tammen. The leaders of the League have been working with us to put an end to all that."

Tammen frowned. "I see."

"How do we know that you speak for the People's Movement, Tammen?" Alayna asked. "You come here alone, unannounced. Why should we commit to anything without hearing from other free mages and from the people you're supposed to represent?"

"Have you always been so suspicious of strangers?" Tammen asked. "Or did something happen to make you that way?"

Alayna narrowed her eyes, but said nothing.

"I appreciate your coming to speak with us, Tammen," Jaryd said, getting to his feet. "I will discuss your offer with the entire Order when we convene again in the morning. In the meantime, do you have someplace to stay here in Amarid, or would you like us to see to making arrangements for you?"

"Thank you, but that won't be necessary." She stood, cast a thin smile at Alayna, and walked to the door. When she reached it, however, she stopped and faced them again. "I hope you'll forgive this imposition, but I've never been to Amarid before and so I've never seen the Great Hall. Would you mind if I took a few moments to look around?"

"Not at all," Jaryd said. "The Hall belongs to all the people of Tobyn-Ser. Take all the time you'd like."

"Thank you." She left the room and began to walk slowly around the Gathering Chamber.

Once she had moved some distance away, Jaryd and Alayna crossed the room so that they could watch her from the doorway.

"You don't trust her," Jaryd said in a low voice, offering it as a statement.

"Not at all. If the leaders of the People's Movement were really interested in an alliance, don't you think they'd send a group consisting of citizens as well as free mages?"

He nodded. "Probably."

Tammen was walking in a slow circle around the central chamber of the hall, looking at the council table, the portrait of Amarid that adorned the chamber's ceiling, the marble floor.

"Well if she's not here representing the Movement, why did she come?"

Alayna shook her head. "I have no idea. But something about her bothers me. I can't say for sure what it is, but I just didn't like her. And did you notice that comment she made about me being suspicious? Who does she think she is?"

He smiled and placed a hand on her shoulder. "I guess she touched a nerve, didn't she?"

"It's not funny, Jaryd. Sartol's the reason I'm so untrusting. And I didn't need her reminding me of that just now."

"I'm sorry."

She shook her head and looked out at Tammen again. "It's all right. I just don't think that we should be too quick to make any deals with her. At least not until we've heard from other free mages."

"I agree."

Tammen had circled the council table and was now near their door again. She glanced at them and smiled. "Thank you," she said. "It's everything I thought it would be."

Jaryd made himself return her smile. "I'm glad to hear it."

The woman looked like she might say more, but then she just started toward the door. When she reached it, she looked at them one last time, a smile still on her face, and left.

"There's just something about her that I don't like," Alayna murmured. "I don't know what it is."

He had slept poorly. He went to bed thinking about the day's debate and all the things he shouldn't have said to Jaryd and Alayna about Myn's dream, and his regrets had followed him into his slumber. Orris had little doubt that his friendship with the two mages could survive almost anything, but he also knew how unfair he had been to them. They needed his support right now, and the Order needed to remain united behind their Eagle-Sage. And notwithstanding the concerns he had expressed in his latest letter to Melyor, he also knew that Jaryd would never have mentioned the girl's dream in the context of this Gathering had he not truly believed that it had been a Seeing.

Even knowing that, Orris wasn't ready to believe that Sartol's spirit was on its way to Amarid. But he was anxious to apologize to both Jaryd and Alayna, and to try to divine with them what Myn's vision might mean.

Indeed, that was what he was considering when he heard the alarm bells on the constable's post begin to ring. A moment later he heard cries going up from nearby, and by the time he was dressed and heading down the stairs of the Aerie, with Kryssan gliding beside him, the bells of the Great Hall and the Hall of the League were tolling.

His heart pounding in his chest, Orris burst out of the tavern into the small courtyard. Trahn and Baden were there as well. Shouts and cries seemed to be coming from all directions.

"Do you smell it?" Trahn asked, turning to look at him.

Orris nodded. "Smoke."

"Yes. And nearby."

The three of them hurried out of the courtyard, through the twists and turns of the alleyways, and onto the main avenue of the city. From there they could see a great black cloud of smoke rising into the morning sky. It was coming from north of where they stood, in another tight cluster of buildings. Plunging back into the alleyways, the three mages soon reached the fire.

It had already claimed one building entirely, an inn from the looks of it, and it had spread to two other buildings, one of them an inn as well, and the other a storefront. There were people everywhere, many of them running in different directions seemingly without a purpose. A few appeared to be attending to the injured, who lay in the narrow street that fronted the buildings. Others had formed a bucket line and were trying desperately to douse the flames, which were quickly engulfing the structures.

There were other mages there as well, three of them, all wearing blue cloaks. Orris recognized one of them as Kovet. The other two, both of whom were older, were healing the burns of those who had been hurt, but Kovet was speaking with a man whose face had been blackened by smoke and who was gesturing wildly toward the buildings.

"Let's go," Orris said, leading Trahn and Baden toward the other mages.

When Kovet spotted him, he stopped talking to the man and just stared, as if not quite certain what Orris intended to do.

"How can we help?" Orris asked, stopping in front of the dark-haired mage. "Are there still people inside?"

Kovet stared at him for a moment longer. "I'm trying to find that out now," he finally said. "This is the innkeeper. He doesn't remember how many rooms he filled last night."

"I went to sleep early last night," the man explained, his voice trembling. "My wife may have sold rooms to a few more. I don't know. She's unconscious. I just barely got her out in time." He cast an anxious glance toward the wounded.

"Go to her," Kovet said. "If there are people inside, we'll get them out."

The man nodded and hurried away.

He faced Orris again and looked at him appraisingly. But before he could say anything, a cry went up from the front of the bucket line.

"There are people inside!" a voice called out.

Orris spun toward Baden. "You stay here and help with the wounded!"

The bald man nodded, and Trahn, Kovet, and Orris sprinted past the bucket line and into the building, with their birds following close behind.

The heat of the flames hammered into Orris like a fist, sucking the air from his lungs and making his eyes water. Fire and smoke were everywhere, and for a dizzying moment he lost his bearings and couldn't even remember where the door was. Then he heard a faint cry and felt Trahn tugging at his cloak.

"This way!" the dark mage shouted, his voice just barely carrying over the roar of the blaze.

With Trahn leading the way, the three of them bounded up the stairs and started kicking open the doors to all the rooms.

The first several were empty, but there was a wall of fire blocking the hallway, and there were voices coming from the rooms beyond it. Shielding their faces with their cloaks, the mages ran through the flames to the far side. There they found three more rooms. One of them was completely burned. There seemed to be a body lying on the small bed, but that person was clearly beyond help.

In the other two rooms, however, the mages found survivors: a young couple in one, and an elderly man and a small boy in the other. The younger man and woman appeared to be unhurt, but the boy had passed out, and the man was coughing continuously.

"Are you hurt?" Orris asked him, hollering to make himself heard.

The man shook his head as another fit of coughing shook his body. "No," he finally managed. "The boy couldn't take the smoke, and there was no way to get out." He gestured at a pile of canvass satchels in the far corner of the room. "I can't carry those myself."

"What are they?"

"My wares. I'm a peddler. The boy's my nephew and apprentice."

Somewhere back up the hall there was a loud crash. The building was starting to collapse.

Orris glanced at Trahn, who shook his head.

"You'll have to leave them!" Orris told him.

"I can't! This is my whole life!"

"I'll carry it!" Kovet said, rushing forward and hoisting the bags onto his back. "You take the boy!" he told Trahn. He looked at Orris. "You make sure the old man and the other two get out of here."

Orris nodded. He helped the man off the bed and wrapping an arm around the peddler's shoulders, led him out the door. Trahn already had the boy in his arms and was wrapping his cloak around the child to protect him from the heat as they started back down the hallway. Kovet was behind them.

The flames in the corridor had spread up the walls and now thoroughly blocked their way.

"Any ideas?" Trahn asked, looking back at Orris and Kovet.

Part of the ceiling dropped to the floor just in front of them, sending up a flurry of sparks. Somewhere below them the building groaned.

"There's no way through?" Kovet asked. "You're sure?"

"I'm sure."

The League mage made a sour face.

"What if we blast through the floor?" Orris asked. "Two of us can jump down and we can hand down these people and the old man's things."

On the other side of the flames, more of the ceiling fell in with an impact that made the floor shudder.

Trahn eyed the walls and ceiling with uncertainty. "I don't think we have much choice. Go ahead and do it."

Reaching for Kryssan, Orris lowered his staff and sent a burst of russet flame through the old wood. An instant later, Kovet's orange flame did the same, and together they shaped a hole large enough to allow them to get through, but not so large that it compromised the stability of the floor.

Orris sat at the edge of the hole and jumped down. Much of the lower floor was engulfed in flame, but they still had a narrow path to the door. He grabbed a chair, placed it beneath the opening, and stood on it, motioning for Trahn to hand the boy down to him.

Within a few moments, the boy, the peddler, and the young couple were all on the ground floor. Trahn jumped down as well.

"Get them out of here!" Orris said. "Kovet and I will take care of the peddler's bags."

Trahn nodded and started leading the others out of the building.

"Hand them down!" Orris shouted to the League mage.

Kovet nodded and started handing down the satchels. But he had only given one to Orris when another crash echoed through the inn. Kovet cried out and burning scraps of wood showered down on Orris through the opening in the ceiling.

"What happened?" Orris called to him.

Kovet didn't answer.

Peering up through the hole, Orris could make out the mage's face. His eyes were closed, and he wasn't moving.

"Fist of the God!" Orris spit.

Jumping off the chair, he raced across the room and bounded up the stairs, taking them three at a time. The corridor was littered with burning beams and charred pieces of the fallen ceiling and Orris had to climb over them just to get back to the wall of fire that they had been unable to cross a moment before. He took off his cloak and balled it up, rather than risk having it catch fire.

"Orris!" he heard from behind him.

He whirled and saw Trahn at the top of the stairs.

"What are you doing?"

"Kovet's hurt. Wait for me below. I'll need to hand him down to you."

Trahn nodded and retreated down the stairs.

Facing forward again, Orris took a deep breath and then leaped into the fire. He felt the flames licking at his face and hands. He smelled his hair burning and he flailed at his back and neck, all the while forcing himself forward. The smoke was so thick that he could see nothing, and his lungs burned for air. And then his leg hit something so suddenly and so hard that he pitched forward, putting out his hands blindly to break his fall.

He landed hard on his shoulder and rolled forward coming to rest on his back with one leg dangling through the hole he and the League mage had made.

"Are you all right?" Trahn called to him.

"Yes," he managed.

He crawled to where Kovet lay and threw his cloak over him, smothering flames that had been climbing up the mage's blue cloak along his legs. When the flames were out, Orris placed a hand on the man's back. He was still breathing, though he had a nasty gash across his brow and extensive burns on his feet and ankles.

He dragged Kovet to the opening in the floor and lowered him to Trahn. Then he jumped through himself, landing heavily and falling to the floor.

"Can you make it?" Trahn asked, hoisting Kovet onto his shoulders.

Orris nodded and scrambled to his feet. He had burns on his hands and no doubt on his face and neck as well. His right leg ached from the fall he had taken upstairs, but he was able to hobble out of the building and into the bright sunshine.

Almost as soon as he stepped into the street, someone threw an arm around him and helped him to a spot several yards from the fire where he could lie down. Once on his back, he started to cough.

It was a long time before he could draw breath normally. When he finally could, he opened his eyes and looked up to see who had helped him. It was Jaryd, and his great bird was standing beside him.

"You almost got yourself killed."

Orris nodded, tried to say something, and found himself coughing again. Kryssan, who was sitting on the ground beside him, nuzzled him gently.

I'm all right, he sent.

"Let me heal those burns," Jaryd said when Orris's coughing had subsided again.

"I'd be grateful."

He laid his hands gently on Orris's face, and for several minutes neither of them spoke. When the Eagle-Sage had taken care of Orris's burns, he turned his attention to the injury to the mage's leg. Orris lay perfectly still during all of this, his eyes closed. He was utterly drained, and as the pain of his wounds slowly subsided he felt himself starting to fall asleep. He forced his eyes open and blinked several times.

"You should rest," Jaryd told him.

"You may need help with the others."

"There are more mages here than we need. And you've done enough already." He sat back, removing his hands from Orris's leg. "That should do," he said. "But I want you to lie still for a while. Understand?"

"Yes, Eagle-Sage," Orris said with mock servility.

Jaryd gave him a grin. He started to stand, but Orris gripped his arm, stopping him.

"Thank you," he said.

"My pleasure."

"And please accept my apology if I offended you yesterday."

Jaryd smiled. "It's all right. Don't worry about it."

Trahn came over and squatted down beside them. "Is he going to be all right?"

"It looks that way," Jaryd answered. "He'll be sore for a while, but I don't think it'll be anything permanent."

"Good." The dark mage looked at Orris. "Kovet seems to be all right as well. Thanks to you."

The Sage's eyes flew to Trahn and then back to Orris. "Kovet? What did he have to do with this?"

"The three of us were helping some people out of the inn and Kovet got hurt. Orris saved his life."

Jaryd gaped at him as if unable to speak, his expression so comical that Orris couldn't help but smile.

"Why are you looking at me like that?" the mage asked. "Do you really think that I would have let him die?"

"No," Jaryd said, after a moment. "But I was thinking that saving him was probably the worst thing you could have done to him. He owes you his life now. It's going to drive him insane."

Orris laughed. "You're right. I hadn't thought of that."

A moment later Alayna and Baden joined them as well.

"Are you all right?" Alayna asked, kneeling by Orris's side.

"Yes, thanks to your husband."

She smiled, but only for an instant.

"What's the matter?" Jaryd asked, looking from Alayna to his uncle.

She ran a hand through her hair. "We've been hearing some strange things from the people we're treating."

"Like what?"

"Several of them have said that they heard a series of loud crashes just before the fires started. And one of them said that he saw a bright blue flash at the same time."

"I'm not sure I understand."

"From the way they described it," Baden said, "I'd have to assume that these fires were started by one or more mages."

"*What?*" Jaryd stood. "Are you certain?"

Alayna nodded. "It's really the only way to explain what they heard and saw."

"You said the man saw a blue flash?" Orris asked, lifting himself onto one elbow.

"Yes."

Trahn exhaled through his teeth. "I can think of at least five mages in the Order and the League who have blue stones."

Jaryd nodded and held up his staff. "Including me."

"What if it wasn't someone from either body?" Alayna asked.

Orris shrugged. "Both the League and the Order are gathered here right now. I think it's safe to assume—"

"There's a free mage here as well. And she has a blue stone."

"It couldn't have been Tammen," Jaryd said. "She's unbound. She wouldn't have enough power to do this."

"Tammen?" Baden repeated. "A young woman? Brown hair, pale eyes?"

Jaryd nodded. "Yes. You know her?"

"Sonel and I encountered her in Tobyn's Wood while on our way to this Gathering. She was still bound then, and she and some of her friends were helping a free town in a dispute with the Temple." He frowned. "What was she doing here?"

"She came to us to propose an alliance between the Order, and the People's Movement?"

Baden's eyes widened. "I find that very hard to believe."

"So did I," Alayna agreed. "I always thought that the mages of the Movement hated the Order."

"I believe they do, but I'm not even referring to that. Tammen was intensely hostile toward Sonel and me, much more so than either of her companions. Even if the Movement had decided to make overtures to the Order, she seems to me a strange choice to represent them. Was she alone?"

"She was when we spoke to her," Jaryd answered. "But there may be other free mages in Amarid."

Baden shook his head. "Very strange indeed."

"She was hostile toward the Order when you met her," Trahn said to Baden, "but did you get the impression that she would do something like this?"

The Owl-Master scanned the street, seeming to take in the charred buildings and the injured. "No," he said at last. "She struck me as impetuous and foolhardy. But I don't think she's cruel. And besides, Jaryd's right: if she's unbound, she couldn't have done this."

Alayna opened her mouth as if to say something. But then she closed it again.

"What is it?" Orris asked.

"It's nothing," she said, shaking her head with a tight smile. "We'll be convening soon, and I'd imagine that none of you has eaten breakfast yet. I know Jaryd and I haven't. Why don't we head back to the Great Hall, and we can all eat there?"

The others agreed, and Trahn and Jaryd helped Orris to his feet. His head spun sickeningly at first, and he squeezed his eyes shut. But after a short while he found that he could open them again without too much discomfort. The bucket line had been unable to save any of the three buildings, but they had kept the fire from spreading beyond them. The injured, it seemed, had been healed. Most were standing, or at least sitting up, and the other mages on the street were standing together in small clusters talking. There was nothing more that they could do.

Orris and his friends started to leave, but before they had gotten very far, Orris heard someone call to him. He turned slowly and saw Kovet limping in his direction. Immediately, Jaryd moved to stand by his side. Orris didn't really expect that Kovet would try anything here, but he found himself tightening his grip on his staff just the same.

"I guess I owe you my thanks," the mage said, stopping in front of him.

Orris felt Jaryd bristle.

"You owe him a lot more than that."

Kovet glanced at the Eagle-Sage and then at Rithlar. "Maybe I do," he allowed, his voice low. He looked away, as if unwilling to meet Orris's gaze. "It took a lot of courage for you to go back and get me."

"Either courage or stupidity."

The mage's eyes flew to Orris's face, and his expression hardened. But then he saw that Orris was grinning, and after a moment he smiled as well. "Yes," he agreed. "One or the other."

"What do you say we call it both?" Orris said. "A lot of the things I've done over the years can be characterized that way. And yet, I think most would agree that some good comes of them anyway."

Kovet seemed to catch his meaning. He nodded slowly, as if weighing his words. "I suppose," he said at last. "I'll keep that in mind."

Orris nodded. "I'd appreciate it."

They looked at each other for another moment or two. Then Kovet turned away and started back up the street in the direction of the Hall of the League.

Orris watched him go, wondering if at last his feud with the League was over. Kryssan nuzzled him again, and he stroked her chin.

"Come on," Jaryd said gently. "Let's get going."

Once more the mages started back toward the Great Hall. But they had only gone a short distance when one of the Great Hall's attendants come into view. She was running, her face flushed and her eyes wide. When she saw Jaryd and Alayna, she stopped.

"Something's happened at the Great Hall!" she said. "Come quickly!"

Without hesitating, the mages sprang forward, running with the woman back to the Hall. Jaryd and Alayna were ahead of the rest, Jaryd's eagle and Alayna's great owl soaring overhead.

When at last they turned a corner and came within sight of the Great Hall, Orris wasn't sure what to make of what he saw. Many of the Hall's attendants—close to a dozen of them, all wearing their bright blue robes—were standing in the street. Jaryd and Alayna sprinted forward, and Orris realized that Myn was there as well, standing between two women. Baden, Orris, and Trahn reached the Hall a few seconds later.

". . . A woman," Orris heard one of the attendants say as he stopped beside Jaryd and Alayna. "The same one who came to see you yesterday. She threatened to kill us all if we didn't leave right away. I didn't believe she really could, because she didn't have a bird with her. But then she made fire fly from her stone, and I got everybody out as quickly as I could."

"You did the right thing, Basya," Alayna said. She had scooped Myn into her arms, and she was embracing her now as if she never intended to let the child go. "Thank you."

"It looks like Tammen was responsible for the fire after all," Jaryd said, looking briefly at Baden and Trahn, and then at Orris. "But I don't see how she could have done all this without a familiar."

"There's something else, Eagle-Sage," the attendant said, sounding less sure of herself now. "The fire that came from her stone was strange-looking. It was unlike anything I had ever seen before."

Alayna stared at the woman, her face suddenly white. "What did it look like?"

The attendant hesitated. "It seemed to have layers: blue and then yellow and then blue again."

"Of course," Alayna said, nodding as if she had known what Basya would say. "Of course."

Orris shook his head. "What? I don't understand."

Jaryd was nodding now as well. "It's Sartol," he murmured, turning to look at the hall. "She was the one in my dream. I should have recognized her."

"What?" Orris said.

The Eagle-Sage shook his head, as if trying to clear his sight. "It's not important. Sartol is here; that's all that matters. Somehow he's used Tammen to escape his binding place and come here."

"But how is that possible?"

"I don't know. But he's in the Great Hall, and he's alone with the Summoning Stone."

22

*I have believed for some time now that we in Tobyn-Ser have been ask-
ing ourselves the wrong question. "Who is our enemy?" it seems to me,
is not what should concern us. By sending us two eagles the gods have
told us that our enemy is formidable. For now, that is all we need to
know. The question that worries me much more is: "How will we
respond when we finally know whom we are to fight?"*

*Assuming for a moment that our conflict is not with either the
Gods' Children or the League, will we be able to put aside the hostilities
that have divided us from them for so long? As I have explained to you in
past letters, our society is riven by petty jealousies and ancient animosities
that cannot be healed overnight. You will tell me, no doubt, that in a
time of crisis we will be able to put aside our differences and unite. I desperately wish to believe that this is true. But I have doubts and I fear the
day when our capacity for trust and forgiveness will finally be tested.*

—Hawk-Mage Orris to Melyor i
Lakin, Sovereign and Bearer of
Bragor-Nal, Spring, God's Year 4633.

If it had been Radomil, Sartol would have killed him on the spot.
Even without knowing the extent to which the Summoning
Stone would augment his power, he never would have doubted that he
could defeat the fat old man. But Jaryd and Alayna were another matter.
He had been Alayna's mentor; he, of all people, had known how strong
she would become. And he still remembered as if it were yesterday how
Jaryd, then new to his power and little more than a pup, had, incredibly,
kept him from killing Baden in the Great Hall all those years ago. Seeing
them there in the Sage's quarters, Jaryd with his eagle—an eagle!—and
Alayna with an owl so much like Huvan, Sartol's last familiar, that seeing it had taken his breath away, the Owl-Master could not help but hesitate. He knew that something had happened; even before he entered
Tammen's body, he had seen the flashing cerylls. But he had never
expected this. How could he have? It almost seemed that the gods
themselves had given Jaryd and Alayna these new birds as confirmation
of the glorious futures hinted at by their first familiars, which had both
been Amarid's hawks.

So rather than chancing a confrontation with, them, Sartol had spoken with them of alliances and politics, and then he had asked their permission to take his little stroll around the Gathering Chamber. He knew that they were watching him from their quarters, wondering who this Tammen was and what she really wanted. So he kept a careful distance from the Summoning Stone, venturing close enough to see if it responded to his presence at all, but not so close that its response would draw their attention. And only then, as he passed by the massive crystal, did he understand what he had to do. For he did see something as he approached it: a brief, faint glimmer of pale yellow light, no more than the flickering of a candle in the dim silver-grey light of morning.

But that was enough. He was still linked to the stone, although he would need to pour more of his power into it before the connection would be strong enough to allow him to control it fully. He needed time with it, uninterrupted time, though not a lot. Within an hour, he would be more powerful than any mage who might wish to oppose him, perhaps any two. Within a day, he would be able to hold off all the mages in Tobyn-Ser. After that, his work would begin in earnest. Nothing would be able to stop him, and the vengeance of which he had dreamed for so long would be his. He had been humiliated in life, reviled in death. But now, in the second life given to him by Tammen's flesh, he would avenge himself on all who had wronged him.

But first, he needed access to the stone.

He had taken little satisfaction in setting the fires. To be sure there had been some pleasure in feeling the Mage-Craft flow through Tammen's body like the waves of Duclea's Ocean. But it had only whetted his appetite for what he knew was coming.

It was a small matter to find his way into the Great Hall afterward. Jaryd and Alayna did just as he had expected, rushing blindly to serve the people without even considering that it all might be a ruse. They were all too trusting, which was why he had come so close to mastering the stone once before. The attendants gave way with almost no fight at all. The one who had greeted him yesterday now informed Tammen that the Eagle-Sage and the First were not there and that she could wait or come back another time. Sartol told her to leave and to take the other attendants and Jaryd and Alayna's child with her or be killed. After he sent a bolt of mage-fire arcing across the council table and into the great stone, she obliged.

For just a moment, Sartol considered killing the child. Jaryd and Alayna had been responsible for all that had befallen him at the end of his life. Taking their daughter seemed to him a suitable punishment. But the last thing he needed was for his two most dangerous enemies to confront him before he was ready, bent on exacting revenge and justice for the death of their child. So he let her live, sending her into the street with the Hall's stewards.

Before he knew it, he was alone with the Summoning Stone. Finally. It had been so easy he had to laugh; only a few minutes had passed since he started the fires.

By the time the constable's alarm bells stopped ringing, telling him that the fire had burned itself out, Sartol was well on his way to mastering the giant crystal. Already it glowed with his ceryll-hue—pale yellow, like the sands of Duclea's beaches at sunset. It would grow brighter, he felt sure of that. One day, not very long from now, it would be as bright as his ceryll had once been, and as the glimmering yellow flame at the center of Tammen's blue stone now appeared. But even now there could be no mistaking the fact that the stone was his.

No doubt Jaryd, Alayna, and their friends knew it the moment they entered the hall.

He had his back turned to the door, and so he heard them before he saw them. Still, without turning, he was able to guess who had come. Besides the Eagle-Sage and his bride, there would be Baden, Trahn, Orris, Radomil, and perhaps a few others whom he would remember from the final battle of his life, when the entire membership of the Order sent him into the realm of the Unsettled.

"Get away from that stone!" Jaryd commanded in a tone that was passably forceful.

"Now why would I want to do that?" he answered, turning slowly to face them. "Ah, Sonel," he added, spotting the tall, green-eyed mage standing next to Baden. "I had forgotten about you." There were eight of them. The ones he had anticipated plus Sonel and Mered, all of them looking much as he remembered, except for Baden, who looked gratifyingly old and feeble. It was more than he had hoped would come, but his morning with the stone had gone well. He felt certain that he could defeat them.

"We know who you are," Alayna said. "You're not Tammen, you're Sartol."

He laughed. "I'm both, actually. But it's not a point worth quibbling over."

"Did you really think we'd let you get away with this?"

"My poor dear," he said, opening his arms and grinning. "You already have."

"You've gotten in here," Baden said, taking a step forward. "And you've admitted to us who you are. Why don't you let Tammen go now? You don't need her anymore."

"Ah, Baden. Always looking after those less fortunate than you. How very noble. I'm afraid though that Tammen is beyond your help. Without me, she'll die. You wouldn't want to be responsible for giving another mage over to Theron's Curse, would you?"

"What is it you want, Sartol?" Jaryd asked.

He shrugged. "Power, immortality, revenge, justice. In other words, the stone, which, as you can see, is already mine."

The eight of them looked toward the great ceryll as one, and though they tried to school their features, he saw their fear.

Again he laughed. "This time you're too late. You stopped me once, but I've beaten you, as I always knew I would."

"You won't have beaten us until every mage in Tobyn-Ser is dead," Jaryd shot back. "And as long as your power is tied to that stone, that will never happen."

"Believe that if you'd like. Perhaps, for a brief time, that will offer a bit of comfort. But not very long from now, you will all be dead. Do you really think that I would have come back here so soon if I hadn't been sure of that?" He grinned again. "I'm dead, remember? Time means nothing to me. If I wasn't sure that I could win, I'd still be just a ghost."

"Then we'll just have to destroy you first," Alayna told him.

"I'd have thought you'd be grateful to me, Alayna. After all, I spared the life of your child. Doesn't that count for something?"

She started to tremble. He could see it, and it made him want to laugh out loud.

"You bastard."

"I'm bored with this conversation," Sartol said. "I have work to do. Leave now, or die, but I'm done talking."

Jaryd and Alayna exchanged a look and the Eagle-Sage gave a single nod. An instant later, all eight of the mages raised their staffs and sent torrents of mage-fire at him. Blue and purple, orange and green, russet and brown, ivory and grey. And even blended into a brilliant white, they were no match for the yellow-and-blue shield that burst from the Summoning Stone. Jaryd and Alayna were strong now—far stronger than he remembered them being—but the others were not, and Baden had grown weak. With barely the effort it had taken him in life to light a fire, Sartol blocked their assault and then sent his power surging back toward them.

They tried to resist him. He felt them gather themselves for a second assault, he saw the strain on their faces and in the corded muscles of their arms. But all he had to do was summon a bit more of his magic, enough to brighten his ceryll on a dark night, and he scattered them to the floor with a concussion that shook the Great Hall to its foundations.

They scrambled to their feet, looking stunned, like children who had just been slapped by an angry parent. And, just like chastened children, they didn't raise their staffs to challenge him again.

"I could kill you all now," he said. "I think I've made that obvious. But I have reasons for wanting all of you to live for just a bit longer. So be thankful, and leave me, before I change my mind."

Again, Jaryd and Alayna looked at each other. Then the Eagle-Sage said something under his breath and the others began to file out of the hall. Jaryd and Alayna, however remained.

"This isn't over yet, Sartol," the Sage told him. "I know you think you've already won, but you haven't. Despite all that's happened between the League and the Order, the League mages will join us when they hear that you're back."

Sartol shook his head. "Fool. Do you really think that a few more mages will make any difference to me at all? I'm no more afraid of Erland than I am of you."

"And what about Cailin?" Jaryd asked.

He narrowed his eyes. "Who's Cailin?"

"The League's Eagle-Sage."

He tried to mask his response. It wouldn't do for them to see any doubt at all on Tammen's face. But this was too much.

"A second Eagle-Sage? I don't believe you." Actually, he was lying. He could see that Jaryd was telling him the truth. He could hear it in the man's voice.

"Fine. Don't believe it. Go ahead with whatever it is you have in mind as if I never even mentioned it. But I assure you it's true. And despite all your bluster and all your threats, I also assure you that before all of this is over, you will be afraid of us. We may only be mages, but the gods have sent us two eagles. They knew you'd be coming, Sartol, even if we didn't. And they gave us the means to defeat you."

"Get out!"

"You can't win, Sartol. You're up against more than just mages and people. The gods themselves are against you."

"*Get out!*" Almost before he knew what he had done, a second bolt of blue-and-yellow fire leaped from the stone, forking at the last instant and crashing into the shields of power they had raised to resist him. Remarkably, their power held, although the force of his blow sent them flying into the walls of the hall. Their birds screamed out and then hopped to where the two of them lay, dazed and bruised.

Slowly, Jaryd climbed to his feet and then helped Alayna stand as well.

"Get out," Sartol said one last time. "Or I swear I'll kill you, even if I have to tear the Great Hall apart in order to do it."

They stared at him for another moment, then made their way out the door. Jaryd was bleeding from a gash on his head, and Alayna was limping noticeably, but that did little to lift his mood.

Two eagles. He had never imagined that such a thing could happen. It defied explanation. *The gods themselves are against you,* a voice in his head repeated, as if to prove him wrong.

He stared at the wooden doors of the Great Hall, seeing once more in his mind how the power he wielded had scattered the mages who opposed him as if they were fallen leaves in an autumn gale. And he smiled at the memory.

"The gods are nothing," he said aloud, turning back to the Summoning Stone and seeing how it glimmered with his ceryll-hue. "Let them oppose me. Before this is over, I'll be stronger than all of them."

Baden rushed forward as soon as he saw them emerge from the Great Hall, Jaryd with an ugly cut on his brow and Alayna hobbled and wincing with pain. He threw an arm around Alayna and helped her to a spot beside the avenue where she could sit and rest. After a morning spent healing victims of the fire, he was tired, as was Golivas, but he didn't hesitate for a moment to begin treating her wound. This much he could still do.

Laying his hands on Alayna's leg, he glanced back over his shoulder to check on Jaryd. Trahn was already healing him.

Baden turned his attention back to Alayna.

"This shouldn't take long," he told her. "I don't think the bone is broken."

"Thank you."

He smiled. "I feel like I've been doing this all morning."

"That's because you have been, Baden," she said, her expression grim. "We're at war now. We may be doing this quite a bit over the next few weeks."

He shuddered, his smile abruptly vanishing. She was right, of course. *We're at war now.*

And as if in response to the echo of her words in his mind, something happened to the Great Hall that chilled Baden's blood. A shield of pale yellow mage-fire, barely perceptible in the sunlight, but unmistakable, suddenly surrounded the building.

"Fist of the God!" Baden whispered. "What's he done?"

"He's made certain that we can't attack him again," Alayna said, staring at the Hall, her expression grim.

"But the power required to do such a thing . . ." He shook his head, leaving the thought unfinished.

"He's an unsettled mage," she said. "And he's mastered the Summoning Stone. Arick knows what else he's capable of doing."

He stared at her for several moments. Then he swallowed and finished healing her in silence.

As soon as he removed his hands from her leg, she started to lift herself.

"You should rest."

She gestured sharply toward the Great Hall and its sheath of yellow magic. "I'll rest later, when all of this is over." She tried to look past him. "Where's Myn?"

"I had Valya take her to the Aerie," Baden said. "She can stay there for now."

"That makes sense," she said, swiping impatiently at the hair on her brow. "Thank you. What about Jaryd? Is he all right?"

"I'm fine," came the Sage's voice from behind them.

Baden stood and helped Alayna to her feet.

"I'm sorry about that," Jaryd said, taking Alayna's hand. "I meant to make him angry, but I didn't realize just how strong he is. I almost got you killed."

She dismissed his apology with a wave of her hand. "It's all right." When he didn't respond she touched his face and made him meet her gaze. "I'm all right, Jaryd. And you didn't do anything wrong."

"I'd like to believe you, but I'm not so sure."

"Why?" Orris asked, joining them. "What happened?"

"I told Sartol about Cailin, about the other eagle. I didn't mean to, but he just seemed so sure of himself. I couldn't help it; I was looking for anything that might shake his confidence."

"I don't see anything wrong with that," Orris said.

The Sage shrugged. "I just wonder if I should have kept it from him. Look what he's done to the Hall. Now he can take as long as he wants to prepare himself. Maybe if I hadn't told him, he wouldn't have done this, and we'd have another chance to fight him before he does whatever he's planning to do."

"Maybe," Baden agreed. "But I think he would have done this no matter what you said."

"I agree," Alayna said.

The Owl-Master looked at her, and then at Jaryd. "How did he respond when you told him about Cailin?"

"He got scared," Alayna answered. "You could see it on . . ." She hesitated and looked at each of them. "Is it his face or hers?"

Baden shook his head. "I don't know. But I do think," he went on, facing the Eagle-Sage again, "that you did the right thing. If he's scared, he might make a mistake. Right now, anything that distracts him from his plans, whatever they may be, works to our advantage."

"You may be right," Trahn said. "But what should we do now?"

It was still strange for Baden to see everyone looking to Jaryd and Alayna for the answer to such a question. For so long, he and Sonel had been the Order's leaders, the ones who guided the younger mages through crises. Even after Radomil became Sage it had remained that way, in part because Radomil himself was more than willing to defer to them in times of trouble. It had taken Jaryd's eagle to bring about a true change in the Order's leadership.

It should have been hard for Baden to accept. He had been at or near the center of power in the Great Hall for many years. And, in all honesty, there were times when it did bother him. It made it easier that this was Jaryd, his former Mage-Attend and his brother's son, whom he loved as his own son. Seeing the Sage standing beside his enormous eagle, Baden could not help but be proud. And it helped as well that on most occasions, Jaryd chose to do precisely what Baden would have done in his place. Just as he did now.

"The first thing we need to do," the Eagle-Sage said, glancing back at the Great Hall again, "is go to the Hall of the League and tell Cailin, Erland, and the rest what's happened."

By this time, they had been joined by the other mages in the Order, who had been informed by their colleagues or the Hall's attendants of Sartol's presence in the Gathering Chamber. Hearing now what Jaryd intended to do, two of the younger mages, Tramys and Orlanne, stepped forward.

"Do you really think that's wise?" Orlanne asked. "We've just had the Great Hall taken from us by one enemy. Do we really want to go and announce our failure to another?"

"The League isn't our enemy," Jaryd said evenly. "Sartol is. If we're to have any chance of defeating him, we'll need the help of every mage in Tobyn-Ser."

"And what if instead of helping us, they choose this moment to try to destroy us? Did you think of that?"

Jaryd opened his mouth to respond, but Alayna stopped him with a hand on his arm.

"You haven't been a member of the Order for very long, Orlanne," she said. "And I know that you were quite young and living in western Tobyn-Ser when Sartol died. So I'll assume that your words are a product of ignorance rather than foolishness."

The young mage's face reddened, but Alayna gave no sign that she had noticed.

"Sartol was my mentor. I've known him nearly all my life. I saw what he did to Jessamyn and Peredur, I saw what the men with whom he allied himself did to Watersbend, and today I saw what he's done to a mage named Tammen, who, for all I know, did nothing at all to deserve her fate. He is more cruel and more ruthless than any person our land has ever known. And now that he has access to the Summoning Stone, he may be the most powerful mage in Tobyn-Ser's history. The mages of the League know of Sartol, even if you and Tramys don't. And regardless of what they think of the Order, when they hear that he's back, they'll realize that Tobyn-Ser's only hope lies in our ability to work together. So if I were you, instead of looking for reasons not to trust the League, I'd start trying to get used to the idea that they're going to be our allies in this war." She swept the street with her glare, as if challenging other members of the Order to speak against Jaryd's proposal. "Our Eagle-Sage has suggested that we go to the Hall of the League. I'd say it's time for us to get going."

She took Jaryd's hand in hers and started walking in the direction of the League's hall. Without a word of protest, the other mages of the Order followed them.

As they walked through the streets of Amarid, a strange silent procession, the people of the city stopped to point and whisper among themselves. Word of Sartol's reappearance had not yet spread, but their march through the streets was already prompting other whisperings.

"They're going to war!" Baden heard one man say.

And another replied, "They're going to fight the League!"

Jaryd seemed to hear that as well, because a moment later he halted and held up a hand, signaling the others to stop as well.

"It might not be wise for all of us to just show up at their hall," he told them. "I'd rather they didn't get the wrong idea. Alayna and I will go on, along with Orris, Baden, Sonel, and Trahn. Radomil," he added, turning to the goateed Owl-Master, "I'd like you to take the rest and talk to the council of city elders about finding us a place where we can convene. The Great Hall is beyond our reach right now, and I'd like to have a place where all members of the Order can discuss matters in private."

Radomil nodded. "Of course, Eagle-Sage." He hesitated. "What shall I say is the reason for our need?"

Jaryd pressed his lips into a thin line and rubbed a hand over his face. "Tell them the truth," he said at last. "With what Sartol has done to the Hall, lying to them would be pointless."

"Very well." Radomil smiled. "Don't worry, Jaryd. They'll listen to you. They must."

Jaryd gripped the man's arm. "Thank you, Radomil."

The small delegation stood in the center of the avenue watching as the portly mage led the rest of the mages away. Then, with Jaryd leading them once more, they walked the rest of the way to the Hall of the League and knocked on the building's large wooden doors.

For several moments there was no response, but just as Jaryd raised his hand to knock a second time, one of the doors opened and a young woman in a long grey robe peered out at them.

"I'm sorry," she said. "The League is in Conclave right now, but . . ."

She fell silent, staring at them in disbelief.

"We need to speak with the League of Amarid," Jaryd told her. "Please tell Eagle-Master Cailin and First Master Erland that Eagle-Sage Jaryd, First of the Sage Alayna, and a small group representing the Order are here."

"B-But they're in Conclave. They're not to be interrupted."

"In this one case I'm sure they'll understand."

"But they're—"

"If you tell us they're in Conclave one more time," Orris said, stepping forward, a fearsome expression on his face, "I'm going to tear your hall apart stone by stone. And believe me, that will be much harder to explain to Cailin and Erland than a simple interruption of their Conclave." He glared at her. "Have I made myself clear?"

The woman nodded and took several steps back away from him before turning to deliver their message. She didn't even bother closing the door again.

While they waited for her to return, Baden looked at Orris and raised an eyebrow. " 'Stone by stone'?"

The burly mage shrugged. "It worked didn't it?"

"Yes," Jaryd said over his shoulder, a slight smile on his lips. "But I'd appreciate it if you'd refrain from threatening anyone else. We're here looking for allies."

An instant later another young woman appeared in the doorway, looking breathless and pale. She wore a blue cloak and carried a staff with a golden stone. But it was only when the eagle appeared beside her, looking almost as large as she, that Baden realized this was Cailin.

"Jaryd, Alayna," she said. "Welcome." She glanced at the others as if to include them in her greeting, but her gaze returned quickly to Jaryd's face. "What's happened?"

The Eagle-Sage hesitated. "It would be best if I could tell all of you at once."

"Of course," Cailin said with a nod. "Come in."

She backed away from the door, gesturing for them to enter. But as they made their way toward the large table that stood in the middle of the League's hall, she fell in beside Orris.

"I know what you did today," she whispered. "I think it may be the most noble thing I've ever known anyone to do."

In the next instant she was gone, hurrying to her place at the far end of the table next to Erland. Baden looked over at Orris and saw that the mage's face was bright red. He almost said something—half a dozen quips about schoolgirl infatuation leaped to mind—but remembering the woman Orris had loved and left behind in Lon-Ser, Baden thought better of it.

"Be welcome in our hall," Cailin said a moment later, standing in front of her chair and smiling at them.

Erland was standing as well, although he eyed the Order mages with an icy expression. And though the other mages of the League shifted their chairs in order to make room at their table for Baden and his companions, they did so silently, the looks on their faces much more like Erland's expression than Cailin's.

Jaryd led his friends over to the table and indicated with a subtle hand movement that they should sit. He remained standing, however.

"Thank you, Eagle-Master, First Master," he said, nodding to each of them in turn. "You honor us with your greeting and by allowing us to join your Conclave."

"What is it that you want?" Erland demanded.

Jaryd regarded Erland coolly for a moment before looking around the table at the other League mages. "Since I first learned that the League had an Eagle-Master," he began in an even tone, "I have vowed that I would do all I could to avoid any conflict that might pit mages of the Order against mages of the League. All of us who serve the land wish to protect it, not to divide it, and I have been steadfast in my belief that the League is not our enemy. Instead, I have maintained that the gods sent these eagles to us so that we would unite when the time came to fight another foe, and I vowed that upon learning of whom that foe might be, I would come to the League and do all that was in my power to convince you to join us in our struggle." He paused, sweeping the room with his gaze. "It is for this reason that my companions and I have come to you today."

"You know who it is?" Cailin said, her voice barely more than a whisper. "You know who we're to fight in this war?"

"I think it's more appropriate," Erland said before Jaryd could respond, "to ask the Eagle-Sage how he can assume that we would consider an enemy of the Order to be our enemy as well."

Baden could see the muscles in Jaryd's jaw tighten, and for a moment he feared that the Sage would fire back a barb of his own. And not too long ago he would have. But Jaryd was Eagle-Sage now, and he responded to Erland's comment with a dignity befitting that title.

"I assure you, First Master," he said, "there isn't a mage in this hall who will want to stand with this enemy. I'm quite confident of that."

"Who is it?" Cailin asked, casting a hard glance at Erland.

Jaryd took a breath. "The unsettled spirit of the traitor Sartol."

Cries of disbelief and denial filled the hall, the loudest as Baden would have expected, coming from Erland.

"That's impossible! Theron's Curse doesn't allow such a thing!"

"Apparently, Sartol has found some way to alter the Curse," Jaryd answered. "Or, more likely, he's managed to escape its limitations. He came to us in the guise of a young free mage named Tammen. But we have no doubt that it's Sartol. He's here in Amarid."

Erland shook his head. "I don't believe you." He looked frightened, however, like a man who knew all too well that he was hearing the truth.

"There's more," Jaryd told them. "He's taken the Great Hall from us. He has the Summoning Stone."

"*What?*" asked Stepan, one of the older mages, who had once been a member of the Order. "How could you allow such a thing?"

"We didn't know yet that this woman was Sartol. The alarm bells started ringing this morning, and we left the Great Hall without a second thought. When we returned, we found Tammen there—or rather, Sartol. A group of us tried to fight him, but with the stone he was just too strong."

"So you think Sartol started the fires?" another man asked. It took Baden a moment to realize that it was the mage Orris had saved earlier that day.

"Yes."

Stepan shook his head. "Arick save us all."

"I don't understand," Cailin said. "What can he do with the Summoning Stone?"

Baden and Erland stared at each other across the table. And for just that brief moment, Baden knew that they were thinking the same thing: how is it possible that a leader of the League could be young enough not to know such a thing?

"Before we defeated him twelve years ago," Erland explained quietly, "Sartol had begun to link himself to the Summoning Stone."

"You mean to make it his?" the young mage asked, a look of fear creeping into her bright blue eyes. "The way one would a ceryll?"

Erland nodded. "Yes. In the days after his death, we who were in the Order at the time decided not to tell anyone about this. We didn't think there was any sense in letting the people of the land know how close he had come to destroying Tobyn-Ser."

Cailin nodded and looked at Jaryd. "So when he returned today, he was able to make the stone his again."

"I don't think it ever stopped being his," Jaryd told her. "He had only been alone with it for half the morning when we returned from the fire, and he already had mastered it enough to fight off eight of us."

"Sartol," Erland said in a low voice, shaking his head slowly. "I never thought we'd have to worry about him again."

"Does that mean that you believe them, First Master?" one of the younger League mages asked.

Once more, Erland looked across the table at the Order mages, his eyes finally coming to rest not on Jaryd, but on Baden. Oddly, Baden understood. There were no old friends here, but perhaps the next best thing was the comfort of an old enemy.

"If this is a trick," Erland said, trailing off and letting the threat hang between them unspoken.

Baden shook his head. "It's no trick. It wasn't easy for us to come to you like this, in need of help and exiled from the Great Hall. We wouldn't be here if the threat wasn't real."

Erland held his gaze for another few moments before giving a reluctant nod. "Yes, Gerwen," he said. "I believe them."

"I'm glad to hear it," Jaryd remarked in a tone seemingly free of irony. "Next we should decide on a course of action. We need to act quickly if we're—"

"With all due respect, Eagle-Sage," another of the young mages broke in, sounding anything but respectful, "you don't set the agenda for our Conclave. Erland and Cailin do."

"Thank you, Vawnya," Cailin said. "But this is now a council of war, and Jaryd has as much right to direct our discussion as I do."

"On whose authority?" Erland demanded.

The young woman glared at him. "Mine. Unless you care to revisit the discussion we had in your chamber the other day."

"No," the Owl-Master said after a brief silence. He glanced around the table and took a long breath. "Cailin's right: this has become a council of war. And in matters of war, particularly against this enemy, we should hear from both Cailin and Jaryd."

The Eagle-Master nodded and faced Jaryd again. "You were saying, Eagle-Sage . . . ?"

Jaryd smiled. "I was saying that we need to act quickly, and I'd add that we need to move beyond the petty jealousies that can be found among mages of both bodies. When all this is over, we're free to go back to being rivals again, but right now that's a luxury we can't afford. For better or worse, the gods chose to give eagles to Cailin and me, and if we're to defeat Sartol, the rest of you will have to respect their choices. I believe that we need to seek the counsel of the Unsettled. Sartol is of their realm, and they may know of a way to defeat him. Cailin, I'd like you to choose two or three mages to accompany us on a journey to speak with the nearest of the Unsettled. And I'd be interested in hearing from anyone who knows which of the spirits is closest to here. I know of none who's closer than Phelan."

He looked down at Alayna and then at Baden, a question in his pale eyes.

"I can't think of anyone," Alayna said.

Baden shook his head. "Neither can I. This is the reason we battled the outlanders at Phelan Spur all those years ago. We decided that he was the closest."

"What about Rhonwen?" Vawnya asked.

Baden frowned. "Who?"

But Jaryd and Alayna were nodding.

"Of course," Jaryd said. "I'd forgotten. Her binding place is in Tobyn's Wood, due south of the mountains."

Cailin looked from Jaryd to Vawnya. "Who is Rhonwen?"

"Rhonwen," Jaryd replied, "was a young mage who entered the Order just a year or two after Alayna and I did. Less than a year after she found her hawk, the bird was killed, by a hunter I think. An accident. And before she could bind again, she was taken with a fever. She died shortly thereafter." He shook his head. "She was the last mage to enter the Order before . . ." He stopped himself, but no one in the hall had any doubt as to what he had been about to say. She was the last mage to join the Order before the sundering of the Mage-Craft.

"You say that her binding place was in Tobyn's Wood?" Orris asked.

Vawnya nodded. "Yes, just north of the top of Phelan Spur. It should be no more than a week's ride from here."

"Then she sounds like the best choice," Cailin said, taking charge of the discussion once more. She looked at Jaryd. "When do you want to leave, Eagle-Sage?"

"Today. As soon as you and the others you select are ready."

She nodded. "Give us until midafternoon. We'll meet you outside the hall."

"All right." Jaryd motioned for his companions to stand. "In the meantime, we'll inform the rest of the Order."

He turned away from the table and led Baden and the rest out of the hall and into the street. There, surprisingly, they found Ursel waiting for them.

"Don't tell me you've found a place already?" Jaryd said.

The mage nodded. "When the elders heard we were in need, they offered the constable's building." She grinned. "It seems the head of the council and the constable are both Order men."

"Has anything happened?" Jaryd asked as they began to walk toward the constable's building, which was in the center of the city, near Amarid's home. "Has Sartol done anything?"

"There's light coming from within the hall, so he must be doing something with the stone, but other than that we really don't know."

Jaryd pressed his lips in a thin line and nodded, but he said nothing, and they walked for some time in silence. After a while, Ursel looked at Jaryd and then glanced back at Baden and the others. "How did your conversation with the League go?" she finally asked.

"Better than I could have hoped," the Sage admitted. "A group of us, Order and League mages both, will be leaving later today to speak with an unsettled mage in Tobyn's Wood."

Her eyes widened slightly. "That's a fine start. I wouldn't have believed such a thing could happen so quickly. You must have been very persuasive."

Jaryd shook his head. "It wasn't me. It was Sartol. The mere mention of his name is enough to convince even the most stubborn mages to put aside their differences."

Baden thought that Jaryd was taking far too little credit for what had just happened in the League's hall, but he said nothing. He was, at this point, consumed with another matter that he fully expected to have to address in the next few moments. So he just walked, holding Sonel's hand in his own, and trying to decide how best to inform Jaryd of the decision he had made.

The constable's building was not a particularly attractive one. It had neither the soothing curves of the Great Hall nor the graceful, lofty spires of the Temple of the Gods located on the edge of the city. The tall bell tower rising from the back of the building was too ponderous to be considered the least bit beautiful. Nor was it an especially large building. Seven years ago, before the formation of the League, such a building would never have sufficed for the Order. But since the Order now consisted of fewer than thirty mages, the building was more than adequate.

They found Radomil and the other mages of the Order waiting for them inside, standing in a spacious room that was otherwise empty.

"I hope this is satisfactory, Eagle-Sage," the Owl-Master said, as Jaryd led Baden and his companions into the chamber. "The constable has promised us chairs and a table, but he said it might take a day or two."

"This is fine, Radomil. Thank you."

"Shall I see to some food before we resume our discussions?"

Jaryd shook his head. "We haven't time. A group of us will be leaving shortly for Tobyn's Wood and the binding place of an unsettled mage named Rhonwen."

As the rest of the mages gathered around them, Jaryd explained what had happened in the Hall of the League and what he and Cailin had decided to do. At first, no one spoke out against the idea, although Baden could tell from the expressions on the faces of Tramys, Orlanne, and some of the other young mages that they still did not relish the idea of entering into an alliance with Erland and his followers.

After several moments, however, Radomil took a long breath. "Forgive me, Jaryd, but do you think it's wise for both you and Cailin to leave Amarid at this time? If Sartol tries anything, we may need an Eagle-Sage to lead us in battle."

"You may be right, Radomil," the Eagle-Sage said, placing a hand on the portly man's shoulder. "But it may take both of us to convince the Unsettled to help us. Besides," he added, a rueful smile on his lips, "I don't think either of us would agree to stay. I'm not willing to give control of this delegation to the League, and Cailin wouldn't trust Erland to represent her."

Radomil nodded. "I see your point," he said quietly.

"We'll return as quickly as we can. Sartol has surrounded the Hall with his magic. I don't get the feeling that he'll be attacking anytime soon. I'm afraid he has something more elaborate in mind."

"Who are you going to take with you?" Orris asked, when the Sage had finished.

"Well, I had hoped that you would come."

The burly mage grinned. "Of course."

Jaryd turned to Alayna, but she shook her head before he could even say something.

"One of us should stay here with Myn."

He nodded. "All right. Then in addition to Orris, I'll take Baden and Trahn."

Baden swallowed. He had been expecting this. "As much as I'd like to go with you, Eagle-Sage, I'm afraid I have to decline."

Jaryd stared at him as if he had just announced that he was leaving the Order to join the League. "Why?"

"This is a younger mage's journey, Jaryd. You need to cross the mountains as quickly as possible, preferably on horseback, and I'll only slow you down."

"That's ridiculous! You know Erland will be going. He wouldn't trust Cailin with something like this. And he's older than you are."

Baden smiled. "Just because Erland is an old fool doesn't mean that I should be, too."

The Eagle-Sage stepped forward and placed a hand on the Owl-Master's shoulder. "Baden, I need you. I need your wisdom and your guidance, just as I always have. Please don't make me do this without you."

"You'll have Trahn with you, and Orris. I'm confident that the three of you have enough courage and wisdom to handle Erland and the Unsettled."

"Never mind Erland and the Unsettled," Jaryd said, his voice barely more than a whisper. "Who'll handle me?"

Baden pulled him close, as much to hide his own tears as to comfort Jaryd. "You'll be fine," he said softly, so that only the Sage could hear. "The gods chose well when they sent that eagle to you."

A moment later he released the mage, although not before giving Jaryd's arm one last squeeze.

"Very well," Jaryd said, pitching his voice to carry. "Orris, Trahn, and I will go. I'm hopeful that we can be back within a fortnight." He turned to Alayna and gathered her in his arms. "Take care of yourself," he told her. "And tell Myn I love her."

She nodded. "I will. If anything happens, we'll use the *Ceryll-Var* to let you know."

Jaryd kissed her and then let her go. "Are you two ready?" he asked, facing Orris and then Trahn.

"Aren't we always?" Orris answered, grinning once more.

The Eagle-Sage smiled in return, and the three of them turned to leave the meeting house.

"Arick guard you!" Baden called to them.

Jaryd looked back over his shoulder. "And you."

A moment later, they were gone, and Baden was left to wonder if he had done the right thing.

Sonel walked over to stand beside him and laced her fingers through his. "That took courage, Baden," she told him in a low voice. "I know how much you wanted to go. I'm proud of you."

He gave her a small smile, but it faded quickly. Sartol had returned, Tobyn-Ser's two Eagle-Sages were on their way to Tobyn's Wood to enlist the aid of the Unsettled, and though Jaryd and Cailin had managed to bring the League and the Order together for the moment, the mistrust that had divided mage from mage for so many years remained. And yet, selfish as it seemed, Baden could not help but wonder in the midst of all this, if he still had a role to play in saving the land.

"I feel old," he said, as Sonel kissed his cheek.

She smiled, the playful soft smile he had come to know so well over the years. "You are old. I am, too." Her expression hardened. "But that doesn't mean we're powerless. This may be Jaryd's war, and Cailin's, but we'll be there at the end. One way or another, we'll be there."

23

As I have sought changes in the ways of the Nal, I have, of course, met with resistance from Overloads, Nal-Lords, break-laws, and even guards under Jibb's command. And though this has been a source of frustration, it has not come as a great surprise. The Nal has worked under one set of rules for a long time, to the benefit of many.

I did expect, however, that my efforts to curb the Nal's excesses would win the support of the Network. I am, after all, a Gildriite, a Bearer of the Stone. As such I thought that Bragor-Nal's Gildriites would embrace me as an ally. I am the first of my people to rise so high in the Nal's hierarchy; certainly I am the first to do so while acknowledging my ancestry. Yet, they have spurned every overture I have made toward them, offering no explanation. I have made it clear to every break-law and lord in Bragor-Nal that the oppression of Gildriites will no longer be tolerated. Acting on my orders, Jibb has ended SovSec's persecution of the Network. And still, they treat me as if I am their enemy. Obviously, I am confused by their behavior. But more than that, I am hurt by it.

—Melyor i Lakin, Sovereign and Bearer of Bragor-Nal to Hawk-Mage Orris, Day 6, Week 12, Winter, Year 3067.

For several days Melyor did little more than sleep. They woke her every few hours to give her more pain medicine and then allowed her to drift away again. She was vaguely aware of certain things: the dull ache in her right thigh, Jibb hovering at her side, doctors moving in and out of her bedchamber. She gathered from what she managed to hear of Jibb's conversations with the meds that while her wound was deep, it was not too serious. She would heal eventually. She had a number of vivid dreams during this time, most of them of the firefight they had just come through. But she also dreamed of killing Marar, and in one especially clear vision, she saw Orris come to her and lay his hands on her leg to heal her.

When she finally did awake, it was night. Jibb was there, of course, sitting at the foot of her bed, a worried look on his round face.

"I was starting to wonder if you'd ever wake up," he said, smiling at her with so much relief that it made her blush.

"How long have I been out?"

"Three days. They had to repair the bone," he added, seeing her reaction. "And you had lost a lot of blood."

"Three days," she muttered. She shook her head and found that doing so made her dizzy. "Has there been any word from Wiercia?" she asked, closing her eyes again.

"No."

"What about Marar? Has he tried to contact anyone in the palace?"

"Not that we know of." He took her hand. "You shouldn't be worrying about all this. Not yet. You need to rest some more."

"Rest?" she said, her eyes flying open once more. "I've lost three days! There's no telling what he's up to now! For all we know he's already recruited someone else to take the place of my driver and Premel." She sat up and glanced around the room, weathering another wave of dizziness. "Where is Premel, anyway?"

His expression soured. "I haven't put him in prison yet, if that's what you're asking."

"Actually, I was wondering if you'd killed him."

He gave a small laugh. "No, not that either."

"Did you talk to Vian?"

Jibb's face abruptly turned pale. "Yes."

"Why did he do it? Who was Selim?"

The security man swallowed. He looked like he was about to be ill. "Selim i Vitor," he said at last. "He was a break-law I killed in the Eighteenth Realm last year during a skirmish. Apparently Selim and Vian were half brothers. Same mother, different father."

"Which is why we never knew," Melyor said, completing the thought. "They had different surnames."

He nodded, but said nothing. Instead, he merely stared at his hands. She could see from the look in his dark eyes how angry he was with himself, and she laid her hand on his arm.

"It wasn't your fault, Jibb. I'm the one who trusted him."

"He says he didn't even care about killing you. It was me he wanted. But that was almost enough to get you killed."

"You couldn't have known. No one could have."

He took a long breath, his eyes flicking in her direction for just an instant. After a moment he gave a small nod.

There was a knock at her door, and one of the doctors walked in.

"You're awake!" he said, a smile on his square face. "Splendid."

340 DAVID B. COE

He sat beside her and gently removed the dressing from her leg, revealing an ugly, raw wound.

Melyor swallowed and looked away.

"You think that's bad," the doctor said. "You should have seen it a few days ago."

"When can I walk again?" she asked, looking at the wall next to her bed as he changed the bandages.

"I'd like to get you on some walk-aids in the next day or two. It'll be a while though before you're running through the tunnels again."

"What does 'a while' mean?"

He stopped working on her leg and took a long breath. "I'd say you'll probably be walking unaided again in four weeks," he replied at last, turning his attention back to the dressing. "Full activity again in six, maybe seven."

"Six weeks?"

"Maybe seven."

She shook her head again. The dizziness was subsiding. "That's unacceptable! I have things to do! Places I need to go!" *I have to kill Marar.*

The doctor said nothing as he finished with her leg, but then he turned to face her. "I'm not repairing a carrier, Sovereign. I'm not tinkering with a thrower. And I'm not making you wait that long for any sort of treatment. I'm merely telling you what your body needs in order to recuperate." He stood. "I can't make you listen to me, of course. And," he added, giving her a disapproving look, "I'm sure you're anxious to get back at whoever did this to you. But I've given you my opinion. If you rush this, you may never move the way you used to."

He nodded once to Jibb and left, closing the door behind him.

"So are you going to listen to him?"

"I haven't decided yet," she said, her tone sullen.

"Melyor—"

"I heard him, Jibb. I'm not deaf, and I'm not stupid. I just need to find a way to follow his advice without giving Marar time to buy himself a new ally in this palace."

"I could take some men, capture him, and bring him back to you."

"And let him see me lying here in bed, like an invalid? He'd die thinking he had won. No, there has to be another way."

"I don't think there is. Not if you're going to stay off your feet."

And in that moment she knew. "But I don't have to stay off my feet," she said, grinning.

"But the doctor said—"

"The doctor said that it would be weeks until I could run again. But he also said that he wanted me on walk-aids in the next day or two."

"So you're going to hobble into Stib-Nal on walk-aids?"

"That's my plan. I just need a little bit of help."

Jibb stood, thrusting his good hand into the pocket of his trousers, and began to pace, as he seemed to do so often these days. "Help? Who could possibly help you with an idiotic stunt like this?"

It was a familiarity she would not normally have allowed, even from Jibb. But these were extraordinary circumstances, and she could hardly begin to imagine how much he had worried about her over the past few days. So she let it go, choosing instead merely to answer his question.

"The Network."

He halted in the middle of her room. "The Network? How can they help with this?"

"Do you remember Gwilym?" she asked, feeling her chest tighten as she mentioned his name. She remembered him as clearly as she remembered her own father. His kind brown eyes, his shy smile, and the quiet confidence and grace with which he carried himself. He had come to Bragor-Nal from the Gildriite settlements in the Dhaalmar, drawn to the Nal by a vision of Orris. And just as her own vision of the mage had convinced her to abandon her life as a Nal-Lord and join Orris's struggle against Cedrych and the Tobyn-Ser Initiative, Gwilym's vision of redemption for Oracles throughout Lon-Ser drove him to journey with Melyor and Orris to Oerella-Nal. There, just outside Shivohn's palace, he died, the victim of an assassin's attack. But before he died, as his life's blood seeped into the Oerellan avenue, he gave Melyor his stone, thus making her a Bearer and changing her life forever.

"You mean the Bearer?" Jibb asked.

Melyor nodded, although she was staring across the room at her stone. It was red now, but it had once been golden brown, back when it was Gwilym's.

"Sure I remember him," the security chief said, drawing her gaze back to his face. "But what does that—?"

"The Network got him all the way through Oerella-Nal and almost all the way through Bragor-Nal without anyone knowing about it, including Shivohn's security, SovSec, and Cedrych. If they can do that, they can get you and me into Stib-Nal."

"It's not the same, Melyor. The Bearer could walk."

"Give me a pair of walk-aids, and I can walk, too."

He shook his head. "This is a bad idea."

"Well, at least that's an improvement. A few minutes ago it was idiotic."

Jibb frowned. "I'm sorry I said that."

"You can make it up to me by finding me someone from the Network."

"How in Arick's name am I supposed to do that?"

"I don't know," she said with a shrug. "You're the head of SovSec; you figure it out."

He stared at her, shaking his head. After a moment he began to smile. "I'm not going to change your mind, am I?"

"You have a far better chance of finding the Network."

"All right," he said, laughing. "But for now I want you to rest." He walked to the door. "I'll have some food brought up to you, then I'll get to work on this. Will that be satisfactory, Sovereign?"

She grinned. "Quite, General. Thank you."

Notwithstanding her confidence in Jibb's abilities, and the blithe manner in which she sent him to find a member of the Network, Melyor knew just how difficult a task she had given him. Years ago, when Cedrych learned that Orris was in Bragor-Nal and in the care of the Network, he sent her to find him. It took her all of her resources and the better part of two days to do so.

Which was why she was truly shocked when Jibb returned to her chambers midway through the following day with a young, wiry, dark-haired woman wearing black trousers, an ivory tunic, and a black overcoat—clothes that marked her as a break-law.

"This is our Gildriite?" Melyor asked. With help from the doctor she had moved to a large cushioned chair by one of her windows, and she shifted slightly now so that she could get a better look at the woman.

"Yes, Sovereign," Jibb replied. "She denies it, but my sources tell me she's a member of the Network. On the street they call her Mouse. She wouldn't give me her real name."

"That's all right," Melyor said. "Mouse will do."

He crossed to where she sat and handed her a scratched, discolored thrower and a blade with a badly worn handle. "She was carrying these."

"Thank you, Jibb. You can leave us for now."

He glanced at Mouse with manifest distrust, but after a moment nodded and withdrew.

Melyor waved a hand at the chair opposite hers. "Please sit down."

The woman just stared at her, unmoving.

"Suit yourself," the Sovereign said with a shrug. She narrowed her eyes, looking Mouse up and down. The woman had a small scar on her chin, and another on her wrist, but they were old. Given the way she stood there in the middle of the Sovereign's quarters—the battle-ready stance, the defiant look in her pale blue eyes, and the slight smirk on her thin lips—Melyor guessed that she had made herself into an accomplished street fighter. In many ways, Mouse reminded Melyor of herself when she was still a break-law. "So you belong to the Network," Melyor finally said.

"No, Sovereign," Mouse answered. "As I told the security goon, I'm no Gildriite. I'm just a poor independent trying to make her way in the Nal."

Melyor raised an eyebrow. "That goon, as you call him, is the head of SovSec, and his sources are seldom wrong."

Mouse shrugged and glanced indifferently around the room. "Well, they are this time."

"Well, let's assume for the moment that they're not."

"But they are."

Melyor smiled thinly. "Humor me."

Their eyes met, and Melyor held the woman's gaze until finally Mouse looked away. "All right," the break-law murmured.

"If I wanted the Network to get me into Stib-Nal, who would I talk to, and how much lead time would you need to get me in touch with that person?"

Mouse held her arms out wide. "How can I answer a question like that? I tell you, I'm not a Gildriite. I'm just—"

"I know," Melyor broke in. "A poor independent, trying to make her way in the Nal."

The woman gave an insolent look and nodded.

"So why aren't you with a gang yet, Mouse?" the Sovereign asked, playing absently with the worn dagger Jibb had given her.

"I don't know," Mouse said with another shrug. "I guess I'm not good enough yet."

Melyor smiled indulgently, and then, with a motion so fluid that Mouse had almost no time at all to react, she lifted the dagger by its blade and hurled it at the woman.

And just as she had expected, Mouse dived to the floor as the blade passed harmlessly over her head, rolled, and came up reaching for her thrower. Or rather, reaching for where her thrower should have been. Melyor was already holding the weapon in her hand, its dented firetube aimed at the woman's heart.

"Easy, Mouse," she said. "Don't do anything foolish."

"Me?" the woman said, her eyes blazing. "You're the one who just tried to kill me!"

"I wasn't trying to kill you. I was just proving what I already suspected. You're a liar. No independent who moves like you do should have any trouble convincing a gang to pick her up. Not unless she wanted to remain an independent. Perhaps as a way of concealing a secret?"

Mouse looked away. "I don't know what you're talking about."

"Stop it. I'm sure you've fooled lots of people over the years, and I'm sure you'll fool many more. But not me. Never me. We're too much alike."

The woman snorted in disbelief.

"How do you think I got started, Mouse? Think for a minute. I've known I was a Gildriite since I was a little girl, and I started my life in the quads when I was fifteen. I was you once. Is that really so hard to believe?"

Mouse stared at her for several moments, saying nothing. Melyor could see that there was a war raging within her, and she understood. Like Mouse, she had spent years hiding her ancestry from everyone she met. It had been a struggle for her even to reveal her secret to Jibb, whom she had trusted with her life for years. What she was asking of Mouse now was far more difficult.

"I thought that you were different," the woman finally said. "I thought that you weren't coming after the Network. They all said, 'She's a Gildriite. She's changing things.' "

It was, Melyor realized, the closest thing to an admission she was likely to get. "I am different. I'm not only a Gildriite," she said, gesturing toward her staff, which leaned against the wall by her bed, "I'm a Bearer."

"Then why are you doing this to me?"

"I'm not doing anything to you, Mouse. The question I asked you before was sincere. I need the Network's help, and so I needed to speak with someone who could put me in touch with them." She shrugged. "You just happened to be the one Jibb found."

"Lucky me."

Melyor grinned. "Lucky you." Again she pointed to the chair in front of hers. "Won't you sit?"

Mouse glanced down at the chair, clicking her tongue. Finally, with a low sigh and a roll of her eyes, she dropped herself into the chair, allowing one thin leg to dangle over the cushioned arm. Melyor had to suppress a laugh; it was like looking at a mirror image of herself.

"Why do you need to get to Stib-Nal?"

Melyor almost went for the bait. It was an impertinent question, one this woman, who was really little more than a girl, had no right to ask. And the Sovereign almost told her so. But that, she was sure, was what Mouse wanted her do. The break-law was looking for reasons not to help her or answer her questions. Melyor wasn't about to give her another.

"Stib-Nal's Sovereign has tried a number of times to have me assassinated." She indicated her bandaged leg with a dismissive gesture. "I got this from his latest attempt. I've grown tired of it, so I'm going to Stib-Nal to kill him."

Melyor had to give Mouse credit. She had expected the woman to gape at her, her mouth open in shock at the Sovereign's candor. But apart from a slight widening of her eyes, Mouse offered no physical reaction at all.

"Sounds dangerous. You sure you're up to it?"

Melyor did laugh at that. "Now you sound like Jibb. But," she added, her mirth fading, "I still want an answer to my question. Who would I need to contact about such a journey, and how long would it take you to get me in touch with him or her?"

"Why should the Network help you?"

"Why shouldn't it?" the Sovereign snapped. "You said yourself that I'm different. I'm a Bearer. Doesn't that count for something? I've stopped SovSec's raids on your hideouts, I've ended the persecution of Gildriites in the Nal—"

Mouse laughed. "If you still lived in the quads, you'd know how wrong you are. The prejudice against Oracles hasn't vanished, it's just gone underground, where it can't be seen from the Gold Palace."

"If you're still being attacked, I want to know who's doing it. I guarantee you, I'll have SovSec all over them within a day."

The woman hesitated. "I haven't seen any attacks. But the hatred is still there."

"I can't change that, Mouse. I can change the rules so that those who hurt Gildriites go to prison, and I can keep SovSec and the lords and break-laws who work for me from persecuting you. But I can't make them think differently. That takes time. And maybe it will help that the Nal now has a Bearer as its Sovereign. Maybe people will see that, and it will start to change their minds. But I can't make it happen overnight."

Mouse smirked. "That's just what I'd expect a Sovereign to say."

"What's that supposed to mean?"

"You can afford to tell the Gildriites in the quads to be patient. You don't have to deal with all that anymore. You're immune to the hatred." She made a vague gesture and glanced around the room. "This place protects you from all that."

"You'd be surprised," Melyor told her, thinking back to the conversation she had with Premel the day she learned of his betrayal.

"What do you mean?"

The Sovereign shook her head. "Never mind. So what you're telling me is that my being a Gildriite and a Bearer doesn't matter to you people because I'm Sovereign now, and that means I don't have to face the prejudice every day. Is that right?"

She gave a noncommittal shrug and looked away. "That's what a Gildriite in the quads might say."

"That's the most ridiculous thing I've ever heard! Do you really think that I can forget what I went through for the first twenty-six years of my life? Do you really think that becoming Sovereign made me any less of a Gildriite than I was before?"

"I don't know. Did it?"

"No, Mouse. If anything it made me more of one, because it meant that I could stop hiding it. Our people have been oppressed for so long that we've come to believe that being a Gildriite means being afraid. But it doesn't. It took me a long time to figure that out. It took the death of the man who gave me that stone. But I know it now, and I'm determined to pass the gift of that realization on to every Gildriite in Bragor-Nal."

"But first you want to kill Marar."

"He's no friend of the Gildriites, Mouse."

"Maybe not, but that's not why you want him dead, is it?"

Melyor started to argue, but then realized that she couldn't. Mouse was right. "What's your point?"

"That maybe you're not so different after all. This all sounds like the old ways to me. This cycle of violence and retribution has been poisoning this land for centuries. It's just the type of thing our people have been trying to avoid since the Consolidation."

" 'Our people,' Mouse?"

The woman blushed to the tips of her ears and looked down at her hands.

"You're right," Melyor said after a lengthy silence. "Maybe killing him isn't the answer."

Mouse looked up. "So I can go?"

Melyor shook her head. "No. I still need to stop him. He's responsible for the death of Oerella-Nal's Sovereign, he's come close to killing me, and he's involved in some sort of campaign against Tobyn-Ser."

That, of all things, got the woman's attention. "What's he doing to Tobyn-Ser?"

"I don't know yet. But I intend to find out. That's one of the reasons I still have to get to Stib-Nal." Melyor took a breath. "Please, Mouse. I need the Network's help."

Mouse looked at her for a long time, her expression neutral. She certainly knew how to conceal her emotions, as did all members of the Network. It was a skill that had been forced upon them by years of fear and secrecy.

"I won't help if you're going to kill him," she finally said. "If that's what you're planning to do, there isn't a man or woman in the Network who'll help you."

"I won't kill him," Melyor said. "I'll find some other way." Seeing the doubt in the young woman's dark eyes, she added, "I swear it on the memory of Gwilym, Bearer of the Stone, whose staff I now carry."

Mouse swallowed, then nodded. "All right." She stood. "Am I free to go?"

Melyor tossed the woman her thrower. "Of course."

She put the weapon in the holder that was strapped to her thigh and started toward the door. "You'll be contacted within two days. We'll expect you to be ready to go on a moment's notice."

"I'll be ready."

Mouse reached the door and put her hand on the door handle. But then she stopped herself and walked to where her blade had stuck in the wall. Yanking it from the wall, she slipped it back into its sheath, in her right boot. Melyor grinned. She still carried her own blade in the same place.

The woman turned and faced the Sovereign. "What if you had been wrong? What if I hadn't been as good as I am and your throw had killed me? Would you have thought, 'Well, no worry, I'll just have my goon find me another Gildriite'?"

"I wasn't wrong. Was I, Mouse?"

"But what if you had been?"

Melyor grinned. "If you hadn't been as good as you are, I never would have tested you. You don't get to be Sovereign by being wrong about people."

"Then how is it that an assassin got close enough to you to confine you to that chair?"

The woman had an unnerving knack for asking difficult questions.

"I've already told you how I knew that I wouldn't kill you, Mouse," Melyor finally said, meeting the break-law's gaze. "You and I are very much alike."

Mouse seemed to consider this for a moment before walking to the door again and pulling it open.

"Mouse," Melyor called just as she was leaving.

The woman paused in the doorway, although she didn't bother turning.

"There may be traitors in the palace. Watch yourself as you make your way back into the quads."

"I always do," the break-law said, pulling the door closed behind her. "I'm a Gildriite."

He had seen her stained with her own blood.

Even when he had thought that he would kill her, he never really imagined that he would see that. In his mind, killing her had seemed a sanitary act—one minute she would be there, he had thought, and the next minute she would be gone. But he had never thought that he would have to see her bleed. She was Melyor i Lakin. She was more than a Sovereign; she was practically a legend.

But he had seen it nonetheless: her blood on her trousers and her ivory tunic. Her blood staining the stone floor of the tunnels. And then, because Jibb was still hurt and there was no one else, he lifted her into his arms—she was impossibly light, almost like a child—and he carried her to the med carrier waiting for them outside the nearest street access. And after the carrier sped away, back toward the Gold Palace, there it was again. Her blood. On his uniform.

Later, after the meds had seen to her and returned her to the palace, Premel had gone to see her in her chamber. Jibb had been there, of course, hovering at her side like an anxious parent as she slept. And though the general had glared at Premel when he entered and then ignored him while he was there, he had not insisted that Premel leave. Perhaps he knew that Premel was there out of concern and respect. Or perhaps he believed that Melyor would have insisted that Premel be allowed to stay. Whatever the reason, Jibb allowed it, and Premel remained, watching the Sovereign as she lay still and pale, looking more vulnerable than he had ever seen her.

Premel had always towered over her, and though he had known for years that she was better with a thrower or a blade than any man in Bragor-Nal, he had never doubted that he was stronger than she. It was only when he saw her in that large bed that he realized how slight she was.

And later still, this very morning, he had seen her on walk-aids for the first time, completing the process that had begun for him a few days before in the tunnels. He would never look at her the same way again. She was no legend; her Gildriite powers didn't make her immortal. She was as human as he. She bled, just like he did.

But rather than diminishing her in his mind, it made her seem braver, more accomplished as a fighter, more brilliant. After nearly ten years, he finally understood why Jibb loved her as he did. And now, at last, he understood fully what an idiot he had been to ally himself with Marar.

Which was why he had been so pleased when Melyor asked him to accompany her, Jibb, and a small contingent of highly trained guards into Stib-Nal. Whatever revenge she had in store for the Sovereign—and Premel understood from Jibb that she no longer intended to kill him—he wanted to be a part of it.

They had spent the better part of the day in carriers, making their way on the Upper from the Gold Palace to the southern tip of Bragor-Nal's Nineteenth Realm. There they met a slight, dark-haired woman, who was, it seemed, a member of the Gildriite Network.

"They sent you, Mouse?" Melyor said, getting out of carrier in the narrow alleyway in which they had stopped. "I didn't think you wanted any part of this."

"I don't," the woman said, her voice flat. "But we all agreed that it would be best if you and your goons know as few of us as possible." She gave a thin smile and opened her hands. "So here I am."

Jibb handed Melyor her walk-aids out of the back of the carrier. She deftly tucked them under her arms and swung herself over to the Gildriite woman. She moved remarkably well on the walk-aids, considering that she had only tried them for the first time the night before. Still, Mouse was not pleased.

"You're using those?" the woman asked.

"Of course. Otherwise, I'd have to crawl, and that might slow us down."

Jibb snickered, drawing a glare from Mouse.

"This is insane," the woman said, facing Melyor again. "We have a swamp to cross, and Stib Grove to get through. You can't do all that on walk-aids."

"You said yourself it's less than fifty quads from here. And if we skirt the foothills," Melyor added, gesturing in the direction of the Greenwater Range, "we won't have to deal with the swamp at all."

"SovSec patrols the foothills. That's not the route we use."

The Sovereign grinned and nodded at Jibb. "SovSec is with us today, Mouse. For this one time, you don't have to hide from them. And you also don't have to show us your route into and out of Bragor-Nal. I thought you'd be pleased."

Mouse blinked, as if this hadn't occurred to her. But a moment later she was eyeing the Sovereign dubiously again and shaking her head. "Don't you have an air-carrier we can use?"

"The air-carrier can't land in the foothills. And even if it could, Marar's people would see it. We have to do this on foot."

"You're crazy," the woman said. "Those walk-aids will add a day to our journey. Probably two. And that's assuming that you're capable of keeping up any sort of acceptable pace, which I doubt."

"Tread carefully, woman," Jibb growled. "That's Melyor i Lakin you're speaking to."

"It's all right Jibb," Melyor said quietly. "What she's saying is true, and we both know it."

The general fell silent, but the look he gave the dark-haired woman could have melted steel.

"Don't worry about me, Mouse," the Sovereign said, facing her again. "You've promised to help me, and I plan to hold you to your word, even if I have to do it with a thrower pressed to your back."

Mouse laughed. "Right. As if you—"

Before she could finish, Melyor lifted her walk-aids off the ground and swung them at the woman simultaneously, so that one caught Mouse on her right temple, and the other crashed into the side of her left knee. The combination of blows knocked the woman off her feet sideways. She landed hard on her side and lay still for a moment, too dazed to move. And by the time she was even able to roll onto her back and look up at the Sovereign, Melyor was standing over her with the butt of one of the aids pressed down on her throat. She wasn't even out of breath. Jibb and the other men were grinning, but Melyor's expression was deadly serious.

"Even with my injury," she said, "I'm faster than you, I'm stronger than you, and I'm capable at any moment of killing you. Never forget that. And never, ever laugh at me. Do you understand?"

Mouse stared up at her for several seconds, giving no response. Finally, she nodded once, never taking her eyes off Melyor's face.

"Good," the Sovereign said. She removed the walk-aid from Mouse's throat, but left it within the woman's reach, as if offering it to her.

After another moment, Mouse took hold of it and pulled herself to her feet. There was already a dark welt forming on her temple.

Melyor turned to Jibb. "Can you get me my staff please, General?"

"Of course," he said, retrieving it from the carrier. He brought it to her, but seeing that both of her hands were occupied with the walk-aids, he hesitated. "Do you want me to carry it?" he asked at last.

"No. Why don't you give it to Mouse? It seems appropriate that the stone should be carried by a Gildriite."

He gave her a doubtful look, but she nodded.

"You don't mind, do you, Mouse?" she asked, glancing at the woman.

Mouse looked from Melyor to Jibb. "No." She faltered, then looked away. "Actually," she said, sounding embarrassed, "I'd be . . . honored."

Melyor looked at Jibb again and nodded a second time. The general shook his head, his frown deepening, but he did as he was told, handing the staff, with its glittering scarlet stone, to Mouse.

"Be careful with that," the Sovereign said, her tone light. "It's the only one I've got."

Mouse smiled. "I will, Sovereign," she answered, drawing a smile from Melyor. "Thank you."

"Let's get going," Melyor said, turning to Jibb. "I'd like to cover a few quads before dark if we can."

"You heard her," Jibb told his men. "Carry sacks on. We're moving."

The general said nothing to Premel. He rarely did these days. But Premel knew that he was expected to do what the other six guards did, so he joined them at the rear of the carrier and flung one of the sacks onto his shoulders. There were only eight packs—no one expected Melyor to carry one, obviously, and she made it clear that Mouse wasn't expected to carry one either.

"She's our guide," Melyor explained. "She's doing us a favor. And there should be plenty of food for all of us, even if we take an extra day."

Again, Jibb did not look happy. Clearly he didn't trust this woman, which made her suspect in Premel's eyes as well. But Melyor seemed to harbor no such doubts. Indeed, despite their confrontation, and the harsh warning Melyor had given her, the Sovereign appeared grateful for Mouse's company. They walked together for the first hour or two of their journey, trailing behind the men slightly—although Jibb hung back near them—and talking. From what Premel could hear of their conversation, it sounded as though Melyor was asking the woman question after question, and that, after being reluctant to answer initially, Mouse grew increasingly talkative.

After some time, however, the strain of using the walk-aids on the soft, uneven ground began to take its toll on Melyor. She fell silent, and though she continued to keep pace with the others, she looked unnaturally flushed. Her face was bathed in sweat, as were her clothes.

Jibb's face was etched with concern, and he glanced back at her with ever-increasing frequency as the afternoon wore on. They were still near enough to the swamp to smell the rank mud. Insects buzzed around them constantly, until Premel was ready to pull out his thrower and try to kill them. But there was a breeze, and the air was mild enough to make the day bearable.

"Sovereign," Jibb finally said. "Perhaps we should stop. It will be dark soon, and we should set up camp for the night."

Premel looked up at the sun, which was just barely visible through the brown haze that hung over the Nal and the mountains. It was maybe an hour past midafternoon. Certainly no more. They had at least two hours of daylight left. But Melyor really did not look good.

"No," she said. Despite her appearance, her voice sounded strong. "I appreciate your concern, Jibb, but I'm fine."

The general nodded, his lips pressed together, and they continued on deeper into the foothills. Conditions improved as they did. The stench of the swamp faded, and there were fewer insects to bother them.

Still, when they finally did stop, close to two hours later, Melyor simply collapsed onto her back, her eyes closed and her chest rising and falling rapidly. Jibb hurried to her side, but she gave a weak grin and waved him away.

"I'm all right," she said breathlessly. "I just need to lie here for a while."

The general shook his head, but he stood again, and started to walk off.

"Where's Orris when I need him?" Melyor muttered under her breath. "At least he could heal this."

Jibb stopped in mid-stride, his whole body seeming to stiffen at the mention of the sorcerer's name. But then he walked on.

"Keep an eye on her," he said as he went past Premel. "If she needs anything, call me. The others and I will get the camp set up."

"I can see to the camp, General," Premel said, turning as Jibb walked by.

Jibb didn't even slow down. "I know," he said over his shoulder. "But I don't want to be near her right now."

The general and the other men had the six sleep shelters set up well before the last vestiges of daylight had vanished. After distributing enough food for an adequate meal, the company began to settle in for the night. Jibb returned to where Melyor was now sitting, to offer her some food and re-dress her wound, but they said little to each other. The general spent most of his time barking orders at Premel and the other guards, and Melyor merely stared off into the night, looking thoughtful and tired. Mouse kept to herself, although she seemed unwilling to stray too far from the Sovereign now that she had been entrusted with Melyor's stone.

When Melyor finally struggled to her feet and hobbled over to her shelter, Mouse followed and took the one beside her, leaving Jibb and Premel to share one that stood a short distance away.

They made good progress the following day, despite Melyor's obvious discomfort. They broke camp at first light, rested briefly late in the morning, and stopped again in the middle of the afternoon. And though the Sovereign once again looked flushed and exhausted, she offered no complaints. She didn't even slow them down.

"How does she do it?" Premel heard Mouse ask, late in the day.

He glanced over at her and realized that she had been talking to him. He hadn't even realized that she was walking beside him.

Premel felt his face color and he quickly faced forward again. "I'm probably the wrong person to ask." *I'm a traitor.* "I really don't know her that well."

"You must know her better than I do. How long have you worked for her?"

He shrugged, feeling self-conscious. "About ten years."

"And you still don't know her?"

Premel looked at her again. She was regarding him with a slightly amused expression and a smirk on her lips. He had seen that look so often during the past day and half that he assumed it was there all the time. Despite the smirk, she was actually quite pretty, although in a hard way.

"Are you mocking me?" he asked her.

"Not at all."

He raised an eyebrow, and she laughed.

"I'm not saying that I'm incapable of mocking you," she conceded. "Or that I won't later. But I'm not mocking you right now."

Premel grinned. "Well, that's reassuring." He looked away again. "The truth is, I don't think anybody knows her that well, except Jibb, and maybe the sorcerer who was here a few years back."

"I've heard about the sorcerer," Mouse said. "People in the Network, still talk about him. Is it true that he and the Sovereign loved each other?"

Premel did know this much. He had been a friend of Jibb's long enough to know what Melyor's feelings for the sorcerer had done to him. But this, he decided, was none of Mouse's business. "Like I said, I don't know her that well."

"Now you're lying," Mouse said. "But that's all right. I probably shouldn't have asked."

They walked in silence for some time, as the sun dipped lower in the western sky. Premel would have liked to talk to her. Jibb hardly spoke to him anymore, and though the men still knew nothing of his treachery, they saw him as their superior officer, not as a friend. He had never been very good around women, however, and Mouse made him feel awkward and unsure of himself. And yet, he was comforted by her company, and she seemed content to walk by his side.

"How did you know I was lying?" Premel finally asked, his eyes trained on the ground in front of him. "There aren't many people who would have figured that out." *Jibb and Melyor never did.*

"I lie every day," she said. "It's a way of life for me. After a while you learn to tell when other people are lying." She looked at him. "Why did you lie to me?"

"I didn't think you needed to know anything that personal about the Sovereign."

"Maybe not. But you know her better than you were letting on, don't you?"

"I suppose," he said. "What I said about nobody really knowing her is true. But to answer the first question you asked me, I think that what drives her to do the things she does, and to do them all so well, is the fact that she's a Gildriite."

Mouse faltered in mid-stride, but only for an instant. "What does that have to do with it?" she demanded, an edge to her voice.

"It's what made her feel she had to succeed. Before she became Sovereign, Gildriites were brutalized in the Nal. They were hunted down by SovSec and break-laws alike."

Mouse shook her head and laughed bitterly. "You all think that things have changed so much."

"You're alive, aren't you?" Premel said, looking at her. "You're traveling in the company of the Sovereign and eight of her security men. Do you really think any known Gildriite would have been allowed to do that under Durell?"

The woman started to respond, but then stopped herself. "You may be right," she said at length, "although the quads still have a long way to go before Gildriites will feel safe there. But I still don't see what that has to do with Melyor, and what she's become."

"You should," came a voice from behind them.

They both turned and saw the Sovereign hobbling toward them. Her face was as red as thrower fire, and her sweat-soaked hair clung to her face and neck. But she was smiling at them.

"I'm sorry, Sovereign," Premel said. "I didn't know you were listening."

"It's all right, Premel," she said, as she reached them. "I probably shouldn't have been."

She didn't stop, so Premel and Mouse started walking again on either side of her.

"But since I was," Melyor continued a moment later, "I thought I'd offer my opinion."

"Which is?" Mouse asked.

"That Premel is right: I'm the way I am because I'm a Gildriite. And you of all people should understand that."

"Ah, yes," the woman said with an exaggerated nod. She looked past Melyor to Premel. "The Sovereign tells me that she and I are very much alike."

"What I actually said," Melyor corrected, "is that she's me ten years ago."

Premel considered this for a moment, and then began to smile. There were differences, to be sure. He would have bet on Melyor in a fight between the two, and by the time she was Mouse's age, Melyor had been a gang leader and well on her way to becoming a Nal-Lord. But in most other respects, the Sovereign had a point: they were really quite similar.

"What are you grinning at?" Mouse asked.

"She's right," he said. "You're her."

The woman halted and shook her head. "No, I'm not," she said. Melyor and Premel stopped as well.

"I know about you," Mouse told the Sovereign. "I know that you killed out of spite and ambition; I know that you never joined the Network, that you chose instead to turn your back on us until you needed our help. And I know that at one time you were going to lead an invasion of Tobyn-Ser."

"Who told you that?" Melyor breathed, her eyes widening.

Mouse bared her teeth in a harsh grin. "It doesn't matter. I just know it. Just as I know that you and I are not at all alike."

"Then why are you helping me?"

"I'm helping you now because the Network asked me to. They thought that maybe if I did, you'd make things in the quads better for us. I told them you wouldn't, that you think it's all fine now, but they insisted, so I'm here. But I'm doing this for my people, not for you."

She spun on her heel and stalked off, leaving Premel and the Sovereign to stare after her in silence. After a moment, the guard looked over at Melyor.

"Sovereign, I—"

"It's all right, Premel," she said in a low voice. She started forward again, her hands white-knuckled as they gripped the walk-aids. "Let's just get this over with."

24

Please do not take what I am about to write the wrong way. I am grateful for the peace that exists between our two lands, and though I am uncomfortable with some of the consequences of the transisthmus trade that has developed in recent years, I see its benefits as well. But I cannot help but be struck by the irony of what I see happening to our land. Twelve years ago, my fellow mages and I fought off invaders from Lon-Ser. Four years later, you and I destroyed Cedrych so that we might prevent future invasions.

Yet every time I walk through Tobyn's Wood and see still more expanses of forest destroyed in the name of commerce, every time I travel into the high country and see mountainsides scarred by miners, I am forced to wonder if our land is any better off than it would have been had we not defeated the outlanders. Yes, the people of Tobyn-Ser are compensated for our trees and our ore—at least some of them are.

And we are not subjugated by anyone. But our land is being ruined. I
believe that with all my heart.

> —Hawk-Mage Orris to Melyor i
> Lakin, Sovereign and Bearer of
> Bragor-Nal, Winter, God's Year
> 4633.

It was worse now than it had been just a few weeks ago, when he crossed through the God's wood with Alayna and Myn. It didn't seem possible really; so little time had passed. But Jaryd could see the difference. The forest was disappearing that fast.

He knew that they had more important things to worry about right now. If they couldn't stop Sartol, the trees would be the least of their concerns. But as their company rode southward toward Rhonwen's binding place, the pain of seeing so many stumps and scarred hillsides tore at his heart like a talon. And judging from the expressions on the faces of Trahn and Orris, he guessed that they felt the same way.

There were six of them in all. Cailin and Erland had selected Vawnya, the young woman who had first suggested that they go to Rhonwen, to accompany them on the journey. She was tall and powerfully built, with long yellow hair and green eyes. She seemed quite comfortable on horseback and she knew the area through which they were riding, having spent much of her childhood near Phelan Spur. Indeed, Rhonwen had served Vawnya's village during her brief time as a member of the Order. According to Cailin, the mage knew just where the spirit could be found.

They had covered the distance to the southern portion of the wood in just five days, and Vawnya seemed confident that they would reach Rhonwen's binding place on this day, before nightfall. But despite their swift pace and the mere fact that League mages and Order mages were journeying together, Jaryd saw little to indicate that the temporary truce he and Cailin had forged might last beyond this journey. Erland had gone out of his way to avoid Jaryd and his friends. Apart from the venomous looks he sent in Orris's direction from time to time, he ignored them entirely. And though Vawnya did not seem to be particularly comfortable with the First Master, she made it quite clear that she preferred his company to that of any mage wearing a green cloak. Jaryd wasn't really surprised, but against his better judgment he had hoped for more.

Only Cailin made any effort at all to bridge the chasm that divided the League mages from those of the Order. She rode with Jaryd, Orris, and Trahn frequently, allowing Erland and Vawnya to ride ahead without her. In the evenings, long after her fellow League mages had gone to sleep, she stayed with Jaryd, Orris, and Trahn, joining in their conversations, or just sitting silently, listening to them. At first Jaryd assumed that she was just building on the friendship that the two of them had forged during their frequent meetings throughout the spring. But he soon realized that Orris was the one who had drawn her into their circle. She rarely strayed from his side as they rode, and at night, as they all sat by the fire, her eyes never left his face.

Under different circumstances it might have been amusing; certainly there could be no mistaking the depth of her feelings for him. And no one who still remembered the power of a first love could help but be moved by the expression in her sapphire eyes. For all her poise and power, and notwithstanding the great eagle that soared above her as she rode through the wood, Cailin was still little more than a child.

But neither could anyone watching Erland when Cailin was near Orris doubt that the First Master would never forgive her for loving a man he believed to be a traitor. What was worse, Jaryd, knowing Orris as he did, could see how uncomfortable the mage was with the attention lavished upon him by the Eagle-Master. Orris was in love with Bragor-Nal's Sovereign. He had been for years, and Jaryd believed his friend when he said that he was incapable of loving anyone else.

No, this was anything but amusing. It should have been. It should have been harmless. Things of this sort happened all the time. But instead, it put everything at risk: their journey to see Rhonwen, the fragile peace that existed between the League and the Order, Cailin's ability to lead the League with Erland's cooperation. Everything. Jaryd could do nothing but watch it all unfold.

Riding through yet another cleared expanse of what once had been woodland, Jaryd held up his hand, signaling to the others that he wanted to stop. Vawnya and Erland were ahead of him, and he called to them as well.

"What is it?" Erland demanded, pulling his mount around so that he was facing them.

"I want to rest a moment."

"Here?" Vawnya asked, scanning the scarred clearing with obvious distaste.

Jaryd pointed to a small, muddied stream that crossed the narrow path between himself and the League mages. "There's water here. My animal needs to drink."

Vawnya and the First Master exchanged a look and then began to ride back to the brook, both of them frowning.

Jaryd swung himself off of his animal, as did the others, and while the horses drank, the company pulled food from their sacks and ate a small meal.

"How much longer?" Jaryd asked Vawnya, breaking a lengthy silence.

The yellow-haired woman scanned the clearing again and gave a small shake of her head. "Not much longer, I think. It's hard to tell with the wood the way it is. I knew this forest when it hadn't been cut. But now . . ." She shrugged.

"You can still find Rhonwen, can't you?"

"Yes, Eagle-Sage," she answered, sounding annoyed. "I'll get you to Rhonwen."

Jaryd sensed Orris bristling beside him, and he laid a hand on the burly mage's shoulder. "Thank you," he said to Vawnya at the same time.

They rested for a few moments more, none of them speaking, or even looking each other in the eye.

Standing there amid the stumps and scraps of shattered trees, Jaryd felt his apprehension deepening. He knew that the company needed to find some way to conceal their divisions from the Unsettled. If Theron and Phelan sensed that the League and the Order were unable to work together, they would be far less likely to help them. And Arick knew that without the Unsettled, the mages of Tobyn-Ser had no hope of defeating Sartol. Yet, the Sage could think of no way even to broach the topic with Erland and Vawnya, much less to reach some sort of understanding with them.

"Are we ready to move on?" Erland asked, his impatience manifest in his voice and stance.

"I suppose," Jaryd said, walking over to his mount and swinging himself into his saddle.

The others climbed onto their beasts as well, but as Erland and Vawnya turned their animals to go, the First Master glanced back over his shoulder, his eyes flicking to Orris and then coming to rest on the Eagle-Master.

"Cailin," he said, "why don't you ride with us for a while?"

"No, thank you, Erland. I'll ride with Jaryd. You're welcome to join us though."

The silver-haired mage cleared his throat and made himself smile. "I just thought that perhaps we three should ride together for a time and discuss how we wish to approach this evening's conversation with Rhonwen."

"That's a matter for Jaryd and me to decide, Erland," Cailin said evenly. "We're the ones bearing eagles."

"Actually," Jaryd broke in, "I think this is a matter we should all discuss." He looked from Cailin to Erland. "That's why Cailin's earlier suggestion was such a good one: why don't we all ride together?"

The First Master's eyes were locked on Cailin. "Stay out of this, Jaryd."

Orris leveled a rigid finger at Erland. "He's properly addressed as Eagle-Sage."

"And you're properly addressed as Traitor!"

"That's enough!" Cailin snapped, sending a bolt of golden fire into the sky.

Erland nodded, his eyes blazing. "That's just the type of display I'd expect from the whore of a traitor."

For an instant no one moved. Then, her face bright red and tears flowing from her eyes, Cailin leaped onto her horse and rode off at a full gallop past Erland and Vawnya and into the forest.

"You bastard!" Orris growled, jumping down from his mount and advancing on the First Master, his hands balled into fists. "I'm going to tear you apart."

Erland lowered his staff, so that his ceryll was aimed at Orris's heart. "Not if I kill you first, Traitor."

Orris stopped in mid-stride.

"Don't do it, Erland," Jaryd warned, leveling his staff at the older man.

"Do you know how long I've waited to do this, Orris?" the First Master asked, as if he hadn't heard Jaryd at all. "Do you know how many nights I've dreamed of killing you?"

"*Erland!*" Jaryd shouted.

But the First Master seemed oblivious to everything and everyone, except Orris. Jaryd had little doubt that he would have killed the mage in the next moment had Vawnya not reached out and placed her hand on Erland's staff.

"Please, don't do this, First Master," she said, her voice steady despite the frightened look on her face.

Erland blinked, then took a breath.

"First Master?"

He looked at the woman and appeared to shudder slightly. But then he nodded. Tentatively, she removed her hand from his staff. He faced Orris again, and the two of them eyed each other for several seconds, saying nothing. Then, as if by agreement, they both looked away at the same time and Orris walked back to his horse and swung himself onto its back.

For what seemed an eternity no one moved or spoke. Jaryd strained his ears listening for the hoof beats of Cailin's horse, but aside from the trickle of the small stream and the distant call of a jay, he heard nothing at all.

"What do we do now?" Trahn asked at last.

"We go on to Rhonwen's binding place," Orris answered before Jaryd could say anything. "And after we've reached it, I'll try to find Cailin."

Erland looked up sharply, as if intending to say something. Instead, though, he just looked away again, the muscles in his jaw clenching like fists.

Orris spurred his mount forward, but when he reached Erland he stopped. "Not that it's any business of yours, but I've never touched her. I've never had any intention of touching her." He kicked his animal forward again and disappeared into the wood.

After a few seconds, Erland and Vawnya followed, leaving Jaryd and Trahn alone in the clearing.

"Erland would have killed him," Jaryd said. "I'm sure of it."

The dark mage nodded. "Probably. But Orris intended no less when he got down off his horse."

"Is that supposed to make me feel better?"

Trahn grinned. "Hardly."

"What am I supposed to do about this, Trahn? Do I keep them apart for the rest of the journey? Do I allow only one of them to come with us when we speak with Rhonwen? Because we can't—"

"It won't happen again, Jaryd," the mage said with such certainty that Jaryd just stared at him.

"How can you know that?"

"I know both of them. And for all their faults, they both love this land too much to let their hatred of each other destroy it."

"But you saw what just happened."

"Yes."

"And you still believe that?"

Trahn smiled and nodded. "I do. Perhaps they needed for something like this to happen. They've been moving toward some kind of confrontation for a very long time, since Orris took Baram from the prison. Maybe even before then. Now that they've had it, maybe they can work together."

"I hope you're right," Jaryd said, starting after the others with Rithlar circling above him.

"So do I."

Vawnya made them stop just a short time later, in a dense, undisturbed portion of the wood. Dismounting and looking around her, she began to nod.

"This is it," she said. She looked at Jaryd. "This is where Rhonwen found her hawk."

The Eagle-Sage wanted to ask if she was certain, but at some point they had to learn to trust each other, and it was up to him to start the process.

"Good," he said instead, climbing off his horse as well. "Well done, Hawk-Mage."

Her eyebrows went up, as if he had surprised her, but a moment later she smiled. "Thank you, Eagle-Sage."

Jaryd looked at the others. "We should find Cailin as soon as possible. The sun will be down soon, and we need to have her with us when we speak with Rhonwen."

"I'll go," Orris said. "I'll find her."

"We'll all look for her," Jaryd told him.

Orris's expression hardened, but after a moment he nodded.

They agreed to split up—Jaryd remarked to himself that it was probably the only thing he could have gotten them all to agree to do—and to meet back at Rhonwen's binding place at dusk. As they started to leave the thicket, however, Jaryd called Orris over.

"I'm sorry," he said quietly. "After what happened earlier, I felt that I needed to send everyone out looking for her."

Orris nodded and gave a small smile. "I understand. And I think I owe you an apology."

"Save it for later. Right now you have to find Cailin. You're the only one who can, because she only wants to be found by you."

The mage stiffened momentarily, but he didn't look away. "I know." He hesitated. "What I said to Erland was true, Jaryd. There's nothing between us. My heart . . . lies elsewhere."

"I know that." Jaryd smiled sadly. "Be kind when you tell her."

"Of course."

Orris turned his horse and steered him into the trees. Within moments Jaryd had lost sight of them.

Taking a breath, the Eagle-Sage turned westward and began his own search. But he had little doubt that what he had told Orris was true: the burly mage was the only one who had any chance of finding the Eagle-Master. The question in Jaryd's mind was whether she wanted to be found at all. He had seen the look on her face as she rode out of the clearing. He had seen the humiliation in her eyes and the tears on her cheeks. She was bound to an eagle, and she led the League; she was strong and wise beyond her years. But she was still young, and Erland had called her a whore.

He knew that he'd find her and that he wouldn't have to go very far to do so. Yes, there was probably a part of her that had wanted to ride as far as her mount would take her. To be sure, there was a part of Orris that wouldn't have blamed her if she had. In the brief time he had known her, however, he had come to realize that she was far more than just a child with an impressive familiar. The gods had chosen well in sending her an eagle, almost as well, he had to admit, as they had in sending one to Jaryd.

So when he spotted her horse through a gap in the trees less than a league from where the company had stopped, he was not surprised. He dismounted and walked forward slowly. The animal was drinking from a small cascade, and hearing Orris approach, he looked up, blinked once, and then went back to drinking. At first though, Orris saw no sign of Cailin.

"Eagle-Master?" he called.

"Go away," came the reply, from much closer than he had expected.

She was sitting on a large rock above the cascade, her arms wrapped around her knees, which were drawn up to her chest. Her hair was falling down around her face, and her eyes were swollen and red from crying. She looked even younger than she usually did.

"I will go away," Orris said gently, "if that's what you really want me to do."

She gazed at him for several moments and then looked down at her knees. "Do you love me?"

He had never been very good at talking about his feelings, especially not with beautiful women. But this struck him as a particularly difficult question to answer.

"Not in the way you mean," he finally said. "I'm sorry."

She began to cry again, and as her body shook with her sobs, she lowered her forehead to her knees.

Orris closed his eyes and shook his head. Jaryd would have handled this better. So would Trahn or Baden, or even Sartol for that matter. Leaving his horse to drink with Cailin's, the mage scrambled up the small rise to the rock on which she was sitting. Her eagle was sitting nearby, and she watched him keenly as he sat beside Cailin.

"I'm sorry," he said again.

"Is it that I'm younger than you?" the Eagle-Master asked, her voice muffled and thick.

"That's part of it. I'm twice as old as you are." He wished that he were exaggerating, but he knew that if anything, he was doing the opposite. "And then some," he added.

She looked at him. Her cheeks were damp, but for the moment her tears had stopped flowing. "That doesn't stop other people. Girls my age marry men who are even older than you. They do it all the time."

"I know that, Cailin. As I said, our ages are only part of it."

"Then what?" she asked, drying her face with the sleeve of her cloak. "Is it me?"

He smiled. "Of course not. Any man in his right mind would fall in love with you."

A single tear rolled down her cheek, but she smiled in return. "Ah, so you're insane."

"There are certainly those who would say so," Orris said with a laugh. He took a long breath. "The reason I can't love you, is that I already love someone else. I have for many years now."

Cailin looked down again. "Oh. I'm sorry," she said in a small voice. "I didn't know."

"There's no reason you should have."

They sat without speaking for some time, she with her eyes trained on the water spilling past the rock they were on, and Orris surreptitiously watching her. After several minutes he sneaked a look to the west so that he might gauge the progress of the sun. They hadn't much time left before they were supposed to rejoin the company, but he was loath to rush their conversation.

"She's probably nothing like me, right?" Cailin finally said, sighing heavily.

"That's hard to say. In some ways you're quite similar, in others you're . . ." He hesitated, then smiled. "You're worlds apart."

"Is she very beautiful?"

"Yes." He leaned forward, peering at her until she had to look him in the eye. "So are you, Cailin."

She gave a shy smile and looked away. "What's her name?"

"Melyor."

She wrinkled her nose. It wasn't a common name here, although Melyor had once told him that it was not an unusual one for girls in the Nal.

"Is she a mage, too?"

Again Orris hesitated. He had no idea how she would respond to learning that Melyor was from Bragor-Nal. Cailin's parents had been killed by outlanders, and though she had been gracious when she learned that it was he who had taken Baram back to Lon-Ser, and had, it seemed, managed to fall in love with him despite his past, this was another matter entirely. Still, he decided, he owed her the truth.

"No," he said. "She's not a mage. She's a Bearer."

The young mage shook her head. "What's a Bearer?"

"A Bearer is someone who's descended from Gildri, one of Theron's followers, who left Tobyn-Ser after the Curse and Theron's death."

She gave him a puzzled look.

"Melyor lives in Lon-Ser, Cailin. She's someone I met while I was there."

Her eyes grew wide. "She's an outlander?"

"Yes. She's the Sovereign of Bragor-Nal." This time it was Orris's turn to look away. "I'm sorry if that disturbs you."

"No, it doesn't. I suppose it might have once, but not anymore." She paused, as if considering what he had told her. "Actually," she went on a moment later, "it makes it easier in a way. We're so different that there's no way I can compare myself to her."

"Well, as I said: you're similar in some ways. You're both strong, intelligent, beautiful women. But I think I understand what you mean."

She sighed again and then hooked her arm through his and rested her head on his shoulder. He stiffened slightly, wondering if she was trying to make him change his mind.

"I'm sorry," she said, lifting her head. "Would you rather I didn't?"

"No, it's all right. As long as you understand that there can be nothing more between us."

She nodded and put her head on his shoulder again. "I do."

He looked to the west again. "We should get back to the others soon."

"I know. Just a few minutes more." She fell silent, but only for a moment. "So how did you meet her?"

Orris grinned and shrugged. "She sent some people to kill me, and things kind of grew from there."

She sat up straight again, smiling. "Really? So if Kovet had been telling the truth, and I had sent those mages after you, I might have had a chance?"

Again he laughed. "I can't say for certain, but let's not try to find out, all right?"

He stood, and offered his hand to help her up as well. As soon as she had gotten to her feet, though, she stepped forward and kissed him softly on the lips.

He frowned. "Cailin—"

"I know," she said, smiling and blushing. "But I just had to do it once."

"Come on," he said, jumping down off the rock and going to his horse. "We need to get going."

She climbed down off the rise and swung herself onto her mount, but once there, she didn't move.

Orris had already started riding, and now he stopped and looked back at her. "What's the matter?"

"I'm not exactly eager to face Erland again."

"I don't blame you, Cailin. But I told him—I told all of them—that it wasn't true, that there was nothing between us."

"It almost doesn't matter," she said. "He had no right to say what he did."

"You're right, he didn't. But he was saying it out of anger at me, not you."

"Well, he has no right to call you a traitor, either."

"Maybe not. But none of that matters right now. You're Eagle-Master, and you need to show him that even if he can't put his anger aside for the good of the land, you can." He smiled. "Now come on. It'll be dark soon."

She returned his smile and nodded, and they started back toward Rhonwen's binding place.

They found the others just as the last rays of sunlight were streaming through the wood. Erland looked up when they emerged from the trees and quickly looked away again. Orris and Cailin exchanged a look, and then Orris shrugged, drawing a grin and a shake of the head from Cailin.

Jaryd approached them, and held the reins of Cailin's horse as she dismounted. "I'm glad to see you, Eagle-Master."

"Thank you," she said, her face reddening. "I'm sorry for riding off like that."

The Eagle-Sage shook his head. "Don't be."

Vawnya walked over to where they were standing and looked from Jaryd to Cailin. "What's our plan?" she asked.

"At this point we don't really have one," Jaryd answered. "We need to find out how Sartol got free of his binding place and what he's done to Tammen. And we need to know if they have the ability and the inclination to help us."

"What if they don't?" Orris asked.

"I'd rather not think about that right now," Jaryd said, meeting Orris's gaze.

Trahn had built a fire, and now they gathered around it to eat a small meal. Orris, however, was not at all hungry, so he merely stood there, staring at his feet and shivering slightly, though he wasn't really cold. He was not a man easily given to fear, but he could do nothing to ease the racing of his pulse or rid himself of the flutter in his stomach. Until their recent encounter with Sartol in the Great Hall, he had never faced one of the Unsettled. He had been unbound when Jaryd, Alayna, and the others traveled to Phelan Spur to battle the outlanders, and he had not had occasion since then to meet one of the spirits.

"There's nothing to be afraid of," Jaryd said, as if reading his thoughts.

Orris looked up, but found that the Eagle-Sage wasn't even looking at him.

"I know that," Cailin answered, rubbing her hands together over the fire. "But I know very little about the Unsettled."

"From the little I know of them," Trahn told her, "it seems that the spirit bears the same temperament as the living mage did. Know the mage, and you know the spirit. Rhonwen was kind and gentle in life, and I expect she will be in death as well."

Orris shivered. This did little to ease his fears. Taking a long breath, he turned away from the fire and gazed into the gathering darkness of the wood. And so it was that he was the first to see Rhonwen's spirit coming toward them.

"Jaryd," he said in an urgent whisper.

He sensed the others turning as well, although he never took his eyes off the approaching light. He heard Cailin draw a sharp breath and felt her move closer to him.

Jaryd stepped in front of them, his eagle by his side. After standing there for a moment, watching as the teal-colored light grew brighter, he turned back and held out his hand to Cailin.

"Come, Eagle-Master," he said, his voice startlingly calm. "This is why we're here."

She nodded, swallowed, and took Jaryd's hand, glancing back over her shoulder at Orris for just a moment. Then the two of them, accompanied by their magnificent birds and followed by the other mages, walked forward to meet the ghost of Rhonwen.

Rhonwen was a stout woman, with a youthful, round face and dark hair that fell to her shoulders. Or rather, she had been in life. It was easy for Orris to see her as merely another person, until her gaze fell upon him and he gasped at what he saw in her eyes. For while the rest of her glowed gently with a soft teal hue, her eyes burned like flames, or, he thought, struck by the incongruity of the image, like the glass-covered lights he had seen in the streets of Lon-Ser seven years ago.

Yet, though she was a ghost, dead for nearly ten years, it was Rhonwen who sounded frightened when she spoke.

"Are those truly eagles?" she asked, her voice sounding both gentle and strong, like the rush of mountain water over a rocky streambed.

"Yes, Hawk-Mage," Jaryd answered. "I am Eagle-Sage Jaryd, of the Order of Mages and Masters and this is Eagle-Master Cailin, of the League of Amarid. With us are First Master Erland and Hawk-Mage Vawnya of the League, and Owl-Master Trahn and Hawk-Mage Orris of the Order."

Rhonwen nodded. "I remember you, Jaryd, and most of your companions as well. I trust Alayna is well."

"Yes," Jaryd said, smiling. "She is, thank you."

The spirit turned to Cailin. "I never met you, but I know of you and how you suffered as a child. I'm sorry."

Cailin nodded, but it took a moment before she seemed able to speak. "Thank you," she finally said. "I'm sorry for you, too."

Rhonwen smiled and opened her arms. "I'm dead. Pity is wasted on me."

"I—I just meant—"

"It's all right," Rhonwen told her, still smiling. "I think I understand."

"And do you remember me as well, Rhonwen?" Vawnya asked, stepping forward.

The spirit's smile vanished. "I thought I did," she said icily. "I remember a child named Vawnya whose hair was yellow like yours. I remember that her parents and mine were once friends. But the Vawnya I knew dreamed of wearing a green cloak, not a blue one. She never would have done anything to weaken the land or the Mage-Craft that protects it. So I have to assume that you and I have never met."

The mage's face blanched. "That's not fair," she whispered.

"Isn't it? Cailin's choice I understand, and I got the sense that Erland was always looking for the quickest path to power."

Orris saw the First Master's jaw clench, but Rhonwen seemed to take no notice of this.

"But you should have known better," she went on. "The Mage-Craft is weaker now than it's ever been, just at a time when it needs to be strongest. Mages like you have doomed the land."

"That's enough," Jaryd said, his voice stern. "We don't have time for this."

Orris winced slightly, expecting the spirit to take umbrage at Jaryd's tone. From all that Jaryd and Alayna had told him of their previous encounters with the Unsettled, Orris had gathered that the spirits did not tolerate the least sign of impudence. Then again, their encounters had been with Theron and Phelan. Rhonwen had died at Jaryd's age, and she had never led the Order. Certainly, she had never been bound to an eagle. So rather than bristling at Jaryd's rebuke, she retreated.

"You're right, Eagle-Sage," she said. "My apologies. I take it you've come to speak to us of Sartol."

"Yes. He's in the Great Hall now. He has the Summoning Stone."

She stared at Jaryd as if he were the ghost and she the living mage. "Fist of the God! Has he mastered it yet?"

"Yes. It didn't take him very long. It seems the stone remained his for all these years." Jaryd indicated the others with an open hand. "We've come here together, united, to ask the Unsettled for help. We don't understand how Sartol has escaped from his binding place. We don't know what he's done to Tammen, or what he's capable of doing to the people of Tobyn-Ser."

"If what you say is true, and he has access to the stone, there's no limit to what he can do." The spirit shook her head. "Arick save you all."

"We need more than your prayers, Rhonwen. We need to know how he's doing this." Jaryd took a breath. "Has he altered the Curse? Is that how he left the Northern Plain?"

"No," Rhonwen said. "That's what makes it so frightening. He's done all this without altering the Curse at all. Any one of us could have done this, if only we had thought of it, and been cruel enough to go through with it."

"What is it he's done?" He sounded so gentle, as if he were drawing information from a child.

"It's difficult to explain in terms you'd understand. The only way Theron was able to explain it to the rest of us, was to convey an image of it." She faltered, shaking her head once more. "He's using Tammen's ceryll," she began again, sounding unsure of herself, "to anchor himself to his binding place."

Jaryd narrowed his eyes. "But he's got her stone with him."

"Yes, I know. But it ties him to the land at his binding place. His power is flowing from his own staff, which remains on the Northern Plain, to her ceryll."

"So that's his weakness," Erland said. "If we can do something to her stone, or if we can interrupt that flow of power, we can stop him."

Rhonwen regarded him coldly. "I suppose," she said at last. "But if he has the Summoning Stone, you'll have no chance of taking Tammen's staff from him. His own staff exists solely in the realm of the Unsettled; you can't reach it. And there is no way to block his power." She looked away. "I suggested such a thing to Theron at one point, and he laughed at me. He said it was impossible."

"Did he say why?" Jaryd asked.

She nodded. "Sartol's power flows through the land like blood through our bodies. Trying to stop his power would be like trying to stop the wind. It's simply too vast."

"Did Theron say that there was any way to stop him at all?" Cailin asked.

"Not unless one of us was willing to do to another mage what Sartol had done to Tammen."

"Which is what?" Jaryd asked.

Orris held himself very still, sensing that they had come to the heart of the matter.

Rhonwen stared at the Eagle-Sage with her glowing eyes, a stricken expression on her round face. "There is no word for it. He's taken everything from her. He resides in her body now; she cannot live without him."

"Can he live without her?"

"I don't know," she said. "But it makes no difference. With the power he now wields, you can't kill her anyway. Nothing can, not even time."

"Do you mean to say he's immortal?" Orris asked. "That's impossible."

"No," Jaryd said, turning to face him. "It's not. Think about it, Orris: Sartol is already dead. He exists as nothing but magic." He looked at Rhonwen again. "That's right, isn't it? All of you are Mage-Craft incarnate."

"Yes."

"So, he himself is an endless source of power. He can keep Tammen's body young forever."

The spirit nodded. "Precisely."

"So it's over," Vawnya said in a small voice. "We can't beat him."

"I refuse to accept that," Jaryd said. "There must be a way."

Rhonwen opened her hands and shook her head. "I'm sorry, Eagle-Sage, but—"

"I want to ask Theron."

The ghost's eyes widened. "Theron?"

"Yes. Tell him Eagle-Sage Jaryd, bearer of his staff, wishes to speak with him."

She looked at his staff, which despite the glowing sapphire ceryll Jaryd had mounted on top of it years ago, still bore black scars from the night Theron placed his Curse upon the mages of Tobyn-Ser. "Of course," she said. "This may take a few moments."

She closed her eyes, as did the lanky, grey hawk on her shoulder, and for several moments nothing happened. Jaryd glanced back at Orris and then Trahn, his expression grave, but none of them spoke. Orris allowed his gaze to stray to Cailin, expecting to find her already looking at him, but instead, she was staring at Jaryd, as if seeing him for the first time. So, too, Orris realized were Erland and Vawnya. In that moment, it seemed, Orris and Trann were the only ones who weren't in awe of him. And that was only because they had realized long ago how special both he and Alayna were. They weren't any less amazed; they were just used to it by now.

In the next instant, Rhonwen opened her eyes again. "He's here, Eagle-Sage," she said, her voice seeming to come from a great distance. "He asks me to convey his greetings to you and your companions."

"Thank him for allowing us to seek his counsel," Jaryd said. He paused, allowing her to do as he had asked. "We need to know if there's any way to stop Sartol," he began again a moment later, "without one of us sacrificing his or her life to allow a second unsettled mage to walk the land."

"First of all," Rhonwen said, after a brief silence, "the Owl-Master says that not even he could defeat Sartol now, not if Sartol has mastered the Summoning Stone. And without that possibility, he knows of no way to defeat him." She looked down at the ground for a moment, before meeting Jaryd's gaze again. "He says that all you can do now is empty the city, perhaps Hawksfind Wood as well."

"You can't be serious," Jaryd whispered.

"I'm afraid I am. He says that Amarid must be abandoned, just as Theron's town of Rholde and the Shadow Forest were abandoned a thousand years ago. As long as his strength is tied to his control of the Summoning Stone, he can only reach so far. At least this way, the people of Tobyn-Ser will be safe."

Jaryd shook his head. There were tears on his face that reflected Rhonwen's teal glow and the blue light from his own ceryll. "Abandon Amarid," he repeated.

Rhonwen nodded. There were black streaks on her face, and Orris realized that they were tears as well. "It's the only way. We made him an outcast among the Unsettled, and now you must . . ."

She trailed off, a puzzled look on her face.

Orris had heard it as well: a second voice riding the light wind that wound through the forest.

"What was that?" the spirit whispered. "It sounded like—"

Before she could finish, she simply disappeared, like a candle extinguished by a sudden draft. The mages stood utterly still, as if unsure of what to do or say. After a moment, Jaryd spun toward Trahn and Orris, his mouth opened. But in that instant Rhonwen returned, looking confused and terrified.

"What's happening?" she asked, panic in her voice. "I don't understand."

"It is he," came another voice, this one deep and distant like thunder from a far-off storm. It was, Orris realized, the same voice he had heard just before Rhonwen vanished.

"This isn't possible," Rhonwen said, sounding desperate.

But on this night, in these times, it seemed that anything was possible. For abruptly, there was a second figure in the wood that glowed as she did, although with a baleful emerald green hue that was as different from Rhonwen's soft teal as lightning is from starlight.

And at the center of this light, stood an imposing man with a long flowing beard and hard, piercing eyes. He carried a dark falcon on his shoulder, but he bore no staff. Because, Orris knew, he had given it to Jaryd twelve years ago.

"Owl-Master!" Jaryd gasped. "How is this possible?"

"It should not be," he rumbled. "The traitor is doing this."

The traitor. Orris had been called traitor for so long that it took him a moment to realize that Theron meant Sartol.

"But how?"

Theron shook his head. "I do not know. He is doing something. He is compelling us to Amarid."

There were others there as well now. Spirits all of them, standing before the six mages in a rainbow of colors like some evil perversion of the Procession of Light. Orris recognized Peredur, his milky white eyes shining like his ceryll. He recognized another man as well, though he had never known this one in life. He was huge and powerful, glimmering like a full moon and standing beside a magnificent silver wolf.

Phelan, Orris thought. *I'm looking at the Wolf-Master.*

There were dozens of them, more than Orris ever would have thought possible. Yet it made sense. This was all of them: a thousand years' worth of unsettled spirits. Before him stood the sum cost of Theron's Curse. And even as they appeared there in the wood, they began to fade, as if they were being pulled back into the night.

"I do not know what he has done, Eagle-Sage," Theron said, his voice sounding even more distant than before, like the retreating cry of a whip-poorwill. "But he has altered my Curse. He wants us for something."

"Can't you fight him?" Jaryd asked.

Theron shook his head. He was dimming rapidly. All of them were, even Rhonwen, who was now no brighter than any of the others.

"There is no fighting him now," the Owl-Master said, in a voice like wind through the limbs of a bare tree. "But do you not see? He has altered my Curse."

"I don't understand."

"Think, Jaryd!" the wind sighed. "If it can be altered, it can be broken! That is the way to beat him; that is the way to save the land, to save all of us! You must undo my Curse!"

They were gone. There was nothing to show that they had ever been there at all. The only light came from the cerylls of Orris and his companions. The only sounds they heard were the embers of their fire settling behind them, and the leaves of the God's wood rustling overhead.

"Undo the Curse," Jaryd said quietly.

Cailin looked at him, the light from her golden ceryll glimmering in her eyes. "Can it really be done?"

"Maybe," Jaryd answered, his expression grim. "But we'd need the Summoning Stone to do it."

25

To answer your question, the reason I never write to you regarding Stib-Nal is that both its Sovereign, an annoying little man named Marar, and its standing in Lon-Ser compared with my Nal or Shivohn's, render it something of an irrelevancy. It is little more than a relic of the Consolidation, a tiny replica of Bragor-Nal that Dalrek, Bragor-Nal's Sovereign at the end of Lon-Ser's civil war, allowed to survive solely so that he could count on a second, decisive vote in the Council of Sovereigns. While Bragor-Nal and Oerella-Nal were rivals, my predecessors continued to count on Stib-Nal's support, but now that Shivohn and I have forged an alliance Marar has lost even that small measure of influence.

In another era, under similar circumstances, Stib-Nal would be swallowed by Bragor-Nal. Its land would become part of our territory, its military and economy would simply bolster our own. But Shivohn and I have pledged to refrain from behaving as our predecessors did. Unless Marar or one of his successors does something truly idiotic, Stib-Nal will remain much as it is today: tiny and weak, but secure.

—Melyor i Lakin, Sovereign and Bearer of Bragor-Nal to Hawk-Mage Orris, Day 1, Week 7, Winter, Year 3067.

Mouse hadn't said a word to her since their confrontation in the foothills. She had barely looked at her. Melyor remained convinced that the Gildriite woman was leading her and Jibb's men to the right place—what choice did she really have?—but she was reluctant even to ask Mouse about their progress.

She still believed that Mouse and she had much in common, that Mouse was a mirror image of Melyor in her youth. But that only made Mouse's loathing more difficult to accept. Had she really turned her back on her Gildriite heritage? She had believed so herself up until the day Gwilym gave her his staff, a final gesture of absolution and surpassing kindness from a dying man. The Bearer had forgiven her, and in doing so, he had forced her to forgive herself.

Yet there had always been a kernel of doubt, a feeling buried deep in the recesses of her mind that she was unworthy of Gwilym's gift. Bragor-Nal's Network had nurtured that doubt in the years since she became Sovereign by refusing to embrace her as an ally. *You may see yourself as one of us,* they had been telling her. *But we don't.* It was much the same message that Mouse had conveyed to her so bluntly the other day.

"I'm doing this for my people," she had said, "not for you."

Melyor had wanted to raise her staff over her head and make fire pour from the stone as she had seen Orris do with his. She wanted to hold the staff out before her, right in front of Mouse's face.

"Look at this!" she wanted to scream. "I'm a Bearer! If this doesn't make me one of you, what does?"

But all she could do was watch Mouse walk away, because the woman was carrying Melyor's stone. And Melyor couldn't help but think that Mouse deserved it more than she did.

Mouse returned it to her every evening when they had set up camp for the night. She said nothing, of course. Most nights their eyes didn't even meet. But she did return it. And each morning, as Melyor picked up her walk-aids, the young Gildriite took possession of it again, as if she, too, thought that she had a claim on it.

On the sixth day after their departure from the quads of Bragor-Nal, as a light rain fell on them from the brown clouds overhead, Melyor's company came within sight of Stib Grove, the small timber stand that separated Marar's Nal from the Greenwater Mountains. Each Nal had a small wood of this sort. It had been the central provision of the Green Area Proclamation of 2899, a complex treaty signed by the Sovereigns of the three Nals that had included an uncharacteristic though tacit acknowledgment that the Nals were being overly zealous in destroying their forests. It had simply required that each Nal set aside a small wooded expanse that was never to be harvested, with the minimum area of each Nal's preserve to be determined by the size of its population. Hence, in theory, Bragory Wood was to be the largest of the three, followed by the Oerellan Green, and finally Stib Grove. As it happened, however, the Oerellan Matriarchy set aside substantially more than their minimum, making their Green the largest in the land.

Stib Grove, however, like Bragory Wood, was no larger than the treaty required it to be. It was barely more than a strip of forest a hundred quads long and twenty wide. In other words, it was no larger than a single Realm in Bragor-Nal.

Seeing the wood, they rested briefly and ate a small meal, before continuing toward the trees. By her own choice, Mouse reported to Jibb now, and he passed word along to the Sovereign. After their rest was over, and they were walking again, the general fell in beside Melyor and told her that the Gildriite thought that they could reach the edge of the grove by nightfall.

"Provided, you feel that you can make it," he added, glancing down at her leg. "If not, sometime tomorrow will—"

"I can make it," Melyor said, sounding more annoyed than she had intended. "My leg's improving," she went on a moment later, hoping to soften her tone. "You should be a med."

A smile flitted across his face and was gone. "I'm glad you're feeling better."

She was better, and not just because her leg was healing. Her arms felt stronger. Going for hours at a time on the walk-aids was getting easier by the day. In spite of everything, she was enjoying being out of the palace and out of the Nal. For the first time in several years she was truly pushing herself, and it felt good.

"Perhaps I should leave you," Jibb said after a lengthy silence.

"There's no need." She paused, searching for something to keep their conversation going. "How are the men holding up?" she finally asked.

"Fine. They're anxious to reach Stib-Nal, finish this, and get back to the palace." He smiled. "But I'm sure all of us are."

Not really.

"But other than that," he said, "they're doing quite well."

"Good."

"I should tell you, though, that a few of them have expressed concerns about Mouse."

Melyor looked at him. "What kind of concerns?"

"They don't trust her. They think that she may try to undermine the mission."

"And do you share their concern?"

He shrugged in a way that told her he did. "I understand it," he said after a moment. He looked at her briefly and then gazed forward, his brow furrowed. "She hates you, Melyor. You must see that."

"Yes. But I don't think she wants to hate me."

"What do you mean?"

"She hates me because she thinks that I've betrayed the Gildriites, that I've done too little to improve life in the Nal for them. But I think that she'd rather see me change than fail. Certainly that's why the others in the Network sent her to help us. And though she might not want to admit it right now, she shares their hope. So even if she hates me, she won't do anything to destroy me. Given the choice between any other Sovereign and me, she'd rather have me."

Jibb raised an eyebrow. "You're certain of that?"

No. She forced a smile. "Fairly."

He was thinking about Vian, she knew. He still blamed himself. But in a way, she realized, he also blamed her for trusting the driver. No doubt he thought she was making the same mistake with Mouse.

"Let's hope you're right," was all he said.

By dusk, Melyor was exhausted. The grove had looked far closer than it actually was, though in the end they did manage to reach it. Marar's palace was less than twenty-five quads away, and now that they were out of the foothills, the terrain promised to be more level. The rain had stopped, though water still dripped from the branches of the grove's trees. Melyor's arms and hands were cramped and sore, but sitting with her back against a wide tree and her eyes closed, the Sovereign could not help but be pleased with the progress they had made.

She wasn't aware that Mouse had approached her until she heard her staff land on the ground in front of her with a thud. She opened her eyes and looked up, but the woman had already turned and started walking away.

"Wait a minute, Mouse," Melyor called.

The Gildriite halted, let out a loud sigh, and turned to face her. "What do you want?"

"What do you want, *Sovereign*?" Melyor corrected.

Mouse stared at her for a moment. "What do you want?" she asked again.

Forcing herself to keep her anger in check, Melyor waved a hand toward the ground in front of her. "Sit."

"I'd rather stand."

"I didn't ask you!" the Sovereign snapped. Enough was enough. "Now, sit."

Mouse peeked back over her shoulder to see if any of the others had heard. They had. Melyor could see that several of the men, including both Jibb and Premel, had stopped what they were doing and were glaring at her. Reluctantly, the woman sat.

"How long until we're there?" Melyor asked.

"Quads or time?"

"Time."

Mouse pursed her lips for a moment. "About a day and a half. At a normal pace we could be there tomorrow night, but we're going so slowly . . ." She shrugged, leaving the thought unfinished.

"When are we likely to encounter Marar's security?" Melyor continued, ignoring the gibe.

"We'll reach wire and mines tomorrow morning. They begin less than a quad from here."

"You know your way around them?"

Mouse nodded.

"And how about his guards? When will we start seeing them?"

"We could start meeting up with some patrols as early as tomorrow afternoon. They don't usually venture farther than ten quads into the grove. By tomorrow night though, they'll be everywhere." She grinned. "That's when the fun begins."

Melyor smiled as well, fighting an impulse to tell the woman once more how similar they were. "Can you get us past them as well?" she asked instead.

"That will be a little harder. I think we can avoid most of them, but it'll slow us down." She looked away. "Chances are we couldn't make the palace by tomorrow night regardless of our pace."

"I appreciate your honesty."

Mouse shot Melyor a look, as if she thought that the Sovereign was mocking her. But seeing Melyor's expression, which was utterly neutral, she looked down again. "You're welcome," she said, her voice barely carrying over the light wind that stirred the branches above them.

Melyor took a breath, steeling herself. Her next question was likely to send Mouse storming off again, but it had to be asked.

"You know, Mouse," she began, "if we do meet up with Marar's men, we'll have to fight them. I know you don't like the idea of killing anyone, but I need to know if we count on your help if we wind up in a firefight."

"There are ways to disable security men without killing them."

"I know that," Melyor said with a nod. "But Jibb's men have been trained to respond in a certain way. I'll see to it that he tells them to avoid killing when they can, but in the heat of a fight, their training may take over."

Mouse regarded her coolly. "Well then, I'll have to get us past the patrols without them seeing us, won't I?"

"That would be preferable, yes. But I still need an answer to my original question."

"What is it you want, Sovereign?" Mouse asked, her voice rising. "Do you want me to say that I'll kill for you? Is that it?"

Melyor shook her head. "Not at all. But I have to know if you'll fight beside us."

"And if I won't?"

The Sovereign looked Mouse in the eye, and neither of them looked away. "If you won't, then you can get us past the mines and wires, and we'll find our way through the rest."

"Do you know the way?"

"I have a pretty good idea of where Marar's palace lies. I may not know the quickest way through the grove, or the safest, but I can get us there."

Mouse shrugged. "If that's how you want to do it . . ."

Melyor closed her eyes. The woman was impossible. "That's not how I want to do it, Mouse," she said, looking at the Gildriite again. "I want you to take us through. But I need an answer."

Mouse stared at her for a moment, then looked back over her shoulder at Jibb and his men. "I never thought that I'd be working with SovSec," she said quietly. She faced the Sovereign again. "For as long as I can remember, SovSec has been my enemy. It's been the enemy of every Gildriite in Bragor-Nal."

"No, it hasn't," Melyor said. "I know that you think of it that way. But for the past seven years, it hasn't been true. I'm not saying it's been your friend, because you wouldn't believe me if I did. But I assure you, SovSec's campaign against the Gildriites ended the day Jibb took control of it. I made sure of it."

"If I were to tell you that I will fight beside you, would you believe me?"

"Absolutely."

"Would the general?"

Melyor hesitated, drawing a grin from Mouse.

"I see," she said.

"Jibb's very protective of me, Mouse. He sees how you feel about me, and it makes it hard for him to trust you."

"It doesn't seem to bother you."

"I understand you better than he does."

The woman raised an eyebrow. "You think you understand me?" But before Melyor could answer, she shook her head and looked away. "Don't answer that. I'm not sure which would bother me more: hearing that you don't know the first thing about me, or finding out that you really do."

Melyor smiled again, but she said nothing.

After a brief silence, Mouse looked at her again. "Don't worry about me. If it comes to a fight, I'll be there beside you."

"That's all I need to hear," Melyor said. "Let's hope it doesn't come to that."

Mouse nodded, then stood. "Do we need to talk about anything else?"

"No. You can go."

The woman stood there for a moment, as if reluctant to walk away.

"Was there anything else you wanted to discuss?" Melyor asked.

Mouse shook her head, though Melyor got the impression that she still had something on her mind. After another moment she turned and started back toward the others.

Melyor watched her go and, doing so, saw that Jibb was watching the woman as well, a dark look in his eyes. As Mouse passed him, he began walking over to Melyor. When he reached her, he knelt and started removing the bandages from her leg. He didn't say anything at first, but Melyor could tell how angry he was.

"What was that all about?" he finally asked her, his voice thick.

"We were just discussing Marar's security and what we could expect tomorrow as we make our way through the grove."

He looked up at her for an instant and then turned his attention back to her leg. "I want you to stay close to me tomorrow, just in case."

"Don't worry, Jibb. I won't let you get hurt."

His head shot up so quickly that Melyor laughed out loud. His face turning a deep crimson, he immediately returned to tending her leg. "I should have left you years ago," he muttered.

"Who would have taken you?"

"I could have just gone to one of Lon's sanctuaries and spent the rest of my days as a cleric."

She laughed again and this time he glanced up at her, a grin tugging at the corners of his mouth. He worked wordlessly for a few minutes more, but as he finished fastening the fresh bandage to her leg, he looked her in the eye, and there could be no mistaking the seriousness of his expression. "All kidding aside, Melyor, I meant what I said before. I want you to stay close to me tomorrow. I know what you think of Marar, but even if he is a fool, he's shown himself to be a dangerous fool. And from what I hear, his men are pretty good."

Melyor nodded, shivering slightly as she did. "All right."

He cocked his head slightly, still looking her in the eye.

"What?" she asked. "I promise. What more do you want me to say?"

"That'll do," he said, smiling and getting to his feet.

He helped her up, and the two of them walked over to the fire, where the others were already eating.

As Mouse had predicted, the company came to the first of the blade wires less than an hour after breaking camp the following morning. SovSec had never resorted to blade wire, because it was a relatively ineffective deterrent for anyone who really wished to enter or leave the Nal. It was little more than a long coil of strong though malleable, razor-sharp metal. Handling the wire was out of the question; it was capable of slicing through flesh and even bone at the slightest touch. On the other hand, thrower fire cut through the wire quite easily, and though this first barrier actually consisted of multiple coils piled on top of each other, strung out to the left and right as far as the eye could see, it presented no real problem for Jibb and his men.

The danger, according to Mouse, lay in the fact that Marar's security men tended to back up the wires with densely spread minefields that could be as much as half a quad wide. So, rather than going straight through the coils, the company waited for some time while the young Gildriite walked along the edge of the wire searching for some sign of where they were to go through.

The men eyed her doubtfully while she searched, but when at last she found what she was looking for, they all crowded around her to see it as well. They opened a space for Melyor, however, allowing her to swing herself through on the walk-aids.

"What have you found?" she asked, standing over Mouse, who was kneeling on the ground, the ghost of a smile on her lips.

The woman looked up at her and then pointed to a small circle of pebbles just beside the wire. It was nothing any of them would have noticed. It could have been random. Which, of course was the point.

Mouse stood and as the men stepped back to let her by, she walked a few more paces along the wire before squatting again. Melyor followed her and saw that there was a second circle there.

"This is where we go through," Mouse said. "There should be a corridor on the far side that lets us get through the minefield."

Melyor stared at the stones for a moment shaking her head. "How could they know this?" she whispered. "Where do they get this kind of information?"

"I don't know," Mouse said. "But when you need information to survive and to protect your family, you do whatever you have to do to get it." She picked up the stones and scattered them around and then returned to the other circle and did the same. "I don't want Marar's men to find those circles when they discover what we've done to their wire," she explained.

She walked back to where Melyor and the men were standing, stopping in front of the Sovereign. "What are you waiting for? Get us through."

"Jibb," Melyor said, not even moving.

Instantly, the general barked an order and his men began carving through the wire with their throwers. They were on the other side in a matter of moments, waiting as Mouse found the Network's markers for the path through Marar's minefield. Once again it was stones, pairs of them this time, laid out on either side of the path at regular intervals. And once again, no one would have noticed them had they not been looking for them.

They crossed through the minefield as quickly as they could, with Mouse and Premel leading the way on either side of the path, their eyes trained on the ground as they looked for the markers. The end of the field was marked by a second pair of circles, which Mouse left intact so they could find their way out again.

Through what remained of the morning and into the early afternoon, they found three more expanses of wire, all of them bordering minefields. But now that Jibb's men knew what they were looking for, finding the paths through took far less time.

"I think that's the last of them," Mouse told Melyor as they cleared the fourth minefield.

"Are you sure?"

"Not completely. But if I'm wrong, it just means that we'll come to more wire. If I'm right, it means that we have to start watching for security patrols."

Melyor looked at Jibb who, as promised, had been right beside her all day. "Better tell the men."

He nodded and whistled once, waving the guards over to where he stood.

As Jibb talked to his men, Mouse handed Melyor's staff back to her.

"You'd best find a way to carry this," she said. "We might need my thrower, and I don't want that thing slowing me down."

"Tie it onto my back," Melyor said. "There's rope in with Jibb's gear."

They were on their way again within a few minutes, walking in a tight cluster with a single scout approximately a quarter of a quad ahead of them, another an equal distance behind them, and a guard on either side about two hundred paces away. They walked as quietly as they could without sacrificing too much speed, and managed, by Jibb's estimate, to cover close to ten quads.

Either by stealth or plain luck, they managed to avoid Marar's men for most of the day. They saw no patrols, although they did occasionally see discarded food wrappers and the remnants of small campfires.

Late in the afternoon, however, the lead scout returned to them, breathless and agitated.

"What is it?" Jibb asked, as the man stopped in front of him.

"A patrol, sir, about half a quad ahead, and heading this way."

The general signaled to two of his men to bring the side scouts back in. "How many men?" he asked, facing the lead scout again.

"I'm not certain. At least half a dozen. Probably more."

"The patrols are usually twelve men," Mouse told Jibb. "Ten with hand throwers and two with bigger ones. All of them have boomers, and all of them carry blades for close fighting."

The general's eyebrows went up. "Thank you."

"I don't want to get killed any more than you do," she said drily.

"I don't want a fight if we can avoid it," Melyor said. "This will work far better if we can surprise Marar."

Jibb nodded. "I agree."

The company retreated until they met up with their rear scout and then cut westward through the trees, moving as stealthily as they could. After some time, they heard voices far behind them, but they could see nothing of the patrol.

"Well done," Melyor whispered to Jibb.

The general nodded. "How are you holding up, Sovereign?"

"I'm fine."

"Are you getting tired?"

She narrowed her eyes. "What's on your mind?"

"If we stop and make camp, and then one of those patrols comes upon us, we'll have no chance to get away. On the other hand, if we keep moving, the patrols will be easy to spot—they've got to have hand lights. We'll see them coming from at least a quarter of a quad. We won't even need scouts."

"No, but we'll need lights, too."

"Maybe not," Jibb said.

He pointed toward the sky, and looking up Melyor saw a half-moon peeking through the trees and the brown haze.

"That should give us some light for the first four or five hours of darkness," Jibb said. "And your stone can provide the rest."

Melyor turned to Mouse, who had been listening. "Can you get us to the palace in the dark?"

"Sure," she said. "As long as I can see the moon I can navigate."

"All right," the Sovereign said, facing Jibb again. "Let's give it a try."

The company almost walked headlong into a second patrol just before dusk, but managed to avoid that one as well. As Jibb had anticipated, however, once the sun went down, the patrols became much easier to spot. And though the moon did not offer much light, it was enough, when combined with the crimson glow of her stone, to keep them from breaking their necks on roots and downed branches. At one point, they found themselves caught between two patrols, and they had little choice but to lie flat on the forest floor with their weapons poised for battle. But when the commanders of the two patrols realized how close they were to each other, they both veered away. Melyor and the others waited until their hand lights were no more than a distant glow to the north and south, then resumed their advance on Marar's palace.

Melyor had expected to be exhausted long before midnight, and to be sure, her arms were sore. But she sensed that the company was getting close to the palace, and rather than being tired, she felt exhilarated, just as she remembered feeling when she was a Nal-Lord preparing for a raid. *No wonder so many of them don't approve of the changes I've been trying to bring to the Nal,* she thought to herself as she made her way through the shadows of the grove. *This is fun.*

They came within sight of the palace two hours after their dangerous encounter with the two patrols. The building was so brightly lit that its glow had begun to seep through the grove some time before. But only when they could actually see the security lights and illuminated windows did Melyor signal for the company to stop.

"How do you want to do this?" Jibb asked in a whisper.

A patrol appeared nearby, forcing Melyor and the others to drop to the ground and keep still until it had passed.

"There's got to be a sub-ground entrance," Melyor said, once it was safe to speak again. "We'll go in that way and fight our way through to Marar's chamber."

Mouse shook her head. "I don't know if that's the boldest thing I've ever heard, or the dumbest."

Another patrol went by. Again they ducked down until the guards were gone.

"I'm afraid I have to agree," Jibb said.

Melyor nodded. "I know it sounds crazy, but I think it will work. I don't think of myself as a disciple of Cedrych i Vran, but he told me something once that I've never forgotten. He said that when you're raiding another man's flat or, headquarters—and I think this works with palaces, too—you're at a terrible disadvantage in almost every respect. Your opponent knows the layout, the vulnerabilities, the strengths of the battleground much better than you do. As an invader, your only advantage lies in your willingness to destroy the building you're attacking. The other side wants to save it—that's their whole purpose. So you have to use boomers and throwers to take the building apart. If you can do that, you can beat them."

"So we're going to destroy the palace?" Jibb asked.

"We're going to tear it to the ground if we have to."

Mouse grinned. "Sounds like fun."

"Premel," Melyor said, turning to the tall guard. "Do you know anything about the layout of the palace?"

Even in the darkness the Sovereign could see the guard's face turn pale, and for just a moment she regretted putting the question to him in front of the others. But there was nothing to be done about that now, and he seemed to realize it, too.

"Yes," he said in a low voice, as the other guards eyed him with curiosity. "Marar's chamber is on the second floor, in the front of the palace, overlooking the gardens and the Nal. That's the area that will be most heavily guarded."

"Good," Melyor said. "Thank you." She looked at the others and smiled at the eagerness she saw in their eyes. She wasn't the only one enjoying herself. "Watch yourselves," she told them. "And watch out for each other. I want all of you coming home with me."

"Even me?" Mouse asked.

Melyor grinned. "Yes, Mouse. Even you."

At first he thought he was dreaming. Sometimes he still had dreams about his days as a Quad-Lord, when he had carried a thrower on his belt and a blade in the studded sleeve of his overcoat. But as the sound of the explosions grew louder and more insistent, he began to emerge from his slumber. And when the boomer went off just outside the door of his outer chamber, he jerked upright in his bed and fumbled for the thrower he kept in the drawer of his night table.

With the weapon in his trembling hand, Marar reached for the security communicator he kept in the same drawer. A moment later, however, he threw the device to the floor without having pressed the shining red button. If there were boomers going off outside his chamber, something must have happened to Gregor and Bain. And anyone else who might have responded to his call for help was either dead or a traitor.

Instead, he got out of bed to crouch and ready himself to fire upon whoever came through his bedroom door. At least that's what he had intended to do.

It was only when he was lying prone on the floor, the back of his head smarting from where he had smashed into the wall and his ears ringing, that he realized another boomer had gone off. There was smoke in the room, and he could hear people shouting in the distance. Occasionally he heard the hiss of a thrower, but the sound was scattered and infrequent. Whatever resistance his guards had given had been broken.

Melyor, he said to himself. This had to be Melyor's doing.

He tried to sit up, but he wasn't even certain he had moved when someone grabbed him roughly, knocked the thrower from his hand, and hoisted him to his feet. He could barely see through the smoke, and his vision was still blurry from the blow he had taken to the head. But then the men who had hold of his arms started to lead him out of the chamber, and one of them said, "This way, Sovereign." And he knew that he had been right.

"Hello, Premel," Marar managed, though he started coughing the instant he opened his mouth.

"How does he know your name, sir?" the other guard asked, just as Marar had hoped he would.

"It doesn't matter."

"I know his name," Marar said, struggling to speak through another fit of coughing, "because he's been working for me since early last summer. Haven't you, Premel?"

The guard said nothing, although his grip on Marar's arm tightened painfully. They were in the corridor outside of his outer chamber now, stepping over rubble and an occasional body on their way to the stairs. Gregor was there, his chest blackened and bloody, his eyes staring sightlessly at the ceiling. Marar's mouth twitched.

The smoke had thinned, and the Sovereign's vision was slowly clearing, allowing him to see what had been done to his palace. The walls were blackened and shattered. As they reached the landing at the top of the stairs, he saw that much of the artwork had been destroyed. Injured security men lay on the stairs and the floor below, but Marar saw only one or two who appeared to be dead. Somehow, Melyor and her men had managed to do all of this without Marar even knowing that they were on their way. He would have liked nothing better than to kill all of them, starting with the beautiful Sovereign, who had to be here, somewhere. But all he had was Premel, so Marar went after him.

"What is he talking about, Colonel?" the other man finally demanded. "Is all of this true?"

Marar made himself grin. "Of course it's true," he said before Premel could reply. "Why do think he's being so quiet?"

"Sir?" the man said, the word coming out almost like a plea.

"Quiet!" Premel commanded. "Both of you! Just shut your mouths! Sovereign!" he called, leaning over the railing. "We have him!"

"We're on our way," Melyor called in reply.

"It's not easy being a traitor, is it Premel?" Marar asked quietly. "Betraying your Sovereign, your general, even the men who serve with you. It must be very difficult."

Marar heard footsteps on the ground floor, people approaching the stairs. He could see the glass doors—broken now, of course—that looked out over his gardens, and he felt an odd rush of relief that nothing had been done to them. Premel was facing forward, his face crimson, but his expression utterly neutral. The other man, a young, square-jawed guard with massive arms and a thick neck, was staring at Premel the way a boy might look at his father upon learning that he was a killer. The man's hold on Marar's arm had grown so loose that the Sovereign briefly considered trying to break away and grab the guard's thrower. But Premel was squeezing Marar's other arm as if he thought it was the Sovereign's throat. Any attempt Marar made to get away would merely give Premel the excuse he was looking for to kill him.

So instead, Marar kept talking. It was, after all, what he did best.

"How much gold have I given you to this point, Premel? I can't remember. Certainly enough to buy yourself—"

Before he could get the rest out, Premel had smashed his fist into Marar's face. The Sovereign's knees buckled, and he would have fallen, but Premel was still holding one of his arms, and the young guard was holding the other. Premel hit him a second time, and Marar felt blood begin to flow from his nose.

"Premel, no!" he heard Melyor call. People were running now, bounding up the steps. But they were going to be too late. Premel was going to kill him before the others ever reached them. There was rage in the guard's pale eyes and he had already pulled his arm back to hit Marar again. The Sovereign flinched and closed his eyes.

"Stop it, Colonel!" the young guard said.

Opening his eyes again, Marar saw the metallic glint of the guard's thrower. The man had it aimed at Premel, who was staring at the weapon, wide-eyed and trembling, his fist still drawn back. Other guards had gathered around them, as had a young dark-haired woman.

"It's all right!" Melyor called to the guard as she came up the stairs, accompanied by a burly man who had to be Jibb. And then Marar noticed something that made his head spin: she was on walk-aids. Melyor had done all of this to him, and she was on walk-aids. Marar felt his stomach heave.

"No, Sovereign," the guard said as Melyor stopped in front of them. "It's not all right. According to Sovereign Marar, the colonel is a traitor."

The other guards stared at Premel as the young one had. Only Melyor and Jibb looked unfazed by the news.

"Actually," Melyor said, smiling thinly and shifting her gaze to Marar, "Marar only thinks this is true. Premel came to the general and me just after Marar contacted him for the the first time. He only took the Sovereign's gold because we told him to."

Marar's mouth dropped open. She was lying. He knew it, because Jibb's expression mirrored his own. But her men had no cause to doubt her.

After a moment, the young guard lowered his weapon. "My apologies, Colonel," he said.

Premel mumbled something, but Marar couldn't make it out. And at that moment he didn't really care.

"You're lying!" the Sovereign said, sounding, he knew, desperate and unconvincing. "Premel betrayed you! He betrayed all of you!"

Melyor laughed. "If he had done that, why would I have brought him with me on a mission like this?"

Marar opened his mouth, then closed it, his fists clenched so tightly that his knuckles hurt.

"Premel, take the men with you and finish securing the palace. Jibb and I will take Marar someplace quiet where we can chat."

Premel nodded, a look of profound gratitude in his eyes. "Of course, Sovereign."

"I'd like to watch this, if I may," the dark-haired woman said.

Melyor eyed her for a few seconds, then shrugged. "Be my guest."

Jibb grabbed Marar by the back of the neck, and with Melyor and the young woman following, steered him into one of the sitting rooms on the far end of the corridor from his chambers. As the woman closed the door behind them, Jibb shoved Marar forward so that the Sovereign sprawled onto an opulent sofa. But rather than coming after him, as Marar had expected, the general then whirled toward Melyor.

"How could you do that?" he railed. "How could you lie like that?"

"I don't want Premel being humiliated," she answered, her voice level. "And I'm certainly not going to let him"—she nodded toward Marar—"decide when and if I should reveal Premel's crimes to the others. That's my decision, and no one else's. Not even yours, Jibb."

"So then it is true," the dark-haired woman murmured.

"That's not to leave this room, Mouse," Melyor said, looking at the woman briefly.

The woman nodded.

The Sovereign swung herself forward on the walk-aids until she was standing over Marar. "As for you, Sovereign, I'd say you're lucky that Jibb and I came when we did. Premel might have killed you."

He sat up slowly and shook his head. "I had the situation under control. That young guard was ready to kill him as a traitor, until you told your little fable."

"Well, then, you are lucky," Melyor said, her tone turning cold. "Because if that had happened, I would have killed you on the spot."

Marar gave a thin smile. "I didn't know you cared so much about him. Perhaps he's a lover? I hope not. That would be terribly disappointing. While sitting here I've been weaving the most wonderful scenarios in my head involving you and your young friend over there."

He glanced at Mouse, his smile deepening

"What did he just say?" the woman said, striding forward.

Melyor held out a hand, stopping her. "Relax, Mouse. He's looking for a reaction. Don't give him one."

"Mouse," Marar repeated. "What a charming name. Are you the Sovereign's pet? Is that why she brought you along?"

"No, you pig. I was her guide. I'm the one who got her past your wires and minefields."

Melyor closed her eyes. "Mouse—"

"Ah, now I see," Marar said. There was only one explanation, really, Who else would be able to help Melyor with such a thing? "You're a Gildriite, a member of the Network."

Mouse grinned. "In the flesh."

"I'll have to remember to punish our Gildriites for their part in this."

The woman's smile vanished as quickly as it had come. "They had nothing to do with it."

"Nothing?" he asked, raising an eyebrow. "I find that hard to believe. Who told you the way through my minefields? Who told you how to avoid my patrols? Only Stib-Nal's Network could do all that. And they'll suffer because of it."

"You bastard! If you—"

"Quiet, Mouse," Melyor said. "He's not going to be able to punish anyone. His days as Sovereign are over."

"I doubt that," he said. "After Wiercia hears of what you did today, she'll have you expelled from the Council. She hates Gildriites even more than—"

The blow came so swiftly, and such force that it took him several seconds to realize that she had struck him with the butt end of one of her walk-aids.

"Is there anything you can't turn into a weapon?" he asked, rubbing the welt that was already forming on his cheekbone.

"If Wiercia opposes me," Melyor said, "I'll install Jibb as Sovereign of Stib-Nal, and she'll never win another vote." She shook her head, her green eyes locked on his. "But I'm confident that it won't come to that. She knows about Shivohn and about the attempts on my life. She'll support whatever I decide to do about you. So I'm trying to decide what that will be. Jibb here wants you dead, as does Premel." She smirked. "And you haven't done anything to make Mouse an ally, either."

Another gibe leaped to mind, but abruptly Marar didn't feel quite as cocksure as he had a few moments before.

He licked his lips. "The Cape of Stars Treaty prohibits executions in cases like this."

"Funny that you should be so concerned with treaties all of a sudden. You've been ignoring the Green Area Proclamation for the better part of a year."

"Yes, but—"

"As I've already told you, Marar, if I choose to kill you, Wiercia won't raise any objections. Although I'll make Jibb much happier if I just give you over to SovSec."

The general grinned darkly, and Marar shuddered.

"On the other hand," Melyor said, "I'd also be willing to consider a simple exile to Abborij."

He stared at her. "You would?"

"I just want to know how you're getting gold from Tobyn-Ser."

"I don't know what you're talking about."

This time he saw the blow coming, although there was nothing he could do to prevent it. Her walk-aid arced up in a blur of chrome, catching him on the temple this time and knocking him to the floor.

"Pick him up," he heard Melyor say.

An instant later, Jibb grabbed hold of him and lifted him back onto the sofa as if he were a child.

"Who's giving you gold, Marar? And what are they getting in return?"

He swallowed. He had been beaten more in this one day than he had since his earliest days in the quads, and he had taken it much better back then.

"You have to understand," he said, "they came to me first—"

She struck him a third time, sending him tumbling to the floor once more.

"Don't lie to me, Marar," she said, sounding bored, as Jibb picked him up and tossed him onto the lounge again. "Who would have known to go to you? Now I don't care how it began, and I don't want any more lies. Either you answer the question, or I'll leave you alone with Jibb for a while." She smiled sweetly. "He's not as gentle as I am."

The general pulled a blade from his belt and started to play with it, his eyes fixed on Marar.

"All right!" the Sovereign said. "All right." He took a deep breath. He had dreamed of riches and power, but there seemed to be little chance that he would have any of that now. And under the circumstances, exile in Abborij sounded rather appealing. "It's coming from their Temples, the Children of the Gods, they call themselves." He licked his lips and looked away. "And in return, I'm sending them weapons."

"Fist of the God!" Mouse breathed.

But Melyor merely nodded. "I figured it was something like that." She turned and started toward the door, with Mouse close behind her. "Bring him along, Jibb. It's time we got out of here. Call for my air-carrier; there's no way I'm walking all the way back."

Jibb gripped him by the neck again and forced him up off the sofa.

"Can I at least bring some of my things?" Marar called after Melyor. "Can I at least bring a bit of gold?"

She stopped in the corridor. "Gold? What are you going to do with gold in prison?"

"B-But you said that I'd get exile if I told you."

"I lied." She turned again and continued toward the stairs. "Be thankful I don't kill you, Marar," she called over her shoulder. "I'd really like to, but Mouse made me promise that I wouldn't."

"Yeah," Mouse chimed in, not even bothering to look back at him. "But at this point I wish I hadn't."

26

I write to you on behalf of Eagle-Sage Jaryd and the entire membership of my Order to request your help in facing this grave threat to the safety of Tobyn-Ser. I know that the Order and the Temple have long been rivals, although I regret that this is so, as does the Eagle-Sage. The Order's relations with the League of Amarid have been strained as well, and yet, even as I write this note, the Eagle-Sage is with First Master Erland and Eagle-Master Cailin on a journey of utmost importance. Perhaps this will give you some sense of how concerned all of us are about Sartol's return.

I know that you will have to discuss this matter with the Keepers of your temples. No doubt you will have to overcome the opposition of many if you are to join our cause; Eagle-Sage Jaryd and I had to do no less before making this request. But I ask you not to delay and not to allow this process to consume too much time. I fear that it will not be long before Sartol seeks to use his vast powers against the people of our land.

> —First of the Sage Alayna, of the Order of Mages and Masters, to Brevyl, Eldest of the Children of the Gods, Spring, God's Year 4633.

Tammen stood before him on the plain, her silken hair stirring in the wind and the hint of a smile touching her lips. He could see Sartol's pale fire burning low in her eyes, like a cooking flame that had been left to die down for the night, but he didn't care. She was there with him. And when she shrugged off her cloak, allowing it to fall to the grass, and then pulled her tunic off over her head and stepped out of her breeches, revealing her perfect breasts and the gentle curve of her hips, he could do nothing but rush forward to gather her body in his arms. Even as he reached her though, even as he felt her soft skin on his hands and arms, and tasted her neck with his lips, he heard her laugh with Sartol's voice, and she burst into flames, searing him. He tried to scream, but there was no air for his lungs. Only fire. Everywhere, fire.

Nodin awoke with a shudder, opening his eyes to see the low wooden edge of the cart and its canvas cover. The sun was shining through the canopy of Tobyn's Wood, casting irregular shadows on the cloth. He could hear birds singing over the hoof beats of the plow horse and the rattle of the wagon, and with an effort he lifted himself onto one arm and gazed out the back of his shelter at the forest and the road on which they were traveling.

"You were dreaming again," Ianthe said from her perch at the front of the cart.

"Yes."

"Of your friend? The one Sartol has taken?"

The healer had shown him little warmth during the course of their journey, and she had asked prying questions like this one almost every day. But she had saved his life—he was quite sure of that—and she had left her village, her people, perhaps even a family, at a moment's notice, just to help him find Tammen. Much as he wanted to tell her to mind her own affairs, he couldn't bring himself to do so. No doubt she knew that as well as he did, which was why she asked such questions in the first place.

"Yes," he said at last. "I was dreaming of Tammen."

"You loved her?"

"Where are we, Ianthe? How long until we reach the Parneshome Range?"

She twisted in her seat to look at him, her pale blue eyes dancing. "What's the matter, Mage? Are you tiring of my company?"

Nodin smirked and looked away, shaking his head. "I'm just anxious to get to Amarid."

"As am I," she said, her expression turning sober.

She faced forward again, leaving Nodin feeling abashed for his thoughtlessness and ingratitude.

"Did you leave a family back there?" he asked.

She glanced back at him again, the sun lighting her grey hair. "Nearly a fortnight together, and suddenly you're interested in my family?"

"Not suddenly. I've wondered since we left. I just wasn't sure you wanted me to ask."

"And today I've given you some sign that I'm anxious to share the particulars of my life with you?"

Again the mage shook his head. "You're a difficult woman, Healer."

That of all things made her smile. "Thank you, Mage."

Nodin laughed, though doing so still caused him great pain.

Seeing him wince, Ianthe clicked her tongue at the horse and pulled on the reins, stopping the wagon.

"It's time I changed those poultices again," she said, climbing back into the cart and kneeling beside him. Her brow was furrowed, as it always seemed to be when she worked her craft, and Nodin could see the concern in her eyes. Some of his burns weren't healing well. She had told him as much the night before. And now, as she gently removed the bandages from his back, she exhaled loudly through her teeth.

"Is it worse?" he asked.

"Yes." She clicked her tongue again and took a long breath. "I'd like to find a mage before we venture into the mountains. You need more healing than I can offer."

"All the mages are in Amarid."

"Not all. Farrek was lucky enough to find you, wasn't he?"

"I believe I was the lucky one."

"I suppose," she said. "You could use some luck again. We need to find a free mage."

"Can you tell me where we are?"

She had been placing new bandages on his burns, and she paused now. "I would say we're no more than two days from the mountains and perhaps twenty leagues from the northernmost falls on Fourfalls River."

Nodin felt a tightening in his chest, and for several moments said nothing. He and Tammen had been near here with Henryk early in the spring. "I know this area well," he told her at last. "Turn toward the river when you can. There are several free towns along its banks."

"All right," she said, resuming her work on his back. "We need more food anyway."

Ianthe was back in her seat a few moments later, calling to the old horse to start moving again. After perhaps an hour they came to a fork in the road, and she steered them toward the river. Eventually, Nodin dozed off, as he seemed to do each day when the healer wasn't tending to his injuries or feeding him.

When he awoke again, the sun was still high in the sky, but the roar of the river told him that they had come a long way as he slept.

"We're coming to a village," the healer said, pitching her voice to carry over the rush of the water. He wasn't sure how she did it. She never woke him with a word, but neither did she ever allow him to lie very long in silence once he was awake. Yet, he had never once seen her turn to check if his eyes were open.

"Thank you," he murmured, blinking his eyes to clear his vision, and yawning. She warned him whenever they approached a town. It was the one courtesy she had extended to him from the start. He had not seen his reflection since his encounter with Sartol, though he gathered from the shocked expressions that greeted him everywhere he and Ianthe went that the burns had disfigured him terribly. There was little for him to do. The worst burns on his face were bandaged already; covering his face any more would impair his breathing and his sight. But still he appreciated the warnings. At least he could prepare himself for what he saw in the eyes of those they met.

As it turned out, there were no free mages to be found in this first town. However, the people there did mention having seen a group of three mages less than a fortnight before. Most seemed to believe that the mages, all of them men, had continued southward. After prevailing upon an innkeeper to give them some food, Ianthe steered the cart back onto the forest road, following the river southward toward the next village.

Darkness fell before they reached it, and they were forced to stop for the night. But they were on their way again with first light and had reached the second village before midday. Once again, the townspeople said that they had seen a group of free mages recently, but that they were gone now.

"It's been no more than a few days," one toothless old woman told them. "They were headed south I think. There are lots of free towns to the south. That's what I told them." And then, glancing at Nodin's face and wrinkling her nose, she had added, "It's about time you changed those poultices, don't you think?"

Nodin had feared for a moment that Ianthe might climb down off the cart and bloody the crone's nose, but instead she merely smiled and nodded, then clicked her tongue at the horse. But for much of the afternoon she muttered under her breath about meddlesome old women who knew nothing of healing.

Late in the afternoon, they still had not reached the next town. The sun had disappeared behind a bank of dark grey clouds, dimming the light in the forest and making it seem closer to dusk than it really was. Ianthe had lapsed into silence, although she continually glanced back at Nodin, the familiar crease in her brow. The mage tried to sleep, but for once, found that he couldn't.

They were still near the river, and lying in the wagon it was hard for Nodin to make out any sounds above the water's tumult. So when he first heard the voices, he dismissed them as creations of his imagination.

But then Ianthe said, "Arick be praised," and called to the horse to halt, and he knew that he had heard them after all.

"What is it?" he asked.

She climbed down off the cart, grinning broadly. "Mages," she said. "Two of them."

She called to them and took several steps down the road until he couldn't see her anymore. He heard them reply, but he could make out nothing of what they said. A few seconds later, he heard footsteps beside the cart and then Ianthe was at the rear of the wagon, peering into the canvas shelter along with two men.

One of them was a young man with curly yellow hair who carried a lean grey hawk on his shoulder and a staff with a pale green stone. There were not many free mages in Tobyn-Ser, but Nodin was certain that he had never seen this man before. His companion, however, Nodin recognized. His name was Ortan, and though his hair had a bit more grey in it than Nodin remembered, he had changed little since their last encounter. He was still an imposing man, broad-shouldered and square-jawed with long hair and dark brooding brown eyes. And he still carried Amarid's Hawk on his shoulder. A free mage, with Amarid's Hawk. All of them had taken it as a sign that perhaps the gods approved of their Movement, and Ortan had become a leader among the cloakless mages.

Under ordinary circumstances, Nodin would have been delighted to see him. But while the stares of strangers shocked by his injuries made him uncomfortable, having Ortan see him like this promised to be humiliating.

"Fist of the God!" the younger man whispered as he stared into the cart at Nodin's injuries. "Who could have done such a thing?"

Ortan placed a hand on the man's shoulder. "It's all right, Shavi." He climbed into the cart and smiled at Nodin. "Hello, friend. My name is Ortan. The healer has asked me to help with your wounds. If it's all right with you, I'd like to take off your bandages and see if there's anything I can do."

"Of course," Nodin said, not meeting Ortan's gaze. "Thank you."

Ortan began to remove the bandages and poultices from Nodin's back, his touch almost as deft as Ianthe's.

"The color of your stone is familiar to me, friend," the dark-haired mage said as he worked. "Have we met before?"

Nodin closed his eyes. *Is my face really so marred?* "I don't think so."

"Well, what's your name?"

"Please," Nodin said, his voice cracking. "I'd rather not say."

He heard Ortan exhale. "I understand. Forgive me."

Nodin began to cry, the tears stinging the burns on his face. Tammen was gone; Henryk was dead. He had no friends left in the world. And now this man was offering him friendship and kindness, and all he could think about was the shame of his disfigurement. "It's me, Ortan," he whispered after several moments. "It's Nodin."

The mage stopped working on his back. "Nodin?" He shifted his position so that he could look into Nodin's face. He looked stricken, as if he had lost a brother. "It is you." He shook his head slowly. "I can't believe it. Shavi and I met up with a friend of yours not long ago."

Nodin felt himself grow cold. "Who?" he asked, shivering.

Ortan frowned. "A woman." He turned to his young companion. "What was her name, Shavi? Do you remember? I remembered it the day we met her, but—"

"Tammen," Nodin said, before Ortan could finish.

Ortan looked at him again. "Yes. That was it. Tammen. She said that you and she had been journeying together, but had separated because you disagreed on how the Movement should proceed."

Nodin was crying again. Merely saying her name aloud hurt him more than anything that she—that Sartol—had done to him. But to know that others had seen her, had spoken with her about him. It was too much.

"She lied to you," he said through the sobs that shook his body so painfully. "Or rather he did."

"He?"

"Sartol."

Ortan's eyes widened. "The traitor?"

"Yes. He's . . . he's inside her. He controls her mind and her body."

Ortan glanced at Ianthe, who was still standing by the back of the cart. The healer shrugged in response.

"You think I'm mad."

Ortan looked at him again. He was smiling kindly, but Nodin could see the doubt in his eyes. "I think you've been through a great deal," the mage said, seeming to choose each word with care. "You're hurt badly. You're feverish. And I think you're grieving as well, although I'm not sure why."

"I'm grieving," Nodin said through his tears, "because the woman I love has been taken from me, and because my closest friend in the world is dead."

"What friend?"

"Henryk. Sartol killed him, just as he tried to kill me. And now he's on his way to Amarid. For all I know he's there already."

"That's where she said she was going," Shavi said, staring at Ortan. "What if he's right? What if that really was Sartol?"

Ortan rubbed a hand across his face. "Then he may have lost a friend, too."

Nodin looked from one of them to the other. "What do you mean?"

"We were traveling with a third mage," Ortan said. "A man named Hywel. He was taken with your friend Tammen and agreed to accompany her to the First Mage's city."

Taken with . . . Nodin closed his eyes briefly, fighting a wave of jealousy. *Perhaps I am mad. She's gone. Hywel is another victim, not a rival.* "I hope your friend survives the journey."

"Is any of this possible?" Ianthe asked. "Could he be telling the truth?"

Ortan looked at Nodin again, studying him as one might an unfamiliar plant or a gem of unknown value. "I'm not certain," he admitted. "Tammen did behave strangely when we met her, but I saw no sign that she was controlled by Sartol. On the other hand, I have no reason to doubt Nodin's claim that she did this to him, in which case she is dangerous, whether Sartol has her in some way or not."

"I tell you he has her," Nodin said. "She wouldn't have done this to me otherwise."

"Either way, Ortan," Shavi said, "we have to go after her. For Hywel."

The older man nodded. "Let me finish seeing to Nodin's wounds, and then we can be on our way."

Nodin gripped his arm. "I have to go with you, Ortan. Please."

"Let's see what I can do for you first. If this really is Sartol, we have need of haste. And you may not be fit for the journey."

Nodin held the man's gaze for another moment, before nodding and looking down. Ortan was right of course. Who knew what Sartol had in mind for the people of Amarid?

In the end, Ortan was able to do quite a bit to ease Nodin's pain and soothe the fever that had settled in the deep wound on his back. It took him all that remained of the day, and several hours more beyond nightfall. And before he finished he had to call upon Shavi to help him. The burns were severe and covered much of Nodin's body, and the fever proved to be quite stubborn. But together, the two mages were able to heal him.

"I wish I could tell you that the scars will vanish, Nodin," Ortan told him when they were done. Nodin was lying beside a low-burning fire, enjoying its warmth, which he had been unable to do since that night on the Northern Plain. "Some of them have faded, and I expect that others will disappear with time. But most will remain. You'll never look as you did. I'm sorry."

"Don't be," Nodin said. "You've done more for me than I ever could have asked. The scars are what I get for allowing my love of Tammen to outweigh my good sense and my friendship with Henryk."

"How did all this happen, Nodin? How did Sartol get close enough to Tammen to do this to her?"

Nodin swallowed, finding it difficult to look Ortan in the eye. "We went to him. Tammen believed that we needed to do something to strengthen the Movement. The Order and the League have more mages than we do, and the Temple has weapons now. We needed something, too. She suggested that we go to the Unsettled, to see if they'd help us. We started with First of the Sage Peredur, but he refused us. Then Tammen suggested Sartol."

"But why? Didn't she know what he had done during his life?"

"She's from Watersbend," he said. "She—"

Ortan raised a hand and shook his head. "No. You don't have to say any more. I understand."

"She truly believed that he'd help us," Nodin said. "She never would have done this otherwise."

Ortan offered a kind smile. "I believe that." He gave Nodin's arm a gentle squeeze and stood. "You should rest now. Shavi and I need to as well. I expect that with a night's sleep, you'll be ready to travel."

"Does that mean you'll be taking me with you to Amarid?"

Ortan grinned. "Is there any way I could stop you from coming?"

"No," Nodin said, grinning as well. "Thank you, Ortan."

The mage nodded, crossed to the other side of the fire, and lay down.

Nodin closed his eyes and listened to the flames, feeling himself grow increasingly sleepy. But before he slipped into a slumber, he heard footsteps nearby. Opening his eyes and turning, he saw Ianthe climbing into the cart.

"Healer," he said.

She stopped and came over to where he lay. "Do you need something?"

"No, I'm fine. But I wanted to thank you for all you've done. If it wasn't for your care," he smiled, "and your foul-smelling poultices, I would have died before Ortan and Shavi could help me. I owe you my life."

She shrugged, her eyes flicking away momentarily. "You owe Farrek your life. He's the one who found you."

"Do you argue with all of your patients, Healer? Or is it just me?"

For a few seconds she offered no response, and Nodin feared that he had given offense. But then she looked away again, a wry grin tugging at the corners of her mouth.

"I argue with everyone, Mage. Even if they're not my patients. It's just my way."

Nodin smiled. "I'm glad to hear that."

They sat in silence for another moment, and then Ianthe leaned forward and placed a hand on his brow.

"Your fever is gone."

"Yes."

"Do you still believe that Sartol did all this to you, that he controls your friend?"

"I'm sure of it," Nodin told her. "I swear it to you on the life of my friend Henryk, whom he killed."

She shivered, as if from a chill wind. "I had hoped that you wouldn't say that. I'd rather that I had made this journey for no reason, than to know that it was all true." She shook her head. "Arick save us all."

He wanted to say something to ease her mind. He wanted to tell her that they'd find a way to stop him. But he had felt the power of the ghost's fire, and he had seen the ease with which Sartol took everything from Tammen and killed Henryk. So he said nothing. She deserved more than lies.

Ianthe remained beside him for another minute of two. Then she rose and walked back to the cart. "Good night, Mage," she said before climbing into it. "I'm glad you're well."

I'm not well, he almost said. *I'm whole again, thanks to you and Ortan and Shavi. But I won't be well until Tammen is free of Sartol.* But again he held his tongue. That was his burden, not hers. She had done all that she could for him.

It had started as a chill, nothing more. A mild fever and a drip from her nose. Two days later she was in bed, too weak to move. Linnea knew little of healing, but she knew her own body. And she recognized that this was the beginning of the end. The disease that had raged within her for the past half year had done its part to wear her down, so that this trifle of an illness, this nothing, could finish her. She had resigned herself to the inevitability of her death long ago, but the irony of this was too much for her.

She cared about nothing anymore, except living long enough to see Cailin one last time. The rest of it didn't matter. Not the eagles or the weapons or the forests. Just Cailin. She had no children of her own, but now, at the end, she finally realized what it was to be a parent.

She had no use for healers anymore, and had told them as much that morning, refusing any more of their ministrations. They were just trying to make her comfortable now anyway, and perhaps delay her death for a day or two. It was all they could do, and she refused even that. No doubt they thought her foolish, and she had to admit that if she truly wished to see Cailin again, she might need their help. But for now, she wanted nothing to do with them.

She sat in her bed, propped up by the pillows they had brought her, watching the day pass by outside her lone window. And she waited for Cailin to come so she could die. Her breakfast sat on the small table beside her bed, untouched save by two fat flies that buzzed around it.

Eventually she dozed off, only to be awakened sometime later by a knock at her door.

"Let me sleep," she said, closing her eyes again.

"Linnea, please," came a man's voice in reply. "It's Brevyl. I need to speak with you."

"I'm dying, Brevyl. Can't you leave me alone?"

The door opened, and the Eldest walked in, a look of worry on his round face. "I'm afraid I can't. Not now."

"Get out of here!" she said, sitting forward with an effort that left her wheezing. "How dare you enter my chamber without my permission!"

Now that he was in the room, he looked uncomfortable, as if he feared that getting too close to her would kill him as well. "Forgive me. But I need to discuss something with you."

"I will not forgive you! Now get out!" She sounded small and a bit insane, but she couldn't help herself. She had never liked this man, nor had he ever given any indication of liking her. And at this point, she was through pretending. "I just want to be alone, Brevyl," she said, falling back against her pillows and closing her eyes. "Can't you understand that?"

"Yes, Linnea. Please believe me when I tell you that I do understand. But this is important."

Something in his tone caught her attention then, making her open her eyes again and look up at him. He held a piece of parchment in his hand, rolled tightly and tied with a bright blue satin ribbon. She stared at it for a moment, then met his gaze.

"What is that?"

He handed it to her. "A message from the Order, from First of the Sage Alayna."

She looked at him for an instant longer before removing the ribbon and unrolling the message.

"Fist of the God!" she said as she began to read. "When did you get this?"

"Just today."

She continued to read, scarcely believing any of it.

"You knew nothing of this?" he asked, as she finished and let the arm holding the parchment drop to her side. "Cailin didn't mention it to you?"

"No. Not a word. I'd imagine that they departed on this journey Alayna mentions as soon as it happened."

He lowered himself into the chair beside her bed, eyeing her intently. "Do you believe it?"

"I think it's more important to ask if you believe it. You're Eldest of the Gods, Brevyl. Not I."

"I don't know what to think," he admitted. "I've had few dealings with the Order, far fewer than you had during your tenure."

"That was a long time ago. I knew Sonel, and Radomil briefly. But I've never even met Jaryd and Alayna."

"Maybe not. But you know the Order. Could this be a ruse of some sort? An attempt on their part to draw us into their conflict with the League?"

"No," Linnea said with a surety that surprised her as much as it seemed to Brevyl. "I don't think they'd lie about something like this. Sartol's treachery was their shame. Sonel felt that the entire membership of the Order was responsible for allowing him to do so much damage to the land, and I always got the sense that others felt the same way. They wouldn't bring all of this up again if it wasn't true."

"So what should we do?"

Linnea smiled. "That, thankfully, is not my decision to make."

"I know that, Linnea. But I'm asking for your advice."

"I'm not sure I can give it, not on something of this importance."

"You're still a part of the Assembly of Keepers," he said. "I'm not asking you anything that I wouldn't ask of the others." He hesitated. "Please, Linnea. I know that you hate me, that you think I've disgraced the Temple."

She winced. She still remembered saying that to him, and she regretted it. Notwithstanding what she thought of him, that had been unfair.

"I need for you to put those feelings aside for a moment," he went on. "This isn't about you and me. This isn't even about the Temple. If Alayna's telling the truth, we could be talking about the survival of every person in Tobyn-Ser."

"In that case," Linnea told him, "I think you've answered your own question."

He blinked. "What do you mean?"

"If the stakes are truly that high, then you have no choice. You must help them."

He stood and walked to the window, seeming to weigh her words. "You may be right, but do you think that I can convince the others of that?"

"I don't know. Hatred for the Order runs deep in the Assembly. And those who haven't served as Eldest don't always understand that there are times when we have to work with the Mage-Craft instead of against it." She almost added that he hadn't helped matters by justifying the purchase of Lon-Ser's weapons with statements about the threat posed to the Temple by the Mage-Craft. But during her years as Eldest, she had done her share to fan those flames as well. In this, she was no less guilty than he.

"Can I count on your help, Linnea? I need to win over as many of the Keepers as I can, and those who won't listen to me will surely listen to you."

All she wanted was to rest, and, when the time came, to die. But what could she do? "Yes. I'll help you."

He smiled. "Thank you," he said, coming forward to reclaim Alayna's note from her bed and starting toward the door. "I need to be going. I should get a message out to the other Keepers as quickly as possible." He paused in the doorway, the look on his round face almost kindly. "Rest well, Linnea. Arick guard you."

She nodded and he began to pull the door closed behind him.

"Brevyl," she called.

He stuck his head back in the chamber, waiting.

"Eldest," she began again, correcting herself. "I should never have said that to you, about you disgracing the Temple. It was presumptuous of me."

He just looked at her for several seconds, as if unsure of what she expected him to say. "Thank you," he murmured at last. He closed the door, and Linnea heard his footsteps retreating across the courtyard.

Closing her eyes once more, she settled back against her pillows and sighed heavily. She was so tired. Cailin would never have understood this, but she was truly ready for death. But it seemed the gods weren't quite done with her yet.

They had been there with him for two days and two nights; vanishing from view with the dawn and then returning at dusk to stand before him like glowing statues. He had managed to bend Theron's Curse enough to bring them to the Great Hall, but to do the rest, to use them as he intended, he needed even greater mastery of the Summoning Stone. So he poured his power into the giant crystal while the ghosts waited for him, wondering, no doubt, why he had brought them to the Hall and what he had in store for them. Theron, their leader in all things, questioned him without pause, at first using the silent communication of the Unsettled, and then, when that failed, turning to the spoken words of the living world. After the first day, the Owl-Master tired of this and Phelan took over. But still Sartol offered no response. He saw no need, and he had more important things to do. But more than that, he took pleasure in making them wait, in leaving them to their silence and their uneasy curiosity. Never mind that they had done much the same thing to him for so many years. He made them wait for the simple reason that he could. And he wanted them to understand that.

On the third night, however, he was ready for them.

Theron was speaking again, asking him, for what seemed the one thousandth time, what he wanted from them, sounding bored and defeated, as if he no longer expected a response. So when Sartol turned to face him, to face all of them, Theron looked shocked.

"Do you really want me to answer that?" Sartol asked, saying the words aloud with Tammen's voice and so denying Theron access to his thoughts. "Do you really want to know what I have in mind for you?"

"We have been asking you for days," the Owl-Master answered, recovering quickly. "Of course we want to know."

Sartol eyed the others. "And what of the rest of you? Are you ready to hear your fate?"

None of them said anything, choosing instead to defer to Theron.

"Don't look to him for guidance," Sartol said. "He's nothing. From this day forward, I control all of you, including Theron."

The Owl-Master raised an eyebrow. "Really? And what do you plan to do with a bunch of ghosts."

"You mean an army of ghosts."

Theron's mouth dropped open, and Sartol felt himself grin. He had waited so long.

"That's right, Theron. You're mine now—all of you are—and I'm going to use you to conquer the land. And by the time I'm done with that, I'll be strong enough to send you across Arick's Sea, so that you can conquer Lon-Ser as well. It's ironic, don't you think, that in the end we'll be the invaders and the outlanders the hapless victims."

"I do not believe it," the Owl-Master said weakly. "The Curse does not allow such a thing."

"The Curse?" Sartol laughed. "The Curse is mine now, too. It allows whatever I want it to. And I've decided that the Unsettled are going to help me rule the land."

"It will never work."

"Of course it will. It's perfect. An army that can't die, that doesn't need to sleep or eat or even rest; an army that I can send anywhere with little more than a thought. The Potentates of Abborij would kill for it."

"We will fight you!" Theron said, his green eyes blazing impressively. "We will not let you do this!"

Sartol smiled, but said nothing. Instead, he drew some of his power from the stone—not much really, barely a fraction of what he now had at his command—and with a single thought, he made Theron raise his glowing arm over his head and hurl a bolt of emerald fire at the portrait of Amarid that adorned the ceiling of the Gathering Chamber. The fire struck the First Mage's likeness in the head, sending smoking fragments of the stone ceiling cascading down onto the council table and the hall's marble floor, and leaving a blackened mark where Amarid's face had been.

For several moments, none of them moved. Then Theron lowered his arm slowly, staring at his fingers with an expression so comical that Sartol had to laugh again. The others merely watched the Owl-Master with stricken expressions, as if they had just learned that Arick was mortal.

"Theron of Rholde," Sartol sneered. "First Owl-Master, author of the dreaded Curse. And yet, not so mighty after all." He regarded the other ghosts, his eyes finally coming to rest on Phelan. "You can't resist me. I'm more powerful than all of you. I'm more powerful than any of you even dreamed of being." He looked back at Theron for just a moment. "Even you, Owl-Master. The stone is mine, immortality is mine, you are mine, and soon, Tobyn-Ser will be mine."

"The gods will not allow this," Phelan said. "Even if we cannot stop you, they will."

"How? With their eagles and the little mages who carry them? I don't think so. Unless Arick himself is ready to fight me, I have nothing to fear. And even if he is ready, I think I can prevail. I've made Theron's Curse my own, and I've mastered the Unsettled. I cannot be killed or controlled. Some would say I am a god. And before this is over, every person in the land will kneel before me, as befits a god."

Phelan opened his mouth to say something more, but Sartol made a small gesture with his hand, denying the Wolf-Master the ability to speak.

"Enough," Sartol said, as Phelan's eyes widened. "I'll be sending you off now, back to the places of your first bindings. It's time we took this war to Tobyn-Ser's people. It's time we began our conquest of the land."

"No!" one of the others cried.

He looked at her, smiling. She was a stout woman, with a lean grey bird on her shoulder and a teal-colored stone on her staff. "I'm afraid so. You shouldn't have cut me off the way you did. You shouldn't have exiled me. I know that it was Theron's idea, and Phelan's, but you're all going to suffer for it. You all love the land, so I'll make you destroy that part of it which you love most." He turned to Theron. "Except you. You never did love the land. Not really, not like them. So I've tried to think of a task for you that you would find equally distasteful."

Theron raised his chin proudly. "And what would that be?"

"Remaining here with me, of course. I have to keep an eye on the others, make certain that they're doing what I want them to do. When Jaryd and Alayna come back, as we both know they will, I'll need someone to deal with them on my behalf." His grin broadened. "You're going to be my champion, Theron."

"Never."

Sartol shook Tammen's head and let out a long sigh. And then, with no more effort than it had taken the first time, he made the Owl-Master lift his hand and blast the council table with green fire. The wood shattered as if it were made of glass, and the chairs around it flew in all directions, clattering across the floor.

Theron glared at him, but that was all he could do.

"You're a tool, Owl-Master. Nothing more. You do what I want you to do, when I want you to do it. And otherwise, you do nothing. This is your existence now. Get used to it." He swept the others with his gaze. "Time for the rest of you to go."

He stepped closer to the Summoning Stone and laid Tammen's hands upon it. And one by one, the other ghosts began to vanish from the chamber until he and Theron were the only ones left. He faced the Owl-Master again and saw that the spirit was watching him with an expression he thought he recognized.

"I can see the envy in your eyes, Owl-Master."

Theron shook his head. "No, Traitor. What you see is contempt, not envy."

"Well, I'm in good company. No doubt you looked at Amarid the same way."

The emerald ghost gave a harsh laugh. "Again, you are mistaken. In spite of everything, I did envy Amarid. He deserved no less. For all your power, you are nothing next to him. And notwithstanding your control over me, I give you my word: I will find a way to destroy you."

"You're welcome to try," Sartol said, turning his attention back to the Summoning Stone. "But you have as much chance of succeeding as Tammen did."

27

As what we in the Order call a migrant, one who wanders the land rather than settling in one particular place, I have become something of a relic. With the Order and the League fighting each other for the loyalties of individual towns throughout the land, more and more mages are choosing to nest, and thus establish themselves as friends and neighbors of the people they wish to serve. At this point, with Baden's decision to build a home with Sonel, I am one of only two migrants left in the Order. As far as I know there are none in the League. The free mages still wander, but I hear that as more towns declare themselves free, even they are starting to settle. . . .

It goes without saying that even those of us who are not tied to one place in Tobyn-Ser by a home or a family have certain parts of the land that we love more than any other. The village of one's childhood perhaps, or the place of one's first binding. For me, that special place is Tobyn's Plain, where I grew up and bound to Pordath, my first hawk. As much as I love the Emerald Hills and the shores of South Shelter, the plain has been and always will be my true home. All of us have a place like that, one that we love more than any other. And all of us, nester or migrant, League mage, Order mage, or free, would give our lives to protect that place from harm.

> —Hawk-Mage Orris to Melyor i Lakin, Sovereign and Bearer of Bragor-Nal, Autumn, God's Year 4632.

They had hoped to return to Amarid as swiftly as they had ridden to Rhonwen's binding place. Jaryd had wanted to start back the night of their encounter with Rhonwen, Theron, and the other Unsettled, but Orris and Trahn had prevailed upon him to wait until morning. The horses needed rest, they had told him. The animals could not be pushed so hard if they were to bear the company through the mountains. In the end, Jaryd relented.

They started north the following morning, commencing their journey with the first silver-grey glimmer of daylight. For two days they pushed themselves—or rather, Jaryd pushed them—until their horses were so exhausted that Cailin had to wonder if resting the night before they left had made any difference at all.

This was not to say that she didn't understand the Eagle-Sage's sense of urgency. It was bad enough that Sartol had mastered the Summoning Stone and altered Theron's Curse for some purpose that she didn't even care to imagine. If her family had been in Amarid, as Jaryd's was, she would have pushed the company every bit as hard.

But the only family she had was gone, and having heard what Rhonwen and Theron had to say about Sartol and the power he now wielded, Cailin could not help but wonder if there was any point at all in trying to stop him. No doubt he would kill anyone who opposed him. So perhaps Tobyn-Ser's mages would be better served by abandoning the First Mage's city, as Theron had said, and devoting themselves to guarding the rest of the land from whatever attacks Sartol contrived. It saddened her to contemplate such a thing—she had come to love the great city. But better to lose Amarid than to sacrifice the lives of dozens of mages in a vain attempt to overpower Sartol's ghost.

She kept such thoughts to herself, of course. She had a feeling that Vawnya might have agreed with her, but she was sure that the others did not. Not Erland or Trahn, and certainly not Jaryd or Orris, whose opinions meant the most to her. So she merely rode, grim-faced and silent like her companions. But her doubts grew.

They rode well past dusk, until the last ghostly glimmer of daylight vanished from the God's wood and Cailin began to wonder if the Eagle-Sage would let them rest at all. Indeed, he might not have, had not Trahn and Orris pulled abreast of him and spoken to him in low, urgent voices. With a reluctant nod, Jaryd raised a hand, signaling to the others that they should stop.

"We'll make camp here," he said simply, swinging off of his mount and walking off alone into the woods.

"Why are we taking orders from him?" Vawnya asked, her tone sullen.

"Because he's Eagle-Sage," Cailin said. "And because any order he gives you comes from me as well."

Vawnya twisted her mouth disapprovingly, but gave a single nod.

"Where's he going?" Cailin asked Orris, after watching Vawnya and Erland walk off to help Trahn gather wood for a fire.

"You mean Jaryd?"

She nodded.

"To reach for Alayna. They never go a night without contacting each other with the *Ceryll-Var*."

"Oh," she said quietly, feeling a sudden twisting in her heart. She wanted to know what it was to share such a bond with someone. She wanted it with the man standing beside her.

Somehow Orris seemed to divine her thoughts, for a moment later he cleared his throat awkwardly and started to walk after Trahn and the others. "We should help them find some wood."

"Of course," she said, watching him move away. But she remained where she was, cursing the ache in her chest and the trembling of her hands.

She was still standing there staring after him when Jaryd returned.

"Where are the others?"

"Gathering wood for the fire." She made herself look at him; she had lost track of Orris's ceryll some time ago anyway. "How are Alayna and Myn?"

The Eagle-Sage allowed himself a small smile. "Fine, thank you."

"Has anything happened?"

"Not that they know of, but it's just a matter of time. She said that there's been some strange light coming from the windows of the Hall, as if there were many cerylls in the Gathering Chamber."

"Or many ghosts," Cailin whispered.

He looked at her, his expression bleak. "Yes."

"Rhonwen may have been right, Jaryd," she said impulsively. "We may have to abandon Amarid."

She caught her breath, expecting him to rail at her. But he surprised her.

"I know that," he said, his voice low as he looked away. "But I'm only willing to do that if everything else fails." He met her gaze again. "You have to do what you think is best for the League, Cailin. I know that. But I need you all and the League mages if I'm going to find another way."

She just stared at him. If Erland had been in her place, she knew, he would have demanded some concession in return for a pledge of the League's support. After all, Sartol had taken the Order's Hall, not the League's. If they were forced to abandon the First Mage's city, it would be the Order's failure. And if with the League's help the Order managed to defeat Sartol, Cailin and her fellow mages would be the heroes. Either way, the League stood to benefit, and as one of the League's leaders, it fell to Cailin to make the most of the situation. But while the color of her cloak demanded that she take advantage of Jaryd's plea, the great bird standing beside her would not allow it. And neither would the friendship she and the Eagle-Sage had forged over the past several weeks. Notwithstanding her own doubts about whether the city could be saved, she knew that she owed it to Jaryd and to all of Tobyn-Ser to try.

"We'll do whatever you need us to do," she told him, as a grateful smile spread across his features. "Regardless of everything else, the League and the Order are allies in this war."

"What about Erland?"

Cailin tried to grin, but she could tell that she only succeeded in grimacing. She could still hear him calling her a whore; she could still feel her cheeks burning with shame. "Leave Erland to me."

Jaryd looked as if he might say something, but instead he clamped his mouth shut and nodded. And a moment later Cailin heard voices and footsteps coming toward them. The others were returning.

None of them said much for the rest of the evening. Vawnya continued to sulk over Cailin's rebuke, Jaryd appeared distracted and worried, Trahn never seemed to say very much, and Cailin, Orris, and Erland refused even to look at one another. When Jaryd finally announced, just a short time after they finished eating, that he was going to sleep, the rest eagerly followed his example.

The second day after their encounter with Rhonwen and the other Unsettled went much like the first. They rode all day with almost no conversation, stopping at nightfall, and eating their supper wordlessly. Even if they had wanted to say anything, they would have been too exhausted to sustain any sort of discussion. They had covered more ground on this day than they had the day before, reaching the foothills of the Parneshome Range by late afternoon, and continuing almost to the base of the first line of mountains. With any luck at all, they would be back in Amarid within three days.

That at least is what Cailin told herself as she drifted toward sleep that second night, forcing herself to think about their journey rather than about Orris, who had positioned himself once again as far from where she lay as he could manage. But when she awoke the following morning, she found herself soaked by a pelting rain and shivering in a fierce wind that swept down from the mountains like an Abboriji army. The other mages were already awake, their cloaks darkened by the rain and their hair matted and clinging to their foreheads, as they scrambled to find some kind of shelter for the horses.

Cailin sprinted to her mount and led him back down the narrow trail to a small cluster of trees, where Trahn was whispering soothingly to his horse and Jaryd's.

Jaryd was there as well, peering out from under the trees, his eyes trained on the thick grey clouds that blanketed the ridge of the mountains like fog on the shores of Duclea's Ocean.

"It's awfully late for this," he murmured in a tight voice. "We never have storms from the north so far into spring."

Cailin glanced at another group of trees about a hundred paces away, where Erland, Vawnya, and Orris stood with their horses. She couldn't begin to imagine what that conversation sounded like.

"It is unusual," Trahn said, "but not unheard of."

"So you don't think Sartol is doing this."

She whirled to face him. "Sartol?" she breathed. "You think he can create storms?"

Jaryd looked at her and shrugged. "I don't know what he can do. He's altered Theron's Curse. We know that. Who knows how deep his powers go?"

"Not this deep," Trahn said with a certainty that Cailin found reassuring. "He may be stronger than any mage who's ever lived, but the elements are ruled by the gods. Even the Summoning Stone can't change that."

The Eagle-Sage took a breath and nodded. "I suppose you're right."

Despite Trahn's assurances, however, the storm might as well have come from Sartol. It raged throughout the morning and into the afternoon. It began to weaken a few hours past midday, and the sky brightened briefly. But then a new bank of dark clouds rolled into view and the rain and winds returned, more violent than before.

Had they simply been riding through Tobyn's Wood, they might have been able to make some progress despite the storm, although admittedly not much. But they needed to cross the mountains, and with the wind blowing so hard and cold in the foothills, none of them had any doubt that even the lowest passes would be impassable. They were stuck where they were for the duration of the storm.

So Cailin thought. But late in the day, the company decided to retreat into the God's wood, which offered more shelter than the small copses of the foothills. Wearily, their clothes soaked, and the muscles in the legs of their mounts quivering with cold, they retraced their steps from the afternoon before and took refuge in the densest grove they could find. Even there, the rain and the wind reached them, but at least they were able to light and sustain a fire, around which they huddled in the gathering darkness.

"We should turn east to the ocean," Erland said, breaking a lengthy silence, "and follow the shoreline around the mountains to Hawksfind Wood."

Jaryd looked over at Orris, a question in his pale eyes.

"It would add seventy or eighty leagues to the journey," the yellow-haired mage said. "And we'd be traveling on sand much of the way, which would slow us." He shrugged. "On the other hand, there'll be new snow in the passes, which could slow us even more."

"How many days?" Jaryd asked.

"Probably three days more to follow the coast."

The Eagle-Sage seemed to consider this for a moment. Then he shook his head. "No. We should wait here. Hopefully this storm will blow through tomorrow, and we'll be on our way."

"Wishful thinking is not a sound basis for leadership," Erland said icily.

"Neither is sarcasm!" Cailin shot back without thinking.

Despite the poor light given off by the fire and their cerylls, Cailin saw the First Master's face shade toward scarlet, and she winced.

"I understand your concern, Erland," Jaryd said evenly. "I may be making a terrible mistake. But storms such as this one are pretty rare this late in the spring, so I do have some reason to believe that it may be short-lived."

Erland was breathing hard, his eyes fixed on the fire, and he did not look up now to meet Jaryd's gaze. But after a moment he gave a single nod.

Now you know how I felt, you bastard, Cailin wanted to say. *Now you know what it's like to be humiliated in front of everyone.*

"So we're waiting out the storm here?" Vawnya asked.

"That would be my preference," Jaryd said, facing her. "But if you have another idea, I'd be glad to hear it."

The woman shook her head. "No. I think that's best."

The Eagle-Sage allowed himself a small smile and looked at Orris and then Trahn. "What about the two of you?"

"I think we're better off remaining here," Trahn said.

Orris nodded. "I agree."

"Cailin?"

"I feel the same way," she said.

"Then it looks like we're staying," Jaryd said. "Let's hope that the storm cooperates."

The others murmured their agreement, and Trahn knelt to place more wood on the fire.

"Cailin," Erland said in a thick voice, "may I speak with you for a moment?"

She made herself look at him. "Of course. What about?"

He frowned. "In private, Cailin."

The Eagle-Master glanced at Orris, but he merely raised an eyebrow and gave a slight shrug.

"Yes, Erland," she sighed, following the older mage as he walked away from the others to another grove a few dozen paces away. Rithel hopped beside her, raindrops rolling off the golden feathers on the back of her neck.

Once they reached the center of the grove, Erland turned, to face her, the glow of his grey stone reflected in his eyes, and those of his round-headed owl. She had expected him to berate her, but when he spoke his voice was surprisingly calm.

"Cailin, you and I need to talk."

"What about?"

He frowned again. "I think you know."

"You mean about the fact that we don't like each other? I thought we had that conversation already in your chambers at the hall."

"Nonsense," he said with a forced smile. "We never—"

"Stop it, Erland," she said. "We wear the same colored cloak, and as circumstances would have it, we both lead the League, but I'm not going to pretend that we're friends."

"I'm not asking you to pretend. I'm just asking you to show me some respect."

She should have held her tongue. Lashing out at him was bound to do more harm than good. But he had shamed her, and she wasn't ready to forgive him. She wasn't sure that she ever would be. So she said the first thing that came to her mind, heedless of the response she knew it would provoke. "You're contradicting yourself, Erland."

His expression hardened. "Fine, Cailin. If you feel that you must insult me as retribution for some injury I've given you, then so be it. But you and I will be working together for years to come, and I expect you to show me some respect when others are present, whether you mean it or not."

"And if I refuse?"

"Don't. Long after your days as Eagle-Master are through, I'll still be leading this body. And you don't want to have the First Master as an enemy."

She gave an exaggerated nod. "Ah yes. I've been meaning to discuss that with you. I'm not so certain that you will be First Master. I've decided that I enjoy leading the League."

Erland gaped at her. "But we had an arrangement. You gave me your word."

"Yes, I did," she flung at him. "And then you called me a whore. Or had you forgotten that?"

He shook his head. "No, I hadn't forgotten. I deeply regret it, Cailin. You must believe me. Orris told me that I was wrong, that there was nothing between you. And I believe him."

"But until then?"

"I see the way you look at him. I know you have feelings for him."

"And that gives you the right to humiliate me?"

"No," he said, his voice low. "It doesn't. But neither does my poor judgment give you leave to renege on an agreement that we entered together in good faith."

She smiled. "You sound frightened, Erland. Don't you think that you can wrest power from me if you want to?"

"I hope that it won't come to that."

"Of course you do. Because you realize that if we manage to defeat Sartol with Jaryd and me leading the land's mages, I'll be able to lead the League for as long as I wish."

The First Master pressed his lips into a thin line. "Any conflict between the two of us can only serve to weaken the League, Cailin. And weakening the League assures Sartol of victory."

"But this is a conflict that will only arise if we defeat Sartol," she reminded him. "It may weaken the League with respect to the Order, but it won't endanger the land."

"Anything that improves the standing of the Order, does hurt the land," he said in a hard voice. "A year ago, you would have understood that. But something's happened to you. That eagle has changed you in ways that I can't begin to fathom. And it makes me very sad."

"You're right: Rithel has changed me. She's made me wiser, and she's reminded me that our oath ought to be to the land, rather than to the League."

"I gave my oath to both of them," he said. "And I intend to honor that oath. If you can't honor yours, perhaps you don't belong in the League anymore."

"You may be right," she agreed, sensing the kernel of an idea forming in the back of her mind. "But for now I plan to remain just where I am."

"So do I."

"Which means we're right back where we began this conversation." She knew as soon as she spoke the words that it wasn't true. The kernel had begun to grow. Things would never be the same again. The League would never be the same. But Erland couldn't know that. Not yet.

"I suppose we are." He took a breath. "I'm sorry for what I said to you the other day, Cailin. Truly I am. For the sake of the League and the land, I will make every effort to show you the respect you deserve. I promise you that."

The League and the land. It occurred to Cailin that he always put the League first, in word and deed. She was amazed that she had never recognized this before. "I make the same promise to you, Erland. For the sake of the land."

If he noticed her choice of words, he showed no sign of it.

"Thank you," he said, smiling. "I think we'll all be stronger for it."

They stood in awkward silence for a moment as the rain continued to fall all around them.

"Well, perhaps we should rejoin the others," he finally said, the strained smile returning to his lips.

She motioned for him to lead the way, then followed him back to where the rest of the company stood around the fire. The others looked up as they approached and made room for them beside the fire, but none of them said anything. And a few moments later, Jaryd lowered himself to the damp ground and curled up just beyond the flames' reach to sleep. The others followed his example, and on this night, for whatever reason, Orris allowed Cailin to sleep beside him.

The storm had yet to pass when they awoke. If anything, it had strengthened, the winds growing fiercer and the rain pouring down on the forest like a mountain cascade.

"It's not too late for us to turn east," Erland said, eyeing the Eagle-

Sage closely, but keeping his tone light. "Even after the storm moves on, those passes are going to be choked with snow."

Jaryd took a long breath, as if fighting to keep his temper in check. "The horses will carry us through," he finally said. "We may lose a day or so, but that's still better than going all the way over to the coast."

"Today perhaps. But what if the storm persists for another day, or two, or even three? What then?"

"If you're so eager to go," Orris broke in before Jaryd could reply, "then go. But the Eagle-Sage has made his decision, and the rest of us have already agreed to abide by it."

"It's all right, Orris," Jaryd said quietly. He faced Erland again. "As I said last night, I know that I'm taking a risk by staying. But I think it's the correct choice. I hope you'll stay with us, First Master, though I'll understand if you feel you must leave."

Cailin suppressed a grin. Erland was not about to set off on his own— no doubt Jaryd knew that as well as she did. And by making the Owl-Master choose to stay, Jaryd was taking away his right to complain about it. Erland seemed to sense this as well, because his face had reddened again, much as it had when Cailin confronted him the night before.

"We're probably better off staying together," Erland said after a brief pause, sounding bitter.

Jaryd nodded. "I think so, too."

The First Master stalked off, mumbling something about seeing to his mount, and Jaryd, Cailin, and Orris shared a smile.

Despite this small victory, however, the rest of the day did not go well. The rain and wind continued relentless and unchanging, until Cailin began to wonder if Erland had been right after all. Another day or two of this, and not only would the company have given up too much time, but the mountain paths would be impassable, even for their mounts.

The mages spoke little throughout the day. Trahn sat by himself, shaping small scraps of wood into figures of men and birds that he said he intended to give to Jaryd's daughter. And Vawnya spent much of the day with her eyes closed, in silent meditation. But the others merely stood around the fire, stomping their feet to keep warm and occasionally setting out in search of more wood. They ate little, though Cailin guessed that the others were as hungry as she was. Their stores of food were getting low, and though they all sent their birds out to hunt, the creatures had little success. Most game birds and small animals had taken shelter from the elements just as the mages had.

Night fell, with no change in the weather. Cailin ate a small meal of cheese and dried fruit and lay down to sleep with Rithel nestled beside

her. She woke with the first grey glimmer of dawn. And hearing the rain
pelting the leaves above her, she felt her heart sink.

"There's less wind," Orris whispered from nearby, sensing somehow
that she had opened her eyes.

"That's something," she said, sitting up to look at him.

"Perhaps. Who knows what it's like up in the mountains."

She made a sour face and nodded.

The others woke up a short time later. Jaryd looked pale and troubled. Cailin could only imagine what he was feeling. Erland, on the
other hand, looked quite smug, although he had the good sense to keep
silent.

The morning passed slowly, and though the winds did not return the
rain remained steady. Near midday, however, the skies began to brighten
and, at long last, the tapping of raindrops on the forest canopy began to
slow.

Immediately their spirits began to lift. Even Erland appeared genuinely pleased. They remained watchful, however. As Jaryd pointed out,
this storm had fooled them once before. But by early afternoon, the
trend was unmistakable: the clouds were breaking up, and once or twice
the sun managed to peek through, illuminating the wood and drawing
steam from the forest floor.

"I've lost track of when the moon is supposed to be full again," Jaryd
said as they climbed onto their horses and prepared to ride. "But regardless, I'd like to ride for as much as the night as we can. We'll light the
mountains with our cerylls if we have to."

Orris nodded and grinned. "I've rested enough in the past two days to
go without sleeping for a week if I have to."

They started out of the grove, but before they had gone even a hundred
paces, Trahn called out Jaryd's name. They stopped again and looked back
at the dark mage, who was sitting utterly still, like a stone statue on his
mount. Beyond him partially obscured by the wood, but drawing nearer,
Cailin saw something that froze her blood and made her tremble.

People. Dozens of them. Perhaps hundreds. They walked slowly,
painfully, in an endless column. Their hair and clothes were soaked from
the rain. Many carried children, who cried or slept or merely whimpered
like animals. Others sat on carts that were pulled by horses or oxen, and
that carried bedrolls, cooking pots, farm tools, and other household
items packed in haste and unprotected from the elements.

"What in Arick's name . . . ?" Jaryd breathed, turning his mount and
steering it over to Trahn.

Cailin and the others followed him.

At the same time, the people at the head of the column spotted the company and rushed forward.

"Mages!" they cried out. And, "Arick be praised!"

They clamored around the mages, all of them shouting at once. Cailin heard the words ghost and fire, and she gathered that they had fled their homes, but beyond that, she could make little sense of what they were saying.

"Please!" Jaryd finally called out, raising his staff over his head and making his sapphire ceryll gleam like a signal fire.

The crowd quieted, although a continuous rustle of voices still reached them from farther back in the column, which stretched on as far as Cailin could see.

Jaryd's eagle had been circling over head with Rithel, and the Eagle-Sage called her to his arm now, wincing as her talons gripped him.

"I am Eagle-Sage Jaryd of the Order," Jaryd said, pitching his voice to carry. "With me are Eagle-Master Cailin and First Master Erland of the League. Can one of you tell us what's happened?"

A flurry of conversations swept through the mass of people at the appearance of his bird, but they quieted quickly and for several seconds no one answered him. Then an older man stepped forward. He had steel grey hair and dark eyes, and there were ugly fresh burns on his arms and his brow.

"If you're Eagle-Sage, then you already know that we're at war."

"Yes," Jaryd answered hesitantly. "But our enemy is in Amarid."

"Your enemy is on Phelan Spur," the man said. "And he is none other than the Wolf-Master himself."

"*What?*" Jaryd seemed to recoil at the very notion of it. "Phelan did this to you?"

"Yes. He destroyed our villages, burned our homes, killed our families and friends."

"That's impossible!"

"I would have thought so as well," a woman agreed, stepping forward to stand beside the man. It seemed to Cailin that they were husband and wife. "We've lived on the spur all our lives. We've encountered the Wolf-Master many times, and he's never done anything like this before. But two nights ago he came to our village and threw white fire into our home and the homes of our neighbors. I saw him kill an entire family."

There were tears on Jaryd's face. "Did he say anything? Did he tell you why he was doing this?"

"What could he possibly say that would justify this?" the man demanded.

But the woman laid a hand on her husband's shoulder, and whispered something to him.

After a moment the man nodded, then looked up at Jaryd. "My apologies, Eagle-Sage."

Jaryd shook his head. "It's all right."

"He told us to leave," the woman said. "He told us that the spur was his now and that if we ever returned, he'd kill us."

The Eagle-Sage looked out over the horde standing before them, and Cailin and the others did the same. He was still crying, as were Trahn, Orris, Vawnya, and even Erland. Cailin wondered what was the matter with her that she should be so stoic in the face of this tragedy. And as if in response to a question, she heard a voice in her mind speak to her. Her mother's voice. *You've seen this before,* it reminded her. *You've lived this.*

"Is this what happened to the rest of you?" Jaryd called out. "Did Phelan do this to all of you?"

Nods and cries of affirmation met his question.

"So this is what he had in mind," Cailin heard herself say.

Jaryd looked at her, and she felt the eyes of the other mages on her as well.

"He's making them fight his war," she went on, keeping her gaze fixed on the Eagle-Sage. "He's using the Unsettled as his army."

"None of this should be possible," the Sage said. There was fear in his grey eyes.

"Theron said that Sartol had altered the Curse," Orris reminded him.

Jaryd turned in his saddle to face the mage. "If what they're saying is true, he's done more than alter the Curse. He's changed the very nature of the Unsettled. Allowing them to appear somewhere other than their binding place is one thing. But Phelan once told me that the Unsettled couldn't interact with our world, at least not individually. They all had to act as one. Apparently, Sartol's changed that as well."

"Perhaps not," Trahn said. "He might not have changed them; he might just be strong enough to impose his will upon all of them, so that he can make them act as one."

Jaryd exhaled through his teeth. "I'm not sure which idea scares me more."

"We need to get back to Amarid," Cailin said. "There's no telling how many other villages have suffered the same fate as theirs." Her eyes met Jaryd's, and it seemed to Cailin that they were both reliving their conversation from a few days before. "It's no longer a question of abandoning Amarid," she told him, as if responding to something he had said. "Sartol can reach us anywhere, so we have to destroy him."

The Eagle-Sage nodded. "If we can."

"What about us, Eagle-Sage?" the man standing before them asked. "What are we to do?"

Jaryd regarded the man sadly, and then looked beyond him to the others standing in their winding column. "We can see to your wounds," he said at last. "But after that, I'm not sure what to tell you. We'll do what we can to win back the spur for you. But until we do, you'll just have to fend for yourselves, or find a town near here that can offer you shelter and food."

The Eagle-Sage started to swing himself off his mount, as did Cailin and the others, but the woman stopped them.

"Save your strength Children of Amarid," she said, raising her voice so that her companions could hear, "and ride as fast as you can to the First Mage's city. There are healers among us who can see to our injuries. I'm a healer myself. And the land has greater need of you than do any of us."

"You're certain?" Jaryd asked, not bothering to mask his eagerness to be going.

The woman nodded. "Go. And may Arick guard you and your companions."

Jaryd lowered his head, as if bowing to her. "May he guard all of you as well, kind woman. As long as people with your courage continue to walk the land, our enemy will never win."

The woman blushed and smiled. "Go," she said again. "Strike a blow for all of us."

The Sage nodded, and the company of mages turned as one and began their long ride back to Amarid.

There were so many who had to go before her. She was one of the newest, and though Sartol was aware of her, and hated her as he hated the rest, she was of little importance compared to others. Phelan was first, of course; Sartol wouldn't have had it any other way. And the traitor seemed to take pleasure in Peredur's suffering as well. But though he took his vengeance on others first, Rhonwen had no doubt that her time would come. She had only to wait.

She was back at the place of her binding. It was night, and she could see Tobyn's Wood. She could hear the distant wash of Fourfalls River and the call of a horned owl. If she tried hard enough, she could even imagine the touch of a cool spring breeze on her skin. But she couldn't move or speak. From what she understood of what Sartol was doing, she knew that he could only guide one of them through an attack at any given time, but he could at least hold the others to keep them from warning anyone. Just as he was doing to her.

She had once compared being unsettled to being trapped within her ceryll, as if the crystal and its light were a prison. But never had the image seemed so apt as now. Only now, rather than merely being inside the crystal, she felt that she was surrounded by it, as though she were an early blossom trapped in a sheath of ice by a late-winter storm. She was utterly helpless.

But it was worse than just that. For though she could do nothing, she could see everything. All that her fellow spirits saw, all that Sartol saw, was conveyed to her as well. When Phelan attacked the fishing village that had been his home, burning homes and slaughtering men, women, and children, she experienced it as if she was doing the killing herself. And when Phelan was done, she found herself in another part of Tobyn's Wood, watching as Peredur destroyed the villages near his binding place. After that she was on the Northern Plain, in the mind of yet another ghost, and then she was in the Emerald Hills. The scene continued to shift throughout the night, but always the visions were the same. People were dying, houses were burning, and the Unsettled were responsible for it all.

Sartol didn't come for her that first night, and when daylight finally arrived, taking her sight, she knew that she was safe for a few hours. Sartol had turned Theron's Curse to his own purposes, but he could not change it that much. He could have made her attack during the day, but he would have been blind, just as she was. So Sartol merely held her and the others, waiting until dusk to resume his war. Even when darkness fell, it was not her turn. There were so many of them spread across Tobyn-Ser, and she had been nothing to him in life. She hadn't even been a Mage-Attend when he died.

Still, in the end, he did come for her, just as he had come for the others. One moment she was alone, unable to move at all, and the next she was walking. And Sartol's voice was in her head.

"Your turn, Mage," he told her, his tone mocking.

I'll fight you. You'll have to force me to do everything.

Laughter filled her mind, reverberating like thunder in the mountains until she thought she would scream.

"I have already forced mages who were stronger in life than you ever dreamed of being. I've already forced Phelan. What makes you think that you can withstand me?"

And as if to prove his point, he made her lift her staff and throw a bolt of teal fire at an ancient oak standing a few yards away. The tree split down the middle, both sides crashing to the forest floor, and within seconds both halves were completely engulfed in flames.

Rhonwen merely stared at what she had done. As a living mage, she had not been capable of such a thing.

"I have made you stronger in death than you ever were in life, Mage," Sartol said, reading her thoughts. "How does it feel to wield such power?"

Had there been anything in her stomach, she would have vomited.

Rhonwen felt herself starting to walk again and she knew that there was nothing at all she could do about it. She knew as well that the others were watching this, seeing it all through her eyes, and that knowledge made it even worse. As did the realization of where they were going. He was sending her west, toward the village that had been her home, and that was still home to her mother.

"I can spare her if you like," Sartol whispered to her, like a lover breathing into her ear. "I can do that small thing for you, but you must ask it of me."

Everything. He was taking everything from her, just as he had done to the others, just as he had done to the woman whose body he was using. Just as he intended to do to all of Tobyn-Ser.

And what could she do but beg?

Yes, please, she sent, feeling the tears pour from her eyes. *Please don't kill her.*

Again he laughed, and Rhonwen wondered if he really intended to spare her mother, or if this was just another cruel game.

She could see the small houses in front of her, and she struggled to break free, to stop in her tracks, to fall to the ground. Anything. Sartol's laughter echoed in her mind.

Reaching the first house, she felt herself raise her staff. She tried to close her eyes, but he didn't even allow her that.

"Consider the others," he said. "They want to see."

She felt a surge of power move through her body like wind through tree limbs. It was a sensation she had not experienced since her death and for just an instant, she found herself savoring it. But when the ball of teal fire that had burst from her staff crashed through the wall of that first home, making the ground shudder, and bringing cries of terror from the people inside, she felt ashamed. *Had Phelan felt this way?* she wanted to ask. *Had the others?*

"No," Sartol told her, laughing once more. "You're the only one."

She walked on, destroying home after home. When the townspeople fled from the burning structures, looking back at her as they ran, their faces distorted with fear and grief, she threw fire at them as well. She recognized a few of them. All of them, she knew, recognized her. Some pleaded, some shouted horrible things at her. And who could blame them? Whatever they thought of her was nothing compared to what she thought of herself at this moment.

"You're doing wonderfully."

Leave me alone! she said to him in a small voice. *Stop talking to me!*

"But I'm so pleased with the work you're doing for me. Surely there's nothing wrong with offering a bit of praise."

She tried to close her mind to him, to silence his voice, even if she could not break free of his will. But his taunts continued, as did her assault on the village.

By the time she came to her mother's home, the entire village had been alerted to her presence. The sky glowed with flame and alarm bells rang from the meeting hall and the Temple of Arick. Her mother was outside the house, but unlike the others, who ran from her in terror, her mother simply stood in the center of the road, staring at her. Tears rolled down her cheeks, and her silver hair hung loose to her shoulders.

"Rhonwen, why?" she asked, her voice quavering.

He's making me do it, Mama. I'm so sorry.

"Because you never came to see me, Mother," he made her say. "Because I've been alone all these years, and you never came to speak with me. Not even once."

It was true: her mother had never come to Rhonwen's binding place. Somehow Sartol had learned that from her. But it was a decision Rhonwen understood. She had died so soon after her father's death. It had all been too much for her mother.

"I meant to Rhonwen. Truly I did. But surely that's no reason for . . ." Her mother gestured at the flames and corpses. "For this."

Of course not, Mama. Don't listen to him. Don't listen to me.

"It's all the reason I need."

Rhonwen was crying again, and she hoped that her mother would see her tears and understand them.

Sartol made her raise her staff again, pointing it at her mother's heart.

You promised! she shouted in her mind.

And at the last instant, Sartol shifted her aim, so that the fire from her ceryll flew just past her mother and hammered into her house, the house of Rhonwen's youth. The force of the blow knocked her mother to the ground, but she was still alive, and as far as Rhonwen could tell, she was unhurt.

A moment later Rhonwen began walking again, carrying her assault to other homes. She could hear her mother calling to her again, but Sartol didn't allow her to turn and look back. And just this once, Rhonwen was grateful.

The attack didn't take very long; it had never been a big village. Within less than an hour, every building was burning and bodies littered the narrow lanes between homes. Mercifully, many of the townspeople had managed to escape into the forest, and Sartol did not deem them important enough to have Rhonwen pursue them.

"We need some witnesses," he told her, sounding pleased with himself. "And it's time you made your way to the next village. I'll be leaving you for a time, but I'll be back soon and we can do this again."

You bastard! She was trembling with rage and grief and disgust at what she had become, at what he had made her. *You sick bastard!*

"Rhonwen!" Her mother's voice.

She felt herself turn, saw her mother standing before her. She was still crying, and there was a dark bruise on her cheek. Apparently she had been hurt by the destruction of the house after all.

"I grow tired of this," Sartol said. "You should tell her to run."

Please! You promised! She had shed more tears this night than she had in all her years as an unsettled mage. And yet they kept falling. *Leave her alone!*

" 'Sick bastard,' am I?"

Her staff rose again, and there was nothing she could do to stop it, or to block the teal fire that flew from her ceryll.

28

As fate would have it, your message regarding the weapons flowing from Lon-Ser to the Keepers of your Temples arrived this very day, just as Jibb's security men were intercepting a shipment of gold from your land that was bound for Sovereign Marar. The next shipment of weapons was already on the merchant ship, but it has been removed and destroyed. As for the Temples' gold, I await your instructions as to what should be done with it. Were I in your position, I would demand that it be given to the people of your land as restitution for what has been done to your forests, but that is merely my opinion.

. . . I am hopeful that by ending the flow of weapons from Marar to your land, we have managed to ease some of the burdens you have described in recent letters, but I get the impression that this represented merely one problem among many. If there is more that I can do, please know that you need only ask. I, too, grow weary of the distance between us, although in an odd way, this episode has made me feel closer to you than ever.

Melyor i Lakin, Sovereign and Bearer of Bragor-Nal to Hawk-Mage Orris, Day 2, Week 11, Spring, Year 3068.

In the days immediately following their successful assault on Marar's palace, Melyor and Jibb managed to get quite a bit of information out of the Sovereign regarding his contacts with Tobyn-Ser's clerics and the operatives he used within Bragor-Nal to deliver gold to Premel. Marar resisted at first, of course. He made no effort to hide his bitterness at being imprisoned after Melyor had hinted at the possibility of exile, and he retreated into a brooding silence for several hours after they brought him back to Bragor-Nal and placed him in one of the Gold Palace's underground cells. But physical pain, and the threat of prolonged torture, had a way of making even the most reticent of prisoners become positively chatty.

In truth, Melyor was reluctant to resort to torture. It had been used against her people for too long, by too many leaders of SovSec. And Mouse, who had asked to be allowed to stay on for a few days until Marar's fate was decided, made it clear that she disapproved of torture just as much as she disapproved of murder.

Fortunately, as they had learned two days before in Marar's palace, the Sovereign had a remarkably low threshold for pain. Jibb barely did more than glare at him, and Marar started babbling on about which merchants he had used to send his gold and who his couriers were here in Bragor-Nal. He had even volunteered the names of his operatives in Oerella-Nal, information Melyor immediately shared with Wiercia. Most importantly, the Sovereign gave them the names of the Keepers of Tobyn-Ser's Temples whom he had contacted by way of Abboriji intermediaries. Those Melyor quickly sent off to Orris, although she knew that it would be many weeks before her letter reached him.

"How did you meet him, anyway?" Mouse asked, after Melyor dispatched her letter.

They were standing in Melyor's office, the midday sun fighting through the Nal's brown haze to light the chamber.

"You mean Orris?"

Mouse gave her a strange look, and Melyor smiled. "That's the sorcerer's name," she added.

"Orris," the Gildriite repeated. "How did you end up as his friend? I know he came to the Nal. I wasn't in the Network yet, but people I know still talk about it."

"I met him," Melyor said, "because Cedrych, who was my Overlord at the time, told me to find him. This, of course, was after I sent Jibb to kill him."

The woman's eyes widened. "You're joking!"

"Not at all. Cedrych was intent upon conquering Tobyn-Ser, and I was to be the leader of his invasion force. It would have put me in line to become Overlord, maybe even Sovereign, and at the time, that was all I cared about. I had a vision of Orris and realized that he was coming here to stop the invasion, and so I decided to have him killed."

Mouse was still staring at her, but her expression had changed from one of astonishment to one of disgust.

"I know what you're thinking, Mouse, but don't judge me too harshly. I had many other opportunities to kill him after Jibb failed, and I didn't take advantage of any of them. In fact, I joined his cause, and as a result I was nearly killed myself by one of Cedrych's assassins."

"So Orris forgave you?"

Again she smiled, remembering how long it took them to trust each other, and how quickly that trust turned into love. "Yes, he did."

Mouse regarded her wordlessly for several moments before turning away and stepping to the window. "So what now?" she asked. "What are you going to do with Marar?"

"Don't you think it's time you forgave me as well, Mouse?"

The woman faced her again. "Me?"

"You, the Network. My people."

"Does it matter to you that much?"

"Wouldn't it matter to you?"

Mouse shrugged, then nodded. "I suppose it would. Truth is, I don't even know anymore what it is we'd be forgiving you for."

"I do," Melyor said, smiling sadly. "And if you give it any thought at all, you will as well."

Their eyes met briefly before Mouse looked away again. But in that one moment, Melyor saw that Mouse did know, that she still remembered their conversation in the foothills.

"So what will it take?" Melyor asked.

"Do you really want an answer?"

The Sovereign gave a small laugh. "I think so."

"Then let me think about it," Mouse said, grinning. "In the meantime, you haven't answered my question yet: what's next for Marar?"

Melyor flexed her leg, which, according to the meds, seemed to be healing quite well. Certainly it hurt less than it had. Then she lowered herself into a large chair. "I'm still not certain. Wiercia is coming here later today so that we can try to decide on something, but I don't think she knows what to do either." She eyed the woman with interest. "Why? Do you have an idea?"

"Not really. I know what I'd do. I'd throw him in prison and leave him there for the rest of his life."

"That would certainly be in the easiest thing to do, but it gets a bit more complicated when you're dealing with Sovereigns. Despite what I said in his palace about his violations of the Green Area Proclamation justifying his arrest, Marar was right: there are procedures for dealing with this sort of thing that are spelled out in the Cape of Stars Treaty. He can't be executed, he can't be placed in a common prison, and he can't be punished unilaterally by the leader of one Nal. I need Wiercia's approval to do anything, and though Stib-Nal carries little weight in the council, their new Sovereign would have legitimate grounds for protest were we to do anything that violated the treaty."

"So are you going to exile him after all?"

Melyor exhaled and shook her head. "I'd rather not. Knowing Marar, it would only be a matter of time before he was stirring up trouble again."

"Sounds like a problem," Mouse said. "I think I'm glad I'm not Sovereign."

There was a knock at Melyor's door before she could answer, and an instant later, Jibb stuck his head into the room.

"Can we—?" Seeing Mouse he stopped and frowned.

"I was just leaving," the Gildriite said, smirking at Jibb as she sauntered toward the door.

"Don't go too far," Melyor called after her. "I'd like to speak with you again later."

Mouse nodded. "All right. See you later, General," she added as she brushed past Jibb.

The security man glared after her for a few seconds and swung the door shut. "I don't like her having the run of the palace," he said. "Who knows what she's learning about our security system?"

Melyor had to keep herself from laughing. True, it was a security man's job to be suspicious, but she sometimes wondered if Jibb was capable of trusting anyone. *He trusted Premel,* a voice in her head said. *And look what happened.* On second thought, perhaps it wasn't so funny.

"I don't think we have anything to worry about," she said, keeping her tone neutral. "If she wanted to do something to me she could have done it on our way to Stib-Nal, or in Marar's palace, or at least a half dozen times since."

"True," he answered without enthusiasm.

"Come on, Jibb. She got us there, just as she said she would, and she fought beside us as effectively and as loyally as any of your men. Hasn't she earned a bit of trust and respect?"

"I guess." He dropped himself into the chair across from where she was sitting. "She is good with a thrower, and she's brave, too."

Melyor raised an eyebrow. That was high praise coming from Jibb. "It seems she's made an impression on you."

He dismissed her comment with a wave of his hand. "It doesn't mean

I like her. She's impertinent and obnoxious, and I resent the way she speaks to you. I'm not sure why you put up with it."

"For the same reason Nal-Lords put up with me when I was younger, and for the same reason I put up with you when we first met. I see her potential; I see qualities in her that could be refined."

He shrugged, as if unconvinced. "Maybe." Then, grinning, he added, "And I was never that bad."

"You might not have been as obnoxious, but you were twice as arrogant."

They both laughed before falling into a brief silence.

"So I understand that you don't like her," Melyor said at last. "But do you think that you could work with her?"

"What? You're not serious."

"Yes, I am."

"You want to bring her into SovSec?"

The Sovereign took a long breath. "I'm not sure what I have in mind. I'd be the first to admit that I haven't thought this through too carefully yet. But she's got talent, Jibb, and it's being wasted out there in the Nal. She should be more than just some independent scratching out a living in the quads."

"That's her choice, and you know it. As an independent she can do more for the Network than she ever could in a gang."

"And working for the Sovereign, she could do even more."

He opened his mouth, shut it, then sat back in his chair. "I see," he said quietly.

"Could you find a place for her?"

The general smiled, and Melyor new that he would. When had he ever been able to deny her anything? "Let me give it some thought."

"All right." She continued to gaze at him, waiting. He had come to her, and she knew why. But she had decided some time ago that it was up to Jibb to initiate the conversation.

The security chief cleared his throat and shifted in his chair. "There's another matter we need to discuss," he began at last. "Now that we've taken care of Marar, we have to figure out what we're going to do with Premel."

"Jibb—"

He raised a hand, stopping her. "I know what you're going to say. You've forgiven him, and you've learned to trust him again. But I haven't, Melyor, and I'm the one who has to work with him every day. He betrayed us, he almost got you killed; he's partially responsible for the deaths of three of my men and the wounding of several more. I can't ignore that, and I can't pretend none of it ever happened." Jibb looked away for a moment. Melyor could see that his hands were shaking. "He deserves to be executed," the general went on, facing her again. "He should at least be jailed."

"So we're just supposed to forget that he saved your life, and that he played an integral role in defeating Marar?"

He didn't answer.

"I can't do that, Jibb. Just as you can't overlook his crimes, I can't overlook the fact that he's atoned for them."

"Saving my life doesn't bring back the men who died in that explosion!"

"I know that," she said quietly.

Jibb stared at his hands for several seconds and took a long breath. "I don't like giving you ultimatums, Sovereign. I think you know that. But if you insist upon letting Premel stay where he is, I'll leave SovSec. I can't work with him anymore."

And in that moment, it came to her. There was a way to satisfy both of them, all of them in fact, and to assure that all for which Melyor had been working would continue.

"What if you didn't have to work with him?" she asked.

He stared at her, a question in his dark eyes. And Melyor smiled.

Premel had dismissed the men from their training a few minutes early today. He had seen Jibb making his way to the Sovereign's office and he guessed from the way the general glared at him that he would be the topic of their conversation. Chances were that this was his last day as an officer in SovSec. Tomorrow everyone would know that he was a traitor, so he figured he might as well give them an easy morning today. Maybe that would soften the reaction a bit. He shook his head and smiled grimly. Probably not.

He was still alone on the training grounds, lost in thought, when the young Gildriite woman spotted him and called his name.

Premel briefly considered making an excuse and retreating to his quarters, but despite her strange manner and the fact that their first conversation in the foothills of the Greenwater Range had ended poorly, he liked her. Besides, this was no time for him to be discouraging would-be friends.

"What are you doing out here?" she asked as she drew near. "Where's everybody else?"

He shrugged. "I let them off a little early today. I was feeling generous." He tried to smile, but in his current mood the humor felt hollow.

"So Melyor still lets you train the guards?"

Premel narrowed his eyes. "What do you mean 'still'?"

"Nothing," she said, her features growing pale. "I just—"

"She told you, didn't she?" He turned away, shaking his head. "I can't believe she told you."

"No one told me anything, Premel. I was with Melyor when she interrogated Marar in his palace. That's how I found out."

The security man glanced at her, wanting to believe what she was saying.

"I'm telling you the truth. Melyor told me nothing. In fact she swore me to secrecy." She shrugged, then gave a slight smirk. "It just never occurred to me to keep it from you."

He couldn't help but smile at that. "Palace politics can be a bit confusing sometimes."

"I guess," she said, the smirk lingering on her face. It occurred to him that it was as much of a smile as he had ever seen her offer. "So why'd you do it?" she asked after a brief pause.

He felt his stomach tighten. "What do you mean?"

"Why did you betray Melyor?"

He pressed his lips into a thin line and stared back at the palace. This was not something he wished to discuss with anyone, least of all her. Yet, there was something about Mouse that kept him from just walking away. Yes, she was pretty, but it was more than that. For some reason, he wanted her to like him, to understand.

"I was wrong to do it," he told her in a low voice. "I never should have."

"That's not what I asked."

He stared at her, as if he could gauge by the look in her eyes just how honest he could be. "Marar was offering me a lot of gold."

"So you did it out of greed?"

Premel frowned. "Are you judging me?"

"I'm trying to understand you."

"Why?"

The woman shrugged. "Was it greed?" she asked again.

"I suppose that was part of it."

"Did you do it because she's a Gildriite?"

I should have walked away when I had the chance. I should have seen this coming. What was there for him to say? She had proven in the foothills that she could tell when he lied. "I did it for a number of reasons," he said.

"And that was one of them."

He nodded. "Yes. I'm sorry."

Mouse gazed at him for a long time, a sad expression in her pale eyes. In that moment, she looked younger than he had ever seen her. "Do you hate my people that much?"

"I thought I did. The truth is, I really don't know anything about your people. Until I met you, the Sovereign was the only Gildriite I had ever known. And so when she started changing the Nal, making it into something I didn't like, I blamed it on the fact that she was a Gildriite. That was how I justified my betrayal."

He had expected the woman to rage at him, perhaps even to strike him. Had their positions been reversed, he would have been infuriated. But she just continued to look at him, albeit sadly. And Premel realized that he shouldn't have been at all surprised. She dealt with blind prejudice such as his every day. There was nothing new in what he had said. People had been treating the Gildriites this way for a thousand years. All of which made him even more ashamed.

"What did she change?" Mouse asked. "What made you so angry with her that you'd turn to Marar?"

He felt his face redden. "It's going to sound foolish to you. At this point it does to me as well. But I resented the fact that she was trying to end the violence. I accused her of making Bragor-Nal too much like Oerella-Nal."

Mouse laughed and shook her head.

"What's funny?" Premel asked.

"My people have been condemning her for years for not doing enough to change the Nal, none more than me. And now I find out that you betrayed her because you think she's changed too much." She shook her head again. "I know she's got more gold than I can imagine, and more power than any other person in Lon-Ser, but I don't think I'd want her job."

Premel started to agree, but in that instant he saw Jibb and Melyor emerge from the palace and begin walking in their direction.

"How would you feel about my job?" he asked. "I have a feeling it's about to be available."

She gave him a sympathetic look but said nothing.

Actually, he knew, his job was the least of his worries. He was a traitor, and in Bragor-Nal, traitors were executed. Still, he felt surprisingly calm as he watched Jibb and the Sovereign approach.

Melyor was still on her walk-aids, but she had become so adept at using them that Jibb appeared to be straining to keep up with her.

"I'm glad to find the two of you together," the Sovereign said as she stopped in front of them. She was smiling, although Jibb looked grim, and though he was afraid to think it, Premel couldn't help but believe that he might not be punished after all.

"Why?" Mouse asked, rising to the bait.

Meylor glanced at Jibb, but the general's expression didn't change. Whatever they had decided, Jibb wasn't entirely pleased.

"How would you like to work for me, Mouse?" Melyor asked. "Or, more precisely, how would you like to work for Jibb?"

"SovSec?" the Gildriite said, looking stunned. "You want me to work for SovSec?"

The Sovereign raised a hand. "Hear me out before you decide. I want to create a new unit in SovSec devoted entirely to the protection of Gildriites. It would work in cooperation with the Network." Her eyes flicked to Premel. "The two of you would run it together, Premel on SovSec's end and you on the Network's end. It would be an equal partnership." Melyor looked at the two of them expectantly, like a kid waiting to open presents on the Festival of Lon. "So?" she asked. "What do you think?"

Mouse exhaled through her teeth. "Me, working for SovSec. I don't know."

"You'd be working for the Network, too, Mouse. You'd be doing more for Bragor-Nal's Gildriites every day than you could ever do in a lifetime as a break-law."

"Why are you doing this?" Mouse asked. "Why would you want to hire me?"

The ghost of a smile touched Melyor's lips. "I'm doing this because I can. I think I've finally found a way to protect the Gildriites of Bragor-Nal. And I want you, because I feel that I've gotten to know you a bit over the past couple of weeks. I've seen the way you work, the way you handle a thrower. I think you can do this." She hesitated, but only for an instant. "I also feel that I owe it to you. I appreciate your help." She grinned. "And I've come to appreciate your candor as well."

Mouse gave a reluctant smile, but quickly turned serious again. "Can I recruit others from the Network to help me?"

"Absolutely."

"And I have complete authority over those I recruit? No interference from you or SovSec?"

The Sovereign glanced at Jibb. "She sounds like you."

Jibb grunted in response. It might have been a laugh, although it was hard to say. His expression remained dour.

"You have authority over your recruits, but you, in turn, take responsibility for whatever they do. If they mess up, you'll answer for it."

"And I'd be working with Premel?" Mouse asked, looking his way.

"Yes," Melyor said.

Mouse raised an eyebrow, and regarded him appraisingly. "I can live with that," she said at length. "I'll do it."

The Sovereign, smiled again and nodded. "I'm glad. What about you?" she asked, turning to Premel.

Premel took a breath and looked directly at Jibb until the general met his gaze. "You're all right with this?"

Jibb frowned, his dark eyes flicking away momentarily. "Would it matter?"

"Yes, it would. If you don't want me in SovSec anymore, I'll resign."

Jibb stared at him for several seconds before looking away again. "I don't know what I want. A part of me would like to see you in prison. Another part of me wishes none of this had happened, and that you could just stay on as my colonel."

Premel said nothing. He just waited.

"The problem is, Premel, I don't trust you anymore. I don't think I can ever trust you again. But Melyor does, and she's my Sovereign. So I guess I have to accept what she decides."

"That's not good enough, Jibb," Melyor said, before Premel could respond. "I told you as much in my office. I may not always be your Sovereign, and I need to know that this arrangement will continue long after I'm gone."

"You never said that!" Jibb whispered, the color abruptly draining from his face. "You never said anything like that!" He shook his head. "What would stop you from being Sovereign?"

The Sovereign shrugged, and this time she was the one who averted her gaze. "I'm not sure. I just know that I don't want to be Sovereign for the rest of my life. There are other things I want."

Even Premel, who didn't know her very well, and who knew even less about the events that had led to her investiture as Sovereign, knew what she meant. The sorcerer. She wanted to be with the sorcerer.

Jibb's face, which had turned white just a moment before, now hardened. "I see," he said quietly.

Melyor took the general's hand. "You've known all along, Jibb. I shouldn't have had to tell you." She tried to smile, but failed. "It won't be for some time yet. I don't even know when. But I have to know that the Gildriites will always be safe. I need you to promise me that."

"But you must know that once you leave, I won't be running SovSec anymore."

She did smile at that. "Of course you won't. You'll be Sovereign."

Looking to Jibb for his response, Premel couldn't help but grin at the irony of it all. He had first betrayed Melyor because he wanted Jibb to become Sovereign, and all this time, she had wanted the same thing. But he could see from the way Jibb was staring at Melyor that the general didn't feel the same way. *I don't want to be Sovereign,* the expression in his eyes seemed to say. *I want you.*

Premel glanced over at Mouse, and then stared down at his feet. Anything to avoid looking at Jibb and the Sovereign.

But after a brief silence, Jibb surprised him. "Well, if I'm going to be Sovereign, I'll need all the help I can get."

Premel looked up again, and their eyes met.

"If you want this position," Jibb told him, "you should take it. I have no objections. I think it's a good use of your talents. And maybe it will teach you a thing or two about Gildriites."

"Oh, I'll see to that," Mouse said.

Melyor laughed, and after a moment Jibb and Premel did as well.

"You're certain?" Premel asked, when their laughter had died away.

Jibb nodded. "But remember: I'll be watching you. If you disappoint me again, even the Sovereign won't be able to save you."

"I'll keep that in mind," Premel said. He looked over at Melyor, who was regarding him closely. But he was most aware of Mouse. Even without looking, he knew that she was watching him as well. And in spite of himself, he smiled. For some reason, all three of them were giving him another chance, and though he had really done little to give offense to the young woman—far, far less than he had done to the Sovereign and the general—he was most grateful to her.

It was a prison. Nothing more, and certainly nothing less. That it was clean and well-lit compared to Bragor-Nal's common prisons, or those in his own Nal, made little difference to Marar. He was a Sovereign, by the gods! He had gold and power beyond the reckoning of every person in Lon-Ser save Wiercia and Melyor. It was ridiculous that he should be treated so. True, he had violated a few provisions of the Cape of Stars Treaty and Green Area Proclamation. But those same agreements contained protections for Sovereigns even in extreme circumstances, protections that Melyor had ignored by taking him from his palace and throwing him into her jail.

He had told her so twice, during each of her two brief visits. And both times she had responded the same way, laughing away his protests and offering to leave Jibb with him so that they might discuss in private the treatment Marar had received.

The next time would be different, he had decided. When she came to see him again, he would demand that she contact Wiercia and arrange a meeting of the council at the Point of the Sovereigns so that the three of them might discuss this situation as equals, as the victors of the Consolidation had intended. Under those conditions, Marar figured, he might have a chance. Both Melyor and Wiercia had to approve of any punishment for his crimes, and they had shown little sign of being able to agree on anything at all. Given that he was guilty of crimes against both Bragor-Nal and the Matriarchy, it was quite possible that their discussions would break down over questions of jurisdiction. And if that happened, he would be freed under the terms of the Cape of Stars Treaty. It wasn't much to hope for, he knew, but it was something.

It had been two days since she last came to see him, and both of her previous visits had come just before dusk. So Marar was not surprised when he heard her voice approaching his cell late that afternoon.

Sitting up on the cold steel pallet on which he had been lying, he straightened the plain blue clothes they had given him as best he could, and passed a hand through the matted tangle of his hair. Then the Sovereign looked expectantly toward the metal door that opened onto this section of the palace prison and waited.

"Good afternoon, Marar," Melyor said, opening the door and stepping into the narrow corridor.

He had vowed not to waste any time. "Melyor," he began firmly, standing as he spoke. "I'd—"

He stopped, his mouth falling open as Wiercia followed the Bragory Sovereign into the hallway. She was dressed, as always, in her crimson robe and hood, and, as usual, there was a slightly mocking smile on her face that broadened when she saw his expression.

"Hello, Marar," she said. "You seem surprised to see me."

He gaped at the two of them, knowing how foolish he must have looked, and yet unable to make himself stop.

"He's speechless," Melyor said with amusement, looking at Wiercia. "If I had known that this was all it would take, I would have invited you to the Gold Palace years ago."

Wiercia laughed, and Marar felt his stomach tightening.

Melyor was still on her walk-aids, but she was dressed for battle as she always seemed to be. She wore the light tunic, dark trousers, and metal-tipped boots of a quad fighter, and she had a thrower strapped to her thigh. Her hair fell to her shoulders in amber waves, and her green eyes shone with the scarlet glow of the stone she carried atop her ancient staff. She was beautiful and mysterious and deadly. He couldn't ever remember seeing her look any different.

Looking from Melyor to Wiercia, Marar couldn't help but be struck by the contrasts between them. Where Melyor was alluring, the Oerellan woman was severe; where Melyor was lithe and compact, like a fighter, Wiercia was solid and imposing. Melyor's clothes reminded all who met her of her violent past as a break-law. Wiercia's robes gave her the look of a cleric, stoic and unflappable. Separately, each was a formidable foe. Together, they were unassailable. And they knew it, just as he did.

"What are you going to do with me?" he asked, abandoning in that instant all the strategies and ploys he had dreamed up over the past few days. "You can't execute me. You can't jail me in a common prison."

"We could leave you in this one," Wiercia said. Apparently there would be no battle over jurisdiction.

"Or in the one at Wiercia's palace," Melyor added, as if to prove the point. "But," she added, addressing Wiercia again, "it seems to me that simple imprisonment hardly fits his crimes."

"It's all you're allowed!" he said, his voice trembling, as it always seemed to at times like these.

"Actually that's not true," Wiercia said. "I took the time to read the provisions of the Treaty dealing with punishment of Sovereigns before I came here today. It's quite specific in what it says we can't do, as you already seem to know. But it's very vague when it comes to describing what we can do. Apparently our options are nearly limitless."

"I don't believe you."

She raised an eyebrow and snapped her fingers. Immediately one of her Legates entered the corridor carrying a worn volume.

"The wording is in here," the Oerellan Sovereign said, as the Legate handed her the book. "Do you want me to read it?"

Marar sat back down on the pallet. "No," he murmured. "Don't bother."

"The problem, Marar," Melyor said, "is that neither of us wants the burden of imprisoning you for the rest of your life. We don't want you in our palace prisons."

He looked up at her eagerly. Perhaps he still had cause to hope. "Exile?" he asked.

"I've been in touch with the Supreme Potentate of Abborij," Wiercia told him. "She doesn't want you."

Melyor leaned casually against the bars of his cell. "I briefly considered sending you to Tobyn-Ser, but they wouldn't have any use for you either, and I wouldn't want to do anything to jeopardize our improving relations with the mages there."

They were toying with him.

"Enough of this!" he said, standing again and starting to pace. "Just tell me what you're going to do, and be done with it!"

"There's really nothing we can do," Melyor said with a shrug. "So we're going to let you go."

He halted in mid-stride, staring from one of them to the other. *"What?"*

"You're free to go."

He shook his head. "This is some sort of joke, isn't it? You're playing games with me."

Wiercia shook her head. "No, we're not."

"You'll have to walk back to Stib-Nal," Melyor told him. "I'm not going to waste my gold paying for an air-carrier to take you home. But the walk's not so bad." She grinned. "I should know."

Nonsense, he thought. I'll hire a boat. Once they know who I am, they'll know that I have the gold to repay them. "That's fine," he said, struggling to keep his glee in check. He took a hesitant step toward the door. "So when can I go?"

Melyor shrugged. "As soon as you'd like." She pressed a red button on the wall behind her, and the door to his cell slid open. "You're welcome to go now."

Still not believing what they were telling him, Marar stepped out of the cell and stood before them. "Thank you, Sovereigns. I'll always remember what you did for me today."

They both nodded, but said nothing. After an awkward moment, Marar turned and started for the door leading out of the prison. His pulse racing, his hands trembling, he allowed himself a smile. After all, neither of them could see.

And at that moment, it all fell apart.

"There is one more thing, Marar," Melyor said, forcing him to stop.

He turned slowly. They were both grinning in a way that froze his blood.

"Wiercia has given me leave to conquer Stib-Nal," the Gildriite said. "After all the trouble you've caused us over the past few months, we agreed that it would best if Lon-Ser had only two Nals rather than three. In return, I've ceded mining rights in the northern half of the Median Range to the Matriarchy."

Marar felt his knees grow weak, and he grabbed the door frame for support. "You can't do that," he said weakly. But really there was nothing to stop them. Any formal declaration of war abrogated the Treaty. Which meant . . .

"You know that we can," Melyor said. "And since Bragor-Nal and Stib-Nal will soon be at war, I'll have to take you prisoner."

At which point, it would be entirely within her right to have him executed.

"Please," he breathed. "I'll do anything you want."

"Anything?" Melyor asked.

He swallowed. Nodded.

"I'll call off the invasion if you'll agree to waive the provision of the Treaty that keeps us from jailing you."

He closed his eyes. A common prison. There was no telling what the inmates would do to him upon learning who he was. Death would be easier. Unfortunately, he was too much of a coward to make such a choice.

"Do we have a deal?" Wiercia asked.

"Yes," he whispered. "I'll waive the provision."

The Oerellan woman pulled a document and a pen from the folds of her robe. He closed his eyes again and muttered a curse under his breath. They had been planning this the whole time. They had known that they had him, and yet they put him through it all: the false hope, the crushing letdown, the humiliation.

She handed him the paper and pen.

"May assassins take you both," he said, signing the document without even bothering to read it.

"They may," Melyor answered. "But they won't be your assassins."

"Will you at least allow me to choose which Nal's prison I'll be going to?"

The two women looked at each other.

After a moment, Melyor gave a shrug. "Sure."

"Thank you. I'll go to the Matriarchy." It wouldn't make much difference, he knew. Break-laws were break-laws. But conditions were said to be better in Oerellan prisons.

"Told you," Melyor said.

Wiercia smiled. "I know, but this is right. I know what he did to you, but he killed Shivohn. Justice demands that we take him."

Melyor nodded. "I hope it brings some comfort to you and your people."

Marar closed his eyes again. Melyor and Wiercia were allies. In the wake of all this, they might even have been closer than Melyor and Shivohn had been. All his planning and all his gold had gone to naught.

Wiercia clapped her hands twice, and four of her guardsmen appeared. "Take him to the air-carrier," she commanded, gesturing indifferently at Marar. "Keep a close eye on him, but treat him with courtesy. He was once a Sovereign."

"Yes, Sovereign," one of the men said.

Two of them took his arms, pinning them to his side firmly, but not too roughly. They led him through the doorway into a wider corridor, and started toward a marble stairway at the far end.

"Marar," Melyor called.

The guards stopped and turned him around.

The woman was grinning again, and he wished he could turn away, rather than hear whatever it was she had to say. The guards, however, would not allow it.

"You should never have gone after Jibb. If you had been content with having Premel kill me, it would have worked. You got greedy, and it cost you everything." Her grin broadened. "Something to think about while you rot in jail."

He stared back at her for a few seconds, before glancing at one of the guards. "Get me out of here," he said.

They turned him again, and led him out of the palace to Wiercia's air-carrier.

You got greedy. Melyor was right. He knew she was right. And, he knew, her words would gnaw at him for the rest of his days, reminding him of how close he had come. Just as she intended.

29

Once more I write to you seeking your aid in a matter of great urgency, and once more I do so on behalf of Eagle-Sage Jaryd. Somehow, through trickery or coercion, Sartol, the enemy of whom I wrote in my last letter, has enlisted the Unsettled in his war against the people of Tobyn-Ser. We are beginning to receive reports of atrocities committed by these spirits against villages near their binding places.

Regardless of how you respond to my previous request for help, I beg you to assist us in our effort to warn our people of this latest threat. Alert the Keepers in every village in Tobyn-Ser as quickly as possible using whatever means you have at your disposal. People have died already. Entire villages have been destroyed. People must understand that even if the spirit near their village has been benign in the past, he or she is not to be trusted now.

—First of the Sage Alayna, of the Order of Mages and Masters, to Brevyl, Eldest of the Children of the Gods, Spring, God's Year 4633.

The fresh snow in the mountains slowed them, but it also captured the glow of the moon and the light the company summoned from their cerylls, allowing them to ride deep into the night. Jaryd drove himself and his companions as hard as their mounts would allow, and though the others had grumbled about the pace he set when they first left Rhonwen's binding place, none of them complained after their encounter with the people from Phelan Spur.

No doubt every night that passed saw renewed attacks by the Unsettled on villages throughout the land. How could they rest?

They reached Amarid late on the fourth night, riding into the great city and through the streets to the constable's building long after the last of the merchants had packed up his wares and retired. Jaryd had contacted Alayna earlier that day to tell her when to expect them, so she was awake, waiting for them in the doorway of the building, her great owl perched on her shoulder. Myn was there as well, looking sleepy but pleased to see Jaryd again.

"She insisted," Alayna said quietly, an indulgent smile on her lips.

Jaryd smiled in return. "Of course." He kissed Alayna and then picked up Myn and kissed her forehead. "I missed you, Myn-Myn."

"I missed you too, Papa," she said, resting her head on his shoulder.

"You need to sleep though, Love, and Mama and I have a lot to talk about."

She lifted her head and looked him in the eye. "Are you going to talk about that man?"

Jaryd felt fear flood his heart like a moon tide. *Arick, give me the power to protect her.* "Yes, we are."

She put her arms around his neck again and held him tight for several moments. Then she scrambled down out of his arms, gave Alayna a hug, and went off with Valya back to the Aerie, where she and Alayna had been staying since Sartol took the Great Hall.

"We should be getting back to the Hall of the League," Cailin said, after they all watched Myn walk away. "Erland and I need to speak with the rest of the League mages about all that's happened since we left. It'll be dawn in another couple of hours. Why don't we meet back here then?"

Jaryd nodded. "All right. I need to speak with the rest of the Order as well. But I have little doubt as to what we'll decide to do. We need to face him, Cailin. We need to try to defeat him now. He's only going to get stronger."

"I agree," Cailin said. "I'll do whatever I can to convince the others."

"If it means anything to you," Erland added, still sitting on his mount, and looking regal in his blue cloak and white beard, "I agree as well."

"Thank you, Erland," Jaryd said, smiling at the man. "It means a great deal."

Erland and Vawnya turned their mounts to leave, but Cailin lingered a moment longer, gazing at Orris and looking like she wanted to say something. But then she turned as well and followed the other two mages.

"I let the others know that you'd be back tonight," Alayna said, taking Jaryd's hand. "They're waiting for you inside."

They walked into the constable's building with Orris and Trahn just a step behind them and Rithlar hopping in front of them.

"Has there been any more news?"

She nodded. "Sartol has removed the shield of power from around the Great Hall. We don't know what it means. We haven't heard of any new attacks, but that means nothing. It wouldn't be like Sartol to stop now."

"Is he still in the Great Hall?" Trahn asked.

"Yes, and Theron's with him."

"You're sure it's Theron?" Orris asked.

Alayna and Jaryd shared a brief smile. "I'm sure," she said. "I'd know that shade of green anywhere."

They stepped into the main room of the building, and the other mages stood to greet them, led, of course, by Baden and Sonel. No one said a word as Orris and Trahn took their places at the table that had been placed there, and Jaryd and Alayna moved to the front of the room.

"Thank you all for being here," Jaryd began. "I know it's late; we'd all rather be asleep. But as long as this war continues, the people of Tobyn-Ser can't rest, so perhaps it's appropriate that we don't either."

"Did you learn anything from Rhonwen?" Baden asked. "Do you know how to stop Sartol?"

"As Sartol took the Unsettled from their binding places, Theron appeared to us," Jaryd answered. "He said that Sartol had altered Theron's Curse, and that in doing so, he had given us our one chance to defeat him." He paused, knowing how this was going to sound. "We must undo the Curse."

The others remained utterly silent, staring at him as if he had told them to darken the sun.

"I wouldn't even know how to attempt such a thing," Baden said at last, his voice barely more than a whisper. "Did he tell you anything more?"

Jaryd took a breath. "No. I assume we'll need to wrest control of the Summoning Stone from Sartol, but beyond that I have no idea what we're to do. All I know is, we can't wait. We should confront him tomorrow."

"Tomorrow?" Trahn asked. "Or tomorrow night?"

"If we wait until night," Baden said, "he can send the Unsettled after us. That could make this a lot more difficult."

Trahn nodded. "True. But if we wait until night, we also give a respite to the rest of Tobyn-Ser, even if just for a time. More importantly, though, Theron uttered the Curse at night; that may be the only time it can be broken."

"Not only that," Alayna added, "but if Theron is there at night, he may be able to help us."

Jaryd looked over at his uncle. "Baden?"

The older mage shrugged slightly. "What they're saying makes sense. Who knows? There may even be some way for the rest of the Unsettled to help us. We should go at night."

"I tend to agree," Jaryd said. "Let's hope the League mages do as well."

"Has Brevyl responded to your request for help yet, Alayna?" Radomil asked.

The First shook her head. "Not yet," she said in a flat voice. "Maybe we'll hear from him tomorrow."

No one responded, and it was clear from Alayna's tone that she held out little hope that the Keepers would come to their aid.

There was little more for them to discuss. They knew almost nothing about Sartol's power and that of the Unsettled now that he had altered the curse. All they could do was confront him and hope that somehow the combined might of the League and the Order would be enough. Yet even after Jaryd adjourned the meeting, all of them stayed, sensing perhaps that this might be their last gathering. They said little, but they seemed to take comfort simply in being together. And when the first light of morning touched the windows of the building, the Order mages filed out into the street to greet the day.

Once more, Alayna took Jaryd's hand. "It's strange to think that by this time tomorrow, all of this will be over. One way or another."

"One way or another," he repeated.

"You don't think we can beat him."

He glanced around them, but no one else appeared to be listening. "I don't know," he admitted. "The Order has never faced anyone this powerful before. I don't even think there's ever been anyone this powerful. We have to defeat him, but I have no idea how we're supposed to do it."

"We'll find a way," she said with such certainty that he actually believed her. "What choice do we have?"

A short time later, as the sun first appeared low over the rooftops of the city, Cailin led the League mages up to the constable's building. Rithlar was standing on the ground next to Jaryd, and seeing Cailin's eagle, she let out a cry that the other bird answered.

"Good morning, Eagle-Sage," Cailin said in a voice that carried to all the mages there. "We of the League of Amarid have come to fight beside you for the people of Tobyn-Ser. Three times, Eagle-Sages have led our land to victory. Today, the four gods willing, you will do so again. We pledge ourselves to your service. What would you have us do?"

Jaryd gazed at her in disbelief. How had she managed to get Erland and the rest to agree to this?

"Eagle-Master Cailin, I . . . I'm overwhelmed."

She smiled, her bright blue eyes sparkling in the sunlight. "This wasn't easy," she said under her breath. "Accept our offer before they change their minds."

"My fellow mages and I gladly accept you as partners in this war," Jaryd said in a voice all could hear. "United, the Mage-Craft can never be defeated."

"Several of the older mages, including Erland, think we'd be wiser to do this at night," Cailin said in a lower voice. "I'm not sure I agree with them, but I thought I'd mention it."

"Actually," Jaryd said, "we came to the same conclusion. I think it makes sense for a number of reasons, but if you're not convinced . . ."

She shook her head. "I'll defer to your judgment, and theirs." She frowned and looked away briefly. "I'm feeling very young today."

"You shouldn't," Alayna said. "None of us thinks of you that way."

Cailin smiled. "Thank you. So we're putting this off until nightfall?" she asked Jaryd.

"Yes. We should gather outside the Great Hall at dusk."

"And until then?"

He opened his hands. "I'm not sure there's any way to prepare for this, Cailin. Rest, do something to make this day special." He looked up into the sky, which was a cloudless, deep blue. "Enjoy the sunshine. Who knows what tomorrow will bring?"

"It will bring victory," Cailin said, as if she had no doubt at all.

"I've been telling him the same thing," Alayna said. "But he won't believe me."

Jaryd smiled at them. "I want to believe you both."

"That's not enough," Cailin said. "You have to believe us. You're leading us. If you don't think we can win, we can't."

He knew that she was right, that they both were. Yet he couldn't shake the feeling that this time was different, that the mages of Tobyn-Ser were faced now with too powerful a foe.

"I'll remember that," he finally said. It was all he could say.

And Cailin frowned, as if sensing his lingering apprehension. "Dusk then?" she asked. "At the Great Hall?"

"Yes."

"All right," she said, turning away to tell the other League mages.

A few moments later all the mages, League and Order, began to disperse, excused for the day like schoolchildren. For just an instant, Jaryd wondered if he was making a mistake, if in fact they should have been preparing somehow.

"You look exhausted," Alayna said. "You should get some sleep."

He shook his head. "I don't want to sleep. Let's find Myn and get out of the city for the day."

"Where do you want to go?"

He gazed up at the sky again. A day like this wasn't to be wasted. Especially now. "Anywhere. Anywhere at all. We'll let Myn decide."

As it turned out, she chose just the place Jaryd would have: Dacia's Lake, the small body of water outside the city in Hawksfind Wood. It was a short ride, but once they were there, it felt as though they were leagues away from the Great Hall, which was exactly what Jaryd had wanted. For a few hours, the three of them merely played and swam and laughed. Rithlar circled overhead for much of the time, reaching for Jaryd occasionally, as if to reassure herself that he was still there, and Alayna's owl slept nearby on an old stump. But for a short while, for the first time in so long, Jaryd and Alayna were husband and wife, father and mother, rather than Eagle-Sage and First.

Late in the afternoon, reluctantly, they climbed back onto their horses, with Myn sitting just in front of Alayna, and they rode back to Amarid. Over the course of the day, Jaryd had not found any reason to believe that the mages would prevail, but he had found a measure of peace, as if the gods had assured him that whatever the outcome of the coming battle, Tobyn-Ser would find a way to survive. *No matter how strong he is,* they seemed to be saying with the sunshine that sparkled on the water, and the warm breeze that stirred the branches of the oaks and aspens surrounding the lake, *he cannot destroy this.* And perhaps, in the absence of true confidence, that was the most for which Jaryd could hope.

They reached the city a short time before sunset and took Myn back to the Aerie, where Valya was waiting. Jaryd and Alayna tried to keep their good-bye casual and lighthearted, but Jaryd could not help but clutch his daughter tightly when his turn came. Alayna had already turned away, so that Myn wouldn't see her tears, and Jaryd had to fight to keep from crying himself.

"It's all right, Papa," Myn said, pulling back to look him in the eye. "I promise. I dreamed last night that we were back at our house. We'll get to go really soon."

He smiled and found that he was crying after all. He almost asked her if it had been a real dream, but he wasn't sure he wanted to know. And at that moment he didn't trust his voice enough to speak. So instead, he kissed her once more, whispered, "I love you," and walked away, with Alayna by his side.

They were among the last to reach the Great Hall. Cailin and Erland were already there with the rest of the League mages, and all but one or two of the Order mages were there as well, standing in a tight cluster around Baden and Sonel.

"We were starting to think you had changed your minds," Baden said, as they stopped in front of him. But then, seeing how red Alayna's eyes were, the Owl-Master's brow furrowed. "Is everything all right?"

Jaryd nodded. "Saying good-bye to Myn was . . . difficult."

Baden frowned sympathetically and placed a hand on each of their shoulders. "I'm sorry."

The last of the Order mages arrived a moment later, and Jaryd beckoned Cailin and the other League mages closer with a wave of his hand.

"I don't have much to say that you all don't already know. I'm not sure what we'll encounter in there. Just take your lead from Cailin and me. If things go badly, and we're lost, fight on as best you can. Our goal is to wrest control of the Summoning Stone from Sartol long enough to break Theron's Curse. If we can do that, we can destroy Sartol and his army."

"How do we do that?" one of the League mages asked.

"I'm not sure," Jaryd admitted. "But if we throw all our might at Sartol—or rather at Tammen, whose body he controls—we may find a way. As soon as we're inside, we should fan out around the Gathering Chamber. Make certain that you have a clear line of attack at Sartol, and," he added, casting an uncomfortable glance at Cailin, "that he can only throw his fire at one or two of us at a time."

"Would the power of two more mages help you with what you have in mind?" a voice asked from behind him.

Jaryd turned and saw three men standing nearby. All three of them carried cerylls, although only two of them had hawks on their shoulders. They wore no cloaks, and Jaryd assumed that they were free mages.

"My name is Ortan," the first one said. He was a large man, with dark eyes and long silver-and-black hair that he wore tied back. He carried Amarid's Hawk on his shoulder; Jaryd had never heard of a free mage binding to one before. "With me are Shavi and Nodin. As you probably gathered, we're free mages. There are more of us scattered across the land; only the three of us are close enough to be of service. But we would be honored to stand with the Order and the League against this enemy."

"We'd be grateful," Jaryd said. He glanced at the other two men. One of them was young-looking and slight, with yellow hair and a pleasant face. But it was the other man, the one who was unbound, to whom Jaryd's eyes were drawn. His face and hands were horribly scarred, his face and head hairless, as if he had walked through mage-fire.

"Nodin?" Baden whispered. "Is that truly you?"

The man nodded, although his gaze dropped. "Yes, Owl-Master."

"Did Sartol do this to you?"

"Yes."

"After he took Tammen?"

Once more, the man nodded.

"I'm so sorry," Baden breathed. "I'm so terribly sorry."

"Jaryd," Alayna whispered, "we can't wait any longer. It's almost dark. The Unsettled will be attacking villages again soon."

"You're right." He looked at Ortan and Shavi. "As I said, we'd welcome your help."

"May I come with you as well, Eagle-Sage?" Nodin asked taking a step forward. He limped slightly. Jaryd couldn't even begin to imagine how he had suffered. "I know I'm unbound, and I'm still weak from my burns. But I loved Tammen, and I think in some small way she loved me, too."

How could he refuse? "Of course, Nodin. We're honored to have you with us."

The man smiled, and, sadly, it made his disfigurement appear even more severe.

"Are there any questions?" Jaryd asked, turning back to the other mages.

No one spoke.

"Then let's go. Arick guard you all, and give us the strength to prevail."

As the mages of Tobyn-Ser started up the marble stairs of the hall, Jaryd looked sidelong at Cailin. "You and I should be on opposite sides, just in case something happens to one of us. You take the right, I'll take the left."

Cailin nodded.

"Where do you want me?" Alayna asked.

He took her hand and held it to his lips. "With me, of course."

They reached the top of the steps, and Jaryd and Cailin, their great eagles on their arms, pulled the doors open and led the mages inside. Jaryd had half expected Sartol to throw fire at them as they entered, but he didn't. Indeed, wearing Tammen's body like a robe, he was leaning over the Summoning Stone at the far end of the Hall, staring into the great glowing crystal as if he could see the coming battle unfold within it. And he was ignoring them, as if their presence there was of no concern to him at all.

Better he should have attacked us, Jaryd thought.

They arrayed themselves around the Gathering Chamber quickly, the Order mages, as it happened, following Jaryd, and the League mages following Cailin, so that an observer might have thought that the mages had come to the Great Hall to do battle with each other.

Rithlar gave a soft cry, and Jaryd reached up to stroke her chin. *Courage, my friend,* he sent. *This is why the gods brought us together.*

Only when all the mages were inside did Sartol finally straighten and look at them, an amused smile on Tammen's face.

"Welcome to my Hall," he said in the woman's voice. He glanced toward the translucent windows for a moment, just as the last golden rays of the sun's light touched the glass. "And just in time, too."

As if on cue, Sartol's ghostly falcon appeared on Tammen's shoulder. And, an instant later, Theron appeared before them, suffused with emerald light, his eyes bright and baleful.

A smile stretched across Tammen's face. "I'm sorry that I can't fight you," Sartol said. "But that's why Theron's here."

Without another word, he turned back to the Summoning Stone. At the same time, Theron took a step forward and raised his fist as if to smite them all.

"You should have come earlier," the Owl-Master said, his gleaming eyes flicking toward Jaryd and Alayna. "Now all is lost."

"Protect yourselves!" Orris heard Jaryd shout, just before Theron's hand came down, sending a wave of emerald fire at them all.

Instantly, Orris raised a shield of power, as did all the mages in the hall except Nodin, whose two comrades extended their power to guard him as well. Yellow and blue, purple and orange, Orris's own russet and Trahn's brown beside him, and dozens of other hues lit the chamber. Together the mages' shields made a wall like a rainbow, with Jaryd's sapphire and Cailin's golden light burning brightest on either end. And though Theron's green fire crashed into their wall with the force of a thousand Abboriji armies, causing the Great Hall to tremble and groan, the shield held.

"Why did you come at night?" Theron rumbled, even as he sent another wave of fire at them. "You knew that he had made us his servants! You knew that he could send us to fight you!"

A third surge of green power crashed into the shield, and Orris felt his arms starting to quiver with fatigue. He sensed Kryssan tiring, and he knew that the familiars of the others would be as well. Their wall of power was still withstanding the spirit's assault, but for how much longer?

"We thought we had to wait, Owl-Master," Jaryd said. "We thought we had to come at night to do what we intended."

That seemed to get Sartol's attention, for Tammen straightened again and came forward to stand beside Theron.

"And what was that?" he demanded.

Orris could see the yellow fire burning in the woman's eyes and the small spot of yellow flame at the center of her blue ceryll, and he shuddered. Whatever suffering Sartol had in mind for the mages who had come to fight him was nothing compared to what he had done to Tammen.

Jaryd did not answer Sartol's question, and a moment later Tammen stamped her foot, like an angry child. Another wall of green flame burst from Theron's hand, this one stronger than the others. Several mages, including Baden, Orris noticed, fell to one knee. But still, their shield did not fail. "Tell me!" Sartol growled.

"We came to destroy you, Traitor!" Jaryd said through clenched teeth, his face bathed with sweat. "What more do you need to know?"

Sartol glanced at Baden. "How does it feel to grow old, Baden? How does it feel to be supplanted by children?"

"These 'children' are wiser than you ever were, Sartol," Baden answered. "And before this day is through, they'll destroy you."

The ghost shook his head and laughed. "You still think there's a way you can win, don't you! You must, otherwise you wouldn't be here!" Her expression hardened. "Now tell me what it is!"

Yet another wall of fire crashed into the mages' shields, this one far more powerful that Theron's earlier attacks. Mages were thrown back against the walls of the chamber, and hawks and owls leaped into the air screaming. Two of the League's older masters lay on the floor for several moments before finally stirring and climbing stiffly to their feet. But once more, their defenses had withstood the assault.

"We can't take much more of this," Trahn whispered hoarsely.

Orris had been thinking the same thing. "I know."

"We won't tell you anything!" Jaryd said, glaring defiantly at Sartol. "No matter how strong you are, you won't make us your slaves."

Again, a grin sprung to Tammen's lips. "I don't need to," Sartol said. "I already have slaves." He turned to Theron. "Tell me what they know. How do they intend to fight me?"

"I will tell you nothing," the Owl-Master's spirit rumbled. He closed his eyes, holding himself perfectly still.

"You cannot resist me, ghost, and you know it! Your mind is open to me."

Theron said nothing, although his brow furrowed as if in concentration.

"Stop fighting me! It's futile!"

But Sartol sounded increasingly desperate.

Theron began to tremble, and he bared his teeth. "Now!" he called out in a strained voice. "Destroy him!"

Jaryd raised his staff and sent a torrent of blue flame at Tammen. In the next moment, every mage in the chamber had joined the attack. Myriad shades of mage-fire converged into one brilliant ball of white fire.

And Sartol blocked them all. With no visible effort at all he sheathed himself in power. Yellow it was, with thin striations of Tammen's blue. And it seemed to absorb their fire, like dry soil soaking up a summer rain.

Theron's hands flew to his head and he screamed in pain with a voice that shook the Hall just as his fire had.

The mages kept up their assault on Tammen, but it did no good at all.

"Tell me what you know!" Sartol commanded calmly.

Theron fell to his knees with an inarticulate roar, his fingers clutching his hair. A moment later he rolled over onto his side.

"Jaryd!" Baden called. "It's doing nothing, and we're taxing our familiars!"

Reluctantly, the Eagle-Sage lowered his staff. The others did the same, and Sartol's shield vanished.

"The Curse," Sartol said, smiling. "You thought you could destroy me by breaking the Curse."

Theron lay utterly still on the floor.

"You killed him!" Erland said, his eyes wide.

"Fool! He's a ghost. He can't be killed, any more than I can! You think you can beat me? You can't even sustain an attack for two minutes without Baden whining about his familiar."

"Perhaps not," someone said from the doorway. "But we can."

Orris turned to look at who had come, and nearly fell over in shock. It was Brevyl, Eldest of the Gods, with twenty men, all of them carrying weapons from Lon-Ser.

Looking at Tammen once more, Orris thought he saw surprise register on her features, and—dare he think it?—just a touch of fear. It lasted for just an instant, however. In the next moment, the familiar sneer returned.

"I had planned to destroy the Temples eventually, Eldest," Sartol said. "But I'm happy to begin today."

Yellow-and-blue fire flew from the Summoning Stone toward Brevyl and his men. But the mages, acting as one, blocked it with another shimmering wall of power.

"Spread out your men, Eldest!" Jaryd called. "But stay behind us so that we can guard you."

The Temple's men quickly positioned themselves along the wall of the chamber as Sartol's fire continued to flow from the stone. When the men began to fire their weapons at Tammen, however, Sartol was forced to raise his own defenses again.

"Do you see that?" another voice cried out. It took Orris a moment to realize that it was Nodin, the scarred mage. "Do you see? There's blue in his fire! Tammen's blue! She's still alive! She still can be saved!"

Sartol looked at the man, Tammen's eyes narrowing. Then her face contorted with contempt. "You!" Sartol said. "You're still alive? That's impossible!"

"Nothing is impossible!" Jaryd told him, drawing Sartol's gaze back in his direction. "You're beginning to see that now, aren't you? Nodin was supposed to be dead, but he's not. The League and the Order and the free mages and the Children of the Gods were supposed to hate one another too much to join forces against you, and yet here we are."

"You're all fools!" Sartol said. "I expected more from you and Alayna, Sage, but I guess I was wrong. You could bring every man and woman in Tobyn-Ser to face me, and still you wouldn't win." A strange look came into Tammen's eyes and she smiled again. "Let me show you why."

She was waiting again. Twice more Sartol had come to her and taken her to a village and forced her to kill and maim. Soon he'd do so again. Rhonwen had begun to sense a rhythm in his assault on the land. She knew that it was almost her turn again.

In a way she no longer cared. She was numb, he had hurt her so badly. It was bad enough that he had made her destroy her village and even the home in which she had spent her childhood. But when he made her raise her staff and kill her mother, he killed her as well, in ways the fever that first took her life never had. She couldn't even grieve anymore. He had denied her the solace of despair. There was nothing left; Sartol had taken it all.

Yet, once more, she realized that he could always find something more to do to her, some other avenue to her pain. Waiting in the darkness, she suddenly sensed that Sartol and Theron were doing battle, that the Owl-Master had found the strength to resist Sartol's will. The effort was in vain. She sensed that even Theron knew this from the start. But by fighting anyway, he seemed to be telling the rest of the Unsettled that they needed to do the same, regardless of the cost.

And just moments after Theron's resistance began, Rhonwen learned how great that cost could be. Pain lanced through her mind like a sword, tearing a scream from her throat that echoed Theron's roar of anguish. Still he resisted, and despite the pain, despite her own grief and what she thought had been her own surrender, she fought to help him. All of them did. From across the land, every unsettled spirit lent their strength to Theron. And it wasn't enough. It wasn't even close.

Abruptly the pain stopped, and a voice whispered to her, to all of them. "When this is over, you'll suffer for what you did tonight."

Rhonwen thought that was the end of it, at least for a time. But only seconds later, she felt herself being transported, just as she had the first night Sartol took her from her binding place to the Great Hall. Suddenly she was immersed in darkness. Even her ceryll went dark, as though it was a candle flame, and Sartol's will a sudden wind. She could see and hear nothing. Only Trevdan's talons on her shoulder told her that she still existed at all.

And just as panic began to claw at her heart, she emerged into the light of the Great Hall. Again. The others were there, too: Phelan and Peredur, Padwyn, whose son, Niall, had once served the land, and Hywel, who was the newest of them all. Theron was there as well, but he was prone on the marble floor, his eyes closed and his mouth open as if in a silent wail. For all she knew, he was lost forever.

But it was only when Rhonwen saw the living mages standing around the perimeter of the Gathering Chamber that she fully understood. *You'll suffer for what you did tonight.* Who could have known that he would find a suitable punishment so soon? As if killing her mother and destroying her home hadn't been enough, now he intended to make her destroy the Mage-Craft. They were his army, his servants. And this was his will.

"You see?" Sartol cried triumphantly, as if to confirm her fears. He waved a dismissive hand at Theron. "Even without the great Owl-Master, I can defeat you. And I don't even need to raise a finger. I command the mightiest army this land has ever seen! They will destroy you!"

Resist him. She heard the voice as a faint whisper, no more than a rustling of wind over plains grasses. But she knew the voice. It was Theron, not lost after all.

How can we, Owl-Master? We've tried, but he's just too strong.

Resist him, Theron sent again. *You must find a way.*

"You failed, Owl-Master!" Sartol crowed, able to hear Theron's voice as well. "You were the strongest of them all, and you failed. How do you expect the rest to stand against me?"

And as if to prove his point, Sartol had them raise their cerylls and throw fire at the mages and the Temple's men. The mages raised their power to guard themselves and the Eldest, but even Rhonwen could tell that the men and women she was fighting were fatigued. They hadn't a chance. The Temple's men raised their weapons and fired at the ghosts, but, of course, the red flames passed right through them.

"Isn't it clear now?" Sartol demanded, laughing triumphantly. "No one can stand against me. Even Lon-Ser will be mine before I'm through!"

But the words came again, faint still, but insistent. *Resist him. You are our last hope. If you fail, the land dies.*

30

Given all that I have written to you about the free mages and about my experiences with the League, you probably think me foolish to even hope that the Mage-Craft can protect our land as Amarid intended. No doubt there are great dangers in the way mages have been divided from one another since my journey to your land. But ultimately I have to believe that the things we share are of greater importance than the issues that divide us. Even if our cloaks are different colors, even if some of us wear no cloaks at all, we all bind to familiars whom we love, we all channel our power through stones that bear our colors. Despite the sundering of the Order, we are all linked by the Summoning Stone. At one time or another we all know the pain of losing a familiar, and at these times, even our fear of Theron's Curse binds us to each other.

So long as these things continue to define the Mage-Craft, I remain hopeful that we will, in times of crisis, find a way to work together for the good of the land. Perhaps I am unwise to think this way; perhaps my colleagues in the Order and I should be trying to determine how we will cope when this hoped for reconciliation fails to occur. But I cannot give up hope. I believe it is better to be a fool than to surrender.

> —Hawk-Mage Orris to Melyor i Lakin, Sovereign and Bearer of Bragor-Nal, Spring, God's Year 4633.

Baden knew that Sartol hated him more than he did any of the others. Their fates had been entwined for many years now, and this was not the first time that the future of the land and their own enmity had come to a crisis within the walls of the Great Hall. In life, Sartol had tried to have Baden executed as a traitor, only to be killed himself by the combined might of the Order when Baden proved that it was he who had betrayed the land. But in death, with the arrival of the Unsettled in the Gathering Chamber, Sartol sought to avenge himself on all of them. And on Baden most of all.

Baden knew this, and so he was not surprised when Sartol sent Phelan to kill him.

"I believe the two of you have met," Sartol called out to them as the Unsettled began to advance on the mages. "Phelan once helped you defeat my plans, Baden. My hatred for him runs almost as deep as my hatred for you. So who else would I choose to kill you?"

Baden said nothing. He merely crouched lower, raised his staff, and prepared to defend himself. Glancing quickly around the chamber, he saw other mages doing the same, and he felt his heart sink. This was not at all like fighting Theron had been a few moments earlier. Rather than one ghost throwing waves of fire at all of them, the living mages of Tobyn-Ser were now slightly outnumbered. Raising a single shield wouldn't work anymore. Now they had to fight for themselves. The young and old, the strong and the weak.

Sartol sent two ghosts against each of the Eagle-Sages, and he sent two after both Orris and Trahn as well. Obviously he knew that at this stage of his life, Baden was not enough of a threat to warrant two foes. Not only was he old, but so was Golivas. Almost any one of the ghosts would have been far more than Baden could handle. But Sartol sent the Wolf-Master, because he wanted to be sure. Because he hated him.

There was a look of profound sadness in Phelan's eyes as he and his wolf came forward to destroy him. Baden still remembered his one encounter with the Wolf-Master as clearly as he did his first binding. It had been a clear summer night on Phelan Spur, and Phelan, working with them on behalf of all of the Unsettled, had helped Baden and his fellow mages defeat the outlanders. Baden could see from the expression on Phelan's face that the spirit remembered as well. *I'm sorry*, the Wolf-Master seemed to be saying. *I don't want to kill you.*

Baden saw flashes of mage-fire out of the corner of his eye and heard cries of alarm from living mages. The battle had begun. Perhaps the last battle the mages of Tobyn-Ser would ever fight. But he dared not take his eyes off Phelan to look. And an instant later, the ghost before him raised the mighty arm holding his staff and threw a bolt of fire at him. White it was, as if the Wolf-Master was Tobyn himself, throwing lightning at the land. Baden met the blow with a curtain of orange power, but he was knocked to the floor so violently that the breath was knocked out of him. Golivas, his glorious white owl, let out a cry as she hovered above him and then swooped quickly to avoid a second stream of fire that was intended for her.

Somewhere in the center of the chamber, Sartol laughed.

Phelan raised his staff again and brought his fire down on Baden's chest like a gleaming hammer. The Owl-Master could do nothing but sheathe himself in magic. And though his power held, barely, the force of the blow forced the air from his lungs a second time. He tried to roll away, but Phelan struck at him before he could. Again and again, the Wolf-Master pounded at him, each blow tearing Baden's breath from his chest, until the mage began to fear that he would pass out. Golivas was above him again, laboring to keep herself aloft. If Phelan decided to strike at her a second time, there would be little she could do to avoid the blow. The Wolf-Master seemed content, however, to continue his assault on Baden.

And with good reason. Baden's power was failing. Every blow weakened him. The orange glow of his shield was fading, the white of Phelan's fire penetrating farther and farther, until it almost seemed that Baden could feel its heat upon him. Each blow rang in his mind like a smith's sledge striking an anvil. But sounds from the chamber still reached him. He heard screams of terror and pain coming from his fellow mages. Men and women he knew were dying. He heard Sonel cry out from beside him, and he couldn't even turn his head to see why.

This is how it's going to end, he thought. *They'll keep striking at us until we're too exhausted to defend ourselves.*

As if to prove him right, Phelan's next blow broke through his power, searing his chest and ripping a scream of pain from his throat. Golivas cried out in response and fluttered to the floor beside him, as if too weak to fly anymore. Somehow Baden was still alive; apparently his shield had managed to absorb most of Phelan's fire. But as Phelan raised his staff to strike him again, Baden knew that this next blow would be the last.

He reached for Golivas, but she had nothing left to give him. So instead of coaxing one last surge of power from her, he merely touched her mind with his. *Thank you, my love,* he sent, *for your strength and your courage.* An image of the Northern Plain entered his mind, the boreal stands of the upper reaches of Tobyn's Wood darkening the horizon. Their binding place. *I remember as well. I've loved you more than any other. Take that with you when I'm gone.*

Then Baden closed his eyes and waited for Phelan's killing blow.

She had made mistakes in her life. Arick knew she had. She had been arrogant at times, dismissive of those who did not wield the Mage-Craft, impatient with those who were less intelligent, or bold, or decisive than she. She had not always treated the people who cared for her with courtesy, and, perhaps as a result, she had few friends. She had known all this for some time, and yet she had done little to change.

It's because of what happened to me, she had told herself time and again, though she knew it was a poor excuse. *It's because of Watersbend.*

But Tammen could think of nothing that she had done to deserve the fate that had befallen her.

Was it that she had allowed Nodin to love her when that love was not returned? Was that enough to warrant this? Or was it simply that she had chosen to trust Sartol despite Henryk's warnings and Nodin's misgivings?

For days after Sartol took her, she repeated these questions in her mind. At first, as she struggled vainly to break free only to find that Sartol's grip on her was complete and unassailable, they were her only outlets for despair and self-pity. Later, when Sartol's abuse began in earnest, when he started to touch her—to make her touch herself—in ways she had never even conceived, she used them as an escape, as if asking the gods "why?" could make her forget what was being done to her.

It was only after he—they?—killed Hywel in the forests below the Parneshome Range, that she stopped asking the questions altogether and closed her mind to everything. After crushing the man's throat with her hand, Sartol had sensed her dismay.

"This is not new to you," he had said, taunting her again. "You killed Henryk, remember? You killed Nodin."

She had not forgotten of course. But with all that had followed, she had not given herself over to the grief that came to her now. Killing Hywel, it seemed, had brought back the horror of what she had done to Nodin.

He was your lover! Sartol said, gleefully, forcing the memories of her night with Nodin to play again and again in her mind. *How splendid!*

Fighting to escape the images of their lovemaking, and then the vision of Nodin flailing wildly at the flames that engulfed his body the following night, which Sartol made her remember as well, Tammen finally resolved to close her mind to everything. There was no escape for her. She knew that now. And if what Sartol had told her that first night on the Northern Plain was true, there would be no death either. Which meant that she would have to endure this for the rest of time, as if she herself was unsettled.

Better then to surrender, to let her mind drift and wither, like autumn leaves freed by a gust of wind, than to continue to fight and suffer each indignity as another defeat. *You cannot fight me,* Sartol told her the night he entered her mind and body. *This body is mine now.* How many times had he proved this to her since then? How many times had Tammen tried to defy him only to find that she could do nothing at all? She would have been better off submitting to him that first night and saving herself the anguish that followed. It had taken far too long, but at last she had learned her lesson. If she could not find comfort in death, she could at least spare herself the pain of being alive.

She was only vaguely aware of their arrival in Amarid and their capture of the Great Hall. Sartol tried to make her watch as the Unsettled began their war against the land, but even then he could not reach her. He could force the images into her mind, but he could not make her see. When the mages came to challenge him, Tammen saw them as if from a great distance, but she heard only whispers of what they said and paid no heed to Sartol's reply. This was their war; she had lost hers long ago.

But then, a voice reached her, insinuating itself somehow into the tiny world that was still her own. It was a voice she knew, although not one that she ever thought she would hear again.

You're dead, she wanted to say. *You can't be here.*

Yet hearing this voice, opening herself to the possibility that it was real, she also heard Sartol's reply. "You! You're still alive?"

And then she knew that it was true, that it really was Nodin, that she hadn't killed him after all.

She allowed herself to see what Sartol saw through her eyes, and so beheld Nodin's ravaged face. *I did this to you.* If it had been possible, she would have cried out, she would have run to him.

Forgive me! she would have begged. *I never meant to hurt you! I'm sorry that I didn't love you!*

Seeing Nodin, she saw the rest of them as well. Nearly every mage in Tobyn-Ser was here. Yet she sensed no fear at all from Sartol. And in the next moment his army of unsettled mages appeared in the Hall, and she understood why. Tammen tried to retreat, to close her mind rather than watch this final battle. But now that Sartol had her again, he didn't let her go.

No, he whispered to her. *You're going to watch. This is our victory, yours and mine. I want you to enjoy it, too.*

There was no escaping it. She couldn't turn away or close her eyes. And in that instant, finally, she understood why she was being punished. It wasn't her arrogance, or her willingness to use Nodin as she had. The gods often forgave greater sins than that. It was simply that she had trusted Sartol to help them. In the end, it was not that she was evil, or even cruel. It was just that she was foolish. For that reason alone, the land was going to perish.

Resist him.

She heard the voice as Sartol did, as the Unsettled did. A whisper, weak and desperate. But while Sartol laughed at Theron's plea, thinking that the Owl-Master was asking the impossible of the other unsettled mages, Tammen knew better. Theron was speaking to her.

I can't do anything, she tried to say. But she couldn't even tell him that.

Resist him. You are our last hope. If you fail, the land dies.

She saw the ghosts advance on the living mages, and despite the hatred she once harbored for the Order, the contempt in which she once held the League, she implored the gods to help them.

You must fight him. You must stop him.

Didn't Theron understand that she was helpless? Didn't he know that Sartol controlled her more completely than he controlled the Unsettled?

Now! Sartol sent.

Immediately, torrents of Mage-Fire flew from the spirits, lighting the Great Hall with shades of blue and red and yellow and green, and crashing into the walls of power raised by the living mages so that the floor of the Great Hall heaved and shuddered as if from an earth tremor. Again and again the ghosts pounded at them. They would never tire, she knew. They would never die. Brevyl and his men were the first to fall—the mages could barely protect themselves. How could they be expected to protect the Eldest and his men as well? And though Tammen had once fought against the Temples, she grieved to see Brevyl and his men die. Then the ghosts turned their attention fully on the mages, and her grief turned to anguish. For it was clear that the mages did not stand a chance again Sartol's army of ghosts. Within moments, several older masters had fallen, unable to summon enough power to guard themselves. Some were consumed by flames, screaming in terror and pain as they burned. Others were blasted with such force that they fell silently, their bodies shattered and still.

Stop this, Theron said to her. *Only you have the power.*

I have no power, she wanted—

Yes, you do!

Tammen fought to control herself. Somehow Theron had heard her. She had spoken to him, and he had heard. Sartol, she realized, was so intent on the battle, and on controlling the actions of every ghost in his army, that he was ignoring her. He still held her. She couldn't move or speak out loud. Certainly she couldn't rid herself of him. But perhaps she could do something.

How? she sent.

Again, miraculously, Theron heard her. *Your ceryll,* was all he said.

She understood.

What? Sartol's voice. Suddenly, he was aware of the conversation she had been having with the Owl-Master, and he moved to crush her once more.

But he was too late. Reaching for her ceryll with her mind, and sensing the flow of Sartol's power from his binding place to her stone, she poured all the power she still possessed into the crystal, much the way she would have if she wanted to brighten the stone. She was unbound, of course—Sartol had seen to that long ago—and her powers were limited. Had he not been distracted by the battle, she never would have been able to do even this much. But he had ignored her for an instant too long, and despite all that had happened, this was still her ceryll. Abruptly, the flow of Sartol's magic stopped.

She heard herself roar with his rage. She saw the army of unsettled mages falter in the midst of their battle and then turn in her direction. She felt him flail at her mind with the power he still possessed, the power that came from the spectral falcon on her shoulder, and she shuddered at the pain. But it was not as it had been.

I'll kill you for this! he told her. *I'll destroy you!*

You killed me a long time ago, you bastard! she answered, knowing that he could hear her, that his control over her was not what it had been. *And now I've killed you.*

The fatigue in her arms and shoulders was overwhelming. Her muscles trembled and sweat poured from her like rain from a storm cloud. The two ghosts were striking at her mercilessly, alternating their assault so that she had no opportunity to rest. Rithel was strong, far stronger, Cailin had to admit, than her beloved Marcran had ever been. But even the great eagle could not endure this forever, any more than she could. And yet, though her entire body ached, and her mind was growing numb from the endless succession of blows, there was little else she could do.

When the spirits suddenly broke off their attack, Cailin suspected a trick. But then she heard Sartol's inarticulate roar of frustration, and she knew that something had happened.

The ghosts turned toward Tammen and started toward her, and Cailin followed them warily.

Theron was on his feet again, and seeing Cailin, he beckoned her forward with a sharp gesture.

"Come, Eagle-Master! We have little time!"

"She's not going anywhere!" Sartol said, leveling Tammen's staff at her.

Cailin raised her staff and prepared to shield herself.

"Fear not," Theron told her. "We will take care of the traitor."

And in that moment the unsettled spirits, who moments ago had answered to Sartol's command, raised a wall of glimmering multihued power that stretched from the Great Hall's marble floor to its domed ceiling. Sartol, standing in the center of this prison of light, roared a second time, and sent volley after volley of yellow fire at the walls of his cell. And nothing happened.

"*No!*" he cried, blasting the walls again and again. "*No!*"

"We can hold him for a time," Theron said. "But eventually he will link himself to the source of his power again. We must act before he does."

Perhaps Sartol heard what the Owl-Master said. Or perhaps he merely realized what he needed to do. But suddenly he fell silent. Closing Tammen's eyes, he raised his staff over his head and then held himself perfectly still.

"He is making the attempt now. Come quickly." Theron looked over at Jaryd. "You, as well, Eagle-Sage."

Jaryd hurried to the Owl-Master's side, and together, Cailin, the Eagle-Sage, and the ghost of Theron strode to the Summoning Stone, with Rithel and Jaryd's bird following close behind.

"Place a hand on the stone," the spirit said. "Both of you." He glanced back at Sartol, who still stood like a statue in the center of the Gathering Chamber. "Make haste!"

Cailin did as she was told, as did Jaryd.

"Now raise your staffs and pour your power into the crystal."

Cailin reached for Rithel with her mind and an instant later, golden yellow fire burst from her ceryll, to be joined a split second later by brilliant blue from Jaryd's. And as their power flowed into the giant crystal, it began to glow, blue at one end, gold at the other, and green in the center where their hues met, so that it seemed as though Theron's fire lay at the core of what they were doing.

"Now the rest of you!" Theron called. "All of you, come here and add your power to the stone!"

"What about us, Owl-Master?" one of the unsettled mages asked.

"No. This is for the living mages only. We are powerless against the Curse. Guard the traitor. That is the extent of what we can do now."

The rest of the living mages, some in blue cloaks, others in green, and three wearing no cloak at all, began to gather around the great crystal and channel their magic into it. Alayna was the first to reach them, followed almost immediately by Trahn and Orris, Erland and Vawnya, and all the others who had survived the assault of the Unsettled.

"Baden!" Jaryd cried out. "Where's Baden?"

He started to pull away.

"Stay where you are!" Theron commanded.

"But—"

"There is not time, Eagle-Sage! We must do this now, before the traitor finds his power again!"

"It's all right Jaryd," came a faint voice. The other mages parted and

Baden stepped forward, supported by Sonel. His cloak was blackened at his chest and his face looked pale and haggard, but he wore a slight smile, and his white owl sat on his shoulder wide-eyed and alert. "I'm all right. Let's end this."

Jaryd smiled broadly and nodded. "Yes, let's."

All of them were there, at least all who were still alive, and their power poured into the stone, so that it glimmered brilliantly with white light, as if it were a star plucked from Leora's sky. And no one's power was greater than Jaryd's and hers. This was what the eagles had come to do. This was their purpose, their destiny. Cailin felt Rithel's power move through her like light through a glass. So vast it was, as if she were holding the sun itself, that she feared she could not contain it. Yet, somehow she did. And Jaryd did as well. And their power, Jaryd's and hers, Rithlar's and Rithel's, bolstered by that of the other mages, seemed to bring the great stone to life, so that the heat of their magic was radiated back toward them. The stone was on fire.

"Jaryd and Cailin," Theron said, looking at them both in turn. "Repeat my words in unison. Say exactly what I say. Do not change anything. Do you understand?"

They nodded.

"The rest of you remain silent and keep your power focused on the stone. We may only get one chance to do this."

He had control of her again, which was the first thing. And though he wasted little time reaching back toward the Northern Plain for the source of his strength, he did make it clear to her that she would suffer mightily for what she had done.

This is but a taste, Sartol told her, searing Tammen's mind with the power he still possessed. *Once I have my full strength again, you'll wish that you'd died at Watersbend.*

He felt her shudder at the pain, and he smiled with satisfaction. She was still struggling against him, but he could hold her, and soon he'd be able to crush her again.

His eyes were still closed, and his mind soared back across the mountains and Tobyn's Wood toward the plain. He heard Theron speaking to the mages. The Unsettled could keep him from attacking Jaryd and his friends, but they could do nothing to keep him from reclaiming his power, and the Owl-Master knew it. He saw the fires burning atop the Emerald Hills.

"Repeat my words . . ." he heard Theron say.

He could see the plain in his mind. He could see the northern peaks of the Seaside Range beyond it, bathed in the silvery light of the rising moon.

"From this night on . . ." Theron said.

And Jaryd and Cailin answered together, "From this night on . . ."

He saw his staff, still jutting out of the earth like a glowing spear. Taking it in his hand, he felt the power surge through him, an ocean of light and fire.

". . . Rest shall be granted to all mages . . ."

". . . Rest shall be granted to all mages . . ."

He stretched his mind back across the land, reaching for the Summoning Stone, which was still his, even with the fire of four dozen mages flowing through it.

". . . Whether they perish bound . . ."

". . . Whether they perish bound . . ."

He could see it, he could almost feel its heat. The massive crystal seemed to be calling to him, reaching back toward him like a gleaming stone hand. It had been his; it would be his again. He had only to grasp—

". . . Or unbound."

". . . Or unbound."

White light exploded in his mind, brighter than a thousand suns. He heard his falcon cry out, heard himself scream with Tammen's voice, and then realized that the scream had come from Tammen herself. He felt the power rush out of him suddenly, as though the gods themselves were pulling the blood from his body. And as the last echoes of Tammen's cry descended to him from the ceiling of the Great Hall, Sartol felt himself being dragged down into an icy, impenetrable darkness. He tried to scream, to grab at something, at anything. But there was no air, no light, no sound. Only the black, which swallowed him like a midwinter sea on a moonless night.

". . . Or unbound."

As soon as the words left his mouth and Cailin's, a blinding white light burst from the Summoning Stone with a sound like the rending of rock. The Great Hall seemed to rise up off its foundations for an instant and then crash down to the ground, sending the mages sprawling to the floor as if they were children's dolls.

For several moments Jaryd lay dazed on the cold marble, his ears ringing, and his eyes open but seeing nothing except traces of the brilliant light that had come from the stone.

Then he felt someone touch his hand.

"Jaryd." It was Alayna, lying beside him.

"Yes," he whispered, gathering her in his arms.

"Is it over?"

"I think so."

He sat up with an effort, and as his sight cleared, he surveyed the Gathering Chamber. The unsettled mages were gone. Theron, Phelan, Peredur, Rhonwen. . . . All of them. They had finally found rest. At the far end of the hall lay the bodies of six mages, the Eldest, and his men. In the middle of the chamber, directly below the portrait of Amarid, which appeared to have been marred by mage fire, Tammen lay unmoving, her eyes staring sightlessly toward the windows above where Jaryd sat.

He turned to look at the rest of the mages, and doing so, beheld something that caused the world to fall away beneath him.

"Fist of the God!"

"What is—?" Alayna froze, gasped. "Arick guard us all," she breathed.

The Summoning Stone lay shattered on the floor, its shards spread in a half-moon around the ancient wooden stand that had held it only moments before. The stand itself was charred in places and broken. Jaryd stood slowly and walked to where it lay. Fragments of the great crystal had embedded themselves in the wood of the stand and in the stone wall behind it. And as other mages began to stir and make their way over to where he was standing, he saw that many of them bore cuts and gashes where pieces of the stone had struck them as well. It was remarkable, he realized, that none of them had been killed.

The Eagle-Sage glanced down at his staff, which once had been Theron's staff. He could still see the blackened edges and thin fracture lines in the wood that were made when the Owl-Master created the Curse. Tonight, in breaking the curse, they had shattered the Summoning Stone, just as Theron had shattered his ceryll a thousand years ago.

Looking up again, Jaryd saw that the others were watching him.

Except one. He heard sobbing coming from the center of the hall, and as the other mages turned to look, Jaryd saw Nodin kneeling on the floor, cradling Tammen's body in his arms.

Jaryd walked to him and knelt beside him, placing a hand on the man's shoulder.

"I wanted to save her," Nodin said, his voice unsteady, and his tears winding a crooked course over his scarred cheeks. "I thought there might be a way."

"I think she was lost the night Sartol took her," Jaryd told him. "I don't think any of us could have saved her. But I think perhaps she saved us."

The mage looked up at that.

"Theron said that Sartol had to find his power again. I think Tammen found a way to stop him, or at least slow him long enough for us to break the Curse."

"You really believe that?"

"Something happened," Jaryd said. "One moment I was on the verge of being killed by two unsettled mages, and the next they were turning on him, and trapping him in the circle of power."

"Phelan had his arm raised to kill me," Baden added. "I may never know why he didn't, but I think Jaryd's explanation makes as much sense as any."

Nodin looked up at the lean Owl-Master, and for several seconds they held each other's gaze. Then Nodin nodded.

"Thank you." His eyes flicked to Jaryd and then back to Baden. "Thank you both."

"Do you know how this all happened?" Cailin asked him. "Do you know how Sartol took her?"

Nodin looked down again and brushed a wisp of hair from Tammen's forehead. "She gave herself to him. She thought he could help the People's Movement."

"But why would she do that? Didn't she know—?"

"She was at Watersbend," Nodin said, his tears flowing again. "She was only a child at the time, but the memory of it seemed to haunt her. Much of her village was destroyed by outlanders. Sartol stopped their attack and killed the men responsible. She didn't care why he did it, and she didn't care that the rest of us thought him a traitor. To her, Sartol was a hero."

Cailin stared at the man, her young face abruptly pale and her lips trembling. "She was at Watersbend?" she whispered.

Nodin gazed back at her. "Yes." He narrowed his eyes. "Were you as well?"

"Kaera. I was the lone survivor at Kaera."

"Of course," he said. "You're Cailin. I should have remembered."

But Cailin didn't seem to hear him. "This could have been me. She's a few years older, and she wears no cloak. But otherwise we're the same."

Nodin shook his head. "No. I wish it were so. Perhaps then she'd still be alive and I wouldn't bear these scars. But the two of you were not at all the same. You and she shared this grief, this nightmare. But it did something to her. Something dark. How else could she have allowed Sartol to take her? The gods never would have given you that eagle if they had seen the same darkness in you."

Cailin seemed to hear the truth in his words, for a moment later the color began to flow back into her cheeks. After a few seconds, she nodded. "Thank you," she said.

"What do we do now, Jaryd?" Orris asked.

Now that the stone is shattered and the Unsettled are gone. Now that there is no Curse to haunt the sleep of unbound mages.

Orris didn't say this; he didn't have to. They all knew what he meant.

Jaryd didn't know whether to rejoice or weep, although he suspected that before this day was over he would probably do both.

"We tell the people of Tobyn-Ser that they have nothing more to fear from Sartol or the Unsettled," the Sage finally said.

"And what about the stone?"

Jaryd shrugged. "The stone is lost. I don't see that we can do anything about it at all. Amarid and Theron brought it back from Ceryllon and altered it so that it was linked to all of our cerylls. I suppose we could bring back another crystal like it, but I wouldn't know how to do what they did."

The other mages stood before him silently, as if contemplating what it meant to have no Summoning Stone. There was nothing binding them to one another anymore. There was no way to summon them all to a Gathering, or inform them of the death of an Owl-Sage. Indeed, without the stone, there was little need for a Sage. Certainly there was no longer any compelling reason for a Sage and First to remain in Amarid. It had always been the Summoning Stone that held them here. It was their responsibility to summon the rest to the First Mage's city in times of crisis. And if the crisis then demanded that the mages go elsewhere, they could use the stone to send a party of mages anywhere in Tobyn-Ser.

"The Mage-Craft will never be the same," Erland said softly, as if he had been reading Jaryd's thoughts. "The stone is lost, the Curse is gone." He shook his head. "I never thought I'd see anything like this."

"Perhaps," Cailin said, "this is a good time to end the feud between the League and the Order. We've defeated an enemy together, and we've lost the ability to respond quickly when the land is in need. To continue our rivalry would be foolish."

Jaryd offered a smile. "I agree."

But she wasn't done, and in the next moment, Jaryd realized that her comments had been meant for Erland more than anyone else. Handing her staff to Orris, Cailin removed her blue cloak and let it drop to the floor.

Erland stared at her, his mouth open. "Wh—What are you doing?"

"I'm leaving the League. You wanted me to relinquish my authority to you once the war was over. I'm doing even more. You won't have to worry about me challenging you anymore, Erland. I'm a free mage now. I serve the land, and that's all."

Orris laid a hand on her arm. "Cailin, maybe this isn't the time."

"Yes, it is!" she said, brushing his hand away. "I've waited long enough. The League is nothing; the land is all that matters. It's time he realized that."

"But if you leave others will as well! The League will be weakened. Surely you don't want that!"

"To be honest, Erland, I don't really care one way or another. Some will stay with you: Toinan, Kovet, Stepan." She stopped abruptly, the color draining from her face once more. "Where is Stepan?" she asked, scanning the hall. After a moment she seemed to remember the dead lying at the edge of the chamber. "Oh, no," she breathed, rushing to where they lay.

She walked among them for a moment, and then with a cry dropped to her knees beside one of them and began to weep.

For some time, no one spoke, although they all made their way over to where she was to see who else had fallen. After several minutes, Orris approached her. He had picked up her cloak, and he tried now to drape it over her shoulders.

"No," she said. "I don't want that."

He hesitated, and then, dropping her cloak, he took off his own and gave it to her.

In all, four League mages died, all of them older. The Order lost two mages. Neysa, a young woman who received her cloak just a year before Jaryd and Alayna received theirs, and Eifion, the oldest member of the Order.

"We should honor them all," Jaryd said, "perhaps with a procession through the city from the Great Hall to the Hall of the League."

"We should include the men of the Temple as well," Sonel suggested. "They came to our aid when we needed them, and they lost their Eldest."

Jaryd nodded. "Very well. Can you get word to them?"

"Of course."

"Thank you," the Eagle-Sage said. He turned to Alayna, took her hands in his, and somehow found it within himself to smile. "Let's go find Myn."

31

In light of the events of this spring, and the loss of the Summoning Stone, we are of the opinion that we can no longer count on the Mage-Craft and the Temples to lead and protect us through times of crisis. We will, of course, still welcome the guidance and service of Tobyn-Ser's mages and Keepers. But we believe that the time has come for Tobyn-Ser's people to take a more active role in the governance of the land. To this end, we hereby request your aid in creating a People's Council. This council would consist of one individual from every village and town in the land, chosen by ballot. Once elected, each member of the council would travel to the Council Assembly, which we hope to locate in a town or village in the southern portion of Tobyn's Wood—someplace that is equally accessible to all. The Assembly would last several months out of each year; long enough to address any matters that warrant its consideration . . .

We understand that to some degree, it is not in the interests of the Temples, the League, or the Order to aid us in this venture. But we are hopeful that in your wisdom and your love of the land, you will look beyond your own concerns to do this for the common good.

> —Open letter to the Order of Mages and Masters, the League of Amarid, and the Keepers of Arick's Temples, from the Leaders of Tobyn-Ser's free towns, Summer, God's Year 4633.

Cailin awoke early the next morning, having spent the night at an inn near the Hall of the League. She didn't like sleeping indoors—she usually slept in Hawksfind Wood during Conclaves. But she had been exhausted nearly to the point of collapse following their battle with Sartol, and had decided to make an exception for this one night.

Thus, at first, she attributed the dark mood that held her when she woke and the strange images sent to her by Rithel, as products of both the previous night's ordeal and the unfamiliarity of sleeping in a bed. She dressed at a leisurely pace, taking time to bathe with the water and scented soaps provided in her room before slipping into her clothes. She put on her cloak as well, before remembering that she had vowed the night before never to wear it again. Taking it off again, she ran her fingers over the embroidery on the sleeves and hood. A part of her wondered if she had been rash to forsake the League, even though she had been considering it since her confrontation with Erland as the rain fell on them in Tobyn's Wood. Stepan would not have approved, she knew, feeling a tightening in her chest, but even he might have understood.

"It was the right thing to do," she said aloud, looking over at Rithel. "Erland and I can't work together. We both know it. It was time for me to leave."

By way of reply, Rithel sent her one of the strange images again. The great bird was soaring high into a clear blue sky, over terrain that Cailin did not recognize.

She shook her head. *I don't understand,* she sent. *What do you—?* And in that moment it hit her.

The war was over, and eagles never remained with their mages in times of peace.

She and Rithel had grown close in the past weeks, but at no time had Cailin loved the eagle as much as she had loved Marcran, her glorious little falcon. Nonetheless, realizing that Rithel was ready to leave her, the Eagle-Master began to cry. The bird hopped closer to her and nuzzled Cailin gently with her enormous beak. An image of their binding entered Cailin's mind, and the young mage smiled.

I'll never forget you, either.

She held out her arm and the bird climbed onto it.

"Come on," Cailin said, wiping her tears away and stroking the eagle's chin. "I'll take you outside."

Seeing her descend the stairs with Rithel on her arm, the innkeeper stepped out from behind the bar and regarded her solemnly. "Many thanks to you, Eagle-Master. You and your League. We feared the ghosts would attack us here before the war was over."

"It was the Order as well," Cailin told him. "If it wasn't for the Eagle-Sage and his mages, Sartol would have destroyed us."

The man's eyebrows went up, but after a moment he nodded. "Would you care for some breakfast, Eagle-Master? I can find some raw mutton for your bird as well."

Cailin fought back another wave of tears. "No, thank you. We'll eat later."

Again the man nodded, and after a brief, awkward silence, he retreated to the bar.

Stepping out into the bright daylight, Cailin caressed the golden brown feathers on the eagle's nape.

Rithel looked up into the sky and cried out softly.

"I know," Cailin said, a dull ache in her chest. "Be well, my love. Arick guard you."

The eagle cried out a second time before hopping off the mage's arm to the cobblestone. Then with a quick step forward, she jumped, and beating the air heavily with her enormous wings, began to rise into the clear blue, crying out repeatedly to Cailin and circling ever higher. After only a few moments she was little more than a dark speck in the sky, and as Cailin watched, it seemed that she was joined by a second bird who circled with her briefly. Then, with one final faint cry, she tucked in her wings, as did the other bird, and they both soared out of sight.

Wiping the tears from her face and exhaling slowly, Cailin walked away from the inn, intending to make her way out of the city and into Hawksfind Wood. Within a few minutes, however, she found herself standing before the Great Hall. She hesitated only for an instant, then climbed the stairs and entered the domed building. As she had expected, Jaryd and

Alayna were there, standing in the middle of the Gathering Chamber surveying the wreckage. The bodies were gone, of course, but the fragments of the Summoning Stone remained, as did its broken stand and the remains of what had once been the council table.

"Good morning," Cailin said, her voice echoing loudly off the ceiling.

They both turned. Alayna's owl sat on her shoulder, but Jaryd's eagle was nowhere to be seen.

"Is yours gone, too?" Cailin asked him.

He nodded. "She left this morning."

"So did Rithel. It feels strange, doesn't it?"

"Yes and no. I was unbound for a long time before Rithlar came to me. So in a way, this feels all too familiar."

Their daughter emerged from one of the back rooms, clutching a small doll in her hand. "Mama! Look what I found." Seeing Cailin, she stopped and smiled. "Hello, Eagle-Master." Her smile quickly vanished, to be replaced by a puzzled frown. "Where's your cloak?"

Cailin glanced at Jaryd and Alayna, smiling shyly. "I got rid of it," she said.

"Are you going to join the Order?"

"Myn!" Alayna said quickly.

But Cailin shook her head. "It's all right. No," she said, facing Myn again. "But I'm not going to be in the League anymore, either."

"Oh," the girl said, nodding sagely. "You're a free mage now."

The three mages laughed.

"Yes," Cailin said. "I guess I am."

"Are you sure that was the right decision?" Jaryd asked.

"Not entirely. But then again, I can't remember the last time I was entirely sure about anything." She laughed, but it even sounded forced to her.

Jaryd and Alayna smiled compassionately, and Cailin looked away, feeling embarrassed.

"I'm not sure it matters anyway," she said, as she started to wander slowly through the chamber.

Jaryd's face seemed to blanch. "What do you mean?"

"I just wonder if we've seen the end of the Mage-Craft as we know it. The stone is lost, the Unsettled have found rest. What if it's all ending? Theron and Amarid are both gone now. Maybe that means that their craft is gone as well."

The Eagle-Sage and Alayna exchanged a look. "I've thought of that as well," he admitted. "It occurred to me that Rithlar may have been my last binding."

"I don't think so," Alayna said. "The Mage-Craft may be changing—

it may be that we can't play the role we once did—but I don't think the gods are through with us yet."

Cailin shrugged, stopping in front of where the Summoning Stone once stood. "I hope you're right."

She lingered there for several moments, absently moving shards of the great crystal with her toe. Then she looked up and forced a smile. "I just realized that you're probably in the middle of something. I didn't mean to intrude. I just found myself in front of the Hall, and wanted . . ." She shrugged a second time. "To be honest, I don't know what I wanted."

"You're welcome here anytime, Cailin," Jaryd told her. "And regardless of whether you wear a cloak or not, we hope that you'll always consider us your friends."

The smile came to her easily this time. "Of course."

She left them a short while later, and making her way to the outskirts of the city, soon came to the Temple of the Eldest. The windows of the Temple were boarded, as they would be for the next forty days, to mark the loss of Eldest Brevyl. And before entering the Temple grounds, Cailin lit one of the tribute candles in the small prayer house at the Temple gate. Then she hurried through the courtyard to Linnea's chambers.

The air in the room was heavy and hot, and it smelled of mage-wort and *shan*. There was an acolyte sitting in the corner, but when Cailin came in, the woman nodded once and withdrew. Linnea was lying in bed, of course, a blanket pulled up to her chin. There were black circles under her eyes, and her pale skin was stretched so tight over her cheekbones that Cailin feared it might rip. But the Eldest smiled when she saw Cailin, and there still seemed to be a good deal of life in her light blue eyes.

"I was hoping you'd come!" she said, her voice barely more than a whisper.

"I've wanted to for some time now. I'm sorry it's been so long."

Linnea clicked her tongue and closed her eyes briefly in a way that seemed to dismiss the apology. "You had more important things to do. They tell me you're a hero."

"We all are." She smiled. "Even Erland."

"I find that hard to believe," Linnea said archly. She indicated the bed with a slight nod. "Sit beside me. Tell me all that happened."

Cailin sat, and the Eldest winced at the movement of the bedding.

"Can I get you anything?"

Linnea closed her eyes briefly, but then opened them and smiled again. "No, Child. I'm fine."

Fine? Looking at her, Cailin felt like crying.

They spoke for some time about the previous night's battle. Linnea peppered her with questions, interrupting often to ask Cailin to elaborate on one point or another. When Cailin was finally done, the Eldest closed her eyes once more, as if resting after an ordeal. But she quickly opened them again.

"Where's your cloak?" she asked, as though she had just realized that Cailin wasn't wearing it.

"I don't wear it anymore. I've left the League."

"When?" Linnea asked, her eyes widening.

"Last night, after we defeated Sartol."

"Erland must have had convulsions!"

Cailin laughed. "He did."

"Did others leave with you?"

"Not that I know."

"They will," Linnea said, with certainty. "Just wait and see." Her eyes scanned the small room. "And what of your eagle?"

"She left me this morning. The war's over. Both eagles are gone."

Linnea regarded her sadly. "So you're unbound again?"

Cailin shrugged, then nodded. "It's not important," she said, not wishing to dwell once more on the loss of her bird and the chance that she wouldn't bind again. "I think the greatest loss was the Summoning Stone."

"You're probably right," Linnea said. "I can't even fathom what it might mean."

Again the Eldest closed her eyes.

Cailin started to stand, moving slowly so as not to move the bed. "I should let you sleep."

"Please don't," Linnea said quickly, although her eyes remained closed. "I don't want to die alone, Cailin. And I don't want some acolyte I don't even know to be the last person who sees me alive."

The mage choked back a sob.

"Come now, Child. You've known this was coming for some time now. Let it come. I'm ready to go."

"But I'm not ready to lose you!" Cailin said, tears pouring from her eyes.

"Would you rather I lived on with this pain?"

"Of course not."

Linnea smiled. "Then let me go. Sit here until the gods come for me, and then let me go. Please."

What could she say? She wiped her eyes and nodded, even managing to smile.

"That's a good girl," Linnea said. "Now tell me again about your fight with the two ghosts. That sounded terrifying!"

They talked well into the night, until finally Linnea fell asleep. Cailin thought about leaving then, but instead she climbed carefully off the bed and lowered herself into the chair beside it. Listening to the Eldest's labored breathing, Cailin soon fell asleep herself, only to wake up sometime later, just as the moon was coming up. It took her a moment to realize what had awakened her. Linnea's breathing had stopped.

Cailin sat gazing at the Eldest's face, which looked fuller and healthier in the moonlight and ceryll-glow than it had in a long time. At dawn, there was a knock at the door, and another acolyte came in. She froze when she saw Linnea's face and then turned to Cailin, a question in her eyes.

"The gods came for her during the night."

The woman sighed. "Now it will be eighty days until the windows are uncovered."

Cailin almost railed at the woman for her callousness. But then she thought better of it. She was young; younger even than Cailin. And to her Linnea had just been a sick old woman. So Cailin merely stood, picked up her staff, and said, as she walked past the woman, "As it should be."

In the days that followed, Linnea's prediction proved correct. Eleven League mages, nearly half the body's membership, shed their cloaks and declared themselves free mages. Not surprisingly, most of those who followed Cailin's example were younger mages, Arslan and Vawnya among them. Several mages of the Order also gave up their cloaks, although not nearly as many. And as a result, the League now had fewer mages than both the Order and the People's Movement.

Cailin only saw Erland twice during this period, the first time at the procession honoring the dead, during which they walked together, leading the League mages through the streets of Amarid, but said nothing to each other. Their second encounter, however, proved more substantive. Early in the morning of the day before she intended to leave Amarid to resume her wanderings, she stopped by the Hall of the League. She wasn't sure why; for some reason, she just needed to see it again. She thought it empty when she entered—everything seemed perfectly still— and she assumed that she was alone.

But as she slowly circled the great table in the center of the hall, she heard a footfall behind her.

"Did you come back to mock me?"

Startled, she turned to look at him. He seemed more stooped than she remembered, and his normally ruddy face appeared sallow and drawn.

"Not at all. I'll go, if you wish."

"You've killed the League, you know."

"No, I haven't. The League still has many—"

"We're old, Cailin. All of us who remain are old. When we die, the League will die with us. You know that."

She hesitated. He was right, and she knew it. "That wasn't my intention."

"Of course it was. You wanted to get back at me. That's why you did it in front of everyone, to humiliate me. Fact of the matter is, I can't really blame you."

"Honestly, Erland—" She stopped herself. There was more truth in what he had said than she cared to admit. "I never meant to destroy the League," she told him at last. "I did it for myself, because I knew that we couldn't work together anymore. And because I was tired of feuding with you."

"But you knew that they'd follow you. You're their hero now."

"I knew some would. I didn't know who, or how many."

He nodded. "I'd like to believe that."

"We won, Erland. We defeated Sartol. That's what matters. That's what you should be thinking about. It took all of us working together. It was your victory and the League's as much as it was Jaryd's and mine."

He gazed at her for several moments, as if weighing her words. Then he nodded again and walked back to his quarters. "Farewell, Cailin," he said from the doorway. "Arick guard you."

"And you, Erland," she answered as he closed the door. She wasn't even sure that he heard her.

She went to the Great Hall a short time later, hoping to find Orris. When he wasn't there, she asked Jaryd where she might find him, and he directed her to the Aerie.

Reaching the courtyard of the inn, she thought that Jaryd had made a terrible mistake. Surely no self-respecting mage would stay at a place like this. But when she stepped into the dingy inn, she was met by an aroma that made her stomach rumble and mouth water, and she decided that Orris might be there after all. A moment later she spotted him in the back corner of the room. He was alone, save for his beautiful white falcon, and he was eating a bowl of hot stew.

"May I join you?" she asked, approaching his table.

Looking up, he smiled, making her heart dance. "Of course."

She sat across from him and they watched each other silently for a few awkward moments.

"I'm leaving, tomorrow," she finally said, cringing inwardly at how awkward and abrupt it sounded.

"I'm sorry to hear that. I hope that our paths will cross again soon."

"Do you?" Too eager. Again, she cringed.

The mage sighed. "Cailin—"

"I know," she said, stopping him with a raised hand. "I apologize."

They lapsed into silence once more.

"Where will you be going?" he asked at last, before taking another mouthful of stew.

"South, I think. It's time people resettled the Shadow Forest and the area around Theron's Grove. I'd like to help with that."

Orris nodded slowly. "That's a fine idea," he said.

She beamed. "How about you?"

He dropped his gaze, hesitating. "I haven't decided. It's a new world, and I'm not certain yet where I fit in."

Come with me! "You'll fit in anywhere you want, I'd think."

He smiled at that, looking into her eyes again. "Thank you."

For a third time, the conversation faltered, and Cailin decided that she was best off leaving before she embarrassed herself further.

She stood and extended a hand. "Good bye, Orris. Arick guard you."

He took her hand in both of his. "And you, Cailin. May the gods keep you safe and bring you happiness."

She gazed at him for a few seconds more before reluctantly pulling back her hand and leaving him. Once outside, she took the quickest route out of the city to the wood. She had intended to spend one last night here before starting south. But it was early still, and she had said good-bye to all the people who mattered. So glancing back across the Larian one last time, she began the slow ascent into the mountains.

She had no cloak or bird, but she was a free mage, and there seemed to be a great truth in that term. For the first time she could remember, probably for the first time in her life, she was utterly on her own. She shivered slightly at the thought, with a touch of fear to be sure, but with excitement as well.

With midsummer approaching and the entire membership of the Order still in Amarid, Jaryd decided, as his last act as Eagle-Sage, to convene the annual Gathering early, and call for the selection of a new Owl-Sage. In the past, that had been a process involving only the Owl-Masters, and it remained true that only masters could be considered for the position. But with the sundering of the Order, the number of masters had grown so small that when Sonel stepped down as Sage, all members of the Order, Hawk-Mages and Owl-Masters, were invited to participate in choosing her successor. Thus, Radomil had become the first Sage since Amarid himself to be chosen by the entire Order.

In addition, the selection of the Order's leader normally revealed ambitions that otherwise remained well hidden. But this year, in the wake of all that had happened, it seemed not a question of who would be chosen, but rather who would agree to serve.

Radomil, who had been Sage before Jaryd's binding to Rithlar, struck Jaryd as the logical choice. But the rotund Owl-Master declined the honor.

"I've served once," he said. "And I'm not sure that I'm suited to the position."

Others assured him that he had done a fine job as Sage, but he refused to be swayed. This began a lengthy discussion of other possible candidates, with Baden, Sonel, Trahn, Mered, who had been Radomil's First, and Alayna mentioned as possibilities.

The phrase, "I've been away from home too long," was repeated so many times over the first two days of the Gathering, that it began to elicit laughter.

At last, on the third and final day of discussion, Jaryd brought up a point that had first occurred to him the night of their battle with Sartol.

Standing during a lull in the proceedings, and clearing his throat awkwardly, he asked, "Do the Sage and the First have to stay in Amarid?"

He had been afraid of the response his question might provoke, and so was surprised when no one said anything at all.

"They always have," Baden answered after a long silence.

"But that was because of the stone, wasn't it? They had to be here in case the other members of the Order had to be summoned to Amarid." He gestured toward the shattered pieces of the stone, which had been gathered into a neat pile next to the broken stand. "That's no longer the case."

Trahn raised an eyebrow. "What he's saying makes sense. One might ask if we even need a Sage anymore."

"Of course we do," Orris said. "I'm still bound to a hawk, so I have nothing to gain from saying this. And I think we'd be foolish to stop selecting Sages and Firsts. We need a leader, someone to guide our debates and represent us in our dealings with the rest of the land."

"I agree," Jaryd said. "But do you think that person has to live in the Great Hall?"

Orris seemed to consider the question for a moment. "Yes, I do. As I said, the Sage is our link to the rest of the land, and to the rest of the world. For the last thousand years, even if a person didn't know the Owl-

Sage's name, they always knew where he or she could be found. I don't think we should change that."

Hearing it phrased that way, neither did anyone else. When they voted on the question a few moments later, every member supported keeping the Sage in Amarid. Which brought them back to the question of who would lead them.

In the end, after the mages discussed the matter for several hours more, Trahn agreed to serve, and Radomil offered to stay on as his First.

"Ilianne has grown quite fond of Amarid," he explained.

Before they adjourned, the mages of the Order agreed unanimously to add one more medallion to the constellation of golden coins that adorned the roof of the Great Hall. Theron's. It was, they all agreed, something that should have been done years before.

After that, there was little left to do, and Trahn declared the Gathering closed, inviting them to a hastily prepared feast at the First Mage's home, to be held later that evening.

Despite the fact that the Great Hall's attendants had only had a few days to prepare, the Procession of Light and the closing feast were the most enjoyable that Jaryd could remember. It was not that the food was any better than usual or that the procession was more spectacular than it was every year. But for the first time in years, there seemed to be no shadows hanging over the Order.

The night of Jaryd's first procession and feast, at which he received his cloak, had been one of the most glorious of his life. And yet, even that had taken place on the eve of the delegation's departure for Theron's Grove. Tonight, finally, the long struggle that began with the outlanders' attacks on Tobyn-Ser was over.

Trahn extended invitations to this feast not only to the people of the city, but also to the League and those free mages still in Amarid. And though Cailin had already departed, and Erland declined to come, several free mages and a few members of the League did attend. The Mage-Craft was still divided—Jaryd had resigned himself to the fact that it probably would be forever—but the rivalries among its various factions appeared to have eased in the aftermath of their war with Sartol. Yes, victory had come at a great cost. Throughout the land, people were grieving for lost relatives and friends. And who could say what the future held for the Mage-Craft now that the stone was gone? But the war was over. Finally, the land could begin to heal itself.

"When will you be leaving?" Baden asked as they ate, looking from Jaryd to Alayna.

"Soon," Myn said, before either of them could answer.

All of them laughed.

Alayna leaned over and kissed the top of Myn's head. "She's right: soon. Tomorrow, if possible."

"What about you?" Jaryd asked between mouthfuls.

"Sonel and I will be leaving tomorrow, too. I miss my home."

Orris laughed. "Listen to him. It's hard to believe he was ever a migrant. I'm going to have to take a look at this house and see what makes it so special."

Baden regarded him with surprise. "I'd like that, Orris. You're welcome anytime."

"Thank you. I'm going to ride with Trahn back to his home when he goes to get his wife. I've always wanted to spend a bit of time in the desert. But after that, I'd like to visit you and Sonel."

"Of course."

"What about us?" Myn asked him, her mouth full of brown bread.

"If it's all right with your mother and father, I'll be coming to you from Uncle Baden's house."

"Sounds great," Alayna said, grinning.

But Jaryd merely stared at his friend, sensing something in the plans he was making. Trahn's home, Baden's, then theirs. And where after that?

Orris looked his way and their eyes met.

"What?" the burly mage asked, laughing again. "You look like you don't want me to visit."

"Not at all," Jaryd said. He shook his head. "It's nothing." If Orris was hiding something, he was doing a fine job of it.

It was a late evening, as the feasts often were. Jaryd and Alayna returned to the Great Hall only an hour or two before dawn, with Myn asleep in Jaryd's arms. Still, they managed to have their sacks packed and their horses saddled and ready by late morning the following day. And after saying their last farewells to Baden and Sonel, Radomil and Ilianne, Orris, and Trahn, they rode out of the city and commenced the long journey back to the shores of South Shelter.

"Do you think it's strange that Orris is coming to see all of us?" Jaryd asked as they rode through Hawksfind Wood.

Alayna shook her head. "Not really. He didn't like to stay with friends while the League was still after him, because he worried about something happening to us. Now that they seem content to leave him alone, he's ready to visit again. It makes sense to me."

"I hadn't thought of that," he admitted. "I guess you're right."

Throughout the afternoon, as they crossed the wood and then started to climb into the foothills, Myn made them sing songs with her and tell her stories. After some time though, Jaryd fell silent, leaving the songs and tales to Alayna.

He couldn't help but think back to what Cailin had said about the possibility that they might not bind again. He had been unbound for so long after Ishalla died, and though the Curse was gone, he did not relish the idea of spending the rest of his life without a familiar. He wanted to believe, as Alayna did, that the gods would continue to send familiars to Tobyn-Ser's mages despite the loss of the stone and the breaking of the Curse. But a part of him wondered.

"What are you thinking about?" Alayna asked quietly, pulling her horse abreast of his. Myn was sitting in front of her, and had fallen asleep.

He gave a wry grin and shook his head. "You don't want to know."

"You're worrying about binding again?"

He nodded reluctantly.

"I really don't think you have to worry. The Mage-Craft has been a part of this land for a thousand years. It's as much a part of Tobyn-Ser as the Seasides or Tobyn's Wood. And as long as there are hawks and owls flying over the plains and forests, and as long as there are people who carry Leora's Gift within them, the Mage-Craft will remain."

He was desperate to believe her. Aside from Alayna and their daughter, there was nothing he loved more than being a mage. And yet, his doubts lingered, like an ocean mist on a cool spring morning.

"You're still not convinced, are you?" She shook her head. "You were a great Eagle-Sage, Jaryd. You're a wonderful husband and father. I see you with Orris and Trahn and Baden, and I see that you're a terrific friend." She shook her head a second time. "But I have never met anybody who's as bad at being unbound as you are."

He laughed a bit too loudly, and Myn started awake.

"What's so funny?" she asked with a yawn.

"Nothing, Love," he said. "You should go back to—"

"Papa, look!" she whispered. She was gazing ahead, pointing at something.

And turning to follow her gaze, Jaryd took a sharp breath.

Just in front of them, perched on a low branch, sat a magnificent owl. It was large and powerfully built, with intelligent yellow eyes and tufts on its head that gave its face a catlike appearance. And it was staring directly at him. It was, he had time to realize, the same type of owl to which Alayna was bound, not that this should have surprised him. *As long as there are hawks and owls,* she had said. *As long as there are people who carry Leora's Gift within them.* She was right after all.

That was his last clear thought for a good while. For in the next instant, a wave of images and emotions crashed down upon his mind like breakers on a sandy shore. And so his new binding began.

Epilogue

As I have told you before, I was greatly relieved to hear of your victory over Sartol and of the pledge made by the Temple's new leader not to purchase any more weapons from Lon-Ser. If you have received my earlier letters, please forgive me for repeating myself. But it has been a long time since I heard from you, and I find myself wondering if you are all right. I worry that perhaps your feud with the League mages is not over as you believed, or that somehow, Sartol proved to be a more resilient foe than you thought . . .

I have come to a decision of some importance that I am eager to share with you, but I am reluctant to do so until I receive word that you are well. Please write to me soon, Orris. I do not want our correspondence to end.

—Melyor i Lakin, Sovereign and
Bearer of Bragor-Nal to Hawk-Mage
Orris, Day 6, Week 2, Spring, Year
3069.

She had been thinking along these lines for nearly a year now, and she had tried on many occasions at least to hint at it, so that Jibb would be prepared. But though he had known since the day they hired Mouse and put Premel in change of Network relations that she didn't intend to be Sovereign forever, he seemed unwilling or unable to accept that her tenure would be ending anytime soon.

Which explained the look on his face now.

"But—" He halted, shaking his head for what had to be the twentieth time. "But what will you do?" he finally asked. "Where will you go?"

She stepped to her window and looked out at the Nal. The air looked browner and heavier than ever. Even the storm that had moved through that morning hadn't cleared any of it. She needed to get out of here.

Melyor had spent almost her entire life in the Nal. She had only left twice, once to escape Cedrych's assassins and once to capture Marar. Not that she was complaining. All in all, the Nal had been good to her over the years. It had given her just about everything she had ever dreamed of having: excitement, power, gold. She was proud of what she had accomplished as Sovereign, of the changes she had brought to the Nal and the improvements she had made in the lives of Bragor-Nal's Gildriites. The process was still just beginning; it wouldn't be completed in her lifetime. But it was still more than many had thought possible. Certainly it was more than other Sovereigns had done.

But with all that she had done, with all the wealth and influence she now enjoyed, she couldn't help the way she felt. The realization had first come to her in the tunnels beneath the Sixth Realm, just before the firefight that nearly killed her. It struck her again during the journey to Marar's palace, when the excitement of their invasion of Stib-Nal was more than enough to offset the discomfort of making the journey on walk-aids. She was bored.

For years, her lone ambition had been to make it to the Gold Palace. And for a time after she got there, she enjoyed running the Nal. But gold could only buy her so much, and despite her power, more often than not, she felt like a prisoner in the palace. After all this time, she had finally come to understand that being Sovereign was a lot less fun than being a Nal-Lord. Not that she wanted to go back to the quads. She just wanted to do something else. And whatever it turned out to be, she didn't want to do it alone.

"I don't know what I'm going to do," she said, finally answering the general's question. She had hoped that she would have heard from Orris by now. What she really wanted was to go to Tobyn-Ser to be with him. But how could she say such a thing to Jibb? Besides, she couldn't very well go without telling the mage that she was coming. "Maybe I'll go to the settlements in the Dhaalmar."

"You're going to live with the Gildriites?"

She faced him again. "There's a part of me that thinks I belong there." She held up her staff. "Certainly this stone does."

"That stone belongs with you, wherever you are. You don't have to give up the palace to deserve it."

She conceded the point with a shrug of her shoulders and turned back to the window.

"When was the last time you heard from him?"

She crossed her arms over her chest, as if to cradle her heart. "It's been a while."

"Have you written to him again?"

She almost told him to mind his own affairs. But she knew how hard it was for him to talk to her about Orris, and so she merely nodded.

"You've told me that he travels a lot. That he wanders the land on foot all year long. Maybe he hasn't been able to get his letters into the hands of any merchants. It's probably as simple as that."

She looked at him over her shoulder and gave a wan smile. "Probably. Thanks, Jibb."

"But until you hear from him again, doesn't it make sense to stay here, where he can reach you?"

He had a point.

"I suppose it does, at least for a while longer."

"And anyway," he said, his tone light, "you wouldn't want to leave me all alone, would you?"

"You wouldn't be alone," she replied with a grin. "You always have Premel."

The rift between Jibb and Premel had persisted for much of the past year, and Jibb still did not trust the security man as he once had. But in recent weeks Melyor had noticed some of the warmth returning to their relationship, as if Jibb had finally found it within himself to forgive Premel for his betrayal.

"Premel," Jibb repeated with a shake of his head. "At this point, Mouse has practically turned him into a Gildriite. In fact, he probably knew I was going to say that before I did."

Melyor arched an eyebrow. "Careful, General. Remember who you're talking to."

Jibb laughed, and Melyor managed to as well. After a few seconds, however, their mirth faded, and they were left staring at each other.

"I'm not ready to lose you, Melyor," Jibb said with unsettling intensity.

She didn't enjoy hurting him, but sometimes he needed to be reminded. "You never had me."

"That's not true. Even if you never loved me, you've been the closest friend I've ever had."

"I'll always to be your friend, Jibb. No matter where I go, or who I'm with."

He looked down. "I know that."

"You know," Melyor said, attempting to change the mood, "as Sovereign you'll be able to have any woman you want."

"You know this from personal experience?"

She gave a coy smile. "Do you really want me to answer that?"

His face turned bright red, and Melyor laughed.

The remote from his speak-screen beeped. "Looks like I need to be going," he said. "Don't move out of the palace before I get back, all right?"

"Fair enough," she agreed.

Jibb let himself out of her quarters, and she returned to the window.

"This isn't my home anymore," she said, staring up at the brown sky. "I'm not even sure I've ever had a home."

She hadn't expected to see Jibb again until the next day, but later that afternoon, as she wandered through the gardens on the west side of the palace, the general approached her, his round face wearing a strange expression.

"What is it, Jibb?"

He stopped in front of her, his brow furrowed. "I'm not sure how best to say this." He took a breath, and then, "I think I know why Orris hasn't contacted you for so long."

Her mouth went dry, and she actually had to remind herself to breathe. "Why?"

And by way of response, the general turned and pointed toward the entrance to the gardens.

There, framed by the marble gate, stood the mage, his yellow hair tied back, just as she remembered, and a beautiful white falcon sitting on his shoulder.

She wanted to run to him, to throw her arms around him. But she was afraid to take even one step. She just gazed at him, and he back at her.

"I'll leave you two," the general said quietly.

"Thank you, Jibb," she whispered.

"Melyor."

She tore her eyes from Orris to look at him.

"I'm happy for you. Truly."

She smiled, feeling a single tear on her cheek. "And I love you for that."

Jibb smiled as well. Then he turned and left the garden.

Facing Orris again, Melyor took a deep breath. "I had wondered what happened to you," she said. It felt strange to be speaking Tobynmir again. She had been writing letters in the mage's language for years, but she hadn't spoken it since leaving Orris at the edge of the Southern Timber Stand eight years ago.

He started to walk toward her slowly, as if unsure of himself. "I'm sorry I didn't get any letters to you. Few merchants come to the isthmus, particularly in the winter and early spring. I did write though. I can show you the letters later."

"You walked? You could have come on a merchant ship."

"Actually I rode." He grinned self-consciously. "I do much better on a horse than I do on the sea."

She gawked at him. "You brought a horse to the Nal?"

"I set him free at a beach on the isthmus, just before the timber stand. He should be very happy there."

He stopped just in front of her.

"I never thought I would see you here again," she breathed.

"I never thought I'd return."

With one last step forward, he gathered her in his arms and kissed her deeply. Melyor had dreamed of this moment time and again, hoping against hope that just once the image would come to her with the weight of a Seeing. She returned his kiss with a passion that had burned within her for more years than she cared to count.

After some time, she realized that Orris's falcon, who had been forced off the mage's shoulder by their embrace, was circling above them, complaining loudly.

She pulled back and looked Orris in the eye. "I do not think your bird likes me very much."

"She'll get used to you."

"Does that mean you will stay with me?"

He kissed her again. "I'm here, Melyor. I spent nearly half the year crossing the isthmus. Doesn't that tell you something?"

Of course it did, though she was almost afraid to let herself believe it. "But why would you leave Tobyn-Ser? I never expected you would do that."

He shook his head, a sad look in his dark eyes. "Things there are changing." He gave a wry grin. "I don't do very well with change."

"Coming here is not change?"

"It's different. I've been a mage and a member of the Order for twenty-one years. And for ten years before that, I dreamed of wearing this cloak. After I left Tobyn-Ser the first time—in fact, because of my leaving—all that it meant to be a mage started to change. I can't even begin to tell you what it was like to see the Order broken, and to know that it was my fault. But even then, the Mage-Craft remained essentially the same. Now, though . . ." He shook his head again. "With the Summoning Stone lost, there's nothing holding us together anymore, there are more free mages than there are Order mages. Too much is different."

She understood only a fraction of what he was telling her, but in a way that was enough, at least for now.

"Besides," he went on, smiling at her again, "I had a very good reason for wanting to come here. Would the Sovereign of Bragor-Nal have need of the services of a mage?"

A reply leaped to mind, one that would have made him blush, but she wasn't sure how to word it in his language. And in any case, she had news for him.

"I want to tell you—" She broke off embarrassed by the difficulty she was having speaking Tobynmir. "I have been wanting to tell you something for a long time. I am not to be Sovereign anymore."

His eyes widened. "Why not?"

She shook her head. "I cannot tell you now. Later, when I can find the words. But it is my choice. I am deciding it."

"I see," he said, nodding. "And what are you going to do?"

"I was going to come to Tobyn-Ser," she said. "I want to see your land. But now you are here."

The mage gave a small laugh. "I guess I should have written."

Melyor smiled and nodded. "So what do we do now? Do you want to return to your land?"

"Not yet." He took her hands in his. "I do someday, Melyor. I want you to see Tobyn-Ser, too. I want you to meet my friends. But I'm not ready to go back."

"Then what?"

"You once asked me to go with you to the Bearer's village."

"To the Dhaalmar?" she asked with amazement, remembering her conversation with Jibb that morning. "You want to go there?"

"Yes," he said. "I think it's time I honored Gwilym in that way. And I think it's time that someone brought the Mage-Craft to the Gildriites of Lon-Ser."

"Do you think that is possible?" she asked, a chill going through her body at the very thought. "Gildri's power left him when he came here. That is what the legend says. And there has been no sign of such power existing among my people since."

"I know that. But Gildri came here a thousand years ago. Think of how much has changed since then."

"But still—"

He held up a hand, stopping her. And a dazzling smile lit his face. "I dreamed it, Melyor. While I was crossing the isthmus, I dreamed of mages in the Dhaalmar."

She stared at him. Wanting to believe him. Afraid to believe him. "Truly?" she asked, her voice so low she could barely hear herself. "A Seeing?"

He nodded.

She shook her head, feeling tears on her face again. "What a marvelous dream."

He smiled, and kissed her once more. "Actually, the best part was that we were together."

About the Author

DAVID B. COE grew up just outside of New York City, the youngest of four children. He attended Brown University as an undergraduate and later received a Ph.D. in history from Stanford. He briefly considered a career as an academic but wisely thought better of it.

David has published two other novels and is the 1999 recipient of the William L. Crawford Memorial Fantasy Award. He lives in Tennessee with his wife, Nancy J. Berner, their daughters, Alex and Erin, and of course, Buddy, the wonder dog. *Eagle-Sage* is the third and final volume of the LonTobyn Chronicle. But David is already hard at work on his next fantasy project.